THE DIAMOND WARRIORS

DAVID ZINDELL

The Diamond Warriors

HARPER
Voyager

An Imprint of HarperCollins*Publishers*
www.voyager-books.co.uk

HarperCollins*Publishers*
77–85 Fulham Palace Road,
Hammersmith, London W6 8JB

www.voyager-books.com

Published by Harper*Voyager*
An Imprint of HarperCollins*Publishers* 2007

1

ISBN: 978-0-00-224761-0 Hardback
ISBN: 978-0-00-224762-7 Trade Paperback

Typeset in Meridien by Palimpsest Book Production Limited,
Grangemouth, Stirlingshire

Printed and bound in Great Britain by
Clays Ltd, St Ives plc

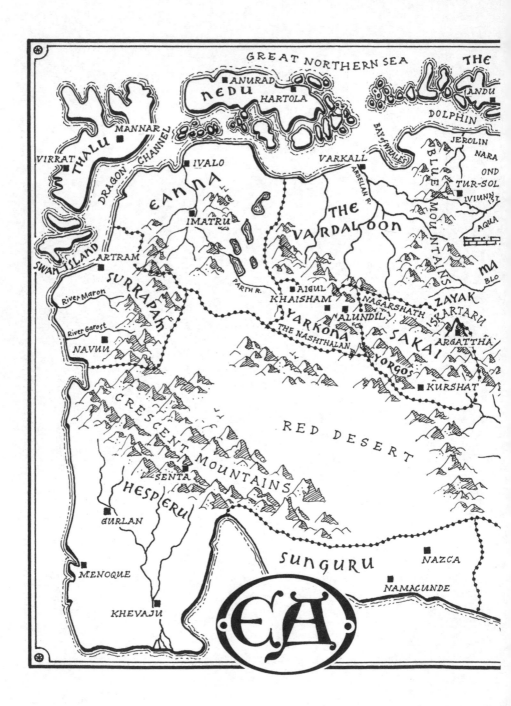

1

On clear summer nights, I have stood on desert sands in awe of the stars. From these countless radiant points, my ancestors believed, comes all that is good, beautiful and true. The Lightstone had its source there. The stars make light itself and that secret, irresistible force which warms angels' hearts and illuminates all things. What man could ever hold this most brilliant of fires? Only one who can endure burning. And one who wills with all his heart that the stars must go on shining forever and can never die.

They shone upon my grandfather and upon Elahad and the ancient Valari who came to earth from other worlds; and still they shone upon *my* world, even though the Great Red Dragon named Morjin threatened to make war upon all Ea's lands and call down that black and starless night without end. In the spring of the fourth year since I had set out to seek the Lightstone and defy Morjin, the stars guided me home. Late into evenings filled with the calls of meadowlarks and the fragrance of new flowers, my companions and I ventured across savage lands, setting our course by Aras and Solaru and the heavens' other bright lights. And at dawn we journeyed toward the Great Eastern Sun: the Morning Star for which my grandfather had named me Valashu. This fiery orb still rose each day over the mountains of Mesh and the dwellings of my people. Where Morjin called my brothers and sisters demons from hell that must be nailed up on crosses or burned alive, I knew them as noble warriors of the sword – and spirit – who remained true Valari. It was upon me to return to them in order to seize my fate and become their king.

On the first day of Soldru, on a warm afternoon, my seven companions and I rode through the Valley of the Swans below my family's ancient, burned-out castle. Our way took us through a thick and ancient wood. Here grew tall oaks and elms through which I had run as a child. Wild grape and honeysuckle twined themselves around the trunks of these great trees, while ferns blanketed the forest floor. Many flowers brightened this expanse of green and sweetened the air: bluets and trillium and goldthread, whose white sepals gleamed like stars. Each growing thing, it seemed, greeted me like an old friend to which I had long ago pledged my life. So it was with the warblers and the sparrowhawks calling out from branch or sky, and the rabbits, voles and badgers who made their abodes beneath them. Our procession through the trees startled a stag feeding on the bracken; just before he sprang away, his large, dark eye fixed on my eyes and called to me as if we were brothers. He did not, I sensed, worry that his forest home might soon be destroyed and the whole world with it. This great being cared nothing for the struggles and aspirations of men, and knew only that it was good to be alive.

'Ah, another deer.' Next to me, from on top of a big, brown horse, my friend Maram watched the stag bounding off through the trees. He was himself a big man, with a thick beard and soft brown eyes which easily filled with worry. 'These woods are still full of deer.'

We rode along a few paces, and our horses' hooves cracked through old leaves and twigs.

'And where there are deer,' he went on, 'there are certainly bears. These huge, brown bears of yours whose like I have seen in no other land.'

I turned in my saddle to look after Daj and Estrella riding behind us. Daj's gaze met mine, and his black curls fell over his face as he inclined his head to me. Although he couldn't have been much older than twelve years, he held himself straight and proud as if he were a knight who knew no fear. Already he had slain more men than had most knights – and sent on as well an evil creature more powerful than any man. Estrella, of an age with him, guided her pony along in silence. Although she could make no words with her throat and lips, her dark eyes and lively face seemed almost infinitely expressive and full of light. Behind her rode Master Juwain and Liljana, who might have been the children's grandparents. They wore the same hooded traveling cloaks that we all did, even Atara, who brought up the rear. This beautiful woman – my betrothed – hated the itch of woven wool against her sunburned skin, for she had lived too long on the plains of

2

the Wendrush with the savage Sarni warriors, who usually wore silks or beaded skins, when they wore garments at all. She was herself a warrior, of that strange society of women known as the Manslayers. As she pressed her knees against the flanks of her great roan mare, Fire, she gripped one of the great, double-curved Sarni bows. A white blindfold bound her thick blond hair and covered the hollows beneath her brows. It was a great miracle of her life that although Morjin had taken her eyes, sometimes by the virtue of her second sight she could still see. If a bear charged out of the bracken at us, I thought, she could put an arrow straight through its heart.

'Bears,' I said, turning back toward Maram, 'rarely hunt deer – only if they come upon one by chance.'

'Like that bear that came upon *you*?' He pointed at my face and added, 'The one who gave you *that*?'

I pressed my finger against the scar cut into my forehead. This mark, shaped like a lightning bolt, had actually been present from my birth, when the midwife's tongs had ripped my skin. The bear, who had nearly killed my brother Asaru and me during one of our forays into the woods, had only deepened it.

'I doubt if it is my fate,' I said, smiling at him, 'to see us attacked here by a bear.'

'Ah, fate,' Maram said, shaking his great, bushy head. 'You speak of it too much these days, and contemplate it too deeply, I think.'

'Perhaps that is true. But we've avoided the worst that might have befallen us and come to our journey's end without mishap.'

'*Almost* to our journey's end,' he said, waving his huge hand at the trees ahead of us. 'If you're right, we've still five miles of these gloomy woods to endure. If you hadn't insisted on this *long*cut, we might already have been sitting at Lord Harsha's table with Behira, putting down some roasted beef and a few pints of your good Meshian beer.'

I cast him a long, burning look. He knew well enough the reasons for our detour through the woods, and had in fact agreed upon them. But now that he could almost smell his dinner and taste his dessert, it seemed that he had conveniently forgotten them.

'All right, all right,' he said, turning his head away from me to gaze off through the trees. 'Why indeed take any chances when we *have* come so far without mishap? It's just that now I'm ready to enjoy the comforts of Lord Harsha's house, it seems that the farmland hereabouts – and the rest of your kingdom – surely holds fewer perils than do these woods.'

3

'It is not my kingdom,' I reminded him. 'Not yet. And whoever wins Mesh's throne, you may be sure that this wood will remain near the heart of his realm.'

Far out on the grasslands of the Wendrush, as we had taken meat and fire with the chieftain of the Niuriu, Vishakan, we had heard disquieting rumors that Mesh's greatest lords were contending with each other to gain my father's vacant throne. War, it seemed, threatened. Vishakan himself told me that Morjin had stolen the souls of some of my own countrymen – and had turned the hearts of others with threats of crucifixion and promises of glory and everlasting life for anyone who followed him. The Lord of Lies had pledged a thousand-weight of gold to any man who brought him my head. So it was that my companions and I had entered Mesh in secret. Twenty-two kel keeps, great fortresses of iron and stone, encircled the whole of the kingdom and guarded the passes through the mountains. But I knew unexplored ways around three of them – and through the country of the Sawash River and past Arakel, Telshar and the other great peaks of the Central Range. And, of course, through the fields and forests of the Valley of the Swans. So it was that we had come nearly all the way to Lord Harsha's little stone chalet without stopping at an inn or a farmhouse.

'The heart of *your* realm,' Maram said to me, 'surely lies with the hearts of those who know you. There can't be many in this district who will fail to acclaim you when the time comes.'

'No, perhaps not many.'

'And there can't be *any* who have gone over to the Red Dragon, despite what that barbarian chieftain said. Surely it will be safe to show ourselves here. After all, we don't have to give out our names.'

I only smiled at this. Even in the best of times, Mesh saw few strangers from other lands. Maram and my other friends would stand out here like rubies and sapphires in a tapestry woven of diamonds. The Valari are a tall people, with long, straight black hair, angular faces like the planes of cut stone, dark ivory skin and bright black eyes. None of us looked anything like that – none of us, of course, except myself.

'As soon as we show ourselves,' I told Maram, 'the word will spread that Valashu Elahad and his companions have returned to Mesh. We should hear what Lord Harsha advises before *that* moment comes.'

We rode on for a while, into a small clearing, and then Estrella, who was good at finding things, espied a bush near its edge bearing

4

ripe, red raspberries. She nudged her horse over to it, then dismounted. Her joyful smile seemed an invitation for all of us to join her in a midafternoon refreshment. And so the rest of us dismounted as well, and began plucking the soft, little fruits.

'These,' Maram said, as he filled his mouth with a handful of raspberries, 'would make a good meal for any bear.'

'And you,' I said, poking his big belly with a smile, 'would make a better one.'

Master Juwain, a short man with a large head as bald as a walnut, stepped over to me. His face, I thought, with his large gray eyes, had always seemed as luminous as the moonlit sea. He looked at me deeply, then said, 'We *are* close to the place that the bear attacked you, aren't we?'

'Yes, close,' I said, staring off through the elms. Then I turned back to smile at him. 'But you aren't afraid of bears, too, are you, sir?'

'I'm afraid of *you*, Valashu Elahad. That is, afraid *for* you.' He pointed a gnarly finger at me as he fixed me with a deep, knowing look. 'Most of us flee from that which torments us, but you must always seek out the thing you most dread and go poking it with a stick.'

I only laughed at this as I reached back to grip the hilt of my sword, slung over my shoulder. I said, 'But, sir, I have no stick – only this blade. And I'm sure I won't have to use it today against any bear.'

Daj, munching on some raspberries, returned my smile in confidence that I had spoken the truth, and so did Estrella. They pressed in close to me, not to take comfort from the protection of my sword – not just – but because such nearness gladdened all our hearts. Then I noticed Atara standing next to the raspberry bush as she held her bow in one hand and her scryer's sphere of clear, white gelstei with her other. The sun's light poured down upon her in a bright shower. Her beautiful face, as perfectly proportioned as the sculptures of the angels, turned toward me. She smiled at me, too: but coldly, as if she had seen some terrible future that she did not wish to share. All she said to me was: 'The only bear you'll find here today is the one that nearly killed you years ago. It still lives, doesn't it?'

Yes, I thought, as my fingers tightened around the hilt of my sword, the bear called out from somewhere inside me – and in some strange way, from somewhere in these woods. Even as Asaru, who had saved me from the bear, still lived on as well. My mother and grandmother, and all my murdered family, seemed to take on life anew in the stems of the wildflowers and in the breath of the leaves of the new maple trees. My father, I knew, would always stand beside me like the mountains of the land that I loved.

Liljana, who could not smile, came up to me and grasped my hand. Her iron-gray hair framed her pretty face, which too often fell stern and forbidding. But despite her relentless and domineering manner, she could be the kindest of women, and the wisest, too. She said to me, 'You've always been drawn to these woods, haven't you?'

Her calm, hazel eyes filled with understanding. She didn't need to call on the power of her blue gelstei to read my mind – or, rather, to know what grieved my heart.

Across the clearing, through the shadowed gloom of the elms, I heard a tanager trilling out notes that sounded much like a robin's song: *shureet, shuroo*. I looked for this bird, but I could not see it. It seemed that this wood, above all other places, held answers to the secret of my past and the puzzle of my future. There dwelled a power here that called to me like a song of fire racing along my blood.

'Drawn, yes,' I said to Liljana. I felt a nameless dread working at my insides like ice water. 'And repelled, too.'

'Well,' Maram said, wiping a bit of raspberry juice from his lip, 'I wish you had been repelled a little *more* that day Salmelu shot you with his filthy arrow. But who would have thought a Valari *prince* would go over to the Dragon and hire out as one of his assassins? And use the filthiest of poisons? Does it still burn you, my friend?'

I pressed my hand to my side in remembrance of that day when Salmelu's poisoned arrow had come streaking out of the trees – not so very far from here. The scratch that it had left in my skin had long since healed, but I would forever feel the kirax poison like a heated iron sizzling deep into every fiber of my body.

'Yes, it burns,' I said to him.

'Well, then perhaps we *should* take greater care here. If a prince of Ishka can turn traitor, then I suppose a Meshian can – though I've always thought your countrymen preserved the soul of the Valari, so to speak.'

I suddenly recalled Lansar Raasharu, my father's greatest lord, who had lost his soul and his very humanity to Morjin through a hate and a fear that I knew only too well. And I said, 'No one is immune from evil.'

'No one except you.'

I felt my throat tighten in anger as I said, 'Myself least of all, Maram. You should know that.'

'I know what I saw during this last journey of ours. Who else but you could have led us out of the Skadarak?'

I did not need to close my eyes to feel the blighted forest called the Skadarak pulling me down into an icy cold blackness that had no bottom. Sometimes, when I looked into the black centers of Maram's eyes – or my own – I felt myself hurtling down through empty space again.

'Do not,' I told him, 'speak of that place.'

'But you kept yourself from falling – and all of us as well! And then, at the farmhouse with Morjin, when everything was so impossibly dark, he might have seized your will and made you into a filthy ghul. But as you always do, you found that brightness inside yourself that he couldn't stand against, and you –'

'It is one thing to keep from falling into evil,' I told him. 'And it is another to succeed in accomplishing good. Why don't we try to keep our sight on the task ahead of us?'

'Ah, this impossible task,' Maram muttered, shaking his head.

'Don't you speak that way!' Liljana scolded him with a wag of her finger. 'The more you doubt, the harder you make it for Val to become king.'

'It's not his kingship that I doubt,' Maram said. 'At least, I don't doubt it on my *good* days. But even supposing that Val can win Mesh's warriors and knights where he couldn't before, what then? *That* is the question I've asked myself for a thousand miles.'

So had I asked myself this question. And I said to Maram simply, '*Then* Morjin must be defeated.'

'Defeated? Well, I suppose he must, yes, but defeated *how*?'

Master Juwain rubbed at the back of his brown-skinned head, then sighed out: 'The closer that we have come to our journey's end, the more sure I have become of what our course should be. I told this to Val years ago: that evil cannot be vanquished with a sword, and darkness cannot be defeated in battle but only by shining a bright enough light. And now, the brightest of lights has come into the world.'

He spoke, of course, of Bemossed: a slave whom we had rescued out of Hesperu on the darkest of all our journeys. A simple slave – and perhaps the great Maitreya and Lord of Light long prophesied for Ea and all the other worlds of Eluru. I couldn't help smiling in joy whenever I thought of this man whom I loved as a brother.

7

It gladdened my heart to know that he was well-hidden in the fastness of the White Mountains – in the safest place on Earth. And guarded from Morjin by Abrasax and the Seven: the Masters of the Great White Brotherhood whose virtues in healing, meditation and the other ancient arts exceeded even those of Master Juwain.

'Morjin retains the Lightstone,' Master Juwain continued, 'but Bemossed keeps him from twisting it toward his purpose. Soon, I think, with Bemossed so well-instructed, he will be able to grasp the Lightstone's radiance, if not the cup itself. And then . . .'

Liljana caught his gaze and said, 'Please don't mind me – go on.'

'And then,' Master Juwain said, 'Bemossed will bring this radiance into all lands. Men will feel an imperishable life shining within them like a star. Truth will flourish. So will courage. Men will no longer listen to the lies of wicked kings and the Kallimun priests who serve Morjin. They will resist these dark ones with their every thought and action – and eventually they will cast them down. Then new kings will follow Val's example here in creating a just and enlightened realm, and they will rebuild our Brotherhood's schools in every land. The schools will be open to all: not just to kings' and nobles' sons, and the gifted. Then the true knowledge will flourish along with the higher arts, as it was in the Age of Law. And as it came to be during the reign of Sarojin Hastar, there will be a council of kings, and a High King, and all across Ea, men will turn once more toward the Law of the One.'

While Master Juwain paused in his speech to draw in a breath of air, Liljana kept silent as she stared at him.

'And *then*,' Master Juwain said, 'we will finally build the civilization that we were sent here from the stars to build. In time, through the great arts and the Maitreya's splendor, men will become more than men, and we will rejoin the Elijin and Galadin as angels out in the stars. And then the Galadin will make ready a new creation and become the luminous beings we call the Ieldra, and the Age of Light will begin.'

Master Juwain, I thought, had spoken simply and even eloquently of the Great Chain of Being and its purpose. But his words failed to stir Liljana. She stood with her hands planted on her wide hips as she practically spat out at him: 'Men, kings, laws – and this *becoming* that keeps you always looking to the stars! Your order's old dream. In the Age of the *Mother*, women and men needed no laws to live in peace on *this* world – no law other than

8

love of the world. And each other. Why become at all when we are already so blessed? So *alive*? If only we could remember this, there would be a quickening of the whole earth, and men such as Morjin wouldn't live out another season. We would rid ourselves of his kind as nature does a rabid dog or a rotten tree.'

Most of the time, Liljana seemed no more than a particularly vigorous grandmother who had a talent for cooking and keeping body and soul together. But sometimes, as she did now in the strength that coursed through her sturdy frame and the adamantine light that came over her face, she took on the mantle of the Materix of the Maitriche Telu.

Atara stepped between Liljana and Master Juwain, and she held her blindfolded head perfectly still. Then she said, 'The Age of the Mother decayed into the Age of Swords because of the evil that men such as Morjin called forth. And Morjin himself put an end to the Age of Law and brought on these terrible times. So long as he draws breath, he will never suffer kings such as Val to arise while he himself is cast down.'

'No, I'm afraid you are right,' Master Juwain said, nodding his head at her. 'And here we must look to Bemossed, too. I believe that he *is* the Maitreya. And so I must believe that somehow he will heal Morjin of the madness that possesses him. I know this is *his* dream.'

And I knew it, too, though it worried me that Bemossed might blind himself to the totality of Morjin's evil and dwell too deeply on this healing that Master Juwain spoke of. Was it truly possible, I wondered? Could the Great Beast ever atone for the horrors that he had wreaked upon the world – and himself – and turn back toward the light?

It took all the force of my will and the deepest of breaths for me to say, 'I would see Morjin healed, if that could be. But I *will* see him defeated.'

'Oh, we are back to that, are we?' Maram groaned. He looked at me as he licked his lips. 'Why can't it be enough to keep him at bay, and slowly win back the world, as Master Juwain has said? That would be a defeat, of sorts. Or – I am loath to ask this – do you mean he must be *defeated* defeated, as in –'

'I mean utterly defeated, Maram. Cast down from the throne he falsely claims, reviled by all as the beast he is, imprisoned forever.' I gripped my sword's hilt as a wave of hate burned through me. 'Or killed, finally, fittingly, and even the last whisper of his lying breath utterly expunged from existence.'

9

As Maram groaned again and shook his head, Master Juwain said to me, 'That is something that Kane might say.'

My friends stood around regarding me. Although I was glad for their companionship, I was keenly aware that we should have numbered not eight but nine. For Kane, the greatest of all warriors, had ridden off to Galda to oppose Morjin through knife, sword and blood, in any way he could.

'Kane,' I told Master Juwain, 'would say that I should stab my sword through Morjin's heart and cut off his head. Then cleave his body into a thousand pieces, burn them and scatter the ashes to the wind.'

Maram's ruddy face blanched at this. 'But how, Val? You cannot defeat him in battle.'

'We defeated him in Argattha, when we were outnumbered a hundred against nine,' I told him. 'And on the Culhadosh Commons when he sent three armies against us. And we defeated his droghuls *and* his forces in the Red Desert – and in Hesperu, too.'

'But that was different, and you know it!' Maram's face now heated up with anger – and fear. 'If you seek battle, none of the Valari kings will stand with you. And even if they did, Morjin will call up *all* his armies, from every one of his filthy kingdoms. A million men, Val! Don't tell me you think Mesh's ten thousand could prevail against *that*!'

Did I truly think that? If I didn't, then I must at least act as if I did. I looked at Atara, whose face turned toward me as she waited for me to speak. Then it came to me that bravura was one thing, while truly believing was another. And knowing, with an utter certainty of blood and breath that I could not fail to strike down Morjin, was of an entirely different order.

'There must be a way,' I murmured.

'But, Val,' Master Juwain reminded me, 'it has always been *your* dream to bring an end to these endless battles – and to war, itself.'

For a moment I closed my burning eyes because I could not see how to defeat Morjin other than through battle. But neither could I imagine any conceivable force of Valari or other free people defeating Morjin *in* battle. Surely, I thought, that would be death.

'There *must* be a way,' I told Master Juwain. I drew my sword then. My hands wrapped around the seven diamonds set into its black jade hilt while I gazed at Alkaladur's brilliant blade. 'There is always a way.'

The silver gelstei of which it was wrought flared with a wild, white light. Somewhere within this radiance, I knew, I might grasp my fate – if only I could see it.

'You will never,' Master Juwain said, 'bring down Morjin with your sword.'

'Not with *this* sword, perhaps. Not just with it.'

'Please,' Master Juwain said, stepping closer to lay his hand on my arm, 'give Bemossed a chance to work at Morjin in *his* way. Give it time.'

A shard of the sun's light reflected off my sword's blade, and stabbed into my eyes. And I told Master Juwain, 'But, sir – I am afraid that we do not have much time.'

Just then, from out of the shadows that an oak cast upon the raspberry bush, a glimmer of little lights filled the air. They began whirling in a bright spray of crimson and silver, and soon coalesced into the figure of a man. He was handsome of face and graceful of body, and had curly black hair, sun-browned skin and happy eyes that seemed always to be singing. We called him Alphanderry, our eighth companion. But we might have called him something other, for although he seemed the most human of beings, he was in his essence surely something other, too. At times, he appeared as that sparkling incandescence we had known as Flick; but more often now he took shape as the beloved minstrel who had been killed nearly three years previously in the pass of the Kul Moroth. None of us could explain the miracle of his existence. Master Juwain hypothesized that when the great Galadin had walked the earth ages ago, they had left behind some shimmering part of their being. But Alphanderry, I thought, could not be just pure luminosity. I could almost feel the breath of some deep thing filling up his form with true life; a hand set upon his shoulder would pass through him and send ripples through his glistening substance as with a stone cast into water. Day by day, as the earth circled the sun and the sun hurtled through the stars, it seemed that he might somehow be growing ever more tangible and real.

'Hoy!' he laughed out, smiling at Master Juwain and me. As it had once been with my brother, Jonathay, something in his manner suggested that life was a game to be played and enjoyed for as long as one could, and not taken too seriously. But today, despite his light, lilting voice, his words struck us all with their great seriousness: 'Hoy, time, time! – it runs like the Poru river into the ocean, does it not? And we think that, like the Poru, it is inexhaustible and will never run out.'

'What do you mean?' Master Juwain asked, looking at him.

Alphanderry stood – if that was the right word – on a mat of old leaves and trampled ferns covering the ground. And he waved his lithe hand at me, and said, 'Val is right, and too bad for that. We don't have as much time as we would like.'

'But how do you know?' Master Juwain asked him.

'I just *know*,' he said. 'We can't let Bemossed bear the entire burden of our hope.'

'But our hope, in the end, rests upon the Lightstone. And the Maitreya. As you saw, Bemossed *has* kept Morjin from using it.'

'I did see that, I did,' Alphanderry said. 'But what *was* will not always be what *is*.'

Atara, I saw, smiled coldly at this, for Alphanderry suddenly sounded less like a minstrel than a scryer.

'Did you think it would be so easy?' he asked Master Juwain.

'Easy? No, certainly not,' Master Juwain said. 'But I believe with all my heart that as long as Bemossed lives, Morjin will never be able to use the Cup of Heaven to free the Dark One.'

The hot Soldru sun burned straight down through the clearing with an inextinguishable splendor. And yet, upon Master Juwain's mention of the Dark One – also known as Angra Mainyu, the great Black Dragon – something moved within the unmovable heavens, and I felt a shadow fall over the sun. It grew darker and darker, as if the moon were eclipsing this blazing orb. In only moments, an utter blackness seemed to devour the entire sky. I believed with all *my* heart that if Angra Mainyu, this terrible angel, were ever freed from his prison on Damoom, then he would destroy not only my world and its bright star, but much of the universe as well.

Master Juwain's brows wrinkled in puzzlement as he looked up at the sky to wonder what I might be gazing at. So did my other friends, who seemed not to be afflicted by my wild imaginings.

'The Seven,' Master Juwain said, turning back towards Alphanderry, 'aid Bemossed with all their powers. And so Bemossed's power grows.'

'So does Morjin's,' Alphanderry said. 'For Angra Mainyu aids *him*.'

'Even so, I believe that Bemossed will resist Morjin's lies and his vile attacks.'

'I pray he will; I fear that he may not. For Angra Mainyu himself has lent all his spite toward assaulting Bemossed's body, mind and soul.'

Master Juwain's brows pulled even tighter with worry. 'But how do you know this? And how can that be? The greatest of the

Galadin have bound him on Damoom, and have laid protections against such things.'

'No shield is proof against all weapons,' Alphanderry said. 'Angra Mainyu has had ages of ages to battle those who bind him. The shield you speak of has cracked. And things will only get worse.'

'What do you mean?'

'Some time this autumn,' Alphanderry said, 'there will be a great alignment of planets and stars. Damoom and *its* star will perfectly conjunct the earth. Toward that day, Angra Mainyu's malice will rain down upon Ea ever more foul and deadly. And *on* that day, if Morjin should prevail and cripple Bemossed, or kill him, he will loose the Dark One upon the universe, and all will be destroyed.'

The sun blazed down upon us, and from somewhere in the woods, the tanager continued trilling out its sweet song. We stood there in silence staring at Alphanderry. And then Master Juwain asked him again, 'But how *could* you know this?'

'I do not know . . . how I know,' Alphanderry said. 'As I stand here, as I speak, the words come to my lips, like drops of dew upon the morning grass – and I do not know what it will be that I must tell you. But my words are true.'

So it had been, I thought, in the Kul Moroth, when Alphanderry had recreated the perfect and true words of the angels – and for a few glorious moments had sung back an entire army bent on killing us all.

'And *these* words, above all others,' he said to us in his beautiful voice. 'Listen, I know this must be, for it is the essence of all that we strive for: *The Lightstone must be placed in the Maitreya's hands.* In the end, of course, there is no other way.'

He had said a simple thing, a true thing, and as with all such, it seemed obvious once it had been spoken. My heart whispered that it must be *I* who delivered the golden cup to the Maitreya. But how *could* I, I wondered, unless I first wrested it from Morjin in that impossible battle I could not bear to contemplate?

I held my sword up to the sun, and I felt something within its length of bright silustria align perfectly with other suns beyond Ea's deep blue sky. My fate, shaped like the dark world of Damoom, seemed to come hurtling out of black space straight toward me. In the autumn, I knew, it would find its way here and drive me down against the hard earth. Despite all my hopes and dreams, I could no more avoid it than I could the blood burning through my eyes or taking my next breath.

'Val – what is wrong?' Maram asked me. 'What do you see?'

13

I saw the forests of Mesh blackened by fire, and her mountains melted down into a hellish, glowing slag. I saw Maram fallen dead upon a vast battlefield, and my other companions, too. Atara lay holding her hands over her torn, bleeding belly, from which our child had been taken and ripped into pieces. I saw myself: as cold as stone upon the reddened grass, unmoving and waiting for the carrion birds. And something else, the worst thing of all. As I stood there beneath the trees staring into my sword's mirrored surface, I gasped at the dread cutting through my innards like an ice-cold knife, and I wanted to scream out against the horror that I could not bear.

And at that moment, in the air near the center of the clearing, a dark thing appeared. Altaru, my great, black warhorse, whinnied terribly and reared up to kick his hooves at the air. I jumped back and swept my sword into a ready posture, for I feared that Morjin *had* somehow sent a vulture or some kind of deadly creature to devour me – either that or I had fallen mad.

'Oh, my Lord!' Maram cried out, drawing out his sword, too.

'What is *that*?' Daj asked, hurrying to my side.

'Hoy!' Alphanderry cried out in alarm. 'Hoy! Hoy!'

Once, Morjin had sent illusions to torment me, but the darkness facing me seemed as real as a river's whirlpool. It hovered over the ferns and flowers like a spinning blackness. My eyes had trouble holding onto it. It shifted about, and seemed to have no definite size or shape, for at one moment it appeared as a smear of char and at the next as a mass of frozen ink. I felt it fixing its malevolence on me. I took a step closer to it and positioned my sword, and it floated closer and seemed to mirror my movements as it positioned itself before me. A vast and terrible cold emanated from it, and seized hold of my heart. It called to me in a dark voice that I could not bear to hear.

'What *is* it?' Daj shouted again.

And Alphanderry, in a voice filled with awe, told him, 'It is the Ahrim.'

I did not have time to speculate on this strange name or wonder at the dark thing's nature, for it suddenly shot through the air straight toward me. I whipped my sword up to stop it. The gleam of my bright blade seemed to give it pause. Like a whirl of smoke, it spun slowly about in the air three feet from my face. Somehow, I thought, it watched and waited for me. I felt sick with hopelessness and a mind-numbing dread. Although it did not seem to bear for me any kind of human hate, I hated it, for I sensed that

14

the Ahrim was that soul-destroying emptiness which engendered pure hate itself.

'Valashu Elahad,' it seemed to whisper to me.

I gripped my sword and shook my head. The dark thing had no form nor face nor lips with which to move the air, and yet I heard its voice speaking to me along a strange and sudden wind. And then, in a flash, it shifted yet again, and its secret substance took on the lineaments of a face I knew too well: that of Salmelu Aradar. It was an ugly face, nearly devoid of a chin or any redeeming feature. His great beak of a nose pointed at me, as did his black and beadlike eyes. I hated the way he looked at me, deep into *my* eyes, and so I brought up my sword to block his line of sight. And his head, like a cobra's, swayed to the right, and I repositioned my sword, and then again to the left as he seemed to seek access in that direction to the dark holes in my eyes. And so it went, our motions playing off each other, almost locked together, faster and faster as it had been during our duel of swords in King Hadaru's hall when Salmelu had nearly killed me, and I had nearly killed him.

'Valashu,' he whispered again, 'I wish you had seen your *mother's* eyes when we crucified and ravished her in your father's hall.'

A dark fire leaped in my heart then, and I fought with all my will to keep it from burning out of my arms and hands into my sword. But my restraint availed me nothing. Salmelu roared out in triumph, and then he was Salmelu no more. The blackness of his being metamorphosed yet again, this time into a thing of scales, wings and a savagely swaying tail.

'The dragon!' Daj cried out from beside me. 'The dragon returns!'

I set my hand on Daj's shoulder, and shouted to Liljana, 'Take the children into the trees!'

I could not spare a moment to watch Liljana gather up Daj and Estrella and carry out my command. The Ahrim, now shaped as a dragon, even as Daj had said, hung in the air before me with an almost delicate poise. It seemed to feed on the fire inside me, and make it its own; in mere moments it grew into a raging, red beast fifty feet in length. I recognized this terrible dragon as Angraboda, into whose belly I had once plunged my sword in the deeps of Argattha. And now Angraboda regarded me with her fierce, cold, vengeful eyes. Then her leather wings beat at the air in a thunder of wind as she flew straight up toward the sun. She grew vaster and vaster and ever darker, and her bloated body blocked out the sun's light and seemed to fill all the sky. She opened her mighty jaws to spit down fire at me and burn me into nothingness. And I felt the hateful fire building inside me, inciting me into a madness to destroy her.

ANGRABODA!

From a thousand miles and years away, I heard myself cry out this name as I readied myself to slay this beast yet again. But dragons cannot be harmed by such fire; only the fulgor of the red gelstei or the stars can pierce through their iron-like scales to a dragon's heart. And so I drew in a deep breath and willed the fire within me to blaze hotter, purer and brighter until I could not hold it anymore, and it poured out into my sword. For one perfect moment, Alkaladur flared with all the brilliance of a star. Maram and Master Juwain cried out in pain at this fierce light. And so did the dragon. Then her jaws closed, and so did her great, golden eyes, and for a moment I thought that I *had* slain her. But the Ahrim, I sensed, might be unkillable. All at once the dragon's immensity dissolved again into a blackness that sifted down through the air like soot. And as it fell to earth, the powdery-like particles of its essence reassembled themselves into the form of yet another man – or rather, a once-bright being who was something more than a man.

'Elahad,' he called out to me in a strong, beautiful voice that carried all the command of death. 'The common murderer who would be king.'

Morjin, for such the Ahrim had now become, stood before me and bowed his gold-haired head to me. His golden eyes twisted screws of hate into my eyes, and I could not look away from him, nor could I lift my sword to block his fearful gaze. From somewhere off in the trees, Daj shouted out in detestation and dread of his old master. Atara, to my right, fitted an arrow to her bowstring and loosed it at him. But the arrow sailed right through his shadowed substance as if it were a cloud.

He paid her no attention, but only continued to stare at me. He appeared as he had been in his youth before his fall: fine of feature, golden-skinned and graceful in his bearing. The compassion in his eyes gleamed almost like gold.

'Morjin!' I shouted out. At last, I managed to raise up my sword.

His smile chilled me. Then he opened his mouth and breathed at me, almost as if he were blowing a kiss. No fire shot forth to scorch me, but only a bit of blackness from which he was made. I lifted my sword still higher, but I moved in vain, for it flowed around my bright blade as oil would a stick. And then his breath fell upon my head and arms, smothering me, blinding me. An unbearable cold burned through my skin deep into my bones. I stood as for an hour inside a lightless and airless cavern, gasping and coughing for breath.

'Valashu Elahad, look at me!' his hateful voice commanded. All at once, the black fog cleared from around my head, and I could not keep myself from staring at him. 'You cannot defeat me.'

My fingers seemed frozen around the hilt of my sword, with all my joints locked and shrieking in pain. I could not even blink my eyes. My heart, though, still beat within me, quick and hard and hurtful, almost as with a will of its own. At last I found *my* will, and I raised back my sword.

'Val, do not!' Atara called out from somewhere near me. 'Do not!'

I could not listen to her. I looked on in loathing as Morjin smiled at me and his features took on their true cast to reveal the hideous man that he had become: sagging flesh all pale with rot, stringy white hair and bloodshot eyes raging with hate. I struck out with my sword then, driving the gleaming point straight into his face. Nothing stopped this murderous thrust; it was as if I drove my sword through pure black air. And yet I felt a resistance to my sword's silustria and its cutting edges, not of flesh and bone, but of spite and pain and cold. I fought this piercing numbness, and pulled back my sword. I stared at it in fury, for somehow the Ahrim's substance had turned it black, like frozen iron. Then I stared at Morjin in horror, for even as I watched, his face became as my own, only blackened and twisted with hate.

'You cannot defeat me,' he said to me again.

Or perhaps it was the Ahrim that spoke these words to me, or myself – I could not tell. But some irresistible force moved the features of the thing standing before me.

There is a fear so terrible and deep that it turns one's insides into a mass of sickened flesh and makes it seem that life cannot go on another moment. I stood there shaking and sweating and wanting to vomit up my very bowels. I knew that the dark thing standing before me had the power to kill me – and worse. But I seemed to have no power over it.

'Val, fight!' Maram shouted out from my left.

I was vaguely aware that he had sheathed his sword and taken out his firestone, for the long ruby crystal caught the sun's rays in a glint of red light. And then, guided by Maram's hand and heart, the crystal drank up the sun's blaze and gave it out as a bolt

17

of pure fire that streaked straight into the Ahrim. I felt the heat of this blast, but the Ahrim felt nothing. The face that seemed so very much my own just smiled at Maram as the black cavern of its mouth seemed ready to drink up more of Maram's fire and his very life – and the lives of Master Juwain and Atara, too.

'Yes, Val, fight!' Atara called out to me, as she stood in a spray of crushed flowers by my side.

I stared at the dreadful thing wearing my face, and I wanted to fight it with every beat of my heart and down to my last breath. But how could I destroy something that was already nothing?

'You know the way!' Atara called to me again. 'As it was at the farmhouse with the droghul!'

I glanced off into the trees, where Estrella stood looking at me. She seemed to have no fear of the Ahrim, but a great and terrible concern for me. I could feel her calling out to me in silence that I must always remember who I really was.

Then the Ahrim moved nearer to me – drawn, I sensed, by my blood and the kirax burning through it. Burning, yes, always hot and hateful, but something in this bitter poison seemed to awaken me to the immensity of pain that was life. And not just my own, but that of the trees standing around me tall and green, and the birds that made their nests among them, and the bees buzzing in the flowers, and everything. But life is much more than suffering. In all the growing things around me, I felt as well a wild joy and overflowing delight in just being alive. This was my gift, to sense in other creatures and people their deepest passions; Kane had once named this magic connection of mine as the *valarda*.

'Valashu,' the Ahrim seemed to whisper to me as it raised up its arm and opened out its fingers to me. 'Take my hand.'

But Atara's words sounded within me, too, as did Estrella's silence and the song of the tanager piping out sweet and urgent from somewhere nearby. I finally caught sight of this little bird across the clearing to my right, perched high in the branches of a willow tree. It was a scarlet tanager, all round and red like the brightest of flowers. In the way it cocked its head toward me and sang just for me, it seemed utterly alive. Its heart beat even more quickly than did my own, like a flutter of wings, and it called me to take joy in the wild life within myself. There, too, I remembered, blazed a deep and unquenchable light.

'Valashu Elahad.'

The Ahrim, I sensed, like a huge, blood-blackened tick, wanted my life. Very well, then I would give it that, and something more.

18

'Val!' Maram cried out to me. 'Do what Atara said! What are you waiting for?'

At the farmhouse, Morjin had been unable to bear my anguish of love for my murdered family. What was it, I wondered, that the Ahrim could not bear? Its immense and terrifying anguish seemed to pour out through its black eyes and outstretched hand.

'Now, Val!' Master Juwain called to me. He stood staring at the Ahrim as he lifted his glowing, emerald crystal toward me in order to quicken the fires of my life.

Kane had told me, too, that I held inside my heart the greatest of weapons. It was what my gift became when I turned my deepest passion outward and wielded the valarda to open *others'* hearts and brighten their souls. As I wielded it now. With Master Juwain feeding me the radiance of his green gelstei, and my other friends passing to me all that was beautiful and bright from within their own beings, I struck out at the Ahrim. Master Juwain believed that darkness could never be defeated by the sword, but he meant a length of honed steel and destruction, and not a sword of light.

ELAHAD!

For what seemed an age, all that was within me passed into the Ahrim in a blinding brilliance. But it was not enough. The Ahrim did not disintegrate into a shower of sparks, nor shine like the sun, nor did it disappear back into the void, like a snake swallowing its own tail. I sensed that I had only stunned it, if that was the right word, for it suddenly shrank into a ball of blackness and floated over toward an oak tree at the edge of the clearing. It seemed still to be watching me.

'You have no power over me!' I shouted at it. But my angry words seemed to make it grow a bit larger and even blacker, if that was possible.

Atara came up to me then, and laid her hand on my ice-cold hands, still locked onto the hilt of my sword. And she said to me, 'Do not look at it. Close your eyes and think of the child that someday we'll make together.'

I did as she asked, and my heart warmed with the brightest of hopes. And when I opened my eyes, the Ahrim had disappeared.

'But where did it go?' Maram asked, coming over to me. 'And will it return?'

Daj came running out of the trees toward me, followed by Liljana and Estrella. All my friends gathered around me. And I told them, 'It will return. In truth, I am not sure it is really gone.'

As I stood there trying to steady my breathing, I still felt the dark thing watching me, from all directions – and from my *insides*, as if it could look out at me through my very soul.

'But what *is* it?' Daj asked yet again. He turned toward Alphanderry, who had remained almost rooted to the clearing's floor during the whole time of our battle. 'You called it the Ahrim. What does that mean?'

'Hoy, the Ahrim, the Ahrim – I do not know!'

'I suppose the name just came to you?' Maram said, glaring at him.

'Yes, it did. Like –'

'Drops of blood on a cross!' Maram snapped. 'That thing is *evil*.'

'So are all of Morjin's illusions,' Liljana said. 'But that was no illusion.'

'No, certainly not,' Master Juwain said. Now he, too, touched his hand to my hands. He touched my face and told me, 'Your fingers are frozen – and your nose and cheeks are frostbitten.'

I would have looked at myself in Alkaladur's shimmering surface, but the silustria was an ugly black and I could see nothing.

'It was so cold,' I said. 'So impossibly cold.'

I watched as the sun's rays fell upon my sword and the blade slowly brightened to a soft silver. So it was with my dead-white flesh: the warm spring air thawed my face and hands with a hot pain that flushed my skin. Master Juwain held his green crystal over me to help the healing along. Soon I found that I could open and close my fingers at will, and I did not worry that they would rot with gangrene and have to be cut off. But forever after, I knew, I would feel the Ahrim's terrible coldness burning through me, even as I did the kirax in my blood.

A sudden gleam of my sword gave me to see a truth to which I had been blind. And I said to Alphanderry, with much anger, 'You *do* know things about the Ahrim, don't you? It has something to do with the Skadarak, doesn't it?'

At the mention of this black and blighted wood at the heart of Acadu, Alphanderry hung his head in shame. And then he found the courage to look at me as he said, 'It was there, waiting, Val. During our passage, it attached itself to you. It has been following you ever since.'

'Following!' I half-shouted. 'All the way to Hesperu, and back, to the Brotherhood's school? And then here, to my home? Why could I not see it? And why could Abrasax not see it – he who can see almost everything?'

Again, Alphanderry shrugged his shoulders.

20

'But how is it,' I demanded, 'that *you* can see it?'

It was Daj who answered for him. He passed his hand through Alphanderry's watery-like form, and said, 'But how not, since they are made of the same substance!'

Master Juwain regarded the glimmering tones that composed Alphanderry's being. He said, 'Similar, perhaps, but certainly not the same.'

I waved my hand at such useless speculations, and I called out to Alphanderry, 'But why did you never tell me of this thing?'

The look on his face was that of a boy stealing back to his room after dark. He said to me simply, 'I didn't want to worry you, Val.'

'Oh, excellent, excellent!' Maram muttered, shaking his head. 'Well, *I* am worried enough for all of us, now. What I wonder is why that filthy Ahrim, whatever it is, attacked us *here*? And more important, what will keep it away?'

But none of us, not even Alphanderry, had an answer to these questions. As it was growing late, it seemed the best thing we could do would be to leave these strange woods behind us as soon as possible.

'Come,' I said, clapping Maram on the shoulder. 'Let's go get some of that roast beef and beer you've been wanting for so long.'

After that, I pulled myself up onto Altaru's back, and my friends mounted their horses, too. I pointed the way toward Lord Harsha's farm with all the command and assurance that I could summon. But as we rode off through the shadowed trees, I felt the dark thing called the Ahrim still watching me and still waiting, and I knew with heaviness in my heart that it would be no easy task for me to become king.

2

We came out of the woods with the late sun touching the farmland of the Valley of the Swans with an emerald blaze. To the west, the three great mountains, Telshar, Arakel and Vayu, rose up as they always had with their white-capped peaks pointing into the sky. Lord Harsha's large stone house stood framed against the sacred Telshar: a bit of carved and mortared granite almost lost against the glorious work of stone that the Ieldra had sung into creation at the beginning of time. We caught Lord Harsha out weeding his wheatfield to the east of his house. When he heard the noise of our horses trampling through the bracken, he straightened up and shook his hoe at us as he peered at us with his single eye. He called out to us: 'Who is it who rides out of the wildwood like outlaws at this time of day? Announce yourselves, or I'll have to go and get my sword!'

Lord Harsha, I thought, would prove a formidable opponent against outlaws – or anyone else – with only his iron-bladed hoe to wield as a weapon. Despite a crippled leg and his numerous years, his thick body retained a bullish power. And even though he wore only a plain woolen tunic, he bore on his finger a silver ring showing the four brilliant diamonds of a Valari lord. A black eyepatch covered part of his face; twelve battle ribbons had been tied to his long, white hair, and in all of Mesh, there were few warriors of greater renown.

'Outlaws, is it?' I called back to him. 'Have our journeys really left us looking so mean?'

So saying, I threw back the hood of my cloak and rode forward a few more paces. I came to the low wall edging Lord Harsha's field. Once, I remembered, I had sat there with Maram, my brother Asaru and his squire, Joshu Kadar, as we had spoken with Lord

22

Harsha about fighting the Red Dragon and ending war – and other impossible things.

'Who *is* it?' Lord Harsha called out again. His single eye squinted as the sun's slanting rays burned across my face. 'Announce yourself, I say!'

'I am,' I called back to him, 'the seventh son of Shavashar Elahad, whose father was King Elkamesh, who named me –'

'Valashu Elahad!' Lord Harsha shouted. 'It can't be! But surely it *must* be, even though I don't know how!'

I dismounted and climbed over the wall. Lord Harsha came limping up to me, and he embraced me, pounding my back with his hard, blunt hands. Then he pulled back to fix me with his single, bright eye.

'It *is* you,' he said, 'but you look different, forgive me. Older, of course, but not so much on the outside as within. And something else. Something has lit a fire in you, like that star you were named for. At last. When you skulked out of Mesh last year, you did seem half an outlaw. But now you stand here like a king.'

I bowed my head to him, and he returned this grace, inclining his head an inch lower than mine. And he said to me, 'You have his look, you know.'

'*Whose* look?' I asked him.

'King Elkamesh's,' he said. 'When he was a young knight. I never saw the resemblance until today.'

I smiled at him, and told him, 'It is good to be home, Lord Harsha.'

'It is good to *have* you home.' His gaze took in Maram and my other companions, who had nudged their horses up to the wall and dismounted as well. And Lord Harsha pointed at Alphanderry and said, 'I count eight of you, altogether, and eight it was who set out for Argattha. But here rides a stranger in Kane's place. Don't tell me such a great warrior has fallen!'

'He has *not* fallen,' I said, 'as far as I know. But circumstances called him to Galda. And as for Argattha, we did not journey there after all.'

'No – that is clear. If you had, we would not be gathered here having this discussion. But where then *did* you journey?'

I looked at Maram, who said, 'Ah, *that* is a long story, sir. Might we perhaps discuss it over dinner? For more miles than I can tell you, I've been hoping to sit down to some of Behira's roast beef and few glasses of your excellent beer.'

At the mention of his daughter's name, I felt something inside Lord Harsha tighten, and he said to Maram, 'It's been a bad year, as you will find out, and so you will have to settle on some chops of lamb or perhaps a roasted chicken. But beer we still have in abundance – surely Behira will be glad to pour you all you can drink.'

He motioned for us to follow him, and we led our horses around his field toward his house. Although I still felt a dark presence watching my every movement, Lord Harsha seemed completely unaware of the Ahrim or that we had fought a battle for our lives scarcely an hour before. As we passed the barn and drew up closer to the house, he called out in his gruff voice: 'Behira – come out and behold what the wind has blown our way!'

A few moments later, the thick wooden door of the house opened, and Lord Harsha's only remaining child stepped out to greet us. Like Lord Harsha, Behira was sturdy of frame and wore a rough woolen tunic gathered in with a belt of black leather. With her ample breasts and wide hips that Maram so appreciated, my mother had once feared that Behira might run to fat. But time had treated this young woman well, for she had lost most of her plumpness while retaining all that made her pretty, and more. Her long hair gleamed a glossy black like a sable's coat, and her large, lovely eyes regarded Maram boldly, and so with the rest of us. I might have expected that she would run out and fall into Maram's arms, but time had changed her in other ways, too. The rather demure and good-natured girl, it seemed, had become a proud and strong-willed woman.

'Lord Marshayk!' she called out to Maram with an uncomfortable formality. 'Lord Elahad! You've come back!'

So it went as she greeted all of us in turn, and then her gaze drew back to Maram. I sensed in her a churning sea of emotions: astonishment; shame; adoration; confusion. I felt hot blood burning up through her beautiful face as she said, 'Oh, but we've much to talk about, and you will all want a good hot bath before we do. I'll go and heat the water.'

And with that she bowed to us, and went back into the house. The explanations for her strange behavior, I thought, would have to wait until we cleaned ourselves. After Behira had filled the cedarwood tub in the bathing room, we went inside the house and took turns immersing our bodies in steaming hot water: first Atara, Liljana and Estrella took a rare pleasure in washing away their cares, and then Master Juwain, Maram, Daj and I. While Master Juwain and Daj were pulling on fresh tunics, Lord Harsha came into the wood-paneled bathing room to inform us that dinner would soon be ready. He eyed the strange, round scars marring

Maram's great hairy body, but did not remark upon them. He seemed to be waiting for a more appropriate moment to tell of things that he was loath to tell and to hear of things that he might not want to hear.

At last, when we were all well-scrubbed and attired in clean clothing, Lord Harsha called us to dinner at his long table just off his great room. As we were about to take our seats, the clopping of a horse's hooves against the dirt lane outside made me draw my sword and hurry over to the door. I said to Lord Harsha, 'We have enemies we haven't told you about, and we are not ready to make our presence known.'

'It's all right,' he said to me as he stood by the window and peered out into the twilight. 'It's only Joshu Kadar – in all the excitement, I forgot to tell you that we've invited him to dinner. Surely you can trust *him*.'

Surely, I thought, I could. Joshu had been Asaru's squire, and he had stood by the horses that day when Salmelu had shot me with his poisoned arrow – and he had served my brother faithfully at the Culhadosh Commons as well.

'All right,' I said, sheathing my sword and leaning it against the side of the table. 'But please let me know if you are expecting anyone else.'

Lord Harsha opened the door and invited Joshu inside. The youth I remembered from the days when Asaru and I had taught him fighting skills had grown into a powerful man nearly as tall as I. He wore a single battle ribbon in his long hair. With his square face and strong features, he had a sort of overbearing handsomeness that reminded me of my brother, Yarashan. But in his manner Joshu seemed rather modest, respectful and even sweet. The moment he saw me, he nearly dropped the bouquet of flowers that he was holding and called out happily: 'Lord Valashu! Thank the stars you have returned! We all thought you were dead!'

He bowed his head to me, then greeted Master Juwain with the great affection that many of my people hold for the masters of the Brotherhood. With perfect politeness he likewise said hello to the rest of our company, but when he came to Maram, I felt the burn of embarrassment heating up his face, and he could hardly speak to him. He gave his flowers to Behira, who put them in a blue vase which she set on the table along with platters of food and pitchers of dark, frothy beer.

There came an awkward moment as Lord Harsha took his place at the head of the table and Joshu sat down in the chair to his right. I had the place of honor at the opposite end of the table, with Maram to *my* right and Atara at my left. It seemed a strange thing for Alphanderry to join us, for he didn't so much sit upon his chair as occupy its space. He could of course eat no food nor imbibe no drink, and soon enough we would have to explain his strange existence as best we could. But as Behira seated herself across from Joshu, it came time for other explanations.

'Well, here it is,' Lord Harsha said, looking at Maram. Lord Harsha was not a man of subterfuge or nuance, and he had put off this unpleasant task longer than he had liked. 'We *did* think you were dead, and too bad for that. And so I had to promise my daughter to another.'

As Behira looked across the table at Joshu, and Joshu lowered his eyes toward the empty plate in front of him, Maram's ruddy face flushed an even brighter red. And he called out, 'But you said that you'd wait for our return!'

Lord Harsha sighed as he rubbed at his eye, and then said, 'We *did* wait, for as long as seemed wise. Longer than a year it was. But you had told us that you were going to Argattha, and so what was there really to wait *for*?'

As Maram fought back his rising choler, he fell strangely silent. And so I spoke for him, saying, 'We had indeed planned to go to Argattha, but in the end we set out on a different quest. My apologies if we misled you. It seemed the safest course, however, for then you could not betray our mission should any of our enemies come here and question you.'

Now Lord Harsha's face filled with a choler of its own. He rested his hand on the hilt of his sword, which he too had leaned against the edge of the table. He said, 'I have taken steel, wood and iron through my body in service of your father and grandfather, and have never betrayed anyone!'

I said to Lord Harsha: 'My apologies, sir. But you know what the Red Dragon and the Prince of Ishka did to my mother and grandmother. Don't be so sure you would be able to keep your silence if he did the same to your daughter.'

Lord Harsha removed his hand from his sword and made a fist. He looked at it a moment, before saying to me, 'No, my apologies, Lord Valashu. These are hard, bad times. You did what you had to do, as we have done. And it's good that we're gathered here together, for this is a family matter, and you and your friends are like family to Sar Maram. And so you should advise him on what our course should be.'

'What *can* our course be?' Maram said. 'Other than this: you promised Behira to me first! And promises must be kept!'

Lord Harsha pressed his hand against his eye patch as if he could still feel the piercing pain of the arrow that long ago had half-blinded him. And he said to Maram, 'On the field of the Raaswash more than two years ago, you promised to wed my daughter, and I still see no ring upon her finger.'

Now it was Behira's turn to make a fist as she set her right hand over her left.

'But I had duties!' Maram said to Lord Harsha. 'There were quests to be undertaken, journeys to be made, to Tria, across the Wendrush – and beyond. And the battles we fought were –'

'Excuses,' Lord Harsha snapped out. 'For three years, you've been making excuses and putting my daughter off. Well, now it's too late.'

'But I love Behira!' Maram half-shouted.

At this, Behira lifted up her head and turned to gaze down the table at Maram. Her face brightened with hope and longing. It was the first time, I thought, that either she or any of us had heard Maram announce his affection for her so openly.

'Love,' Lord Harsha said to Maram, 'is the fire that lights the stars, and wc should all surrender up our deepest love to the One that created them. And a father loves his daughter, which is why I promised Behira to you in the first place, for every hour I had to bear my daughter's talk of loving *you*. But everyone knows that such love matches often end unhappily. *That* kind of love is only for the stars, not for men and women, for it quickly burns out.'

At this, I reached over and took hold of Atara's hand. The warmth of her fingers squeezing mine reminded me of that bright and beautiful star to which our souls would always return. I did not believe that it could ever die.

'Are you saying,' Maram asked Lord Harsha, 'that a man should not love his wife?'

On the wall above the table hung a bright tapestry that Lord Harsha's dead wife had once woven. He gazed at it with an obvious fondness, and he said, 'Of course a man should come to love his wife. But it is best if marriage comes first, and so then a man does not let love sweep away his reason so that he loses sight of the more important things.'

'But what could be more important than love?' Maram asked.

And Lord Harsha told him, 'Honor, above all else.'

'But I had to honor my duty to Val, didn't I?'

Lord Harsha nodded his head. 'Certainly you did. But before you went off with him, you might have married my daughter and given her your name.'

'But I –'

'Too, you might have given her your estates, such as they are, and most important of all, a child.'

As the look of longing lighting up Behira's face grew even brighter, Maram closed his mouth, for he seemed to have run out of objections. And then he said, 'But our journeys were *dangerous*! You can't imagine! I didn't want to leave behind a fatherless child.'

Lord Harsha sighed at this, then said, 'In our land, since the Great Battle, there are many fatherless children. And too few men to be husbands to all the widows and maidens.'

All my life, I had heard of the ancient Battle of the Sarburn referred to in this way, but it seemed strange for Lord Harsha to give the recent Battle of the Culhadosh Commons that name as well.

'Sar Joshu himself,' Lord Harsha continued, 'lost his father and both his brothers there.'

Joshu looked straight at me then, and I felt in him the pain of a loss that was scarcely less than my own. I remembered that his mother had died giving him birth, while his two older sisters had been married off. Joshu had inherited his family's rich farm lands only a few miles from here, and who could blame Lord Harsha for wanting to join estates and take this orphan into his own family?

'Sar Joshu,' I said, looking down the table. I studied the two diamonds set into the silver ring that encircled his finger. 'Before the battle, my brother gave you your warrior's ring. And now you wear that of a knight?'

Sar Joshu bowed his head at this, but seemed too modest to say anything. And so Lord Harsha told us of his deeds: 'You came late, Lord Valashu, to the fight with the Ikurians, and so you did not witness Sar Joshu's slaying of two knights in defense of Lord Asaru. Nor the lance wound through his lung that unhorsed him and nearly killed him. In reward for his valor, Lord Sharad, Lord Avijan and myself agreed that he should be knighted.'

Now I could only bow my head to Joshu. 'Then Mesh has another fine knight to help make up for those who have fallen.'

'Nothing,' Joshu said, 'can ever replace those who fell at the Great Battle.'

I thought of my father and my six brothers, and I said, 'No, of course not. But as I have had to learn, life still must go on.'

'And that,' Lord Harsha said, 'is exactly the point I have been trying to make. Morjin's cursed armies cut down a whole forest of warriors and knights. It's time new seeds were planted and new trees were grown.'

I considered this as I studied the way that Joshu looked at Behira. I sensed in him a burning passion – but not for her.

'Sar Joshu,' I asked, 'have you ever been in love?'

He looked down at his hands, and he said simply, 'Yes, Lord Valashu.'

As Behira took charge of finally passing around the roasted chickens, blueberry muffins, mashed potatoes and asparagus that she had prepared for dinner, it came out that Joshu had indeed known the kind of all-consuming love that makes the very stars weep – and he still did. It seemed that he had been smitten by a young woman named Sarai Garvar, of the Lake Country Garvars. But a great lord had married her instead.

'My father was to have spoken with her father, Lord Garvar, after the battle,' Joshu told us. Although he shrugged his shoulders, I felt his throat tighten with a great sadness. 'But my father died, my brothers, too, and so it nearly was with me. And so I lost her to another. Everyone knows how bitter Lord Tanu was when the enemy killed his wife during the sack of the Elahad castle. So who can blame him for wanting to take a new wife? And who can blame Lord Garvar for wanting to make a match with one of Mesh's greatest lords?'

Lord Tanu, of course, had been not only my father's second-in-command but held large estates around Godhra, and his family owned many of the smithies there. As Joshu had said, who could blame any father for wanting to join fortunes with such a man?

'But Lord Tanu is *old*!' Behira suddenly called out as she banged a spoonful of potatoes against her plate. She seemed outraged less for Joshu's sake than for Lord Tanu's new wife. 'And Sarai is only my age!'

'Here, now!' Lord Harsha said, laying his hand upon her arm. 'Mind the crockery, will you? Your mother made it herself out of good clay before you were born!'

Behira looked down at the disk of plain earthenware before her, and she fell into a silence. And I said to Joshu, 'Then if any man should appreciate Maram's feelings in this matter, it is you.'

'I do,' he agreed, nodding his head sadly to Maram. 'But Lord Harsha is right: how can any man's feelings count at a time such as this?'

29

Although I sensed his sympathy for Maram, there was steel in him too, and great stubbornness. I knew that, having lost one prospective bride, he would not easily surrender what Lord Harsha had rightly deemed as a good match.

For a while we busied ourselves eating the hearty food that Behira had prepared us. For dessert, she brought out a cherry pie and cheese, and made us chicory tea as well. But Maram wanted something stronger than this – stronger even than the black beer that he had been swilling all through dinner. And so he announced that he had to retrieve a gift from the barn; he nudged my knee beneath the table to indicate that I should follow him.

We stepped out into a warm spring night full of chirping crickets and twinkling stars. We lit the lantern that Lord Harsha had given us, then went into the barn, with its smells of cattle and chicken droppings. We rummaged around in the saddlebags that we had placed on the straw near our horses' stalls. And Maram said to me, 'This is not the homecoming I had imagined.'

I nodded my head at this, then asked him: 'But can you really blame Lord Harsha for wanting what is best for Behira?'

'*I* am best for her!' Maram half-bellowed. Then his voice softened as he said, 'I love her – this time, I'm really sure that I do.'

I tried not to smile at this, and I said, 'But you *have* put off the wedding, again and again. Some might take this as a sign that you don't really want to marry her.'

'That doesn't mean I'm ready to let that little squire take her!'

'Sar Joshu,' I told him, 'is a full knight now, and a good man.'

'I don't care if he's a damn angel! He doesn't love Behira as I do, and she doesn't love him! Will you help with this, Val?'

I thought about this for a while then said, 'You're my best friend, but what I *won't* do is to help you make Behira into an old maid.'

'But I *will* marry her, if I can, as soon as our business here is done – I swear I will!'

'*Will* you?'

He found his sword resting upon a bale of hay, and drew it out of its scabbard. He laid his hand on the flat of the blade and said, 'I swear by all that I honor that I will marry Behira!'

I gripped his wrist, and urged him to sheathe his sword. Then I pointed at the bottle of brandy that Maram had pulled out of his saddlebags and set on top of the hay, too. I took his hand and placed it on the bottle.

'Swear by all that you *love*,' I told him, 'that you will marry her.'

'Ah, all right then – I do, I do!'

'Swear by *me*, Maram,' I said, looking at him.

In the lantern's flickering light, Maram looked back at me, and finally said, 'Sometimes I think you ask too much of me, but I *do* swear by you.'

'All right then,' I said, clapping him on the shoulder. I retrieved the lantern from its hook on one of the barn's wooden supports. 'I will do what I can. It may be that there is something that Sar Joshu desires much more than marriage.'

We went back into the house, and Maram presented the brandy to Lord Harsha as a gift. He told him, 'It's the last of the finest vintage I've ever tasted, and I've been saving this bottle for you for at least a thousand miles.'

'Thank you,' Lord Harsha said, holding up the bottle to the room's candles. Then, with a wry smile, he asked, 'Will you help me drink it?'

After Behira had retrieved some cups from the adjacent great room and Lord Harsha had poured a bit of brandy into each, I gave them presents, too. For Behira I had silk bags full of rare spices: anise, pepper, cardamom, clove. To Lord Harsha I gave a simple steel throwing knife. He hefted it in his rough hands and promised to add it to his collection of swords, knives, maces, halberds and other weapons mounted on the wall of his great room. When I told him the story behind the knife, he sat looking at me and shaking his head.

'This was Kane's, and he wanted you to have it,' I said to him. 'When we were made captive in King Arsu's encampment, one of Morjin's High Priests made Kane cast the knife at Estrella and split an apple placed on top of her head.'

Lord Harsha's hand closed around the knife's handle as he regarded Estrella in amazement – and concern.

But Estrella remained nearly motionless nibbling on a gooey cherry that she had plucked from a slice of pie. Her large, dark eyes filled with a strange light. In the past, she had suffered greater torments than that which the Kallimun priest, Arch Uttam, had inflicted on her. It was her grace, however, to dwell in the present, most of the time, and here and now she seemed to be happy just sitting safe and sound with those she loved.

'Well, you have stories to tell,' Lord Harsha called out, 'and we must hear them. Let's drink a toast to your safe return from wherever it was that the stars called you.'

So saying, he lifted up his cup, and we all joined him in drinking Maram's brandy.

'All right,' he said, 'it's clear that you haven't come home just to see Maram happily wed to my daughter.'

It came time to give an account of our journey. I said that we had set forth into the wilds of Ea on a quest to find the Maitreya. Many parts of our story I could not relate, or did not want to. It wouldn't do for Lord Harsha – or anyone – to learn the location of the Brotherhood's school or of the greatest of the gelstei crystals that they kept there. Of the terrible darkness I had found within myself in our passage of the Skadarak I kept silent, although I did speak of the Black Jade buried in the earth there and how this evil thing called out to capture one's soul. Likewise I did not want to have to explain to Behira that the round scars marking Maram's cheek and body had been torn into him by the teeth of a monstrous woman called Jezi Yaga. Nothing, however, kept me from telling of our journey through the Red Desert and crossing of the hellish and uncrossable Tar Harath. Behira listened in wonderment to the story of the little people's magic wood hidden in the burning sands of the world's worst wasteland – and how this Vild, as we called it, had quickened Alphanderry's being so that he could speak and dwell almost as a real man. She wanted to hear more of the Singing Caves of Senta than I could have related in a month of evenings. At last though, I had to move on to our nightmarish search through Hesperu: nearly the darkest and worst of all the Dragon kingdoms. It was there, I told Behira and her father, in a village called Jhamrul, that we had come across a healer named Bemossed.

'With a laying on of his hand,' I said to Lord Harsha, 'he healed a wound to Maram's chest that even Master Juwain could not heal. In Bemossed gathers all that is best and brightest in men. It is almost certain that he is the Maitreya.'

Lord Harsha sipped his brandy as he looked at me. He said, 'Once before you believed another was the Maitreya.'

Truly I had: myself. And the lies that I had told myself – and others – had inexorably brought Morjin's armies down upon my land and had nearly destroyed all that I loved.

'Once,' I said to Lord Harsha, 'I was wrong. This time I am not.'

Now Lord Harsha took an even longer pull at his brandy as his single eye fixed upon me. And he said to me, 'Something *has* changed in you, Lord Elahad. The way you speak – I cannot doubt that you tell the truth.'

'Then do not doubt this either: when it is safe, the Maitreya will come forth. The Free Kingdoms must be made ready for him. And *our* kingdom, before all others, must be set in order. It is why I have returned.'

'To become king!' he said as his eye gleamed. 'I knew it! Valashu Elahad, crowned King of Mesh – well, lad, I can't tell you how often I've wished that day would come!'

Then his face fell into a frown, and the light went out of him. 'But after what's happened, how *can* that day ever come?'

I noticed Joshu Kadar studying me intently, and I asked, 'Then has another already been made king?'

'What!' Lord Harsha said. 'Have you had no news at all?'

'No – we entered Mesh in secret, and have spoken to no one.'

'Likely, it's good that you haven't. There are those who would not want you to gain your father's throne. I can't think that they would resort to a knife in the back, but as I said, these are bad times.'

'Bad times, indeed,' I said, looking down the table at him, 'if you would even speak of such a thing.'

'Well, with your father having sired seven sons, I never thought I would live to see such a day: Mesh's throne empty, and at least three lords vying to claim it.'

I let my hand rest on my sword's hilt, and I said, 'Lord Tomavar, certainly.'

Lord Harsha nodded his head. 'He is the greatest contender – and he has become your enemy. He blames you for what happened to his wife.'

I looked down at my sword's great diamond pommel glimmering in the candlelight, and I thought of how Morjin's men had carried off the beautiful Vareva – most likely to ravishment and death. How could I blame Lord Tomavar for being stricken to his soul when I already blamed myself?

'Too many,' Lord Harsha told me, 'still believe that you abandoned the castle out of vainglory. And then told the baldest of lies.'

'But that itself is a lie!' Joshu Kadar called out. His hand pressed against his chest as if his brandy had stuck in his throat and burned him. 'Everyone who knows Valashu Elahad knows this! I have spoken of this everywhere! Many of my friends have, as well. Lord Valashu, they say, led us to victory in the Great Battle and should have been made king.'

'He *should* have,' Lord Harsha agreed with a sigh. 'But on the battlefield, five thousand warriors stood for Lord Valashu, and eight thousand against, and that is that.'

'That is *not* that!' Joshu half-shouted. It must have alarmed him, I sensed, to speak with such vehemence to a lord knight who might become his father-in-law. 'If the warriors were to stand again, they would acclaim Lord Valashu – I know they would!'

Lord Harsha sighed again, and he poured both Joshu and himself more brandy. And he said, 'If the warriors were free to gather and stand, it *might* be so. But we might as well hope that horses had wings so that we could just fly to battle.'

He told us then that Lord Tomavar had made many of the knights and warriors who followed him swear oaths of loyalty in support of his kingship. In order for them to stand for another, he would have to relieve them of their oaths. So it was with Lord Tanu and Lord Avijan, the two other major contenders for Mesh's throne.

'Lord Avijan!' I called out, shaking my head. This young lord resided in his family's castle near Mount Eluru just to the north of the Valley of the Swans. 'My father was very fond of him and trusted no man more.'

'And no man is more trustworthy,' Lord Harsha said. 'Of all Mesh's lords, none has spoken more forcefully in favor of your becoming king. But when you went off with your friends and did not return, he thought you must be dead, as everyone did. He never wanted to put himself forward against Lord Tomavar and Lord Tanu, but we persuaded him that he must.'

'*We*, Lord Harsha?' I said to him.

I felt the blood and brandy heating up his rough, old face as he said, 'Myself, yes, and Lord Sharad and Sar Jessu – and many others. Almost every warrior around Silvassu and the Valley of the Swans.'

'Then have you taken oaths to support Lord Avijan?'

Lord Harsha rubbed at his face to hide his shame. 'We *had* to. Otherwise we would have come under Lord Tomavar's boot, or Lord Tanu's. In any case . . .'

'Yes?'

'In any case, only one can become king, and we all agreed that no one deserves the throne more than Lord Avijan.'

I remained silent as I squeezed the hilt of my sword, and I felt Maram, Master Juwain and Liljana looking at me.

'No one, of course,' Lord Harsha went on, 'except yourself. But we all thought you would never return.'

I gazed at him and said, 'But I *have* returned.'

'That you have, lad,' he said. 'And Lord Avijan would release us all from our oaths and be the first to stand for you. But Lord

Tomavar commands six thousand warriors, and another four thousand follow Lord Tanu, and they will surely oppose you if you come forth.'

Although Atara, sitting near the middle of the table, kept her face still and stern, I could almost feel her heart beating in time with my own. I wondered if she had foreseen this moment in her scryer's crystal sphere or what might befall next.

'Will Lord Tanu and Lord Tomavar,' I asked Lord Harsha, 'oppose me so far as to go to war?'

I would rather die, I thought, than see Meshians slay Meshians.

'Who can say?' Lord Harsha muttered. 'These are bad times, very bad. And since the Great Battle, Mesh is weaker, much too weak. New trees we need to stand in the ranks and face our enemies, but we'll be a whole generation growing them. Our enemies know this. Already, it's said, the Waashians are looking for a way to attack us. And the Urtuk already have: they invaded through the Eshur pass last fall. They weren't many, only a thousand, and they might have been just testing our strength – and so Lord Tomavar's army threw them back easily enough. And then there is Anjo.'

'Anjo!' I said. 'But Anjo has never threatened us.'

'No, and that is exactly the point: Anjo hasn't had a real king in two hundred years, and can threaten no one. Her dukes and barons still battle each other bloody. You will not have heard that only two months ago, the Ishkans annexed Adar and Natesh. And King Hadaru still looks for other of Anjo's domains to bite off. Lord Tanu has vowed that this must never happen to Mesh.'

'And it must not!' I told him.

'No – and so Lord Tanu has said that Mesh must have a new king, and soon, if we don't want to wind up like Anjo. Lord Tomavar has said the same thing. They have each demanded that the other stand aside, and have made threats.'

'But if they make war upon each other,' I said, 'then they *would* make Mesh like Anjo!'

Lord Harsha shrugged his shoulders as his face fell sad and grave. He muttered into his cup of brandy: 'These are bad times, the worst of times, so who can blame an old man for wanting to see his daughter well-wed and give his grandson his first sword? Now, in your father's day, and your grandfather's, no one would ever have thought that –'

'Lord Harsha,' I said, with greater force. 'Will Lord Tomavar and Lord Tanu take up arms against *me*?'

With a jerk of his head, Lord Harsha downed the last of his brandy and sighed out, 'I don't know. Lord Tanu will be cautious, as always. Once he makes up his mind about something, though, he can strike fast and hold on like a bulldog. And Lord Tomavar . . .'

'Yes?' I said.

'Lord Tomavar is burning for vengeance now. Full of the blood madness, do you understand? His warriors captured thirty of the Urtuk – and Lord Tomavar accused them of helping Morjin escape across the steppe with Vareva. And so he had them hacked to death.'

'But that is not our way!'

'No, it is not,' he said. He let loose an even deeper sigh. 'And so what will he do when you come forth to claim your father's crown? That I don't *want* to know, lad.'

The sound of steel forks against earthen plates full of pie rang out into the narrow room, and echoed off the stone walls. I noticed Liljana concentrating all her attention on Behira and Joshu, while Master Juwain looked at me as if admonishing me to find a way of peace in a world full of hate and vengeful swords.

'What needs to be decided,' Lord Harsha finally said to me, 'is what *you* will do. Will you go to war for your father's throne, Valashu Elahad?'

Would I draw my sword against my countrymen, I wondered? I sat considering this while I gripped Alkaladur's hilt. As Lord Harsha had said, only one man could be king of Mesh.

'There must be a way without war,' I said to Lord Harsha, and everyone. 'If I could step aside and see Lord Avijan crowned king, I would. Or even Lord Tomavar or Lord Tanu. But from what has been said here tonight, this is not possible.'

'No,' Lord Harsha agreed, 'such a grace on your part might only make the situation worse.'

Atara, who had said little all during dinner, now drew forth her sparkling crystal, and told us: 'Neither Lord Tanu nor Lord Tomavar will ever be king. Nor Lord Avijan. It must be Val – or no one.'

I tried not to smile at Atara's seeming assurance. Most of the time, she refrained from saying such things. I could not tell if her words were a true prophecy or whether she wished the mere force of her statement to bring about the future that she willed to be.

I drew my sword a few inches out of its scabbard, and the flash of silustria warmed my blood. And I said, 'It *must* be me. I never wanted this, but what other choice is there?'

'But Val,' Maram said, 'what will you do? Coming forth now

will be *dangerous* – even more dangerous than we had thought. And what if Kane's worries prove out, and you find that some of your countrymen have joined the Order of the Dragon?'

At the mention of this secret society of blood drinkers and murderers who followed Morjin, Lord Harsha said, 'It is bad enough to know that Prince Salmelu went over to the Red Dragon, and is now a filthy priest who calls himself by the filthy name of Igasho. For even *one* Valari in all the Nine Kingdoms to turn traitor this way is a disgrace.'

He tapped his sword and said, 'Despite what I said earlier, I won't believe that any man of Mesh would ever dishonor himself so – I *won't*! And the warriors of the Valley of the Swan are as true as diamonds.'

'Yes,' Maram agreed with a nod of his head, 'but will they be true to *Val*?'

'Nine of ten will be – perhaps more.'

'But what of Lord Tanu, then? His army is only a two-day march away. And Lord Tomavar? How long would it take him to lead his six thousand here – a couple of days more?'

How long, indeed, would the hot-headed Lord Tomavar need to march his army from the northwest down across our small kingdom?

Lord Harsha frowned at this as he rubbed the lines creasing his face. He had never been a quick thinker or a brilliant one, but once he decided on a thing, his reasoning usually shone with good common sense.

'We had thought,' I said to him, 'that we might send out a call to those who would follow me to assemble at my father's castle.'

Lord Harsha slowly shook his head at this. 'That won't do, lad. The castle is all burned out, and it would take a week even to get the gates working again. And Lord Tanu might move before you had enough warriors to man the walls.'

He drummed his thick fingers on the table as he looked at me.

'What do you suggest then?' I asked him.

'Let's do this,' he said, looking at Joshu Kadar. 'Sar Joshu and I will ride out tomorrow and gather up those we absolutely trust. We'll escort you to Lord Avijan's castle, where you'll be safe. And then we'll put out the word that Valashu Elahad has returned to Mesh. Two thousand warriors have sworn oaths to Lord Avijan, and another thousand, at least, look to the weather vane to see which way the wind will blow. Let's see how many will declare for you.'

I thought about this for a while as I traded glances with Maram, Master Juwain and Liljana. Atara inclined her head toward me. Then I told Lord Harsha: 'Very well, then, it will be as you have said.'

Our decision so stirred Joshu that he whipped forth his sword and raised it up toward me. 'Tomorrow morning I will speak with Viku Aradam and Shivalad and a dozen others! I know they'll all ride with you, Sire!'

This word seemed to hang in the air like a trumpet's call. And Lord Harsha banged the table with his fist, and turned his angry eye on Joshu.

'Here, now – that won't do!' he snapped. 'You may call Lord Valashu "Sire" when the warriors have acclaimed him, but not before!'

Joshu bowed his head in acquiescence of Lord Harsha's admonishment. Lord Harsha, as he should have known, was a stickler for the ancient forms, and he believed that a king must always draw his power from the will of the warriors whom he led.

'All right, then,' Lord Harsha said as he stood up from the table and picked up the brandy bottle. He went around the table filling up everyone's cup. He returned to his place and raised his own as he said, 'To Valashu Elahad – may he become the next in the unbroken line of Elahad kings and protect our sacred realm!'

After we had clinked cups and sipped our brandy, Behira stared across the table at Joshu and said, 'Then tomorrow you'll ride off again?'

At this, Joshu turned toward me. I sensed that he didn't want to wed Behira half as much as he burned to take his revenge for what had happened upon the Culhadosh Commons. As our eyes met, I felt a bright flame come alive within him.

'I must serve Lord Valashu,' he told her. 'There will be war – if not against Lord Tanu or Lord Tomavar, then against the Waashians when Lord Valashu becomes king. Or the Urtuk will invade in force, and the Mansurii with them. Perhaps Morjin himself will march against Mesh again. And when he does, I must ride with Lord Valashu.'

'If he is your king, then you must,' Lord Harsha agreed. 'And so must I. And that is why we should arrange a wedding while we can.'

I felt Maram's knee pressing against mine beneath the table, and I said to Lord Harsha, 'I am afraid there *will* be war. Why not let the question of your daughter's marriage wait until greater matters are settled?'

'Do you mean, wait until one of Morjin's knights puts a spear through Joshu's other lung?' Lord Harsha said bluntly.

As my father had once told me, sometimes problems worked out best if left alone. And death solved all of life's problems.

'Or Sar Maram,' Lord Harsha said. 'I would no more see him lying bloodied on the battlefield than I would Sar Joshu.'

In the dark corner of the room above Maram's head, I caught a sense of a deeper darkness. The Ahrim, I knew, followed Maram as it did me.

'I understand your concern,' I said to Lord Harsha, 'and I will do what I can to ease it. Do you know of the estate my family holds along the Kurash River?'

'The lands by the Old Oaks?' Lord Harsha said. 'Five hundred acres of the best bottomland?'

'Yes, those,' I said. 'It shall be my present to Behira at her wedding.'

Lord Harsha nodded his head at this as he regarded me. Ever a practical man, he said, 'You're even more generous than your father, lad. But suppose that neither Sar Joshu nor Sar Maram survive what is to come? Suppose – may the stars forbid it – that you yourself do not?'

'Then,' I told him, 'let these lands be held in dower for Behira to whomever she might marry.'

'Generous, indeed!' Lord Harsha called out. Again he lifted up his cup. 'Well, let us drink to that!'

At this, Maram smiled at me in gratitude. We raised our cups, even Master Juwain, though he would drink no intoxicants. Behira, however, sat still and stolid, refusing to touch her cup.

'What's wrong?' Lord Harsha asked her.

And in a clear, strong voice, she said, 'What if I don't want to marry?'

Lord Harsha sat in a stunned silence staring at her. 'Not marry – what do you mean?'

'I mean, father, that I'm not sure I want to marry anyone.'

Her words struck Lord Harsha speechless, and he glared at her.

Then Behira looked down the table at Liljana, and caught her eye. Usually Liljana stayed out of such business, but something in Behira must have moved her, for she said, 'There are other things a young woman can do besides marry.'

Her words caused Lord Harsha to turn his black blazing eye upon her. And he commanded Behira, 'You won't listen to such outlandish talk!'

But he wasn't the only one in the Harsha family who could summon up the more wrathful emotions. Behira shook her head at her father and without warning exploded into what might have been a tantrum if it hadn't been so well-reasoned: 'Oh, won't I? And why not? Why *must* I marry? Because *you* want grandsons, father? More meat to skewer on our enemies' swords? I won't see my children killed this way – I won't! All this talk tonight of people dying and noble men defending Mesh while I wait and wait yet again for Maram or Joshu or someone else to return someday and favor me with their precious seeds – as if I'm no more than a field of dirt to plant them in! Well, what if I don't *want* to wait?'

Lord Harsha, utterly taken aback by this outburst, stared at her and said, 'But if you don't marry, what do you think you will do?'

Behira looked at Atara sitting quietly as well-balanced and straight as one of her arrows. And Behira said, 'The Sarni women, some of them, become warriors.'

'The Sarni are savages!' Lord Harsha shouted. Then I felt shame burning his face as he looked at Atara and said, 'Forgive me, Princess!'

'It's all right,' Atara said with a cold smile. 'Sometimes we *are* savages – and worse.'

'Do you see?' Lord Harsha said to Behira. 'Do you see?'

Behira turned to look down the table at me. Then she told her father, 'I see a man who would become King of Mesh, and *not* be content merely to keep the roads in good repair and hold feasts. If Lord Elahad wins the throne, then there *will* be war – a war such as we've never seen. And we Valari women are supposed to be *warriors* aren't we? With the whole world about to spill its blood, you can't just expect us to sit around and hope for our men to return and bestow upon us babies!'

Lord Harsha forced himself to breathe in and out ten times before he made response to this: 'Our women *are* warriors: warriors of the spirit. Who teaches our children to meditate, and so ennobles them with the grace and power of the One? Who teaches them to tell the truth? It's the truth I'll tell you now, as your mother would have if she were still alive: our women are the keepers of the very flame that makes us Valari.'

Behira placed her hand across her breast as she looked at me and said, '*This* flame burns for a better world, as it is with Lord Valashu. Whatever spirit I have, I wish to use in his service helping him to win. *Then*, father, it might be safe to wed and bring a child into the world.'

Lord Harsha, who had finally borne too much, banged his fist against the table and thundered: 'You will wed *when* I say you will and *whom* I choose as your husband!'

At this, Behira burst into tears. But she soon gathered up her pride, and stood up from her chair. With an almost violent clacking of the crockery, she began stacking up our dirty plates. And she announced, 'I'm going to do the dishes, and then go for a walk outside. Atara, will you help me? Liljana?'

Without another word, these three very willful women cleared the table and then disappeared into the kitchen, shutting the door behind them. Their voices hummed beyond it like the buzzing of bees from within a hive. Then Lord Harsha gazed at me with accusation lighting up his eye.

'You *have* returned, Lord Elahad, to lead us to war,' he said, 'for now there is war even in my own house. These are *bad* times indeed – the worst times I've ever seen!'

For a while he sat sipping his brandy and rubbing at his temple. Then I smiled and said to him, 'Tomorrow I'll talk with Behira – it will all come out all right. There is always a way.'

'Hearing you say this,' Lord Harsha told me, 'I do believe it.'

'I am no scryer,' I said, 'but your family *shall* have the lands that I spoke of, and you shall have many grandchildren as well.'

'I want to believe that, too,' he sighed out, reaching for the brandy bottle. 'Well, let us make a toast to children then.'

The fiery taste of brandy lingered on my lips that night long after we all had left the table and had gone off to our beds. For hours I lay tossing and turning and dreaming of children: Behira's brood of boys and girls playing happily in Lord Harsha's wheatfields, and Daj and Estrella and the son or daughter whom Atara would someday bear for me. All the children in the world. Although it seemed a vain and vainglorious thing to imagine that their future and very lives depended upon my deeds, the painful throbbing of my heart told me that this was so. Tomorrow, I thought, and in the days that followed, I must do that which must be done in order to become king and finally defeat Morjin. Even if it seemed impossible, I must believe that there was always a way.

3

Lord Harsha and Joshu rode out early the next morning. Along with my companions, I whiled away the hours resting and reading and eating the good, hearty foods that Behira prepared for us. As promised, I took her aside and tried to reason with her. I reminded her that Valari ways were different from those of the Sarni, and that the Valari women have never marched into battle. A sword, I told her, would always be a man's weapon, while a woman made better use of her soul. And I had need of her father's sword and all his concentration on the task at hand. I asked her to give her word that she would not anger her father by openly decrying marriage or refusing to wed. If she helped me in this way, I said, I would help her in whatever way I could. We clasped hands to seal our agreement. And then she went off to ask Atara to teach her how to work her great horn bow and fire off her steel-tipped arrows.

We waited all that day, and a little longer. The following morning, just before noon, Lord Harsha returned at the head of fifteen knights whose great horses pounded the little dirt lane into powder. All had accoutered themselves for war: they bore long, double-bladed kalamas and triangular shields and wore suits of splendid diamond armor. I recognized most of them from the charges emblazoned on their surcoats. Sar Shivalad bore a red eagle as his emblem, while Sar Viku Aradam's surcoat showed three white roses on a blue field. I stood with my friends outside Lord Harsha's house watching them canter up to us in clouds of dust. As they calmed their mounts and the dust cleared, a sharp-faced man called Sar Zandru pointed at me and called out: 'It *is* the Elahad! He lives – as Lord Harsha has said.'

He and the other knights dismounted, then bowed their heads

to me. They came up to clasp my hand and present themselves, where presentations were needed. I knew some of these knights quite well: Sar Shivalad, with his fierce eyes and great cleft nose, and Kanshar, Siraj the Younger, Ianaru of Mir and Jurald Evar. Others had familiar faces: Sar Yardru, Sar Barshar and Vijay Iskaldar. Sar Jessu and I had practiced at swords when we were children running around the battlements of my father's castle; I had last seen him at the Culhadosh Commons leading his warriors into the gap in our lines that might have destroyed the whole army – and Mesh along with it. For his great valor and even greater deed, he should have been rewarded with a ring showing four brilliant diamonds instead of the three of a master knight. But only a Valari king has the power to make a knight into a lord.

'Valashu Elahad,' he said, stepping up to me and squeezing my hand. He was a stocky man whose lively eyes looked out from beneath the bushiest black eyebrows I had ever seen. 'Forgive me for pledging to Lord Avijan, for I would rather have given my oath to you – as we all would.'

'There is nothing to forgive,' I said, returning his clasp. I brought his hand up before my eyes. 'I only wish I could have given you the ring you deserve.'

When I praised him for saving Mesh from defeat in the Great Battle, he told me, 'But I only fought as everyone did. It was *you* who had the foresight and courage to let the gap remain open until our enemy was trapped inside. You have a genius for war, Lord Valashu. I have told this to all who would listen.'

'And you have the heart of a lion,' I told him, looking at the red lion emblazoned on his white surcoat and shield. 'I shall call you "Jessu the Lion-Heart," since I cannot yet call you "Lord Jessu."'

He smiled as he bowed his head to me. The other knights approved of this honor, for they drew out their kalamas and clanged their steel pommels against their shields. And they called out, 'Jessu the Lion-Heart! Jessu the Lion-Heart!'

I looked around for Joshu Kadar, but could not see him. When I asked Lord Harsha about this, he told me, 'The lad has gone off to retrieve his armor and his warhorse, and should meet up here soon.'

He told me that he had preserved my armor, and Maram's too, and he led the way inside his house up to his room. There, from within a great, locked chest, he drew out three suits of armor reinforced with steel along the shoulders and studded with bright diamonds. After we, too, had accoutered ourselves, Lord Harsha

43

handed me my old surcoat, folded neatly and emblazoned with a great silver swan and seven silver stars. He said to me, 'You'll want to wait, I suppose, to wear this?'

'No,' I said taking it from him. I pulled it over my head so that the surcoat's black silk fell down to my knees, with the swan centered over my heart. 'I am tired of skulking about in secret, as you said. I will go forth beneath my family's arms.'

Lord Harsha smiled at this. At the very bottom of the chest, he found a great banner also showing my emblem. He said to me, 'There is no force that can molest us between here and Lord Avijan's castle, and so why not ride as the Elahad you are? In any case, the news that you have returned will spread through all Mesh soon enough.'

When we went back outside, we found that Joshu Kadar had arrived decked out in heavy armor and bearing on his shield the great white wolf of the Kadars. It came time to say goodbye to Behira, for she would be staying home in order to milk the cows and hoe the fields – and, I guessed, to take up one of Lord Harsha's swords and practice the ancient forms out in the yard, since there would be no one looking over her shoulder in disapproval of such an unwomanly act.

'Farewell,' Behira said to Maram, standing by his horse with him and clasping his hand. She gave him a blueberry tart that she had baked that morning. 'This will sustain you on at least the first leg of your new adventure.'

'I pray that it will be my *last* adventure,' he said, squeezing her hand. 'Just as I pray that someday you *will* be my wife.'

Behira smiled nicely at this as if she wanted to believe him. She had little gifts as well for Joshu Kadar and her father, and for the children. Master Juwain and Liljana had brought our horses and remounts out from the barn into the yard. Atara sat on top of Fire, while Daj climbed up onto a bay named Brownie and Estrella rode a white gelding we called Snow. They formed up behind Lord Harsha and the fifteen knights – now seventeen counting Joshu Kadar and Maram. Lord Harsha insisted that I take my place at the head of the knights, and so I did. Then, in two columns, we set out down the road.

We had fine weather for travel, with a warm, westerly wind and blue skies full of puffy white clouds. Bees buzzed in the wild-flowers growing along the barley and wheat fields, and crows cawed in the cherry orchards. After turning past a farm belonging to a widow named Jereva and her two crippled sons, we made our way east toward Mount Eluru and the white-capped peaks of the Culhadosh range that shone in the distance. The ground rose steadily into a hillier country, and after six or seven miles, the farms began giving way to more orchards, pastures full of sheep and cattle, and patches of forest. The road, like every other in Mesh, had been made of the best paving stones and kept in good repair. Our horses' hooves drummed against it in a clacking, rhythmic pace, and we made good distance without too much work. Twenty-four miles it was from Lord Harsha's farm to Lord Avijan's castle, straight through the heartland of what had once been my father's realm. And at nearly every house or field that we passed, men, women and children paused in their labors to watch us pound down the road.

At the edge of a pear orchard, a hoary warrior raised his hand to point at my father's banner streaming in the breeze as he called out to his grandson: 'Look – the swan and stars of the Elahad!'

He was too old and infirm to do more than wish us well, but we came across other warriors who wanted to take part in our expedition. Those who owned warhorses – and whom Lord Harsha or the other knights could vouch for – I asked to join us. By the time the sun began dropping toward the mountains behind us, we numbered thirty-three strong.

About eight miles from Lord Avijan's castle, we turned onto a much narrower road leading north. This took us through a band of pasture with the Lake of the Ten Thousand Swans to our left and the steep slopes of Mount Eluru rising almost straight up to the right. In one place, only a strip of grass ten yards wide separated the sacred mountain's granite walls from the icy blue waters of the lake. Lord Avijan's ancestors had built the Avijan castle farther up through the pass in a cleft between two spurs of Mount Eluru's northern buttress. In all the world, I could think of few castles harder to reach or possessing such great natural defenses.

We approached the castle up a very steep and rocky slope that would have daunted any attacking army. A shield wall, fronted with a moat and protected by many high towers, surrounded the castle's yards and shops, with the great keep rising up like a stone block beneath the much greater mass of Mount Eluru behind it.

Lord Avijan, followed by a retinue of twenty knights, met us on the drawbridge that was lowered over black waters. He had decked himself out in full armor, and sat upon a huge gray stallion. His blue surcoat showed a golden boar. He was a tall man with a long, serious face that reminded me of a wolfhound. At twenty-six years of age, he was young to be a lord, but my father had found few men in Mesh so skilled at leading a great many knights in wild but well-organized charges of steel-clad horses.

'Lord Elahad!' he called out to me in a strong, stately voice. 'Welcome home to Mesh – and to my home. My castle is yours for as long as you need it. And my warriors and knights are yours to command, for as you must have been told, they have taken oaths to me, and it is *my* command that they should support you in becoming king.'

This, I thought, was Lord Avijan's way of apologizing for a thing that he had no need to apologize for. A proud and intelligent man with little vanity, he came from a long and honored line of warriors. His grandfather had married my great-grandfather's youngest sister, and so we counted ourselves as kin. This distant tie of blood, however, formed no basis for his claim on Mesh's throne. That came from his skill at arms, his coolness of head on the battlefield and his good judgment off it – and the way he inspired courage and loyalty in the men whom he led.

'Thank you, Lord Avijan,' I told him. I nudged Altaru closer to him so that I could clasp his hand. 'But it is my wish that you release your warriors from their oaths. I would have them follow me, or not, according to their hearts. And then, if it is my fate to become king, they may make their oaths to me.'

Lord Avijan bowed his head at this, and then so did the knights lined up in the tunnel of the tower behind him. They drew out their kalamas to salute me, then struck them against their shields in a great noise of steel against steel. And one of them – a knight I recognized as Tavish the Bold – cried out: 'You *will* become king, and we will follow you to the end of all battles, oaths or no oaths!'

Lord Avijan then invited all of us to a feast. After we had ridden into the castle and given our horses to the care of the stableboys, we settled into whatever rooms or quarters that Lord Avijan had appointed for us. Half an hour later, we gathered in Lord Avijan's great hall, on the first floor of the keep. Many long tables laden with roasted joints of meat and hot breads filled this large space; many stands of candles had been set out to light it, and hundreds of little, flickering flames cast their fire into the air. The great wood beams high above us were blackened with generations of soot. A hundred knights and warriors joined us there, for word of my arrival had gone ahead of me. Many of these tall, powerful men I had known since my childhood. I paid my respects to a master knight named Sar Yulmar, and to Sar Vikan, whom I had led into battle at the Culhadosh Commons. Also to Lord Sharad, a very tall and lean man with hair as gray as steel, who had taken command of Asaru's battalion after my brother had been killed. He had gained great renown at the Battle of Red Mountain against Waas, and fourteen years before that, at the Diamond River, where the Ishkans had practically murdered my grandfather. Despite his years, he had a gallant manner and didn't mind taking risks in the heat of battle.

We all filled our bellies with good food that night, and then it came time to fill our souls with good conversation. We might have hoped for many rounds of toasts, entertaining stories told and minstrels singing out the great, ancient tales. But as Lord Avijan's grooms went around filling and refilling the warriors' cups with thick, black beer, our talk turned toward serious matters. Soon it became clear that our gathering would be less a celebration than a council of war.

After Lord Avijan's young children had been sent off to bed, he and I came down off the dais at the front of the room where we had taken the table of honor. I insisted that all present should be honored equally that night, and so near the center of the hall I found a table littered with empty cups and spilled beer, and I leaned back against it. Lord Avijan, Lord Harsha and others gathered around informally, sitting on tables or the long benches nearby – or standing all crowded-in close. Atara sat on one side of me as if she were my queen, while Maram pressed his huge body up against my other side. Master Juwain and my other companions took their places at the other end of the table. More than a few of the warriors looking on must have thought it strange that we included Daj and Estrella in our discussion, but that was because they did not know these two remarkable children.

'Let me say, first and last,' I told the warriors gathered around me, 'that you do me a great honor in coming forth for me after all that has happened – and in such perilous times. I will never forget this, and no matter what befalls, I will stand by you to my last breath.'

'You will stand as king – that is what will befall!' Sar Vikan barked out. He, himself, stood a good few inches shorter than most Valari, but what he lacked in height he made up in the power of his thickly muscled body. His square-cut face seemed animated with a rage of restlessness streaming through him. 'When Lord Tanu and Lord Tomavar hear that you have returned, they will surely step aside.'

'They will *not* step aside!' Lord Sharad said. He leaned against the table opposite me, and pulled at one of the battle ribbons tied to his long, gray hair. 'Let us, at least, be clear about that.'

'Then we will *make* them step aside!' Sar Vikan snapped as he grasped the hilt of his sword. 'Just as we will make known the truth about Valashu Elahad – at last. Who, hearing this, will try to hold his warriors to oaths made under false knowledge and great duress?'

'Well, lad, it is one thing to hear the truth,' Lord Harsha said, 'and another to take it to heart. Here's the truth that *I* know: Lord Tanu has hardened his heart to the plight of our kingdom, and Lord Tomavar has lost his altogether – and his head!'

Although he had not spoken with humorous intent, his words caused the fierce warriors standing around us to laugh. But any levity soon gave way to more serious passions as Lord Avijan said, 'If we allow it, Lord Tanu and Lord Tomavar will tear the realm apart – that has been obvious from the first. But we *must* not allow it!'

'But our choices,' protested Sar Jessu, who was sitting next to him, 'are growing fewer. And things between Lord Tomavar and Lord Tanu are only growing worse.'

'Truly, they are,' Lord Avijan said. 'And all over mere matters of marriage.'

These 'mere' matters, it seemed, had fairly exploded with pure vitriol. The first, and ostensibly the most trivial, concerned a brooch. Lord Tanu's cousin, Manamar Tanu, was the father of Vareva, whom Lord Tanu had arranged to marry to Lord Tomavar in order to strengthen the bonds between these two prominent families. Now that more than a year had passed since Vareva's abduction, according to our law, Manamar had declared Vareva dead. He had asked Lord Tomavar for the return of a beautiful diamond brooch that his wife, Dalia, had given to Vareva as a wedding gift. Manamar held that the marriage agreement called for the return of this brooch should Vareva either die or produce no issue. The brooch, he said, had passed down in Dalia's family for generations, and Dalia now wished to give it to her second daughter, Ursa. But Lord Tomavar claimed that the law was vague concerning such declarations of decease, and said that in any case his beloved Vareva could not be dead. The brooch, he said, was dear to him, and he would not surrender it unless Manamar Tanu took it from him by the victor's right in battle.

'Lord Tomavar challenged Sar Manamar to a duel!' Lord Avijan said. 'In effect, he did. For the time being, Lord Tanu has forbidden

Sar Manamar to go up against Lord Tomavar. But if he wishes for a cause of war, he has only to let his cousin impale himself on Lord Tomavar's sword.'

'And *that*, I fear,' Lord Harsha said, 'would be the result of such a duel. I was there at the tournament in Nar twenty years ago when Lord Tomavar won a third at the sword.'

'Twenty *years* ago!' Joshu Kadar called out from behind me.

'Don't let Lord Tomavar's age fool you, lad. We old wolves might get longer in the tooth with the years, but some of us get longer in the reach of our swords, too. I've seen Lord Tomavar's kalama at work, and there are few knights in all of Mesh who could stand up to him.'

Here he looked at me, and so did Lord Avijan and everyone else. In Nar, only two years before, I had won a first at the sword and had been declared the tournament's champion.

'A brooch,' I said, 'a simple brooch.'

It seemed the most foolish thing in the world that two families could tear themselves apart over a piece of jewelry – and take a whole kingdom along with it.

'Well,' Lord Harsha said, 'it *is* a diamond brooch, said to be made of the finest Ice Mountain bluestars – haven't we Valari always fought each other over diamonds?'

'That we have,' Lord Avijan said sadly. 'But Meshians have never fought Meshians.'

'And now Zenshar Tanu is dead – just two weeks ago on Moonday,' Sar Jessu put in. 'And so who can see a chance for peace?'

This was the second matrimonial matter that Lord Avijan had spoken of. Some years before, Sar Zenshar Tanu, Lord Tanu's youngest nephew, had married Lord Tomavar's niece, a headstrong young woman named Raya. During the Great Battle, Sar Zenshar had taken an arrow through his leg. Although the arrow had been successfully drawn and Raya had cared for him with great devotion, the wound had festered and had poisoned his blood. Sar Zenshar, to the horror of all, had taken a whole year rotting, withering and dying. After the funeral, as Zenshar had neither father nor brothers, Lord Tanu had taken charge of Raya and her children. But Raya had declared that she would not live under the command of a man who had become her uncle's enemy. And so in the middle of the night, she put her children onto the backs of swift horses and fled through the Lake Country and the Sawash River Valley to Pushku, where Lord Tomavar had his estates. And so she had broken the final chain that linked the two families together.

'The whole Tanu clan,' Sar Jessu said, 'is outraged over what they are calling the abduction of Zenshar's children. They've put out the word to their smithies, and are refusing to sell swords to anyone who would follow Lord Tomavar.'

The best swords in the world, of course, have always been forged in Godhra, and every Meshian warrior aspires to wield one and invest it with his very soul.

'And worse,' Sar Jessu went on, 'the Tanus have pressured the armorers not to sell to the Tomavar clan. The Tomavars have no diamond mines of their own, or so the Tomavars whine, and so how can they make their own armor?'

'Diamonds, always diamonds,' Lord Harsha muttered. 'It's been scarcely two years since we nearly went to war with the Ishkans over Mount Korukel's diamond mines.'

'But Valashu Elahad,' Joshu Kadar said to him, 'returned with the Lightstone and cooled the Ishkans' blood!'

At this, Sar Shivalad and Sar Viku Aradam and other knights gazed at me as if they were looking for something within me. I felt the whole room practically roiling with strong passions: wonder, doubt, elation and dread.

Lord Avijan bowed his head to me, then said, 'The Elahad did return, it's true, but now that the Lord of Lies has regained the Lightstone, the Ishkans' blood is rising again. Already they have taken a part of Anjo, and have defeated Taron in battle.'

And this, as he was too kind to say, had been the inevitable result of my failure in Tria to unite the Valari against Morjin.

But I must never, I told myself, *fail again.*

'Pfahh – the Ishkans!' Sar Vikan called out to Lord Avijan. 'You think about them too much.'

'King Hadaru,' Lord Avijan reminded him, 'remains a merciless man – and a cunning one.'

'Yes, but he has been wounded, and some say the wound rots him to his death.'

'Some do say that,' Lord Avijan admitted. 'But I would not hold my breath waiting for the Ishkan bear to die.'

The story he now told angered everyone, and saddened them, too, for it was only a continuation of the ancient tragedy of our people. After the conclave in Tria where I had slain Ravik Kirriland before thousands, the Valari kings had lost faith in me – and in themselves. Seeing no hope for peace, they had fallen back upon war. Old grievances had festered, and new ambitions fired their blood. In the course of only a few months, Athar had attacked Lagash, while King Waray of Taron had begun plotting against Ishka and King Hadaru. King Waray had tried to help the duchies and baronies of Anjo unite against Ishka – with the secret agenda of trying to make Anjo a client state and so strengthening Taron. But King Hadaru had sniffed out King Waray's plans, and had marched the strongest army in the Nine Kingdoms into Taron. He defeated King Waray at the Battle of the Broken Tree, where a lance had pierced him. As punishment he had not only annexed part of Anjo but was now demanding that King Waray surrender up territory as well – either that or a huge weight of diamonds in blood payment for the warriors that King Hadaru had lost.

'But has King Hadaru,' I said to Lord Avijan, 'made any move toward Mesh?'

'Not yet,' Lord Avijan said. 'Surely he waits for us to weaken ourselves first.'

'It is a pity,' Sar Vikan said, 'that we *didn't* make war upon the Ishkans on the Raaswash. Then we might have weakened *them*.'

I felt many pairs of eyes searching for something in *my* eyes, weighing and testing. And I said to Sar Vikan, 'No, that is not the war we must fight.'

'But what of Waas, then?' Lord Avijan asked me. 'There bodes a war that we might not be able to avoid.'

I turned toward the hall's eastern window, now dark and full of stars. In that direction only twenty-five miles away across the Culhadosh River lay Waas, where I had fought in my first battle at the Red Mountain. King Sandarkan, as Lord Avijan now told us, burned to avenge the defeat that my father had dealt him. He said that there were signs that King Sandarkan might be planning to lead the Waashians in an attack against Kaash.

'If they do,' Lord Harsha said, 'we must aid them. It is a matter of honor.'

How could I disagree with him? King Talanu Solaru of Kaash was my uncle, and Kaash was Mesh's ancient ally, and so how could ties of blood and honor be ignored?

'We *cannot* march to Kaash's aid,' Lord Avijan said, 'if we are busy fighting ourselves. Surely King Sandarkan is counting on this. Surely he will defeat the Kaashans, for they are too few, and then he will annex the Arjan Land and extract a promise from King Talanu that Kaash won't come to *our* aid if Waas then attacks us.'

Joshu Kadar slapped his hand against his sword's scabbard and said, 'But we defeated Waas handily once, and can again!'

Lord Harsha sighed at this and said, 'Little good that will do us, lad, for we'll only weaken ourselves further, and then King Hadaru *will* surely lead the Ishkans here.'

'Or else,' Lord Avijan said, 'Waas won't attack alone but will ally with the Ishkans to put an end to Mesh once and for all.'

'At least,' Lord Sharad added, nodding his head at me, 'that is our best assessment of matters as they now stand.'

For a few moments no one spoke, and the hall fell quiet. Everyone knew that, from more than one direction, Mesh faced the threat of defeat. And everyone looked to me to find a way to escape such a fate.

'When you left Mesh last year,' Lord Avijan said to me, 'you could not have known how things would fall out. But you should not have left.'

I stood away from the table behind me to ease the stiffness in my legs. Then I looked out at the knights and warriors standing around me, and said, 'My apologies, but I *had* to. There are things you don't know about. But now you must be told.'

With everyone pressing in closer, I drew in a deep breath and wondered just how much I should divulge to them? I thought I might do best to conjure up some plan by which we Meshians might prevail against the more familiar enemies: the Ishkans and the Waashians, the Sarni tribes in their hordes of horse warriors – even ourselves. And so save ourselves. But I had vowed never to lie again, and more, to tell the truth so far as it could be told. Were my fellow warriors strong enough, I wondered, to hold the most terrible of truths within their hearts? In the end, either one trusted in men, or did not.

'For thousands of years,' I said to them, 'Mesh has had enemies. And where necessary we defeated them – all except one. And *his* name is Morjin.'

'But we defeated him at the Sarburn!' Sar Vikan called out.

'Three thousand years ago we did,' Lord Avijan said. 'With the help of all the Valari kingdoms.'

'And at the Culhadosh Commons!' Sar Jessu cried out to me. 'Upon your lead, we crushed an army that outnumbered us four to one!'

His words caused most of the warriors present to cry out and strike their swords' pommels against the tables in great drumming of steel against wood. Then I held up my hand and said to them,

'Those were great victories, it is true, won by the most valorous of warriors. But they were *not* defeats, as the Red Dragon must be defeated. He has other armies, and greater than the ones we faced. What good does it do to strike off a serpent's head if two more grow back in its place?'

I told them then of our journey to Hesperu and of our triumphant quest to find the Maitreya. A great light, I said, we had found in the far west, but along the way we had endured great darkness, too. Morjin had wrought horrors everywhere – and now was planning to work the greatest of evils: to loose the Dark One upon Ea. I feared that this doom would prove too great a terror for many of the warriors staring at me to contemplate. Who really wanted to believe, or *could* believe, that the whole world – and the very universe itself – might be destroyed down to the last grain of sand?

'As always,' I said to them, 'Morjin remains the true enemy.'

My words gave the warriors pause. All through Lord Avijan's great hall, I saw brave men looking at each other in a dreadful silence.

'For now,' I continued, 'the man called Bemossed, who must be the Maitreya, keeps Morjin from using the Lightstone to free the Dark One. But he needs our help, as we need his.'

At this, a white-haired warrior named Lord Noldashan turned to me and said, 'You appear to know things that it seems would be hard for any man to know. May it be asked how you have come by such knowledge?'

'Only through great suffering!' Maram called out from beside me. 'And through great fortune, if that is the right word.'

Because it pained me to think of the torture that I had led Maram to endure in the Red Desert, and in other places, I laid my hand on his knee and squeezed it. And then I said to Lord Noldashan, and the others: 'It was Kane who told me about the Dark One named Angra Mainyu. And I do not doubt his word, for much of what he related is hinted at in the last three books of the *Saganom Elu*.'

'An old book,' Lord Sharad said with a smile. 'Almost as old as Lord Noldashan – and myself.'

But Lord Noldashan, it seemed, could not be moved from his intense seriousness. He nodded at Master Juwain, and called out in his raspy voice: 'The Brotherhood teaches that much of what is written in the *Valkariad* and the *Trian Prophecies* can be taken in different ways. And even more so with the *Eschaton*. How, then, should we take this doom that Lord Valashu's companion has told of? This Kane is a mysterious man – and an outlander, as we should not forget.'

'He is the greatest warrior I have ever known!' Lord Sharad called back. 'I was there when he slew the Ikurians beneath the Mare's Hill, and I have never seen a sword worked so!'

'Lord Sharad tells true,' Sar Vikan said. 'I fought near Sar Kane, and when his blood is up, he seems less a man than an angel of battle.'

Upon these words, I struggled to keep my face still and my gaze fixed straight ahead. I hoped my companions, too, would keep the secret of Kane's otherworldly origins.

'Man or angel,' Lord Noldashan said, 'Sar Kane might well have come by his knowledge through great quests, with a true heart, and yet have learned things that are *not* true.'

'They *are* true!' I suddenly called out. The force of my voice seemed to strike Lord Noldashan and others as with the blow of a war hammer. I fought to control myself. In some dark room of Lord Avijan's castle, I sensed, perhaps even in the great hall itself, the Ahrim waited for me – and perhaps for everyone. 'Angra Mainyu still dwells on Damoom, and he turns his dark gaze on Ea. But even if he were only legend, there is still Morjin. *He* exists, as we all know. And so do his armies.'

The men standing around me considered this. Then Lord Sharad looked at me and said, 'I think I have to believe what Kane has told, though I am loath to. But why hasn't Kane returned with you from your last quest to tell us himself?'

'Because,' I said, 'he has gone into Galda.'

'Galda! But why?'

'Because,' I told him, 'we heard that Morjin might have gone there.'

And this, I said, was a consequence of our battle with Morjin and his creatures in Hesperu. I explained more about the worst of the enemies that we had faced on our quest: the three droghuls that Morjin had sent to destroy my companions and me. As with any ghul made from a man, I said, Morjin seized the droghuls' minds and caused them to work his will, as if they were puppets being pulled by strings. But the droghuls were particularly deadly, for Morjin had made these dreadful beings from his own flesh, in his likeness, and had imbued them with a part of his power. After we – actually young Daj – had slain the third of the droghuls, a rumor had shot across the world that Morjin himself had been slain. And so Morjin had been compelled to come out of the

54

stone city of Argattha to show himself and prove that he still lived. He had gone through the Dragon Kingdoms one by one, finally leading an army from Karabuk into Galda, where brave knights had revolted against Morjin upon the false news of his death.

'Kane,' I told Lord Sharad, 'went down into Galda so that he might take part in the rebellion.'

'You mean,' Lord Harsha said with a distasteful look, 'he went to put an arrow into Morjin's back, if he can.'

I smiled sadly at this. 'Kane would be more likely to use a knife. But, yes, he went to Galda to slay Morjin – *if* he can. And if Morjin is really there.'

'And if he is not?' Lord Avijan asked me.

'Wherever Morjin is,' I said, 'his plans will go ahead unless we do kill him. What happened in Hesperu has delayed him, but no more. Already, it is said, he has ordered a great fleet up from Sunguru and Hesperu to attack Eanna. If it takes him a hundred years, he will conquer Ea's free lands one by one until he has the Nine Kingdoms surrounded. But it will not take him a hundred years.'

As I paused to take a sip of beer, a half dozen speculations and arguments broke out among the warriors standing around me. The hall filled with the stridor of angry and confused voices. And then Lord Avijan turned to Maram and asked, 'You are from Delu – will the Delians fight if the Red Dragon attacks them?'

'Will we *fight*?' Maram called out. 'Of course we will! Ah, that is, a *few* knights and diehards will fight, while my father tries to make terms. He is no fool, and he'll no more want to stand isolated against the Red Dragon than would any other king – even, I might add, King Iadaru or King Waray, or any of the Valari kings.'

Here he glanced at me as if wishing that I would proclaim that Mesh would never go alone against the Red Dragon. But I looked down into my beer and said nothing.

'And what of the Sarni tribes?' Lord Avijan asked, turning toward Atara. 'Has the Manslayer had news of her people?'

Next to me, Atara nodded her head at this, and her white blindfold moved up and down like a signal banner. 'The Kurmak will *never* make terms with Morjin, so long as Sajagax is chief – and I think my grandfather still has a good few years left to him. He will call for the other tribes to ride with him in battle, if battle there must be. The Niuriu might join with him. Perhaps the Danladi, too, and the central Urtuk. I cannot say about the Adirii, for their clans are divided. But I believe that the Manslayers will decide for Sajagax, should the Red Dragon ever attack him.'

She did not add that the fierce women warriors of the Manslayer Society, who came from all the tribes, favored making Atara their Chiefess, and Atara would certainly lead them in aid of Sajagax, if she could.

Now Master Juwain let out a long sigh as he clamped his gnarly hands around his beer mug – filled with apple cider. And he said, 'There are other ways of opposing the Red Dragon than through war.'

While the warriors listened with the great reverence they held for Masters of the Brotherhood, Master Juwain told them of much the same plan for the peaceful defeat of Morjin that he had put forth two days before in the wood where we had fought the Ahrim.

'The Maitreya,' he said, 'will light a fire in men's hearts that the Red Dragon cannot put out. In the end it will consume him.'

'This is our hope,' I added. 'But the Maitreya must first live long enough to pass on this flame.'

'The Maitreya!' Sar Jessu cried out, looking at me. 'Always, the Maitreya! Once, we believed that *you* were the great Shining One.'

At this, a hundred warriors stared straight at me. I, too, had shared in their delusion. In truth, I had engendered it.

'We believed,' Sar Jessu went on, 'that the Maitreya would lead us to victory. But now we don't want to believe in miracles – it is enough to believe in *you*.'

Again, the warriors around me struck their swords against the wooden tables.

Then Lord Harsha's single eye swept around the hall as he regarded the warriors sternly. And he reminded them, 'The Shining One *will* come forth, as has been promised in the *Trian Prophecies* and the *Progressions*. Is he, then, the man Bemossed that Lord Elahad has told of? I would like to believe he is. But whoever he is, flame or no, we must look to our own swords for our defense, as we always have!'

So saying, he whipped free his long, shining kalama, and saluted me. Lord Avijan inclined his head to him, and said, 'That is my thought, too. But what, indeed, is the best course for defending Mesh?'

'There is only *one* course for us,' Sar Jessu called out. 'And it is as Lord Valashu has said: we must stop Morjin!'

'But stop him *how*?' Sar Shivalad said, turning his great, cleft nose toward Lord Harsha. 'That is the question we must decide.'

'That it is, lad,' Lord Harsha said. 'And here I'm in agreement with Master Juwain. Let us make Mesh strong again, as it was in the reign of King Shamesh. Then let us remember that we have destroyed or thrown back every army that tried to invade our land – even Morjin's.'

'But what of the Lightstone?' Sar Shivalad asked him.

And Lord Noldashan broke in, crying out, 'Let Morjin keep it! It is a cursed thing, and it nearly destroyed our land!'

His vehemence stunned me, and I looked from Lord Noldashan to his son, Sar Jonavar, beside him. He was a tall, well-made knight, perhaps a few years older than I, and he stood gripping his gauntleted hand around the hilt of his sword as he looked at me in great turmoil.

'No, it is just the opposite,' I said to Lord Noldashan. 'The Lightstone holds marvels and miracles. In the hands of the Maitreya –'

'It nearly destroyed *you*!' Lord Noldashan shouted. 'Do not dream of leading us on impossible expeditions to win it back!'

'Do not,' Lord Sharad said, moving closer to Lord Noldashan, 'speak to Lord Valashu so. Remember why you've come here!'

'To make Valashu Elahad King of Mesh!' Lord Noldashan said. 'Not to follow him on a fool's mission!'

'I would follow him to the end of the earth!' Lord Sharad cried out.

'And I!' Lord Jessu said.

'And I!' Joshu Kadar said.

'So would I,' Sar Vikan said, drawing his sword, 'if it meant a chance to put *this* through Morjin's neck! I would think that Lord Noldashan, of all knights, would want his vengeance!'

As Lord Noldashan faced Sar Vikan and moved his hand onto his sword's hilt, I remembered that Lord Noldashan had a second son, Televar, whom I did not see anywhere in the hall.

'Peace, honored knight!' I said to Lord Noldashan as I held up my hand. 'Let us sit together and drink our beer – and cool our heads!'

'Peace!' Lord Noldashan cried out. 'Have you *truly* returned to bring peace, Lord Elahad? Or only to bring more blood, as you did a year ago when you practically called down the Red Dragon upon us?'

'Do not speak to Lord Valashu so!' Lord Sharad said again. 'Remember yourself, Lord Knight!'

'I remember,' Lord Noldashan said with a rising anger, 'whole streams on the Culhadosh Commons running red with our warriors' blood!'

'Pfahh, blood!' Sar Vikan spat out. 'When has a *true* warrior been afraid of spilling it?'

The moment that these words left Sar Vikan's mouth, his face tightened in horror, as if he could not believe that he had spoken them. But it was too late. Quick as a bird, Lord Noldashan drew his sword five inches from its scabbard before Lord Avijan and others closed in and managed to clamp their hands around Lord Noldashan's arm.

'*This* warrior,' Lord Noldashan said to Sar Vikan as he struggled against those who held him, 'would not be afraid to see *your* blood spilled here!'

His challenge filled my belly with a sickness as if I had eaten splinters of iron. As other warriors came up to restrain Sar Vikan from drawing his sword and setting off an inescapable duel, I felt many people looking at me. Maram and Master Juwain – and my other companions, too – were clearly distressed to witness things falling out so badly. I felt them wondering what I wondered: why had we returned to Mesh at all if we could not even keep my own countrymen from killing each other?

'Stop!' I called out to Lord Noldashan and Sar Vikan. 'Let go of your swords! We are all one people here!'

My voice fell upon them with the force of a battering ram, stunning them into motionlessness. But it did not, I sensed, touch their hearts.

Lord Avijan finally let go of Lord Noldashan, and he said to me, 'Lord Noldashan has cause for grieving and grievance, and few men more. And he raises an important question, Lord Elahad: is it your purpose to go against Morjin or to protect Mesh?'

'But they are the same thing!' I called out. 'Mesh will never be safe so long as Morjin draws breath!'

I looked around the hall at the tens of warriors weighing my words. The older ones such as Lord Noldashan and Lord Harsha, had grown to manhood in an era when the Sarni and the other Valari kingdoms posed the greatest threat to Mesh. They held a more cautious sentiment, shared by such prominent warriors as Lord Tanu: that Mesh had repelled Morjin once, and could again if we had to. They believed that the Dragon, as with bears, would be likely to leave us alone if we left him alone. Although they would fight like angels of battle, to use Lord Sharad's words, if Morjin *did* try to invade our land again, they had no liking to march out of Mesh to make war against him. Others, such as Lord Avijan, desired vengeance for Morjin's desecration of Mesh and believed that he must somehow be defeated, though they, too, feared to seek him out and bring him to battle. A smaller number of men – and these were mostly younger knights such as Joshu Kadar, Sar Shivalad and their friends – burned with the fever of our generation to annihilate Morjin from the face of the earth and make the world anew.

'Morjin,' I finally said to Lord Avijan, and to everyone, 'must be destroyed. How that is to be remains unclear. But until he *is* destroyed, we will never bring peace to the world.'

'*You*,' Lord Noldashan said to me, 'if we follow you, will bring only death.'

I could tell from the grave faces of such prominent warriors as Lord Kanshar and Sar Juladar, even Lord Harsha, that many of the men gathered in the hall feared that Lord Noldashan had spoken truly – as I feared it even more. But I must, I thought, at all costs hide my disquiet. The gazes of a hundred warriors burned into me, and I thought that I must gaze right back at them, bravely and boldly, and betray not the slightest doubt or hesitation. Every moment that I stood among them, in field, forest or a great lord's castle, with my every word or gesture, I must surround myself as with a gleaming shield of invincibility. How, I wondered, was this possible? How had my father ever managed to last a single day as king?

Lord Noldashan stared straight at me, and continued his indictment: 'You *would* bring death, I think, Lord Elahad. Even as you brought it to Tria – and so destroyed all hope of an alliance of the Valari. And without an alliance, how could you ever hope to destroy the Red Dragon?'

In Tria, I thought, we had been so close to uniting. The Valari kings had nearly had the very stars within their grasp. But in the end, I had failed them.

'How many of our warriors fell at the Great Battle?' Lord Noldashan went on. 'How many of our women and children died at the Red Dragon's command?'

From somewhere in the hall I caught a sense of the great darkness that pulled me always down. Again, I saw my mother and grandmother nailed to planks of wood. And again, I saw a great grassland covered with tens of thousands of broken and bleeding bodies.

'How many, Lord Elahad?' Lord Noldashan asked me. 'How many of our people must die for your impossible dream?'

I tried to speak then, but I could not, and so I took a sip of beer to moisten my bone-dry throat. Then I looked at Sar Jonavar standing in close to his father, and I said to Lord Noldashan, 'You had another son, didn't you? Did he fall at the Commons?'

'He fell before the Great Battle,' Lord Noldashan told me. 'If that is the right word. For in truth, Morjin's men crucified him.'

Many standing in the hall knew the story that Lord Noldashan now told me: that when Morjin's army had invaded and laid waste the Lake Country, Lord Noldashan's two sons had been out on a hunting trip in the mountains to the north. After waiting as long as he could for them to come home, Lord Noldashan finally rode off to join the gathering of the warriors. But Televar and Sar Jonavar had never received my father's call to arms. They returned to find that Morjin's army had swept through the Lake Country, and that Morjin's men were about to burn their farm to the ground. The two brothers then fell mad. In the ensuing battle, Morjin's soldiers captured both of them – along with Lord Noldashan's wife and two daughters. They crucified all of them, and left them for the vultures. Two days later, after Morjin's army had moved on, a neighbor had found Lord Noldashan's family nailed to crosses. Miraculously, Sar Jonavar still lived. The neighbor then summoned help to pull Sar Jonavar down from his cross and tend his wounds until Lord Noldashan could return.

As Lord Noldashan finished recounting this terrible story, his raspy voice choked up almost to a whisper. I did not know what to say to him. I did not want to look at him just then.

'Once they called you the Maitreya,' he said to me. 'But can you bring back the dead? Can you keep my remaining son from joining the rest of my family?'

He doubts, I thought, feeling my heart moving inside me like a frightened rabbit, *because I doubt – and that is the curse of the valarda. But how can I not doubt?*

How could I, I wondered, ever defeat Morjin if I first must accomplish an impossible thing? The most dreadful thing in all the world that I could not quite bring myself to see?

I finally managed to make myself face Lord Noldashan. In the anguish filling up his moist, black eyes, I saw my own life. Then a brightness blazed within me again. In truth, it had never gone out. I remembered how, in Hesperu, in the most terrible of moments, Bemossed had clasped my hand in his and looked deep inside me as if he could behold the brightest light in all the universe.

'You have spoken of the dead,' I said to Lord Noldashan. 'And we have walked with the dead, you and I.'

I looked around at the hall's stone walls, hung with banners and shields and the heads of various animals that Lord Avijan and his family had hunted: lions, boars and elks with great racks of antlers spreading out like the limbs of a tree. Above an arch of one of the corridors giving out onto the hall, Lord Avijan had mounted the head of a white bear. It looked exactly like the beast whose will Morjin had seized and sent to murder Maram, Master Juwain and me in the pass between Mount Korukel and Mount Raaskel: the great ghul of a bear that I had killed with my old sword.

'There are the dead, and there are the *truly* dead,' I told Lord Noldashan. 'When Morjin would have turned *me* into a ghul, the man I call the Maitreya gave me his hand and pulled me back into life. There, I found my mother and grandmother – my brothers, too. And my father, the King.'

I stepped over to him and his son, and I felt his whole being wincing inside even as his back stiffened and he stared at me.

'So long as we don't forget,' I said to him, 'so long as we live, truly and deeply, with *passion*, they cannot really die. And neither can we.'

I laid my hand on the gauntlet covering Sar Jonavar's hand, and eased it off. A circle of reddish scar marred the back of his hand and his palm, which seemed slightly misshapen, as if the bones had been pushed apart. I grasped his hand then, gently, and I felt something warm and bright pass from me into him, and from him into me. He looked at me with tears in his eyes as he said, 'My apologies for not fighting with you at the Commons. The greatest battle of our time, and I missed it.'

Then I removed his other gauntlet so that he wouldn't have to hide his shame, which was really no shame at all.

'Sometimes,' I said to him, 'the greatest battle is just to go on living.'

At this, he clasped his other hand around my arm and smiled at me.

I felt the blaze that burned inside me grow even brighter. I looked at the men gathered around me: Lord Harsha, Lord Avijan, Lord Sharad, Sar Jessu and Sar Shivalad and all the others. And they looked at me.

They are afraid, I thought. *The greatest warriors in the world, and they are afraid.*

I could feel how their dread of Morjin tormented their very bodies and souls. And then, for the first time in my life, I opened my heart to these grave men whom I had always revered. I moved over to Lord Sharad and set my hand upon his chest, where I could feel the hurt of his old wound where an Ishkan lance had once pierced him. I touched Sar Viku Aradam's shoulder, which I sensed must have been split open, perhaps by an axe or a sword. And then on to grasp the stump below Vishtar Atanu's elbow and rest my hand on Araj Kharashan's mangled jaw. And so it went as I walked around the hall to honor other warriors and knights, Sar Barshan and Sar Vikan and Siraj Evar, touching my hand to heads and arms and faces and nearly every other part of a man's body that could be torn or cut or crushed.

I drew strength from my friends, looking on: from Liljana, who had gazed into the horror of Morjin's mind, and now could not smile; from Estrella, who could not speak; from Maram, who had been burned to a blackened, oozing crisp in the hell of the Red Desert. And from Atara, who could not look at me with her eyes, but somehow communicated all her wild joy of life despite the most terrible of mutilations.

Then my fear suddenly went away. I knew with an utter certainty of blood and breath that I had something to give these warriors who had come here to honor me. The light inside me flared so hot and brilliant that my heart hurt, and I could not hold it. I did not *want* to hold it within anymore, but only to pass it on, through my hand as I pressed it against the side of Sar Yardru's wounded neck, and through my eyes as I looked into old Sar Jurald's eyes, still haunted by the deaths of his sons at the Culhadosh Commons. And with this splendid light came the promise of brotherhood: that we would never fail each other and would fight side by side to the end of all battles. And that there was no wound or anguish so great that we could not help each other to bear it. And most of all, that we would always remind each other where we had come from and who we were meant to be.

That was the miracle of the valarda: how my love for these noble warriors could pass from me like a flame and set afire something bright and inextinguishable in them. At last, I returned to where Lord Noldashan stood, staring at me. I pressed my hand to his, and felt it come alive with an incendiary heat.

'I am sorry,' I told him, 'for your family.'

For a long time he stood looking at me as if wondering if he could bring himself to say anything. His eyes seemed like bright black jewels melting in the light of some impossibly bright sun. Finally, he seemed to come to a decision, and his breath rasped out: 'And I am sorry for yours. I should not have said what I said. You are not to blame for what Morjin did to our land. In truth, it is as Sar Jessu has told, that without you, the battle would have been lost. I know this in my heart.'

I squeezed his hand, hard, and held on tightly to keep myself from weeping. I did not succeed. Through the blur of water filling my eyes, I saw Lord Noldashan gazing at me with a terrible, sweet sadness, and so it was with Lord Harsha and Lord Avijan and many others. But within them, too, burned a great dream.

'You are *not* to blame for Morjin's deeds,' Lord Avijan affirmed, inclining his head to me. 'As for your own deeds, we shall honor them in the telling and retelling, down to our grandchildren's grandchildren – and beyond, when our descendants know of Morjin only by the tale of how we Valari vanquished him, leaving to legend only his evil name.'

Sar Vikan then came forward and said to Lord Noldashan, 'Well, sir, *I* am certainly to blame for what I said to you. I wish I could *un*say it. But I since I cannot, I will ask your forgiveness.'

'And that you shall have,' Lord Noldashan said, clasping his hand. 'As I hope I shall have yours for forgetting that we are brothers in arms.'

At this, Lord Harsha called out his approval, and so did Sar Jessu and dozens of other warriors.

Then Lord Noldashan turned back to me as he laid his arm around Sar Jonavar's shoulders. 'Despite my misgivings, I came here tonight because my son has great hope for you. And because I loved your father and Lord Asaru. An oath, too, I gave to Lord Avijan, but he has released me from it. What, then, should I now do?'

'Only what you must do,' I told him.

Lord Noldashan continued gazing into my eyes, and then said, 'My head speaks one thing to me, and my heart another. It is the right of a warrior to stand for one who would be king – or not to stand. But once this one *is* king, no one may gainsay him.'

I felt something vast and deep move inside Lord Noldashan. Then he glanced at Lord Sharad, before looking back to me and smiling grimly. 'Very well, then, Lord Elahad, I will follow you *past* the very end of the earth, to the stars or hell, if that is our fate.'

As he bowed deeply to me, a hundred warriors drummed the hilts of their swords against the tables. Then Lord Avijan stepped forward, and held up his hand. He called for fresh pots of beer to be brought up from his cellar. When everyone's cup had been filled anew, he raised his cup and cried out: 'To Lord Valashu Elahad, heir of the Elahads, Guardian of the Lightstone, and the next king of Mesh!'

I sipped my thick, black beer, and I found it sweet and bitter and good. I smiled as Alphanderry came forth and everyone hailed this strange minstrel. Tomorrow, I thought, we must meet in council again to lay our plans for my gaining my father's throne – and for Morjin's eventual defeat. But now we had a few moments for camaraderie and cups clinked together, and singing songs of glory and hope far into the night.

4

In that time of year when the wild asparagus growing along the hillsides and roads reached its peak and the lilacs laid their sweet perfume upon fields and gardens, the call for warriors who would support my claim to Mesh's throne – and perhaps much more – went out into every part of the land. They came to Lord Avijan's castle, in twos and threes, and sometimes tens and twenties, riding up in full diamond armor and bearing the bright emblems of their families. Most of them lived in the country near the Valley of the Swans and Mount Eluru, but many also arrived from the north, in the mountains near the two Raaswash rivers, and from the southern highlands below Lake Waskaw. Fewer hailed from the hills around Godhra, for there Lord Tanu held sway, as did Lord Tomavar in the Sawash River valley and its three largest cities: Pushku, Lashku and Antu. But a warrior had the right to give his oath to whom he wished, and at least ten men from Pushku had braved Lord Tomavar's anger by rallying for me. And fifty-two men – led by the long-faced Lord Manthanu – had journeyed all the way from Mount Tarkel above the Diamond River in the far northwest.

Soon the number of warriors overflowing the grounds of Lord Avijan's castle had swelled to more than one thousand. Lord Avijan's stewards worried about finding food for this growing army. But as the Valley of the Swans between Silvassu and Lake Waskaw held some of Mesh's richest farmland, to say nothing of woods full of deer, it seemed that no hour passed without a few wagons full of barley, beef and salted pork rolling up through the pass between Mount Eluru and the sparkling lake below it.

My companions and I kept busy during this period of waiting. While Master Juwain and Liljana tried to further the children's education, contending with each other as to exactly which subjects they should teach Daj and Estrella, and how, I greeted the arriving warriors one by one. The most distinguished of them joined Lord Avijan, Lord Harsha and other great knights in taking council where we discussed the strengths and weaknesses of Lord Tanu and Lord Tomavar. Although I asked Maram to attend these meetings, he insisted on attending to the matter of exploring the capaciousness of Lord Avijan's beer cellars. As he put it, 'These countrymen of yours drink like an army of parched bulls, and I'd at least like a little taste of beer before it's all gone.'

Although Master Juwain had practically given up lecturing him about the evils of strong drink, Liljana kept scolding him whenever she had the chance. On the third day of our stay at Lord Avijan's castle, she took Maram aside and said to him, 'We all know that bad times are coming. You should spend your days helping Val, as we all try to do – either that or learning more about your firestone.'

Now that Bemossed kept Morjin from using the Lightstone, or so we prayed, those of us possessing gelstei found ourselves free to discover new depths and powers of these ancient crystals.

'Bad times *are* coming,' Maram said to Liljana, 'and that is exactly the point. The only way to fight the bad is with the good, and right now I can think of nothing better than to fortify myself against the evils of the future with some good Meshian beer.'

He might have added that beautiful young women would have served best of all to drive back his fears, but in the overcrowded castle he never knew when Lord Harsha might come around the corner of some cold stone corridor and take him to task for mocking his professed love for Behira.

Of all of us, I thought, Atara had the hardest work with her gelstei, for the kristei's deepest virtue was said to be not merely the seeing of the future but its creation. But how could a single woman, through the force of her will alone, contend with Morjin's great fury to destroy all who defied him, to say nothing of his master, Angra Mainyu?

At one of our councils, after she had told Lord Manthanu of her grandfather, Sajagax's, strategy to persuade a few Sarni tribes to oppose Morjin, Lord Manthanu asked her to give the assembled warriors a good omen. They had talked that evening of cutting apart Morjin's best knights with their fearsome kalamas, and their spirits were running high. Atara did not wish to discourage these brave men, but neither would she speak anything but the truth.

And so, in her scryer's way, she told them: 'Then it will be as you wish, and your swords will cleave the armor of even the best knights of Morjin's Dragon Guard.'

She did not, however, reveal how many of them might live to fulfill this gruesome prophecy, and they could not bring themselves to ask her.

But it is not the way of fortune to progress in one direction forever: the cresting wave crashes into sand even as day passes into night. On the seventh of Soldru, after a long day of hunting, sword practice, councils and feasting on roasted venison, I retired to the rooms that Lord Avijan had appointed for me in the southern corner of the keep. They gave out into a small garden full of herbs, roses and bushes heavy with lilac blossoms. I sat on one of the stone benches there to listen to the crickets chirping and watch the stars come out. It was the only place in Lord Avijan's castle where I could find a space of solitude and listen to the whisperings of my soul.

Some time before midnight, with the moon waxing all silvery and full, Liljana found me there walking along the lilac hedges. Although she had brought me some tea, I could tell at once that serving me a soothing drink had little to do with the purpose of her visit. As she set out the pot and cups on one of the tables near the garden's great sundial, I could almost feel her willing her hand not to tremble. Even so the cups rattled against the hard stone with such force that it seemed they might break.

'What is wrong?' I asked her, taking her by her arm and urging her to sit down with me.

'Does there have to be anything wrong,' she said, 'for me to bring you a little fresh chamomile tea?'

'No, of course not,' I told her. 'But something *is* troubling you, isn't it?'

She nodded her head as she took out her gelstei. In the light of the moon, I could barely make out the blue tones of this little whale-shaped figurine. And then she said to me, 'I have terrible tidings.'

Something in her voice pierced me like an icy wind.

'What tidings?' I asked her. Without thinking, I grabbed hold of her arm. 'Are the children all right? Is Master Juwain?'

'They are fine,' she told me, 'but –'

'Is it Kane, then? Has word come of his death?'

It did not seem possible, I thought, that this invincible warrior who had survived countless wars in every corner of the world over thousands of years had finally gone back to the stars. Nor did I wish to believe that Maram, in a drunken stupor, had stumbled down the stairs after exiting some young woman's bedchamber and broken his neck. Most of all, I could not bring myself to think of any violence harming even a single hair of Atara's head.

'No, we're all safe here tonight,' Liljana said to me. 'But others, in places that we had thought were safe, are not. Or so I think.'

Her round, pretty face could hide a great deal when she wished, and she could hold herself calm and careful even when delivering the most disastrous of news. Such was her training as the Materix of the Maitriche Telu. It occurred to me for the thousandth time how glad I was to have this wise and relentless woman as my companion and not my enemy.

I sat on my hard stone seat breathing deeply and waiting for her to say more. I looked around at the roses and lilacs of the starlit garden for sign of the Ahrim – and then back at Liljana to see if she might tell me that this terrible thing had gained some dreadful new power. I reminded myself that if I would rule over Mesh, I must first and always rule myself.

'I came to tell you tidings,' she said to me again as she rotated her little figurine between her fingers, 'but I cannot tell you with absolute certainty that these tidings are true.'

'You speak more mysteriously,' I told her, 'than does a scryer.'

She would have laughed at this, I thought, if she had been able to laugh. Instead she said to me, 'Perhaps I should have just spoken of what I know, with my very first breath, but I wanted to prepare you first. I don't want you to give up hope.'

My heart seemed to be having trouble pushing my blood through my veins. Finally I said to her, 'Just tell me, then.'

'All right,' she said, drawing in a deep breath. 'I believe that the Brotherhood school has been destroyed.'

I gazed straight at her, trying to make out the black centers of her eyes. I felt as bereft of speech as Estrella.

'It would have happened around the end of Ashte,' she told me.

I continued gazing at her, then I finally found the will to say: 'You mean the Brotherhood school of the Seven, don't you? But no place in the world is safer! Morjin could not have found it!'

I thought of the magic tunnels through the mountains surrounding the Valley of the Sun, and I shook my head.

'But he *has* found it,' she told me as she covered my hand with hers. 'Somehow, he has.'

'But the Seven, and those that came before them, have kept

the school a secret for thousands of years. And Bemossed has had scarcely *half* a year of sanctuary there. How *could* Morjin suddenly have found it?'

The answer, I thought, was built into the very words of my question. Bemossed, contending with Morjin for mastery of the Lightstone over a distance of a few hundred miles, touching upon the very filth of Morjin's soul, must somehow have drawn down Morjin upon him.

'Is he dead, then?' I asked Liljana. 'Have you come to tell me that Bemossed is dead?'

'I came to tell you *not* to give up hope,' she said, squeezing my hand. 'And so if I knew the Shining One was dead, how could there be hope?'

I considered this for a moment as I looked at her. 'But you cannot tell me that he is *not* dead.'

She sighed as she held up her crystal to the lanterns' light. 'I cannot tell you very much for certain at all.'

She went on to say more about her personal quest to explore the mysteries of her blue gelstei and gain mastery over it. In the Age of the Mother, she told me, in the great years, the whole continent of Ea had been knitted together by women in every land speaking mind to mind through the power of the blue gelstei. The Order of Brothers and Sisters of the Earth had trained certain sensitive people to attune to the lapis-like crystals, cast into the form of amulets, pendants, pins and figurines. Some had gained the virtue of detecting falseness or veracity in others' words, and these were called truthsayers. Others found themselves able to speak in strange languages or remember events that had occurred long before their birth or give others great and beautiful dreams. Only the rarest and most adept in the ways of pure consciousness, however, learned to hear the whisperings and thoughts of another's mind. No one knew why those most talented at mindspeaking had always been women. With the breaking of the Order into the Brotherhood and that secret group of women that became the Maitriche Telu, men had almost completely lost knowledge of the blue gelstei while any woman possessing even a hint of the ability to listen to another's thoughts was reviled as a witch.

'I *know* that the time is coming,' Liljana said to me, 'when the whole world will be one as it was in the Age of the Mother. We will make it so: those who still keep the blue gelstei or have the will to try to attune themselves to one, whether they hold the sacred blestei in hand, or not. I have not spoken to you of this, but I have been trying to seek out these women. If we could pass important communications from city to city and land to land at the speed of thought, we would gain a great advantage over Morjin.'

I nodded my head at this, then said, 'Assuming that he himself does not have this power.'

'He is a man,' she huffed out with a wave of her hand as if that said everything.

'He is a man,' I said, 'who somehow managed to control his three droghuls' every thought and motion from a thousand miles away.'

'Yes, *droghuls*,' she said. 'Creatures made from his own mind and flesh.'

'Kane,' I said to her, 'believes that Morjin keeps a blue gelstei.'

'Even if he does, and is able to project his filthy illusions through it, that does not mean that he can speak mind to mind with other men.'

Some deep tension in her throat made me look at her more closely as I said to her, 'Only men dwelled at the Brotherhood's school. How, then, did you come by your knowledge of its destruction?'

'It was Master Storr,' she told me. 'I believe he kept a blestei.'

I remembered very well the Brotherhood's Master Galastei: a stout, old man with fair, liver-spotted skin and wispy white hair. A suspicious man, who spent his life in ferreting out secrets, whether of men and women or ancient crystals forged ages ago.

'I was casting my thoughts in that direction,' she continued. 'I *know* I touched minds with him – it was only an hour ago! When the full moon rises and the world dreams, that is the best time to try to speak with others far away. Somewhere to the west, on the Wendrush, I think, the moon rose over Abrasax and Master Storr – perhaps the other Masters as well. And, I pray, over Bemossed. They were fleeing.'

She went on to explain that she had only had a moment to make out all that Master Storr wanted to tell her.

'Somehow Morjin must have learned the secret of the tunnels,' she said, 'for he sent a company of Red Knights through one of them – right down through the valley. There was a battle, I think. A *slaughter*. The younger brothers tried to stand before the Red Knights while the Seven escaped.'

I pressed my finger to the warm teapot as I said, 'But how *could* they escape? Only one tunnel gives out into the valley – surely the Red Knights would have guarded the entrance.'

'I can't say – you know how strange those tunnels were. Perhaps there was another entrance. Or another tunnel.'

I thought about this for a few moments. 'But did the Red Knights pursue the Seven? And did Bemossed escape with them?'

'I don't know. I couldn't *see* that in Master Storr's mind.'

'But wouldn't he have wanted to tell you that particular tiding, above all others?'

'Of course he would have – I think.' Liljana rubbed at her temple as she looked down at her little blue stone. 'Speaking with another this way is not like sitting down to table to have a chat with a friend. At least, I don't think it is. There has been no one to teach me this art, and I'm really like a child playing with matches. And Master Storr is even more artless than I. He is only a *man* – and a very confused one at that. At least he seemed so when we managed to attune our two gelstei. We had only a moment, you know. A single moment and a flood of images, as in a dream, fire and blood and bewilderment, you see, trying to make sense of it all. To really *hear* what was in Master Storr's mind. It was like trying to drink from a raging river. In fact . . .'

Her voice died off into the sound of the crickets chirping somewhere in the garden. I waited for her to say more, but she only gazed up at the white disk of the moon.

'In fact,' she said in a trancelike rush of words, 'if I am to be completely truthful with you, as I always try to be, I have to consider the possibility that what I touched upon in Master Storr's mind *was* a dream.'

'A nightmare, you mean,' I said, taking a deep breath of air. I looked at Liljana. 'Then it is possible that nothing of what you told me actually happened.'

'No, it *happened* – of course it did. I know it in my heart.'

Here she pressed her hand to her chest and then reached out to pour the tea into our cups.

'It might indeed have been a nightmare,' she told me. 'But if so, then Master Storr was dreaming of these terrible things that Morjin did to the Brothers and their school.'

'But how do you know that Master Storr wasn't just dreaming of that which he most feared would befall?'

'I don't *know* how I know – I just do. There is a difference. It is like the taste of salt versus the description of saltiness. But since I can't expect you to appreciate this, as a mindspeaker does, I thought that I should tell you all.'

I sat sipping my tea and hoping that the chamomile might drive away the burning ache in my throat. I gazed at the clusters of the lilacs on the bushes along the garden's wall. It was strange, I thought, that even in the intense light of the moon, their soft purple color had vanished into the darker tones of the night.

'Have you tried again?' I said to Liljana as I looked up at the sky. 'We have hours of moonlight left, don't we?'

'I have tried and tried,' she told me. 'And then tried thrice more. But Master Storr, I have to tell you, is not much of a mindspeaker – whether or not he dreams or wakes. And neither am I.'

'Once,' I told her, 'you looked into a dragon's mind. And into Morjin's.'

'Yes, into his. But he burned me, Morjin did,' she said with a terrible sadness.

'I know he did,' I told her. 'But before he did, there was a moment, wasn't there? When you *saw* the great Red Dragon, and he saw you. And was afraid of you, as it was with the dragon called Angraboda.'

'He was afraid,' she admitted. 'But I was terrified.'

'Terrified, perhaps – as much as you ever allow yourself to be. But that has never kept you from looking into dark places, has it? Or going into them.'

Now she took a turn sipping her tea before she finally said to me, 'I'm not sure I want to know what you mean.'

I reached out and took hold of her hand. I glanced at her gelstei, then asked her, 'Now that Bemossed has driven back Morjin's mind from your crystal and given its power back to you, have you ever thought of using it to try to look into *Morjin's* mind again?'

She suddenly snapped her hand from my grasp, and covered up her gelstei. She said, 'But I have promised never to look into a man's mind without his permission!'

'Yes, you have,' I told her. 'But Morjin is more a beast than a man, or so you have said. You wouldn't keep that promise for *his* sake.'

'No, I wouldn't,' she agreed, squeezing her blue stone. 'But what you suggest is so *dangerous*.'

Truly, I thought, it was: like a double-edged sword, Liljana's talent could cut two ways. If she touched minds with Morjin, he could tear from her some essential knowledge or secret as she could from him. And Morjin could again ravage her mind, or do to her even worse things.

Even so, I stared at her through the wan light and said, 'I have to know, Liljana.'

'No, no, you don't,' she murmured, shaking her head.

'I have to know if Bemossed still lives,' I said. 'And Morjin would know that, if anyone does.'

'Yes, *Morjin*,' she said.

I felt her throat burning as with a desire for revenge, even as her soft eyes filled with pleading, compassion and great hope. I did not pursue my suggestion that she seek out the foul, rat-infested caverns of Morjin's mind. Although I suspected that she herself might dare to contend with him mind to mind once more, someday, this impulse must come from her, according to her sense of her own power – otherwise Morjin might very well seize her will and make her into a ghul. If I loved her, I thought, how could I violate her soul with any demand that might lead toward such a terrible fate?

'I'm sure,' she said, suddenly warming toward me, 'that I would have felt it in Master Storr's mind if Bemossed had been killed.'

I did not know if that was true – or if she only wanted it to be true, and so believed it. But I needed her to tell me that Bemossed still lived, and make *me* believe it. And so she did, and so I loved her, for she was almost like my own mother, who had been able to make me believe in most anything, myself most of all.

'My apologies,' I told her, 'for bringing up the matter of Morjin.'

She waved her hand at this, and looked at me deeply. 'Don't give it another thought.'

'I think about little else. I know it is upon me to face him – someday, somehow. But first, I'm sorry to say, I wanted you to find out where he is the most vulnerable, as it was with Angraboda. Or even to put a little poison in his mind and let it work.'

The look in her eyes grew even warmer and brighter as I said this. She almost smiled, then. That was her magic, I thought, to love me despite my weaknesses and darkest dreams. She was like a tree with very deep roots, and something about her seemed to enfold my life with all the vitality of fresh running sap and a crown of shimmering green leaves.

'If *I* were Morjin,' she said to me, 'I would not want *you* as my enemy.'

'If you were Morjin,' I told her, 'the world would not need Bemossed to restore it.'

Although she could not smile, she could still frown easily enough, which she now did. 'The Sisterhood, I should tell you, has always taught that it will be a *woman* who will bring new life to the world – even as a mother does with a child. I admit that it is strange for me to think of Bemossed as the Maitreya, though I don't see how he cannot be.'

I couldn't help smiling at this. Each Maitreya throughout the ages had been a man, as the *Saganom Elu* had told, and never, I thought, had a man been born into the world as splendid as Bemossed.

'He will come here,' I told her. 'If you are right and the Brotherhood school is destroyed, Bemossed will want the Seven to bring him here.'

'But how do you know that?'

In answer, I drew my sword from its scabbard, which I had set down by the side of the table. Alkaladur's silver blade shimmered in the light of the stars.

'I *know*,' I told her, echoing the words that she had spoken to me. 'They will try to make their way here, to these mountains, and so Mesh must be made safe.'

'Then you will do what you must do to make it so. As you always *do*. I saw that in you the first time we met.'

I smiled again as I looked up at the stars. To Liljana, I pointed out Valura and Solaru – and then Icesse, Hyanne and the other stars of the Mother's Necklace, high in the sky in this season of the year.

'If Alphanderry is right,' I said, 'about Damoom's star conjuncting the earth this fall, we have so little time to accomplish what we must accomplish.'

'But we *do* have time, still.'

'Time,' I said, gazing at the bright silustria of my sword. 'Already, a thousand warriors have answered Lord Avijan's call. And in another six or seven days, there will be a thousand more.'

'And you will win them as you did the others,' Liljana told me. 'And then somehow, Lord Tomavar and Lord Tanu.'

'I must win them. Or win *against* them. Otherwise, Bemossed might as well try to find refuge in Argattha as here.'

'But what is your *plan*, Val? You have yet to confide it to me.'

My sword glistered with the lights of the constellations shining above us – and seemed to await the clusters of stars soon to rise. And I said to Liljana, 'That is because I still don't know. Ask me again in another week.'

'All right,' she said to me, 'but for now, why don't you finish your tea and try to sleep? Tomorrow can only bring you better tidings than I did tonight.'

Liljana, though adept at many arts, proved to be no scryer. Late the next morning, a messenger galloped up to the castle bearing tidings that no one wanted to hear: Lord Tanu had assembled his men and had marched out of Godhra along the North Road. Four thousand warriors he had called up to fight for him on foot, while three hundred knights rode beneath his banner. Only yesterday, this army had crossed the Arashar River and passed through Hardu, and was now making its way toward Mount Eluru and Lord Avijan's castle where many fewer warriors so far had gathered to me.

5

This news set the castle into a fury of activity. Lord Avijan immediately sent out emissaries to speak with Lord Tanu. He ordered the castle's walls manned and extra provisions brought inside. Then, some hours later when he deemed all was secured, he summoned the greatest lords and knights to a war council in his great hall.

'Lord Tanu has moved more quickly than even I would have thought possible,' he told us.

I sat at one end of the great table at the front of the hall facing Lord Avijan at the other. In between us along one side of the table were Lord Harsha, Lord Sharad and Lord Noldashan – Sar Jessu and Sar Vikan, too. My companions took their places along the table's other side with Lord Manthanu, a thick and jowly man who had arrived only the day before. This great knight regarded me with puzzlement clouding his long face; he pulled at one of the battle ribbons tied to his long gray hair as if wondering if the tides of war would sweep him away so soon.

'It is upon me,' Lord Avijan said, looking up the table at me, 'to see to the defenses of my lands and my castle. As it is upon us to advise you, Lord Elahad. But if you are to be king, in the end you must decide what we should do about Lord Tanu.'

I inclined my head to him, then said, 'To begin with, we don't know why Lord Tanu is marching up the North Road.'

'He isn't on his way to invade Ishka!' Sar Vikan called out.

I smiled at this as the others laughed grimly. Then I said, 'It seems that there is little doubt as to *where* Lord Tanu is leading his army. But we don't yet know his intentions.'

'To raze Lord Avijan's castle and see you murdered!' Sar Vikan cried out again. 'And all of us who support you. *That* is his intention!'

'Here, now!' Lord Harsha said, banging the table with his hand. 'There's no need for such talk! Lord Tanu is no murderer, and he is certainly not so stupid as to waste his army trying to take this castle.'

At this, Lord Sharad studied the keep's thick walls, and said, 'If not take it, then perhaps lay siege.'

I slowly nodded my head at this as I looked at Lord Avijan. I asked him, 'How long could you hold out against Lord Tanu's army?'

'Not so long as we could have a few days ago,' Lord Avijan said. He pointed out into the hall, whose many tables would soon be filled with hungry men eating their dinner. 'A thousand warriors have answered your call, Lord Elahad, and that is a great many to feed. Our stores might last four months.'

'Four months!' Sar Jessu said. His thick black eyebrows pulled together. 'That is a long time to lay siege. Lord Tanu might give up.'

'He *won't* give up,' Lord Avijan said. 'No knight in Mesh is more tenacious. You have fought under him, and should know that.'

'Then even if he doesn't, anything might happen in the meantime,' Sar Jessu said. 'Lord Tomavar might move against Lord Tanu. Or the Waashians might move against all of us.'

Here Sar Jessu turned toward me, and so did Lord Avijan, Lord Harsha and everyone else. And I told them, 'We cannot afford to wait four months – not even one. Whatever we do, we cannot remain holed-up here behind these walls. That is what Lord Tanu wants.'

Sar Vikan, a fiery and impulsive man, called out to me, 'But you have said that you don't know his intentions!'

I looked at Atara, whose blindfolded face was like a clear glass giving sight of the future. I looked at Liljana, whose relentless gaze reminded me that I must always try to look into my enemies' minds and try to think as they did – even as my father had taught me.

'My apologies for misspeaking,' I told Sar Vikan. 'But surely, as Lord Harsha has said, Lord Tanu will not waste his men attacking the castle. Therefore his strategy must be to keep us immobilized here – and to divide Lord Avijan's forces.'

'*Your* forces, now, Lord Elahad,' Lord Avijan said.

'We shall see,' I said, inclining my head to him. 'Lord Tanu can encamp his army outside the castle and block the pass leading to it. He would keep the rest of your men from joining us. And threaten them. Would they then still keep their oath to you?'

'Certainly they would!' Lord Avijan said. 'They are good men, with true hearts!'

Sar Vikan, who now finally saw the line of my argument, asked Lord Avijan, 'But if you released them from their oaths, as you released us, in such circumstances, would they then pledge their swords to Lord Elahad?'

At this, Lord Avijan looked down at the table and said nothing – and so said everything.

'Lord Tanu *would* divide us,' Lord Manthanu said to me in his deep, gravely voice. 'And that might be the end of your chances, Lord Valashu. In my district, many warriors remain unpledged to anyone – as it is throughout Mesh. They wait to see what you will do. A victory of any sort will encourage them. But a defeat . . .'

He did not finish his sentence, nor did I wish him to. I did not want to think in terms of *victory* over my own countrymen, if that meant driving them down with swords.

Lord Noldashan rubbed at his tired eyes and said to me with a deep anxiety, 'If you won't stand to be besieged, does that mean that you will take the field against Lord Tanu?'

'If he does,' Lord Sharad said boldly, 'Lord Elahad will find a way to outmaneuver our enemy as it was at the Culhadosh Commons!'

'We'll cut down any of Lord Tanu's men who stand against us!' Sar Vikan called out.

At this, Lord Harsha banged his fist against the table and shouted, 'Enemy! Cut down! Have none of you listened to what Lord Valashu has been saying these last days? We cannot weaken ourselves so!'

Both Lord Sharad and Sar Vikan looked down in shame. Then I said to them, 'No one can blame you for letting such great spirit impel you toward battle. But this must *not* be against Lord Tanu, nor Lord Tomavar – not if we can help it. So long as I am alive, I will *not* see Meshian slaying Meshian.'

Lord Avijan, perhaps the most intelligent and purposeful of the warriors at the table, asked me, 'If you won't stand a siege nor take the field, what will you do?'

At this fundamental question, I noticed Master Juwain looking at me keenly – along with everyone else. And I said, simply, 'I will talk with Lord Tanu. Tomorrow, I will ride down into the pass, and try to reason with him.'

All during our council, Maram had remained uncharacteristically quiet. I worried that his beer guzzling had finally addled his wits. But now he licked his lips as he looked at me and said, 'But Lord Tanu will be bringing his whole damn army through that pass! You can't ride down into that river of swords! It's too dangerous!'

I smiled at this, and I said, 'We shall fly a banner of truce, and Lord Tanu will have to respect that. In any case, Sar Maram, I have to know.'

'Know what . . . *Lord* Elahad?'

'I must know what Lord Tanu truly intends.' I paused to draw in a breath and look around the table. 'Is *he* willing that we should slay each other just so that he might become king?'

Much later, after we had eaten dinner and I finally had a chance to speak with my companions about the destruction of the Brotherhood school, Lord Avijan's emissaries returned to the castle in the dead of night. They made report of Lord Tanu's intentions – or rather, his stated purpose in marching toward Mount Eluru. Lord Tanu, they said, had taken it upon himself to ensure Mesh's safety. And so on the morrow, he would arrive to inspect the soundness of Lord Avijan's castle, with or without Lord Avijan's leave.

The next morning, as I had promised, I made ready to go forth and speak with Lord Tanu. I asked my friends to accompany me. Although we would be riding under a banner of truce – along with Lord Avijan, Lord Harsha and the other knights who had become my war counselors – I did not want to chance the children's safety in the midst of many angry men with quick and deadly swords. Daj protested my decision, reminding me of how he had slain the third droghul and taken far greater risks before: 'Estrella and I rode with you all the way to Hesperu, and back, and you won't allow us to ride a couple more miles?'

Estrella brushed the curls from her dark, liquid eyes, and she looked at me as if to tell me once more that our lives were bound together, and wherever I went, she must go as well. In her quiet, sweet way, she could be a very willful girl – now almost a young woman. Even so, I had to tell her that she must remain in the castle.

In the cool air blowing off the mountains, we rode out of the castle's south gate and down the narrow road that cut through the green hills and meadows toward the pass. I took the lead, with Lord Avijan at my one side and Sar Vikan at my other. To this fierce knight, perhaps the most bellicose of all the men in my train,

I had appointed the task of holding up the white banner of truce. Just behind him rode Sar Joshu Kadar, who had taken charge of the banner showing the silver swan and seven stars of the Elahads. Then came Lord Harsha, Lord Sharad, Lord Manthanu and Jessu the Lion-Heart – followed by Lord Noldashan and his son, Sar Jonavar. I had asked other five other young knights to join us, too: Sar Shivalad, Viku Aradam, Sar Kanshar, Siraj the Younger and Jurald Evar. My companions kept pace with them only a few yards behind, with Atara pushing her horse to an easy trot in the rear. Although we expected no attack from this direction, nor at all, Atara could whip about in her saddle and fire off an arrow at any pursuer in the blink of an eye.

Our course took us into a long taper of grassy land wedged between the Lake of the Ten Thousand Swans to our right and Mount Eluru to our left. As we moved further into the pass, this taper grew narrower and narrower. Finally, we came to that place where the road cut through a band of grass only ten yards wide. There we came to a halt. We had a nearly perfect day to wait for Lord Tanu and his army. The sky above us shone a deep and dazzling blue, with a few white clouds moving slowly along a cool breeze. This slight wind, however, failed to ripple the lake's silvery waters, which had fallen as clear and still as a mirror. In its perfect sheen, I saw the reflection of Mount Eluru: a great and nearly symmetrical cone of green, tree-covered slopes, blue rock and white ice pushing straight up into the heavens.

After some time had passed and the sun rose over Mount Eluru's eastern ridgeline, Maram rode forward to speak with me. As we had no privacy at the head of fourteen diamond-armored knights, we urged on our horses a few dozen more yards, and closer to the lake.

And then Maram held up his firestone to the glaring sunlight, and said, 'Do you remember the Kul Moroth? A single blast from this, and I filled up that damn pass with enough rocks to stop an army.'

He looked up at the smooth, steep slopes of Mount Eluru above us; they were not so steep, however, that any of the few large rocks or boulders sticking out of the ground could easily be dislodged and rolled down into the pass.

'I think I see the direction of your worries,' I said to him.

'Do you?' he said, pointing his firestone down the road through the pass. 'At Khaisham, I used this to set men on fire, like torches. But never again. I *won't* use this against men, Val.'

'You won't have to,' I said to him. 'There will be no violence here today.'

'Oh, no? Why can't I believe that? I have a bad feeling about you meeting Lord Tanu here.'

I waved my hand at this. 'You have had other bad feelings before.'

'Yes, I have,' he said. 'And most of them have proved out even worse than I had feared.'

'It will be all right,' I told him. 'I have known Lord Tanu all my life, and he is a man I can reason with.'

'Is this a day for *reason*, then?' He shook his head then gazed at me. 'I will not summon fire out of this stone, but ever since Liljana told you about Bemossed, you're practically burning up with this rage to become king. That makes a bad situation urgent. And urgency, in my sad experience, too often leads to violence.'

I laid my hand on the diamonds encrusting his arm. 'We have faced more urgent situations before.'

'Perhaps,' he said, 'but one never knows about these things. A mole's little hole can trip a horse and break a man's neck. A single match can set a whole grassland on fire. What might a few ill-considered words do? It is all too much, do you see? Alphanderry told us, in effect, that we had until this fall to succeed or fail, once and for all. *I'm* telling you, Val, that I don't have it in me to go on any longer than that, as we have gone through one hell after another these past three years.'

My hand tightened around his arm, and I smiled at him. '*You* say that? The man who crossed half the Red Desert by himself to save me?'

'I *do* say that!' he called out as he pulled away from me. He looked at the knights gathered behind us with the flag of truce barely rippling in the soft wind. 'We could *die* here today, as easily as anywhere. Your Sar Vikan and Sar Jessu seem eager enough to draw swords.'

'It will *not* be a day for swords,' I reassured him as I patted Alkaladur's scabbard, slung on my back. Then I added, 'At least, not kalamas.'

'Well, if it *is*,' he said, staring at Jessu the Lion-Heart, 'I won't be of much use. Not against *Valari* knights. And they know that.'

'What do you mean?'

'I mean, your countrymen all see me as a complainer and a coward.'

'No, you are wrong – it is just the opposite,' I told him. 'You

81

have succeeded in two great quests. And taken a second in wrestling at the tournament and a third in archery. And above all, you slew half a dozen Ikurians at the Culhadosh Commons. To my people, you *are* a true Valari knight. They regard you as a hero, Maram.'

Maram thought about this as he studied Sar Shivalad, Sar Kanshar and Viku Aradam, who sat bunched together and looking back at him. And he muttered, 'Well, if they *don't* see me as a coward, they should. It can't be long, you know. Today, or tomorrow, or at the next *urgent* situation, whatever it is, I'll finally have had enough. I'll turn my back and flee, as any sane man would, and then your people will finally see what Sar Maram Marshayk is made of.'

'No, Maram, you are –'

'It is too much!' he said to me. 'Do you understand? Too, too damn much! I don't want to be *anyone's* hero.'

And with that, he wheeled his horse about, and rode slowly back to rejoin the others.

Then I took my place again at the head of the column of knights jammed into the pass. After perhaps a half an hour, I caught sight of a sparkling light ahead of us. Soon the knights of Lord Tanu's vanguard came closer, and the sun's reflection off their diamond armor shone with an eye-burning brilliance. I could not, at this distance, make out Lord Tanu's face, but I could see quite clearly his black, double-headed eagle banner held high and the same emblem emblazoned on his surcoat. As well I made out the charges of his two greatest captains: the red bull of Lord Eldru and Lord Ramjay's white tiger. I estimated the number of knights riding behind him at three hundred, which accorded with our reports. And behind this mass of mounted men with their long lances and triangular shields marched the rest of Lord Tanu's warriors, some four thousand strong. I could see practically the whole of the army, strung out around the curve of the lake like a mile-long strand of diamonds.

Lord Tanu, of course, had an equally good view of us. He must have seen Sar Vikan's white banner clearly enough, for he made no move to deploy his warriors into a battle formation, nor did he change his slow and relentless march toward us. The silver bells tied to the boots of the thousands of warriors that he led sent a high-pitched jingling into the air. This eerie sound, tinkling out with a terrible beat, had often unnerved the enemies of the Valari. And sometimes the Valari themselves. I remembered hearing it before on the battlefield of the Red Mountain in Waas. I reminded myself that we faced no enemy, but only proud Meshian warriors who should be as brothers to us.

I could almost feel Maram sweating in his saddle behind me and the hearts of my companions beating more quickly as Lord Tanu rode forward. For a moment it seemed that he and his entire vanguard might keep on going and try to sweep us from the pass down into the lake. At the last moment, however, at a distance of only ten paces, he stopped his horse and held up his hand to call for a halt. The three hundred knights behind him ceased their march, as did the thousands of warriors behind them.

'Lord Valashu Elahad,' he called out to me formally in his sawlike voice, 'we had heard that you had returned to Mesh, though we hoped you never would.'

Lord Tanu sat on a big horse as he regarded me with his small, black, deep-set eyes. At nearly sixty years of age, he still retained the suppleness and strength of a much younger warrior. Although not large in his body, his fighting spirit and skill at arms had almost always led him to prevail against his foes. He had a tight, sour face that did nothing to hide his irascible temperament. I had known this man all my life. I remembered my father telling me why he had chosen Lord Tanu as one of the two greatest captains of his army: because he was quick of mind and fearless in battle and as steady as a rock. My father also had counted on Lord Tanu always to tell him the blunt and painful truth.

'It would have been better,' he said to me, 'if you had stayed in exile in whatever land you found to give you shelter. Your presence here is only a disturbance. And your purpose is vain – and *in* vain. We have heard of your call for men to gather to your standard. Promises to defeat the Red Dragon you have given, and people believe you. You remain a firebrand who incites impossible dreams.'

I could feel the knights near me waiting for me to gainsay him. But I did not wish to dispute him word for word and assertion with counter-assertion. And so I said to him, 'My father always valued your counsel, Lord Tanu, hard though it sometimes might be to hear. But he would *not* have appreciated your claim to his throne.'

I sensed Lord Tanu's face flushing with a hot surge of blood as he lowered his eyes in shame. Then, at his right side, Lord Eldru angrily shook his head. Long white hair flowed out from beneath his winged helm, and his stern, wrinkled face showed a great round scar where an enemy spear had pierced his jaw down through his throat and nearly killed him at the Culhadosh Commons. Finally, he spoke for Lord Tanu, saying, 'Would your father have thought *you* more worthy of the crown? You, who deserted the castle in defiance of your father's command?'

Next to him sat the iron-haired and iron-faced Lord Ramjay, and Sar Shagarth, a large master knight sporting a thick mustache and black beard rare among the Valari. They nodded their heads in agreement as Lord Eldru recited the same indictments that had been made against me after the Great Battle: that five years previously, in Waas, I had hesitated in slaying the enemy, and so could not be trusted to lead men. And that two years ago, in Tria, in a fit of wrath, I had slain the innocent Ravik Kirriland, who was *not* my enemy, and so I should be doubly mistrusted. And that on the Culhadosh Commons, my taking command of Lord Eldru's reserve and waiting to attack had put the entire army at risk and should be taken as a proof of my recklessness.

'A year ago,' Lord Eldru said to me, 'you left Mesh for lands unknown, and in that time, nothing has changed.'

Because I had previously defended my actions to these men, to little effect, I decided to let the past remain the past. But I must, I thought, at all costs speak for the future.

'Everything has changed,' I told them. 'To begin with, we have found the Maitreya.'

Lord Tanu finally looked at me again as his harsh voice whipped out: 'So you say, Lord Valashu. As you said once before when *you* claimed to be the Maitreya.'

'Every man,' I told him, 'deserves a chance to be wrong once in his life. But I am not wrong about Bemossed.'

As I went on to tell of this man who had worked miracles of healing and other wonders, Lord Tanu listened intently. I held nothing back in my description of how Bemossed had given new life to a dying boy and had faced down Morjin's ghul – and so overcame Morjin himself; I spoke with all the power and truthfulness that I could summon. My love for Bemossed, I thought, if not my words, touched something inside Lord Tanu and cracked open a hidden door. But he immediately tried to slam it shut again.

'Maitreya or not,' he said, 'your claim for your latest quest has little to do with the problems that Mesh faces – nor does it help men to see the way clear to their solution.'

At this, Lord Avijan took umbrage, pointing at the knights behind Lord Tanu and calling out, 'Is *this*, then, your solution to a divided realm? That you should march uninvited into my lands at the head of an army?'

'If I had made request,' Lord Tanu countered, 'would you have made invitation?'

I felt the steel inside Lord Avijan heating up, as with a sword plunged into a bed of hot coals. He did not, however, let his anger cause him to misspeak. He merely stared at Lord Tanu and said with an icy calm, 'You are always welcome in my castle, Lord Tanu. We will always try to keep a room open for you – though I'm sorry to say we cannot accommodate four thousand men.'

'We heard that you accommodated a thousand easily enough, with more expected,' Lord Tanu told him. 'Such a gathering of warriors, so close to Waas, might cause King Sandarkan to worry that you are about to attack him. Indeed, my counselors worry that this might provoke him into attacking *you*.'

Here he nodded at Lord Eldru and Lord Ramjay, who nodded back.

Then Lord Avijan, forcing down a grim smile, said, 'One would think that your four thousand warriors pose an even greater provocation.'

'Perhaps they do. But at least if King Sandarkan is so provoked, we will have the strength to turn him back.'

'I see,' Lord Avijan said. 'Then you marched here unheralded as a show of strength?'

Lord Tanu smiled sourly at this. 'You understand, then. We must show King Sandarkan that Mesh's warriors remain ready to march to any part of the realm at a moment's notice and defend it. And *we* must know that our castles remain in good repair so that we can mount an effective defense, if need be. Your castle is critical to Mesh's security.'

'Then you have my assurance,' Lord Avijan told him, 'that my castle is in excellent repair. Her gates are strong, and we've plenty of oil to heat up and pour down upon attackers – plenty of arrows, too.'

Lord Tanu nodded at this as he pulled at one of the ribbons tied to his long hair. He looked at Lord Eldru, and then at Lord Ramjay and Sar Shagarth. Finally he turned back to Lord Avijan and told him, 'Surely you can understand that we must see this for ourselves.'

His insistence angered Sar Vikan, who shook the white banner of truce at him, and shouted, 'See for yourself then as you stand beneath the battlements and bathe in burning oil!'

I tried to keep my face stern and still as Lord Avijan held up his hand to quiet him. Then Lord Avijan told Lord Tanu: 'You do not have the right to inspect my lands, or my leave to cross them. And you do not have the right to be king.'

A quiet fell over the knights gathered on the road, and the only sound to be heard was the flapping of a swan's wings far out on the lake. Then Lord Avijan said that Mesh must have a king who could unite the whole of the realm and then gain victory over the other Valari kingdoms – or win an alliance with them – in order to oppose Morjin.

At this Lord Tanu nodded his head at Lord Avijan, and said, 'Your arguments are good ones, but it is not Valashu Elahad who should be king. He will only divide the realm further, for the reasons that have already been stated. Also, he is too taken with heroics. And he is too young.'

Lord Harsha, from on top of his horse behind me, barked out, 'You have known Lord Valashu all his life, and you still don't know him. And you don't know *yourself*, if you think you should be king in his stead.'

'My failings are many,' Lord Tanu fired back, 'and thank you for reminding me. Even as I grieve King Shamesh's death, I wish that Lord Asaru had lived to wear his father's ring. Or any of his brothers, save Lord Valashu, I would have wished see as king rather than myself. But fate is fate, and the world turns on. What are we to do? Lord Tomavar, as we all know, is too proud to be king. Too quick to take insult, too eager for glory and he loves war too much. A fine tactician, yes, but he is weak in strategy, and he does not listen to others' counsel, and so what hope have we that he will lead us to victory in the wars soon to come? And you, Lord Avijan, have too little support to be king. Other claimants have less. Therefore it is upon me to take up a mantle I never sought.'

As the wind rose and bent the grasses along the side of the road, I sensed that he was speaking the truth – at least the truth as he saw it. Lord Tanu had realized all his ambitions as one of Mesh's most renowned warriors and greatest lords: commander of half of my father's army. My father had always counted him among the most faithful of his knights. I thought that he had no deep, driving desire to become king. But he was one of those men who reasoned relentlessly and flawlessly from unquestioned premises to reach a perfectly logical result that was dead wrong.

'Only one man,' he said, looking at me, 'can be Mesh's king.'

Each time he uttered this word, I sensed, he added another iron bar to the prison that he was building for himself.

'Only one,' I agreed, gazing back at him. I felt within myself a great power to use the valarda simply to batter down the doors of his will and bend him to my purpose.

'Don't look at me like that, Lord Elahad!' he said to me. 'As I have the best claim, it is upon me to do whatever must be done to make Mesh safe.'

He shot me a hard, pugnacious look, but I felt a hint of fear burn through him as well. I finally turned my gaze away from him. Battering down doors, I remembered, was Morjin's way, not mine.

'Four thousand three hundred warriors,' I said, pointing behind him, 'follow you. But five thousand stood for me upon the Culhadosh Commons.'

'My claim is not solely of numbers. Do not delude yourself into thinking the warriors wish you to be king. Go back into exile, and Mesh will be the better for it.'

'You speak for the warriors,' I said, 'but they have voices of their own. And wills. Release them from their pledges to you, and let them stand for whomever they will, and we shall see who will be king.'

Lord Tanu's face tightened at this, and he told me, 'At the Culhadosh Commons, five thousand stood for you – and eight thousand against. They have stood, and that is the law. It is decided.'

'No law prevents them from standing again.'

'It is pointless, Lord Elahad.'

'Let the warriors decide,' I told him.

Lord Tanu glanced behind me at Master Juwain, Atara and Liljana, and seemed to be looking for Kane, as well. And he said, 'You keep strange company. You have a strange way about you, and nothing is stranger than the story people tell about you merely looking at the Alonian lord in Tria and somehow causing him to die.'

I gazed at the many knights gathered behind Lord Tanu. 'I have not returned to Mesh to cause *anyone* to die – except Morjin and those who follow him. Release your warriors from their pledges to you that they might decide whether or not to follow me against the Red Dragon!'

Lord Tanu slowly shook his head at this like a bull preparing to charge. Then he called out to me: 'Remove yourself from this road, and leave Mesh.'

I glanced down at the road's paving stones, and I said, 'My ancestors built this road, and my father saw to its maintenance.

He would have wanted me to inspect it, when the time came. And he would *not* want me to ride off just because Lord Vishathar Tanu commanded it.'

Now Lord Tanu stared at me, in anger and dread. He pointed along the strip of land behind me, and barked out, 'Our army marches through this pass!'

'And here I stand!'

So saying, I dismounted, then gave my horse to the care of Sar Kanshar. I took a few steps toward Lord Tanu, out onto the bare road away from Sar Vikan and Joshu Kadar and the other knights accompanying me. They looked at me as if I had fallen mad, but I felt a great hope surging in them as well.

'We *will* march,' Lord Tanu said to me, 'whether you stand or fall!'

I feared that I *would* fall, and soon. If Lord Tanu pressed his knights to move forward, jammed together in the narrow pass, one or more of their horses would inevitably knock me over, and then other horses would trample me to death.

'If we cannot ride past you,' Lord Tanu shouted, 'we shall ride over you! I am not bluffing!'

'Neither am I!' I called back to him.

My reason told me that only I could be king of Mesh and find the way to defeat Morjin. But my heart cried out that if I died, I still might pass on the sacred sword of my dreams to others who would carry on the fight. Somehow, in the end, they would prevail. They *must* prevail, though it seemed impossible. Just as it seemed impossible that Lord Tanu would really command his knights to ride over me. Lord Tanu, though, did not make threats wantonly; I knew that he *would* let his knights' horses drive me down to the road's hard stones.

'One last time, Lord Elahad, I'll tell you to get off this road!'

I felt him steeling himself to press his knees against his horse and urge the great beast forward. Just then, from behind me, I heard the slap of boots against stone, as of someone running hard. I turned to see Estrella darting and weaving among the knights gathered behind me as she practically sprinted toward me. Daj followed close at her heels. I was never to learn how these two children found their way out of the castle; it seemed that once they had escaped, however, they had run the whole distance down to the pass. Estrella rushed up to my side, and threw her arms around me as she stood against me gasping for breath. Daj found his way to my other side, and his chest worked so hard to draw in air that it seemed his lungs might tear open. They looked up at Lord Tanu in defiance – and in fear, too.

'What is this?' Lord Tanu cried out to me. 'Some trick of yours?'

In answer, I could only shake my head at him.

'It is said,' Lord Tanu cried out, 'that these children accompanied you on your quest.'

In the way he gazed at Estrella, and then Daj, I wondered if he felt more keenly the loss of his two grandchildren, slaughtered when Morjin's Red Knights had ravaged my father's castle.

'Well, *this* is no place for children,' he continued. 'Get them off the road!'

I moved to take hold of them, for I would not see either of them trampled to death, even for the sake of my dream. But then Daj took hold of my leg even as Estrella tightened her grip around my waist. Then, with a great and heavy sigh, Maram dismounted, too, and came forward to stand by me. So did Liljana, Master Juwain and Atara. At their show of courage, the knights behind me could do no less, and so Lord Avijan took his place on the road, along with Lord Harsha, Joshu Kadar, and everyone else.

'*I* will remain with the Elahad!' Joshu Kadar shouted, staring at Lord Tanu. He had no liking for this old man who had taken his young lady love away from him. 'You *won't* drive us away!'

'I will remain, too!' Sar Shivalad called out.

Estrella, locked on to me, gazed at Lord Tanu with no less defiance.

'What *is* this?' Lord Tanu cried out. 'Must we ride over *all* of you?'

In the warmth of Estrella's face pressed against my chest I felt her will to stand and die wherever I stood. So it was with my other companions and the knights who followed me, even Maram, who pressed up behind me and clasped his hand around my arm. Their hearts seemed to beat in unison like a single, great drum. In the immense silence that sounded out along the road above the lake, I gazed at Lord Tanu. And *my* heart filled with a wild and anguished love of life.

'Ride, if you must,' I said to him.

For a long time, he sat on top of his great warhorse staring down at me. He appeared at once sad, fearful and weighed down with a bittersweet longing. My companions drew in closer to me. I felt their élan passing into me and gathering in my eyes with a painful brightness. Lord Tanu stared and stared at me, and at last, a door inside him opened. Then *his* eyes grew all moist and glassy, like the waters of the lake.

'I might have been wrong about you,' he forced out in a harsh, thick voice. 'I had thought you were vainglorious, like Lord Tomavar.'

He looked from Maram to Atara, and then at Lord Harsha, Lord Avijan and Joshu Kadar, still holding up my banner with the swan and stars. Then he said to me, 'Too many adventurers are careless of their own lives, and those of others. But it might be that you are more like your father and grandfather. They would gladly have *given* their lives for the men who followed them – and did.'

I bowed my head at this, then so did Lord Tanu and everyone else. After a few moments, Lord Tanu turned to Lord Eldru and said, 'Let us not ride any farther up this road today.'

He nodded at Lord Ramjay and Sar Shagarth, who nodded back at him. Then Lord Tanu said to Lord Avijan, standing a few paces from me: 'We will take your word that your castle is well defended. But you should prepare your warriors to march forth from it within the week.'

'And why is that?' Lord Avijan asked him.

'Because,' Lord Tanu said, looking at me, 'we shall call for a gathering of all the warriors in Mesh – even Lord Tomavar's. Let it be as Valashu Elahad has said: all who have made pledges should be released from them. Let the warriors decide who shall be king!'

At this, Sar Vikan let loose a great cheer, which Jessu the Lion-Heart and Sar Shivalad and the other knights near me picked up and amplified, calling out: 'Let the warriors decide!'

The knights who had pressed up close behind Lord Tanu must have sympathized with this sentiment, for they too repeated this cry. And then, like a command passed across a battlefield, the warriors drawn up in columns along the road shouted out that they should be allowed to stand for a new king. Their thousands of voices boomed out across the lake like a stroke of thunder.

'Very well, then,' Lord Tanu said, bowing his head to me. 'Until the gathering, Lord Elahad.'

'Until then, Lord Tanu,' I said, bowing back to him.

It was no great work for Lord Tanu to call for his captains to turn his army about and begin marching back down the road, with the vanguard following those who marched on foot. We watched them go as they had come, a great mass of men and horses pounding at the road's stone. When they had disappeared from our sight around the curve of the mountain, I looked down at Estrella, still clinging to me, and I said to her, 'It was *you* who led the way out of the castle, wasn't it?'

At this, she happily nodded her head as if she thought her action should have pleased me. Then Daj spoke for her, saying, 'We *couldn't* let you face Lord Tanu alone. He might have killed you!'

I tried to smile at him as I swallowed against the lump in my throat. Then Maram gazed down into the pass and muttered to me, 'Do you see how it goes, then? We survive another *urgent* situation, only to be to be forced into yet another. A gathering of the warriors, indeed! Three armies will be at this gathering – and Lord Tomavar, I think, will be quicker to have his warriors draw swords than to release them from their pledges.'

At this, Sar Vikan stepped up to Maram, and clapped him on the shoulder. 'If that is the way of things, then I shall have the pleasure of fighting by your side again. Which of Lord Tomavar's knights can stand against Sar Maram Marshayk?'

As Maram rolled his eyes at this and let out a soft groan, Lord Avijan came over to me. 'Which of *Mesh*'s knights will fail to stand for Valashu Elahad as king?'

For a while we remained there above the deep, blue lake feeling very glad for our lives – and not a little amazed that our small force had been able to turn back Lord Tanu's army without a single sword flying from its scabbard. I thought about Lord Avijan's words to me. Of all the questions in my life, at that moment, it was the one I most wanted to be answered.

6

It took more than a week for Lord Tanu's emissaries to ride across Mesh and arrange with Lord Tomavar a time and place for the gathering of the warriors: On the 21st of Soldru we were to converge on a great open meadow to the west of Hardu along the Arashar River. This field, where the Lake Country gave way to the Gorgeland at the very heart of the realm, was almost exactly equidistant from Mount Eluru, Godhra and Lord Tomavar's stronghold in Pushku. Other claimants to the throne – Lord Ramanu, Lord Bahram and Lord Kharashan – would have to make longer journeys. As they had no hope of becoming king, however, few worried that they might take insult in not being given equal consideration. It had proved hard enough to persuade Lord Tomavar to attend the gathering. In the end, however, his innate character drove him straight toward this historic confrontation. Perhaps he suspected that Lord Tanu and I would join forces against him, and he wanted to forestall such a combination. More likely he simply assumed that he could go among Mesh's warriors and win them to his banner with his bravura, a few quick smiles and a great show of strength.

As the spring deepened toward summer, warriors who had pledged to Lord Avijan continued riding up to his castle. By the ides of Soldru, almost all of these had arrived. Of course, there would always be a few who would miss the call to gather. As had happened with Sar Jonavar a year before, they might be away on hunting trips or meditation retreats deep in the mountains. These two or three dozen men, though, would not significantly diminish our forces, which Lord Avijan counted at more than twenty-three hundred. In combination with Lord Tanu's army, I thought, we *would* slightly outnumber the six thousand warriors said to be pledged to Lord Tomavar.

At dawn on the 18th we finally marched out of the castle and down to the pass. I led forth with Joshu Kadar flying my banner beside me. A hundred and fifty knights on horses came next, followed by more than two thousand warriors stepping along at a good pace. At the rising of the sun, their full diamond armor glittered with a fiery brilliance. My companions had leave to ride where they would, and most of them remained within the vanguard near me, though from time to time, Atara would drop back behind the marching columns to check on the wagons of the baggage train and to look for enemies in that direction. Or perhaps, I thought, she just wanted to gain a few moments of solitude riding behind the whole of our army. Although we had no reason to fear attack, a lifetime of discipline drove me to keep everyone moving in good order. My army, almost ten times the size of the greatest force that I had ever led, needed no extraordinary urging to negotiate the excellent roads leading down to Hardu. My father had always said that half the skill of commanding an army was just to keep men moving from one point to another and then seeing them lined up in good array for battle – but only half, and much the lesser half at that.

Our first day's march took us down the North Road a good part of the way to Hardu. On the second day we passed through this little city of waterwheels, mills and breweries, and we crossed over the Victory Bridge spanning the fast-flowing Arashar River. There we turned onto a smaller road paralleling it. It led north and west, behind the tree-covered slopes of Mount Vayu, and through some rolling green pastures toward the Gorgeland farther to the north. In the trough between two low hills, we came across acres of grass ablaze with blue and red starflowers. I knew of no other place on earth where these glorious things grew. A few miles farther on, however, where the road led away from the river, the flowers gave way to fields of long-bladed sweetgrass and the many sheep and cattle that grazed upon it.

At the end of the day, in a stretch of country where the hills flattened out a bit, we came upon the place of the gathering. This was a broad meadow perhaps a mile across. Acres of tents dotted the grass. Its center, though, had been kept clear, with many banners of truce flapping in the wind almost like great swans' wings. According to our agreement with Lord Tanu's emissaries, everyone was to encamp around a central square. Already Lord Tomavar's army, marching from Lashku in the west, had settled in to the west of the square, while Lord Tanu's four thousand men made camp to the south. Fanning out above the square's northern perimeter I made out the standards of Lord Ramanu, Lord Bahram and Lord Kharashan. They commanded four hundred, two hundred and a hundred and fifty men respectively. Other warriors and knights – those who had not given their pledges to any lord – set up there as well. Most of them had arrived without tents of their own, and so I had a hard time counting their numbers. If Lord Avijan was right, though, more than two thousand of these free warriors, as they called themselves, would assert their right to stand or not for any lord wishing to be king.

We made our way down to the expanse of meadow east of the square, scarcely four hundred yards from the roaring Arashar River. There we set up our camp, with neat lanes at regular intervals running down the lines of our tents. I had inherited my father's campaign pavilion: a great, billowing expanse of black silk embroidered with the silver swan and stars of our ancestors. My companions would sleep within tents next to mine, as would Lord Avijan, Lord Harsha and my other counselors. I did not like being so close to the river. Although we would not have to haul water so far as Lord Tanu's or Lord Tomavar's men, everything I knew about strategy warned me against taking a position with a river or lake at my back. If the worst befell and a battle *did* break out, we would have little room to maneuver against what might prove a much greater force.

'But I will not let it come to that,' I promised Maram that evening as we gathered around one of our campfires to eat some roasted lamb. 'And neither Lord Tanu or Lord Tomavar will break the truce.'

'No, of course they won't,' Maram said between bites of bloody meat. 'If it becomes obvious that the warriors want you as king, Lord Tomavar will march off beyond the bounds of the truce – and then turn and attack you farther down the river.'

For a while, after dinner, I stood at the edge of our encampment staring out across the square. Lord Tomavar stood with his knights in his encampment, staring back at me. Although the distance was too great to make out the features of his face with any clarity, I could see the black tower of the Tomavars emblazoned on his white surcoat. I sensed his black eyes seeking out my own and warning me not to oppose him.

As we had also agreed, we spent the night in our own encampment, with the warriors ordered to remain near their campfires, and so it was with Lord Tomavar and Lord Tanu and their men.

Although most of us had friends or kin in the other encampments, we had foes, too, and it wouldn't do to let a little casual mingling lead to arguments that might very well end in swords drawn and warriors lying dead in pools of blood.

Despite Maram's gloom, which he assuaged with cups of both beer and brandy, the night passed peacefully, and the next day dawned with clear blue skies and abundant sunshine. Lord Tomavar sent his emissaries across the square to the various encampments to call for an immediate conclave. But Lord Tanu would not be moved from his original plan: tomorrow would be the 21st of Soldru, and we must allow time for the last of the free warriors to arrive. The conclave, he said, must not begin before then.

Already, though, as Liljana pointed out, a sort of informal conclave had gotten underway. The news of the gathering had gone out to every corner of Mesh, and beyond. According to a long tradition, women and boys from Hardu arrived bearing food and drink for the warriors of our armies, and blacksmiths came up from Godhra to shoe horses and repair weapons or armor. Others, from Mir or the Diamond River clear across the realm, merely wished to be present at the choosing of a new king. They joined the throngs who set up little tents or made cookfires on the outskirts, around the warriors' encampments. By late morning, it seemed a city of Meshians had sprung up overnight from the pasture's thick grass.

A handful of outlanders also attended the gathering. On a trip down to the river, I saw five merchants from Delu and a dozen evacuees, from Galda and faraway Surrapam, who sought refuge in our land. From the Elyssu came a herbalist searching for rare botanicals, and this adventurous man incvitably found his way to consult with Master Juwain. A traveling troupe from Alonia, Nedu and points farther west decided to seek its fortune in entertaining the waiting warriors. They misjudged, however, the mood prevailing among those who had journeyed to this place: tense, wary and deadly serious. Few, it seemed, wanted to watch a juggler toss colored balls into the air or an acrobat walk across a tightrope – at least not yet.

Late in the afternoon, five warriors of the Manslayer Society arrived asking for the great *imakla* granddaughter of Sajagax. They rode their steppe ponies from Lord Tanu's encampment down the rows of tents into ours. Their leader, a stout, ebullient woman named Karimah, I knew from two campaigns across the

Wendrush. She could be quick with a drawn knife or a bow and arrow – and even quicker to smile and bandy words, with friend or foe. When Atara came forth to greet them, Karimah laughed out with great gladness and urged her horse forward so that she could kiss Atara's hands and face. She leaned her head down close to Atara's and spoke words that I could not hear. Then Atara went to saddle Fire. After leading this beautiful mare up to where I stood with Karimah and the others, she told me, 'We must hold a conclave of our own. We shall try to be back by dinner.' Without any further explanation, she rode off with her sister Manslayers. A burning disquiet worked at my throat as I watched them make their way through the many people ringing our encampment. Then they crested the hill to the north above the river, and disappeared.

And so Atara did not witness the miraculous event that stirred warriors in every encampment to break off their sword practice and rush to the edges of the square. From out of the south, along the crowded central lane running through Lord Tanu's array of tents, a single rider appeared and made his way into the square. His close-cropped white hair gleamed in the sun almost as brightly as a steel helm. The lines of his sun-browned face – at once savage and beautiful and burning with a strange grace – had been set like cracks running through stone. His large, powerful body flowed with the movements of his nearly spent horse. He wore no armor, but only trousers and a torn, tainted shirt. A red arrow stuck out of his back. Whether this color came from the dyes that the Red Knights use to stain their arrows or from the man's own blood was hard to tell. He seemed to give this deadly shaft of wood no thought, however, but only rode on toward our encampment with a rare ease and unquenchable will. His contempt for pain and what could only be a mortal wound amazed the tough Meshian warriors who looked upon him. Sar Vikan, straining to see at the edge of the square, suddenly cried out, 'Look! It is Kane! Sar Kane has returned!'

'Sar Kane!' someone else shouted. And then half a hundred voices picked up the cry: 'Sar Kane has returned! Bring a litter for Sar Kane!'

But my old friend would not be carried so long as he had the strength to command his own motions. And strength he still possessed, in an overflowing abundance that stunned those who watched him ride up to me. He sat tall and straight in his saddle, as if some vastly greater hand had sculpted him from a burning rock. Dressed in rags, dirty, bleeding, the air hissing out of the hole torn into his lung, Kane managed to look more regal than either Lord Tanu or Lord Tomavar – or, I imagined, myself.

'So, Valashu,' Kane said as he stopped his horse before me. 'I did *not* come back too late.'

He dismounted, and I rushed forward to embrace him as best I could without disturbing the broken arrow embedded in him. His large, hard hands, however, thumped against my back without restraint. At last he stood away from me. His bright, black eyes drank in the delight in *my* eyes. And with a savage smile, he growled out, 'Ha – but it is *good* to be back! Let us go somewhere we can talk.'

Just then Master Juwain, followed by Liljana, Maram, Estrella and Daj, pushed through the throngs of knights surrounding us. Master Juwain hurried up to Kane and looked at him gravely. 'First, I should draw that arrow.'

'No – the arrow remains where it has been for four hundred miles, and will still be there when you need to go to work on me. But right now, I've tidings that must be told.'

I led the way toward my pavilion then, and Sar Vikan, Lord Avijan, Sar Shivalad and others cleared a path for us. Although Kane walked with all the smooth power of a tiger, I could almost feel the agony of the arrow grinding against his ribs and searing his lungs. My companions and I went inside my huge tent, where Alphanderry joined us in a splash of glittering lights. Daj pulled the flaps closed behind us. We sat on one of the carpets there, in a circle, as if gathering around a fire on one of our campaigns. From one of the braziers heaped with hot coals, Master Juwain removed an iron pot full of hot water and prepared Kane a cup of tea that would help keep the blood inside Kane, or so he said.

'I've *bad* tidings from Galda,' Kane told us without further ado. 'The revolt has failed. Gallagerry the Defiant defies no one anymore: the Dragon Guard captured him, and the Red Priests crucified him. His followers are being hunted down. And Morjin . . .'

Here he paused to take a sip of tea as he grimaced in pain. Then he continued, 'I was not able to determine if it *was* Morjin who led the Dragon Guard and the Karabukers into Galda, or only one of his droghuls. I *think* it was he. All of Galda reeks with his stench. The Galdans are gathering their armies again – exactly why, no one would say. But everywhere I heard soldiers speak of marching forth on a great crusade.'

He took another sip of tea, and stared into the dark liquid of his cup. And he muttered, 'So, *my* crusade failed, eh? Everyone except myself captured or killed.'

'Everyone?' Maram said, looking at him. 'Do you mean your knights of the Black Brotherhood?'

In answer, Kane just stared at him in a dark, dreadful silence – and that was answer enough.

'Then you had to flee,' Maram prompted him, 'so that you could tell us this news?'

Kane shook his fearsome head. 'With my men held captive and Morjin still on the loose, I would *not* have fled. But there is something that I learned that overruled these considerations.'

Here he looked straight at me, and added, 'There is something that has been sent to destroy you, Valashu. A dark thing, so damned dark – you cannot know.'

At this, I stared into the corner of the tent, where I could feel an emptiness pulling at me. Then Alphanderry, sitting across from Kane, recounted our battle with the Ahrim in the woods near Lord Harsha's farm and our speculations as to its nature. He said, 'It followed us all the way from the Skadarak, and so we thought it must *be* some part of the Skadarak.'

'No,' Kane said, 'the *Ahrimana* is something worse – much worse.'

He moved to take another sip of tea, then looked up at the tent's roof as if his eyes could pierce the black silk to gaze at the heavens.

'So, it came *through* the Skadarak,' he told us. 'From far, far away it came. The Dark One, Angra Mainyu, sent it from Damoom. It is all his malice and spite, the very shadow of his soul. In a way, his herald.'

'His herald!' Maram cried out. 'But it was so powerful! It nearly killed Val!'

At this, Kane looked at me as he shook his head. 'This you must know about the Ahrimana: it has no power, of its own. But the power you give it, which it seeks out as a leech does blood, *that* power can burn you like hellfire and utterly destroy you.'

Upon speaking these words, Kane's immense strength finally seemed to fail him. Air bubbled out of his back in a sprinkling of bright red blood as if he could no longer will his veins to keep his life's essence within him. His eyes closed, for a moment, and he seemed ready to topple over.

'That is enough for today,' Master Juwain said, going over to Kane. He positioned his small body against Kane's side to prop him up. 'I don't know how you learned of what you have told us, or how you could ride four hundred miles with an arrow in your lung. But I've got to draw it, now, or even *you* might be destroyed.'

Kane slowly nodded his head at this. Then I called for a litter, and Kane had to consent to being carried from my pavilion into Master Juwain's smaller and starkly furnished tent. There, with Liljana's help and that of two other healers, Master Juwain went to work with his gleaming steel instruments to draw the barbed arrow from deep within Kane's flesh. This difficult surgery nearly killed the unkillable Kane. Finally, though, with a great spray of blood, Master Juwain pulled free the arrow. He used his green gelstei to stop the ferocious hemorrhaging and heal the terrible wound torn into Kane. Finally, he helped Kane drink a tea that would make him sleep.

'I shall stay with him the rest of today and tonight,' Master Juwain told me. He looked over toward his own bed, where Kane rested with his eyes closed. 'Liljana will stay, too. But there is no need for you to remain here – you must have many things to do.'

I did indeed have matters to attend to, though none so important as seeing Kane restored to himself. I waited by his side all the rest of the afternoon, through dinner and late into the evening. And then as the night deepened and the stars came out, Atara finally returned with news of her own. She stepped into Master Juwain's tent, and came over to kiss Kane's forehead. She smiled sadly as if she had looked upon his still form a thousand times. Then she said to me, 'May I speak with you alone?'

I nodded my head at this. We went outside and walked along the rows of campfires, where warriors gathered drinking beer and telling of deeds at the Culhadosh Commons, and other battles. Joshu Kadar and a few knights kept a vigil outside my pavilion. No one seemed bothered that I should hold council inside alone with Atara. I closed the flaps behind us, and went around this large space lighting the many candles in their stands. They cast little, flickering lights on the long council table and the tent's walls and ceiling. Atara and I sat facing each other on a red carpet at the center of the tent.

'We are as alone as we can be,' I said, gazing at the blindfold that bound her face. 'What is troubling you?'

Atara cocked her head as if listening for eavesdroppers along the walls. 'It might be better if we took a walk in the hills.'

I laughed softly at this, and told her, 'Joshu Kadar and Shivalad, to say nothing of Lord Avijan, would never allow that. Now that the gathering has begun, they look for assassins everywhere. They don't even like me to walk around our own encampment alone.'

Atara smiled grimly at this, then her deep, dulcet voice grew even lower. 'It is beginning, Val. At last, this terrible, terrible future that I have seen for too long is upon us.'

I moved even closer to her, and covered her hot, long hand with mine. Outside the tent came the sound of crickets chirping and men chanting out the ancient epics. Inside, it was nearly so quiet that I could hear the drumbeat of Atara's heart – and my own.

'Kane,' I whispered to her, 'said that in Galda, people spoke of a great crusade. I didn't think Morjin could be ready to order forth his armies so soon.'

She drew out her scryer's crystal, and she pressed this sphere of white gelstei against her forehead. 'I don't know that he is. But he makes ready *something*. Out on the Wendrush. Karimah told me that the Zayak have crossed the Blood River, the Janjii, too. It can only be that they have gone to join with the Marituk. From the south, there have come reports that the Tukulak are making common cause with the Danyak and Usark.'

'Kane always said,' I murmured, squeezing her hand, 'that Morjin would try to unite the Sarni before falling against the Nine Kingdoms.'

Atara smiled sadly as she cupped her clear crystal in her free hand. 'He will *never* unite all the Sarni – not so long as my grand-father can pull a bow. Sajagax has called for the tribes to join with the Kurmak in alliance against Morjin.'

'Is this the news that Karimah brought you?'

'Yes, in part.'

'Sajagax,' I said, remembering, 'is a great man. But most of the tribes favor Morjin, do they not?'

'Yes, most,' she told me, nodding her head. 'But not the Niuriu, nor the central Urtuk. Nor the Adirii, most of the clans, and prob-ably not the Danladi. And then there are the Manslayers.'

At the mention of these most willful of warriors, drawn from every Sarni tribe, I gazed at Atara and waited for her to say more.

'My sisters,' she told me, 'will not keep allegiance with their tribes – this has been decided. The Manslayers are to be a tribe of our own. But what my sisters could *not* decide when they met at the council rock a year and a half ago was whether to go to war against Morjin. Only a chiefess, my sisters say, can lead them against such an enemy.'

I listened to her deep breathing for a few moments. Then I said, 'But the Manslayers have no chiefess.'

'No, they do not – not yet. But there is to be another gathering, in the Niuriu's lands, where the Diamond River joins with the Poru. We are to choose a chiefess.'

I bowed my head to her. 'You, then?'

'That is Karimah's hope. And Sonjah's, and Aieela's – and others'.'

I looked over at the long table where my father had once sat at council with his most trusted lords. And I said, 'For you to be Chiefess of the Manslayers – that would be a great thing.'

'That is what Karimah tells me,' Atara said with a sad smile. 'If the Marituk, with the Zayak and Janjii, attack my grandfather, we could ride to his aid.'

I looked around for a pitcher of water so that I might ease the aching in my throat. And I said to her, 'Then you have already decided, haven't you?'

She slowly nodded her head. 'I cannot allow the Kurmak to be trampled under. *We* cannot, Val.'

'*I* cannot let you go,' I said, wrapping my hand around her hand even more tightly. 'I need you here, beside me.'

She brought my hand up to her lips, whose softness seemed to burn against my fingers. Then she told me, 'I shall stay with you until you become king.'

'*Will* I become king, then?'

'Only you know that. Isn't that what you want?'

'Does it matter what I want?' I asked her. I gazed into her gelstei as if I could see within its sparkling clarity not only the shape of future events but the calamities of the past. 'Once, I wanted nothing more than to climb mountains and play the flute in the company of my family. And to marry you.'

'And now?'

I blinked against the burning in my eyes, and turned away from her crystal because I could not bear what I saw there. And I said, 'After Morjin murdered my mother and grandmother, and my brothers, everything seemed to burn away. Everywhere I looked, at myself most of all, I could see only fire. I *was* this fire, Atara. You know, you must know. I thought only of murdering Morjin, in revenge. As I now think only of destroying him. Everything that he is – even his memory in the hearts and minds of those he has deluded. I can almost hear the wind calling me to do this, and the birds and the wolves and every child that Morjin's Red Priests have ever nailed to a cross or put to the sword. Sometimes, it seems the very world upon which we sit cries out for me to put *my* sword into him.'

She positioned her head fully facing me, then she said, 'Do you remember the lines from the *Laws*?'

She drew in a breath, and then recited from the twenty-fourth book of the *Saganom Elu*:

> *You are what your deep, driving desire is:*
> *As your desire is, so is your will;*
> *As your will is, so is your deed;*
> *As your deed is, so is your destiny.*

I smiled at this, as Kane might smile at a whirlwind sweeping down upon him. And I asked her, 'Have you seen my destiny then?'

'I have seen your desire,' she said to me, taking hold of my hand again. 'I have *felt* it, Val – I can't tell you how deeply I've felt it, this beautiful, beautiful thing that burns me up like the sweetest of fires. It is *not* to do this terrible deed that you dream of. Not just. A marriage you would make with me, you have said. A child we would make together, *I* have said. But I will not see him born into *this* world.'

I stared down by my side where I had set my sword. 'But what other world is there?'

'Only the one that you dream of even more than you do Morjin's death.'

'Oh, *that* world,' I said, smiling. 'That impossible world.'

She smiled back as if she could really see me. 'What was it that your father used to say?: "How is it possible that the impossible is not only *possible* but inevitable?"'

'He was a wise man,' I told her. 'He would have wanted me to believe it is inevitable that I will marry you. That this is not just my own desire, but the will of the world.'

'That is a beautiful, beautiful thought,' she told me.

'But it will never be, will it? Not unless we defeat Morjin. And *that* will never be if I keep you from aiding Sajagax.'

She held up her clear gelstei before me. 'Very little of the future is set in stone, but I can tell that you cannot prevail against Morjin alone, without the help of the Sarni tribes.'

I considered this as I drew out the handkerchief that I always kept close to me. I unfolded it, and I gazed at its center, at the single long, coiled, golden hair, no different from any of Atara's other hairs.

And I whispered to her, 'One chance for victory, you said, as slender as this hair. And one chance only that I will marry you.'

'One chance,' she said, squeezing her crystal. 'And I must *make* it be. And so must you.'

I felt a stream of fear burn down my throat as if I had swallowed molten silver. And I asked her, 'Will I ever see you again?'

She smiled in her mysterious way, and said, 'The better question might be: will I ever see *you* again? As the king you must be?'

'Tomorrow will be the test of that,' I told her.

'No,' she said with a wave of her hand, 'I do not mean King of Mesh, but King of the World. And *not* this world, as Morjin wishes to rule, but a true king, of starfire and diamond, such as has never been before on Ea.'

I considered this, too, then said, 'I am not sure I know what you mean.'

'I am not sure that I do either,' she said. 'But I once told you that I can never be the woman I have hoped to be until you become the man you were born to be. The one I have always dreamed of.'

Because her words cut at me, I pressed my fist against my chest. 'But I am who I am, Atara. And I am just a man.'

'And *that* one I have always loved, with all my heart, with all my soul,' she told me. 'The man who is just a man – and an angel, too.'

At this, I looked off at the walls of the tent, hoping that no one *was* listening in on our words. 'You shouldn't speak that way of anyone, not even me.'

'No, I shouldn't, should I?' she said. 'But I can't help myself, and never *have* been able to. Most people take too little upon themselves; a few take too much. They look in the mirror and behold a giant, immortal and invincible. I was always afraid of being one of these. I wanted to make everything *perfect*. Or, at least, to see things come out as they should. And that is why, when I look at my fate, and yours, I want to laugh or cry, and sometimes I don't know which.'

'But *why*, then?' I said, not fully understanding her.

And she grasped hold of my hand and said, 'Because that is the strange, strange thing about our lives, Val. It might really be upon *us* to save the world.'

She started laughing then, and so did I: deep, belly laughs that shook the whole of my body and brought tears to my eyes. I drew Atara closer, and kissed her lips, her forehead and the white band of cloth covering the empty spaces where her eyes used to be. And

I whispered in her ear: 'I will miss you so badly – as the night does the sun.'

'And I will miss you,' she told me. 'Until I see you again in the darkest of places, where it seems there is no sun – only Valashu, the Morning Star.'

She kissed *me* then, long and deeply, and I didn't think she would have cared if anyone had heard the murmurs of delight and fear within our throats or had seen us sitting with our arms wrapped around each other for what seemed like hours. At last, though, we broke apart. Atara said that she had to go feed her horse and prepare for a long journey. And I must prepare to meet my fate – or make it – when the sun rose on the morrow.

7

On the twenty-first day of Soldru, early on a morning of blue skies and brilliant sunlight, I put on my diamond armor and girded my sword at my side. When I came out of my pavilion, my companions and counselors stood on the crushed grass of our encampment's central lane waiting for me. I nodded at Lord Avijan, tall and grave, and resplendent in his blue surcoat emblazoned with its golden boar. Likewise I greeted Lord Harsha, Lord Sharad, Lord Noldashan and others. Maram also had donned a suit of diamond armor, as had Kane. My invincible friend stood between Atara and Liljana as if ready to ride on a pleasant outing in the countryside – or to go to war. His harsh face radiated anticipation, wrath, joy and his fiery will to crush anyone who opposed him. I had thought that he must spend the next few days or weeks recuperating from his dreadful wound. I should have known better. According to what Liljana later told me, Kane had awakened before dawn calling for a haunch of bloody meat. He had drawn great strength from this savage meal, hour by hour regaining his nearly bottomless vitality. With a new adventure now at hand, he seemed ready to battle any or all of Lord Tomavar's knights on my behalf.

'So, Val,' he said to me with a nod of his head, 'this is the day.'

With Sar Shivalad, Sar Jonavar, Sar Kanshar and Joshu Kadar acting as my guardians, I led forth down the lane and into the square. The two thousand warriors and knights who had originally pledged to Lord Avijan stood drawn up in full battle armor along its eastern side. The sun poured down upon their neat, sparkling ranks. So it was with Lord Tanu's men and Lord Tomavar's, at the southern and western edges of the square. Along the northern perimeter, the Lords Ramanu, Bahram and Kharashan had arrayed their smaller forces in three separate groupings, next to a veritable mob of the two thousand free warriors. Into the square's four corners crowded the women, children, old men and a few outlanders who had come to witness the day's events. I reminded myself that they must be evacuated from the field at the first sign of trouble.

I walked straight out to the center of the square with my companions, and so it was with the other lords who would be king. I paid little heed to either Lord Bahram or Lord Ramanu, or even Lord Kharashan, a thick, bullnecked old warrior whose square face showed little guile. Lord Tanu stood to my left with Lord Eldru, Sar Shagarth and the grizzled Lord Ramjay slightly behind him. A small, dark, dangerous-looking man, Lord Tanu's cousin, Lord Manamar, had joined them as well.

Straight across from me waited Lord Tomavar. I had not seen him since the year before at the Culhadosh Commons, and he still looked much the same: very tall, with great broad shoulders and long arms used to swinging a sword. His white surcoat, draped over his heavily-muscled body, showed the black tower of his line. Grief still tormented his long, horsey face, which he positioned facing me square-on as if in challenge. I liked his eyes, for they were deep and quick and shone with a ready courage. My father had valued him greatly as the finest of tacticians and a warrior who inspired his men to fight with a terrible ferocity. And I knew that he had esteemed my father, though it seemed he held only grievance and suspicion toward me.

'Lord Valashu Elahad,' he said, greeting me formally, 'I should like it made known from the beginning of this gathering that you do the warriors great insult in asking them to stand for you again, where they have already stood *against* you.'

His words, carried by his loud, deep, powerful voice, blasted out into the square. His rage and deep anguish stunned me. So did the fury that darkened his black eyes. He took advantage of my silence to try immediately to preempt my bid to become king.

'Lord Tanu!' he called out, turning to his right where Lord Tanu stood with Lord Manamar and his other captains. 'We have marched in many campaigns and fought in many battles together. Your men trust you, even as King Shamesh did, and all those who know you. If I should be struck down here today by a bolt of lightning, is there anyone in Mesh who would make a better king? It is in recognition of your services to our land and your prowess as the greatest of knights that I would like to honor you. Command your warriors to pledge to *me*, and I shall make you Lord Protector of Mesh and Lord Commander of my army!'

Lord Tomavar's captains – Lord Vishand, Sar Jarval and the elegant Lord Arajay Solval – pressed up close behind him as if they could not quite believe what they had just heard. They seemed as surprised as the rest of Lord Tomavar's warriors, drawn up across the square. It seemed that Lord Tomavar's offer to Lord Tanu had been an inspiration of the moment, based upon Lord Tomavar's keen instincts and his reading of Lord Tanu.

'Lord Protector, you say!' Lord Tanu cried out. He tried not to let his amazement show on his tight, sour face. 'And Lord Commander of *all* the army?'

'Second only to myself,' Lord Tomavar told him. 'The command of all the infantry shall be yours.'

As the infantry in our army outnumbered the cavalry by more than ten to one, it was a magnanimous offer.

'Command your warriors to pledge to me,' Lord Tomavar said again, 'and we can bring an end to this conclave, here and now!'

If Lord Tanu did as Lord Tomavar asked, then more than ten thousand of the nearly sixteen thousand warriors gathered around the square would stand for Lord Tomavar, and he would become king.

'Val,' Maram murmured at my shoulder, '*do* something, before it is too late!'

Slightly behind Maram stood Daj, Estrella, Master Juwain, Liljana and Atara. And Kane, who growled out, 'So, it's a *deal* that this Tomavar would make!'

As a tactic, Lord Tomavar's offer to Lord Tanu was bold and brilliant, and I could feel Lord Tanu nearly burning to incline his head to Lord Tomavar. In the moment before he commanded his muscles to move and changed the future forever, I called out to him: 'Lord Tanu – you have promised to release your warriors from their pledges so that they may stand for whom they will!'

Lord Tanu, always a thoughtful man, regarded me deeply as the tension flowed down from his jaws into the rest of his compact body. For the moment, it seemed that he could not speak.

'Lord Tanu,' Lord Ramjay shouted out in his lord's stead, 'has made no such promise! He has said only that he agreed with you that the warriors should be released from their pledges. Well, perhaps they *should* be, if no solution other than war can decide who should be king. But Lord Tomavar has proposed an honorable way out of our troubles.'

I heard murmurs of assent ripple up and down the lines of men behind Lord Tomavar and then pass even to Lord Tanu's warriors, drawn up in their ranks ten deep. And then the fiery Sar Vikan, standing with the others in my escort, cried out: 'You speak of honor, but Lord Tanu has said that the warriors should decide who will be king! By the lake, Lord Ramjay! In front of you and many who are gathered here, Lord Tanu said this thing!'

'He *did* say it,' Lord Ramjay agreed. 'And it *shall* be the warriors who will choose our king. They have given their pledges of their own free will, and if Lord Tanu then asks them to stand for Lord Tomavar, that, in the end, is nothing but their will, and is the very essence of honor.'

For a while, various knights and lords gathered in the square bandied words back and forth. And all the while Lord Tanu stared at me as I did him. I felt my heart pushing my blood through my veins up into my hot, hurting face. I felt Lord Tanu's blood rushing through him, too. I did not want to think that Lord Tanu would equivocate and try to take Lord Ramjay's ignoble way out of his promise to me. In the end, as my father had said, either one believed in men, or not.

'Lord Tomavar!' Lord Tanu finally said, turning to this great lord. 'Your proposal is fitting, fair and indeed generous.'

He paused to take in a breath of air as he looked up at the grinning Lord Tomavar. Lord Tanu's face seemed to sour even more, if that were possible. Then he continued, 'But it comes too late – I have indeed given my word to Lord Elahad that the warriors should be free choose our king.'

'You *have* promised that,' Lord Eldru said, glaring at Lord Ramjay.

'And the warriors should choose *you* as king!' Sar Shagarth said.

'Lord Tanu for king!' a hundred warriors standing behind Lord Tanu cried out all at once. 'Lord Vishathar Tanu for king!'

Lord Manamar Tanu, the father of Lord Tomavar's abducted wife, cast Lord Tomavar a dark, angry look, and muttered, 'Why should we, in any case, negotiate with a man who won't even return a brooch to its rightful owner?'

As a strategy, Lord Tomavar's offer to Lord Tanu had been a poor one and had ultimately failed. It antagonized not only me and the men whom I led, but many of Lord Tanu's followers as well. And worse, Lord Tomavar had betrayed his essential weakness: he sought Mesh's kingship with such desperation that he was willing to stoop to bargaining like a merchant rather than relying on sound arguments and force of character to win the warriors.

'All right then!' Lord Tomavar shouted. 'Do you think *I* have any cause to fear the judgment of the warriors? Let it be as you have said! Let them stand for a king, here and now!'

Lord Tanu positioned himself like a ram before a furious bull. Even as Lord Tomavar's face grew darker, hotter and angrier, Lord Tanu stared at him stubbornly as if he had ice in his veins.

'We all can agree to that,' Lord Tanu called out to Lord Tomavar. 'Release your men from their pledges, that they can stand for whom they will!'

But Lord Tomavar only shook his long, heavy head at this. 'My men gave their pledges of their own will, and so they have already chosen who should be king.'

'Yes, they chose – but in diffcrent circumstances. The times have changed.'

'The times are as they have always been! And they demand a king, tested in many battles, loved and trusted, who can *lead* his warriors. To glory and victory!'

As he said this, his warriors behind him let loose a great cheer – though it seemed not so great as Lord Tomavar might have wished.

'We cannot,' Lord Tanu said, 'allow a king to be chosen this way, with two fifths of the warriors pledged to you, and everyone else standing free.'

Lord Tomavar turned to glare at me then. And he shouted, 'I *won't* allow my warriors to stand for *this* one! They call Morjin the Lord of Lies, but Valashu Elahad deceives men into following him!'

A dark fire leaped in Kane's eyes at this, and my fearsome friend stepped forward as he grasped the hilt of his sword. And he snarled at Lord Tomavar: 'Say it to my face, Gorvan Tomavar, that I am a man who has been *deceived*!'

In horror of what might soon occur, both Master Juwain and Maram grasped one of Kane's arms and eased him backward. Lord Tomavar tried to ignore the furious Kane. He continued staring down his long nose at me.

'I *won't* let my men stand for the Elahad,' he reaffirmed. 'Not *this* Elahad.'

He whipped about to look at Manamar Tanu and bellowed: 'And I *won't* return the brooch! It belongs to Vareva, and my beloved wife is not dead!'

'The Red Dragon,' Lord Manamar said in a venomous voice, 'took my daughter more than a year ago, and so we must assume that she *is* dead – or worse. Return the brooch, Lord Tomavar!'

'You ask me to send diamonds to *you*,' Lord Tomavar snapped, 'when you command your smithies to cease shipments of diamond armor to *us*?'

'It is not the same thing – return the brooch!'

'You may have it,' Lord Tomavar said, grasping the hilt of his sword, 'when you pry it from my dead fingers!'

'I should like nothing better!' the small, deadly Lord Manamar said. His hand, too, locked onto his sword. 'Tell me you are willing, and we shall settle this matter here!'

Now it was Lord Tanu's turn to cool things down. He grasped Lord Manamar's arm and pulled his bellicose cousin a few paces back from Lord Tomavar. It might have been thought that Lord Tanu would want Lord Manamar to put his sword through Lord Tomavar's neck, and so remove at least one contender to the throne. And Lord Tanu *might* have wanted this. But the most likely outcome of a duel between the two lords would see a flash of angry swords and Lord Manamar's head rolling bloody across the grass.

Lord Tomavar, with a great show of restraint, relaxed his hand from the hilt of his sword. He stood proud and too obviously pleased with himself, and he strode back and forth before his warriors in their gleaming ranks as he called out to them: 'Do you see? Do you see the madness that Valashu Elahad has brought upon our land?'

He turned to pace toward Lord Tanu's warriors as he continued his tirade: 'A brooch, your Lord Manamar wishes returned to him. My wife I *demand* be returned to me! How did it come to be that the Red Dragon stole the most beautiful woman in the world from me? How is it that many of you have lost brothers, sons and fathers in battle? And seen your daughters and wives slaughtered in the sack of the Elahad castle? It is because Valashu Elahad called down the Red Dragon upon Mesh! As he now calls down discord upon this field! Is this the man you would stand for as king?'

I knew that I must make a riposte to this, and soon. But Liljana was quicker with words than I. She had spent a whole lifetime manipulating men in service of her secret purpose. I sensed her will to provoke Lord Tomavar into talking himself into a trap.

'And what would you do, mighty Lord,' she said to him in a voice as sharp and precise as an acupuncturist's needles, 'to see Mesh restored and your wife returned to your arms again?'

Her calculated ridicule drove him to a fury. And he bellowed out: 'I would make Mesh strong, and lead her against our enemies! The Waashians we could defeat without too great a loss. And

110

then, if need be, the Ishkans. And so we would gain great glory! And so the Valari would *have* to follow us, to the war against Morjin. We *shall* have our revenge! We shall storm the Black Mountain again, and this time, we shall triumph! We shall take all of Morjin's treasure, and *I* shall take my most beloved of treasures back!'

As Lord Tanu had observed in the pass, Lord Tomavar was a poor strategist. Everyone standing at the center of the field listened to him with doubt beginning to work at their hearts. The warriors in the front lines of each of the forces crowding the square took in his words and passed them back to the deeper ranks. I heard some shouts of acclaim, but even more grumblings of dismay. Once, at the very end of the Age of Law, at the Battle of Tarshid, Morjin had destroyed an army of Valari assaulting his stronghold inside Skartaru, the Black Mountain. The six thousand survivors, many from Mesh, he had crucified. It was the worst defeat in all the history of the Valari, and the minstrels still sang of it with mourning and lament.

Lord Tomavar, perceiving that the tide of the warriors' sentiments might be turning against him, moved quickly to the offense by attacking me: 'And what would Valashu Elahad do if you stand for him as king? Only this: he would fail you as he did before and leave your wives and daughters to be ravished!'

I knew that I must respond to this calumny, without hesitation and in a clear, strong voice so that the warriors could hear the truth of things. I knew that I had this power, to open my heart to men and speak straight from my soul. What *would* I do if made king, I wondered? Only this: I would use all my power and call upon every particle of my being to defeat Morjin. Strangely, Lord Tomavar's blood burned with same desire as mine to see Morjin brought down, even if his plan to do this was folly – and even if he dreamed too much of revenge and glory.

'If you stand for me as king,' I started to say to the fifteen thousand warriors assembled around the square, 'I will –'

'He will betray you!' Lord Tomavar cried out, interrupting me with an unforgivable rudeness. 'As he betrayed all of us at the Elahad castle! How could our women and children have been slaughtered like animals? How *could* they? It is only because Valashu Elahad deserted the castle! Out of his criminal pride! And then lied about it, putting the blame on Lord Lansar Raasharu, a great and noble man, whom King Shamesh loved and trusted as much as he did myself!'

111

'No, that is not true!' I cried out. 'I thought my father was dead and that my brother had summoned me, and I wanted only to –'

'You wanted to usurp your own father! By gaining glory on the battlefield, you hoped your renown would lead *you* to stand before the warriors! In place of your father, killed in the very battle you brought down upon us!'

His words drove me to a fury. I felt my spleen pouring out poisons into my blood and a sick heat tormenting my brain. A terrible pressure built inside my throat. I opened my mouth to draw in air and deny his vile accusations. And in that moment, the Ahrim struck. It came out of nowhere, a boiling blackness that fell over my face and eyes. For three long, bitter beatings of my heart, I could not hear nor could I see. And then the Ahrim's icy cold substance seemed to gather about my neck. It clamped down, hard, like a iron fist, squeezing the very breath from my throat with such a crushing force that I could barely speak:

'My . . . father,' I gasped out, 'I . . . loved . . . like . . .'

'Do you see?' Lord Tomavar called out, pointing at me. 'He chokes on his own lies!'

I wanted to kill him, then. He stood glaring at me in his dark, doubting manner, and I wanted to whip free my sword and plunge the point straight through his slanderous mouth. And then I recalled a much darker encounter with a much greater enemy, far away. In Hesperu, with the help of my friends and a great, good man, for one shining moment, I had managed to transmute my hate into something beautiful and bright. I felt this grace still warm and alive somewhere inside me. It made me believe in myself. This certainty of power and purpose had nothing to do with the delusion that I might be infallible or the destined Maitreya, but only that like any man I could keep the evil inside myself at bay and exert my will to do the right thing.

'Lord . . . Tomavar!' I gasped out. 'Your . . . heart . . .'

I must not, I told myself, regard this man as my enemy. My father had believed in him and trusted him, and so must I. All men, as I knew too well, could be driven mad by hatred and a rage for revenge.

'Your . . . heart,' I tried to tell him again.

But my desire to see him healed was not enough. The Ahrim only tightened its hold upon me, and I could not speak. And so I took a step closer to him, holding out my hand. I thought only of resting it upon his chest, and trying to drive away his doubts, as I had with the warriors in Lord Avijan's hall. Lord Tomavar's hatred, though, ran deeper than a gorge cut into the earth; I could touch neither it nor him. The anguish in his black eyes warned me to stay away from him even as he drew his sword from its scabbard, and nearly cut off my hand.

'Stand back, Elahad!' he cried out. 'Don't try your trickery on me!'

'He draws!' Sar Vikan called back from beside me. 'Lord Tomavar draws on Lord Elahad! A challenge has been made!'

According to the laws of the Valari, any warrior who drew his sword on another made an irrevocable challenge to a duel.

'He draws!' Sar Vikan called out again. The thirst for blood I heard in his voice made me sick. 'Let them fight, here and now, sword to sword! Let honor be satisfied!'

His words were like a flaming brand held to spilled oil. Lord Sharad, who had never liked Lord Tomavar, called out, 'Let them fight! Let honor be satisfied!'

And then Sar Jessu and Sar Shivalad and half a thousand warriors standing behind me called out that Lord Tomavar and I must face each other sword to sword, and thousands of Lord Tomavar's own men called out the same thing – along with even many of Lord Tanu's men. So did Lord Ramanu's men call for a duel, and Lord Bahram's and Lord Kharashan's followers and the mob of free warriors to the north. Their voices thundered out into the square:

'Honor! Honor! Honor!'

'Fight! Fight! Fight!'

Lord Tomavar stared at his long, gleaming kalama as if in horror of what he had done – but also in great gladness, as if relieved of a terrible burden. I tried to give him a way out of the bottomless chasm quickly opening up before us. I gasped out, 'A . . . mistake. Put . . . away . . . your . . . sword.'

But sometimes there can be no going back. Lord Tomavar's great head swept right and left as he listened to the roar of the warriors: 'Honor! Honor! Honor!'

'Let honor be satisfied!'

'Fight – let them fight!'

'A duel to the death! Let the victor be king!'

At last, Lord Tomavar looked at me. And he shouted out: 'I will *not* put away my sword! I call upon you to draw *your* sword, so that we might settle this matter honorably. Let it be as the warriors say: let the victor be king!'

A great cheer seemed to shake the very earth. And I forced out a few, choked-off words: 'But . . . I . . . won't . . .'

'You *must* accept the challenge,' Sar Jalval shouted on Lord Tomavar's behalf. 'Or else be called a coward! And if coward you be, then leave this field now, and let no man in Mesh give you salt, bread or fire!'

Now it seemed that almost every warrior or knight gathered about the square shouted out that this must be. I heard the men loyal to me crying out, 'Lord Valashu Elahad – Champion, Champion! The Elahad for King of Mesh!'

This is not my will, I thought. *This is not only my will*.

Then Lord Avijan stepped forward and said to Lord Tomavar, 'Fight, if you must, but your duel will not settle who sits on Mesh's throne. The warriors still must decide who will be king.'

Lord Tomavar, whose mind could race as swiftly as a greyhound when pressed, considered this only for a moment. 'All right then, let this be the way of things: Lord Elahad will ask your warriors to stand for me if I am the victor in our duel. And if Lord Elahad prevails, my warriors shall be free to stand for him.'

Lord Tomavar gambled like a player rolling the dice. But it was a fair enough game. If I fell beneath Lord Tomavar's sword, then the two thousand men who marched behind my banner, standing for Lord Tomavar, would give him the edge over Lord Tanu. Even if many of them refused this realignment, then Lord Tomavar still might find that most of the free warriors would support him, and give him the numbers he needed. And if I put my sword into Lord Tomavar, then I still might hope to win his warriors – and many others.

'All . . . right,' I choked out, accepting Lord Tomavar's challenge. 'Let . . . it . . . be.'

I made it known to Lord Avijan that he should go among our warriors and tell them of what we had decided here. Then, surrounded by my guardians, I walked off the field to return to my pavilion, where I would remove my armor and prepare for the duel. My companions all came with me. When we stood alone beneath my tent's glowing black silk, Kane growled out to me, 'So, it's come to *this*, then! Well, kill him quickly, Val. Ha – I should have killed the Tomavar for you when *I* had the chance!'

I put on my best tunic and belted it. Then Master Juwain took out his green crystal and held it to my throat. After a while, he sighed out to me: 'I'm afraid my varistei has no power over the thing that attacks you. At least, I can't sense how it might be driven away. Are you any better at *all*?'

'No . . . not . . . better,' I whispered.

'The Ahrim might indeed choke you to death. Perhaps you should withdraw from the duel.'

'No . . . impossible.'

'Then perhaps you should wait until your airways clear and your voice returns.'

I shook my head at this. 'No . . . time.'

Just then Lord Avijan came into the pavilion and announced: 'The warriors did not want to do as you have asked them, Lord Valashu. But since *you* asked them, they are willing. Though none of us can bear to see Lord Tomavar become king.'

'Thank . . . you,' I croaked out.

'How did it come to this?' Lord Avijan said to me. 'This is no time for you to lose your voice! If only *all* the warriors could but have heard you, they would know that you speak the truth.'

At this, for no reason that I could understand, Liljana drew out her blue gelstei and looked at it strangely.

'Well,' Lord Avijan said, 'things are as they are. The warriors do not believe they will have to stand for Lord Tomavar. Neither do I. Everyone remembers what you did at the tournament.'

At the great tournament in Nar two years before I had defeated Lord Dashavay, the greatest swordsman in the Nine Kingdoms, to become that year's champion.

'I've always said,' Lord Avijan continued, 'that duels are a plague upon our people. *This* one, it seems, however, must really be fought. And so, may you fight like the heroes of old, Valashu Elahad, and send Lord Tomavar back to the stars!'

With that, he clasped my hand and went back outside to make arrangements with Lord Tomavar's seconds for our duel.

Then I whispered, 'I . . . must . . . not . . . kill . . .'

I pressed my hand to my throat, burning as if I had inhaled a lungful of the Red Desert's fiery dust. I seemed to be losing my power of speech altogether.

'Lil . . . jana,' I gasped.

I tried to make her understand that she should use her blue crystal to take the words off the top of my mind and speak them for me – but to delve no deeper into my more private thoughts. She nodded her head in agreement with this. Then she positioned her little whale figurine near my temple. We waited for her to speak.

'Val says,' she told everyone, 'that he must *not* slay Lord Tomavar.'

At this, Daj looked at me, amazed, and then turned to Estrella, who smiled as she nodded her head in agreement. But Master

Juwain only seemed puzzled, even as Kane scowled and Maram took hold of my arm.

'You *have* to kill him,' he told me. 'It's a barbaric thing, and I agree with Lord Avijan, but that's the way of you Valari and your damned duels.'

'So, Val – so,' Kane said.

I looked at Liljana, who had closed her eyes. And then she told my other friends: 'Val must *not* come to the kingship over Lord Tomavar's dead body. Meshians must not slay Meshians. And Valari must not slay Valari!'

'But you Valari have *always* slain Valari!' Maram called out to me. 'Ever since the Star People came to earth and Aryu slew Elahad!'

'Never again,' Liljana said. 'The Valari must be as brothers, and sisters – or else Morjin will destroy us all.'

'As Val has said,' Atara intoned, nodding her head, 'so it must be.'

Although she seemed almost icy cool in her manner, I could sense her terrible fear for me.

'But Val,' Maram said, squeezing my arm more tightly, 'what will you do? You can't just walk back out on that field and cross swords with Lord Tomavar in the hope that he will apologize, or just give up. If you do, he'll destroy *you*!'

I swallowed hard against the burning dryness in my throat, and I heard Liljana speak my words: 'There must be a way – there is always a way.'

At this, Kane picked up my scabbarded sword where I had set it on the council table. He pressed it into my hand as he growled at me, 'There *is* a way! Strike this into Tomavar's damn heart!'

'No,' Liljana told him, as I shook my head.

'Do it, damn you! Do what must be done!'

'No, I must not kill him,' I heard myself say – and Liljana, too.

Then Daj, afraid for me, stepped up to Kane and said, 'But Val has *advantages*. He is younger than Lord Tomavar, and quicker.'

'So what if he is?' Kane snapped. 'Tomavar is older and more experienced.'

'But Val has the better sword!'

'And Tomavar the longer reach.'

'But Val was Champion! I *saw* King Waray put the gold medal around his neck.'

'Did you see Val fight Lord Tomavar at *that* tournament?' Kane asked, looking down at Daj. 'When men cross swords, who lives or dies can turn on a glint of the sun off of cold steel.'

'But Val *can't* die!' Daj said. 'He can't! He's the best swordsman on all of Ea, and no one has ever stood up to him.'

Kane, of course, *had* stood up to me, and more, but Daj did not need to comment upon this, as Kane had no vainglory that must be fed.

'Val has faced many in battle,' Kane agreed, 'and most of them no longer move. But none of his enemies, save Salmelu, has been Valari. As *most* of the men Tomavar has killed have been.'

'But I *know* Val can kill Lord Tomavar!'

'And I know it, too,' Kane told him. 'But he must *fight* to kill. If he only defends against Tomavar's attack, trying to tire him, he'll throw away all his advantages. So, his life, too. Sooner or later, Tomavar's sword will cut its way through. Then *he'll* kill Val, and that is that.'

The tent grew quiet then, for it seemed that Kane had pronounced a sentence of death. I could only shake my head at this, and whisper, 'There . . . must . . . be . . . a . . . way.'

As I clasped my hand to my throat, I prayed that this might be so.

8

After that, I swept up my sword and led the way back out into the square. When we reached its center, the various knights and lords gathered there had already formed themselves into a great circle. Lord Harsha stood there waiting for me, and Lord Sharad, Lord Manthanu and my other counselors. Sar Jonavar and Sar Shivalad took their places there, too, as with the rest of my guardians. They joined Lord Vishand and those who followed Lord Tomavar. At the edge of the circle, I bowed my head to Lord Eldru, Lord Ramjay, Sar Shagarth, and Lord Manamar, who had accompanied Lord Tanu. Lord Tanu himself had agreed to oversee the duel. He stood inside the ring of honor with Lord Tomavar, and his seconds: Sar Jalval and Lord Arajay Solval. Lord Avijan would act as *my* second, as would Maram, who bitterly regretted this honor, saying to me, 'I had to stand by once in this capacity as Salmelu nearly cut your head off. Don't make me watch Lord Tomavar put his sword into you!'

Despite his protests, he stayed close to me as Lord Sharad and Lord Noldashan stepped aside for us to enter the circle. My other companions – Kane and Atara excepted – had to stand outside it since they were not warriors. Although Daj objected to this, citing his deeds in battle, Lord Tanu directed him to wait farther out on the grass with Liljana, Master Juwain and Estrella. No child, he said, could be part of the ring of honor, and I breathed deeply in relief to see him walk over to Estrella and take her hand as they waited for the duel to begin.

'A challenge has been made!' Lord Tanu called out in his crabby, high-pitched voice.

Maram and I, with Lord Avijan, stood facing him on his left, while beside us to his right gathered Lord Tomavar, Sar Jalval and

118

Lord Arajay Solval. Lord Tomavar had already drawn his kalama, which he passed on to Maram. It took Maram only a few moments to wipe down the long, shining blade with a brandy-soaked cloth. Then I unsheathed Alkaladur, whose shimmering length of silustria needed no cleansing. Even so, I handed it to Lord Avijan, who gave it to Lord Arajay so that the rituals could be completed.

When our swords had been returned to us, Lord Tanu directed us to close our eyes for a few moments of meditation. Then he called out to the ring of knights surrounding us: 'Are the witnesses ready?'

I watched as many grim-faced men nodded their heads.

'Are the combatants ready?'

Lord Tomavar's eyes grew as cold as balls of obsidian. 'I am ready to live or die.'

'And I, too,' I said, looking at him.

Lord Tanu now motioned for Maram and the other seconds to rejoin everyone else in the circle, and he did so as well. And then he called out: 'A challenge has been made and accepted. You must now fight to defend your honor. In the name of the One and all of our ancestors who have stood on this earth before us, you may begin.'

As Lord Tomavar drew back his sword and faced me across twenty feet of crushed grass, the thousands of warriors and others gathered around the square grew so quiet that I could almost hear their breathing. *My* breath came hard and heavy, forced through the painful chute of my throat. I drew back my bright blade behind my head, waiting. I felt my heart driving at my chest like a great, mailed fist. The kirax burning along my blood sent shoots of fire into every part of my body. I did not know which I feared more: Lord Tomavar killing me or me killing him.

For a while we circled each other, measuring distances and feeling each other out. Lord Tomavar moved with a practiced grace that chilled me. Though he might be a complicated man, with his willingness to sacrifice himself for his warriors in battle at odds with his overweening conceit, none of this conflict or any other showed in the easy, natural way that he stepped right or left, or shifted his sword about. Indeed, even his torment over his missing wife seemed to have melted from his mind. I had rarely seen anyone so relaxed, as if he didn't care if he lived or died. He flowed over and around the little bumps of the lawn almost like water.

Then something inside him suddenly tightened, as with the pull of a man's body on the rope of a grappling hook. He sprang at me in a whirl of bright and furious steel. I jumped back a few paces to avoid the slice of his sword. It was barely enough, for his long arms and legs gave him a great reach, and his sword's point streaked through the air only an inch from my face. Again, he cut at me, and again I moved out of the way, and then we met each other in a clash of his steel blade against Alkaladur's shimmering crystal. Middling old he might be, but the years hadn't robbed him of his strength. The shock of the blows that he struck against me ran through my sword with a terrible force and nearly shattered my arm bones. I struggled to turn my blade right or left and beat aside his ferocious attack. The sound our swords clanging against each other rang out into the morning air like bells.

'He is cut!' someone at the edge of the circle called out, pointing at me. 'The Elahad has been cut!'

'First blood to Lord Tomavar!'

As if a signal had been given, Lord Tomavar stood back from me, breathing hard. He stared at my face. I pressed my hand to my forehead, wet with blood. By wild chance, it seemed, his sword must have reopened the lightning bolt scar etched into my skin. So intent had I been on keeping myself from getting killed that I hadn't even felt the wound.

'Val!' Kane called out to me. 'Val!'

He didn't have to say anything other than my name for me to know what he meant: I could not go on fighting like this. In a way, I was not really fighting at all, but only fencing with Lord Tomavar. He certainly sensed this. He stared at the blood dripping down my forehead. And then, like a wolf incited to kill, he came at me again.

And again we cut and thrust and moved across the grass in a frenzy of whipping arms and straining legs. Once, twice, thrice, we came together in a clash of steel against silustria, sprang apart, then clashed again. My breath burst from my lungs and nearly caught in my throat. My arms ached with a smoldering flame. Ten times I avoided the edge of his blade by a hair; ten times its point burned past my neck, my chest, my eyes, by the whisper of a breath. Each time his muscles tightened and bunched to unleash his fury at me, I felt the pain of it in my own body a moment before he moved. But my gift of valarda would not save me forever. Sooner or later, as Kane had said, Lord Tomavar's sword would cut its way past the silvery arc of mine, and that would be that.

'Val!' Kane cried out again.

I could feel Kane's savage soul calling for me to kill Lord Tomavar. But even as Lord Tomavar's kalama nearly cleaved my head in two, I knew that I could not kill him. I could not even wound him and then break off fighting, as I had with Salmelu in King Hadaru's hall, for that unwanted mercy had only brought down upon me shame and King Hadaru's wrath. All duels were to the death – so said the ancient codes of the Valari. Only the life's blood could satisfy honor, unless of course the challenger had a change of heart and formally apologized to the challenged. But such miracles were as rare as the rising of the sun at midnight.

'Val!'

We battled on and on beneath the heat pouring down from the sky and the eyes of thousands of warriors. I could only hope to exhaust Lord Tomavar so that he collapsed and broke. But it seemed that I must break first. My sword, once so light, now grew as heavy as a mallet made of lead. Every muscle in my body burned with a terrible, deep fire. My belly knotted and spasmed as I fought for breath. I coughed, hard, against the dark thing choking my throat. Most duels lasted only seconds, but my desperate combat with Lord Tomavar had already gone on longer than any duel in living memory – so I heard someone cry out from afar.

'He is cut again! The Elahad is!' another knight shouted. 'Second blood as well to Lord Tomavar!'

I could barely feel the new wound where the edge of Lord Tomavar's blade, as we locked together face to face, pushing and sweating and straining, had bloodied me. Amazingly – unbelievably – the steel had cut open my forehead again. Drops of blood flew out into the air as I twisted my head out of the way of one of Lord Tomavar's vicious thrusts; more blood found its way into my eye, stinging and half-blinding me. I knew that I could not go on this way much longer.

'Fight, Lord Elahad!' I head Joshu Kadar cry out. 'Kill Lord Tomavar, if you would be king!'

His words seemed to enrage Lord Tomavar. And shame him, too, for he would gain little honor in slaying an opponent who refused to slay him. And his shame touched upon some deep guilt, whether of his failure to prevent Morjin from ravaging my father's castle or his betrayal of my father in trying claim his throne, I could not say. But I felt building inside him a guilt and grief so terrible that he desired death – and wanted to kill *me* in order to drive it back. Up to this point, he had fought with a cool and fluid fury, as flawless in execution as any Valari warrior could hope for.

But now hate broke through his blood and poisoned his eyes. He swung his sword at me, again and again, as might a madman, in a shocking burst of anger and steel; he attacked with such recklessness and rage to kill that there could be no defense – other than to attack him back.

'Valashu!'

Then, in the slash and burn of Lord Tomavar's sword, his immense anguish cut me to the heart, and his hate became my hate – and something more. Deep beneath my throat built an immense, black storm, as within a small room and wholly contained by it. At its center raged a whirlwind.

'Strike, now!'

At last, when I opened the door to hate's brilliant reflection and its ultimate source, lightning flashed and drove away the dark thing choking me. As Kane had called for, I struck Alkaladur straight into Lord Tomavar's heart: but *not* the gleaming length of silustria that I gripped in my sweating hands, only the blade made of a finer and brighter substance that men called the Sword of Truth. I found my voice again, and shouted out to him words that rang out like thunder: 'I did not usurp my father! I did not betray the castle to Morjin! And I am sorry about your wife! You have my promise that I will do all that I can to help get her back!'

Lord Tomavar stood ten feet away from me across the blood-dewed grass. He gasped for breath, and pressed his free hand to his chest as if he might drop of a blood stroke. His sword dipped down toward the ground. The madness, I saw, had gone out of his eyes. Then he called back to me in amazement: 'You speak truly, Lord Elahad! I know you do!'

In the ring around us, the knights and warriors stared at him, stunned.

'I was wrong to say what I did to you!' he shouted. 'I should not have challenged you! I give you my apology, freely, that all should hear and know: I, Gorvan Tomavar, have wronged you, and am in your debt!'

Now Lord Vishand, Lord Avijan and Lord Harsha – and many others – looked at Lord Tomavar as if struck dumb with shock. Hundreds of warriors gathered around the square closest to us, as they finally understood what was happening, let loose cheers of relief and wonderment. I saw Maram choking back tears and Atara smiling mysteriously. Kane simply stood like one of the shining mountains to the east. Above all of us, the hot morning sun blazed down.

'And I should not have challenged you for your father's throne!' Lord Tomavar continued. 'Please forgive me!'

And with that, he cast his sword upon the grass. He stepped up to me. Then he knelt down, and bowed his head as he broke out sobbing. All standing around him stared at this extraordinary sight as if they could not believe what they saw.

'A challenge has been made, and a challenge has been withdrawn,' Lord Tanu finally cried out, stepping inside the ring. 'Honor has been defended and satisfied. The duel is over.'

As the knights surrounding us broke apart and regrouped into twos and threes and Master Juwain came up to bandage my cut head, Lord Tomavar looked up at me through his dark, moist eyes. And he asked me, 'Will you really help me find my wife?'

Before I could answer him, even as the warriors picked up his words and passed them back through the ranks edging the square, a tall figure dressed in a hooded traveling cloak stepped onto the field. A glint and jangle of metal hinted at steel mail concealed beneath woven wool. I wondered at the audacity of this person. By the agreement of the truce, only Lord Tanu's or Lord Tomavar's counselors, or my own, were to be allowed into the square. At the quick approach of this intruder, who might have been a rogue knight, Sar Jalval drew his sword and stepped in front of Lord Tomavar as if to protect his lord.

'Your wife needs no finding!' a high-pitched and angry voice cried out. Then the knight pulled back the hood of the traveling cloak – and the helmet of mail beneath that. 'At last *I* have found *you*!'

Before us, shaking out her long, raven hair, stood one of the loveliest women in the Morning Mountains. She was tall, with flawless skin the color of dark ivory and large, dark eyes that shone like twin moons. In her, I thought, gathered all that was best and brightest of the Valari people.

'Vareva!' Lord Tomavar shouted, pushing himself up to his feet. 'You are alive!'

He made a move to cross the grass and embrace her, but Vareva clasped her hand to the sword belted to her side and cried out, 'Stay back, my lord! Stay back – please!'

Lord Tomavar halted his charge and stood staring at her, utterly stupefied as if someone had smashed a mace into his brains. Everyone on the field gathered around us and made a second ring of warriors acting as witnesses that day. Lord Manamar Tanu gazed at his daughter, clearly chagrined and confused as to what he should do.

'But how did you come to be here?' Lord Tomavar asked her. 'And how long have you been back in Mesh?'

'Long enough to hear that you had taken up arms against the son of the man you revered and called "Sire."'

'But, dear wife, there are things you don't understand,' he huffed out. 'Things have happened that you know nothing about!'

Her pained gaze fell upon him with a strong brew of emotions: ire, grief, resentment and adoration. Then she called out in a clear voice: 'I know this: that Valashu Elahad did not desert the castle as you, and others, have accused! I was there, you know. Before the castle fell and they killed almost everyone and took the rest of us away, I heard Lord Lansar Raasharu say that King Shamesh was dead, and that Asaru was now king and had sent Lord Raasharu to summon Val. Valashu Elahad speaks the truth! Lansar Raasharu *was* a ghul! I heard Morjin say this himself! To his filthy priests, in the Stone City, that foul, foul beast of a man boasted that he had suborned the noblest man in Mesh!'

Her words stunned the warriors, knights and lords standing around her. No one had ever dreamed that Vareva – or anyone else – would ever return out of Argattha to confirm the truth of what had happened in my father's castle on that most terrible of days.

'You were in the . . . presence of the Red Dragon?' Lord Tomavar finally stammered out to her.

'I served him in his throne room,' Vareva said, with loathing and shame burning up her face. 'Morjin took great pride in sporting his Valari slaves. As he did in boasting of how he had deceived everyone in Tria. Everyone in the world, almost, accuses Valashu Elahad of slaying an innocent man! But Ravik Kirriland was no innocent! He was a Kallimun priest, sent to murder Atara Ars Narmada!'

At the mention of this perfidy, of which Kane had told my friends and me many months ago, Atara bowed her blindfolded head toward Vareva.

'And so all the defamations people have made against Lord Valashu are false!' Vareva cried out. 'And everything that he has said is true!'

As she had spoken, I noticed Liljana holding her blue gelstei out toward Vareva with one hand while pressing her other hand to her temple. Then far out across the field, deep within the ranks of Lord Tomavar's men, an unseen warrior cried out: 'Valashu Elahad has told true! Lord Tomavar's wife confirms this! I can hear her words plain as a robin's song!'

Then others standing even farther back, out of easy reach of a spoken voice, made murmurs of amazement that they could understand Vareva as well. All at once it seemed as if all fifteen thousand warriors gathered around the square were affirming this and nodding their heads. Later, I would overhear men speaking of a miracle: of how they heard the voices of us at the center of the square clearly and distinctly, as if we stood right next to them. It would seem that Liljana had discovered a new power of her blue gelstei.

'Dear Vareva,' Lord Tomavar said, 'I am sorry. I give you my apology, as I did to Lord Valashu.'

I felt the hearts of more than ten thousand Valari warriors beating as one, and suddenly changing directions in their passion, as with the shift of a great flock of birds in flight. I wondered if Lord Tomavar could sense this as well.

'But why, dear wife,' Lord Tomavar continued, gazing at Vareva, 'did you not come forth sooner and speak of these things?'

'I was about to,' Vareva told him, 'when you drew on Lord Valashu. Then it was too late. I did not think that your pride would allow you to apologize, even if you knew the truth of things.'

At this, Lord Tomavar bowed his head in shame.

'Then, too,' Vareva continued, 'I knew that Lord Valashu would defeat you, as how could he not? I *wanted* him to, don't you see? Because how can I be your "dear" wife, or any wife at all, after all that has *happened*?'

It seemed that Lord Tomavar could not bear to look at her, and so he stared at my sword instead. His black eyes grew brighter and sadder as he studied his reflection as if finally seeing himself as he really was. Then he looked at me, and I felt his heart opening to the vast sea of suffering that Vareva held inside herself. I had a strange sense that he had come alive, in some small part, to my gift of valarda.

'I am sorry,' Lord Tomavar said again, finally turning back to Vareva.

'And I am sorry, too,' she said to him.

'I am sorry – but tell me that you no longer love me, then!'

'I cannot tell you that!' she cried out. 'But what is love against the dark thing that eats at all of us? That waits inside like a beast?'

Lord Tomavar's eyes brimmed with tears as he gazed at her

with a rare tenderness. Then she broke down sobbing. After she had regained control of her spasming belly, she gasped out to him, 'I always said that you had the soul of an angel! But I *hated* you for losing it and going against Lord Elahad. It was as if you were already dead! And why did you leave me to Morjin? You should have come after me! You *should* have! Valashu Elahad went into Argattha once, and *he* would have come after the woman he loved!'

At this, Lord Tomavar turned back to gaze at my sword again. So great was the grief ripping through him that I knew he wanted to die. But his pride would not let him take his own life or cast it away. Earlier he had spoken of a debt to me, and debts must be repaid. And he owed Vareva more than his life.

'I cannot undo what has been done,' he called out in a deep yet quavering voice. 'But I *can* do, now, what *should* be done – it is all that anyone can do.'

So saying, this very flawed man, whose essential nobility and faithfulness my father had always counted on, drew himself up tall and straight, and moved over to me. He set his hand upon the flat of my sword and cried out for everyone to hear: 'I stand for Valashu Elahad as king! I call for every warrior who has pledged to me to be free to stand as well!'

He turned toward Vareva yet again. His gaze burned with a promise that he would try to redeem himself in service to me. And more, with a plea to win her back as his wife.

'I stand for Valashu Elahad, too,' Vareva said, taking a step toward me.

'You cannot!' Sar Jalval called back from the ring of men around us. 'You are a woman, and no warrior!'

'I *am* a warrior!' Vareva shouted at him. She drew forth her sharp, shining sword. 'My father taught me how to use this! With it, I slew three of Morjin's guards and made my escape! Many there are standing upon this field who have not slain so many of our enemy!'

Everyone looked at Manamar Tanu then, and this fierce knight nodded his head as he admitted, 'It is true – I instructed my daughter in the sword. I should not have, but she was always a willful girl, and I could not refuse her.'

He paused a moment, then added, 'But she is right about who should be king of Mesh. I stand for Valashu Elahad, too!'

He drew his sword and moved over to me. Then Lord Tanu freed his bright kalama and called out to me, 'I was *very* wrong

126

about you. And so *I* will stand for you as well. All who have pledged to me are free to stand for you, as they will!'

I stood waiting for someone, or anyone, to speak.

'Valashu Elahad!' a powerful voice brayed out. I turned toward Lord Ramjay, Lord Tanu's greatest captain. On the field of the Culhadosh Commons, after the battle, he had spoken against me the most strongly. 'In Tria, with this secret sword you carry inside, you slew a man who has proved to be *not* an innocent – so Vareva Tomavar has told us. If you become king, what will you do with this great power of yours?'

I looked at Alkaladur, shimmering in the sunlight. And then, as I held this beautiful blade in one hand and my handkerchief containing Atara's golden hair in my other, I heard my voice crack out like thunder: 'Only this: I will call upon every particle of my being to defeat Morjin! And I will call upon you. You are Valari, descended all from Elahad himself and his brethren from the stars. *We* are brothers and sisters, warriors of the sword and the spirit. If our spirits are one, then the very fire of the stars shall be ours. If *we* are one, even if there is only one chance in all the universe of what we most desire, we shall set our sight on that and nothing else, and make it be.'

I told them, too, that if fate called me, I would die for them, as all must die for their dream.

For a while it seemed that no one moved. Liljana's blue crystal carried my words out for all to take in, not just with their ears but with a deeper sense. My passion to fight Morjin became *their* passion, not because I struck it into them as I had the truth with Lord Tomavar, but because they opened their hearts to me. Did the valarda, I wondered, dwell within all women and men, waiting to be awakened?

'Very well!' Lord Ramjay suddenly shouted as he drew his sword. 'Then I, too, will stand for Valashu Elahad!'

'And I!' Sar Shagarth shouted back.

'And I stand for Valashu Elahad!' Sar Jalval and Lord Vishand called out, as with one voice.

For a while, Liljana's crystal gave me to hear hundreds of conversations that had broken out around the square like the rumbles of a storm. I listened as warriors recounted my victories where I had led in battle: over Baron Narcavage and his assassins in King Kiritan's garden; over Morjin and his guards in his throne room when my friends and I had claimed the Lightstone; over the rogue Akhand clan of the Adirii tribe on the Wendrush; over the treacherous Duke Malatam and his five hundred knights at Shurkar's Notch in Alonia; and, of course, over Morjin's three armies at the Culhadosh Commons, which many now claimed that we won only because of me. Then Lord Tanu, finally deeming that enough had been said, held up his hand and called for the warriors to make their way to the various edges of the square: north, if they would stand for either the Lords Ramanu, Bahram and Kharashan; south if they favored Lord Tanu; west for Lord Tomavar; and east if they wanted me to be king. The warriors, however, ignored him. As one, almost all of them, from every direction, broke ranks and rushed into the square, crying out, 'Valashu Elahad – Valashu Elahad for king!'

As they pressed in closer, Lord Tanu turned about estimating numbers. And then he shouted: 'It is done! The warriors acclaim Valashu Elahad as our king!'

'Valashu Elahad!' ten thousand men called out at once. 'The Elahad for king!'

'Elahad! Elahad! Elahad!'

Then Lord Arajay Solval looked down at my bare hand, still gripping my sword, and he said, 'But there is no ring!'

I, too, looked down at my hand. In Hesperu, Kane had broken apart my lord's ring for its four diamonds so that we might purchase a slave named Bemossed. Every king of Mesh, for ages, had worn on his finger a ring of five brilliant and perfect diamonds.

'Lord Elahad,' Lord Solval announced, 'cast down his father's ring upon the Culhadosh Commons, and so there is no ring!'

'No, you are wrong!' Lord Harsha's gruff voice blared out. He stepped closer to me, and reached out his fist. When he opened his hand, everyone could see sparkling at its center my father's old ring. 'I kept this on that terrible day against *this* great day, which I always hoped would come.'

So saying, after I gave Kane to hold my sword, Lord Harsha grasped my hand and slid the ring down upon my finger. It fit perfectly. I held up my hand for everyone to see the five bright diamonds, once worn by my father and my grandfather's grandfathers.

'With this ring,' Lord Harsha intoned, repeating the ancient formula, 'go forth in the name of the Shining One as King of Mesh and never forget from where you came.'

'Valashu Elahad!' Lord Avijan shouted. 'King of Mesh – King Valamesh!'

'Valamesh! Valamesh!' thousands of warriors cried out. 'King Valamesh!'

128

Kane gave me back my sword, which I held blazing up to the sun. Then the warriors and knights all drew their swords and pressed in closer to me, not as a mob, but arrayed as ring around ring around sparkling rings, like those that circle the great planet Shahar. They pointed their swords up toward mine, and the reflection of bright steel off of silustria cast a cone of silver and light up into the sky.

And the acclaim continued with shouts that seemed to shake the very earth: 'Valamesh! Valamesh! Valamesh!'

After what seemed a long time, the warriors quieted and broke their circles to allow my friends to pass. Estrella danced up to me with great delight filling her lively face, while Liljana came closer and kissed my hand. Straight across from me, Atara stood as proud as a queen, smiling and weeping, without tears. Kane beamed like the very sun. As for Maram, he shouted for a whole barrel of brandy to be opened so that we might celebrate the moment.

'But what shall I call you now?' he said to me. '"Sire" is how I addressed *my* father, and "Valamesh" has a strange ring to it.'

'Call me "friend,"' I said to him, smiling and clasping his hand.

Then Joshu Kadar, standing nearby, bowed his head to me and said, 'I shall call you the "King of Swords!" To fight as you did today – that was the most wondrous swordwork I have ever seen!'

Kane, hearing this, nodded his head at me. 'So it was.'

A king, my father once said, lived in order to fulfill his duties, and my first was a happy one. I motioned for Sar Vikan and Sar Jessu to come closer. I took out two silver rings that I had reserved for this moment; each shone with four diamonds, and were the rings of lords. After bidding Sar Vikan and Sar Jessu to take off their old rings, I slipped these new ones in turn down around their fingers. Then I called out, 'Only a king can make a master knight into a lord, and it is long since time that both of you received these rings. Stand and be recognized! Lord Vikan Arval! Lord Jessu the Lion-Heart!'

Many warriors struck their swords together and cried out, 'Vikan Arval, Jessu the Lion-Heart, Lords of Mesh!'

Now many women and children from Hardu, Lashku and Godhra, and other towns, began making their way through the circles of soldiers in order to honor me. A few of the outlanders who had set up camp here also pressed in for a better look, even though Sar Shivalad and Sar Kanshar and my other Guardians kept them at a good distance. One man, however, would not be discouraged by the fence of swords surrounding me. He pushed himself right up against the flat of Sar Shivalad's kalama, and called out to me in a strong, deep voice, 'King Valamesh, indeed. As you desired, Valashu Elahad, it has come to be.'

Then he threw back the hood of his traveling cloak to reveal a fine, weathered face as dark as chocolate and wreathed in wavy white hair and a great flowing beard. He had the wisest eyes I had even seen.

'Grandfather!' I cried out. 'You are safe!'

I motioned for Sar Shivalad and Sar Jurald to lower their swords. Then Abrasax, the Master Reader and the Grandmaster of the Great White Brotherhood whom his intimates called "Grandfather," stepped closer to me. Others of his ancient order accompanied him: Master Virang, with his deep almond eyes and whimsical old face; the stolid Master Storr, whose title was Master Galastei; Master Nolashar, the Music Master; Master Yasul and Master Matai. I did not see Master Okuth among them, and my first fear would soon be proved true: that on their perilous journey from the Valley of the Sun where Morjin's men had destroyed their school, the Seven had now become only six.

'Master Okuth,' Abrasax said by way of explanation, 'died so that your friend might live.'

And with that he stepped aside so that Bemossed might come forward. The man I had befriended in Hesperu looked at me with the same large, luminous eyes that haunted my dreams. His face, soft yet handsome, had lost none of its gentleness, though deep lines creased his dark skin, especially across his forehead, tattooed with a black cross marking him as one of the despised Hajarim. But no man on Ea, I thought, could be more revered or more welcome in Mesh than he.

'Bemossed!' I called out, rushing up to embrace him. 'You *are* alive!'

'And you are a king!' he said, bowing his head to me. The smile that broke upon his face seemed as natural and bright as the sun.

Then Vareva stepped over to us, and she said to Bemossed, with relief and familiarity, 'We came just in time.'

'Thank you for leading us here,' he told her, turning his smile upon her.

Master Juwain, edging closer, looked from Abrasax to Vareva and then at Bemossed. 'I can see that there are stories that must be told – why don't we go somewhere we can tell them?'

It was a good suggestion, but the fifteen thousand warriors surrounding us would not allow it. When it became known who

Bemossed was, Lord Noldashan cried out: 'It is the Maitreya! He has come to honor King Valamesh!'

Then many, many voices, those of warriors and those of women, children, too, shouted out: 'The Maitreya! The Maitreya! The Maitreya has come!'

Once again, the warriors raised up their swords and sent a dazzling radiance out into the square. Bemossed, however, standing next to me, fairly shone with a deeper and finer light that seemed to fill up the whole world. Then his smile grew even brighter as his clear, sweet voice called out along with thousands of others':

'Valamesh! Valamesh! Long live King Valamesh!'

9

For the next three hours, I put my lips to many cups of brandy raised up to acknowledge the many men who insisted on toasting their new king. I walked among my warriors, looking into their eyes and asking their names. Too, I gathered Joshu Kadar, Sar Shivalad, Sar Kanshar and the other knights whom I had come to call my 'Guardians.' Now that they had made me king, in honor of their greatest aspirations, I formally declared them to be the 'Guardians of the Lightstone.' Then it came time to adjourn to my pavilion. My companions all followed me inside, along with Abrasax and the Masters of the Brotherhood. Bemossed, of course, came with them, and I invited Vareva to speak with us as well. I sat at the head of the long council table, with my companions on one side facing the Seven and Vareva on the other. Bemossed took his place at the end of the table opposite from me.

'I still can't quite believe that you are alive and safe here,' I said to him. I gazed at his bright, restless face, and it seemed that I could not get enough of looking at him.

'But I *can* believe that you are now king,' he said with a smile. 'Even when you first came to me in your guise as a poor flutist, it seemed that you must be something more. We've come a long way from Hesperu, haven't we?'

'We have,' I agreed, glancing at the ring that sparkled around my finger. 'And *you* have come a long way from the Valley of the Sun. What happened, friend?'

As Bemossed rubbed at his tired eyes, his gaze seemed to turn inward. I sensed in him many troublesome things: shame, grief, dread and an overwhelming sense of failure. He finally looked at Abrasax to speak for him.

'We had hoped,' Abrasax said in his clear, forceful voice, 'that we had more time. But in the end, the Red Dragon proved too clever. And too powerful.'

He told us, simply, that Morjin had at last discovered the location of the Brotherhood's school that he had been seeking for so long. Then one of Morjin's Kallimun priests had led a whole battalion of soldiers and a company of the terrible Grays into the lower reaches of the White Mountains. This priest – whose name was Arch Igasho – had managed to unlock the secrets of the tunnel that gave into the Valley of the Sun. Then Morjin's men had fallen upon the school with fire and steel and all the evil power of the black gelstei wielded by the leader of the Grays.

'They cut down everyone who tried to reason with them,' Abrasax told us in a heavy voice. 'And they burned everything that could be burned. They found the library, and put torches to the books.'

Master Juwain, nearly stricken by this terrible news, asked him, 'But they can't have burned the *vedastei*!'

At the mention of these magical books, made of some sort of gelstei that could call ancient knowledge to its crystal pages as of light out of thin air, Abrasax sadly shook his head. And he told us, 'The fire grew so hot it melted the vedastei's crystal. There is nothing left but ashes.'

I stared down at the floor of my tent. With the burning of the millions of books of the Library at Khaisham and now this even greater desecration, it seemed that Ea had suffered a burning away of wisdom that might plunge the whole world into a Dark Age without end.

'But how could you have verified this?' Master Juwain said to Abrasax. 'Surely you did not remain to *see* the books destroyed?'

Abrasax's thick beard and hair seemed like a corona of white as he nodded his head for Master Storr to speak. Master Storr sat staring down at his liver-spotted hands. His old, fair face, burned red from his recent travels, grew tighter and tighter as if he could not bring himself to answer Abrasax's silent request.

Then finally he looked up and told us: 'We *did* see the books destroyed. With this.'

So saying, Master Storr, the Brotherhood's Master Galastei, drew forth a sphere of white gelstei no different than Atara's. And he said to us in his tight, fussy voice: 'We managed to rescue many of the gelstei. I haven't a scryer's ability to see into the future. But sometimes I have seen things far away in space – or not so very

133

far away. This crystal gave sight of what the Red Dragon's men did to our school.'

He held up the clear ball to the light streaming through the pavilion's black silk. I was afraid that if I looked into it too deeply, I would see writhing flames and men screaming in agony.

'You must have taken a blue gelstei, as well,' Liljana said to him. She held up her little whale figurine. 'I *know* I touched minds with you through this.'

Master Storr nodded his head slowly. 'That was a stroke of good fortune, I think. I wanted you to know that Bemossed was safe.'

Master Juwain sat looking at the clear crystal in Master Storr's hands. 'But what of the Great Gelstei then? Are *they* safe?'

In answer, Master Matai, an Old Galdan whose white curls fell over a browned, noble face, drew out of his pocket a small, translucent sphere, ruby in color. Master Virang kept a similar stone, tinted golden-orange, while Master Nolashar, the Music Master, had a yellow sun stone, which he raised up gleaming above the council table. I feared that with Master Okuth's death his green heart stone had been lost, but it was not so. Master Storr held it in keeping for the Brotherhood's new Master Healer, whoever that might be; he also still guarded his own purple stone. Master Yasul's mahogany skin cracked into dozens of lines as he smiled and showed us a round, azure gelstei. Abrasax, of course, kept the last and most powerful of these seven stones: a clear bit of crystal no bigger than a marble. In his hand, it seemed insignificant, as did the crystals of the others. But I couldn't help thinking that with great gelstei similar in kind, if not size, at the beginning of time, the Ieldra had summoned a beautiful music that sang the very stars into creation.

'At least, then, Grandfather,' Master Juwain said to Abrasax, 'you have preserved your greatest treasures.'

Abrasax's wise, worn face grew sad beyond bearing as if he had lived not just a hundred and forty-seven years but a million. 'No, our greatest treasures lie dead in the Valley of the Sun. Most of our Brothers fell beneath the soldiers' swords. And those who were captured, Arch Igasho ordered crucified.'

Now Master Juwain bowed his head in shame and grief. It seemed that he had almost forgotten his quest to escape the ideals and abstractions of his head in order to feel with his heart.

Abrasax closed his hand around the Seventh, as his gelstei was called, and he put it away. Then he said, 'We had hoped the moment would never come, but we had prepared for it a long time. Our Brothers all died believing their sacrifice was to the good. And we should believe it, too.'

Here he looked at Bemossed, and smiled sadly. Kind, the Brotherhood's Grandmaster might be, and compassionate, too, but I felt a will as hard as diamond buried deep inside him. It seemed that he could accept the sacrifice of others – and even encourage it – if that served his highest purpose. It was a lesson, I thought, that a king must take to heart.

'But how,' Maram asked, 'did *you* escape, since only one tunnel leads in and out of the valley? Surely the soldiers would have guarded it.'

'Indeed, they did,' Abrasax said. 'But we slipped past them, so to speak.'

He looked at Master Virang, the Meditation Master, who showed us one of his mysterious smiles. I remembered how, when my companions and I had first come into the Valley of the Sun, this small and lively man had somehow concealed the school's buildings from our sight. It seemed just possible that through his great control over his mind, and that of his enemies, he had somehow cast a cloak of invisibility over the Seven and Bemossed, and caused the soldiers not to see them.

'Let us say,' he told us by way of explanation, 'that most men cannot keep their attention where they should. And so they do not see what they should see. And so we were able to hide in plain view of the soldiers – so to speak.'

'As you hid today, out beyond the square?' I asked him.

Master Virang shrugged his shoulders as he touched the wool of the cloak enfolding him. 'For *that* we needed little more than *this*.'

His words caused Kane to scowl, and my savage friend said, 'All right – keep your secrets, then. But tell us this: how did Igasho get through the tunnel? Did Morjin give him a gelstei that unlocked it?'

'He must have,' Master Storr said. 'As he must have given him another gelstei that gave him sight of our school.'

'Ha – I wouldn't have thought that the damned Igasho, as he calls himself now, could have such skill with such stones.'

Arch Igasho had been born Prince Salmelu Aradar of Ishka into one of the most ancient and noble of Valari lines. All through his youth, he had trained at the sword like any other Valari warrior. But somehow his soul had sickened, and he had surrendered both sword and soul to Morjin. My blood still burned with the kirax that Salmelu had fired into me with his assassin's arrow. In reward for his service, Morjin had made Salmelu a full priest of the Kallimun, and then elevated him again and again.

'You mustn't underestimate this man,' Abrasax said to Kane and me. 'He nearly destroyed you in Hesperu. As he nearly killed all of us – as he did our Brothers.'

'Ha!' Kane said again. 'Igasho is a traitor and a worm, for he lives on Morjin's droppings when he could have been a king in his own right. He *failed* to kill Val with his damned arrow, as he did in Hesperu – even as he did with you.'

'He did,' Abrasax agreed, 'but each time he came very close. The Red Dragon must hope that the next time he will succeed.'

'In a way, he *did* succeed,' Master Storr said. 'Our school is destroyed, and some of the brightest souls of our generation. Our books are ashes. Morjin would count this as a victory.'

Abrasax made a fist as he fought for words that must have been hard for him to say: 'Books can always be rewritten and new generations will arise to replace the old. No treasure is beyond being restored. Except one, I fear. This age is almost over, and if it comes to an end without the Maitreya taking the Lightstone in his hands, then *all* will come to end, forever. For Bemossed, it has been so close – as close as that hair you keep folded in your pocket, Valashu Elahad.'

I looked at Atara, sitting straight and motionless to my right. I did not know how Abrasax had learned of this great treasure I kept close to my heart, Master Reader of the Brotherhood though he might be. Then this very perceptive man let out a pained breath as he told us of how Bemossed had almost died.

'Our young friend,' Abrasax said, 'was already weak from fighting Morjin for too long. Our struggle to escape the valley weakened him further, and our flight through the mountains even more. And that was not the worst of things.'

'What could be worse than that?' Maram asked. Then his face seemed to drain of blood as he answered his own question: 'The Grays, then – the damn Grays!'

'The Grays indeed,' Abrasax told us.

He went on to say that these soulless men, whose eyes were as hard and dead as pieces of stone, had listened for the murmurings of Bemossed's mind and had followed him for many days through the mountains and then out onto the grasslands of the Wendrush. And all the while their leader had used a black gelstei to suck away the very fires of Bemossed's life so that he had sickened nearly to his death.

'It was that way when the Grays pursued us across Alonia,' Maram said with a shudder. 'At the end of things, they put their cold claws into our minds so that we couldn't move. And then came to suck out our souls!'

Maram, I thought, remembering, spoke dramatically but not inaccurately.

'Only Kane's coming saved us then,' Maram told Abrasax. 'But I should think that the powers of the Seven would have saved *you*.'

'We do have our skills,' Abrasax said with a note of mystery shading his voice. 'Which is why we are even here to tell you how Master Okuth saved Bemossed's life at the sacrifice of his own.'

I remembered very well old Master Okuth's iron-gray hair and heavy head resembling that of an ox. But it seemed that he had possessed the soul of an angel. For as the Seven had fled with Bemossed barely beyond the knives of the Grays and swords of Igasho's men, Master Okuth had employed all his powers to keep Bemossed from failing and falling off his horse. And at the end, when Bemossed could go no further, Master Okuth had used his green heart stone to pour his own life fires into Bemossed as if giving him his own blood. This greatest of all kindnesses had killed Master Okuth – even as it gave Bemossed the strength to go on.

'We buried Master Okuth in the Sarni way,' Abrasax said, 'on a knoll above the Astu River. And then we rode on.'

'But how did you escape then?' Maram asked. 'From the *Grays*?'

Abrasax pulled at his white beard as if deciding how much he should tell us. Then he nodded his head for Master Nolashar to speak.

In answer, Master Nolashar took out a flute little different than the one I had once given to Estrella. Although he wore his hair cut short, like Kane's, and he now practiced with this instrument rather than the sword, he had been born a Valari many years ago – into which land he had never said. His large eyes gazed with great intensity out of a stark and stern face. Yet deep down he seemed a happy man, as why shouldn't he be? For he had spent most of his life in the study of music, which had been my first and greatest dream.

'The Grays,' he said, 'listen for the sounds of the soul in the minds of those they hunt. Other sounds can overwhelm these and confuse them. In particular, music.'

Maram gazed at him with doubt coloring his face. 'Are you telling us that you threw the Grays off your trail by playing your *flute*?'

'No, Sar Maram, I am *not* telling you that. There are many ways of making music.'

The tones of his smooth voice hinted at much more than he would say. Had he, with his bright sun stone, led the Seven to call up enchanting melodies out of their gelstei and cast this unearthly music across the steppe to madden the Grays? Or a vastly deeper sound that might have utterly deafened them? It seemed that Master Nolashar, too, liked to keep his secrets.

'Let us just say,' he told us, 'that in the end the Grays and soldiers rode in one direction, while we rode in another.'

I nodded my head at this, then looked down the long table at Bemossed. He sat as within a cloud of melancholy, and seemed to hold on to this dark mood as he might an old friend. I felt torment and self-doubt eating at his insides, and I thought I knew why.

'Master Okuth,' I said to him, 'was a very good man.'

'He was like my father!' Bemossed said with tears filling his eyes. 'As I *think* my father must have been. He died trying to protect me, too.'

'And that was surely the best thing he ever did. As he would have wanted to tell you. And so with Master Okuth.'

Bemossed looked down at his long hands, which had performed so many loathsome tasks during his years as a despised Hajarim slave. Then he said, 'In Hesperu, they flavor wine with oranges, cloves, pepper and honey. Fire wine, they call it. It is like an elixir of the angels – I was allowed to taste it once, and I got drunk on it. That is how it was with Master Okuth. He gave me his life! Even as it emptied from him, I felt it filling me up, like fire, so hot, so sweet. And now his bones lie cold and picked white on the grass of the Wendrush while here I sit with my blood still beating sweetly through me.'

'Fathers,' I told him, remembering, 'die for their sons. That is life.'

'No, that is death,' he murmured to me.

'Master Okuth would not have wanted to hear you say that.'

'No, Valashu – I know you are right. And I know I must honor Master Okuth in living, as best I can, as I was born to do. It is just that . . .'

His voice vanished into the quiet of the tent; from outside came the muffled cries of many men drinking and celebrating.

'What is it, friend?' I asked him.

He seemed to fight back some deep dread inside him, and a warmer thing, too. Then he said, 'It is just that one shouldn't pour wine into a cracked vessel.'

At this, Abrasax and the other masters looked at him with deep concern. So did my companions, and so did I.

'Once,' I said to him, 'I thought wrongly that I was the Maitreya. And people therefore thought wrongly of me that I would be without flaws. But, like any other man, I was only –'

'No, I am not speaking of *common* faults. Jealousy, stubbornness, uncertainty – these I know as well as anyone.' He paused to draw in a long breath as he looked at me. 'But there is something else. Something that I can't even tell you because I can't quite see it myself. A *wrongness*. The Maitreya, you call me, the Shining One. But I can't always hold this light that I should be able to hold. I can't always *be* it, even though it is always there and in some strange way I can't ever *not* be it. And when I can't, there is a kind of darkness, inside the light. It goes on and on, forever. It . . . is hard to describe. But Master Okuth knew, I think. And Morjin.'

'Morjin!' I called out, nearly shouting.

'I have fought with him for what seems forever,' he said. 'It is killing me, Valashu!'

I sensed something dark and dreadful pulling at him inside, and he seemed immensely tired and older than the twenty-three years he supposed himself to be. Then I remembered lines from an old verse:

> *The Shining One*
> *In innocence sleeps*
> *Inside his heart*
> *Angel fire sleeps*
> *And when he wakes*
> *The fire leaps.*
>
> *About the Maitreya*
> *One thing is known:*
> *That to himself*
> *He always is known*
> *When the moment comes*
> *To claim the Lightstone.*

The Maitreya he must be, I thought. He *must* be. But I wondered if circumstances – and my own desperate purpose – had forced him to take on this mantle before he had fully awakened. The verse hinted at a kind of quickening and self-knowing that would occur only when the Maitreya set hands upon the Lightstone. It tormented me that in losing the Lightstone to Morjin, I might have kept Bemossed from his fate.

'You are safe here,' I told him, not quite knowing what to say. I looked down at my new ring, and then pointed in the direction of the square outside the tent. 'As safe, now, as anywhere on Ea. Fifteen thousand warriors stand ready to fight to the death to protect you.'

'King Valamesh,' he said to me with a forced smile, 'I do not want a single warrior to fight and die for me.'

'Nor I,' I told him. 'But I will never let Morjin harm you.'

'Is that power now yours, great King?'

He sat gazing at me, then he drew out of his pocket a small, shining bowl that had been made in the image of the Lightstone. It was an ancient work of silver gelstei, tinted gold; through the power of this vessel Bemossed could sense the vastly greater power of the distant Lightstone and contend with Morjin over its mastery.

'Every day,' he told me, 'I wake up and take this cup into my hands, and my battle with Morjin begins anew. At night, when I am able to sleep, I keep it close to my heart as I fight with him in my dreams. Every hour, every minute – every moment that I push against his will, he harms me.'

I sat gripping the hilt of the work of silver gelstei that had been given to me. Liljana kept her blue gelstei safe, as did Master Juwain his varistei, and my other friends their stones. Only through Bemossed's struggle with Morjin, I knew, could we use our gelstei without Morjin wielding the Lightstone to pervert and control them. As only Bemossed's sacrifice kept Morjin from freeing the Dark One from Damoom.

'You must be strong,' I said to him. I heard myself speaking as a king, and I hoped Bemossed would not hate me for that. 'As you truly are – as strong as steel.'

'You do not understand,' he said, looking down at his cup.

His long lashes were like dark curtains falling over his eyes. And I told him, 'In Senta, in the Singing Caves, I listened as the Morjin of old lamented his murdering of an angel: his best friend. And more than once, Liljana has touched minds with the Beast.'

'You do not understand,' Bemossed said again, now looking up at me. 'It is not his mind that I must face. It is his soul. And the crack through *it* is so black and deep it could swallow up the stars. It goes on and on forever.'

Something inside him seemed bruised, as if he had taken too many blows from a mace. I drew in a deep breath as I listened to swords clashing in practice rounds and men singing outside. And I said to him: 'It will not be forever that you must fight Morjin this way. I returned to Mesh just so that you would not have to fight him alone.'

'Fifteen thousand warriors have acclaimed you, and that is a great thing. But Morjin, it is said, commands a million men.'

I looked down at my sword, and I said, 'We *will* prevail over Morjin. There must be a way.'

'Not *that* way,' Bemossed said, pointing at Alkaladur.

'You have only to be strong a little longer,' I told him, not really wanting to hear his words. '*We* must.'

'Yes, friend, we must.'

I drew my sword a few inches from its scabbard so that I might see its gleaming blade.

'You would still kill him,' he said to me. 'Kill him and cut the Lightstone from his hands.'

'And you would still heal him,' I said, looking up at him.

'And why not? He is a man like any other.'

'No, not like *any* other.'

'His deepest desire is to be made whole.'

'No – not his *deepest* desire.'

'He *is* a man,' he told me, 'even as you are.'

'No, he is a beast.'

Bemossed rubbed his tired face as he stared off toward the roof of the tent. Then he said to me: 'Somewhere on Ea, there is a man who has been faithful, dutiful and kind all his life. A *good* man, Valashu. And for no reason that anyone else can see, his soul will sicken and then one day something within him will break. He might strangle his wife in a jealous rage or even slay his best friend arguing over the rights to a stream dividing their lands. And ever after, set out on a life of murder and outlawry. *That* man, I tell you, is more dangerous than Morjin would be if only he turned back to the light.'

Now I had to consider what Bemossed had told me. Finally I said to him: 'But he won't turn back, and that is what is so terrible about Morjin. He *likes* doing evil.'

Bemossed said nothing to this as he looked at me. His hands tightened around the silver gelstei called the False Lightstone.

'I think,' I said to him, pointing at the cup, 'that you have already begun trying to heal him through *that*.'

He nodded his head to me. 'As this touches upon the Lightstone, it opens upon Morjin's soul.'

'And so the reverse must be.'

His eyes grew sad and anguished as he said, 'Yes, I know that is how Morjin found me and the Brothers' school.'

For a while he descended into that dark, watery part of himself from which he took too great a comfort. Then he looked over at Estrella, sitting quietly as she fairly drank in each of his words. She smiled at him, as if his essential goodness couldn't help but make her happy. Her warm, lively face seemed to remind him of the incredible brightness of his own being and draw out of him something even warmer.

'Don't be afraid for me,' he finally told me. He seemed to brighten like a sunrise, for that, too, was his power and delight. 'As you said, there is always a way.'

Now he, too, smiled, and I wondered that I had ever worried that Morjin might find a way to destroy him. He sat up taller and straighter as a new strength poured into him from some secret source. His radiant face made me recall the three signs by which a Maitreya might be recognized: steady abidance in the One; looking upon all with an equal eye; unshakable courage at all times.

I felt my heart beating out great bursts of my life as I looked at him, and he looked at me – and looked deep *inside* me. At last, he asked me: 'What ails *you*, Valashu?'

I glanced around the tent for any sign of the dark thing that had hounded me since my return to Mesh. Although I could not see it, a black cloud seemed to hang over my head no matter which direction I turned to look toward the future. I had not wanted to speak so soon of my deepest affliction and add yet another stone to the great weight pulling Bemossed down. But the time had come, I saw, when I must tell of the Ahrim.

'It is like a great nothing,' I said to Bemossed and the Masters of the Brotherhood, 'that holds more power than *everything*: all the suns and stars across the universe.'

Bemossed listened as I described my battle with the Ahrim in the wood near Lord Harsha's farm, and then my struggle to speak out the truth of things not an hour ago. He turned the whole of his awareness upon my words, the dread breaking from my eyes, the anguish in my heart. Who could not love a man who put aside his own sufferings in order to uplift another? As Bemossed's whole being seemed to grow brighter and brighter, I realized the essential thing about him: that he must find a way to heal those he cared about – either that, or die. And that he could bring the most splendid of lights to others, but not to himself.

'I am sorry that I said you did not understand what it is like with Morjin,' he told me. 'In the end, I think, we face the same evil.'

Abrasax nodded his head at this. Then he said to me, 'This thing you have told of remains unknown to us. But it is clear that you must fight it even as you did Morjin in Hesperu.'

'I will fight Morjin with *this*,' I said, unsheathing Alkaladur and holding it shining up toward the apex of the tent.

Abrasax smiled at this in his mysterious way. Then he asked me, 'Can you tell me in truth that the sword you hold in your hand and the one you carry inside are not the same?'

'Of course they are not the same,' I said, looking at Alkaladur's luminous silustria.

'Perhaps not the same, then. But not entirely two, either.'

I thought about this as I gazed at the blade that had been named the Sword of Fate. I knew that in some strange way, Abrasax must be right.

'I have said many times,' he told me, 'that Morjin will never be defeated through force of arms alone. But there must be a way to defeat him – even as you did Lord Tomavar.'

At the sound of his voice, my sword grew brighter.

'Can that be?' I whispered. 'Can that truly be?'

'It *must* be,' Abrasax told me. 'I can see no other hope for victory.'

My hands tightened around the diamonds set into my sword's hilt. And I shook my head. 'But Morjin is *not* Lord Tomavar.'

'No, he is not. But you will not fight him alone.'

He turned to look at Bemossed, and so did I. Then he continued, 'You and Bemossed have seemed at odds today. But you must remember that you are as brothers, and *do* fight the same battle. He will help you, if you let him, Valashu. As we will help him.'

I met his gaze and thought of the seven Great Gelstei that he and the other Masters of the Brotherhood kept. I wanted to believe what he told me.

'The time is coming,' he said, 'when everything and all of us will be put to the test.'

Here he nodded at Alphanderry, who occupied one of the table's chairs, not as a man of flesh and blood pressing against wood, but rather as a gleaming substance contained by it.

'Your messenger's warning to you concurs with what we know,' he went on. 'Master Matai?'

143

He turned to the Brotherhood's Master Diviner. Despite his years, Master Matai seemed possessed of an innocence and a great gratitude for the wisdom his discipline had brought him. He said to us: 'I have been plotting the movements of the heavens all my life. The planets and stars all gather toward a great moment. If my calculations are correct, then the alignment that your friend told of will occur on the eighth day of Valte.'

On that day, he said, Ea and Damoom would perfectly come into conjunction with Agathad where the greatest of the Galadin dwelled by the silver lake known as Skol. Then out of Ninsun, at the center of the universe, the Ieldra's radiance would pour out in a golden light upon these three fated planets, whether in creation or destruction not even the angels could say.

'There is nearly infinite power in the Golden Band,' Master Matai told us. 'And if Morjin can use the Lightstone to seize upon it and free Angra Mainyu, then . . .'

He did not finish his sentence. He did not have to state, one more time, the danger hanging over Ea and all of Eluru: that if Angra Mainyu were loosed upon the universe, a dark age lasting forever would descend upon all the stars, and the Ieldra would be forced to put an end to their glorious creation.

'I cannot believe that will ever be,' Abrasax said, looking at me. 'I *must* believe Ayondela Kirriland's prophecy: "The seven brothers and sisters of the earth with the seven stones will set forth into the darkness. The Lightstone will be found, the Maitreya will come forth, and a new age will begin."'

He nodded his head as if in agreement with one side in an ongoing argument that he held with himself. Then he said, 'The first half of the prophecy has already come to pass, for who can doubt that a new age will soon begin, whether for good or ill? *I* do not doubt the final part of the prophecy: "A seventh son with the mark of Valoreth will slay the dragon. The old world will be destroyed and a new world created."'

'But, Grandfather,' Maram said, 'a scryer's words are like a cat's eyes: they can change colors, depending on how one looks at them. Val has *already* slain the dragon. A real dragon, of flesh and blood and fire. In Argattha, he put his sword into Angraboda's heart, and killed that monster.'

'But is that the dragon of which the prophecy speaks?' Abrasax asked him.

'You tell me!'

'I shall tell you this,' Abrasax said, pointing at the bandage that

Master Juwain had plastered above my eye. 'Val has been cut on his forehead, in the same place, yet a third time in his life. The mark of Valoreth, indeed! We should all take great hope from this miracle. As we should pay close attention to the ordering of the lines of Ayondela's prophecy: "The Lightstone will be found, the Maitreya will come forth" – and only *then* will the dragon be slain. But slain *how*, I ask you? Not, I hope, by a sword through Morjin's heart. Not by *that* sword, which Val holds in his hands. I pray it will be as Bemossed has said: that Morjin can be aided to turn back to the light. And if he can be, then the Dragon will truly be slain, for Morjin's evil self will perish, and the Great Red Dragon will be no more. And Morjin will stand radiant and good, as he was born to be.'

For a while we all sat quiet and unmoving at my council table. The sun's fierce rays pierced through the thin, woven fibers of my tent. Outside, men were singing out the verses of the old epic that told of Aramesh's defeat of Morjin.

Then Kane stood up and began pacing back and forth like a tiger locked in a cage. Beneath his taut, sunburnt skin, his muscles bunched and relaxed in rhythm with the pounding of his savage heart. At last, he paused by Abrasax's chair, and fixed him with his black, blazing eyes.

'So,' he said. His voice rumbled up out of him like molten rock from a crack in the earth. 'You reopen the old argument. The old, old argument.'

Only a day before, Master Juwain had pulled an arrow from his lung; the immense vitality pouring out of him suggested that he had forgotten this insult to his flesh. But I sensed him reliving grievances as ancient as the stars – and much else, too. His eyes grew clear and bright, and sad, and I saw looking out through them a strange and ancient being.

'There was a man,' he said. His voice flowed out rich, deep, fiery and pained. 'Ha – a man who had once *been* a man. A warrior of the spirit, for he lived in obedience with the One's law that the Elijin are not permitted to slay. He, too, believed that a great soul could be turned back toward the light.'

As the afternoon lengthened and it grew warmer inside the tent, my friend who was now very much a warrior of the sword spoke of the ancient ages long before the Star People had come to earth. He told us of Asangal's fall as the damned angel called Angra Mainyu – and the great War of the Stone that had resulted when Angra Mainyu stole the Lightstone to challenge the will of the

Ieldra. Half of Eluru's Elijin and Galadin, known as the Daevas or Betrayers, had followed Angra Mainyu into exile, while the others called themselves the Amshahs: they who would preserve the Law of the One. They remained with Ashtoreth and Valoreth on Agathad, which some called Skol. There, led by the immortal Kalkin, they worked to drive the poison from Angra Mainyu's heart. Some of what he told us the Galadin's messenger, two years before, had confided to my companions and me in a stone amphitheater outside of Tria. And now, as Kane paused to look at Alphanderry and asked him to sing for us, a very different messenger recited lines from the ancient verse:

> When first the Dragon ruled the land,
> The ancient warrior came to Skol.
> He sought for healing with his hand,
> And healing fire burned his soul.
>
> The sacred spark of hope he held,
> It glowed like leaves an emerald green;
> In heart and hand it brightly dwelled:
> The fire of the Galadin.
>
> He brought this flame into a world
> Where flowers blazed like stellulars,
> Where secret colors flowed and swirled
> And angels walked beneath the stars.
>
> To Star-Home thus the warrior came,
> Beside the ancient silver lake,
> By hope of heart, by fire and flame,
> A sacred sword he vowed to make.
>
> Alkaladur! Alkaladur!
> The Sword of Love, the Sword of Light,
> Which men have named Awakener
> From darkest dreams and fear-filled night.
>
> No noble metal, gem or stone –
> Its blade of finer substance wrought,
> Of essence pure as love alone,
> As strong as hope, as quick as thought.

Valarda, like molten steel,
Like tears, like waves of singing light,
Which angel fire has set its seal
And breath of angels polished bright.

Ten thousand years it took to make
Beneath their planet's shining sun;
Ten thousand angels by the lake:
The souls poured forth their fire as one.

In strength surpassing adamant,
Its perfect beauty diamond-bright,
No gelstei shone more radiant:
The sacred sword was purest light.

Alkaladur! Alkaladur!
The Sword of Ruth, the Healing Blade,
Which men have named the Messenger
Of hope of angels' star-blessed aid.

In ruth the warrior went to war,
A host of angels in his train:
Ten thousand Amshahs, all who swore
To heal the Dark One's bitter pain.

With Kalkin, splendid Solajin
And Varkoth, Set and Ashtoreth –
The greatest of the Galadin
Went forth to vanquish fear of death.

And Urukin and Baradin,
In all their pity, pomp and pride:
The brightest of the Elijin
In many thousands fought and died.

Their gift, valarda, opened them:
Into their hearts a fell hate poured;
This turned the warrior's stratagem
For none could wield the sacred sword.

'None could wield it!' Kane suddenly called out, interrupting
Alphanderry. 'The Dark One waited for the Amshahs to open their

hearts, in ruth – even in love. But *he* was ruth*less*, eh? And so he drove all the vileness of his spirit into them, and slew those who could be slain.'

I felt the blood pounding in his face as his eyes filled with a black and bitter thing. I had a hard time believing that my furious friend could once have been Kalkin: the Elijin lord and mighty warrior told of in the verse.

He saw me looking at him, and moved over to my chair. Without any care that I now might be king, he reached out to lay his hand upon my chest. And to Abrasax, he said, 'We call that within Val's heart a sword. Of light, of love. But it has other names, eh? The soul force, the valarda, the fire of the stars. So, *Alkaladur*. The Elijin possess it, too, and in greater measure, for they are greater beings; in the Galadin it truly blazes as brightly *as* the stars. If they, in their thousands, could not turn back Angra Mainyu, why should you demand of Val that he must strike his sword of light into Angra Mainyu's creature?'

Abrasax considered his response only a moment before he answered him: 'Because it is wrong, even for men, to kill. And because in harming others, we harm ourselves.'

According to his ideals, he had elucidated the highest of principles. But for me, the valarda was no theory on how to live, but the very agony and heartbeat of life itself. And death. Atara had once told me that on the day I killed Morjin, I would kill myself. I feared that she might be right.

'Your way,' Abrasax said to Kane, 'has always been the sword – whether of silustria or steel.'

'Not *always*,' Kane reminded him.

At this, Abrasax bowed his head as if to honor Kane. Then he told him: 'But you can never defeat Angra Mainyu this way. He was the greatest of the Galadin, and so you cannot even harm him.'

'No, I cannot – not that way.' Then quick as a breath, Kane drew his kalama from its sheath. 'But I *can* destroy Morjin this way. Or Val can. And so the Lightstone might be regained and given to the Maitreya.'

He looked at Bemossed sitting quietly at the end of the table, and so did everyone else.

'I will not,' Bemossed told him, 'have men go marching out to war on my account.'

'On *your* account,' Kane growled out, 'men will come here marching to war, whether you will it or not.'

148

He went on to tell us what he had learned in Galda: that armies gathered and everywhere men spoke of Morjin and the coming great crusade.

'I am almost sure that Morjin went to Galda,' he told us. 'To put down the rebellion, yes, but even more to drive the Galdans to war. Now that Bemossed has come here, which he will certainly learn, he will send soldiers to hunt him down. He cannot allow the Valari to unite around such a great light. But he *won't* strike straight at Mesh, with a small force, as before. He will march with all his armies, and surround the Nine Kingdoms. And then he will annihilate the Valari, once and for all.'

His words clearly distressed Abrasax, who pressed his fingers against the snowy hair covering his temple. He seemed to be fighting a battle within himself – I guessed between discretion and the telling of the truth. In the end, truth prevailed.

'After we eluded the Grays,' he told us, 'we fled across the Wendrush into the Niuriu's lands. There we learned evil tidings.'

He pressed his fingers into his neck below his ear. Those of the Brotherhood, I knew, were masters of revitalizing the body through touching upon critical points where the body's deep flames whirled.

'The Red Dragon,' he told us, 'has conquered Eanna. He sent a great fleet up through the Dragon Channel. It defeated the Eannan navy. His Hesperuk and Sungurun armies then landed outside of Ivalo in the west, while King Ulanu and his soldiers attacked up from Yarkona in the southeast. They split the kingdom in two, and finally brought King Hanniban to battle – and nearly destroyed him. On the eighth of Ashte, this was. King Hanniban has fled with a thousand of his men to Alonia. It is thought that the Red Dragon might next send his armies there.'

'So, that is the way of things, then,' Kane said. 'With Eanna gone, there's nothing to stop the Hesperuk fleet from sailing straight through the Dolphin Channel into Tria.'

'But that is exactly the Beast's plan!' Vareva called out. For all the time we had sat together, this strong, lovely woman had remained quiet, listening politely to all that transpired. Now, however, she told us of things that she had too long held inside. 'In Argattha, one of Morjin's priests said this! They called him Arch Yadom – sometimes Lord Yadom. It was said that Morjin trusted no man more.'

My jaws clenched as I looked at Vareva. I remembered too well the filthy torturer of whom she spoke: a man with a long skull and hooked nose that made him seem like a vulture.

149

Kane, always alert for subterfuge, caught Vareva in his dark gaze. 'Morjin trusted no man more, and this I believe. But then why should *we* trust what Arch Yadom told *you*? Perhaps this is exactly what he wanted you to believe – and to tell us.'

'Are you saying that the Beast *allowed* me to escape?'

'How else do you think you found your way out? Of *Argattha*?'

Vareva shook her head so violently that her long, black hair whipped into the face of Master Matai, sitting beside her. And she called out, 'No, no, no – I *know* Lord Yadom would not let me escape. He was in love with me! A vile priest of the Kallimun, it is true, and it was a vile and twisted love, if I can even call it that. But when he was drunk, he used to whisper things to me. And at other times. He told me that if I didn't do exactly as he said, he would split me in two – as Morjin planned to split the Nine Kingdoms in two! After Morjin conquered Alonia, the Dragon Armies would march south to –'

'All right,' Kane growled, cutting her off, 'then Yadom must have let you go at Morjin's command.'

'No, you don't know how it was!' Vareva slammed the flat of her hand against the table with such force the wood rang out. 'After Arch Yadom was done with me, I was to have been given to Morjin. He had prepared a torture for me – he would not say what and so ruin the surprise. It was some new kind of crucifixion, I think. He had promised to show all his priests what he planned for the Valari.'

Kane stared at her hard, without compassion, or so it seemed. I sensed Vareva holding back her tears as she stared right back at him. Finally I stood up and grasped Kane's arm.

'Enough!' I said to him. 'What Vareva has told us agrees with the Grandmaster's tidings and your own guess as to Morjin's strategy.'

'So it does. But what if Morjin has a deeper strategy, eh?'

Again, he turned to look at Vareva. Then I gripped his arm even more tightly and called out: 'Enough, Kane! She has suffered enough!'

It turned out that after Vareva's escape from Argattha, she had walked straight across the burning grasslands of the Wendrush for more than four hundred miles. She had eaten insects or carrion, when she could find it, and when she couldn't, nothing at all. Miraculously, she had neither drowned crossing rivers nor been devoured by lions or bitten by poisonous snakes. But even as she had drawn within sight of the Morning Mountains, her tide of fortune had turned the other way, for she had been captured by warriors of the Yarkut clan of the eastern Urtuk – the very same clan which had once cut off my uncle, Ramashan's, head and sent it back to Mesh in a basket to show their contempt for all Valari emissaries. The Yarkut had held a fierce debate over what to do with Vareva. Some of their warriors called for her to be held for ransom, while others fought for the right to take her as a concubine; a few warriors wanted nothing more than to burn her at the stake and make wagers as to how long it would take her to scream. It was even as she faced these dire circumstances that Abrasax and the other masters, with Bemossed, had also approached Mesh's mountains.

'Thank you, Sire,' Vareva said as she bowed her head to me. She cast Kane a long, angry look. 'I *have* suffered enough at the hands of men, but no more. I do not know what would have happened to me if the Brothers, and Bemossed, had not come along.'

It turned out, too – this is the story as Vareva told it – that Bemossed and the others had walked right into the Yarkut's encampment as if out of a mirage. Bemossed had stunned the Yarkut's headman, Barukurk, by simply asking for Vareva to accompany him and the Seven on their journey. The fierce Yarkut warriors whispered that Bemossed had somehow laid an enchantment on Barukurk. A few of them told of how Barukurk couldn't help staring at Bemossed; he was like a captive, they said, who had been staked out with his eyelids cut off beneath a blazing sun. Barukurk had then stunned *everyone* by giving Bemossed a ring of gold, and escorting Varveva, the Brothers and Bemossed to the very foot of the mountains.

'It is a time for miracles,' Vareva said. Then she clasped the hilt of her sword as she turned to bow her head to Kane. 'But I agree with my King's old companion. They will never come to pass unless we can keep the Shining One safe.'

Abrasax's great head nodded, too. But he did not so much bow in agreement with this as he did look down in defeat. At last he turned to gaze at me. 'I think, then, that you have decided on war, King Valamesh.'

'War, yes,' I said to him. I looked at the deadly weapon I still held in my hands. I looked down the length of the table at Bemossed, so trusting, so bright and utterly vulnerable. 'But a war of the sword or a war of the spirit, I do not know.'

After that, we concluded our council. Soon I would have to go

151

back outside with the others to rejoin the festivities. It should have been the greatest day of my life, full of song and celebration. For the first time, however, I felt the great weight of kingship fall upon me. I gazed at the five bright diamonds set into the ring my father had once worn, and I heard a voice whispering to me that I would yet kill many more men with my sword on the long and seemingly endless road to war.

10

Early the next morning, with the sun's first rays warming the mountains' white ridgelines to the east, Atara and her sister Manslayers made ready to leave on their journey. I said goodbye to her down by the river behind our encampment. I stood holding her for what seemed an hour, listening to the rushing waters ring against great, smoothed boulders. Finally, she stood back from me and said, 'You have gained what you sought . . . King Valamesh. I am so proud of you.'

I looked back at my warriors' thousands of brightly colored tents flapping in the morning breeze. And I said, 'I have gained what I sought, yes. But not what I most wanted.'

'And what is that, truly?'

'You know,' I whispered to her. 'You have always known.'

'And *you* have always had what you most desired,' she said as she took my hand. 'As you always will.'

I gripped her warm fingers in mine as I gathered up the courage to say to her: 'I am afraid that I will never see you again.'

'But you will!' she told me with a smile. Then her face fell beautiful and grave. 'You must. The important question is: will *I* see you again? Will I, Val?'

And with that, she kissed my lips with a desperate blaze of passion, as fiery as the rising sun. Then she adjusted her blindfold, grabbed up her bow and mounted her horse. I watched her ride off with the other Manslayers who had come to Mesh to take her away.

Later, I sent out envoys to each of the other Nine Kingdoms: Ishka, Waas, Kaash, Anjo, Taron, Athar and Lagash. They were to tell the Valari kings that the Maitreya had come forth and that the Valari must at last unite behind this Shining One. I had little hope for the success of their missions. My plea must surely fall upon deaf ears, I thought, for only two years before I had made a similar argument – with the assertion that *I* must be the Maitreya.

By strange chance, even as one of my envoys pounded down the road leading east toward Kaash, an envoy from that kingdom rode toward the west and found his way into our encampment. Lord Zandru the Hammer seemed astonished to discover that I had returned to Mesh to be acclaimed king only the day before. When I learned the purpose of his visit, I immediately called for a council in my pavilion. I invited to sit at my table the greatest lords in Mesh: Lord Harsha, Lord Avijan and Lord Sharad – Lord Jessu and Lord Manthanu, too. And Lord Noldashan. I did not yet know what place Lord Tanu and Lord Tomavar would take in my army, and yet no important strategy could be discussed without them. And so with Lord Eldru and Lord Ramjay, and even with Lord Ramanu, Lord Bahram and Lord Kharashan. The Seven, now only six, I also asked to hear Lord Zandru's tidings. My companions, of course, would not leave my side. As for Bemossed, he had now become the bright star around which all peoples and events on Ea would whirl. I would never allow him to leave *my* side.

Lord Zandru, a huge, barrel-chested man with long arms like those of an ape, sat opposite me at the end of the table. He had a face as blunt as the black war hammer emblazoned on his white surcoat. His words, too, for an envoy, were blunt, for he wasted no time getting to the point of his mission, calling out in a deep, almost braying voice: 'King Valamesh, Lords of Mesh – Kaash needs your help!'

He told us that after two years of threats and feints, King Sandarkan had finally ordered Waas to complete preparations to make war against Kaash. There was to be a battle, Lord Zandru said, for King Talanu Solaru – my mother's eldest brother – would not cede to Waas the Arjan Land taken from Waas generations before. But at that time, Kaash had been strong and Waas weak. Now, as Lord Zandru told us, the Kaashans had lost too many warriors in battles against the Atharians, and so were few while the Waashians were many.

'King Talanu can probably put the battle off until mid-Marud,' Lord Zandru told us. 'But it *will* come to battle, and we will lose. And so we will lose the Arjan Land anyway. But all Kaash's lords and warriors agree with King Talanu on one thing: it is better to lose some dirt and rocks, and a little blood, than our honor.'

At this, Lord Tomavar rapped his lord's ring upon the edge of the table with a sharp clack as if to command everyone to look at him. It might have been thought that after his defeat the day before, he would have hidden himself inside silence. But as always, he liked to charge into the heart of the battle, whether of swords and spears or words.

'Lord Zandru!' he called out. 'Not two years ago, Mesh lost more than four thousand warriors because Kaash would not help us – and whole rivers of blood! Why, then, should *we* help *you*!'

'Because,' Lord Avijan said to him in his cool, controlled voice, 'we can. And more, because we should. After King Sandarkan has safeguarded his rear against Kaash, he will be free to ally with the Ishkans and turn against us.'

'Damn the Ishkans!' Lord Ramjay said.

'Damn the Waashians, too!' Lord Kharashan called out. 'They killed my boy at the Red Mountain!'

For a while, as everyone drank cups of chicory coffee and the day deepened toward night, I let these battle-hardened warriors speak their thoughts and debate strategy. I said very little, while my companions said less and the Seven and Bemossed nothing at all.

Finally, I held up my hand for silence. Everyone looked at me. It was my duty as a king to listen to my counselors and consider their words. But it was also my duty to rule.

'We cannot know,' I said, 'how the day would have gone at the Culhadosh Commons if the Kaashans had come to our aid. But is there anyone here who wished that they would *not* have come? As we looked to them, they now look to us, with desperate hope. As they failed us, with good reason, are we to look for better reason and so fail them?'

Lord Tomavar banged his whole hand against the table as he practically shouted: 'But they *did* fail us, reason or no, and so I say that we should see to our own –'

I looked at Lord Tomavar then. As I had in the square outside the day before, I looked deep inside him, and suddenly his face reddened as he fell into a shamed silence.

'My apologies, Sire,' he said, bowing his head to me. 'When I see a breach in the lines in front of me, I can rush in too quickly.'

'And so you helped my father win more than one battle,' I told him. Then I nodded at Lord Zandru. 'But the Kaashans, please remember, are not our enemies but our allies. And that is why we shall help them.'

As Lord Zandru's face brightened, I explained that we would

need every ally that we could find for the great struggle soon to come. Every lord at my table bowed his head in acceptance of this.

'Very well . . . Sire,' Lord Tanu said. His crabby old face seemed to have trouble forcing out this last word. But once he had spoken it, he seemed to accept its reality as he must the changing of summer into autumn. 'We have the warriors already gathered. And so since we *have* decided upon this campaign, let us march east with all due speed.'

Lord Harsha sat rubbing his single eye, then sighed out to Lord Tanu, 'Well, speed we might all wish for, but an army doesn't march on air. We've made no plans for such a campaign. We've set in no stores.'

'How long would it take to gather them?' I asked him.

'I don't know – a week, maybe more.'

'And maybe less,' I told him with a smile, 'if Lord Harsha was given the charge of gathering them. Do what you can, old friend. As Lord Tanu has said, we must march like the very wind.'

I stood up then to adjourn our council. Kane took me aside, and growled in my ear, 'So, we march to Kaash – and Kaash is a hundred leagues that much closer to Galda, eh? Where Morjin still might be!'

He fell silent as Maram came up to us, too. Then Maram said to me, 'It's finally begun, hasn't it? This is the end, then, the last day of peace I will ever know. Well, Val, then I promise you that *I* will not fail you and will remain with you until the ugly, bitter end. The very, *very* end.'

After that, in the days that followed, there seemed little to do except to go about the countryside buying up beef, pork, barley, wheat, peas and other provender with which to victualize our army. We had to put in whole mountains of hay for all our hundreds of horses, and find wagons to carry this great mass of supplies. Lord Harsha proved as patient and efficient in finding food as he had been in growing it. On the second day, when I saw that he had much more talent for this task than I, I left it all to him. Then I set myself a task which nearly everyone told me would be impossible.

'I would meet the men who pledged to you,' I told Lord Tomavar. We stood with my other counselors by the side of the square watching hundreds of warriors drilling at their nightly sword practice. 'And your men, too, Lord Tanu. And yours, Lord Avijan. Every warrior who would march with me, I would learn his name.'

My father, it was said, had known five thousand warriors by name.

And so that evening I retreated to my pavilion while Lords Tomavar, Tanu and Avijan – Lords Kharashan, Ramanu and Bahram, as well – set to organizing the fulfillment of my unusual request. The call came for the warriors to line up outside my tent, and this they hastened to do with a great curiosity and rare enthusiasm. I stood inside ten feet back from my tent's opened flaps as the warriors entered, one by one. The first man to greet, Yarkash the Bold, hailed from Lashku, and had strongly supported Lord Tomavar until a couple of days before. He was a tall, thickly-muscled knight, with a scar nearly splitting his chin in two. He wore his diamond battle armor, and bore a bright sun emblazoned upon his surcoat. I stood with my sword drawn, and he approached me with quick, sure strides. Then he stopped before me, and with a form that we had arranged, he drew his sword and said to me: 'Sire, I am Yarkash Jurmanu, son of Suladar Jurmanu. I pledge my sword to you, in life and in death.'

I pressed my palm to the flat of his blade, and bowed my head in acceptance of his service. And then I said to him: 'I am Valashu Elahad, son of Shavashar Elahad. And I pledge *my* sword to you, in life and in death.'

I held out Alkaladur for him to touch as well. Maram and Master Juwain, looking on, both drew in a quick breath at this, for in all the time that I had kept this sword, I had allowed no one to put his flesh to it – except my enemies, in wounding or death.

As Yarkash the Bold turned about to exit my tent, another warrior stepped forward. He came up to me and said, 'Sire, I am Kanshar Sharad, son of Evar Sharad, of Pushku . . .'

And so it went. I could spend only a fraction of a minute with each warrior, for there were not enough minutes in a day to allot to each of them, and I had more than fifteen thousand warriors to greet. I stood for hours that night until the muscles in my legs burned with the strain of it. Twice, I broke to drink some tea and take a few moments of rest in my chair at the head of the council table. Then I returned to my new duty, listening to my warriors' pledges: 'Sire, I am Juval Eladar . . .'

When morning warmed the roof of my tent with a black sheen, I stepped over to the entrance. I looked out to see a glittering line of warriors stretched out down the lanes of the tents of my encampment, across the square and through the lanes of Lord Tomavar's men's tents. And then out across the grasses of the meadow beyond. I could not see the end of the line, for it disappeared behind the edge of a low hill.

At this, I summoned Lord Tomavar and Lord Tanu and said to them, 'This will not do. All the warriors beyond the square – let them stand down. See to it that they are called up only as the warriors ahead of them finish making their pledges. We have a long day ahead of us.'

That day was long indeed – one of the longest of my life. And yet its hours did not suffice for me receive all my warriors' pledges. The sun reached its crest in the cloudy sky at high noon, and then dropped behind the mountains to the west, and still my warriors lined up outside my tent. When it began raining that night – big drops of summer rain that splatted against the earth and thousands of tents with a nearly deafening sound – I considered calling for everyone to break off and take some rest. But Lord Harsha informed me that our army's provisioning was nearly complete, and I did not want to delay our march. And I would not, I said, march until I heard the names of all my warriors.

And so the men of Mesh stood in the pouring rain, gaining a few moments of respite only when they stepped dripping inside my tent to face me. Their names seemed to pour from their mouths in an irresistible torrent of sound: 'Dovaru Elsar, Yulsun of Pushku, Bashar the Brave, Juradan Nolarad . . .' I heard no grumbles, even from those who had stood in the rain the longest. The warriors seemed as eager to honor me as I was to honor them.

'It is a great thing that you do,' Master Juwain said to me as I sat drinking coffee during one of my breaks. 'But you cannot continue on like this. Already, you have stood here more than a day.'

'These warriors,' I said to him, 'will march with me for many days. And then stand in line against our enemies, and many will die. And you say that I cannot continue?'

Later, long past midnight, I fought to hold myself up straight and keep my eyelids open against the burning dryness there. With every name spoken to me, my sword seemed to flare a little brighter, sending stabs of recognition deep into me. The silver gelstei, Master Juwain had once told me, could quicken all the powers of the mind, especially memory. Although it seemed impossible that I could remember each of my warriors, or even a tenth of them, I had a strange sense that my sword's silustria was drinking up their names and holding on to them the way it did the stars' light.

Late on the afternoon of the following day, with many more men still to greet, a warrior who stood out from all the others came up to me. Indeed, this warrior was no man at all, but rather one of Mesh's greatest women: for it was Vareva. How she had acquired the suit of diamond armor poorly fitted to her womanly body, I did not know. Perhaps, I thought, she had forced Lord Tomavar to purchase it for her. She wore the two swords that all Valari warriors bore: a bright kalama and the shorter tharam, which she kept sheathed. I looked long and deeply as she held her kalama out to me and said, 'Sire, I am Vareva Tomavar, *daughter* of Manamar Tanu. I pledge my sword to you, in life and in death.'

'And I pledge my sword to you,' I told her, 'in life and in death.'

I saw the warriors behind her staring at her in anger. Then I drew in a deep breath and told her, 'Many will disapprove of what has just passed between us. They believe that a woman cannot be allowed to be a warrior. But a great man once said this to me: "Does one let the sun shine? No one *lets* a woman become a warrior."'

'Then, Sire, I will march with you to the end of –'

I saw a bright hope come alive in her eyes, but I could not allow it to consume her. And so I held up my hand to silence her. 'You are what you are, and even your king must respect that. As you must respect your king. Men are only what they are, too, and all those who have stood before you and remain behind you will not bear to see you march with them to war. It is not the Valari way.'

She bowed her head to me, but then stood up straight and proud as she told me, 'That has not *been* our way, Sire, it is true.'

'You cannot change what is,' I said to her. 'A man faces battle more bravely for knowing that his woman is safe at home.'

'The warriors,' she informed me, 'say that no man of Mesh is braver than Valashu Elahad. He, whose woman has fought by his side in many terrible battles across the length and breadth of Ea.'

I blinked my burning eyes as I looked at this formidable woman. I had to keep a good grip on my sword to stop my legs from trembling, so that I didn't fall down.

'Atara Ars Narmada,' I said to her, 'has vowed to forsake marriage so long as she remains a warrior.'

'I, too, would make such a vow, Sire.'

'But that is not our way. That is not how a Valari woman serves her people.'

'How *should* I serve, then, Sire? By staying in Mesh and bearing Lord Tomavar's children?'

'A child, from you, would be a great and beautiful thing.'

'Thank you, Sire. But I want nothing more than to put *this* into Morjin's filthy creatures, and that would be an even greater thing.'

So saying, she thrust her sword toward the wall of my tent.

I shook my head at this. 'You cannot change the nature of things. When a man dies in battle, a woman might remarry and continue to bear children, and nothing is greater than this life. But when a woman dies, *all* her children that she might have brought forth die with her as well. And if many women die, her people will die.'

I hoped that Vareva might see the sense of what I said to her, for I was too tired to argue with her, and many more warriors stood lined up outside my tent. But Vareva, who had often defeated me at riddles and word games when we were children, seemed not very tired at all, and she had the better argument:

'It is not the Valari way, you say, that women should go to war,' she told me. 'Or else our people will dwindle and begin to die. But, Sire, *this* war will be a war to the death for the whole Valari people. *I* know, for I have heard Morjin himself talk of making whole forests into crosses. If we do not fight this war down to the last breath of every man – *and* woman – we shall lose. And then the Valari will be no more.'

I felt *her* impassioned breath spilling over my face like fire. I could find no logic to dispute her. And yet I could not, I thought, allow her to march with the army.

'You *are* a warrior,' I said to her, 'and let no one doubt that.'

I called for Joshu Kadar, one of the knights standing by my side that afternoon, to bring me a wooden box full of rings. I took out one of them – the smallest, set with a single, bright diamond – and I slipped it around Vareva's finger. She seemed delighted to be honored this way.

'Wear this ring,' I said to her, 'that all may recognize a true Valari warrior.'

Lord Avijan and Lord Jessu – Sar Shivalad and other knights, too, who happened to be present – reluctantly rapped their rings against the hilts of their swords in a great sound that nearly drowned out the patter of the rain. Vareva gazed in wonder at the ring encircling her finger; I sensed that she valued it much more than the diamond brooch over which Lord Tanu and Lord Tomavar had nearly gone to war.

But then her happiness seemed to melt away as I said to her, 'I cannot take every warrior with me, and so leave Mesh defenseless. Many will remain, and you must be one of them.'

At this, she had no choice but to bow her head in acceptance of what I had said.

'But I charge you with a task,' I said to her. 'Other women feel as you do. Behira Harsha, for one. I fear they will train at arms

160

no matter what their king says. Seek them out, then. Train them as warriors against the day we all fear will come.'

Vareva looked at me with hope brightening her face again. 'Thank you, Sire. I shall train a whole battalion of warriors such as the world has never seen!'

Then she turned about and left my tent, and another warrior came forward to tell me his name. And another, and another after that, and then a thousand others. And so the day passed into yet another night.

The next morning, to the sound of birds chittering in the meadows, Maram came into my tent. He bulled his way past the warriors lined up at the entrance and indicated that he wished to speak with me. We stepped off into the corner, where he murmured to me: 'Two full days and one whole night – and here you still are! You cannot continue this way!'

'I *can* continue!' I told him.

I had to fight the urge to lay my hand upon his huge shoulder for support.

'Ah, well, maybe you can,' he said, looking deep into my eyes. 'But you *shouldn't*. It is too much – too, too much.'

'I have faced worse trials before, Maram. *We* have.'

'At need, we have. In the Red Desert, you drove yourself harder than any man would a slave – even as you drove me. And it kept us alive. But this isn't necessary.'

I looked off toward the tent's entranceway, where I could see a dozen men in diamond armor standing miserably in the rain.

'Some might say,' he told me, 'that this is only a new king's vanity. A great show without true meaning.'

'Do *you* say that, then?'

'I? No, I don't, and I am a man who knows about vanity. But I *do* say that you are overzealous. Nearly killing yourself to prove your worthiness as a king.'

I fought to keep myself from yawning and rubbing the sleep from my dry, itching eyes; I fought not to go over to my canopied bed and collapse into unknowingness.

'And more,' Maram went on, 'this desperate learning of names has the taint of thaumaturgy. As if in holding on to one of your men's names, you can magically keep him from dying when his time comes.'

His words worked their way into my hot, pounding brain, and I found myself forced to consider them. Finally, I said to him, 'You know me too well, old friend.'

'Then break off and sleep! Just this one day! And tomorrow finish your task, or the next!'

I slowly shook my head at this. 'A day will come when I must face Morjin. On that day, I will not be able to break off and sleep, no matter how tired I am.'

'But you can't prepare for *that* like *this*. It is madness to –'

'The day *will* come,' I said to him again. 'And when it does, no matter what I do, many of the men I have greeted in this tent will die. But how many, then? If it is not to be *all* of them, then I fear that we will have to fight such as the Valari have never fought before. As *men* have never fought. We are so few, and our enemy is so many. We cannot defeat them through force of arms alone – this the wisest of the wise has told me. All we will have, in the end, is our spirits. And if our spirits are to be as one, and we are to die for each other – and live! – then I must know who my warriors are, and they must know me.'

Maram, suddenly understanding, nodded his head to me. He sighed, long and deeply, as he looked at me. Then he drew his sword and with great sadness said, 'Sire, I am Maram Marshayk, son of Santoval Marshayk, of Delarid. I pledge my sword to you, in life and in death!'

After he had gone, I spent the rest of that morning, afternoon and evening as I had the days before. It seemed to me that I must have spoken with fifteen million men, and not fifteen thousand. I finally summoned Lord Tanu, and asked him, 'How many more?'

'Nearly a thousand, Sire.'

'And is that all, then?'

Lord Tanu hesitated as his old face tightened with weariness. It seemed that he had slept little, either, over the past days.

'There are only the warriors,' he said to me, 'who refused to stand for you on the day you were acclaimed – eighty-nine of them. It was thought that you wouldn't want to know *their* names.'

As a king, of course, I now had the right to command every man in Mesh, and not just those who had acclaimed me. But I would rather lead them. And so I said to Lord Tanu, and to Lord Avijan and Lord Sharad also present and bending over the map table: 'It takes courage to stand against the enemy in battle. But it takes a deeper and truer courage to stand out by keeping to one's convictions when almost everyone is taking a different course. I do not know why the men you have spoken of failed to stand for me. Their reasons are their reasons. But *those* men I especially

162

want to honor. I can tell you that when battle finally comes, none will stand more valiantly.'

As I had requested of Lord Tanu, he made it be. I endured the last hours of my vigil greeting the last of my warriors. I learned the names of those who had refused to stand for me but now must follow me to war: Ianadar Elshan, Yarsar Balvalam, Juvalad the Elder, Marsavay of Mir . . . and all eighty-five others.

At last, there came a moment when the open flaps at the front of my tent revealed only the campfires of my army flickering in the dark and the vast, starry sky. I stepped outside beneath these glistening lights. I had spoken with more than fifteen thousand men. As I pointed my sword toward the bright heavens, I felt a brighter thing burning behind my eyes, and I knew that all fifteen thousand of their names blazed somewhere inside me.

It was a moment of great triumph. I dared to think, for one shining instant in time, that my warriors and I could wield our swords as one and utterly vanquish Morjin. I *willed* this to be, with all the might of my mind and the force of my heart.

And then I chanced to think of Atara riding blindly across the plains somewhere in the dark world to the west. In my utter exhaustion, fighting the leaden pain in my eyes and to keep from collapsing onto the trampled grass, I let my desire to defeat Morjin descend into a wrath for vengeance. I saw myself gouging out *his* eyes as he had Atara's; I wanted to repay him death for death, and hate for hate. I longed for this one, last battle to the very bottom of my soul. I knew that this terrible urge was as beneath me as I should be beyond it. But I couldn't seem to help it. It came welling up through me like a dark dream through sleep. And in that terrible, terrible moment – an eyeblink in time   the Ahrim attacked me.

Like a filthy blanket steeped in poison, it fell out of nowhere down around my head. It closed in over my face, nearly smothering me; it burned my eyes like acid. And then the light of the stars disappeared, and I found myself standing alone inside an utter blackness.

11

Somehow, I managed to stumble back through my tent and to find my bed. I fell onto it. Given all that had occurred over the past four days, none of those present – Lord Avijan, Lord Sharad and Joshu Kadar – thought this strange. I asked Lord Avijan and Lord Sharad to leave me. Then I bade Joshu Kadar to go find Master Juwain.

Alone in my tent, I tried to summon the fierce light inside myself by which I had twice driven off the Ahrim. But either I could not find it or else my life fires had burned too low. I pressed my hands against the pain stabbing into my eyes, and then opened them. I could not make out any of the things of my pavilion: the council and map tables; my small clothes chest and a larger one full of treasure; the candles in their stands and the braziers full of hot coals. All was lost into a blackness as total as a cave's deepest depths.

There came a moment when I despaired. I shook my head from side to side in a wild, terrified fury. But it did nothing to dispel the Ahrim. I seemed only to find within myself a deeper blackness inside the blackness, if that were possible.

Finally, Master Juwain came into my tent and knelt by the side of my bed. He asked me, 'Val, what is wrong?'

I turned my head toward the sound of his voice and said, 'I am blind.'

I tried to explain what had happened. I asked him for his help. Only a few days before, however, he had tried to use his green gelstei to heal my afflicted throat, to no avail.

'What attacks you is beyond my power to drive away,' he told me. 'Beyond the power of our friends, as well. That, I think, has been proven. But on that first day in the woods, it seemed that in opening yourself to what power we *do* possess, it helped you find your own.'

I nodded my head at this. 'But on that day, Atara had not left me.'

'True – and I can only imagine how much her love for you strengthens you. But you have two friends, now, who weren't with us in the woods.'

'Kane,' I murmured. 'Bemossed.'

'Indeed. Kane seems to know things about the Ahrim. And Bemossed is Bemossed.'

Again, I nodded my head. 'Please summon them, then. And Liljana. Maram, too, of course – and the children. I want all my friends by my side.'

At this, Alphanderry somehow came into being within my tent – or so Master Juwain told me. I could not see him any more than I could Master Juwain or anything else.

'And please ask Joshu Kadar to come back inside,' I said to Master Juwain. 'He will have to know what has happened to me, but no one else must.'

'But what of Abrasax and the other Masters?'

'All right,' I said, 'bring them with you, too, but no one else.'

The Guardians standing outside my tent during that watch – Sar Jonavar, Sar Shivalad, Sar Kanshar and Siraj the Younger – must have thought it strange that I summoned my old friends to me so late at night. But kings must sometimes take council at odd hours, and so I hoped that my actions would cause my warriors no suspicion or distress.

A little later, everyone I had sent for gathered by my bedside as I had requested. Kane pressed his rough old hand to my forehead, taking care to avoid the plaster that Master Juwain had set over my reopened scar. And he told me, 'I know less about the Ahrimana than you might hope. It partakes of Angra Mainyu's being – this I have said. It has *escaped* from Damoom, where the Baaloch is still bound, eh? And so I must wonder if anything can bind *it*. I think not. At least not here on Ea. For in a way, the Ahrimana has not really escaped at all, but merely made its way from the darkest of the Dark Worlds to one that has been falling into shadow for a long time.'

'But two times, now,' Master Juwain said to him, 'Val *did* drive it away.'

'So,' Kane said. 'So he did – through the light of the sword he holds inside himself. When it blazes brightly enough, the Ahrimana can no more abide it than Angra Mainyu can the radiance of Star-Home.'

'But it is dead within me,' I said to Kane. 'Either dead or blackened like a piece of charred wood. I cannot find it.'

'That is because,' Kane said in a pitiless tone that chilled me, 'your blindness is not just of the eyes but the soul.'

Abrasax, usually a much kinder man, took my hand in his and said to me, 'You must somehow open your third eye so that your other two might see. In this, we can help you perhaps a little, but no more.'

I sensed him and the other Masters taking out their seven Great Gelstei in order to call forth the fires along my spine's seven chakras and brighten their flames. Although their magic gave me new strength, it failed to lift the blindness from me.

I heard Kane draw in an angry gasp of breath. Then his great regard for me filled his voice as his manner softened and he said, 'So dark – so damnably dark. I have said that Ea is almost a Dark World, and it is. But there *are* bright things here, and the soul of Valashu Elahad is only one.'

I sensed him looking at Bemossed then. Even through my panic at having been blinded, I felt the vast weight of expectation that people had fastened around Bemossed's neck like a collar made of lead.

Then Bemossed pressed his warmer and softer hand to the side of my face. And out of the darkness above me, he told me: 'I had dreams just before Master Juwain woke me. The most evil of dreams yet. I could *feel* Morjin, all his twisted desire. Somehow, he lends his power to the Ahrim and guides it. And sics it on Val as he might a hound. He has learned that Val has become a king – I am sure of this. And he is desperate to destroy him.'

After that, with infinite gentleness, Bemossed touched his fingers to my closed eyelids, to my temples and the back of my head. For more than an hour, he tried with the full force of his soul to heal me. But he could not drive the Ahrim away.

'I am sorry, Valashu,' he said to me at last. 'I have told you before that I can't really heal people. Only, somehow and sometimes, help them to heal themselves.'

His words seemed to touch off deep emotions in Kane, who said, 'So, it's not *healing* that Val really needs – it's freedom from that filthy thing!'

I heard him pick up my unsheathed sword, which then he pressed into my open hand. 'The Sword of Sight, this is called. In the end, it might be that you, yourself, will have to see your way free.'

I closed my hand around Alkaladur's diamond-set hilt. It seemed strange how I could feel the shape of the swans carved into its black jade through the skin of my palm. Still lying flat on my back, I gripped my sword with both hands and pointed it straight up toward the roof of my tent and the stars beyond.

And through the dark came a softly glowing white light. I could see the faint, flaring outline of my sword's blade against a wall of blackness.

'There is something!' I cried out, to Kane and my other friends. 'There is something!'

I managed to lever myself up and rise from my bed. Then, after nearly knocking over a brazier, I found my way to the center of the tent. I told everyone to stand clear, then I swept out my sword toward the south, west, north and east. It flared even more brightly. A band of silver shimmered before my eyes. It was the only thing in all the world that I could see.

And then, as if lightning flashed out of a dark night, I knew a thing. I called out to my friends: 'I must go there.'

'Go *where*?' Kane said to me.

'To the wood,' I told him. 'The place where the Ahrim first found me.'

'There? But why? There's nothing *there* but deer and trees.'

'I don't *why*, Kane. I only know that I must go – and go now!'

At this, Maram came over and grabbed my arm. 'But you can't go *now*! You are beyond being exhausted. Go back to bed, eat a good meal, drink a little brandy, sleep. Who knows? – you might wake up to find the Ahrim gone.'

I shook my head at this. 'No, it will *not* be gone. And there is no time. We will march in two more days, and I cannot lead my men to war if I am blind.'

'At least wait until dawn,' Maram said to me. 'It's nearly pitch black outside.'

I thought of Atara again, and I suddenly sensed at least a small part of what her life had become. And I told Maram, 'For me, it will still be dark in the morning. And it is better that we should go now, that the warriors will not behold their king's blindness.'

I issued commands then. It was Abrasax who came up with the story that we would tell everyone to explain my headlong rush out into the black of night: I was to go on a meditation retreat into the mountains in order to seek a vision toward victory. My friends, along with the Seven and Bemossed, were to help prepare me for a great battle. In its way, it was true enough.

Joshu Kadar led my great stallion up to the very opening of my tent. I tried not to fumble as I mounted him; I sat on Altaru's great back with all the sureness that I could muster. My friends had their horses brought up, too. So did the Abrasax and the rest of the Seven. Although Sar Jonavar and the other Guardians on duty that night must have thought it strange to see us prepare for an outing at such an hour, they said nothing. Neither did Lord Avijan, still awake, who came out of his tent nearby. I was now their king, and they did not like to question me.

I left it to Maram and Kane to lead the way out of our encampment, with me riding close behind them, and the others following me. As we proceeded down the lanes that I could not see, I felt the eyes of many men looking upon me. I prayed that they would not be able to make out the staring emptiness of *my* eyes – or at least would not wonder at it if they did. I had feared that I would not be able to ride blind. I needn't have. Altaru, always so aware of my every nuance of motion and the fires of my heart, seemed to sense my impairment and that he would have to see his way through the night for both of us. I told him simply to follow Maram and his big brown horse, and this he did. All I had to do was to keep my legs wrapped around his sides and not fall off.

It was strange journeying through the dark. The dark was nothing, in itself, and yet it seemed to envelop me like an evil substance that I could feel with every particle of my being. Every motion and shift in location seemed a threat to my very life. I had to fight my urge, again and again, to call for a halt so that I might find a little peace in stillness. How, I wondered, had Atara ever learned to bear her blindness? How could anyone? Never, not even in the lightless tunnels of Argattha, had I felt so vulnerable. I wanted nothing more than to go back to my bed and lie there in safety beneath the blankets that my mother had once embroidered – and to remain there for the rest of my life.

We rode at a decent pace for a couple hours back along the route we had taken from Lord Avijan's castle. The sun finally rose and warmed my face. Its light, however, failed to touch my eyes, even slightly. I heard birds' wings beating the air above flower-scented fields, and then the drumming of our horses' hooves as we crossed the bridge over the roaring Arashar River. Twice I dozed, and only the snap of my head dropping down to my chest kept me from falling off Altaru's back. After the third time that I nodded off, in the lake country outside of Hardu, Maram insisted that we stop so that I could rest. I slept for a couple of hours in a fallow wheatfield off the side of the road. It seemed that I had found one good thing, at least, in being blind: that I would be able to sleep as easily during full day as I could at night.

And then it came time to go. Kane, who had taken charge of our little expedition, shook me awake and said to me, 'For you it might make no difference, but I want to find my way into these woods of yours while it's still light enough to see.'

Our course took us along the excellent North Road, up through Silvassu and below my family's burned-out castle that I could not see. Despite my sleeping break, we made excellent time, covering a distance of nearly five miles each hour. So it was that early in the afternoon, we turned down the smaller roads leading past many farms to the wood that I sought. The closer that we came to this place where I had fought a bear so many years before, the brighter my sword flared. This length of almost infinitely sharp silustria remained the only thing that I could see.

Alkaladur, I thought as I pointed it in front of me. *The Sword of Fate.*

Although Maram, riding ahead of me, said very little and Kane even less, I knew that we must be close to my wood. We rode through a stand of birch trees that seemed familiar to me. I sensed them from the sound of the wind across their papery bark and by their fermy fragrance. Each kind of tree, I suddenly realized, as with the animals, had its own smell. I knew that the wood of great oaks and elms where Salmelu had fired his poison arrow into me must be close, scarcely a mile from this spot. There, too, the Ahrim had found me and nearly killed me with the even more terrible poison that afflicted my soul.

'We might do best to enter the wood,' I heard Maram say to Kane, 'as we did that day when I went hunting with Val and Asaru. But that would take us past Lord Harsha's farm, and as badly as I would like to see Behira, I don't think it would serve for *her* to see Val in such a state.'

We paused then, and I heard the horses of the Seven and my friends come up behind me. I heard them gathering in together, and I had to suppose that no one had lagged behind. I found myself able to pick up the little boy smell of Daj and Estrella's sweeter scent, as well as the rosewater perfume that Liljana often wore. But I was a man, and not a hound, and whether or not Abrasax and Master Storr and the others had kept pace with us, I could not say – at least until their voices announced their presence.

'I remember that day,' Joshu Kadar said to Maram from out of the darkness behind me. 'I waited for hours at the edge of the wood by Lord Harsha's farm while you went after your deer. But surely we could enter it from a different direction.'

'Surely we could,' I said, pointing my sword to the right of the birch trees. My sense of direction burned like an arrow through my blood as strong as ever. 'If we go straight that way, we will come to the place where the Ahrim attacked me.'

'Ah,' Maram said to me, 'I still can't see how it will avail us to go back *there*.'

'I can't either, Maram,' I told him. 'I am sorry.'

'But what if the Ahrim only draws more power from that dark, damned wood? What if it finds a way to blind the rest of us?'

The radiance sparking off my sword seemed to pull me forward as might the twinkling of the North Star. And I said to Maram, 'I can find my own way from here, if I must. I would ask no one to come with me.'

'Ah, well, you might not *ask* it then. But what kind of a man would let his friend go stumbling off blindly through the trees?'

And then Joshu Kadar said to me: 'I have pledged my sword to you, in life and in death, Sire. Please let there be no more talk of you going on alone.'

I smiled at this, then nodded my head to Kane that we should continue.

As we left the road and entered the forest, we moved more slowly, letting the horses pick their way through the bracken. I left it to Kane to determine if we should dismount and walk, should the undergrowth become too thick or the downed, dead trees threaten to break the horses' legs. But all of our horses, I thought, had become used to journeys through the forest. So had I. It seemed to me that I had spent nearly my entire youth walking through this one, or others. I could not see the tall oaks, elms, maples and chestnuts that I knew lay beyond the birch grove. I could not make out their two stories, dark lower down and a lighter green where their leaves bushed up against the sky. But I could almost feel their hugeness and the great streams of life that coursed through them. I could smell the humus of the forest floor and bear droppings full of raspberry seeds and many flowers. Bees buzzed from some honeysuckle hanging on a tree nearby, and I heard a woodpecker knocking its needle-like bill into the bark of another farther away.

All my senses, save my sight, seemed to have come fully alive here.

As Kane led on, taking his bearings from the direction in which I pointed my sword, I perceived Alkaladur's blade gradually warming to a brighter silver. It almost drove back the blackness clinging to the trees and holding fast about my head.

'I think we are close,' I heard Maram say to Kane, and me. 'It can't be much farther – maybe just past that rotting log.'

Behind me, I heard Liljana murmur soft reassurances to the children, and behind them, Abrasax announced that the trees here exuded a more powerful aura than those of any he had ever encountered. And then, fifty yards farther on, I heard Maram call for a halt.

'There's something strange here,' he said.

I, too, felt what he felt, and perhaps even more strongly. The air suddenly grew denser and moister, and seemed to waver with a charge as if lightning might strike out at any moment.

'Val – I feel sick to my stomach. It's as if a fist is driving into me and keeping me back.'

As it turned it out, when we gathered in close to discuss things, we all felt a deep and silent force working at our bodies and souls like an ocean's tide pushing us back the way we had come.

'It was this way,' Master Juwain said, 'with the Vilds.'

I remembered vividly the three magic woods that we had found in Ea's wild places: in the great tract of the Alonian forest and on the grasslands of the Wendrush and in the burning waste of the Red Desert. It did not seem possible that another Vild could exist in the middle of Mesh, surrounded by farms and men who had hunted all through these woods many thousands of times over thousands of years.

'Kane,' I called out, 'you once said that at least five Vilds still remained somewhere on Ea. Can one of them be *here*?'

'Not that I know,' he said with a strange tightness in his voice. 'At least, not that I remember.'

I could almost hear Master Juwain rubbing the back of his bald head in intense cogitation. He suddenly said to me, 'In the three Vilds, we have found great power and great healing. Perhaps, in your forays here, you sensed the presence of a Vild within this wood, even if you were never aware of it. And have now sought it in your blindness.'

His thoughts, it seemed, almost exactly mirrored my own.

'Let us go on then,' I said. 'Into that very place where it seems the hardest to go.'

The silver streak of my sword pointed us deeper into the woods. More than once, the force pushing at us almost caused me to turn my sword to one side or the other, or lower it altogether. But I kept a hold of it, and we continued moving through the great, silent trees.

'Do you see anything?' I heard Maram say to Kane. 'Does *anyone* see anything? There are only trees here, just as there always were, and one tree is like another!'

I smiled at this, for not even two oaks that grew from a pair of acorns would be like each other – to say nothing of the immense oaks of Ea's Vilds that were like no other trees on earth. I felt sure that we must be close to these living giants that grew out of the forest floor. I wondered why no one seemed able to make them out.

'Wait!' Maram shouted. 'There is *something* ahead of us – I can almost see it!'

I, however, could could not. Trapped within a cloud of blackness as I was, I wondered at the nature of sight, itself. How did anyone, or anything, really see? Vision could not merely be a matter of light filling up the eyes with colors and shapes, or else *my* eyes would behold a sea of green all around me. When my grandfather had taken me hunting as a young boy, he had taught me how to look for fire moth caterpillars, whose form and hue exactly matched that of the twigs they hid among. Detecting them, he had told me, required patience, concentration and a training of the mind behind the eye. Had it been this way for Atara, too, searching among millions of possible futures for the one that might hold life for the earth?

True seeing, I thought, could not be possible without a *will* to see. One must learn to look behind surfaces and the usual expectation and habits of the eye and mind. There must be a sensitivity to nuance, a drive toward something higher and deeper, the sudden perceiving of things in a new light – and a sort of astonished touching of the real. To see the unseen required a freshness of the mind and a cleanness of the spirit. And seeing, as my grandfather had told me, was much of what the One had created us to do. What did the *One* will us behold? Above all, the infinite depths and delights of the One's creation and the immense glory of life that filled even the tiniest of seeds as they sent up through the earth green shoots that fought their way higher and ever higher toward that brilliant and beautiful star in the sky that men had named the . . .'

'Maram!' I heard Kane shout out from ahead of me. 'Can you see me? Can you *hear* me?'

With the breaking of Kane's voice into the peace of the woods, the darkness suddenly lifted from me. It was as if the door to a dungeon had been flung open: I blinked against the burning stabs of light that drove into my eyes. It took me many moments before everything began to clear. Then I gasped in awe to see that we had somehow left the wood to find ourselves in a grove like unto no other that I had ever seen. The trees around us, with their silver bark and golden leaves, all were astors but much taller and more magnificent than their cousins in Ea's other Vilds. They grew not like the trees of most woods, crowded together crown to crown, but rather spaced apart allowing a clear sight of the blue, sun-filled sky. Few bushes spread out above the forest floor, carpeted with old leaves and patches of grass, but flowers grew everywhere.

'Maram!' Kane called out once more. And then: 'Liljana! Daj! Master Juwain!'

I whipped about in my saddle, looking around me. I could see none of our friends whom Kane had named, nor Joshu Kadar, Master Matai, Master Nolashar, Master Yasul or Master Storr. Of the Seven, only Master Virang and Abrasax himself seemed to have found their way into this new place. As had Bemossed and Estrella, but no one else.

Or so I thought until I saw Alphanderry suddenly take form to stand in a spray of crimson flowers almost as bright as his mysterious being, which seemed somehow much more luminous and real than it had ever been before.

Kane saw me looking about, and called to me: 'You can see again!'

'Yes,' I told him, 'the Ahrim left me suddenly. I think it is gone.'

I cast about trying to sense it, perhaps hiding in the lee of one of the great trees. But the brightness of this wood made even shadow seem light.

'But what happened?' I said to Kane. 'Where are the others?'

Beneath the silvery bough of one the astors high above us, we gathered to hold council: Kane, Abrasax, Master Virang, Bemossed, Alphanderry and myself. And Estrella. Although our passage into these wondrous trees had not cured her of her muteness, she could say more with a smile and a brightening of her eyes than most people could with a whole stream of words.

'So, *this* happened,' Kane said. 'I was looking for the Vild, and suddenly found myself within it.'

'So it was with me,' Abrasax said. The intense sunlight seemed to set his white hair and beard on fire. 'I was looking, as a Master Reader is trained to look. There should be an *aura* to any Vild, different from other woods. And then, of a moment, instead of the wood where the Ahrim attacked Val, I saw *this.*'

Off through the silver and golden shimmer of astor trees, I noticed gardens of emeralds and diamonds that the Vild's people cultivated, along with dozens of other gems and even gelstei themselves. Birds as bright as parrots flew from tree to tree. Timpum – in all their swirling, scintillating, many-colored millions – hung about nearly every branch, twig and leaf. Never had I seen these luminous beings blaze so brilliantly.

It turned out that all of us had experienced a sort of ripping away of our bodies and souls to find ourselves suddenly riding our horses through this glorious wood. Even Kane, who must have experienced almost everything that could be experienced, seemed distressed. Estrella, however, simply gazed up in wonder above the trees at the fiery red sun. She evinced no fear at how she had come to be in this place; in truth, she seemed utterly at home here, as in some strange way she did everywhere.

It was Bemossed who asked the questions that pressed most keenly on all our minds: 'But where are the others, then? Did they remain behind? And if so, why?'

At this, Kane shrugged his shoulders then scowled at the sky. Not even Grandmaster Abrasax, wise in all lore, had an answer for him.

'And if they *did* make their way here,' Bemossed continued, 'is it possible that they came out into a different part of this wood?'

No one knew. The Vild seemed to spread out for miles around us in all directions. So open were the spaces between the giant trees that one could say that no path led through them – or that a thousand did.

'We must search for our friends then,' I said. I turned toward Kane. 'You have the most woodcraft, and so it might be best if you . . .'

I did not finish my sentence. For at that moment, from behind a tree nearby, a small, muscular man stepped out to greet us. He had the leaf-green eyes and curly hair of many of his people, whom I had first known as the Lokilani and Kane called by their more ancient name: the Lokii. He wore an emerald necklace which hung down upon his brown-skinned chest and a skirt woven of some kind of gleaming fiber, but nothing else. I expected him to speak with that strange lilt to his words, as had the other Lokii in the other Vilds. Instead he addressed us in an almost formal manner, as might an envoy sent from a great king.

'Valashu Elahad,' he said, stepping closer, 'you have come here again – and now as King Valamesh. Allow me to present myself: my name is Aukai.'

Although he did not bow to me, for such was not the Lokii's way, he might as well have. I dismounted then, and so did the others. And I said to Aukai with astonishment: 'But how do you know who I am? For I never *have* come here before.'

At this, he just smiled. And then his hand swept out, pointing through the trees as he said, 'There is a forest beyond here that the Forest sometimes touches upon. You have come *there*, three times now, at least, for that is your fate. As you have come here.'

'But how do you know this, then?'

'I know because I *know*. And because it was foretold.'

'Foretold by whom?'

Aukai looked from Abrasax to Master Virang, and then at Bemossed before his gaze finally settled on Kane. And he said to me, 'The messenger told of your coming, Valashu Elahad.'

'And what messenger is this?'

'Her name is Ondin.' He paused as he looked at me more deeply. 'She is of the El Alajin.'

'One of the Elijin, *here*!' I said. 'But they are not permitted to come to Ea!'

Aukai used his bare toe to dig at the golden leaves spread out over the earth. And he said to me, 'But you do not now stand on Ea.'

At this, I looked up at the sun, almost as deeply red as a ruby. And I said to Aukai, 'But where *do* we stand, then?'

'In the Forest, of course.'

'Yes – but *where* is the Forest?'

In the third Vild, I had fallen into a magic pool only to emerge dripping wet upon the Star People's world of Givene. I wondered if once again I had made a passage to the stars.

'The Forest,' Aukai said to me, 'is where it is. Sometimes it is one place, and sometimes another. But *always* it is where one wills it to be.'

Abrasax, I noticed, paid keen attention to Aukai's words, and so did Master Virang. Bemossed, though, looked up at the sun. To my amazement, it now shone as yellow-golden as the sun I had known all my life.

'I am sorry,' Aukai said to me, 'I have confused you, and I did not mean to. But some things are hard to explain. Let me try again.'

He drew in a breath of the wood's bracing air as he watched Estrella touching a small, five-pointed flower. Its white petals radiated a soft white light, and we would later learn that the Lokii named this wonder as a stellular.

'In truth,' Aukai told us, 'it might be most accurate to say that the Forest always just *is*. And it always is upon the world you call Ea. But it also exists upon Lahale, where the El Alajin dwell.'

He paused to let us consider what he had said. Kane, I saw, stared at Aukai so intently that I could feel the raw, red hammering of his heart.

And then Master Virang asked the question that anyone, and not just a Master of the Brotherhood, would wonder at: 'But how can your wood be two places at once?'

'In the same way that your thoughts can dwell with two things at once,' Aukai told him. 'And your awareness, and your will. Above all, your *will* to be aware. That was how all of you found your way here.'

He told us that the attainment of a certain awareness would allow one to perceive the Forest and enter it. In a way, one called the Forest into the world and 'set' it either on Ea or Lahale.

'Then would it be possible,' Master Virang asked, his almond eyes sparkling, 'for one of us to set the Forest on Lahale and walk out onto the world of the Elijin?'

Aukai looked at Kane for a moment before he said, 'It would be *possible* – someday, perhaps, if a man attained the awareness of the Immortal Ones. But not I, nor my people. Nor you, I think.'

'I think not, too,' Master Virang said sadly. 'But clearly the Elijin whom you call Ondin can set the Forest on Lahale. Can *all* of their order?'

'All who wish to. But why should they come to *our* Forest, or call it to them, when theirs is even brighter and spreads out across almost their whole world?'

'Why, indeed,' Master Virang said as he watched the light of the stellular fill up Estrella's hand with its warm sheen. And then he asked: 'But if the people of Ea cannot pass to Lahale, can the Elijin pass to Ea?'

'Some can. But it is difficult.' Aukai sighed as he seemed to look through the trees for the wood in which the Ahrim had attacked me. 'To set the Forest on Ea requires entering into a lower awareness, and only some of the El Alajin are willing to put themselves in such jeopardy. And even those the Shining Ones have forbidden to walk upon Ea.'

I thought of my friends, whom I feared we had left behind, on Ea. I asked Aukai about this.

'They have not entered the Forest, that I know,' Aukai said. 'I do not think they will. It was foretold that seven of you would come, and seven of you are here.'

'Seven,' I said, watching Altaru browse on a bit of grass, 'and our horses, too.'

I thought it strange that an animal should be able to pass into the Lokii's wood, but then I recalled that it had been my wise, black stallion who had found his way (and ours) into the first of the Vilds. Altaru's awareness, I thought, in its own way might be higher than that of most men – or at least deeper and more primeval. But that did not explain how my other companions' mounts had managed to 'set' the forest so that they could enter it as well.

Aukai did not have a very satisfactory explanation for this. All that he could manage to tell us was: 'When a man and horse move together, there must be a sharing of awareness. Or perhaps your horses, being as one with you, were able to enter the Forest with you. I do not really know.'

I nodded my head as I considered this. Then I asked him, 'There was a thing attached to me even more completely than was my horse. A dark thing. And yet it seems not to have made the passage to this place.'

'Yes, the Ahrimana,' Aukai said with great distaste. 'For a long time, it has wandered the world, seeking entrance to the Forest. But it cannot bear to behold the trees here. And much else. And so it can never enter the Forest. It is bound to Ea, and finds its home most readily in the darkest of places.'

I did not like to consider the implications of his words, although they accorded closely enough with what Kane had told me.

'But come,' Aukai finally said, holding out his hand to me. He smiled at Bemossed and Estrella, and the rest of us. 'Your other companions will be waiting for you when the time comes for you to leave. Now is the time for other things. You must eat and restore yourself. And then speak with the El Alajin.'

It seemed that we had no better choice than to go where Aukai beckoned us. He led the way through the great astor trees, and my friends and I led our horses by their reins as we walked along in wonder. I felt so glad at being able to see again that I almost forgot the exhaustion that weighed down every particle of my body. Our journey, though, took us a good seven miles, or so I guessed, and by the time we neared the end of it, I was almost sleeping on my feet. The weariness cramping my stomach and other muscles made me doubt if I would be able to eat any of the foods that Aukai's people had prepared for us.

However, as in the other Vilds, the Lokii set out a feast of the most delicious things. On a large lawn within a great circle of astors, we met the rest of Aukai's people: some five hundred men, women and laughing children, who had come here to greet us. As we had before, we sat at one of the leaf-woven mats that served as tables. Aukai presented to us some of the most honored of the Lokii: a man named Kele, and three small but striking women: Anouhe, Sharais and Eilai – and others. Anouhe had a spray of wispy white hair and an air of kindness about her that reminded me of my grandmother. We ate of the bounty of the Forest, and then afterward Anouhe passed around a bowl full of golden timanas. These sacred fruits, which the astors bore only once every seven years, afforded lasting visions of the Timpum to all who tasted them who did not then die from the power and beauty of the experience. Daj and Estrella, of course, as children, were still not permitted to put their teeth to the timanas, but Abrasax and Master Virang took great wonder from what they ate and then beheld. And I took great strength from a clear, sweet drink that Anouhe poured just for me: the sap taken from a young astor tree. Miraculously, like a cool wind blowing everything clean, it drove away my body's weariness and cleared the haze from my head. When it grew dark and the stars came out, I almost didn't want to sleep – for the fifth straight night. But sleep I must, as Anouhe told me, for on the morrow Ondin would come to the Forest, and I must face her with a freshness of the eye and the spirit.

I awoke just after dawn to find the glade nearly deserted. The sun's golden light warmed the leaves of the astors and illumined the forms of my friends resting beside me. All except for Kane, that is. He stood watching over us as silently as the silver-barked trees all around us. Off perhaps fifty paces, Aukai and Anouhe gathered at the center of the glade as if waiting for someone. From a bush nearby, a lark sang out its morning song.

My friends and I then roused ourselves and bathed in a nearby stream. I put on a clean tunic embroidered with the silver swan and seven stars of the Elahads – and of my distant ancestors long before Elahad had come to earth. We breakfasted on some fresh fruit. And then we walked out into the center of the glade to join Aukai and Anouhe.

Abrasax, who had a mind every bit as sharp and curious as Master Juwain's, asked Aukai, 'Will the Elijin come here into this place as we did into the Forest?'

'She will come into the Forest as you did,' Aukai told him. 'But into what part of it, not even the Immortal Ones can know. And so, most likely, we will have to wait for Ondin to walk here.'

And so wait we did. While the trees around us brightened with whole flocks of birds and uncountable numbers of Timpum, we looked for the great Elijin to appear. The summer sun, sometimes yellow and sometimes red, rose above the crowns of the trees. The glade filled with a warm and vivid light.

And then, from out of the east, I saw a white form moving against the woods' colors of silver, gold and green. Ondin, I knew this must be, a women who was also something more – and yet she walked toward us with an animal grace that hinted of great power. Then she stepped closer, and I thought rather of a water-fall flowing across smooth rocks and sparkling in the sun. By the time she entered the glade so that I could look upon her in all her glory, she seemed more like the sun itself: brilliant, beautiful and beaming out all the hope and warmth of life.

She carried herself perfectly straight, though perfectly naturally and without obvious effort. She wore nothing more than a white gown, which covered her tall, lithe body from neck to knee. Her long hair, black as jet, fell down past her shoulders. Her aquiline nose seemed to split the sun's rays and scatter this radiance across her face so that her ivory skin gleamed. I could not say that in the loveliness and symmetry of her features she was more beautiful than the most beautiful of Valari women: Vareva or my mother, for instance. But in Ondin gathered a power and grace that seemed otherworldly in its perfection. It stunned my eyes and caused me to stare at her in wonder.

As Ondin drew up close to us, Aukai took charge of making the presentations. Then Ondin spoke to each of us in turn, pronouncing our names in her rich, ringing voice as if to honor us. I could not keep myself from staring at her, for I felt sure that I had seen her before, if only in my dreams.

'Grandmaster Abrasax,' she said, smiling at him. 'I have hoped my path would cross yours.'

She seemed even wiser than this wisest of men. I could not

guess her age: she might have been thirty years old – or thirty thousand.

'Alphanderry – famed minstrel,' she said, addressing the sparkling form of my old companion as if he were a real man. And then, more mysteriously: 'You have come so far, and have only a little farther to go.'

Then she turned to Kane. After gazing at him deeply, she uttered a single name that seemed to echo through the glade and the vast, open spaces of time: 'Kalkin.'

Kane, his black eyes blazing, clamped his hand to his sword's hilt as he suddenly thundered at her: 'Do not call me by that name!'

'I call you as you *are*,' she told him in a voice that rang out sweet but sure, 'and not as you wish you could cease to be.'

I had never known anyone or anything able to intimidate Kane. But as Ondin stared back at him with eyes every bit as black and brilliant as his own, I felt a strange fear come alive within him. It seemed that he could not bear to look upon her. And so he stared down at his hard, clenched hand as if in disappointment and dread.

Then Abrasax, trying to be kind, said to Kane, 'Bright she is, indeed, but no more so than you. In truth –'

'Say no more!' Kane snarled at him. 'I won't hear it, do you understand?'

Abrasax bowed his head to Kane, then looked at him as if he *did* understand my savage friend's most terrible wounds.

Ondin did not press matters with Kane – but neither did she let his dark mood gloom her. She finally turned to me, and her smile was like a honey tea warming my heart. And she said to me, 'Valashu Elahad, ni al'Adar – you have changed.'

I stood still gazing at the marvel of her, as did everyone else. Abrasax, I thought, the Brotherhood's Master Reader, might have spoken of the perfect progression of the fires that whirled within each of Ondin's chakras, the colors of each ingathering and then strengthening each other so as to cast a brilliant aura about her being. I, however, had no such talent. Even so, I could not help sensing her splendor, for it seemed at once both numinous and utterly real.

'You speak,' I said to her, 'as if you had seen me before – and not in a scryer's visions.'

I wondered how Ondin – and Aukai – seemed to know so much about me and the world of Ea beyond this Vild.

'But we *have* met before!' Ondin said to me.

'Where, then? In the dreamworld?'

'No, here. In this very place. When you were seven years old.'

I stared at her as if she had told me that I really had wings and could fly.

'You do not remember, I know,' she said. 'But it is time that you *should* remember.'

She nodded at Anouhe, who now held a wooden cup full of a bright green liquor that might have been the juice of crushed grass. Anouhe gave the cup to Ondin, who inhaled its fragrance and then handed it to me.

'There is no danger in this,' Ondin told me, 'but only remembrance. Drink, Valashu, and know what has truly been.'

Because I wanted to solve the mystery that Ondin had presented me – and because I trusted her – I put the cup to my lips and took a drink. The liquor tasted at once sweet and peppery, cool and bitter. I could not guess from what fruits or plants Anouhe had brewed it.

Upon swallowing, the liquor streaked like fire straight down through my insides. Before it even reached my belly, it seemed, I *did* feel myself flying, as if a catapult had flung me straight up into the sky's empty space. There came a moment of blinding brilliance. And then, as if a fireflower had opened inside my mind fully formed, I remembered what Ondin had hinted to me:

On my seventh birthday, my father had taken me on my first hunting trip into the woods behind Lord Harsha's farm. Two of my brothers, Asaru and Yarashan, had come with us. They had each put arrows into the same deer at the same moment, and then argued over whose had killed it. And as they stood beneath the elms disputing with each other and my father judged their deeds, I had wandered off. I made my way deeper into the woods, drawn by the call of a scarlet tanager – and something else. I remembered thinking that I could walk to the end of the woods and right up the slopes of Mount Eluru to the very stars. Instead, I had somehow walked straight into the Forest. Now, as I looked around the glade at the silvery astor trees and the glowing stellulars, I relived my wonder at beholding this magical place for the first time sixteen years before.

'I *did* come here!' I shouted in astonishment. I looked at Aukai. 'You were here! You taught me how to listen to the animals, and call them to me!'

Aukai smiled hugely as he nodded his head and whistled like a wood thrush.

'And you,' I said, turning to Anouhe, 'gave me a drink that you told me would keep me from dying, should I ever take any wounds that became infected.'

She, too, smiled as I pressed my hand to my side where Salmelu's sword had driven through me during our duel. I noticed that Abrasax, Master Virang and Bemossed were looking at me in amazement.

'And you,' I said, bowing my head to Ondin, 'were waiting for me here. You played the flute with me and taught me three songs! You told me that music would quicken my spirit.'

I remembered leaving the Forest and walking away from it holding the flute that Ondin had given me: the very same one that I had years later passed on to Estrella. This beautiful girl smiled as she now took out this slip of wood and held it up to the shining sun.

'And it has quickened it,' Ondin said to me. 'As much else has, too. You have such a bright spirit, Valashu Elahad. So bright, and so strong.'

'But why did I forget this place?' I asked her. 'And forget *you*?'

Ondin looked down at the Cup of Remembrance, as she called it, that I still held in my hand. Then she nodded at Anouhe to take it and told me, 'Because I asked this wise one to give you to drink from the Cup of Oblivion.'

'But why?'

'Because,' Ondin explained, 'in looking upon the glory of this place, you did not want to return to *your* woods. And since you *had* to return, we took away your memory of the Forest so that it would not haunt you.'

'But *why* did I have to go back? I might have remained here and spent my whole life making music with the birds.'

Ondin smiled at this. 'You said the same thing when you were seven years old. But you had to go back to Ea to fulfill your fate, which you would have found impossible to do if you lamented the darkness all around you while always longing for the brightness of the Forest.'

'My fate, you say? But what do you know of that? Can not a man make his own fate?'

I noticed Ondin looking at the sword I had strapped over my shoulder, and I felt its weight pulling at me.

'Your fate,' she told me, 'was to fight – and fight you have done.'

'Yes, I have. But always with an eye toward the end of war, when I would have time to make music again.'

'And that time is coming. When war shall end, or all things shall end. And you have your part to play in that.'

'Yes, but *what* part?' I asked her.

I was never to know if Ondin possessed the gift of looking into others' minds as Liljana could. But she seemed able to look into my soul – and those of Abrasax, Master Virang, Bemossed and Kane. She seemed to sense, all in a moment, the nature of the argument that divided us as to how Morjin must be fought.

'You are Valashu ni al'Adar,' she told me, 'descendant of the Lightstone's first Guardian and one of the first Valari. And the Valari were once warriors of the spirit, and must be again.'

'Others have told me that,' I said to her. I drew out my bright blade from its sheath. 'But fate, it seems, has also called me to be a warrior of the sword.'

'So it seems,' she said, smiling at me. 'But not just *any* sword.'

I pressed my hand to my chest and said, 'That which I hold inside myself is not enough to defeat Morjin as people wish.'

'No? Do you *know* that, Valashu? I have come here to tell you that the true Alkaladur has not yet been fully forged. And so no one has ever wielded it as it should be wielded.'

I thought of the great War of the Stone that the angels (and many Valari) had fought across the heavens for a million years, and one of its most terrible moments: when the Amshahs, led by Kalkin, had tried to touch Angra Mainyu with a splendid light and return him to the Law of the One. In an amphitheater outside of Tria, one of the ghostly Urudjin had recited these verses to us, and more recently, Kane:

> *In ruth the warrior went to war,*
> *A host of angels in his train:*
> *Ten thousand Amshahs, all who swore*
> *To heal the Dark One's bitter pain.*
>
> *With Kalkin, splendid Solajin*
> *And Varkoth, Set and Ashtoreth –*
> *The greatest of the Galadin*
> *Went forth to vanquish fear of death.*
>
> *And Urukin and Baradin,*
> *In all their pity, pomp and pride:*
> *The brightest of the Elijin*
> *In many thousands fought and died.*

Their gift, valarda, opened them:
Into their hearts a fell hate poured;
This turned the warrior's stratagem
For none could wield the sacred sword.

Alkaladur! Alkaladur!
The Brightest Blade, the Sword that Shone,
Which men have named the Opener,
Was meant for one and one alone.

Kane, the very warrior spoken of in the verse, stared at Ondin with bottomless black eyes full of pain. And I said to her, 'If the tale is a true one, then all the angels, even Ashtoreth herself, could not together forge what you call the true Alkaladur. Angra Mainyu turned the force of their souls back upon them! And slew all those who could be slain! And so why should you speak to me as if *I* can have anything to do with Alkaladur's forging, much less wielding it as you desire?'

She watched the sun's light play on my sword's silver blade, and she said to me, 'But you must know that you must have *something* to do with its forging. As all who follow the Law must. There will come a day when the Amshahs, in our millions, will again strike the soul force into Angra Mainyu's heart.'

As she spoke these words, Kane ground his jaws together, and his whole being seemed to writhe with fire.

'But you failed once,' I said to Ondin. 'Why, then? Why couldn't the ancient Maitreyas heal Angra Mainyu?'

'That is not known,' Ondin told us sadly. 'But the great Maitreya, who will lead all worlds into the Age of Light, has yet to come forth.'

At this Estrella's large deep eyes seemed to catch up Bemossed's brightness and give it back a hundredfold. Then everyone else looked at him, too.

And Ondin, feeling the weight of our expectation, said to us, 'I am the messenger of Ashtoreth, but not even she knows who this great Maitreya will be. All we can say is that the Maitreya has not yet quickened and come into his power.'

Her words did not distress Bemossed. He smiled at Ondin as if at least one person existed who understood him.

I thought again of the verse's refrain:

Alkaladur! Alkaladur!
The Brightest Blade, the Sword that Shone,

Which men have named the Opener,
Was meant for one and one alone.

'Then the great Maitreya,' I said, 'must the one for whom the
true Alkaladur was intended. The verse tells that none of the
ancients could wield it.'

'None could,' Ondin said, with even greater sadness. 'Just as *you*
have not yet learned to wield the sword you hold in your hands.'

I raised up my silver sword a little higher. And I said, 'But what
does *this* have to do with *that*?'

'No one knows. Perhaps no one.' Ondin turned to look at Kane.
'You forged Valashu's sword and gave it its name. Why did you
call it Alkaladur?'

For a long moment, Kane stood in a cold silence staring at me
and what I held in my hands. Then he snapped at Ondin, 'So, it's
a sword, of silustria, most luminous of all substances – as the true
Alkaladur was to be a sword of light. What else *should* I have called
it, eh?'

'You make a mystery out of your creation,' Ondin told him.

'So what if I do, then? Creation, itself, is mysterious, eh?'

Ondin gazed at him, then finally turned away to touch her finger
to my sword's blade. She said to me, 'Ashtoreth sent me to tell
you that this must somehow be used in the battle against Angra
Mainyu and Morjin.'

She lifted her hand away from my sword and set it down upon
my tunic over my heart. 'And *this*. And *you* must find the way to
use them.'

'But I do not know how!'

'You said that, too, when you were a boy learning the songs I
taught you. You will learn how.'

'But who will be my teacher then? Will *you* leave the Forest
and remain on Ea?'

'No, Valashu – you know I cannot.' She looked at Bemossed.
'But you will have the greatest of teachers. You will come into
your power when the Maitreya comes into his.'

I gripped my hands more tightly around Alkaladur's hilt; I could
almost feel the sun's light coursing through it.

'You will face Morjin, soon,' she told me. 'And then, if you are
a warrior of the spirit and a true king, you will find a way to
forgive him. You must desire his healing and only good for him –
even his happiness. And in the end, with all your heart, you must
find a way to –'

'No!' I cried out. 'I will *slay* Morjin, for that is my fate!'

'But Valashu, you cannot know –'

'I *do* know!' I shouted at her. 'Ashtoreth and all the Galadin, and you, yourself, might be capable of finding inside such a benevolent and selfless soul force. But I am not so noble!'

'You are –'

'I am not the one who can do this thing!' I shouted at her.

Her face grew stern as she looked at me. 'You are King Valamesh.'

I pointed my bright blade straight toward the heart of the sun. 'Yes, I am now King of Mesh – and *this* is my sword. And Morjin is my enemy.'

Ondin just smiled at this, with an immense sadness that flooded over me like the tide of the sea. Then she said to me, 'You are right: that is your sword. And its inscription was graven there for you.'

'What do you mean?' I asked, angling the sword slightly so that the light played over the silver blade. Its surface gleamed as unmarked as the most perfect of mirrors. 'Alkaladur bears no inscription!'

'Does it not?'

I gazed more deeply at my sword. 'If it *does*, then time has worn it away.'

'From *silustria*, Valashu?'

My sword's silustria, I knew, was so hard that not even thousands of years of its immersion in the sea had left the slightest mark upon it.

'But what is inscribed there?' I asked her.

'I do not know *what* is inscribed there. Only *that* it is inscribed there.'

'Inscribed *how*, then? I can see nothing.'

'No? Can you not? Then *look*, Valashu!'

Kane, three paces from me, stood still as a mountain as he gazed at my sword.

Then I looked, too. I looked at the smooth, shining silustria with a will to see behind its surface and the habits of my eye and mind. I must, I thought, let my the whole of my awareness blaze forth. I must drive myself to perceive something deeper within the silver gelstei and to grasp it with all the force of my soul in a sort of astonished touching of . . .

'It flares!' I cried out. 'The letters – they flare!'

From within the sword's bright surface near the hilt, curved glyphs suddenly leaped out from the silustria with an even brighter light. They formed and flared like etchings made from a silvery flame: *Vas Sama Yeos Valarda . . .*'

Abrasax, almost without thought, translated these words from the ancient Ardik:

> *With his eye of compassion*
> *He saw his enemy*
> *Like unto himself*

As he spoke, I studied the luminous glyphs graven into my sword near the hilt – but leaving the patch of silustria nearest it unmarked.

Then Ondin said to me, 'With *your* eye, Valashu. Look! There is more to the inscription.'

I looked at my bright sword with all the power I could find within myself to look. But the patch of silustria beneath the inscription remained as smooth as glass.

'I cannot see anything else!' I said. 'What are the lines, then?'

'I cannot tell you. It is known only that the sword's maker inscribed six lines.'

Here she turned toward Kane and asked him, 'Can *you* tell us what they are?'

Kane shifted his attention from my sword to Ondin, and gazed at her with a fierce, deep longing. He seemed to fight back tears with a terrible savagery toward himself. I sensed in him, however, no desire *for* her, as a man desires a woman, but only the keenest of urges to behold her as she truly was and to embrace that luminous part of her hidden so deeply from his sight.

'So, I cannot tell you,' he finally said. 'I have forgotten them.'

Ondin nodded at Anouhe, still holding the cup of green liquor. 'Then perhaps *you* should drink from her cup.'

I felt something flash inside Kane, and I feared that he might strike out at Ondin. Instead, in a voice both gentle and anguished, he said, 'No – it would not help.'

Ondin took a step closer to him, and with a sad smile, touched his face. I stared at the two of them in amazement. I had never seen Kane let anyone make free with his person or tender him this sort of kindness.

'Someday,' she told him, 'you *will* remember.'

Then she withdrew her hand and looked back at me. She tapped her finger just above the hilt of my sword. 'Just as *you* will find the last three lines inside yourself, and then see them written here.'

She drew in a long breath of the glade's flower-scented air. 'The time is coming, Valashu. Ashtoreth bids me to tell you that just as Angra Mainyu has sent the dark thing to attack you, the Ieldra will shower upon Ea their blessed light.'

Abrasax, who seemed as well-schooled in astrology as the Brotherhood's Master Diviner, pointed up into the sky to the left of the sun. 'The Golden Band still strengthens. Never have I seen it flare so.'

To most people, most of the time, the radiance that the Ieldra sent out to all worlds of the universe remained invisible. Now, however, Abarasax aimed his finger at a patch of cloudless sky far beyond which lay Ninsun at the center of all things. And suddenly, I thought, I beheld what he did: the sky's blueness seemed to break open to reveal the deeper color behind. It was glorre, the one color that possessed the qualities and attributes of all the others while shimmering with its own marvelous and unique splendor.

Without knowing why I did what I did, I raised up Alkaladur straight toward this band of glorre. My sword's silustria grew almost clear then. It seemed to draw down the onstreaming glorre and drink it in. And then, as with the flash of lightning, my sword showered out a brilliance of this color. Its radiance fell upon all of us, and brought a gleam to our eyes and hope to our hearts.

To Alphanderry, it brought much more. We all watched in wonder as he stood near my glistering sword as beneath a waterfall. He raised back his head and opened his mouth as if he wanted to let the Ieldra's light run down his throat deep into his being. His hands closed about the glorre-filled air, almost as might a real hand of flesh and blood. At last, I lowered my sword, and the glade returned its more usual hues of silver, gold and green. But Alphanderry did not return to the same substance he had been. He laid his hand on top of my hand, and the warmth of his skin burned me; I felt hard bones beneath, and the blood of life streaming through him all warm and good, and I shook my head in astonishment because I knew that somehow he had been made again as real as any other man.

'It is a miracle,' Bemossed said, putting his hand to Alphanderry's wrist. 'A true miracle – and not the kind that men say I make.'

'As it has been promised, Minstrel,' Ondin said to Alphanderry, 'you have been restored to yourself.'

Alphanderry – and all of us – bowed our heads in awe.

Then Kane, his eyes filling with tears, moved over to Alphanderry and embraced him. His hands thumped with great force and sound against Alphanderry's back as he cried out: 'My little friend, my little friend! Ha – you *are* alive!'

Thus did Alphanderry, killed in the pass of the Kul Moroth, rejoin his companions of old, and both Kane and I wept without restraint.

Then Ondin told us that her work here had been completed and that she must go. 'And you must, too,' she said to me.

I knew that I must. I asked her, 'But what of the Ahrim, then? It will be waiting for me when I leave these woods, won't it?'

Ondin nodded her head at this. 'It will always be waiting for you, Valashu. Just as *we* will be waiting for you to defeat it, once and for all.'

We both looked at the flaming inscription sealed into my sword's silustria. Then she smiled at me and added, 'Farewell, mighty King. Until we meet again.'

Without another word she inclined her head as if to bid us all goodbye. Then she turned and walked from the glade as she had come.

Kane, now exultant, moved over to his horse, where he retrieved the mandolet that he had inherited from Alphanderry. He gave it into Alphanderry's hands and said, '*Now* you can play this again!'

And play Alphanderry did. For the rest of that morning, as we took one last meal with Anouhe, Aukai and a few other of the Lokii, Alphanderry plucked the strings of his mandolet as he sang out in his poignant, beautiful voice the very lyrics which had brought down the wrath of Morjin's men in the Kul Moroth: *La valaha eshama halla, lais arda alhalla* . . .

Now it brought only smiles to our faces.

12

It proved less difficult to leave the Lokii's Forest than it had been to enter it. The seven of us came out into the woods where we had left our companions – but a quarter mile farther to the east. We heard Maram and the others shouting for us through the oaks and maples. We shouted back at them, and soon met up near a great silver maple tree.

'What happened?' Maram bellowed out to us. 'One moment, we were all riding along together, and then the next . . .'

His voice died off into the twitterings of the birds as he gazed at me. 'Val! You can see again!'

As I sat on top of my horse beneath the maple's pointed and shining leaves, I could see perfectly Maram's heavily bearded face, happy with relief. Through the greenery of the trees, I could make out some red clusters of sumac nearly a hundred yards away. I could not, however, detect any sign of the Ahrim.

'Then you are free,' he said, 'and you . . .'

Again, Maram stopped speaking as he looked at Alphanderry sitting on top of his horse as he plucked at his shiny mandolet. And then Maram shouted, 'Alphanderry! Is it really *you*? What *happened*?'

Abrasax took charge of giving an account of how we had come to enter the Lokii's wood and our meeting with Ondin. Maram – along with Master Juwain, Liljana, Daj and Joshu Kadar – listened in wonderment to his words.

'Strange,' Master Juwain said, pulling at his ruined ear. 'Everything you have told us, so strange. And strangest of all, perhaps, is this matter of time. It seems that you spent nearly a whole day with the Lokilani, but to us, you went missing only moments ago.'

He had no explanation for this mystery, nor did Abrasax, Master

Virang or any of us. But Daj seemed more interested in something else. He said to us, 'Each of the Vilds seems larger on the inside than the outside, in whatever part of the world we have found them – but how can that be?'

No one could explain this, either. And no one wanted to venture a guess as to how we seven had entered the Vild while our other companions had been left behind. Liljana, however, saved the better part of her amazement for the miracle of Alphanderry's return. She nudged her horse up to his, and leaned over and planted a loud, smacking kiss on his cheek. 'You are as alive as you ever were, and who knew that the Ieldra had such power? But, since you *do* live and breathe, you'll soon be hungry again, just like any other man. So why don't we leave these woods and find a place where I can cook you a good meal?'

On our way back to the army's encampment, that evening and part of the next day, Liljana had more than one chance to prepare sustaining foods and serve Alphanderry once again. We rode back across the middle of Mesh, down the North Road and through Hardu, crossing the Arashar River in midafternoon. I looked for the Ahrim through wood and glen and along the roadside for every mile of our journey. Although I could find no sign of it, I felt its presence lurking behind nearly every tree, bush and farmhouse.

Our entrance into the camp created a stir. A rumor, it seemed, had circulated among my army that I had been stricken blind. As I rode down the lanes of tents toward my billowing, black pavilion, I did my best to dispel it. Warriors in their thousands lined my way to greet me; I met eyes with as many of them as I could, and I called out hundreds of names: 'Ramaru of Ki; Barshan Nolaru; Skymar Yuval; Juladan the Bold . . .' I knew then, to my amazement, that I had not stood inside my tent for days greeting these men in vain. They now greeted *me* in high spirits, and I guessed that they would pass around a new rumor: that my quest for a vision had been successful, and soon I would lead them out of Mesh to war.

We marched at dawn on the 26th of Soldru, a day of intense sunshine and bright, blue skies. The captains of my army – Lord Tanu, Lord Tomavar, Lord Sharad and Lord Avijan – gave me a report of our numbers: ten thousand and eighty-nine men. Although more than fifteen thousand had stood for me in our encampment's square, I had to leave many behind for Mesh's defense. And many warriors were too old or too crippled with old wounds, taken at the Culhadosh Commons and at other battles, to set out with us.

It was a smaller army than most that my father had fielded. I thought, however, that we would fight just as well, and perhaps even better, since we would be contending not just for our own lives but those of our people – and perhaps everyone in the world.

I led forth, with Joshu Kadar riding beside me and holding the Elahad banner, with its silver swan and stars. Lord Avijan's companies of knights formed my vanguard, nearly four hundred strong; their gleaming shields showed blue bulls and golden eagles and hundreds of other charges against fields of white, black or red. I assigned Lord Sharad's three hundred cavalry to guard our rear. They would have a boring, dusty duty of looking after the many wagons in our vulnerable baggage train – more wagons than I would have guessed that Lord Harsha could have assembled and filled with supplies considering the short notice that I had given him. Between the train and the vanguard marched the Meshian foot: more than nine thousand warriors clad in brilliant diamond armor. With each step, the jangling of the silver bells fastened around their ankles rang out in a great, nerve-piercing sound. Lord Tanu commanded seven battalions of them, and Lord Tomavar likewise. Although Lord Avijan still mistrusted Lord Tomavar, and had argued against giving him such an important command, I kept faith with my father's judgment in this. As much as possible, I wished to preserve the order of battle that had led us to victory at the Culhadosh Commons.

Maram and Kane, of course, rode with me in the van, while Master Juwain and Liljana kept pace with Abrasax and the other Masters of the Brotherhood farther back. It seemed odd that they should accompany us on our way to battle. But I could not bear to leave Bemossed ill-guarded in Mesh, and where the Maitreya went, they would go as well. I told myself that each of the Seven possessed skills that we might need – if only I could prevail upon these willful old men to employ them in my service. One last time, I tried to persuade Daj and Estrella that they would both be better off taking up residence at Lord Harsha's farm with Behira. But they persuaded me – with the sheer, soaring force of their spirits – that they must follow me to the end of our road. They feared their own deaths, I thought, much less than I did. In the end, king or no, I had to relent. I knew the limits of my power.

Our route took us back through Hardu, and then down the North Road (here called the South Road) through Godhra. In this city of smithies, the smoke from thousands of coal fires filled the air and stung our eyes. Many people turned out to watch us march

192

past. They cast roses upon the warriors and shouted out their blessings. It seemed that all of Mesh now knew what we intended to accomplish, and why.

It was fifty miles, altogether, down the good road from Hardu to the Sky Pass in Mesh's southernmost mountain range. We made this distance in three days; I might have pressed my army to even greater speed, but I did not want to tire my men too sorely at the very beginning of our campaign. Then, too, the road from Godhra climbed steeply up to the pass, and with the wagons full of stores and creaking slowly along, the oxen had a long, hard work of pulling them. No other way out of Mesh took a traveler up so high. By the time we reached the great stone kel keep guarding it, the terrain about us was all barren tundra, ice, rocks and snow. Some clouds formed up, and it rained upon us: icy pellets of water that caused ten thousand men to wrap themselves tightly in their cloaks. We were all glad, I thought, after we had descended the pass and came out into the broader – and drier – valley below. But there, at the end of the valley, where the foothills gave way to the rolling grasslands of the Wendrush, we found ourselves at the very edge of the country claimed by the Sarni's Mansurii tribe: one of Mesh's oldest and fiercest enemies.

We made camp with the mountains to our backs on this foreign soil. I ordered our rows of tents to be surrounded by a moat and earthen stockade. My warriors had a bitterly hard time employing picks and shovels to break through the steppe's tough sod to the black earth beneath. But I would not needlessly expose my army to attack by the Mansurii's horse archers. On another campaign across the Wendrush, two years before, I had discovered just how vulnerable even the best knights in the world could be to armor-piercing arrows fired at a distance by the galloping Sarni. In truth, I knew I took a great chance in leading my men through this land. But only one other route led to Kaash, and that would have taken us through Waas.

'And we can't cross Waas, if we are to surprise the Waashians,' I overheard one warrior telling another that night around one of our many campfires. 'I'd rather risk a battle with the Mansurii, who might never notice us, than call down the Waashians to face us on their own ground.'

It pleased me that my captains had passed along my intentions to the warriors. I wanted each of them to understand our strategy so that they could march into battle like men, instead of ants, even as they fought like killer angels.

That night, in my pavilion, I gathered with my captains and other lords around my map table. I traced my finger along the curve of the mountains, bending north and east up toward Waas, and then back south and around to form Kaash's border with the Mansurii. If we marched straight for Kaash, we would have a journey of ninety miles across the open spaces of the Wendrush. If we kept within easy retreat of the mountains, however much safer that might be, we would add miles to our journey.

'Will spending a few extra days really bring us to Kaash too late?' Lord Tanu asked.

'It might,' Lord Zandru told him. His long, apelike arm swept out toward the map. 'I have said that King Talanu can probably maneuver and delay things until the middle of Marud. But King Sandarkan might be able to bring him to battle sooner.'

'Then time is of the essence,' Lord Sharad said.

'In any case,' Lord Tomavar added, 'cleaving the mountains near Waas might not prove so very safe: what if we are spotted?'

As had become my habit, I let the lords of Mesh speak from their hearts. In the end, though, I had to speak from mine, as well as follow it – along with ten thousand men.

'Tomorrow,' I told them, 'we will send out riders to look for the Mansurii. Even if their warriors detect us, it will take them some time to assemble their clans and attack us. If we move quickly enough, we could reach Kaash before they call up their full strength.'

'How quickly, then?' Lord Harsha asked me, gazing at me with his single eye.

'Three days,' I told him. 'Four, at the most.'

'But, Sire, the wagons are still nearly full,' he told me. 'The oxen will have a hard time of things, and the men almost as bad. You'll march their legs off.'

Kane answered for me then. He caught up Lord Harsha in his fierce gaze and growled out, 'March their legs off? Ha – that's better than *cutting* them off when they rot from the filth that the Mansurii spread on their damn arrows!'

We set out early the next morning across the trackless steppe, driving the oxen as hard as we dared. The wagons bumped and lurched over the grassy, uneven ground. The jangling of the warriors' silver bells drove up flocks of birds and herds of gazelles bounding from our path. In the distance, lions roared, though none of us in the vanguard or farther back had the privilege of laying eyes on these noble beasts. But neither did we, or our outriders, espy any of the Mansurii, and we all gave thanks for that.

Along our way, Estrella stopped to pick some white yarrow growing in sprays across the sun-seared grass. She bound them up and gave them to Bemossed. She could not explain, in words, the purpose of her gift. But those of us who knew her understood well enough: she tried in her own quiet way to inspirit him. For even as my warriors marched forth to distant battles, Bemossed continued fighting his nightly and hourly battle with Morjin. This great struggle seemed to wear away at him. No matter how much good food Liljana tried to urge into him, he had little appetite, and seemed to be growing thinner. His flesh hung dark and bruised beneath his eyes, and he rode along under the hot sun as if trying to bear its fiery weight upon his shoulders.

Alphanderry, as well, tried to cheer him. Especially at nights, around a blazing campfire, he took out his mandolet and played stirring, ancient epics. He composed songs of his own, singing straight to Bemossed's soul. This helped, a little. What nourishment Bemossed failed to find in salted beef or barley bread, he seemed to take in music. I remembered the songs that Ondin had taught me so many years before, and I added my voice to Alphanderry's, and we sang out ancient harmonies that pleased the warriors and finally brought a gleam to Bemossed's eyes. I remembered that the Ieldra, at the beginning of time, had sung the whole universe into being, and on those star-filled nights on the steppe with the lions roaring and ten thousand warriors singing along with us about the miracle of creation, all things seemed possible.

During the days and nights of our march to Kaash, I reflected often on the words etched into my sword: *Vas Sama Yeos Valarda*. What would it mean truly to see my enemy as myself? What would I do if I could? I wondered, with every mile of grass that my great stallion trampled beneath his hooves, at the powers of my sword – and even more at the deepest impulses of my soul.

Three days and a morning it took us to cross the pocket of grassland pressed up against the curve of the Morning Mountains between Mesh and Kaash. Our luck held good. Our outriders sighted not a single Mansurii warrior, nor did I lose any of *my* warriors to sunstroke, exhaustion, the flux, or any of a hundred other maladies that strike down men on the march. Three oxen, only, dropped beneath the great weights they pulled. Lord Harsha had them butchered and roasted, and my tradition-loving Meshian warriors put tooth to this fresh meat with much greater gusto than they had exhibited toward the antelope and gazelles that the hunters had brought in.

Lord Zandru the Hammer, riding a large white gelding, steered us straight toward the opening in the southwest curve of the mountains known as the Lion's Gate. Tall, white-capped peaks rose up to either side of this narrow and rocky gap. The Kaashans had built a great fortress on a hill overlooking the Lion's Gate. Lord Zandru, with Lord Avijan, Lord Noldashan and other knights, rode up to this heap of stones to inform the fortress' commander that the Meshians had come to answer Kaash's call. The commander – a Lord Yulsun – seemed both surprised and delighted to learn this news. He opened the Lion's Gate to our army, in a manner of speaking, and we encamped that night on pasturage along a river to the north of the fortress.

Lord Yulsun, according to protocol, invited my captains and me to take meat in his fortress. But because I did not want to leave my men, I invited into our encampment Lord Yulsun and as many of his warriors as could leave their duties. I had my council table set up on the grass outside between four blazing fires, and there I sat at dinner with Lord Yulsun, Lord Zandru and my captains and the other greatest lords of Mesh.

Lord Yulsun, a spare, old warrior who had lost one eye and part of his cheek bone from a Mansurii arrow, wasted no time in niceties. He was hard, blunt man used to speaking his mind.

'King Valamesh,' he said, addressing me with a grave formality, 'no one in Kaash expected you to gain your father's throne. And for you to march to our aid at a moment's notice, when we failed to march to yours – this is a very great thing. Who would have thought it possible?'

'Sometimes,' I said, thinking of my father, 'it seems that everything is possible.'

'Perhaps it is,' he told me, 'for the one who gained the Lightstone out of Argattha and tried to bring our people together in alliance. But then King Shamesh was a great man, and so why should we not expect even greater things of his son?'

I bowed my head to acknowledge his kind words. And I looked around the table at my captains, and I told Lord Yulsun: 'We cannot let Waas defeat you. Our two kingdoms have been allies for ages, and we cannot let your misfortune of two years ago break that bond.'

'I wish King Talanu were present to hear you say that! Your uncle would be proud of you, Valashu Elahad, if you don't mind *my* saying that. And pleased to see you leading ten thousand men. With our six thousand, we will surely outnumber the Waashians. If you can move quickly enough, we have a great chance to defeat them once and for all.'

He told us that King Sandarkan's Waashians were marching down from Charoth, and that King Talanu had called up nearly every available warrior to throw them back. Their armies were to meet in battle along the west bank of the Rajabash River just south of a village called Harban.

'I scouted that place two years ago,' Lord Zandru said to Lord Yulsun. 'It is a *good* battleground, with a pasturage of ten miles along the river, and almost two miles wide, rising up to the forest beneath Mount Ihsan.'

In Kaash, most mountainous of the Nine Kingdoms, clear and level ground on which a battle could be decently fought was almost as rare as water in the middle of the Red Desert.

'Has a date been set for the battle yet?' Lord Zandru asked.

'Yes,' Lord Yulsun told him, nodding his head. 'The sixteenth of Marud.'

Lord Zandru turned to me. 'King Valamesh – it is a hundred miles from here northeast to Harban. Tomorrow will be the fifth, will it not? And so that gives us eleven days to cover a hundred miles.'

Lord Zandru, in his zeal to lead reinforcements to his king, neglected to mention the obvious, which Maram now pointed out: 'Ah, but you're speaking of *mountain* miles, aren't you? It might be a hundred miles for a bird to fly from here to Harban, but how far is it *really*?'

In the mountains, as my father had taught me, over rugged terrain that bent and twisted, rose and fell, a hundred miles' journey equaled twice or thrice that of a route taken across flatter country.

Lord Zandru had no numbers to offer to Maram, but he did try to encourage him, saying, 'There is a road that leads from the Lion's Gate through the Ice Mountains to the Rajabash River.'

'The Ice Mountains – oh, excellent!' Maram said. 'I suppose the peaks there did not acquire their name by accident? No? I thought not. Well, I hope it is a *good* road.'

'As good as any in Kaash,' Lord Zandru told him. He turned toward me. 'If the weather holds, you should have time to make the march and meet up with your uncle south of Harban. When the Waashians learn of this, they will either have to retreat back to Waas or face defeat.'

'Defeat,' I murmured. It had come that time in our meal when the plates of food were taken away and pitchers of beer set on the table. 'But can there be a defeat without *defeat*?'

'What do you mean, King Valamesh?' Lord Zandru asked, fixing me with a puzzled look.

'Is the road you spoke of the only one that leads to Harban?'

'Well, no – there is a track around the backside of Mount Ihsan that gives out to the north of Harban. But you could never get a wagon over it, and even the horses would have a hard work of that route.'

'But it *is* passable, is it not?'

'It is – but why would you want to *pass* that way? It would add twenty miles to your journey.'

'Oh, no!' Maram said to me with sudden understanding. 'I hope you're not thinking what I *think* you're thinking . . . Sire. Isn't it enough to defeat the Waashians? Or turn them back?'

'No, it is *not* enough,' I said. 'Not nearly enough.'

I turned to look at Kane, sitting to my right. His black eyes glistered with the same fire I felt blazing inside me.

'Tomorrow,' I said to Lord Zandru, 'I would ask you to lead us toward Harban and the track that you have told of. We must march like the very wind.'

We all drank to that; in short order Maram downed not only one large mug of beer, but three more as well. His voice had begun to thicken as he came up to me and said, 'All right, my daring friend, tomorrow we *will* march – the beginning of the last leg of the march we've been making toward that place that we're loath to speak of. You know where I mean. That very, inevasible, inevitable place. I can *see* it, can't you? Well, I've promised to follow you there, and I will.'

With that he drank another mug of the golden-brown Kaashan beer, and then another. The Kaashan and Meshian knights regarded his capacity for holding his drink with great respect, and Maram took an obvious pride in this. But they would respect him even more, he must have known, if he stopped himself from drinking himself into a stupor that would slow him down the next day or impair his ability to fight. And so, finally, knowing himself as well as he did, he pushed his froth-stained mug away from him. And in his loud, beery voice, he announced: 'I've drunk to our commitment to reaching the end of the road, and that *is* the end . . . for me. For Maram Marshayk, the end of brandy and beer. This promise I make, upon my honor, in respect of yours: Sar Maram will take no more drink until Morjin is defeated!'

Lord Noldashan and Joshu Kadar – and many others – cheered Maram's sacrifice, and not a few made similar pledges of their own. But I had already marched with Maram for too many miles to take too much encouragement from his new vow. I caught Master Juwain looking at me as if to ask: 'Can a fish give up swimming in water?'

The next morning, Lord Yulsun sent a messenger galloping ahead of us to inform King Talanu to expect us on the battlefield near the ides of Marud. Then I commanded my captains to form up the warriors, and I led them out of the Lion's Gate and up the road toward Harban.

For the next nine days we marched at a brutal pace. The road, while not quite as sound as those that my father had maintained, was built of good stone and well-drained against the frequent summer rains that came up and drenched the forest spread over most of Kaash. The road led around the curves of high mountains, through green, grassy valleys and up and over the sides of tree-covered hills. The Kaashans made a hard living from the farms carved out of this rugged country, and had little food to spare a foreign and hungry army. But what little they had, they gave to us in order that we might preserve our stores for our march and the coming battle. In village after village, they welcomed us with open hearts and cheered us on; in a little town called Yarun, they urged upon us leaves of the khakun bush. The bitter green leaves, when chewed, would impart great stamina and strength to a man, or so they said.

Great strength we all needed. While I tried to take care with my men's feet, to say nothing of their legs, we had to keep driving forward, even if a hundred or more warriors dropped by the way. But so tough and well-trained were the men I led that only a few could not bear up under the constant pounding of boots against stone. And Master Juwain, inside his creaking wagon that a team of oxen pulled along, using his green gelstei freely, was able to heal them and restore them to their battalions. He, himself, drove himself nearly to exhaustion. When the power of his varistei faded and then failed him, he relied on needles to lance the blood blisters afflicting my men's raw feet and the herbs and ointments that he employed to great effect. Abrasax, I thought, and the other Masters of the Brotherhood took note of his devotions, and they must have seen in him the same rare skill for healing that had perished with Master Okuth when he had sacrificed his life for Bemossed.

199

Maram, true to his word, touched no spirits in all those long days. But finally, on the evening of the 13th when we came to a village called Anan beneath the slopes of Mount Ihsan, he had great trouble resisting the brandy that the villagers broke out and poured for us. He took up a cup of his favorite drink and held it for a long few moments beneath his nose. Then he made a great show of passing it along as he called out, 'Morjin is certainly not yet defeated, and neither are the Waashians. And so I suppose the fragrance of this blessed liquor will have to sustain me until they are.'

The road through Anan, I saw, curved off east through a forest of elms, beeches and oaks as it made its way up around the white, rocky hugeness of Mount Ihsan at the heart of the great peaks of the Ice Mountains. We might yet follow it, and so meet up in good time with King Talanu's forces by the Rajabash River. Or we might take the track that Lord Zandru pointed out to my captains and me at the edge of Anan. It led higher up around the western and northern buttresses of Mount Ihsan, through stands of aspen and spruce, and carved into bare earth, or so Lord Zandru told us.

'But one horse only and no more than two men at a time can make their way up this,' he said to us. 'You will be half a day even getting your army moving forward, King Valamesh.'

'Thank you,' I said, pointing off to the left, 'but that is the way we must go.'

'It will be a long two-day march to the battlefield – if the weather is good. And weather or no, the men will have to sleep in the woods off the side of the track, where they can.'

'Very well – then tonight we shall pitch our tents here on the best ground that we can find and take as much rest as we can.'

'But what will you do tomorrow, King Valamesh? With your baggage train?'

I summoned Lord Harsha and said to him, 'Will you see to it that the wagons are taken up the road that they might be waiting for us by the Rajabash?'

His single eye burned with discontent. 'I will if I must, Sire. But that will bring us out behind the Kaashan lines, and I will have to ride with them on the day of the battle, and not with my countrymen.'

'On that day,' I told him, bowing my head to Lord Zandru, 'the Kaashans will *be* as our countrymen.'

Then I issued orders that my warriors each take only enough food for the two-day march around Mount Ihsan. And their weapons and armor, of course. Everything else – the tents, extra clothing and food – would have to make the journey with Lord Harsha and the baggage train.

Marud's fourteenth day gave us a morning of crystal-clear air and the scents of the evergreen trees and flowers wafting down from Mount Ihsan's slopes. To the sounds of ten thousand men strapping shields and swords over their backs, horses stamping and snorting, and water poured on campfires sending up a hissing steam, I mounted Altaru. To the protests of Lord Avijan, Sar Shivalad and Joshu Kadar, and other knights in my vanguard, I insisted on leading forward at the very head of the long column of our army. I rode straight through Anan and onto the track that pushed through the dense woods to the northeast. Four hundred mounted knights kept close behind me, followed by Lord Tomavar's and Lord Tanu's nine thousand foot, and then the three hundred knights of Lord Sharad's rear guard. Although it did not take half the morning to get everyone moving up the track, as Lord Zandru had feared, it took long enough, and I soon found my army spread out for more than three miles along it behind me.

For most of the rest of the day, our march through the summer woods might have seemed a pleasant hike, if not for the gradual rising of the track and our urgency. Birds in great numbers called out to each other from branch to branch, and deer and elk had the good sense to go bounding off through the trees so as to avoid our hunters' arrows. The sound of thousands of boots grinding against stones swelled outward through the forest and echoed off walls of bare rock around those steep parts of the mountain where few trees would grow. I did not fear my men giving the alarm. Almost no one lived in these wilds of Kaash, and those who did would never betray us to the Waashians. Even so, I commanded my men to remove the bells from around their ankles. Although I thought it unlikely that King Sandarkan would send any scouts down this path from the north, I did not want the tinkling of silver to alert them from afar and give them more time to escape from Kane and other knights whom I would have to send after them.

We camped that night off the side of the track, on semi-level ground beneath great trees or perched precariously on rocky slopes, even as Lord Zandru had said. Our luck had held good. The evening began warmly enough, or rather, with as much warmth as ever found its way to Kaash's high mountains. Our small campfires gave us good comfort, and we scarcely needed to wrap ourselves in our cloaks except for the hardness of the stony earth beneath us. But then, a couple of hours after midnight, a storm blew in. Dark clouds devoured the moon and stars, and a cold rain fell upon us like waves of the icy sea. Then, we desperately needed our cloaks, and more. The rain doused our fires and left us in nearly total blackness. Many of my men had to endure this misery in whatever spot they had laid down that night, for movement along the slopes above or below the track might prove fatal. I, however, had the good fortune of encamping with my friends on a saddle of earth almost perfectly flat. The few trees above us gave us little protection against the slanting rain. But at least we didn't have to worry about an icy torrent sweeping us down the side of the mountain.

'Ah,' Maram said to me as we sat huddled together for warmth, 'I'm tired, wet and cold. So *damn* cold – I've never been this cold before.'

He spoke in low tones so that Sar Shivalad, Joshu Kadar, Siraj the Younger and my other Guardians huddled nearby could not hear him. But Kane, Liljana, Master Juwain, Daj, Estrella and Alphanderry, pressed up close, must have made out his every word, despite the great noise of the rain. I heard Alphanderry chuckling with amusement, and sensed Kane smiling through the dark even as I did.

And then Liljana's voice cracked out into the nearly-drowned air: 'You were as cold as a man could stand when we crossed the Crescent Mountains into Eanna, and then in the Nagarshath, too. And last year, coming down from the White Mountains into Acadu.'

'Yes, yes, I was,' Maram's voice spilled out into the rain. 'But this is worse.'

'Why is it that each hardship you endure is worse than the last?'

'Why indeed? I suppose that is the nature and perversity of suffering: the more we endure, the more we are *able* to endure, if you know what I mean. And so the more we must suffer, and do. In the end, we become nothing more than a single, raw nerve utterly exposed to all the world's outrages. Even if a *strong* nerve, it is true. And so it is the very strongest among us who must live through the worst of hells.'

I thought about this as I listened to Kane's deep, disturbed breathing beside me. Had I ever known a man so strong or who had endured such incredible torments? Then I looked through the dark for Bemossed, who was trying to sleep with the Brotherhood's Masters only twenty yards from us, but I could not see him.

'And that is why,' Maram added, 'a man needs a bit of brandy at such times to numb his nerves. Ah, one might even say that the strongest of men need the strongest of brandy.'

'Drink if you must, then,' I told him. 'I'm sure you must have a bottle stowed in your saddlebags.'

'*Must* I? Well, I suppose I have. But I have also made a vow.'

'Which you have broken before, at lesser need.'

'So what if I have? A vow should be like a signpost that keeps a man pointed on the right path, and not a dungeon's cell imprisoning him. That being said, I *won't* drink so long as there are men spread out in this damn rain with nothing to warm them. I *won't* ease my own suffering only to watch as others freeze to death.'

I smiled at this and told him: 'The warriors you speak of are men of the mountains. They won't die tonight.'

'No? Well, perhaps they won't *quite* die. But they'll wish they did. And then, the day after tomorrow, supposing that we can get down off this damn mountain, we'll have to face the Waashians. And then . . .'

He did not finish his sentence. His words died into the pounding of the torrential rain.

Somehow we did all survive that bitterly cold night. In the morning, still freezing in the pouring rain, my men marched onward again with nothing more to put into their bellies than a little dried beef and cold battle biscuits. I led the way along the treacherous track. We had to go much slower, especially around the slopes of Mount Ihsan's great buttresses, for the track in many places became little more than slips of mud hiding stones that could turn a man's ankle or lame a horse's hoof. Lord Zandru did not have a good memory of this route, but he offered his anticipation that the track would dip down into more level country after only a couple more miles of snaking through some of the mountain's steepest terrain.

I placed much hope in this, for our delay had already put to the question our timely arrival on the battlefield south of Harban. And then, after I had ridden Altaru up and around another sparscly wooded saddle, I came out suddenly upon one of Mount Ihsan's steepest slopes. And my hope washed away. For I saw ahead me, for a stretch of about half a mile, that the entire side of the mountain had come down in a rockslide that had completely buried the track.

I dismounted and stood on a large shelf of earth gazing in despair ahead of me. Lord Zandru dismounted, too, and came up to me; so did Lord Avijan, Lord Noldashan, Kane, Liljana and my other friends.

'This is the end, then,' Lord Zandru sighed out. He was one of those men who are quick to see in any event the worst possible outcomes. 'We have taken a chance and lost.'

'No, there must be a way,' I said. 'There is always a way.'

The rain seemed suddenly to beat down even harder. It did not take much of an eye to see that even a mountain goat would not have dared the mud and rocks spread out above and below the track – or rather, where the track had once been.

'I can't see any other way,' Master Juwain said to me, scanning the steep and rugged side of the mountain. 'Unless you turn the army around and go back a few miles and try bushwhacking across the ground lower down. But that would take another day, at least, and the horses could not negotiate such terrain in any case.'

'No, we can't go back now,' I told him. I grasped the hilt of my sword to give strength to my trembling hand and stop the shivering ripping through me. And then a thought came to me. 'Perhaps we can clear a path.'

'Through *that*?' Lord Zandru said, pointing at the mass of sodden earth churned up ahead of us. 'It would take a thousand men working with picks and shovels for three days. And then who is to say another slide wouldn't bury your army as it marched past?'

My men, I thought, *could* build a good route along this slope, for my father had well-trained them to such work, as he had me. But Lord Zandru was right about one thing: we did not have enough time.

'Maram!' I called out. 'Could *you* clear a way? With your firestone?'

Maram, always eager for a chance at heroics that did not cost him too much effort or risk of his life, strode over to stand beside me. He took out his great red gelstei, nearly a foot long. Raindrops broke like a waterfall against the ruby crystal.

'I don't know,' he shouted through the rain. 'I haven't used it very much since Argattha – and never for so great a work as this.'

He glanced back at the dull diamond gleam of ten thousand men spread out in a line for three miles across the rocky buttresses of Mount Ihsan. Then he glanced up at the dark, closed-in sky.

'In any case,' he said, 'there is too little light. I'd be lucky to get a few sparks out of my stone, let alone the fire needed to melt through rock.'

'You could try,' I said to him. 'With a firestone no bigger than yours, Telemesh built the way between Mesh and Ishka.'

Maram must have clearly remembered the day that we had

passed through the mile-long Telemesh Gate, melted out of the rock between Mounts Raaskel and Korukel, for he smiled hugely. Then he said, 'But it took Telemesh six days to cut his channel, or so it is said.'

'Telemesh,' I told him, 'boiled into the air a good part of a mountain. You have much less to do: merely to clear away a little mud and a few rocks.'

Again, he looked out at the collapsed slope ahead of us. Then he nodded his head and called out: 'Very well – I shall try! Stand back, now! Stand back as Maram Marshayk makes a new path!'

Maram stood at the edge of the shelf, perhaps four hundred yards from the place where the track disappeared into the mass of the rockslide. He gathered in all his concentration as he pointed his crystal at the collapsed slope. Then he let loose a stream of fire at it.

The flames that he summoned from his gelstei, however, while much more than a few sparks, were much less than was needed to melt anything larger than a pebble. After half an hour of such fruitless work, he threw up his hands in frustration.

'There is too little light,' he said again, looking up at the sky. 'This is hopeless.'

Master Storr, the Master Galastei, stepped up to Maram then. He had his sopping cloak pulled tightly around his old, freckled face. He told him, 'I have made a study of the firestones. Although I have not been so fortunate as to have one to work with, much is written about them in the old texts. You say it is too dark, that your crystal cannot drink in the sun's fires, and so give them back. But what of the fires of the earth?'

He spoke, of course, of the telluric currents that burned most heatedly beneath Ea's mountains – the very same earth fires that Morjin would use to free Angra Mainyu.

'I'm sure,' Master Storr told Maram, 'that you could learn to summon them, with our help.'

He explained to Maram that the 'feel' of the telluric currents would be more subtle than that of the sun's blazing rays. And so Maram would have to open himself to these deep flames and pass them up through his body into his firestone.

'Now is the time,' Abrasax added, moving closer to Maram. 'You must not let the currents get caught up in that overly-worked second chakra of yours.'

Maram rested his hand just above his belt: the very place in his body from which he had summoned those fires that had too often gotten him into trouble. Then I remembered lines from a verse that he had composed:

> But 'low the belly burns sweet fire,
> The sweetest way to slake desire.
> In clasp of woman, warmth of wine
> A honeyed bliss and true divine.
>
> I am a second chakra man;
> I take my pleasure where I can;
> At tavern, table or divan –
> I am a second chakra man.

'This is surely a day,' Abrasax told him, 'for opening *all* your chakras. And we shall help you.'

As at the Brotherhood's school, the Seven positioned themselves around Maram. With Master Okuth dead, Abrasax asked Master Juwain to stand in his place. He gave him Master Okuth's old gelstei: the emerald crystal that was one of the seven Great Gelstei. Each of the other Masters held one of these ancient stones toward Maram.

What followed was no exercise or mere discipline designed toward the perfection of Maram's body and being. The whole world, it seemed, depended on what now transpired. I watched as the various gelstei came alive in the Seven's hands; their radiating colors, I imagined, found a perfect resonance inside each of Maram's chakras. I wondered if Abrasax could perceive a river of light, like a rainbow, flowing inside him? Whatever invisible fires filled Maram, the flames that suddenly erupted from his red crystal split the air for all to see. The heat of this lightning burned the very rain into steam.

'It flares!' Daj cried out, pointing at Maram. He kept back from Maram with Lord Avijan, Sar Shivalad and others. 'As it did when Maram scorched the dragon, it flares!'

The thousands of warriors held up back around the curve of the mountain must have wondered at these unexpected fireworks.

'All right then!' Maram cried out. 'Stand back! Stand back, I say!'

He, himself, could not heed his own warning. He planted himself at the edge of the shelf, gripping his firestone in both hands as if holding on for his life. His crystal brightened to an almost blinding crimson color as fire continued to pour out of its point in what seemed a dense and incredibly hot stream. Maram directed it against the mass of the rockslide. Mud and stones, in nearly an instant, melted and ran down the slopes in a glowing orange lava. The water in the ground heated into steam and exploded up into the air like a boiling fountain. It carried with it tons of hot grit and ash, which the wind and rain washed back upon us. All standing upon the shelf soon found themselves coated with this grime. The very earth seemed to hiss, crack and scream as Maram directed his terrible fire at it.

So thick did the cloud of ash and steam grow that he had to cease his efforts occasionally to let it subside – else we would all have choked to death. And Maram would not have been able to see where to lay his flames. Three times these flames nearly got out of control and threatened to consume us all in an explosion that might have sundered the very mountain. Such, the ancients warned, was the power of the firestones. But all the while that Maram swept his red crystal back and forth along the mountain's slope, Kane stood by him holding in his hand his dark crystal. It damped the worst of the firestone's burning light and kept it under control. For just such a purpose, as Kane had told us, the ancients had fabricated the black gelstei.

At last, after some hours, Maram lowered his red stone and looked out upon his work. After the rain had swept the air clean, we could all see the channel he had cut along the mountain's side. It seemed a path made of solid rock.

'Behold!' Maram's voice boomed out like thunder. 'Behold and rejoice: Sar Maram's Passage!'

He seemed well-pleased to name his creation, and even more pleased with himself. We all rejoiced then, as he had suggested. We gave thanks, too, for the driving rain, which sizzled off the hot rock along Maram's newly-made track, even as it cooled it enough so that men could move down it without burning their feet.

So it was that Maram cleared the way for our army to continue on around Mount Ihsan and come out behind the Waashians at the Rajabash – if only we could now drive ourselves to march quickly enough.

13

It is impossible for a man, burdened by more than fifty pounds of armor, weapons, clothing, water and food, to run more than a short distance. Even so, I pressed my warriors to such a fast walk that others might have called it a run. For all the rest of that day, I led my army around the slopes of Mount Ihsan. We had some good luck when the rain stopped in the late afternoon. We must have covered ten miles of some of the Morning Mountains' most rugged terrain by the time dusk fell upon the world. When we came out into the forested hills northwest of Harban, we were all so exhausted we were ready to crawl off beneath the trees and drop onto the bracken. But we could not sleep just yet. The Kaashan and Waashian armies would meet on the battlefield early the next morning, and we still had another fifteen miles to march in order to reach it.

The track that we had been following, as Lord Zandru told us, found its end in Harban. From there, a good road led down along the Rajabash to the proposed battlefield. But we could not set out on this route, for surely King Sandarkan would have left warriors behind in Harban to secure his rear. Therefore we needed to march cross-country – and now at night.

Lord Zandru found a woodcutter who knew of a track that would take us a good way through the forest toward the battlefield. When the moon and stars came out, we had just enough light to make our way through the ghostly trees. Lord Zandru, after dropping back to observe the heavy motions of Lord Tanu's and Lord Tomavar's warriors as they trudged along, said to me, 'Your men are already spent, and even if you come to the battlefield in time, they won't be able to fight.'

'They won't *have* to fight,' I told him. 'But only appear *ready* to fight.'

Lord Avijan, hearing this as we rode along through the starlit trees, turned to Maram and said, 'If the warriors cannot lift their shields and work their spears, then you can strike down our enemy with that sorcerer's stone of yours.'

'*Could* I?' Maram asked, taking out his firestone and holding it up to the thin light sifting down through the crowns of the trees. 'Ah, I suppose I could. But I *won't*. You see, I've taken a vow never again to burn men with its fire.'

I commanded my army to halt only once that night, for a break of half an hour. It was a dangerous thing to do, for it seemed that no one could remain awake to rouse the others when the time came – no one, that is, except Kane. I wondered for the thousandth time at his inexhaustible vitality. He seemed no more tired by our mountain's passage than he would have been after a walk in the woods.

Just after dawn, we came out into the pastureland along the Rajabash, below Harban but to the north of the battlefield. Now that we marched in the open, I commanded Lord Tanu and Lord Tomavar to keep a tight formation and to be ready to deploy from columns into lines at a moment's notice. We hurried across the rolling, grassy ground full of sheep and cattle. I sent outriders ahead of us. King Sandarkan's scouts would probably spot them, as they surely would our thousands of warriors before we drew up close enough to fall upon the Waashians' rear. But by then it would be too late.

I led my army's vanguard down along the Rajabash River, gleaming an icy blue off to our left. Our hundreds of horses churned up the dew-damp grass. Behind them marched Lord Tomavar's and Lord Tanu's warriors, now wearing their ankle bells again. The tinkling of silver spilled out into the cool morning air.

At last, I urged Altaru up and over a hummock, and saw the battlefield spread out below us. About two miles away, King Talanu had drawn up his army into glittering lines that stretched from the Rajabash across the pasturage, where he had anchored them against a wooded hill. A half mile closer to us gathered the Waashians. Their diamond armor gleamed as brilliantly as did that of the Kaashans and my own warriors. But King Sandarkan had arrayed them in an unusual and desperate formation: as a huge, open square, fronted by perhaps three thousand foot and as many on each of the other three sides. He had posted cavalry on each point of the square, and the most forward of these knights faced the Kaashans while those in the rear had their lances pointed toward us.

In short order, I saw to it that my army deployed as did the Kaashans, from the river in the east to the hills in the west. I rode with the vanguard to the right, pressed almost up against the hills; the rear guard took up its post to protect my army's left flank along the river. Then we advanced. Our drummers beat their great war drums and added to the thunder that the Kaashans' made; the jangle of thousands of silver bells spread out across the valley. Our warhorses, eager for battle, let out terrible whinnies. Yard by yard we moved down the meadow closer to the Waashians. In truth, we closed in upon them like a jaw of diamond and steel that would soon tear into them and grind them against the Kaashans' lines.

The battle, however, never took place. King Sandarkan now held an impossible position; his army's square formation gave evidence that his outriders had indeed warned him of our approach – but too late for him to retreat. And now, when he beheld my men's numbers, he must have realized that it would be hopeless to fight. As I had intended as far back as Mesh, he would have no choice but to surrender and ask for terms. If he did not, he and his entire army would be annihilated.

It did not take long for him to send out a herald holding up a white banner of truce. I saw another such gallop out toward the Kaashans' lines. I halted my men to receive the herald. We spoke for a few moments, and then I sent him back to his king – and sent one of my own to King Talanu, as he did to me. In this way, with heralds racing back and forth across the battlefield, we arranged a parley of the three kings and their captains down by the river.

I asked Lords Avijan, Sharad, Tanu and Tomavar to come with me, as well as Kane and my other friends. I asked Bemossed and the Seven, too. And, of course, Lord Zandru. It would be an unusual company for such a meeting, but these were unusual times.

King Talanu ordered a great canopy set up above the banks of the raging Rajabash and three chairs placed beneath it in the shade of the sun. I watched him ride out from his lines toward this meeting place. My uncle was now an old man – almost too old to hold a horse's reins and wield a sword, let alone command an army. Despite the pains of his joints and old wounds, however, he held himself proud and straight as if he would let nothing in the world bend him. He was thick through the shoulders and chest, as my brother Karshur had been, and I had never known a man with such large, strong hands – except, perhaps, for Sajagax. Nineteen brightly-colored battle ribbons festooned his shining white hair, and I knew of no other warrior in the Morning Mountains who sported so many. Over his diamond armor, he wore a bright blue surcoat showing the white tiger of Kaash.

'Greetings, Nephew!' he called out as our horses drew closer to each other. 'Welcome and bless you, honored King Valamesh!'

I dismounted and would have helped him do the same if he hadn't waved me off. I could feel a sharp stabbing pain in his shoulder, elbow and crippled right foot as he struggled down from his horse. Two men – Prince Viromar and Lord Yarwan – hovered near him, but he eschewed their attentions. With difficulty he walked over beneath the canopy and sat down in the middle chair. He beckoned for me to take the one to his right.

'This is a great day,' he said to me. 'Perhaps the greatest in Kaashan history since Kaash and Mesh threw back the invasion from Delu a thousand years ago.'

At the time he spoke of, Delu had been nearly the strongest Kingdom on Ea instead of one of the weakest. In fact, it had been one of Maram's own ancestors, King Kasturn, who had led Delu to her age of ascendence. Maram seemed to take an uneasy pride in this, for he hung back behind me with my captains and other friends, and he gazed at King Talanu with conflicting emotions lighting up his face.

'I have things to tell you before King Sandarkan arrives,' King Talanu said in his straightforward way. 'First, I regret with all my heart not marching to Mesh when your father called for us to come. I did not think we could arrive in time – and we *couldn't* have, as events proved. But more, King Sandarkan made maneuvers against Kaash, and I felt that I couldn't let him ravage my kingdom. I was wrong. No Valari, not even King Sandarkan, would commit the atrocities that Morjin did against Mesh. It took the torture of my own sister and too many of your countrymen for me to see that Morjin is our true enemy. Even though I *knew* it, in my heart, I was afraid to fight him.'

Here he placed his great, scarred hand across his chest and looked at me. And his captains, standing behind him nearer the river, looked at him with the poignant reverence they held for their old king.

'Anyone who knows the Red Dragon,' I said to my uncle, 'is afraid to fight him. But what other choice do we have?'

'What choice, indeed? At least we won't have to fight the Waashians, though I must tell you that many of my knights looked forward to washing their swords in our enemy's blood.'

Behind me I could almost feel my other uncle, Prince Viromar, directing his rancor toward the Waashians in their diamond block out in the middle of the field, and so it was with my cousin, Lord Yarwan, a bold-looking man with a great hawk's nose and a bloody eye for vengeance. And with several other of the Kaashan lords standing there, too. All of us, I thought, waited to see how long it would take King Sandarkan to force himself to ride out and face his defeat.

'But it is best to avoid bloodshed, as I have always said,' King Talanu told me. He shifted about in his chair the better to look into my eyes. 'When Lord Yulsun's messenger arrived to tell us that you were coming, we all rejoiced, for victory seemed at hand. But I must tell you that when your Lord Harsha confirmed that you had taken the route around the mountain, many despaired.'

Lord Harsha, standing off to my right as he conferred with Lord Tanu, bowed his head to me as if to inform me that our baggage train had arrived safely behind the Kaashans' lines.

'We nearly despaired as well,' I said to him. Then I told him something of our journey and Maram's great feat in cutting a way across Mount Ihsan's slope.

'A great feat, indeed,' King Talanu said. 'And I mean the whole of your march: it will go down as one of history's great ones. As will this victory today. What you have done is both brilliant and bold.'

I bowed my head to him, and looked at Maram, Master Juwain, Master Storr and Abrasax. 'I have had great help from great companions.'

Then I turned to gaze off down by the river, where Kane stood talking to one of the men who had ridden out with King Talanu from the Kaashans' lines. This stranger wore a stained traveling cloak instead of diamond armor, and was too short and thick to be a Valari. Although I could not get a good look at his face, he seemed familiar to me.

'Ah, at last!' Maram's voice boomed out as he pointed toward the Waashians' army. 'He comes!'

From between the warriors forming one wall of the Waashians' square, a short column of knights rode out across the field. A herald flying the white banner of truce kept pace with another holding up King Sandarkan's standard: two crossed silver swords against a black field. King Sandarkan, a tall, reedy man, wore a black surcoat emblazoned with the same charge. Three of his captains – Lords Telsar, Rayadan and Araj – followed behind him.

King Sandarkan led them straight up to our canopy, where he dismounted and sat down on the chair to King Talanu's left.

My uncle spent only the barest moments dispensing with the formal politenesses. He greeted King Sandarkan, as did I, and he asked after the health of King Sandarkan's family. Then he barked out at him in his gruff, old voice: 'Are we agreed that you have come to surrender?'

King Sandarkan's thin face tightened with such tension that it seemed his skin collapsed around his bones. And then he gritted his teeth and forced out, 'I am here to offer my army's surrender.'

'Good. Then let us agree upon the terms.'

'Let us agree,' King Sandarkan said, in his dry, raspy voice, 'but I can tell you that I will never ask my warriors to surrender their swords or their armor.'

'That has not been asked, and may not be. But you must know that you are in no position to insist on the point.'

'My army,' King Sandarkan said, pointing out into the field, 'still holds position. And we will fight to the death before giving up our swords.'

'We are met here so that we might avoid needless deaths. But since you have made your surrender, you must know that you must give up *something*.'

'What is it you want, then?'

'First,' King Talanu said, holding up a blunt finger, 'that Waas pay Kaash a weight of diamonds to compensate for the expense of my kingdom being threatened and having to prepare for battle these last two years.'

'How great a weight?'

'A bushel of bluestars. Or three hundred bushels of armor-grade whites.'

'Very well, then.'

King Talanu pulled at one of the ribbons tied to his long white hair as he studied King Sandarkan. He said, 'Second: You will agree to make common cause with Kaash if there should be war between Kaash and Athar. Eight thousand warriors you will agree to lead to Kaash's defense.'

'Very well – Athar is Waas's enemy, too.'

'Third,' King Talanu said, 'you will recognize Kaash's reclaiming of the Arjan Land. You will sign a paper stating that the Arjan Land is to belong to Kaash until the end of the world – or until the Star People return to earth.'

Now King Sandarkan hesitated. His long, predatory face fairly trembled with old grievances and desires. He shouted out: 'But the Arjan Land is *ours*! My own ancestors shed their blood so that –'

'This term,' King Talanu said, cutting him off, 'is not subject to dispute. Every warrior you have led onto the field today will shed his blood if Waas's king does not agree to it.'

King Sandarkan closed his eyes as he breathed in deeply in a meditation exercise. Then he finally looked at King Talanu, and he croaked out, 'Very well – the Arjan Land is yours.'

I sensed my uncle wanting to smile in triumph. But he would not allow himself such petty gloating. Instead, he bowed his head to acknowledge King Sandarkan's great sacrifice in giving up at long last the Arjan Land. Then he delivered his fourth term: 'During the course of your reign and for so long as you live, you shall forswear waging war upon Mesh.'

Now King Sandarkan turned to gaze at me with black, burning eyes full of jealously and resentment. And he called out to King Talanu: 'No other Valari king has been asked to accept such terms!'

And King Talanu looked at me as he told him: 'No other Valari king has so underestimated his enemy and let himself be trapped to face total defeat.'

I could feel King Sandarkan's face burning. His long limbs bent like those of a praying mantis as he pointed at me and said, 'Very well – so long as I live, Waas will not make war against Mesh.'

He drew in five deep breaths and asked King Talanu: 'Are those all your terms?'

'They are,' King Talanu said.

King Sandarkan bent forward as if readying himself to stand up and flee from this place of shame. And then King Talanu held out his palm toward King Sandarkan. 'But we are not finished here.'

'How not, then?'

King Talanu looked at me, and then back at King Sandarkan. He said, 'King Valamesh has marched here at great sacrifice and risk, and it is he whom Kaash must thank for victory. Therefore he has the right to demand of you his own terms.'

In response to King Talanu's logic, King Sandarkan stared at me with a smoldering resentment.

'Very well,' King Sandarkan said. 'What does Mesh's new king *demand* of Waas?'

While I sat there deep in thought, studying King Sandarkan's craggy, troubled face, Kane came up to me. He had no compunction in interrupting a conclave of kings.

'I must speak to you,' he told me. The fire in his dark eyes put an urgent heat into my own. 'This cannot wait.'

'*We* cannot wait,' King Sandarkan said, glaring at him, 'while this rogue knight whom the Elahad calls his friend delays matters here.'

'Please excuse me, King Sandarkan,' I said with all the politeness that I could find. 'Kane is not given to alarms, and I must hear him out.'

So saying, I stood up and walked with him down to the river. He presented the man he had been speaking with, and I suddenly realized where I had last seen him: in Mesh, after the Battle of the Culhadosh Commons. He wore a suit of steel mail beneath his cloak; his broad, heavily bearded face seemed to bear only hardness and threat. Kane gave his name as Hadrik. He did not have to say outright that Hadrik was a Master of the Black Brotherhood, which Kane employed to oppose Morjin and achieve his deepest purpose.

'Hadrik has come up out of Galda,' he said to me. 'He thought to find me in Mesh, and followed the track of your army here.'

Hadrik bowed his head to verify this. Then, in a voice as raw and rageful as any that I had ever heard, he told me what he had told Kane: 'Morjin left Galda late in Ashte to return to Argattha – I have spent the lives of my last ten men proving this. He moves, the Dragon does! The hour of our doom has finally come.'

As if he could not bear another word of speech, he shook his head as he turned and stalked off down to the very edge of the roaring water twenty yards farther down. He was a strange man, I thought, and one of the deadliest-looking I had ever seen.

'He is the last of his kind,' Kane said, nodding at him. 'All the others perished in Galda's torture chambers or nailed to crosses.'

He hung his head as if staring down through the earth and the turbid sediments of time. Then he looked up at me with his black, blazing eyes. 'So. So, Valashu. This *is* the hour. On the third of Ashte, Morjin called up the Uskadans to Argattha. On the day that you became king, he ordered the armies of Uskudar and Sakai to march north, toward Alonia. He leads them in the open, as of old! The Zayak and Marituk tribes ride with him, the Janjii, too. He has broken the Long Wall. Perhaps with fire, perhaps by opening up the earth – I do not know. As we speak, he marches up the Poru toward Tria.'

My heart drummed at the triple-time against my chest bones. And I gasped out, 'To *Tria*! But why he would spend his forces against the Alonians when they would do his work for him fighting among themselves? Unless he cannot wait.'

'So – he cannot.'

'Then he will have sent his fleet from Eanna, with the armies of Hesperu, Sunguru and Yarkona embarked upon his ships. Morjin will take Tria, then, and make it safe for them to land.'

'So – he will.'

'Five armies Morjin will then command – and how many men? Four hundred thousand? Five?'

'So,' Kane murmured, gazing at me.

'Then it will be as you said,' I told him. 'Morjin will attack down the Nar Road and invade the Nine Kingdoms.'

'So, just so. And I have worse news to give you. He will try to *split* the Nine Kingdoms in two, as we discussed in Mesh.'

He told me then the rest of the tidings that Hadrik had ridden so far to tell him: that upon the news of my coronation, Morjin had ordered a great fleet bearing the armies of Galda and Karabuk to prepare to set sail across the Terror Bay and land in Delu. The Dragon Lords would easily defeat Delu's army in battle – or more likely cow King Santoval into surrendering without a fight. And then, after forcing King Santoval to swear allegiance to Morjin, they would incorporate Delu's army into theirs and attack the Nine Kingdoms from the east.

'Your people's lands,' Kane said to me, 'will be caught between a hammer and an anvil. Even if by some miracle you *do* lead the Valari to make alliance.'

'Who leads the enemy's force?' I asked Kane.

'Karabuk's own king, Mansul the Magnificent.'

'And how many men does he have?'

'With the Galdans, perhaps a hundred and fifty thousand. If he can defeat Delu, he will have eighty thousand more.'

I stood by the gushing river considering this. Then Kane said to me, 'You have been thinking of mounting a raid into Galda and slaying Morjin, haven't you?'

'Yes,' I told him, staring at the river's spray. And then, 'Can we be sure of Hadrik, that Morjin has truly left Galda?'

'We can be sure. Morjin marches on Tria. And then soon, surely by summer's end, he will turn east and south toward the Nine Kingdoms.'

'With his army of half a million men?'

'So, Val.'

'And if I united the Valari and marched against Morjin, then

King Mansul's force would attack unopposed across the Nine Kingdoms and take us from the rear.'

'So.'

I pressed my hand against the newly-made scar cutting my forehead as I contemplated what seemed to be an impossible situation. I felt myself trapped, even as King Sandarkan was. But my warriors and I faced an enemy who would never offer us terms.

'There must be a way out,' I said to Kane. 'There *must* be.'

And with that, I returned to the canopy and sat back down with King Talanu and King Sandarkan. I said, 'As always, we Valari dispute with ourselves while our real enemy endeavors to destroy us.'

Then I related the news that Hadrik had brought.

'Unless we act immediately,' I said, 'the Galdan and Karabuk armics will invade Delu, and Delu will fall.'

King Sandarkan, glad for any distraction from his present woes, stabbed his bony finger into the air as he said, 'If what that rogue knight told is true, Delu will fall no matter how we act. But that is not our business.'

'Not our business!' I cried out.

'No,' he said, 'the Valari must look to the good of the Valari.'

'But Morjin would destroy the Valari!'

King Sandarkan cast his resentful gaze upon me. 'The Red Dragon would certainly destroy *you* – and Mesh. But that is not really Waas's business either, is it?'

My throat choked up with such anger that I shouted at him: 'How can you be so blind? Perhaps Morjin *will* fall against Mcsh first. And then aftcr he slaughters my countrymen, he will turn toward *you*. And Ishka and Taron, Anjo and Athar, Lagash and Kaash. The whole world, King Sandarkan!'

'That has always been your claim,' he said to me. 'Beneath the spur of such terror, you sought to elevate yourself as the Maitreya to gain lordship over the Valari. And when that failed, you put forth an outlander slave as the Shining One.'

Now he stabbed his finger at Bemossed, waiting with the Seven behind us.

'I have put forth no one,' I told him. 'Bemossed is who he is, and his calling does not depend on what we do or do not do.'

'What *shall* we do then, King Valamesh?' he said to me. 'The Red Dragon has sent envoys to each of the Nine Kingdoms. Gifts of diamonds and gold they have brought. They have brought, too, Morjin's assurance that his dispute is with Mesh and Valashu Elahad alone. He gives a pledge of friendship to any kingdom who supports him in war against Mesh – or at least pledges in return not to intervene in that war.'

I could not believe the words that I was hearing. I fairly shouted at King Sandarkan: 'But Morjin is the Lord of Lies! Don't tell me you believe him!'

King Sandarkan looked to his left, at the lines of the Kaashan army still standing in the warm sun, and then to his right, at my warriors. He said, 'At such times as these, one must believe what one *must* believe. In any case, the Valari, even in alliance, do not have the power to stand against Morjin. Therefore each Valari king must come to terms with Morjin and arrange a peace.'

'A peace?' I cried out. 'For a month or a year, until Morjin decides to turn on you and nail all your countrymen to crosses?'

'What do *you* propose then . . . King Valamesh?'

'To fight! Now, that we have been given such a rare chance! We know the Galdan fleet's plans, but they do not know that we know.' I pointed east, past the Rajabash at the pointed white peaks gleaming in the distance. 'We have three armies gathered here. Just over those mountains lies Delu. We can march across them and take our enemy by surprise.'

King Sandarkan laughed at this. 'That is a desperate chance, a fool's chance. What if we are discovered? And even if we are not, King Mansul's armies will still outnumber us five to one.'

'We can still win!' I called to him. I turned to my uncle and said, 'King Talanu – if Mesh were to march for Delu tomorrow, will Kaash join us?'

My uncle looked at me for a long time, and the deep creases cutting his forehead and face made him seem a thousand years old. Then he told me, 'King Sandarkan is right: what you propose is a desperate chance.'

He sighed as he grasped the hilt of the sword that he had set down by his chair. 'But it is our only chance. If we *can* defeat Morjin's eastern armies, then perhaps the other Valari kingdoms will join us in facing Morjin's main force as they come at us from the west.'

This, too, was my hope. For a long time I had known that I must win a great victory to have any chance of uniting the Valari.

'You dare too much,' King Sandarkan said to King Talanu. 'Even as your nephew does.'

'I *do* dare,' King Talanu told him. 'In truth, I *like* the thought of Kaash marching to Delu's rescue. And having the Delians be in our debt.'

'But you can't defeat Morjin's eastern armies! You will die with the Elahad on the march – or at the end of your road, in a desperate battle.'

'I will die soon in any case,' King Talanu said, shrugging his great shoulders. 'And it is good for a warrior to die in battle.'

'An *old* warrior can say that with good courage. But what of your men? Are you willing to see your young men cut down?'

'Better that than mounted on crosses when Morjin burns and ravages through the Nine Kingdoms.'

I caught King Sandarkan's gaze and said to him, 'At the Culhadosh Commons, Morjin's forces badly outnumbered us, and we *still* prevailed.'

'At great cost. But it *was* a great victory, even so.'

King Sandarkan looked at me more deeply. I felt doubt working at his insides and the slow burn of an awe that he seemed to fight down.

'In Delu,' I said to him, 'we can win an even greater victory. *We* can, King Sandarkan. With Waas's army joining those of Kaash and Mesh, we might just have enough strength.'

I felt this as a blazing certainty deep within my blood. I sensed it all hot and fiery within King Sandarkan, too. Did my most urgent passion communicate itself to him through my eyes and the pounding of my heart? Or more tangibly, through the valarda? Or did King Sandarkan, along with many Valari, hold his own gift sleeping inside him?

And then I felt King Sandarkan turn away from himself and his innate greatness as his face tightened with calculation. 'You ask for Waas's aid. What is Mesh willing to give in order to have it?'

'What *can* I give you other than hope for the future? And a chance for life?'

He smiled thinly at this. 'Perhaps I should have asked you this: what is King Valamesh willing to *give up* in the way of demands here today?'

He might as well have slapped my face, so keenly did I feel the blood burning my cheeks. I immediately hated myself for shouting at him: 'Mesh could *demand* of Waas levies to march to Delu! Instead of *asking* for an alliance!'

'*Could* Mesh demand this of Waas?' King Sandarkan said, his own face growing hot. 'If we cannot come to terms here, then battle there must be. And you will certainly prevail *here*, King Valamesh. But tell me: are you willing to spend your men's lives for such a victory?'

I looked behind me at Lord Harsha, whose bright single eye stared at King Sandarkan; Lord Avijan and Lord Sharad regarded him, too. I looked out toward the gleaming lines of my men still standing in the sun. I knew that I could not hide very much from Waas's crafty king.

'No, I am not willing,' I told him. 'I will never again be the cause of any Valari killing another Valari.'

I took a deep breath, and held it for a count of ten as Master Juwain had taught me. Then I said to King Sandarkan, 'If you are to march with us, it cannot be because of what I have demanded – or *not* demanded. It can only be because you know it is the right thing to do.'

The glimmer in King Sandarkan's dark eyes told me that he *did* know it was right. All that was good and noble within him urged him in this direction. But still he hesitated.

'King Sandarkan,' I murmured to him.

With my deepest sense, I reached out to feel inside his heart for that unbearable tension where fear and fearlessness, weakness and will, hung poised in a delicate balance. I had only, I knew, to touch him lightly in order to push him one way or the other.

'King Valamesh!' he suddenly shouted at me.

When I wielded the valarda to open others' hearts and brighten their spirits, my gift became a sacred sword named Alkaladur. But what should I call this terrible force when desperation drove me to seize hold of a man's heart and choke his very soul?

No, I told myself, *I must not make men into ghuls*!

But it was too late. Like a whisper setting off an avalanche, I felt my will to move King Sandarkan to a right action loose a cascade of raging emotions within him. His own will to push back at me suddenly hardened and grew as unmovable as a mountain.

'King Valamesh,' he asked me, 'do you then offer me a free choice of marching with you to Delu, or not?'

I gritted my teeth against the pain I felt stabbing through my throat. Then I told him, 'Yes, a choice – I do.'

'Then freely,' he snarled at me, 'I tell you this: I will not put my men at such peril. What king who loved his warriors would?'

With a look at King Talanu and then again at me, he said, 'Now, unless you *do* have additional terms to demand of me, I should like to lead my men off this field and begin the march back to our home.

'No, I have no terms to demand,' I told him. 'Go back to Waas.'

King Sandarkan made no farewell either to King Talanu or

myself. He stood up with a jolting abruptness. With his captains, he rode back toward his army still standing in its square formation at the center of the field.

And then my uncle said to me: 'Some men, even Valari kings, are ignoble.'

I took in the gleam of King Sandarkan's emblem, with its two silver swords. What would it be like, I wondered, truly to see my enemy as myself?

Then I said, 'No, King Sandarkan is noble enough, even if he doesn't know it. But how should I expect him to call up his nobility when I can't even find my own?'

In the face of the great defeat that I had just suffered, I knew that this question would torment me on the long road to Delu, and beyond.

14

After the Waashians had left the field to begin their march back to Waas, my army and that of King Talanu remained encamped by the Rajabash River. For four days, I rested my exhausted men while Lord Harsha worked with King Talanu's quartermasters to ensure that we would have enough stores for our journey into Delu. Along the river for three miles, the warm summer air filled with the smells of beef being smoked over oak fires and new battle biscuits roasting. Lord Harsha grumbled that he could not calculate how many provisions our two armies would need because he did not know how far or for how long we must march.

'We will march as far as we must,' I told him one evening as the men gathered around their campfires and listened to Alphanderry sing. 'We will march until Morjin is defeated, and if our provisions run out, we will have to find more along the way.'

The feeding of our armies was only one of my concerns; as the day approached when we must set out upon the road, the question arose as to who should lead them.

'You are the eldest,' I said to King Talanu in my tent later that evening. 'You have fought in a score of battles and have led your warriors in almost as many.'

'I *am* the eldest,' my uncle said. 'But I think I am *too* old.'

In truth, my uncle was much the most ancient of the Valari kings. My mother's father, King Yuravay, had sired him nearly seventy-five years before.

'There is still good wisdom here,' he told me, tapping a gnarled finger against his head. 'But my brain does not work as well as it once did. And therefore I am not so clever or quick.'

He looked around at Lord Sharad and Lord Tanu and my other

captains, and at Prince Viromar and Lord Yarwan and his captains, too. Then he said to me: 'What you propose to accomplish will require both quickness and cleverness, and more, daring and brilliance. These are qualities that *you* possess, King Valamesh. And have put to good use defeating the Red Dragon's forces again and again.'

I bowed my head to acknowledge his honoring of me.

'And therefore,' he continued, 'it is *you* who should lead our armies. And those of the other Valari kingdoms, if ever you can unite them. Once you almost did.'

None present disputed his assertion that I should be warlord of the combined armies of Kaash and Mesh. To seal the new covenant between us, King Talanu called for brandy to be poured into everyone's cup. Everyone toasted my new status then – except for Maram, who loudly reaffirmed that he would touch no spirits until Morjin stood defeated.

'And that great day,' Maram called out as if trying to convince himself more than the grim warriors around him, 'will surely come now that King Valamesh leads the Valari!'

But I, of course, now led only a fraction of the Valari. And although on the morrow I would ride at the head of two armies into Delu, I still did not know where I must lead them.

After King Talanu had returned to his encampment and my captains went off to their beds, I requested that my friends hold council with the Seven to help decide this matter. We took our places at my long table, where Liljana served us tea instead of brandy. I sat sipping from a small blue cup as I looked from Master Juwain to Kane and then at Abrasax.

'I told King Sandarkan,' I said to everyone, 'that we know the plans of the Galdan fleet, but that is not quite true. Hadrik rode from Galda to inform us that the Galdans will soon sail, but he did not know when. And he did not know where our enemies' armies will land.'

I wished that Hadrik had agreed to sit at our council. But this strange knight seemed loath to bear the company of other human beings. I might have tried to command his presence here, but I was not his king, and he called no man master, not even Kane. He roamed our encampment like a lone wolf, and I did not know what role he would play on our march to Delu – that is, if he consented to ride with us at all.

'The *where* and the *when*,' I said to Abrasax, and to everyone. 'If we knew *that*, we would gain a great advantage over our enemies.'

'As to the *where*,' Maram said, swirling his tea in his cup, 'we might make a good guess. Surely our enemy will make use of the beaches along the White Coast.'

He, born of Delu, spoke of that stretch of white sand beaches that began about a hundred miles southwest of Delarid and ran for seventy miles back toward the Morning Mountains and Delu's border with Kaash.

'Even if they do,' Kane said, 'we don't know *which* beach to concentrate on.'

'But we can send out scouts,' Maram said. 'Val can lead the armies as close as he can, and when the scouts make report, we can fall upon our enemy in a lightning stroke.'

I smiled sadly at this because I knew that I would not be likely to bring up our armies very close to our enemy's landing point – not if we had to cover seventy miles of beaches. The lightning stroke that Maram envisioned would degenerate into a slow thrust that our enemy would see coming from miles away.

I turned to Master Matai, sitting next to Abrasax, and I said, 'Can the Master Diviner help us?'

Master Matai's golden skin gleamed in the soft light given off by the stands of candles around the tent. So did his soft brown eyes as he regarded me. 'You ask a good question, King Valamesh: *can* I help you? *Can* I, really?'

'So,' Kane said to him, 'you must keep a kristei, or make use of the Master Galastei's stone. What futures have you seen in your crystal sphere, eh?'

'I am a diviner, it is true,' Master Matai said with a grave formality. 'But I am no scryer. And even if I were and could tell you exactly which beach the men you call your enemy will embark upon, should I then point it out to you so that you can fall upon them with your swords?'

'They are the *enemy*!' Kane snarled out.

'They are men,' Master Matai said, 'who are compelled to fight beneath the Red Dragon's standard. And many of them are from Galda, which I once called home.'

While I remained quiet out of respect for the immense tragedy that had befallen the once-proud kingdom of Galda, Kane wasted not even a glimmer of a tear on useless sentiment. He said to Master Matai: 'Compelled, ha! Your own Brotherhood teaches that all men and women may choose between the light and the dark. In the end, our wills are free!'

'Our wills *are* free,' Abrasax said, intervening on Master Matai's behalf. 'And we do have to choose between the dark and the light. But that choice is difficult at times of twilight, when all the world seems as gray as an ice-fog.'

Then he went on to reaffirm the Brotherhood's ancient stand against war.

'Master Matai,' he told us, 'should not have asked if we *can* help Valashu Elahad. But rather, *may* we? Are we permitted to?'

'You've helped before,' Kane said.

'We helped him to find the Maitreya,' Abrasax said, nodding at Bemossed, who sat at the end of the table between Estrella and Liljana. 'We helped him to recover from his wounds, to his body and soul.'

'And so helped him to become king. And now that he *is* king, you shilly-shally in helping him to fulfill his purpose *as* a king.'

'And what is that purpose?' Master Storr broke in. 'To bring on a war that will burn up the world?'

'No,' Kane said. 'To fight a war that is not of our making, that we cannot avoid. And then, in victory, to end war once and for all.'

I sat quietly feeling the drumbeats of my heart. Kane spoke of my deepest dream almost as if he had made it his own.

'To kill then, in order to end killing?' Master Storr asked.

'Is it better to avoid killing and so bring on annihilation?'

'But do you not see how your way is impossible?'

'Do you not see that men must fight, when they *must* fight? It is what we were born for!'

Master Storr shook his head at this. 'We were born to know the peace of the One. And to honor the Law of the One. And that law says that men must not kill other men.'

'No – it says that the *Elijin* must not kill!'

'Thus, from your own mouth, you damn yourself.'

Kane's eyes caught up the red glow of the candles as he growled out, 'So – then I am damned!'

'As *you* choose,' Master Storr said to him. 'But we of the Brotherhood have devoted ourselves to walking the path of the Elijin and the Galadin, and so we must accustom ourselves to their laws. As with those for mortal men, they are simple.'

'Simple, ha! Nothing about this universe the Ieldra created is simple!'

Master Storr, Elder of the Brotherhood and honored Master Galastei of the Seven, was rich in lore and wisdom and full of years – and even so, Kane looked upon him as if he were a child.

The two men might have gone on arguing through the night if Abrasax had not held up his hand for a truce.

'We have a hard choice to make,' he said, 'and this will not help.'

He looked at me then, and his eyes seemed to hold whole universes inside. It gave me great hope that although Abrasax tried to live by simple principles, he never interpreted them simply.

'As I have said,' he told me, 'twilight is now upon the world, and we must do our best to see our way through it. We have many miles still to go on our march. Let my brothers and me confer along the way. When we come to Delu, we shall tell you if we will help you.'

I bowed my head to him, then gazed at Bemossed sitting within a deep silence at the other end of the table. He spoke no words to me that night, nor to anyone else, but his soft, pained eyes seemed to ask me how much longer I could go on killing when I knew that this violence must inevitably turn back upon myself and those I loved?

The next morning, the armies of Mesh and Kaash set out for Delu. I led forth with the Guardians and my friends riding in the van near me, and we kept to the same formation as we had in our crossing of the Wendrush. Behind the rear of the Meshian army, King Talanu and his captains rode at the head of the Kaashans. There might have been a better way to organize and move our combined forces, but I thought that my countrymen and our allies would do best fighting alongside their own people, and to be captained by lords whom they knew and trusted. Like a two-headed man, it might prove harder to coordinate this union of warriors who must go into battle as a single army. I had immense faith, however, in our army's other head. King Talanu remained a *king*, and so would not simply receive my commands as must Lord Tanu or Lord Tomavar. But neither, I knew, would he lead his warriors in a way that contradicted me or mine. With every mile farther that we marched along the Rajabash River, with every pause to confer with each other or take our meals together at our nightly encampments, I came to know my uncle better, as he did me. As the days passed and we pushed our way into the eastern mountains of Kaash, I had a strange sense that King Talanu's will was becoming as my own.

For five days we kept to the good road that followed the winding course of the Rajabash, which flowed mostly north toward Waas. Our way took us through thick forests beneath high mountains. At a town called Antas, we came to the Char, a tributary of the Rajabash, and there we turned almost due east. King Talanu came forward to speak with me and to point out the road through the Char Valley that would lead us part of the way to Delu. At the valley's end, he said, we would find it a hard road of steep grades and bridges over swift rivers; three passes we must cross, though none so difficult as the route that my warriors had taken around the back of Mount Ihsan.

And so for the next nine days we labored on toward the east. The forest here showed many willows and maples of a kind that I had never seen. Flowers, in the warm Marud sun, bloomed along the roadside and from bushes beneath the overhanging trees. Many animals dwelt here: raccoons and badgers, rabbits, skunks and deer. King Talanu claimed that these eastern reaches of his realm were a hunter's paradise, and I saw no reason to doubt him. But as the mountains grew more steep and rugged, this rough land became a wilderness where even hunters must take care where they tread. And my warriors, I thought, were a whole army of hunters in search of men instead of beasts.

The weather favored us, for we endured no heavy rains or unbearable nights. The men marched as hard as they could without wearing themselves to the bone. We suffered no mortal accidents on the rough roads leading over chasms and winding up across broken rock. One unfortunate incident occurred on our descent from Mount Makara. One of my warriors, Sar Aragar, keeping pace at the head of Lord Tanu's columns, managed to turn his boot in a pothole and sprain his ankle. Joshu Kadar happened to be riding in the vanguard not far ahead of him, and he immediately offered to bear Sar Aragar back to the wagons on the back of his horse. But this displeased Lord Tanu, who stood before Joshu Kadar and said to him: 'When battle comes, you'll be off with the cavalry and won't be able to take time helping fallen foot warriors. Sar Aragar can wait by the side of the road for the wagons to catch up to us.'

'But there is no need for him to wait!' Joshu Kadar called out. 'Let me take him back to Master Juwain before the swelling grows too great!'

'Sar Aragar's companions can wrap the wound,' Lord Tanu told him testily. He looked out at the patches of snow covering the tundra around us. 'And cool it, too.'

'But Lord Tanu, there is no need for such austerity and –'

'No need? What does a young knight know of *need*?'

Joshu wisely broke off his dispute with Lord Tanu. After all, he bore only two diamonds in his knight's ring while Lord Tanu was a lord of great renown who commanded nearly half my army. Then Joshu came forward to complain of Lord Tanu's callousness.

'The man has no heart,' I overheard him say to Sar Shivalad. 'It is a crime that such a nasty old bag of bile should have wed my Sarai!'

I remembered that, after the Culhadosh Commons, Lord Garvar had given young Sarai Garvar in marriage to Lord Tanu instead of to Joshu. I felt Joshu's hot, throbbing jealousy almost as my own. But I could not allow his passions to turn poisonous and deadly.

'Lord Tanu,' I said to Joshu that night in my tent, 'is a true Valari and so has heart enough. My father always said that of all his captains, Lord Tanu had the greatest talent for forging men as hard as diamonds. We will need all this hardness, and more, before very long. As I need Lord Tanu. And so I must ask you to stay away from him before your quarrel results in a duel.'

'Very well, Sire,' Joshu said to me, reluctantly bowing his head. 'You may be sure that I will stay as far from him as I can, on the march or the battlefield. But do not expect me to weep if our enemy cuts him down.'

If discord lurked always among my warriors as it did all Valari, and indeed all men, at least I could give thanks that no worse arguments broke out among them. I knew that while Lord Tanu might not be moved to easy pity for Sar Aragar, he would gladly throw himself at a dozen of our enemy in order to protect him if the need arose. Most of my warriors, I knew, felt that way about most of their companions, even the Kaashans who would line up in battle by their sides. And so we marched across the mountains toward Delu, and on the brightest of days with the sun shining down warm and good upon us, we were like thousands of brothers who must soon fight and die as if we were one.

At last, late on the seventh day of Soal, we came to a bridge over the Ianthe River, which marked the border of Delu. On the other side of this clear water rose yet more mountains, though slightly less high than those of Kaash.

That night in my tent my friends and I again met with the Seven. And again Bemossed fell into a troubled silence as Abrasax spoke for the other masters: 'We have decided that we must help you after all, Valashu Elahad. We do evil, we fear, in putting a sword into your hand. But it might prove an even greater evil to refuse you.'

He went on to say that just as there could be no real distinction between matter and the numinous force that animated it, so men could not always keep separate a war of the spirit from a war of the sword.

'You asked Master Matai if he might be able to divine the *where* and the *when* of the landing of the Galdan fleet,' he told us. 'Although we can have no certain knowledge of this, we have been able to formulate a good guess. Master Matai?'

Abrasax turned toward the Master Diviner, who said, 'The *when* of the landing will depend on that of the fleet's sailing. And that date, I feel in my heart, *is* nearly certain.'

He went on to tell us that he had spoken with the aloof Hadrik as to the Galdans' and Karabukers' preparations for war. Hadrik had offered his calculation that the Galdan fleet could not possibly have made ready to sail before the middle of Marud.

'And the fleet,' Master Matai told us, 'must sail from Tervola, for no other port can accommodate such a gathering of ships. And so our enemy, as you call them, will have to sail up around the Ram's Cape and then cross the Terror Bay, at this time of year, mostly against wind and tides. Ten days such a journey will take, perhaps twelve – more if there are storms. But the Galdan sea captains will do everything they can to avoid such storms. As I should know, for my father's father commanded a bilander named the *Maiden's Hope*.'

Master Matai's fine face broke into dozens of radiating lines as he grew more thoughtful and seemed slightly embarrassed. 'And the captains will almost surely seek for fair weather by casting for good omens.'

'Ah, will they go to a haruspex then?' Maram asked. 'Who could think to find clues to the future in the bloody guts of a slaughtered goat or some other poor beast?'

'No, they will *not* go to a haruspex,' Master Matai told him, smiling as he shook his head. 'And neither will the fleet's diviners practice hydromancy or sortilege. No, certainly not. They will look to the stars, even as we do.'

He paused, then added, 'But not *quite* as we do. In Galda, outside of our schools, they practiced the Old Eaean astrology – and still do. It remains more superstition than studied art. In employing that system, which posits the earth as the center of all things, I have found a strong omen most propitious for sailing: when Argald covers Belleron, with Elad on the ascendent. Which occurred on the second of Soal.'

'Five days ago,' I said. 'If the Galdan astrologers also found this omen, then do you believe that the fleet would have waited to sail?'

'It is too strong for them *not* to have found it. And followed it. And so, yes, I believe they would have waited.'

'Then if you are right, the fleet will make landfall in another five days – perhaps seven. Therefore we must cross Delu, nearly a hundred miles, in five days.'

Through mountains and across hills, I thought, this march might nearly kill my men.

'We can always hope for a great sea-storm,' Maram put in.

I looked down the table at Estrella, sitting within a deep calm, as she often did. I remembered how, with the aid of a blue gelstei that she had gained from the Lokii, she had summoned a storm in the middle of the Red Desert. But I did not think that even this strangely powerful girl could direct a storm at an unseen fleet of ships across hundreds of miles.

'The only storm we can count on,' I said to Maram, 'is that of our spears and swords when we surprise our enemy. And so we *must* reach the sea by the 12th, at the latest – if Master Matai is right.'

Here Master Juwain, whom the Seven had asked to join them, looked at me and said, 'I believe he is, Val. We have all of us given this much thought.'

'But sometimes,' Liljana said to him, citing his greatest fault, 'you think *too* much.'

She did not need to add that in the Skadarak, Master Juwain had been seized by a terrible temptation to steal Liljana's gelstei and force his way into Morjin's mind.

'It is true, I know,' Master Juwain said. 'Sometimes I've wanted to suppose that I could divine the Red Dragon's plans and outthink him.'

He sighed and took a sip of tea. 'And that is the path of pride and ruin. It might prove even worse, however, to suppose that the Red Dragon will always outthink us. He is not so brilliant as he thinks he is.'

He took another sip of tea as he looked from Kane to Bemossed, then added, 'In his powers, he might be greater than anyone else in this tent. He *might* be. But when we put our minds together, to say nothing of our spirits, I believe that we can penetrate his plans.'

'Yes, by determining the *when* of the fleet's sailing,' I said, bowing my head to Master Juwain and then Master Matai. 'But what of the *where* of its landing?'

At this Master Matai cracked a bright smile and said to me, 'Now we enter into the realm of legend and supposition. But legend, if accepted unquestioningly, can gain the force of what is real. And supposition, if carefully constructed, can be a set of steps leading to the truth.'

Then he went on to relate a bit of history and tell us where he thought the Galdan fleet would land: 'In the year 1610 of the Age of Swords, Darrum the Great of Galda led a fleet to invade Delu. And King Alok Arani sailed forth with the Delian fleet to meet them in a great sea battle in the Terror Bay. It is recorded that they fought to a draw, though both sides claimed victory. The Delians lost a greater number of ships, while the Galdans lost King Darrum – to a fire arrow that pierced his eye, it is said.'

Master Matai took a slow sip of tea as if he had all the time in the world to relate his story. I waited for him to continue, as did Kane, Liljana and the rest of us.

'It is also said,' Master Matai finally told us, 'that the Galdans did not bear King Darrum's body back to Galda nor did they sink him into the sea. Instead, a Galdan ship named the *Sky Dragon* landed in secret on Delu's White Coast. The Galdans buried him beneath the sands there. They said that if Darrum the Great could not conquer Delu in life, he might yet in death. For the place where his bones lay, they said, would ever after be Galdan soil. And someday, the Galdans would come to this place and claim it for their own.'

Maram, who could stand the suspense no longer, fairly shouted at Master Matai: 'Well, where on that forsaken coast *is* this place? You must know, or you would not torment us so!'

Master Matai took yet another sip of tea as if relishing the discipline of patience. Then he told us, 'If the legend is true, they buried King Darrum between two great rocks rising up from a broad, flat beach.'

'The Pillars of Heaven!' Maram said. 'When I was a boy, I stood beneath them! The beach from which they arise is called the Seredun Sands.'

Upon his pronouncement of this name, something inside me clicked as with a key perfectly fitting into a lock.

'The Pillars of Heaven, indeed,' Master Matai said. 'In Galda, for ages, the soothsayers have foretold that one day, Darrum the Great's spirit would return to guide the Galdans. It is said that an army marching through the Pillars over King Darrum's bones will gain invincibility and the greatest of victories.'

I nodded my head at this, then asked, 'And where on the White Coast is this Seredun Sands?'

'Near its midpoint, a few miles to the north,' Master Matai said.

I closed my eyes for a moment, calculating distances and time. Then I looked at Master Matai and Abrasax, and each of the Seven, and I told them, 'Thank you. Then tomorrow we will set out for this beach.'

I did not give voice to my fears for what might befall upon these distant sands, nor did I imagine that Abrasax and the other good Masters of the Brotherhood would wish to hear them.

The next day, just before dawn, I sent envoys riding over the Ianthe River toward King Santoval Marshayk's palace in Delarid. As soon as my army entered his kingdom – the Delians would call it an invasion – alarms would be sent out in any case. I wanted King Santoval to know the general course that my army would take and why we marched.

'Is that wise?' Maram said to me as we stood before the bridge over the Ianthe. 'My father's court is full of those sympathetic to Morjin. I'm ashamed to tell you that the Way of the Dragon has put down some very deep roots in my homeland's poor soil. My father, himself, will certainly fear Morjin more than he does the Galdans – or you. And so *someone* will certainly send word to Morjin of our plans.'

'Yes, someone will,' I told him, 'no matter what we do. Our army cannot move through Delu unnoticed. But if Master Matai is right, the Galdans are now likely five days at sea. We must hope that in the next five days, Morjin will not have time to learn of what we intend. Or if he does, that he will not be able to inform King Mansul.'

'Always,' Maram said, 'we seem to find ourselves in circumstances in which fate forces us to hope too much.'

'Is it too much, then, that when the odds favor us, the dice should fall our way?'

'No, my friend, it is not – not unless Morjin breathes his foul breath upon them.' He sighed then shook his head. 'But at least we can count on one thing: my father will oppose neither our army nor our enemy. He will wait to see how things fall out between us.'

'If we gain a victory,' I said, 'we can hope that he will join us.'

'We can *hope* that,' he told me. 'But that, it seems to me, truly is wishing for a miracle.'

After that, I led our army into Delu. No garrison guarded the passage into this realm, nor did the local lords send any knights or soldiers to oppose us. For hundreds of years, there had been peace between Delu and Kaash, and the Delian kings could not afford to spend any force protecting such a wild frontier. Few people lived in this mountainous region, and those who did kept to themselves and tried to mind their own business. They might have fled at the approach of an army marching out of a foreign land, but we Valari had never pillaged or raped, even in the worst of wars. Then, too, I sent out envoys through the countryside to inform the poor farmers and hunters that we would not requisition supplies but would pay good gold and silver for whatever food and forage the local Delians could sell us. In this way, we gained their good will and acquiescence to our purpose, if not their friendship.

The roads we found to take us toward the east had nearly crumbled into dirt tracks or sheets of scree, but at least we were able to get our wagons down them. The first day of our passage through Delu proved the most difficult, for we had to work our way up and over a pass known as the Eagle's Nest. On the other side, however, the Morning Mountains lost elevation with nearly every mile, and soon fell off into a succession of lines of old, worn hills. As the land grew ever more gentle, the rises were blanketed in black ash, oak, chestnut and red poplar while through the valleys grew beech, walnut and elm. Wild grape hung thick about the trees' trunks, and it was the time of year when the plum trees grew heavy with their purple fruits. Maram, often riding alongside me, remarked that Delu was a fair land that had a sad, violent history. He might, I thought, have been speaking of Ea herself and all the misfortunes of the last eighteen thousand years.

The next four days we spent in our rush to the sea. Urgency drove us to pound forth over rocky roads and fairly swim our way through slips of mud and around bogs. Twelve wagons suffered broken wheels or axles, and we had to abandon them. And my men *truly* suffered, mostly from cramping muscles, shin splints and bleeding feet; no matter how hard they might be, men were still made of flesh that could too easily be exhausted, broken or worn by wet boots right off their bones. Forty-six warriors had to fall out of their columns on the third day of our march, and by the fifth day, another hundred and twenty. I could not, however, simply abandon *them*. We cleared out stores from another two dozen wagons, inside of which the wounded rested and waited for Master Juwain and our other healers to attend them. It was a measure of my warriors' spirits, I thought, that to a man they pleaded with Master Juwain to make them whole and ready for the day of battle.

On the 11th of Soal, I sent outriders to the east to scout the countryside ahead of us, all the way to the sea. That night, as we made camp in a valley full of walnut orchards and potato farms, one of these riders returned with good news – and bad.

'Sire,' a young knight named Sar Galajay said to me in the relative quiet of my tent, 'the sea is close: less than half a day's march from here. We found the place called the Seredun Sands and the Pillars of Heaven. And great rocks they are, black as coal and rising two hundred feet above the beach. Such white sands! I've never seen their like! It is a *perfect* place for a battle! The beach is half a mile wide and stretches north and south for as far as the eye can see. Three hills block the way to it. If we are careful, they will cover our approach. The enemy would have no sight of us, only . . .'

His voice died into the crackling of many fires and the other sounds of our encampment. I waited for him to go on, and he added, 'Only, there is no enemy! Nothing but empty sands and the wind blowing them into little mounds like sugar.'

'Thank you,' I said to him, nodding my head. I tried to fight down my great disappointment and make good of his news. 'Then the hardships of our march have not been in vain. Surely our enemy will make landfall tomorrow or on the day after that.'

Sar Galajay did not gainsay my optimistic words or point out that Master Matai might have been wrong and our enemy might land far to the north or south of the Seredun Sands – or indeed, might have come ashore already. While Lords Sharad, Tanu, Harsha and Tomavar looked on, Sar Galajay tried to pick up on my forced high spirits, saying to me, 'We are hoping you are right, Sire. Sar Siravay and Sar Torald remain in the hills above the beach, watching for our enemy's approach.'

Later that night, I stood around a fire with Kane and Bemossed, and others, listening to Alphanderry sing. He gave the warriors verses from an ancient epic to inspirit them and ignite their valor. He praised the warriors' true essence, which shone the same in all men and women, as it did within the One, and could never be extinguished:

Who takes up sword to rend and slay,
Cut men from life like sheaves of hay?
To feel, in blood, the noblest need,
With honor do the dreadful deed?

'Tis evil killing men in war,
Reduce their dreams to pain and gore,
But worse to suffer evil kings
To make free men their underlings.

They truly live, thus they are free
Who know their immortality;
The soul abides, its sacred light
Shines on through death forever bright.

Brave warriors neither fear nor mourn:
The blessed flame is never born,
Within its blaze all living lies,
It always is and never dies.

No sword nor axe nor lance nor mace
Can violate the soul's true face,
No dart can pierce nor knife nor spear,
So fight, with honor, do not fear . . .

I had never heard Alphanderry sing so powerfully before. His voice seemed to call down the very fire of the stars. When he had finished and put away his mandolet, Bemossed stood in deep contemplation, staring at him. And then he finally murmured to me: 'Do you really think there will be a battle, Valashu?'

'Yes,' I told him, 'I do.'

Kane's savage face gleamed in the firelight as he turned toward the east and sniffed the air. 'So, there *will* be – I can smell it coming, even as I can the sea.'

My senses were not so keen as his, nor were Bemossed's. But he possessed an exquisite sensitivity to life that Kane seemed to lack. He looked for Kane through the night's gloom, and he asked him, 'Are you not afraid then?'

'Have you listened to none of Alphanderry's song?' Kane replied. 'Ha, afraid! – of what, then? Death?'

'No – of living. At having to survive yet another battle.'

'Ha!' Kane growled out again. 'You might as well ask an old

wolf if he fears killing and filling his belly with good meat and his blood with new life so that he can run across the snow all night and then stand howling at the splendor of the moon!'

Even as he spoke these words, his eyes filled with deep lights, and he gazed out at the disc of silver rising above the wooded hills in the eastern sky. I wondered if this same bright orb shone down upon a fleet of ships sailing at this moment straight toward us.

'Your way,' Bemossed said to him, 'is war, while mine must be of peace.'

'What *peace*, then?'

'The peace of the One. The stillness of the moon and stars that we must learn to bring to men, here on earth.' He turned toward me to meet my gaze. I had never seen a man who seemed so tired or old deep inside his soul – in some ways, older even than Kane. 'Valashu, is there no way to stop this battle?'

I thought of Morjin and how he had clawed his fingers into Atara's eyes; I thought of my mother and grandmother nailed to wooden planks, and of my brothers who had been speared and cleaved upon the Culhadosh Commons. Then I said to Bemossed, 'Only if my heart can be stopped from beating.'

'But what if you gain the advantage over the Galdans and the Karabukers, forcing them into a bad position as you did King Sandarkan? Could you not force them to surrender?'

'Our enemy's army,' I told him, 'is ten times the size of ours. With such numbers, they will never surrender.'

'You do not know that.'

'I *do* know,' I told him. 'If King Mansul surrendered to such a force of Valari, Morjin would crucify *him*.'

'But what if you could persuade the Karabukers and Galdans to change sides? And so add another 150,000 men to your army?'

'The Dragon's soldiers, changing sides!' I cried out. 'Impossible!'

Bemossed moved a step closer to me, and I could almost feel his soft breath falling over my face. Something vast and irresistible moved within him then, and the force of his words struck me like a whirlwind: 'Nothing is impossible, King Valamesh. There must be a way – how often have you, yourself, said this?'

There must be a way to end war, I told myself for the ten thousandth time. *But how?*

As I gazed at Bemossed, the tiredness seemed to leave him, and he smiled at me. His face seemed even brighter than the moon. In that moment, I wanted to believe that all things were possible. But then I chanced to lay my hand on the hilt of my sword, and

I felt a terrible power coursing through it, and me. And I said to Bemossed, 'I am sorry, but we cannot avoid this battle. If I called for our enemy's surrender, we would give up our surprise. Our enemy would kill many of us, too many, perhaps even all, and our cause would be lost.'

As I told him this, the weariness came over him again. He slumped as if his sinews had been cut. He gazed at me, and I wondered if he regarded his dispute with me as yet another exhausting battle that must be fought, as he must ever contend with Morjin.

'King Valamesh, they call you now,' he said to me. 'King of Mesh. But what will it take, friend, for you to behold your true realm?'

Then he excused himself, and went off to his tent. For another hour, I stood talking with Kane about stratagems for war. I tried to sleep after that; perhaps I spent a short while in a land of dreams. Just before dawn, however, I was awakened by the hoofbeats and panting of a horse galloping up to my pavilion. I came out to greet Sar Siravay, a much-scarred warrior with ten battle ribbons tied to his long hair. And then he told me that he and Sar Torald had sighted the ghostly white sails of our enemy's ships far out upon the moonlit sea.

15

At dawn, we marched east, straight toward the beach that my outriders had described. Our course took us through a valley and then through a cleft in the forested hills. Late that morning we came out into a long dell, where three low hills stood between us and the sea. From a woodcutter, one of my outriders had learned their names: Tirza, to our left, on the north, and Urza in the center. To our right rose the largest of these hills: a roundish mass sparsely covered with some oaks and bushes. Magda, the locals called it.

I dismounted and climbed to the top of this hill, along with Kane and my captains, as well as Prince Viromar and Sar Yarwan. At its top, we peered out from behind trees to study the beach below. My outriders had made an accurate report of it. To the north, perhaps a mile beyond the slopes of Tirza, two immense black monoliths rose up from the white beach sands. I guessed that they must be made of basalt or some other hard rock. I wondered if the Galdans long ago had really buried King Darrum between them. I wondered, too, if the Galdans would soon try to pass through these Pillars of Heaven, for as I saw, Master Matai's divination had proved true and now much of the Galdan army had already put ashore.

Across a distance of half a mile, I looked out upon a confusion of tens of thousands of men crowding the beach like ants. They gathered in groups of ten or twenty, and seemed without organization. Casks and crates of supplies had been strewn about the beach; I saw men breaking open the crates with hammers and emptying their contents into packs that they would bear on the march. Other men stood knee-deep in water at the shore's edge, coaxing whinnying horses down the gangplanks of rowboats. None of these beasts had been fitted with armor; indeed, only a few of the men had yet donned their suits of mail or steel-enforced leather, for our enemy clearly did not expect to do battle that day, and perhaps not even that week. Shields stood piled in heaps, and spears had been stuck down in the sand in rows. Many of the soldiers wore nothing more than tunics, with their swords nowhere near at hand. A good thousand of them stood naked in the shallows, bathing in the waters of the Terror Bay, where hundreds of ships lay anchored with their white sails gleaming in the sunlight. Travel at sea, as I knew, could be a cramped, foul affair, and so who could blame these soldiers for trying to get clean?

The Karabukers, tall, black-skinned men who favored the spear above the sword, had disembarked on the beach to our left across from Tirza and the northern half of Urza. They were grouped in no better array. I could not make out a single, formed unit in all this manswarm and piles of weapons and gear. I looked for the standards of the Karabukers' lords and captains, but of course they were hard to distinguish. In all the Dragon Kingdoms save Sunguru, not even the most renowned knight or lord was permitted to bear his own arms. The common soldiers wore yellow garments showing clusters of small red dragons, while King Mansul himself would be draped in a golden surcoat emblazoned with a three-quarter sized dragon. I wondered if the enemy's king had led the way ashore, or still remained aboard his ship. Although such masses of men were difficult to count, I estimated that at least nine tenths of both the Karabukers and Galdans had made landfall.

Without a word, I motioned to my captains and the Kaashans to follow me down the back slopes of the hill. We met up with King Talanu about half a mile to the west, along the banks of a little stream. We held council on horseback, and I described to King Talanu what I had seen from the top of Magda. Then we quickly laid our plans for battle.

'Many of the Galdans on the other side of that hill,' I said to King Talanu, pointing up at Magda, 'invaded Mesh at Morjin's command two years ago. My warriors would do best fighting them. But are you willing to go against the Karabukers?'

'I am,' he told me, fingering the hilt of his kalama. 'But the Karabukers outnumber the Galdans, while my warriors are fewer in number than yours, King Valamesh. Will any of yours be willing to join me?'

I nodded my head at this. King Talanu's suggestion was the logical solution to the situation we faced, but I wanted him to come to it on his own and give voice to it, that it should not seem that I was commanding him.

'They would be honored,' I told him, 'to march with you.'

We arranged that Lord Sharad's cavalry and most of Lord Tomavar's battalions would form up with the Kaashans behind the gap between Tirza and Urza. The rest of the Meshian cavalry, which I would lead with Lord Avijan, and Lord Tanu's infantry along with two battalions of Lord Tomavar's, would take position between Urza and Magda. Then, upon a signal, the two halves of our army would debouch from the two gaps between the hills and fall upon our enemy.

'What you propose, Sire,' Lord Tanu said to me, 'will require precise coordination. Our two forces will have to charge from either gap at full speed in column, and then deploy into line obliquely over a distance of nearly a mile so as to meet up in front of the middle hill.'

He made a sour face as he pointed at the tree-covered Urza rising above the stream.

'If any battle lord in the Morning Mountains,' I said to him, 'can lead such a maneuver, it is you, Lord Tanu.'

Then I turned to Lord Tomavar and added, 'And you.'

At this, Lord Tomavar's long face broke into a huge smile, so glad was he to be acclaimed. He seemed almost to have forgotten that he had nearly become King of Mesh instead of me.

'Sire,' he said to me, 'the strategy is a bold one, but our two forces *must* meet, and quickly. As soon as the first of us emerges from between the hills, our enemy will spot us and give the alarm. We cannot afford to let any part of their army form up and force a wedge between us.'

'No, we cannot,' I said, stating the obvious. 'What do you suggest?'

I knew that Lord Tomavar, famed as Mesh's finest and most daring tactician, would propose a solution to the problem at hand, and I had a fair idea of what that would be.

'Do not,' he said, 'deploy all our cavalry to guard our flanks. Instead, lead half of them at a charge at our enemy's center. Strike terror into their heart, and keep them from organizing. That will give Lord Tanu and me time to close up our lines and advance.'

I noticed King Talanu staring at me, along with Prince Viromar, Lord Sharad, Lord Avijan and many others. If I took Lord Tomavar's advice, I would find myself galloping straight toward the most dangerous part of the battlefield. I did not pause to wonder if Lord

Tomavar harbored a wish that I might be killed; his plan, after all, was only what *I* had planned from nearly the moment when I had laid eyes upon our enemy. In any case, a king, a Valari king, must go first into the deadliest part of a battle, if that is where fate calls him to go.

'Very well,' I said to him. I turned to Lord Sharad. 'Then will you help guard the Kaashans' flank?'

'Yes, Sire,' he said, bowing his head to me.

'And you, Lord Avijan,' I said to the man who had championed my kingship. 'Will you guard *our* flank?'

'I will, Sire,' he told me with a quick smile.

Now I nudged my horse over to my uncle, King Talanu Solaru, who had perhaps survived more more battles than any warrior in all the Nine Kingdoms. I said to him, 'It falls to us then to lead the attack against our enemy's center. Let us meet by the sea and fight our enemy side by side.'

He nodded his head at this, and we clasped hands and looked into each other's eyes.

'At the signal, then, we shall charge,' he said to me. 'But King Valamesh – are you sure of this signal?'

Was I sure? I wondered. *How could I ever be entirely sure of my best friend*?

I glanced at Maram, bunched with the other knights of my vanguard against the base of Urza. He sat on his horse drinking from a waterskin. From the gleam of his eyes and the greed with which he sucked at this container, I knew that he had somehow filled it with brandy. In watching me watch him, I saw that he knew that I knew he had once again broken his vow. He seemed not to care. With battle only minutes away, he was doing all that he could to fortify himself so that he could carry out his duty.

'Sar Maram!' I called to him. 'King Talanu would like to know if you will be able to get a little fire out of that crystal of yours?'

As everyone turned to look at Maram, he put away his water-skin. He took out his long, red gelstei and shook it in the air. 'No, I will not get a *little* fire out of this. I will burn the very sky! Wait and see, King Talanu! Watch and marvel!'

It came time to move our forces into the gaps between the hills, and this my captains and King Talanu's did. The terrain and the trees gave us good cover. With Sar Galajay riding beside me, I led Lord Tanu's battalions and Lord Avijan's cavalry between Urza and Magda. Only with difficulty did these seven thousand men crowd into this rocky space. Indeed, a good part of my force had to queue up behind the vanguard in a line that stretched nearly back to our baggage train and encampment. There, the Seven would wait with Liljana and the children. There, Master Juwain and the other healers would prepare the healing pavilion to receive the wounded, laying out their gleaming steel knives, clamps, arrow pullers and saws.

Altaru, fitted with steel armor that protected his neck, throat, chest and hindquarters, carried me between the hills rising steeply to either side. Hundreds of other horses clopped their hooves against the stony ground as the knights of the vanguard moved into position through the trees. I feared that this thunderous sound would carry out to the unseen beach beyond. Lord Tanu's warriors marched behind the vanguard in good order. I had commanded them to leave their ankles free from their silver bells – until just after Maram gave the signal to attack. If the noise of our approach did not give us away, I feared that the flash of our diamond armor would. And so, as the beach and our enemy came into view between the trees ahead of us, I called for a halt. It would be better to have to charge an extra hundred yards than to expose ourselves too soon.

I waited on horseback on a bare patch of ground listening to the distant crashing of the sea; near me gathered Maram, Kane, Lord Avijan and many others, including my Guardians: Lord Vikan, Sar Jonavay, Sar Shivalad, Siraj the Younger and Joshu Kadar. I knew that King Talanu must at this moment be forming up *his* knights in the gap between Urza and Tirza. I tried to give him all the time I could to make ready. I stared out at the dots of thousands of Galdan soldiers scattered and clumped across the beach. I listened to the wind whipping sand over sand, and I prayed that none of our enemy would look our way just yet and cry out that they were under attack.

'Maram!' I finally whispered, looking at the man with whom I had journeyed so many miles. 'Are you ready?'

Maram sat on top of his big horse, holding his red gelstei in place of a lance or sword. He wore a full suit of diamond armor, however, and bore a small triangular shield emblazoned with his new coat of arms: a golden bear against a blue field. His face had fallen all waxy and white as if he had lost his courage. He belched, twice, and seemed in danger of losing his breakfast as well.

'Ah, *am* I ready?' he said, as if addressing the sky. 'How can a man ever *truly* be ready for such work as lies ahead of us today?'

I could feel him swallowing back the acids that burned his throat.

He looked at me then as if beholding a corpse, and his terrible fear became my own. I thought of Atara, standing over my grave and weeping. I prayed that I would live through the day so that she did not have to suffer the anguish of my death.

Atara, Atara, I thought, *where are you now?*

Kane, sitting on his horse by my side, gripped his long lance with a savage glee. He seemed to revel in the strange joy of suffering life's anguish again and again.

'All right,' I finally said to Maram. 'Give the signal!'

With yet another belch, Maram aimed his crystal at the sky above the beach. We all waited for fire to streak out of its pointed end.

'Nothing!' I heard Sar Shivalad murmur. 'The gelstei still sleeps!'

For a while, as the sun rose higher above us and sent arrows of fire streaking down through the air, Maram tried to get a flame out of his crystal. But nothing seemed to wake it up.

'Sire,' Lord Avijan said, upon riding over to me. 'Perhaps we should have the trumpeters give the call.'

To our left, the rocks and trees of Urza stretched for almost a mile to the gap between this fat hill and Tirza, where King Talanu's force gathered. I doubted if the blare of a hundred trumpets could carry so far up and around it.

'No,' I said to Lord Avijan, 'Sar Maram will not fail us – you will see!'

Again, Maram shook his red firestone at the sky. But still the crystal remained as cool as a ruby.

'Maram,' I whispered. 'Concentrate on what Abrasax and the Seven taught you about moving your own fires up through your chakras.'

'What do you think I *was* concentrating on?'

'Who can know?' I told him. 'But perhaps you were thinking how you might never see Behira again – or any other woman.'

'Well – what if I was?'

I smiled at this, even beneath the stares of the knights of the vanguard and the many warriors massed behind them and waiting to charge across the beach. And I said to Maram, 'Why don't you think of that woman, then? The one your heart has always burned for?'

It was not Maram's heart that usually flared with his fierce desire for a woman. But now, with death so near, he closed his eyes to look for that glorious and fiery place within him. And then, a few moments later when he opened them to gaze at his red gelstei, a great gout of flame streaked out of it like lightning to fill up the sky.

'The signal!' someone cried out. 'Sar Maram gives the signal!'

Above the beach, the sky itself seemed to have caught fire, as its blueness burned away to an incandescent crimson. Tens of thousands of our enemy jerked their heads back to gaze up in wonderment and fear.

'Bells on!' I heard someone call out from the columns of warriors behind the cavalry. There came that eerie jangle of thousands of men fastening their silver bells about their ankles.

Now Maram's crystal finally fell quiet again. But King Talanu and his knights on the other side of the hill could not have failed to see its fire.

'Attack!' I shouted, pointing my long lance straight ahead of me. 'For your brothers who fell at the Culhadosh Commons, for Mesh, for Ea – attack!'

As I put my heels to Altaru's flanks and urged my huge horse forward, I noticed that Bemossed had disobeyed my command to ensure his safety and had come up from our encampment. He stood up on the side of the hill, out of the army's way. From this perch between two gnarled oak trees overlooking the beach, he would have sight of the entire battlefield.

It took only moments for Altaru to pound across the rough terrain between the hills and come out of the trees upon a stretch of grassy ground that fronted the beach. The wind whipped through my helmet and vibrated the swan feathers forming its crest. I led my hundreds of knights veering left toward the center of the army stretched out ahead of us, even as Lord Avijan and his knights moved off in a flanking maneuver to our far right. From out of the woods between Urza and Tirza a mile away, I saw King Talanu burst forth in a gallop toward the beach. The white tiger emblazoned on his surcoat shone in the sun. He, too, led his knights on a charge toward our enemy's center.

The Galdans and Karabukers now began running in every direction, colliding with each other and cursing, shouting and grabbing for their armor and weapons. I could feel waves of terror washing across the beach.

'Valari!' I called out as loudly as I could. 'Today the Valari fight as one!'

Soon my knights and I came to the upper reaches of the beach. Our pace slowed as our horses' hooves worked for purchase against the soft, shifting sands. Sar Galajay, riding near Joshu Kadar who

244

held up my standard with its swan and stars, seemed discouraged at this – and surprised. This man of mountains might have looked upon the beach from afar, but he had never tried to run across one or make his horse do so. He must have realized, in a moment, that this beach would not be a perfect place after all to engage a battle.

'The Valari!' came the cry from across the beach. 'Arm yourself! The Valari are upon us!'

Arrows loosed by our enemy's archers whined through the air; one of them clacked against the diamonds covering my chest and another pinged off my helm. And still another found a joint in Viku Aradam's armor and stuck out of his shoulder. He bore the shock of it in silence. But these feathered shafts flew at us in sparse numbers, for most of the Galdan and Karabuk archers scrambled to find arrows at all and had time for only a couple of volleys before we pounded right up to them.

'The Valari!' I heard men shouting. 'Form up against the Valari!'

But we gave our enemy no time to form up; we galloped straight toward the disorganized mass of men frantically trying to bring spears or shields – or even hammers – to bear against my knights.

'The Diamond Warriors!' someone cried out. 'They come! Look! Listen!'

From behind me came the ringing of hundreds of thousands of silver bells. I turned quickly about in my saddle to see the Kaashans and Lord Tomavar's battalions deploy across the beach, exactly as we had planned. I smiled to see the black tower emblazoned on Lord Tomavar's white shield. He led his warriors in a near-run to close ranks with Lord Tanu's force spreading out from between Urza and Magda. And then my knights and I fell upon our enemy, and I had no time to look at anything except the spears, axes and swords sweeping toward me in a circle of death.

I lost my lance almost immediately through the chest of a huge Galdan soldier, who stood naked except for one boot that he had managed to pull on. He screamed and cut at the lance with a short sword that he had found in the heaps of weapons around him. I screamed, too, silently, at his terrible, piercing anguish, and I nearly fell from my horse even as the soldier fell, ripping the lance from my hands. I drew Alkaladur then. Its flaring silustria cast a brilliant silver radiance across the beach. It made the Galdans gasp out in fear even as it gave me strength to endure the agony being wreaked upon men all around me.

Kane, to my side, had already drawn his kalama. His face had fallen into a mask of fury. The Galdans, almost all on foot, tried to flee from him, but they had nowhere to run. He swung his sword, once, twice, thrice, and then again and again. More men screamed, and founts of blood reddened the air. A single Galdan knight, who had donned a helmet but no other piece of armor, rode at Kane across the powdery sand, and he tried to impale Kane with his lance. Kane easily parried his thrust, then almost casually cut off the knight's arm. A good kalama, if wielded with skill, can cut through steel mail, and what it could do to unarmored flesh was terrible to behold.

Some of the Galdans grabbed up pikes and tried to stab me or knock me off the back of my horse. Maram killed one of these with a vicious lance thrust through the eye. The Black Knight, Hadrik, riding behind him, killed another with his lance. Then Sar Shivalad, Sar Kanshar and a few other of my Guardians came up closer and worked a quick slaughter with their swords. Our enemy, hacked and hopelessly disorganized, fell in tens and twenties all around us.

After a short while of such bloody, frenzied work, Joshu Kadar pointed toward the northern part of the beach and cried out an alarm, 'Sire, the Karabukers! Beware!'

I swung my sword and cut right through the shaft of a pike that one of the Galdans thrust at me; then I cut off his head, and I turned to look up the beach.

'To the King!' Joshu cried out. 'Protect King Valamesh!'

Thirty Karabuk knights, in tight formation, had appeared as if from nowhere, and were forcing their way through the mass of their own companions as they made their way straight toward me. They were long of form and both graceful and powerful in their movements; their hard black hands gripped lances even longer than the ones my knights wielded. They wore a heavy armor of mail and plate. It seemed a miracle that they had found the time to accouter themselves so completely; I guessed that they must be knights of King Mansul the Magnificent's Black Guard, who stood always ready to guard King Mansul or cut down his enemies.

Although I had hundreds of my own knights at my call, my charge across the beach had carried me too far into the Galdans' ranks, and so too few of my knights could quickly come forward to meet this new threat. The Karabukers might have ridden down Maram and the half dozen Guardians nearby me, perhaps even Kane. But their greater weight of armor, both encasing their bodies and fastened to their mounts, slowed them and caused their horses to sink more deeply into the white sands. And even as Joshu Kadar cried out once again, 'To the King! To the King!' another king and his knights rode to my defense. I looked to the left through a fence of flashing weapons to see King Talanu and Zandru the Hammer – and fifteen other Kaashan knights – working their way forward. They intercepted the Karabukers moments before our enemy fell upon us.

'We meet, King Valamesh!' my uncle cried out to me through the tangle of men, horses and crates between us. 'Now let us fight our enemies together!'

So saying, he pushed his lance point straight through the face of the Karabuk knight nearest to him. I heard the point embed itself in bone and snap off. Old my uncle might be, and slow of movement, but he still possessed great prowess at arms and retained most of his old strength. He was cunning as an old wolf, too; he had not survived ten bloody battles solely by chance.

'Careful, Sire!' Lord Zandru called out to him. 'Stay close to us!'

Lord Yarwan, too, seemed concerned at his king's wild attack of the Karabukers. But King Talanu was in no mood to be cautious. He cast down his broken lance and drew out his kalama. Then he pointed this long sword at the largest of the Karabuk knights, and cried out, 'Forward, forward all, and fight! This is the day! This is the day! Do you not *see*?'

The urgency in his voice caused me to look at his adversary more closely. This huge knight bearing down on him looked as if he must stand seven feet tall. Black ostrich feathers crested his shining helm; within this steel covering, his implacable black face and dark brown eyes seemed intent upon destroying King Talanu. In his huge hand, he bore a great lance, the longest I had ever seen a knight wield.

'Sire!' the sharp-eyed Joshu Kadar called out to me. 'Look at his emblem! The dragon!'

I stared across the corpse-strewn sands to gaze at this great knight's shield, emblazoned with a three-quarter sized red dragon.

'It is King Mansul!' Joshu cried out again. 'Let us slay him!'

But neither he nor I nor any of my Guardians could get close enough to execute Joshu's exhortation, for at that moment, many knights of King Mansul's Black Guard fell upon us. I had all that I could do to keep their lances from tearing me open.

And so I did not witness most of King Talanu's combat with King Mansul. I learned later that both the Kaashan knights and the Karabukers held back to allow the two kings to fight to the

247

death, one on one. Just after I ducked beneath a lance thrust and buried my silver sword inside the chest of a particularly strong Karabuk knight, I chanced to look over at King Talanu. Somehow, he had gained position on King Mansul. For a moment, King Mansul sat on top of his huge warhorse unbalanced, with his lance thrust too far forward into empty air. My uncle worked inside his reach then. For a blessed moment, he gained the speed of a much younger man, and he whipped his sword at King Mansul's neck. The edge of King Talanu's kalama bit through the steel bevor hanging down from King Mansul's helm, and then through skin, muscle, blood vessels and bone. King Mansul's head went flying though the air and smacked down onto the beach. Then the hoof of a nearby horse chanced to crunch down upon it and so bury it in the soft sand.

'The King is dead!' one of his Black Guard cried out. 'King Mansul is dead!'

Upon this shocking sight, most his knights lost heart. Then *my* knights, those Guardians closest to me and others such as Lord Noldashan, Sar Omaru and Jessu the Lion-Heart, closed in upon them, and we used our lances and long swords to slaughter them down to the last man.

'King Talanu has slain Mansul the Magnificent!' Lord Zandru shouted out. 'Long live King Talanu!'

Lord Yarwan and other Kaashans picked up this cry, roaring out, 'Long live King Talanu! Long live King Talanu Solaru!'

And then, in our time of triumph, as our knights rampaged through the center of the Karabuk and Galdan armies to dispirit our enemy and keep them in disarray, a Galdan archer managed to sneak up close to King Talanu. He loosed his arrow at nearly zero range, right through King Talanu's neck. Lord Yarwan almost immediately cut down this man. He looked on in horror – as did we all – at the bright red blood that spurted from around the arrow lodged in my uncle's flesh.

'I am killed!' King Talanu choked out to Lord Yarwan. His hand closed about the arrow that had cut his neck artery. Somehow, he kept seated on his horse. 'Prince Viromar is to be king after me. Bury me on the beach, facing the sea. I always wanted to look upon the sea.'

He gazed out beyond the ships at the ocean's gleaming waters. For a moment, his eyes grew as bright as the sun's golden shimmer. Then he gasped out to Lord Yarwan: 'This is a *good* death!'

As his eyes closed and he slumped in his saddle, Lord Yarwan and several other Kaashan knights hurried forward to take up the weight of his body. They eased my uncle's still form over the back of Lord Yarwan's mount so that Lord Yarwan could lock his hand on this brave king and keep him from falling off onto the beach.

With our enemy trying to flee from my knights, I had a moment to survey the battlefield. I turned to look for the Kaashan infantry and Lord Tomavar's men – and those of Lord Tanu. The closer sound of steel swords clanging against steel merged with the rhythmic ringing of thousands of warriors' silver bells on the beach behind me. Upon covering most of the distance to the water's edge, the two halves of our army now joined in a single, glittering diamond line nearly two miles long. The line advanced, spears pointing forward, at a quick pace across the sand.

'Back!' I shouted to my knights. I did not want my men to be caught here by the water in what was about to occur. 'Back, through our lines!'

A few of our enemy, who must have thought that we had lost heart, cheered to see my knights and me turn our mounts and gallop back toward the wall of warriors rushing toward them. A dozen archers fired arrows at us, but no one stood in our way to try to stop us. It took only moments for our horses to pound back up the beach. Our lines opened to allow our columns of knights to pass. Lord Yarwan gave King Talanu's body into the keeping of two of his knights. We turned to watch our warriors knit up their lines and come almost within striking distance of the Karabukers and Galdans.

'Shall we remain in reserve in case our enemy makes a break-through?' Lord Yarwan asked me.

'No one is going to break through our lines today,' I told him. I pointed at the center of our advancing infantry. At its front, Lord Tomavar and Lord Tanu marched with their men, and I heard my two grizzled captains barking out commands. I said to Lord Yarwan, 'Let us instead reinforce our cavalry.'

Lord Yarwan nodded at this. Then he gathered up his Kaashan knights, and they rode off around the rear of our army to join with the other Kaashan cavalry and Lord Sharad's knights who had now fallen upon the Karabukers at the far north of the beach. I led my knights south, to throw in with Lord Avijan and his knights, protecting our army's right flank. But even as our lines of diamond-clad warriors finally closed with our enemy, I saw that our encirclement of their two armies was complete, and it would be *they* who would need protection from us.

What followed then beneath the blazing, noontime sun was less a battle than a slaughter. With Lord Avijan's cavalry already pushing their lances through the barely-armored Galdans, I led my hundreds of knights into the clumped masses of our enemy attempting to engage them. Most of the Galdans tried to run away, back up the beach or toward the water. But too many of their fellow soldiers blocked their way; they scrambled around the sands trying to bring their weapons to bear in too small a space. A few soldiers reached the water's edge. My knights pushed their mounts splashing through the shallows, and they used their kalamas to cut them down, filling the sea with cleaved bodies and ropes of blood. Meshian archers, called up from the rear, shot down even more of our enemy as they tried to climb into skiffs and escape to the ships floating offshore. So, I imagined, things must have gone to the north, where Prince Viromar and Lord Sharad would be hacking apart the Karabukers.

With his eye of compassion . . .

Along the gleaming lines which Lord Tanu and Lord Tomavar commanded, their warriors worked an even greater horror. The whole art of Valari infantry tactics is in using the spear, shield and razor-sharp tharam to try to open holes in the enemy's line. Then wedges of warriors can work their way through and use their kalamas to cut down their foes from their unprotected flanks or even from behind. Today, however, the Galdans and Karabukers never managed to form up a single line. In places, little walls and blocks of our enemy tried to stand and fight. But part of a wall is no real wall at all, and frantic men packed together like cattle can make little use of the weapons they wield – supposing they have been able to arm themselves at all.

It did not matter that our enemy outnumbered us ten to one. As the Meshian and Kaashan cavalry fell at them from the south and north, as our lines of warriors drove the bellowing mass of men back toward the sea, less than a tenth of them at any moment could actually try to meet my warriors' spear thrusts with their own. Most of the Galdans and Karabukers could do nothing more than to push at their companions from behind and wait for them to fall. And then, at the last, when they stood exposed to the furious Valari warriors protected head to ankle in suits of diamonds and swinging their murderous kalamas, to die. And die they did. Without the proper complement of weapons, shieldless and un-armored, terrified and utterly disorganized, they died by the hundreds and then the thousands. Their blood soaked into the white beach sands and turned it pink. Their screams drowned out the ringing of my warriors' bells and the crashing of the sea.

'This is hell!' Maram shouted to me. He rode beside me, pushing his horse forward into the crowds of Galdans before us. Nearly every time his sword whipped out, another of our enemy fell shrieking to the sand. 'Let us take their surrender, as Bemossed suggested!'

'No surrender!' a dozen men shouted out in response. 'No surrender!'

These voices, however, came not from my grim warriors, mad for revenge, but from the Galdans themselves. Outmatched and doomed they might be, but they still fought bravely. And they fought to the death.

'No surrender!' Kane now snarled out from my other side. He swung his sword in a tremendous blow that cleaved through the head of a Galdan standing beneath him and then into the shoulder of another packed in next to him. 'No quarter! Kill them all!'

Then he unleashed a rain of death upon our enemy so terrible in its fury that even the most battle-hardened of my warriors looked on in awe. I never sensed that Kane *liked* thrusting his sword through men's flesh or wreaking upon them the most bitter of agonies. But he had been born to fulfill a purpose, and he had a terrible love of his fate. It was both his grace and his curse to find a bit of heaven within the bloodiest of hells. And so he wielded his sword with a savage exaltation, and he killed his enemies without pity or pause.

At last, no one stood before him – or indeed before the knights around me or any other Valari warrior on the field. A few of our enemy fled across the shallows in frantically-rowed skiffs; we could not prevent their escape into the ships that had brought them here, nor that of the small fraction of their army that had never come ashore. The greatest part of the Karabuk and Galdan armies, however, nearly a hundred and fifty thousand men, lay dead in hacked and twisted heaps upon the beach. The incoming tide lapped over their bodies. The waters of the Terror Bay ran red with their blood.

. . . he saw his enemy like unto himself.

'Valari!' a knight shouted out from nearby me. I turned to see Lord Avijan holding up his bloody sword. 'Victory to the Valari!'

Ten thousand warriors picked up his cry: 'Valari! Valari! Valari!'

Then Viku Aradam, who had fought the whole battle with an arrow embedded in his shoulder, raised up his sword toward me and called out: 'King Valamesh! Victory to King Valamesh!'

251

I sat on Altaru at the water's edge as I gasped for breath and tried to keep my huge warhorse from trampling our fallen enemy. Now, across the entire length of the beach, both Meshians and Kaashans pointed their swords toward me. With one voice, the thousands of warriors of both armies called out: 'Valamesh! Valamesh! Victory to King Valamesh!'

Soon I would learn of the Valari who had fallen that day upon the Seredun Sands: sixty-three killed and slightly more than twice that number wounded. Lord Harsha called this the greatest victory in all Valari history, if not in the criticalness of its result, then in a brilliant defeat of our enemy at little cost. I, however, took little joy from the acclaim that he and many others wished to shower upon me. For even two hundred Valari killed and wounded were too many, and as for our enemy, they had still been men, had they not?

I thought about this as I gazed across the beach to that vantage point on Magda's wooded slope where Bemossed had stood during the entire course of the battle. From half a mile away, I could not make out the features of his face. I felt, however, the sickness that gripped his belly and devoured his soul. He seemed stricken to his very core. For a long time then, and from different directions, we stared out at the evil thing that my warriors and I had done.

16

L later that day, we buried King Talanu at the north end of the beach between the black rocks called the Pillars of Heaven. I never learned if King Darrum the Great's bones lay interred there, too. But in consideration of the fallen Valari that we placed beneath the ground nearby and the blood that they had shed, we would always regard the Seredun Sands as Valari soil.

The Karabukers and the Galdans we did not bury, for there were too many of them and we were too exhausted. My warriors and I watched their ships sail away with the remnants of their army. Perhaps, I thought, once we had marched off, they would return and make proper graves for their countrymen.

Although I wanted to leave that place of death as soon as possible, I had matters to attend to, and so did the warriors of my army. We kept our encampment behind the three hills, which blocked the sight – and smell – of the beach. Within an hour, I sent envoys riding northeast up the coast toward Delarid to tell King Santoval Marshayk of what had happened here. I sent envoys to the west, as well: to Athar, Lagash and Taron, and all the Nine Kingdoms. I wanted the whole world to know that a handful of brave Valari had utterly destroyed one of the Red Dragon's great armies.

I spent most of that evening with the wounded in the healing pavilion speaking with them and learning of their deeds. I gritted my teeth as I watched twelve warriors lose their hold on life and make the journey to the stars. The healers stood helpless to keep them from going over. Even Master Juwain could do nothing for them.

'I dare not use my gelstei,' he said to me much later outside the healing pavilion. He gripped his green crystal as he gazed off to the east. The moon's light showed three peaceful hills covered with bushes and dark trees, but no hint of the beach beyond them. 'With Bemossed fallen ill, all of us should keep our crystals quiet.'

Master Juwain then led the way into Bemossed's tent, lit with candles. Kane, Daj, Estrella, Liljana and Alphanderry all gathered around his still form. Abrasax and the other masters of the Seven stood above them. Bemossed lay on his sleeping furs with his eyes open; he seemed to be staring up at the flickering flame shadows dancing across the tent's ceiling. But I sensed that he stared at nothing.

'Has he spoken yet?' Master Juwain asked Liljana.

Liljana shook her head. In her hands she held a cup of soup that she had been unable to get Bemossed to swallow.

'He won't speak,' Liljana said. 'He won't eat and he won't drink.'

'He just *lies* there,' Daj added. 'It's as if something has sucked out his soul.'

Something has, I thought. *Someone has.*

'Some men,' Kane said as he rested his hand on Bemossed's curly hair, 'cannot bear battle.'

'You mean *slaughter*,' Liljana snapped at him. She bent down to kiss Bemossed's forehead. 'This *man* has battled Morjin night and day for months. And for all we know, battles him still, even at this moment.'

Master Juwain held his gelstei over Bemossed's chest. Then he sighed and said, 'We can only hope that is so. I fear that he might be lost in the gray land between worlds. Until we do know, however, we must assume that Morjin has gained the freedom to use the Lightstone – and therefore that we *cannot* use our stones.'

'We cannot *not* use them,' Kane growled out as he stroked Bemossed's hair. 'At least not for long. And we cannot allow Bemossed to remain half-dead, not unless we are willing to throw our victory away and watch Morjin set fire to the world.'

Abrasax, his white hair nearly brushing against the top of the tent, held out the clear stone of the seven Great Gelstei entrusted to his keeping. 'That fire might take a while to ignite. We might yet have time.'

'And we might not!' Kane said. 'How long, when the moment comes, will it take for Morjin to open the gates to Damoom? So, less than a flash of an instant.'

'But what can we do?' Abrasax asked him. 'Other than that which we are doing?'

'I don't *know!*' Kane half-shouted. 'That's the hell of it: not knowing what to do!'

After that, I went inside my pavilion to write a letter to the grandfather of Sar Dovaru Andar, who had died protecting Lord Avijan from the Galdan pikemen. I knew old Lord Andar well for he had been friends with my grandfather.

I sat for a long while at my council table, staring at the sheets of white paper laid out before me. A bottle of black ink seemed to wait for me to pick up my quill and dip it down into the dark liquid. But what should I say to the crippled Lord Andru, who had already lost two sons and a daughter in Morjin's invasion of Mesh? That Sar Dovaru had died a good death, fighting his enemy lance to spear and recklessly throwing himself forward against three Galdan pikemen? And that in dying he had been spared becoming the executioner of their nearly unarmed countrymen?

I should have known better than to immerse myself in the darkness that waited always inside me. For just as I allowed myself a moment of despair at the depravity of man, the Ahrim found me. This greater darkness seemed to come out of nowhere and fall upon me like an ice-fog. It concentrated all its essence in my right hand. I felt my flesh freezing, my fingers curling into my palm in agony. Arrows of ice drove up my arm, through my shoulder and deep into my chest. I gasped for breath. Then there came a tingling and a fierce burning, as of a limb being thawed after suffering frostbite. A terrible fire burned my muscles and blood. The heat of it seared into my nerves and then seized hold of them.

My hand, of its own will it seemed, gripped the quill and pushed its point down into the ink bottle. And then pressed the quill to the first sheet of paper. My fingers moved, and I began to scratch out words that were not of my making. I knew then whose will it really was that caused me to write a message to myself so full of lies and hate:

My Dearest Valashu,

> *This will be my last letter to you. Time, as you must know, is running out. The world turns, and carries us both toward that moment in time that the diviners have long told of. Soon, all debts will be settled and justice meted out. The Great One, the Marudin, will rule the stars. The golden future will open before us.*
>
> *You still must wonder at your part in the new ordering of the world. You have proved yourself, many times, a murderer. How few months has it been since you took the life of my son? And then burned my beloved daughter to her death? And now the blood of Karabuk's and Galda's finest soldiers, in all their thousands, stains your hands. What*

shall be the fate of the one who led his henchmen to murder them?

Shall I mete out murder in recompense? I shall, I shall: every one of the men you incited to wreak such slaughter upon my dutiful soldiers shall be put to the sword or crucified. The other Valari will not come to your rescue. I have given them diamonds that they might reflect upon my unbreakable word of friendship – and my adamantine resolve to punish my enemies. Do you think King Waray, or even King Mohan or King Hadaru, will risk seeing the children of their lands mounted on crosses? Did you really hope that they paid heed to the desperate dreams of Valashu Elahad?

Know that, on your account, I have already punished the Trians. The city fell to my armies five days ago; but too many of its subjects took up swords in secret against me. The blame for their rebellion and their chastening falls upon you. You, who brought the Lightstone into their city and claimed to be the Maitreya. You incited their illicit hope and turned their sight away from the true Maitreya. Lord Morjin, they should address me, the Lord of Light. After today, they shall. For I have burned Tria to the ground, and the light of this conflagration shall be seen across Ea as a signal of the future: those who stand against me shall be utterly destroyed, along with all they possess. And their ashes shall be the fertile soil out of which will grow a new civilization and a new order for all who remain alive.

Many, however, in all righteousness, must be sacrificed to bring about this new world. The grandfather of the woman you think you love has called for the Sarni tribes to take up arms against me. I shall tear out Sajagax's liver with my own hands and feed it to my hounds; his head I shall mount on a pole. Thus to those who have let Valashu Elahad incite them to defy me! Atara Ars Narmada, you will want to know, has taken on the title of Chiefess of the Manslayers. She shall soon be slain by one who is much more than a man. The last time I had this vixen under my thumb, I took her eyes; this time I will flay her alive and make a cloak of her skin. Tell me, Valashu, will you want to clasp her close to you then?

As for the Hajarim slave whom you harbor, he is a false Maitreya and an abomination who keeps the true Shining One from using the Lightstone – and therefore keeps the world in darkness. I shall punish him above all others, except yourself. I swear to you that you will live to see him crucified. And his agony shall become yours, multiplied a thousandfold.

Even as my fingers forced the quill to form these hateful words, I tried to command myself to stop writing. I could not. I sweated and ground my teeth and fought against the burning spasms of my muscles. The Ahrim now seemed to have seized control of my arm and most of my body. I could not stand up away from the table, even though I trembled to flee from my tent. I could not even draw my sword to cut off my own hand and the stream of lies that poured from the quill in swirls of black ink. All I could do was to stare down in horror at what I wrote:

Do not think that what I have done and still must do has not caused me infinite suffering. But it is you who have made me do it. Have I not said before that our fates are bound together as one? And that you and I are as brothers?

True, we are brothers who have come to hate each other. But joined to hate, as left hand to right, is always its opposite; can you deny that we have developed a terrible affection for each other, as well? How much poorer would the world be, I wonder, if Valashu Elahad had not come forth as the greatest of evils that gives birth, in bitter opposition and war, to the greatest of good? And how much less a man would you have been, you should wonder, if I hadn't sought to end your cursed life at every turn?

And so it is from my great affection for you that I will make this pledge: when at last you are defeated in battle and you are brought before me, I shall not have you crucified. A murderer you are, and you do deserve death, no man more so. But since you have already murdered your own soul, what more can the Red Dragon do? Only this: you will live, even as you live at this moment, transcribing my message to you. You shall serve me, all the days of your life. I shall not permit you to take your own life. Is it not fitting that he who has opposed me the most strenuously should be made to write down my words and then to proclaim them to all the world? You shall be my herald, Valashu. My most beloved ghul. Men will listen to you. And they will fear you, even as they do me, for you will take up the hammer and nails and crucify my enemies as if they were your own. And together we shall bring peace to the world.

Please reflect on this as you write on and on into the night. Do not lament that you once possessed a will of your own; it has only betrayed you and all those you loved. Your fate is to serve, as we all must. The world has far more need of you as its subject than as a would-be Maitreya and a King of Kings.

Faithfully, Morjin, King of Sakai, Lord of Ea and Lord of Light

In coming to the end of this despicable letter, I hoped that the Ahrim – or Morjin – would let go its hold upon my hand. But then I gripped the quill even more tightly. With my left hand, I reached out to pull another sheet of paper from the stack before me. I did not know what additional words Morjin might wish me to transcribe. A confession of my guilt as to the butchery of the Galdans and Karabukers? Denunciations of my friends and the captains of my army, accompanied with their death sentences? Or perhaps a credo proclaiming a new purpose for the Valari people in pledging their swords to the true Maitreya? Whatever Morjin wished me to write, I fought against his distant hand with every nerve fiber in my body and all the strength of my own. Sweat poured in rivulets down my face and neck and soaked into my tunic, and every muscle in my body quivered as with an over-tightened bowstring. I could not lift my finger a hair's-breadth away from the quill; I could scarcely keep my mind thinking those thoughts that I wished it to think.

And then I heard someone enter my tent and come up beside me. Although I could not turn my head to see who it was, I felt his presence as a fresh, sea wind that drives away the stench of death after a battle. A hand, long of palm and with delicate, tapering fingers, laid itself down on top of my hand. Immediately, I felt the cold burning through my muscles leave me. The Ahrim seemed to vanish along with it, like smoke into the sky. I finally looked up to see Bemossed gazing at me.

I would never know how he had managed to arise out of the catalepsy sickening him. Had it been, I wondered, through the Master Juwain's healing arts or the strengthening virtue of the Great Gelstei that the other masters of the Seven wielded? Had the goodness of Liljana's soup finally found its way deep into his body or one of Alphanderry's songs called to his soul? Or had Estrella's quiet but fierce love awakened him? He did not speak of this to me. Although he seemed weaker and more tired than ever in his flesh, a fire had come into his soft eyes. I sensed a terrible resolve burning through him and a vast will to make this be.

'Valashu,' he said to me, 'I must speak with you.'

I drew my hand out from beneath his and stared at it. I said to him, 'You have driven away the Ahrim!'

With great sadness, Bemossed shook his head. 'No, it was not I – I have no power over that thing.'

'But it is gone!' I said, flexing my fingers. 'You *do* have power over it!'

258

'No,' he told me with a shake of his head. 'Only power over you.'

He smiled at me, but there was no joy in him, only oceans of pain. Then he added, 'No, that isn't right, either. I have no power *over* you. But I can help you to be free.'

At this, I dropped the quill onto the new sheet of paper. It left scrapes of black against white.

'I *am* free,' I told him. 'Free from that evil thing.'

Bemossed bowed his head at this, and his smile grew deeper. 'That is good, friend. But the question that we should ask ourselves is not what we are free *from*. Rather, it is what are we free *for*?'

'Surely,' I said, reaching out to grasp the hilt of my sword, 'we are free to make our fate. Or, at least, to meet it bravely.'

'You would meet Morjin, wouldn't you? And his army?'

'They have burned Tria!' I told him, looking down at the letter that I had been forced to write. 'If Morjin tells true, they have done this terrible thing. Now he will march on the Nine Kingdoms to do the most evil work of all!'

'Then you will not turn back from the road that *you* march down?'

'You know what I dream – how can I?'

'And you know what I dream, too,' he told me. 'And so how can I watch men slaughter men ever again? How *can* I, Valashu?'

That was all he said to me that night, and for many days after that. In the morning, while everyone went about the business of breaking camp, he took up his post on the east slopes of Magda overlooking the sea. He stood watching as I led the Meshian vanguard out from between the hills onto the corpse-strewn beach. Then came Lord Tanu at the head of our foot warriors, and Lord Tomavar, and then the Kaashans in their masses of knights and glittering columns. True to King Talanu's wishes, the Kaashans had acclaimed Prince Viromar as their new king. That morning he rode beside me so that we might hold council as we marched north up the great highway of the beach. His standard, showing a white eagle against a blue field, flapped and cracked in the stiff wind blowing off the sea. The great noise of our army – the snorting horses, creaking wagons and jingling bells – drove away most of the gulls working at the fallen Galdans and Karabukers. I did not know until the last if Bemossed could bring himself to join us on our march. But as I led my thousands of men toward the Pillars of Heaven to the north of the beach, I looked back to see Bemossed come down from his post and mount his horse. Then he galloped forward to rejoin Liljana, Daj, Estrella and Alphanderry riding behind the vanguard.

I was the first of the Valari to pass between the great black monoliths rising up toward the sky. Then came Viromar Solaru, now King Viromar, and the rest of our army. I did not know if these strange rocks held any magic or if marching across King Talanu's grave might inspirit my warriors. I prayed, however, that my army might somehow gain invincibility and go forth toward the greatest of victories.

Abrasax, looking back at the devastation of the beach, his face all gray and grave, spoke only these words to me from the *Book of Battles*: '"From out of the darkest dark, the brightest light. From the worst of evil, the greatest of good."'

For all that day and part of the next we journeyed north across the hardpacked sands of the beaches of Delu's southern coast. Then, at a point where the coast slanted off northeast toward Delarid, we turned northwest to cross Delu's lowlands and cut the Nar Road some fifty miles away. Morjin, I thought, would leave a burning Tria behind him and march down the Nar Road from the opposite direction, perhaps to attack the Nine Kingdoms through Anjo and Taron. Our journey to the Seredun Sands had taken the Meshian and Kaashan armies far afield, and we had need of haste if we were to keep Morjin's soldiers from ravaging across the Morning Mountains and destroying the Valari armies one by one. My hope was that when we passed into Athar, the Valari kings would begin to join us, one by one. And then inevitably, some-where, we would meet Morjin in a great battle where the Valari would once again fight together *as* one.

It took us three days of tramping through some rich farmland to reach the city of Nagida astride the Nar Road. The umber foothills of the eastern ranges of the Morning Mountains rose up ten miles to the west of Nagida's red brick buildings. To the east, a hundred and seventy miles down the Nar Road, lay the white stone city of Delarid and King Santoval's magnificent palace, said to be the second grandest on all of Ea. I had sent an invitation to King Santoval, requesting that he lead his army forth and meet up with mine at Nagida. As his men would have a longer distance to cover than would mine, I was prepared to wait some days to welcome Delu's eighty thousand soldiers to our great purpose of defeating Morjin.

'He won't come,' Maram told me for the twentieth time as we made camp. 'He hates to leave the company of his concubines.'

'He *must* come,' I told him. 'I know he will come.'

King Santoval's army, however, true to Maram's prediction, never made the journey from Delarid, nor did King Santoval himself. In his place, he sent an envoy, Prince Adamad, a cousin of Maram. Prince Adamad, a large, florid-faced man wearing jeweled rings on seven of his fingers, rode up to our encampment along with half a dozen others of his retinue. He dismounted in front of my pavilion, and made a great show of bowing to me and my battle-hardened captains. In a voice as smooth and sweet as orange oil, he called out to me: 'King Valamesh the Victorious, Champion of the Tournament at Nar, Hero of the Great Quest, Guardian of the Lightstone! – know that my lord, King Santoval Marshayk, sends his greetings! And his everlasting gratitude for your valor and that of your men in defeating the invaders from Galda and Karabuk! You have done Delu a great service! It shall never be forgotten! In recognition of your deeds, King Santoval has created a new honor just for you: that Valashu Elahad shall ever after be known as the Friend of Delu and Savior of the Realm!'

So saying, he presented me with a golden wand set with emeralds and topped with a cut diamond as large as a horse's eye. Wings, like those of an eagle and covered with diamond dust, projected out from the sides of the wand. It was a gaudy thing of great value but little beauty. I stood holding it and looking at Prince Adamad.

'Please convey my thanks to your lord for this,' I said, squeezing the wand. 'But it would be an even greater honor to see King Santoval again – and to march with the king and his men to war.'

Prince Adamad's face seemed to lose a little of its color. His smile lacked warmth as he said to me: 'War *is* upon us now, and all free men from all the Free Kingdoms must do all that men can do to throw back our enemy.'

'Good!' I called out. 'Then when can I expect King Santoval to join us here?'

'Unfortunately, he is ill, and so he had to send me in his place.'

I looked at Master Juwain, waiting nearby, and I said, 'What ails your king? Perhaps we can be of help.'

'Oh, it is just the flux, and nothing that our own healers can't cure. But it will keep my lord from taking the field for some time.'

'But we haven't much time!' I told him. 'The Red Dragon has burned Tria! We must march west to meet him, and soon. If King Santoval is too ill, is there another who would lead the army here?'

Prince Adamad cast me a long, hard look from beneath his heavily-lidded eyes. He looked even harder at Maram, standing next to me.

'Prince Tymon commands the army in the king's absence,' Prince

Adamad said. 'But I must tell you that he has been forced, from strategic necessity, to keep the army close to Delarid.'

I stared right back at him and said, 'Please tell me why.'

'Why, in case the Galdans and Karabukers return. Our diviners believe that more armies might be summoned from Galda.'

At this, Kane stepped forward. I felt him restraining himself from grabbing Prince Adamad's jeweled tunic and shaking him. 'Return, ha! There's no one left *to* return. We destroyed our enemy, nearly down to the last man!'

'So it is said,' Prince Adamad coughed out. He looked at Kane as he might an uncaged tiger. 'But the Red Dragon seems always able to summon up new armies. King Santoval has determined that Delu can be of greatest service to the Free Kingdoms – and of course, to the Valari – if we guard the gateway to the west and prevent any of the Red Dragon's armies from marching on your rear.'

He looked at Lord Avijan and then Lord Harsha, whose single eye seemed to shine upon Prince Adamad like a star. The prince smiled with much nervousness at Lord Tomavar, Lord Tanu and King Viromar, who watched him with the concentration of a falcon.

Now it came Maram's turn to confront Prince Adamad. He said to him, 'If you believe what you just told me, you are even more a fool than my father – and he is more a coward than I had thought possible!'

Maram's words failed to chasten Prince Adamad, or even embarrass him. He drew himself up stiffly, and with the relish of nastiness declared to Maram: 'You have no father, now. You wear diamond armor and the sword of a Valari knight; you have given your allegiance to a Valari king. Where the Valari march, you will march as well. And where they fall, so will you. King Santoval will make no prayers over your grave.'

'So be it,' Maram said. I could feel him holding back tears – of anguish and rage. 'But at least I will lie in the company of *men*.'

Prince Adamad made no response to this, nor did any of the other Delians in his retinue. Then Maram shouted at them: 'Is there no one of our land who will *fight*?'

Prince Adamad said nothing to this, either. Then he bowed to me and told me, 'My lord and all of Delu wish you well on your journey. King Santoval will send provisions to speed you upon it. The Savior of the Realm will always have Delu's blessings.'

He bowed once again, then mounted his horse and rode off with the others of his embassy. I stood watching them disappear down the road to the east. I gripped the golden wand of victory that King Santoval had sent to me. Then I turned in the opposite direction and said to King Viromar: 'It seems that those who should have been our allies have abandoned us. Will Kaash still march with Mesh?'

Prince Viromar, whose face seemed harsher than that of an eagle, smiled and told me: 'To the end of the earth, if that is our fate. It will be as that fat prince said: we Valari will march together.'

I, too, smiled grimly. Then I cast the golden wand down to the dirt at my feet, and clasped King Viromar's hand.

It was our fate, however, that the Delians did not completely desert us in our time of need. Just before nightfall, from the north, a renowned Delian warrior known as Prince Thubar led five hundred mounted knights and three thousand foot soldiers into our encampment. Prince Thubar, a great bull of a man and yet another of Maram's innumerable cousins, met with King Viromar and my captains and me outside my pavilion, where the wand of triumph still lay on the ground. Prince Thubar looked down at it, and said, 'I had heard that King Santoval ordered a victory baton made. And that he has betrayed you, King Valamesh. But you might, even so, wish to keep the baton in recognition of your men's sacrifice for Delu and your great victory. My countrymen, across our land, know of what you did, and we *do* honor you. Those who would not be made cowards by their king have come here with me in proof of this honor, that we might pledge our swords to your cause.'

So saying, he drew out his single-edged sword, only slightly less long than a kalama. I bowed my head to him, and pressed my hand to the flat of his blade. I picked up the golden wand. Then I walked with Prince Thubar out to the edge of the encampment where he had ordered the Delian cavalry and infantry to draw up in neat ranks and columns. The Delian knights wore a good mail armor reinforced with steel plate; the infantry, though, had only thin sheets of bronze sewn to padded leather to protect them. I wondered at the fighting quality of these men. But I could not doubt their spirits, for they stood here not only in defiance of Morjin but of their own king.

'You must know where we march,' I told him, 'and how desperate is our hope of victory.'

Prince Thubar only smiled at this as if I had suggested to him a particularly challenging game. His hand swept out toward his small army, and he said, 'We are all desperate men – as are all who know what the Red Dragon will do to Delu if you fail.'

'We *must* not fail,' I told him. 'But even if we defeat our enemy, will you not find it dangerous to march back down this road again? Will not King Santoval regard your pledge to me as treachery and rebellion?'

'It is no treachery,' he told me, 'to serve one's lord by fighting that lord's enemy, even if he has foolishly forbidden it. And as for rebellion, if ever my men and I do return home, King Santoval would incite open revolt in trying to punish those who risked their lives for Delu.'

I nodded my head at this, then smiled. 'All right then – you shall march with the Valari, and let no one say that the Delians are afraid of Morjin!'

We clasped hands at this, and then I invited Prince Thubar to take dinner with my captains and me in my tent. As we made our way back toward the center of our encampment, with its many cooking fires sending up smoke plumes into the sky, Kane took me aside. And he said to me, 'Three thousand foot and half a thousand knights this Delian prince brings us – some will count us fortunate for adding to our army, eh? But how many of them have made secret vows to the Order of the Dragon?'

'None, we must hope,' I told him. 'I trust Prince Thubar – and his judgment of his men.'

'Would you stake everything on such trust? If an assassin fell upon you or Bemossed, then . . .'

He lapsed into silence. His black eyes seemed to gather up the darkness of the falling night.

'Once,' I said to him, clapping my hand against his shoulder, 'you told me that you were an assassin of assassins. With you by my side, I will have no cause to fear any of Prince Thubar's men. Nor even Morjin's.'

Kane smiled, showing his long, white teeth. 'Still, it is a chance.'

'It *is*,' I agreed. 'But too much caution, now, will be worse than too much audacity.'

Kane, I sensed, must have agreed with this, for he turned to stare at Prince Thubar's soldiers as if defying any of them to move against me.

In the morning, we began the march across the eastern range of the Morning Mountains. The white peaks pushing into the sky ahead of us did not rise so high as those of the White or even the Crescent Mountains. Even so, they were steep and rugged, blanketed in thick forests, and the passage through them might have proved arduous if not for the ancients who had built the Nar Road.

This band of brick and stone wound through valleys and around the sides of mountains at an easy grade for most of its miles; it spanned gorges and rivers in great, arched bridges that still stood in good repair after many centuries. It made me wonder at the glories of the past ages; what would it be like, I asked the wind blowing off the glaciers above me, if all roads on Ea could be made as well as this one, and connect every realm to every other in a free passage of people, goods and knowledge?

For ten days, the men of Mesh, Kaash and Delu and our thousands of horses pounded up the road while our wagons' iron-rimmed wheels ground on and on. Little of Soal's heat found its way into these heights. It rained often, and twice great storms seemed to come out of nowhere and shake the very mountains in lightning flashes and earsplitting cracks of thunder.

My warriors' spirits held good and true. At night over blazing campfires, Meshians mingled with the Kaashans without quarrel, and both armies of Valari welcomed Prince Thubar's Delian soldiers with politeness if not a quick and easy warmth. Too many times in the past, when Delu had been strong, we Valari had had to throw back the invading forces of one ambitious Delian king or another. Memories could no more easily be expunged than ink set into white paper. Still, I thought, new memories could be written. Toward this end, I invited Prince Thubar to sit at my table during our councils, and for my Valari warriors to share food and song with the Delians. I marveled at the capacity of these strangers for feasting and drinking, laughing at crude jokes and weeping at sentimental stories – and then being able to rouse themselves from their beds after staying up half the night throwing dice. Master Juwain reminded me that different peoples practice different ways, and I thought that two peoples could hardly be as different from each other as the Delians and the Valari. The ways of these effusive, sensual men were completely at odds with those of the Morning Mountains, but we would march together with a single purpose – and fight side by side when the time came for battle.

Just before we reached the frontier to Athar, smallest of the Nine Kingdoms in size if not in deeds, two envoys sent from afar intercepted my army. Many of my men shook their heads in wonder at them, for they were Sarni warriors and women at that: Sonjah and Aieela of the Manslayer Society. I had met them once in Mesh nearly two years previously: just before Morjin's armies ravaged my homeland. Now, as then, they had been sent bearing tidings.

I dismounted and walked with them away from the vanguard

through a pasture at the side of the road. Kane came with me, and King Viromar and Prince Thubar – and others. Sonjah, dressed in steel-studded leather and wearing gold bangles about her heavy, naked limbs, seemed as barbaric as any Sarni man. So did Aieela, who was younger and slighter of build, though more fearsome in her aspect, for she glowered at men from out of a scarred face and would not deign to speak to them. Both she and Sonjah wore quivers full of arrows and gripped double-curved bows in their hands. They seemed awkward on foot, away from their horses.

Sonjah, tall and serious, stood before me and looked me straight in the eye without bowing. As with Liljana, she seemed to have been robbed of the ability to smile.

'Valashu Elahad,' she said to me. 'King Valamesh, as they call you now – greetings once again. We have ridden a long way to find you.'

'Greetings,' I told her. 'But how *did* you find me here? You must have set out on your journey before we turned north and west on ours.'

Sonjah's blue eyes danced with lights even if her mouth remained as stiff as an old piece of leather. Then she said to me, 'Atara, the *imakla* one, told that you would be coming up this road on this day. We Manslayers have chosen her Chiefess. She asked us to inform you of this.'

I inclined my head to acknowledge her service in making such a dangerous journey – for it is always a great chance for a Sarni warrior to brave the lands of the Valari. I did not, however, admit that I already had news of Atara's new honor. I thought it unwise to tell anyone except my friends of Morjin's letter to me.

'Is Atara well?' I asked.

'She is well enough,' Sonjah said. 'She recovers from a saber wound gained in battle with the Marituk.'

I fought to keep my heart from racing and the blood from draining from my face. I said, 'Then are the Manslayers at war with the Marituk?'

'Not yet. It was a skirmish only. The Marituk test the Manslayers' strength – and that of the Kurmak with whom we have allied.'

'Brave women,' I said, looking from her to Aieela. 'If you have allied with the Kurmak, then you have pitted yourself against Morjin.'

At this, Sonjah spat on the ground, then shrugged her shoulders. 'It had to go one way or the other. Morjin has sent gold to each of the tribes, or tried to. He will buy what allies he can, or win them through fear. But some remain unafraid.'

'The Manslayers,' I said.

Although Sonjah held her face expressionless, Aieela smiled savagely in her place.

'We, yes,' Sonjah told me. 'And Sajagax. He is a great warrior and a greater chieftain, perhaps the greatest Sarni since Tulumar – and I thought I would never say such a thing of a Kurmak. I might have hoped that we Urtuk would take the lead against Morjin, but my tribe remains divided, and so the honor falls to Sajagax and all those who would answer his call.'

'Then his call *has* been answered?'

Sonjah strummed her thumb across her bowstring, and nodded her head. 'It has, and the tribes gather to his standard.'

'Which tribes, then?'

'So far, the Adirii and the Niuriu. We expect the Danladi to ride soon. Perhaps the Urtuk beyond the Poru. And perhaps my people as well.'

It seemed strange to hear Sonjah speak of the eastern Urtuk this way, for I knew that her first allegiance must lie with the Manslayers and only secondly with the clans and kin of her homeland.

Lord Tanu, who stood next to me, cast his suspicious old eyes on Sonjah. He had led his warriors in more than one battle with the eastern Urtuk, and was not inclined to trust anyone from this tribe so readily.

'If the Sarni gather openly against Morjin,' Lord Tanu said, 'then Sajagax invites Morjin to move against him.'

Sonjah shrugged her shoulders again. 'What must be, must be.'

'But Sajagax,' I said, 'has no hope of winning such a contest! Most of the Sarni will side with Morjin. And the Red Dragon already marches at the head of an army hundreds of thousands strong.'

Sonjah pointed at the long line of warriors strung out on the road behind us. 'There march three armies, not so strong in numbers, but they are mostly Valari. And more Valari you will find in the lands through which we have ridden. Atara has spoken of this.'

Again, I felt my blood rushing through me. 'Has she foreseen an alliance of my people, then?'

'Who has *not* foreseen this, King Valamesh? But it is one thing to see it, and another to make it be. This, Atara says, lies in your hands. And in your heart.'

I stood breathing in the scent of grass as I gazed off across the pasture to the west. I said, 'We *will* make an alliance – and then we will march across the Nine Kingdoms to where Sajagax and the Sarni gather!'

My words caused Sonjah finally to smile. Her even, white teeth gleamed in the sunlight as she laughed out, 'Atara told that you would say that. Sajagax, too, has declared that you would not fail him. He has sent the call to every free kingdom in your name.'

'In *my* name!' I called out.

'In the name of King Valamesh. Sajagax knows that the Free Kingdoms will not come to the aid of the Kurmak and their allies, for the sake of Sajagax.'

'But will they come for *my* sake?'

'Sajagax says yes. That once, you nearly forged an alliance of the Free Kingdoms. And that now, if Sajagax believes in you, the free kings and all their peoples will have to, as well.'

I looked toward the west as the wind blew across my face. Sonjah turned that way, too, and when she gazed upon Bemossed standing in close on the grass nearby, her smile widened.

'Sajagax also says,' she added, 'that warriors from across the world will come to honor the true Maitreya.'

I heard the awe in her voice as she said this, and so must have Bemossed. After looking long and deeply at the deadly bow that she held, he walked off by himself farther into the pasture.

'A great battle we will fight, King Valamesh!' Sonjah said to me. 'You are the rightful Guardian of the Lightstone, and you will cut it from Morjin's hand! And then give it to the Shining One! It is said that the light of the Cup of Heaven will resurrect the dead!'

I felt sure that Bemossed overheard her speak these words, and that he doubted if the Maitreya, even wielding the Lightstone, could have such power. And that he remained resolved that no one should ever die for his sake, not even in one inevitable and final battle.

'Where,' I asked Sonjah, 'does Sajagax wait for the Sarni to gather?'

'Where the Rune River turns south toward the Snake. On the plain beneath the rocks of the Detheshaloon.'

Upon her pronouncement of this name, something inside me seemed to darken as of a sky during a storm. I felt a whirlwind tear through me and lightning split me open.

'The Detheshaloon,' I murmured. I gripped hold of my sword to give me strength. I knew then that this must be the place that Atara had seen in her terrible visions.

'We are to take you there, if you are willing,' Sonjah told me. 'Sajagax will be waiting for you there. And, I hope, Atara.'

The whole world, I thought, waited for the Valari to march to this killing plain in the middle of the Wendrush. I remembered Alphanderry's warning to me in the wood where the Ahrim had first struck; I thought again of Master Matai's calculation of a great alignment of planets and stars on the eighth of Valte. The whole universe, it seemed, waited upon a single, fiery moment when all time and history would be fulfilled.

'We are willing,' I told Sonjah, speaking for my captains and my warriors looking on from the road. 'Let us march to this Detheshaloon!'

At this, Sonjah clasped hold of my hand and smiled at me again. But her sunburnt face held no mirth or humor, only a grim acceptance of what the Sarni allied with Sajagax and the Valari must try to accomplish against the armies of the Red Dragon.

17

And march we did. Sonjah and Aieela were both glad to turn their steppe ponies around and to ride at the head of our armies west, back toward the Wendrush. At a cup-shaped gap between two rounded mountains, later that day, we came to the pass guarding the frontier to Athar. As I had sent envoys ahead to warn King Mohan of my intention to lead my army through his realm, the Atharians stationed at the fortress overlooking the pass took no alarm from my thousands of knights and warriors. Even so, the Atharians seemed loath to let two strange Valari armies and a few battalions from Delu just march across their kingdom, no matter how noble our stated purpose. King Mohan resented our passage much more bitterly, as we discovered four days later.

Near the eastern reaches of Athar, in a rolling country of green pastures and orchards, King Mohan led the Atharian army forth from Gazu to meet mine coming up the Nar Road. His knights and warriors had donned their diamond armor and their silver ankle bells. He arrayed his cavalry and his battalions of foot in gleaming lines on either side of the road. To continue our journey as we had come, we would have to march straight between thousands of warriors pointing their long spears at us.

King Mohan sat on top of a white stallion, waiting along with his captains at the road's center. He, too, wore full battle armor, which included a great helm bearing a single black ostrakat plume. His golden surcoat gleamed with a great blue horse; a banner held by one of his knights displayed this emblem as well.

I rode forward alone to meet with him, as he did me. We stopped with our two horses facing each other across a couple of yards. King Mohan's small, compact body fairly trembled with a barely

270

contained passion for strife. He was a hard man and sharp in his purpose, like a piece of flint chipped into the shape of an arrow-head. A terrible pride deformed his fine and noble features as he stared at me.

'King Valamesh,' his whiplike voice cracked out without pause for greetings or niceties, 'you have entered my realm without my leave, and that is an act of war.'

Some men take their measure of other men by the forcefulness with which their foes are willing to oppose even the most casual aggression. King Mohan, I thought, gave his grudging affections only to those who were willing to risk everything by standing up to him.

'It *is* an act of war!' I called back to him. I heard his captains behind him and his warriors lined up nearby draw in deep breaths in surprise at my words. 'As you know, we march to war against the Red Dragon and all who follow him. We cannot turn back! We cannot let anyone, not even the Valari's most fearless king, turn us back. And so it would have been dishonest to ask for your leave if we were not willing to accept your refusal. Your blessings, however, we do ask for. And even more, your warriors and their swords.'

King Mohan gripped his horse's reins in his hard, little hands as he stared at me for a long time. He finally looked away from me, at the thousands of warriors lined up for miles behind me. It would, of course, be just as disastrous for him to provoke a battle here as it would be for me.

'Any man,' he told me, 'who would go up against the Red Dragon has my blessings, for Morjin is a false king and a crucifier who should be punished for his crimes. I see that now. And so I will let you pass through Athar unhindered. I will give you grain for your army. The swords of *my* army, though, you may not have, for they are needed elsewhere.'

'No need in all the world, at this time, can be so urgent as defeating Morjin.'

'That has always been your will.'

'Not mine alone: it is the will of the world.'

'So you say. So you have always said, as you have always spoken of the world's fate as if it is your privilege to interpret it for others.'

'Morjin,' I half-shouted, 'has burned Tria! At this moment he marches down the Nar Road toward the Nine Kingdoms! What is your sword *for*, and those of your warriors, if not to fight him?'

'My sword,' he said, laying his hand on the hilt of the kalama strapped to his side, 'is for fighting my enemies. I have many.'

'No enemy is an enemy like Morjin.'

'*Is* Morjin my enemy? Or only yours?'

'A king might ask that question if he has been given diamonds and gold to deny the truth concerning such an enemy!'

At this, King Mohan's blood rose, and he drew his sword half an inch from its scabbard. His face knotted in fury as he shouted at me, 'Are you saying that I have taken the Crucifier's bribes?'

'Have you?'

'No! And a true king, if he be Valari, would not ask another king such a question!'

King Mohan trembled on the brink of drawing free his sword. I knew that my anger had driven me to wrong him. And so I told him, 'My apologies, King Mohan. I never thought that you, of all Valari, *would* accept such a tainted treasure.'

'You should not think that of *any* Valari. Not even King Waray would sully himself so. We know, now, who and what Morjin really is.'

'If you *know* this, then why not join with us?'

'You mean, join with *you*. Your purpose has not changed, has it, King Valamesh? You would still be warlord of the Valari.'

'I would have us make an alliance, yes. Can you not see that is our only hope?'

'I can see well enough,' he told me. He looked past me toward the knights and my friends in my army's vanguard; I turned to watch him meet eyes with Bemossed. 'Once, you put yourself forth as the Maitreya. And now, another.'

'I did not know who the Maitreya was,' I said. 'I did not know *what* he is. I did not know . . . myself.'

King Mohan looked back at me. I felt his scorn battle with deeper emotions within him. 'Again, you hint at your fate. What title, if you vanquished the Red Dragon, would you take for yourself? King Valamesh, Lord of the Valari and Emperor of Ea?'

'I would take nothing except the Lightstone so that I might guard it with my life, all the days of my life, for the Maitreya!'

Once more, King Mohan's eyes flicked toward Bemossed and then back at me. His voice softened as he said, 'I think you speak the truth. Still, it is one thing to purpose to vanquish Morjin and another thing to do it.'

'We *can* vanquish him!' I called out. 'If the Valari unite, and go out on the Wendrush to meet Morjin as he marches –'

'If we *did* unite,' he snapped out, cutting me off, 'we should remain behind our mountains and force Morjin to battle on bad ground for his armies. We can kill half his men coming through the passes!'

'No,' I told him, 'we must answer Sajagax's call, and meet at the Detheshaloon.'

'Unite with the Sarni savages? Why?'

'Because that is where we must face Morjin. That is where the battle must be.'

That is where it will be, I thought. *That is where our children's children will say it has always been.*

King Mohan, who was more perceptive than people suspected, looked at me strangely. 'Again, as always, you follow your fate, don't you? Instead of the basic principles of warfare that your father must have taught you?'

'I remember everything that my father taught me,' I told him. 'And this above all: that in the end, a king must follow his own heart.'

King Mohan tried to hold my gaze, and I felt his black eyes burning. He turned his head to look at his warriors lined up in silence at the side of the road. They looked back at him with a great weight of devotion and expectation. I knew that they must have heard of the slaughter of the Galdan and Karabuk armies at the Seredun Sands.

'It must be said,' King Mohan finally told me, 'that your father taught you well. And that no one will ever doubt the *heart* of King Valamesh.'

I bowed my head to him, and said, 'Join us, then! No one ever doubted King Mohan's heart or those of his men – or their swords!'

King Mohan pointed at King Viromar, wearing the white tiger of the Solaru line and sitting on his horse ten yards behind me. He said, 'Kaash, as always, joins with Mesh.'

King Mohan, of course, had no love of his neighbor to the south. It had been only eight years since King Talanu had fought King Mohan and the Atharians to a draw at the Battle of Sky Lake. And long ago, in the year 841 of the Age of Swords, Athar had met its greatest defeat when King Sarjalad led an alliance of Kaash, Mesh and Waas to crush the invading Atharians under King Saruth at the Battle of Blue Mountain.

'And now Delians,' King Mohan said, pointing at Prince Thubar, 'march with Valari.'

I did not remind him that Athar, in its bid for glory and empire during the reign of King Saruth, had conscripted Delian levies into its army. Who knew better than an Atharian Athar's long and bloody history?

'Why must things always be so *complicated*?' King Mohan spat out.

And I answered him, 'What is so complicated about free men joining freely to defeat a great evil?'

'But who is *really* free?'

'You are,' I told him. I pointed west, back along the road behind him. 'You have only to give the command, and your warriors will gladly follow you to where they must go.'

'But my warriors,' he said, pointing toward the north, 'must go *that* way.'

I turned to look along the line of his finger. To the right of the Nar Road, half a mile behind him, stood a small town and a much smaller road that ran across the rounded green pastures toward King Kurshan's realm of Lagash.

'It is fate,' he said, smiling bitterly at me. '*My* fate, and Athar's.'

Athar's dispute with Lagash also went back to the Age of Swords – and perhaps farther. It had continued on and on through the centuries in one bloody war after another. Only thirty years before, both Athar and Lagash had accused each other of violating the rules of Sharshan: the formal battles that we Valari waged against each other as a lesser evil than total war. More recently, after I had failed to unite the Valari in Tria two years ago, King Mohan and King Kurshan had drawn swords on each other on their journey home.

'You come too late,' King Mohan told me. 'King Kurshan and I have already agreed to meet in battle ten days hence on the field of Arantu outside of Osh.'

'You must make a new agreement, then! I have sent envoys to King Kurshan. Surely once he has learned of what Morjin intends, he will join with us to oppose him.'

King Mohan shook his head at this. 'Your envoys will not reach him. It is said that he has gone to meditate in the mountains, and will speak with no one until the day of the battle.'

'Not even myself? If I were to ride up into Lagash?'

'Can you afford to waste so much time?'

I thought about this as I felt the world beneath me whirling around the sun. 'All right – then you must send envoys to King Kurshan informing him that you have marched with us. They will reason with King Kurshan when he comes down from the mountains.'

Now King Mohan slammed his sword back into his scabbard and called out, 'But King Kurshan will not *reason*! He will declare that Athar has once again broken Sharshan – then he will use that as an excuse to ravage and burn Athar!'

'He will not!' I called back to him. 'He is a man of honor. And he is Valari. When he learns that you have led your warriors out to meet Morjin, and why, he will follow with Lagash's army.'

'So you dream, King Valamesh. But how can I take such a risk? For my kingdom? For my *people*?'

'How can you risk letting Morjin *crucify* your people?'

King Mohan's black eyes filled a wild ferocity, like that of a leopard trapped by hunters on all sides. Then he snapped out: 'Morjin has never made a threat against Athar – and King Kurshan has never *stopped* making threats!'

'Morjin's very existence is a threat – you face none worse. Come! Help me to end it!'

I nudged my horse closer to his and extended my hand to him. But he shook his head and kept his hand clamped around the hilt of his sword.

'How can you ask me to do this?' he called to me.

Because, I thought, feeling the fire of his eyes, *I know what is in your heart. And you know what is in mine.*

At that moment, with my hand still held open in midair, with Bemossed looking on with all the ardor of the sun, I felt something deep and irresistible rend King Mohan apart. It was, I knew, the valarda. I had always sensed that this mysterious power lay waiting to be awakened in everyone.

'Come with me!' I called to him again. 'Let us throw down Morjin!'

All my warriors lined up behind me down the road seemed to echo my plea to King Mohan; so did *his* warriors, waiting to either side of us, in the silence of their eyes and the drumming of thousands of hearts. How could King Mohan turn away from this terrible but beautiful force?

'What is it you *want*?' I said to him.

'You *know* what I want!' he shouted back. 'You and yours go forth to fight the battle of the ages! And what a fight you will make! The minstrels will sing of you, for ages! You will lose, but so what? Your warriors will die, but that is war. In dying for each other, though, they will feel their spirits blaze like the stars, and they will know they are *alive*. And that, King Valamesh, is what I truly want.'

275

He removed his hand from his sword, and regarded it with his fierce, dark eyes. 'But it is what I may not have. Kings, if they love their lands, do not do as they *want* to do, but only as they *must*.'

And what King Mohan thought he must do, as he had said, was to protect his land by marching off to the wrong battle. And his warriors must follow his will, even as he submitted himself to his own sense of honor and duty.

Two roads, north and west, lay before him, and as with King Sandarkan, I wanted to push out with the force called Alkaladur and nudge him onto the one leading to the meeting with Morjin. But I could not bring myself to commit this violence. I could only look at him and tell him what my father had once told me: 'King Mohan – your heart is free!'

'Yes,' he said with a seething bitterness, 'free to follow this will of the world that you have spoken of, but never my own.'

'No – *always* your own,' I said to him. 'Don't you see? In the end, they are one and the same.'

I waited for him to apprehend this, to feel it like a fire deep in his heart. Instead, he inclined his head to me and forced out: 'I am sorry, but I have given my word. I must go where I must. I wish you well on your journey, King Valamesh.'

I did not want to believe that King Mohan had refused to join with me; why, I wondered, had I failed yet again? There seemed nothing to do now except to continue on, as King Mohan had said. I could only hope that he would change his mind and follow after me.

And so I returned to my vanguard, and then led my army up the road between the assembled lines of King Mohan's warriors. As we marched past, the Atharians began striking their spears against their shields and crying out acclamations to honor us. I did not want to think that even King Mohan would punish them for breaking discipline that day.

Later, after we had passed through Gazu, with its many buildings of ironwood and white granite, Master Juwain rode up beside me. He must have doubted the success of what I intended to accomplish, as many in the columns behind us now must have as well. Even more, he must have questioned Abrasax's decision that the Seven should help me to wage war. But he refused to dwell in the dark. And so he pointed up the Nar Road and said, 'There are other Valari kings.'

I clenched my teeth as I squinted against the late sun. Then I said, 'I came so *close*.'

'King Mohan,' he said, 'is a hard man, and even more, a willful one. But it may be as you said, that in the end he will see where his will should lead him. Give it time, Valashu.'

'But that is just it, sir,' I said to him. 'I have no more time.'

That, however, was not quite true, for some three hundred miles and many days of hard marching still lay between my army and the plain of the Detheshaloon. We crossed over into Taron early the next afternoon. At a bone-jolting pace, we passed through a rich countryside of apple orchards and farms growing barley and rye. We bought supplies from the Taroners, who were generous with their prices. Then, nearly a week after my meeting with King Mohan, we made our way up into the Iron Hills outside of Nar. This ancient city, largest in the Nine Kingdoms, spread out on the other side of these red hills to the north and west. Its many smithies cast a bitter black smoke into the air. The stinging of my eyes and the reek of hot iron made me instantly recall the three other times that I had journeyed to Nar, where King Waray for many years had plotted to make himself the greatest king and Taron the greatest kingdom in the Morning Mountains.

King Waray arranged for my army to encamp near Nar's northern outskirts, on the Tournament Grounds laid out on a greenway of many acres. Then he invited me and my friends, though not my captains, to a meeting at his palace, which was built on the side of a hill overlooking the city's southern districts. He invited as well King Viromar. Although Taron had never been particularly friendly with Kaash, King Waray must have wished to charm Kaash's new king, as he had so many others. He would be glad to have Kaash's help against Waas, for he had long had ambitions against King Sandarkan's domain.

King Waray received us on a lawn giving out onto a stream flowing down through a wild green past the palace. Some of us sat on rocks above the stream; others stood to appreciate the view of the city below. Three of King Waray's advisors joined us: Lord Jurathar, Lord Marjun, and the very tall and very muscular Lord Stavaru. King Waray also invited his only child: a daughter named Chantaleva. Many called her beautiful, with her jet black hair and finely sculpted features. I thought her too thin and too pale, as her delicate skin seemed almost bone white. She took a quiet pleasure in pouring the coffee that King Waray's attendants brought out to us, but she had few words to offer anyone.

King Waray stood with his back against a large rock with the rest of us arrayed around him. After I had told him of what had transpired since I had become king and marched with my army out of Mesh, he rapped his king's ring with its five diamonds against his coffee cup and said, 'King Valamesh – no man could be more worthy of succeeding your father, whom I felt fortunate to call my friend. If he is looking down from the stars, he would rejoice at your great victory in Delu, as everyone who knows of it must.'

King Waray, a strikingly handsome man with a broad forehead and radiant eyes, spoke as always with the steel knife of his true thoughts and intentions concealed by a handkerchief of silk. His voice spilled out through his long, high nose as through a trumpet, even as it seemed to rumble and catch deep within his throat. It could be as sweet as sugared wine – and as deadly as poison.

'But it is a pity that you failed to persuade King Mohan to ally with you,' he continued. 'War, among our people, has always been the tragedy of our people. Athar's quarrel with Lagash couldn't help but lead to war, once you failed in Tria to bring the Valari into alliance.'

King Waray, of course, knew that I hadn't come up to his palace that day just to drink a good Galdan coffee and to appreciate the view of smoky Nar from these wooded heights. He had always resisted my leadership of the Valari – as he did now.

'*That* war could be helped,' I told him.' I stood across from him with my boot pressed up against an exposed tree root. I looked very hard for his innate nobility within his gleaming eyes. 'King Mohan *wanted* to make alliance. And might have, but for his fear of King Kurshan.'

And how often, I wondered, had King Waray spoken to King Mohan of King Kurshan's design to build a great fleet of ships and so strengthen his realm in order to threaten King Mohan's? And all under the guise of friendship and *averting* war?

'*That* fear,' he said to me, 'is reasonable enough. For how long has King Kurshan been readying his army for an attack against Athar?'

'Only as long as he has feared that King Mohan would attack him.'

'That concern, too,' King Waray said, 'is not without foundation. I have reasoned with King Mohan many times, trying to find a way to make a permanent peace between Athar and Lagash.'

I tried not to smile at this. I said, 'You are a reasonable man.'

'I like to think I am. And that others speak of me that way, too.'

'Then can you not *reason* with both King Mohan and King Kurshan one last time? I must march west with my army tomorrow, but if you sent fast riders east to Athar and Lagash, there is still time for you to help persuade their kings to put aside war and join us at the Detheshaloon.'

'To avoid *their* war, you mean,' he said, tapping his cup. 'Only to join *you* in making a much worse war against the Red Dragon.'

'What comes is not of my making.'

'Is it not? If you hadn't put yourself forward as the Maitreya, if you hadn't lost the Lightstone to Morjin, we might have made alliance two years ago and kept the Dragon from marching on the Nine Kingdoms.'

I tried to quiet the wild, hot rush of blood through my veins. I asked him: 'Do you mean, *you* might have organized the alliance and led it?'

King Waray took a sip of coffee, then waved his hand at my question as if shooing away a biting fly. 'Many have spoken of me as warlord of our people, but I think that it is perhaps less important *who* leads us than *that* we are led. I would see even King Hadaru take command of our armies, if that was the only way to stop the Red Dragon.'

My heart beat hard with a sudden surge. 'Then you *will* support an alliance?'

King Waray flashed me a brilliant smile, and said, 'I always have. It was always just a question of how to bring it about.'

'The way to bring it about is simple: send word to Athar and Lagash that Taron will not tolerate a war just beyond her border. Inform King Hadaru that you have joined with Mesh and Kaash. When Athar marches after us, so will Lagash. Then King Hadaru will have no choice but to lead the Ishkans out against Morjin. As Ishka goes, so Anjo will have to follow. Perhaps even King Sandarkan will be persuaded to make alliance as well.'

After I finished speaking, King Waray stood gazing at me. His counselors waited near him, ready to support him in whatever line of reasoning or debate he might pursue. I hated it that so much should depend upon this one conniving king who had always positioned himself at the center of Valari affairs. And then King Waray said to me, 'You have given this matter a great deal of thought.'

'I have thought of little except Morjin's defeat for a long time.'

King Waray, like a duelist evading his opponent's sword and then circling, turned his attention to Abrasax, Master Matai and the others of the Seven. He said to Abrasax: 'We of the Nine Kingdoms had long heard that secret Masters ruled the Brotherhood, but until today I had thought this a legend. I have to say that it is strange to see *Brothers* supporting an Elahad as the Valari's warlord. What of the Brotherhood's rule forsaking wine, women and war?'

Abrasax's corona of white hair and beard gleamed in the sunlight as he said to King Waray, 'The spirit of our rule has led us to see that forsaking war is a good thing but ending it forever would be even better.'

'I see,' King Waray said, glancing at me. 'The Elahad's dream.'

He smiled at he turned toward Maram, who sat on a fat rock imbibing his coffee with too much relish. I wondered if he had somehow persuaded one of the attendants to add a little brandy to it.

Then King Waray asked, 'But is not fighting a war to end war something like hoping for sobriety by drinking dry every cask of wine in the world?'

Before Abrasax could answer, Maram put in, 'Ah, well – there must be a bottom to everything.'

Abrasax only smiled at this. Then he looked at King Waray. He, too, could circle around an opponent, though the sword he wielded was not one of steel. He seemed to look down deep into King Waray, and he said, 'What ails you, lord? What has made you so cynical?'

King Waray's face darkened in anger, but he could not hold the Grandmaster's kindly gaze. He turned to Master Juwain, and said to him in a sweet but pinched voice: 'Am I to understand that your order has made you its Master Healer? Was that your reward for removing gelstei from the school here without my leave?'

A couple of years ago, King Waray had closed down the Brotherhood's school in Nar, in part because of Master Juwain's necessary indiscretion. It seemed that King Waray had never forgiven him this slight defiance – and, as it happened, for other things.

'We made Master Juwain the Brotherhood's Master Healer,' Abrasax said, 'because on all of Ea there is none more worthy.'

'Is there not?' King Waray said. He held his hand out toward Bemossed, sitting on a rock with Estrella at the edge of the stream. 'But what of this one that King Valamesh, with the Brotherhood's blessing, has now put forth as the Maitreya?'

Bemossed stood up to address King Waray, saying much as he had before: 'I am no healer, as Master Juwain is, for I know little of his art. But sometimes, a kind of light that heals passes through me, and then –'

'And then,' King Waray said, interrupting him, 'I suppose people are miraculously made well. If true, you are too modest.'

'It *is* true,' Master Juwain said. 'His power far exceeds my own, and he would make a better Master Healer than I if he didn't have other work to do.'

'And you,' King Waray told Master Juwain, 'aspire to modesty, too. I believe that someday you will succeed, for you have much to be modest about.'

I could almost feel Master Juwain's misshapen ears burning with shame; King Waray's daughter, Chantaleva, looked at Master Juwain as she let out a little cough. She coughed again, this time harder, and Estrella got up and went over to her. Estrella's dark, quick eyes seemed to ask permission of the princess as she laid her hand on Chantaleva's chest.

Bemossed, upon noticing this, stepped up to Chantaleva, too, and rested his hand on top of Estrella's. Then he said to King Waray, 'Your daughter is cachetic – it is the white plague, isn't it?'

At this, Lord Jurathar looked at the immense Lord Starvaru in surprise, while old Lord Marjun studied King Waray's angry face. And King Waray shook his long finger at Master Juwain as he snapped at him: 'You promised, upon your honor as a *healer*, to keep this confidence!'

'But I have, King Waray!' Master Juwain said. 'I have told no one – not even my order's Grandmaster.'

Abrasax nodded his head to confirm this. It now came out that Master Juwain, on his mission to Nar two years before, had attempted something more profound than purloining gelstei, and that was the healing of Princess Chantaleva. As King Waray saw things, Master Juwain had failed. Even though, in truth, he had not failed completely.

'There is no cure for the white plague that I know,' Master Juwain said. 'Morjin bred this disease with the aid of a green gelstei two thousand years ago, and I hoped to use *my* gelstei to undo its hold upon the princess. I am sorry that I could not.'

'But it seems you kept the disease from progressing,' Abrasax said. 'At least, from progressing too quickly. How many can live with the white plague eating at them as long as the princess has?'

Chantaleva's face seemed to grow even paler. I did not think that she had made her peace with her inevitable death. And from the look of adoration and dread with which King Waray favored her, I knew that his fear for his daughter was even greater than her own.

'My apologies,' King Waray said to Master Juwain with a real warmth flowing out of him. 'We must be grateful for the time that my daughter has had. But I would give a barrel of diamonds to anyone who would give her a long and happy life.'

I said nothing to this declaration, and did not question King Waray as to where these diamonds might have come from. At least, I did not question him, with words. But I thought that King Waray sensed my doubt of him, for his belly tightened up as if he had eaten tainted meat, and he fell back upon his habit of evasion and scheming.

'My daughter is dear to me, and I possess no greater treasure,' he told me. 'I would give my own life and claim upon my kingdom to see her made well, but if she *were* healed, well, then I would have to see her married and leave my house. A king, a *father*, can take consolation in this loss only by seeing his daughter wed to the most worthy of men, and one who could make her happy.'

He smiled at me, and his handsome face seemed as bright as the sun.

'A worthy man, indeed,' he continued, repeating himself as he looked at me. 'A great warrior who will sire grandchildren great not just in their prowess at arms, but strong and bright in their spirits. Such a son-in-law I have always longed for, one who might stand by my side in accomplishing the greatest dreams of our people.'

I looked right back at King Waray. I gathered that he was offering Chantaleva to me as a wife, if only I would support him as the Valari's warlord.

'Of course, it is true,' he said, 'that my daughter might *not* be healed, and then she would have only a few more years to live, as might I. And so the rule of Taron would have to pass to the man I called my son.'

Now I noticed Chantaleva gazing at me – not in desire of me as a husband, I thought, but only from a gnawing wish that somehow I might help her to live long enough to see her children grow up healthy and strong.

'A true treasure,' King Waray said as he regarded his daughter with what seemed a deep love. 'The greatest of all treasures.'

I did not know what to say to him. Certainly I could not consider marrying Chantaleva, sick or well. But neither did I wish to antagonize King Waray with too blunt a refusal. It was then that Liljana, who had remained quietly seated all this time, came to my rescue by drawing his aggression toward her.

'Your daughter is indeed beautiful,' Liljana said to King Waray. She had her hand buried in her pocket, and I sensed her grasping her gelstei. 'Any king would be proud to have her as a wife. Or any prince. I am sure that Prince Issur looks forward to being just the son-in-law of whom you have spoken.'

King Waray's eyes grew dark with a quick and sudden rage. He must have realized that his deepest maneuvering had been exposed. He did not, however, attribute this uncovering to its correct source, for he turned from Liljana to Master Virang, and pointed his finger at him as he called out: 'You are the Brotherhood's Meditation Master, aren't you? Have you then turned from the most profound of arts to reading minds? It is said that the Brotherhood keeps the ancient blue gelstei, once used by the accursed witches of the Maitriche Telu.'

As King Waray glowered at Master Virang, Liljana managed to keep her face as still as a mountain lake. No hint of emotion rippled upon it.

'Many things are said of the Brotherhood,' Master Virang called out with his almond eyes twinkling. 'But I had never heard that we could read minds.'

'Then you must keep spies at your schools in Ishka. You should not heed too closely the rumors they report or share them with King Valamesh's companions and confidants.'

Liljana might have smiled at this, if she had been able to smile. Instead, she looked at King Waray and said: 'It is certainly no rumor that King Hadaru made battle against Taron in response to your conspiring against him – and that you lost this battle. And that King Hadaru was pierced with a lance and the wound still festers. As many do, you wait for him to die, don't you?'

King Waray looked at Liljana with a sudden new understanding – and dread. He must have finally suspected that she might be one of the witches he had just decried.

'And what do *you* know of this . . . Lady Liljana Ashvaran of Tria?'

King Waray turned all the considerable force of his person upon her in a blaze of his black eyes. But Liljana would be cowed by no man, and so she answered his question with another: 'What did it take for you to make the peace with Ishka?'

'Only the blood of too many of my warriors!'

'And also your promise of your daughter's hand in marriage to Prince Issur – is that not so?'

'Yes!' King Waray cried out.

'And your support of King Hadaru as the warlord of the alliance?'

King Waray took a step away from his rock, and he clapped his hands across his temples as he shouted at her: 'Witch! Mindreader! Leave me alone!'

But Liljana had not finished with this vain, manipulative king. She said to him, 'King Hadaru does not know that your daughter is ill, does he? No doubt you hope that he dies before this is discovered. And then, with your daughter wedded to the new and inexperienced king of Ishka, you would use all your influence to –'

'*I* should lead the Valari!' King Waray cried out. 'It is what I have striven for all my life!'

In the silence that fell over the rocks around him, the rushing of the stream seemed as loud as the ocean. King Waray stared at Liljana with such a deadly intensity that he did not immediately notice Bemossed pressing his hand against Chantaleva's chest. He turned just in time to behold the radiance that passed from Bemossed's hand into Chantaleva. I might have thought that it would take some days, at least, for this healing force to work upon her. Within moments, however, the color returned to her face, and she stood breathing more easily as she stared at Bemossed in awe.

'I am well!' she cried out. She bent to kiss Bemossed's hand.

'But how do you know?' King Waray asked, going over to her.

'I *know*!' she said. She clasped Bemossed's hand to her chest. 'There is no more pain *here*.'

And upon her utterance of this word, I felt a sudden new pain come alive within King Waray's chest.

'Maitreya!' he called out to Bemossed. He bowed his head, then declared, 'I shall give you *two* barrels of diamonds.'

'Thank you, King Waray,' Bemossed told him. 'But I would not know what to do with such wealth.'

'What is it that you want, then?'

In answer, Bemossed looked at me in a deep and painful silence.

'That, surely, must be obvious,' King Waray continued, answering his own question. 'You would see Valashu Elahad lead the alliance.'

'To lead it, yes,' Bemossed said. 'But not to war.'

'But war is nearly upon us. What will you do?'

'I will fight,' Bemossed said mysteriously. 'As all must fight.'

'I don't understand,' King Waray said.

But Bemossed did not enlighten him. He just gazed down at the city below us, where Nar's white Tower of the Sun rose up almost as high as the surrounding hills.

'What will *you* do?' I asked King Waray. 'Will you support the alliance? And not just with words, but with your warriors and your own sword?'

King Waray stood considering this. Around him gathered Abrasax and the others of the Seven, who had their hands thrust down into the pockets of their robes. Though none of them looked at King Waray, I could sense their deep concentration upon him; I sensed as well that Master Juwain, and not Abrasax, guided the Seven in directing the power of their hidden gelstei at King Waray.

'I *will* support it!' King Waray finally said to me.

'Good!' I called it. 'Then who is to lead?'

King Waray thought about this for a few moments. Then he said, 'When we Valari first came to the Morning Mountains, we made our homes in Mesh. Mesh has always been at the forefront of our affairs. And it was a Meshian, King Aramesh, who defeated Morjin at the Sarburn.'

He paused as he looked at me, and I waited for him to say more. Once, in the silver shimmer of my sword, I had seen that one, and only one, could unite the Valari. The wind flowing across the world from the west seemed to whisper his name to me.

'And that is why,' he went on, 'that this time, the king who leads us must *not* be from Mesh. We Valari have failed, too many times. Even Aramesh failed to defeat Morjin once and forever. I am sorry, Valashu Elahad, but the Valari will not follow you.'

For ages, I thought, the Valari had suffered two opposing impulses: to elevate Mesh and the Elahads as exemplars of all that was most truly Valari, and to tear down my kingdom and my family out of jealousy.

'They would follow me,' I said to King Waray, 'if you did. Will you?'

He stood straight across from me looking at me deeply, and I knew that he wanted to say yes. Something, however, kept him armored inside his ambition and pride as with a breastpiece made of steel plate. I knew that within my heart I held a sword that could cut it open.

Kane waited to my right with his hand poised near a very different kind of sword. His black eyes seemed to ask me if I wanted him to draw it and slay this recalcitrant king.

'How *can* I follow you?' King Waray said to me.

I looked past him, down across Nar, where the green, wooded plain of Taron vanished into the west of the world. King Waray had spoken truly: I *did* have a dream, and I saw a way to make it be. But, always, men opposed me. And not just evil ones such as Morjin and the Red Priests of the Kallimun, but foolish kings such as Sulavar Jehu Waray. He had his own ideas for the world, and for himself. I knew that if only I could eliminate such men, I could accomplish the greatest of things. That, however, was Morjin's way, and too often, Kane's. I knew that I could never allow him to put King Waray to the sword. And neither could I use the true Alkaladur to destroy King Waray's will so that he would give his consent to what I desired. If I did, with him and with others, then soon I would kill my own soul and make myself like unto Morjin.

'How can you not help me to fight our enemy?' I asked him.

If I could not wield the sword within me to rule King Waray, much less to slay him, then at least I could hold it before him like a shining silver mirror. And what might he see as he stood there gazing into my eyes? I thought that he, too, had a secret dream, which was to ally the whole world as one so that Chantaleva's children might grow up to pursue meditation and music and all the higher things. He would make a better world, cleansed of hideous diseases such as the white plague. He might, too, behold himself as I sometimes could: that his immense pride concealed a haunting sense of his basic flawlessness; that his refusal to tell an outright lie suggested a long-forgotten love of truth; that all his intrigues sprang from his quest for a deeper ordering of the world.

I thought, too, that he might come alive to his own compassion and open himself to all the immense suffering around him – if only I could open *myself* to him.

'King Waray,' I said to him, holding out my hand, 'let us join our forces together!'

I felt his urge to reach out and press his palm against mine. Then, at the last, he looked away from me, down at the ground. And he said, 'Perhaps we should first wait to see if Morjin really does march his armies toward the Morning Mountains.'

At this, Daj jumped up from his rock to face King Waray. Daj usually had a great respect for rank, even that of false kings such as Morjin. Now, however, he shook his fist at King Waray and cried out, 'If you won't help Val, Morjin will win! What is *wrong* with you! How can you call yourself a *king*?'

For what seemed a long time, I stared at my empty hand. Then I pulled my arm back and closed my fingers around the hilt of my sword.

'This council,' King Waray said, glaring at Daj as his face flushed with anger, 'is over.'

He drew in a deep breath, then looked at me and added, 'You should consider long and well before you take this boy with you to war. You should consider taking *anyone*, King Valamesh.'

He paused to regard Bemossed. 'Especially this man. He might really be the Maitreya.'

After that my companions and I, with King Viromar and the Seven, rode back down from King Waray's palace into Nar. At a tree-lined curve along the winding road, Daj pushed his horse up to me and asked: 'How can the Valari kings keep spurning you? How *can* they, Val?'

King Viromar, riding just behind us, had remained as faithful as anyone could be. He cleared his throat as he looked at Daj and said, 'Some of them, at least, must hope that now that Morjin possesses the Cup of Heaven, he will leave the Nine Kingdoms alone.'

He fell silent for a moment, then added, 'They must think that Morjin's quarrel was only with Valashu Elahad.'

I smiled at this with great bitterness. I said, 'No, that is not why the Valari refuse me.'

'Why, then?' Daj asked.

'Because,' I told him, 'I broke their hearts.'

I stopped Altaru and turned my huge warhorse around in the middle of the road so that I could speak with my friends. 'In Tria, we almost made an alliance. And so in coming an inch from a great dream, the Valari kings have had to tell themselves that it would have been a nightmare.'

But Master Juwain, for one, would not accept my condemnation of myself. He told me, 'You have not failed, Val. King Waray might yet come to his senses.'

'Do you really think so?'

Master Juwain nodded his head and said to me, 'King Waray suffers from a sad malady: he experiences the world and other people as does any other man. But because his heart chakra has been blocked, he cannot *feel* anything of what he experiences very deeply.'

'And so,' Abrasax explained, looking at Master Virang, 'we employed the great crystals to open *all* his chakras, and particularly that of the heart.'

I thought of Master Juwain using the dead Master Okuth's green stone on King Waray, and *my* heart warmed, slightly.

'All that happened today,' Master Juwain told me, 'might yet work a slow magic on King Waray. Give it time, Val.'

I ground my teeth together as I saw the moments of my life running out like grains of sand through an hourglass.

And then Maram, sitting on top of his big horse, turned to Liljana and accused her: '*You* opened up King Waray like popping a cork out of a bottle! But you *promised* that you would never, without permission, use your gelstei to look into anyone's mind!'

'How many times have *you* broken your promise to forsake brandy?' she countered. 'When the need is great enough, exceptions must be made. King Waray needed to be pushed by the truth of what he has done. I thought it would save Val from pushing in his way, as he is loath to push.'

I did not know whether to thank her or to take her to task for what she had done. Kane, though, could not abide her violation of King Waray. He sat on his horse glaring at her, and I did not like the look that burned through his black eyes.

'But what shall we do now?' Maram asked. 'Since we haven't the strength even to consider going up against Morjin?'

I closed my eyes as I gripped the hilt of my sword. Then I told him, 'We will march on. If the warriors consent, tomorrow we will march toward Anjo and then cross over the mountains. And we will join with Sajagax and the other Sarni tribes.'

'And then?' Maram asked.

'We will wait – and hope for the magic that Master Juwain has spoken of.'

'You mean, hope for a miracle.'

I tried not to let my terror show as I forced myself to smile. And I said to him, 'There is always hope.'

As I turned my horse back around and looked out at the cloud-darkened sky to the west, I prayed that the words I had spoken would not prove to be a lie.

18

The next morning, with the wind blowing in rain clouds from the west, I called for the warriors of Mesh, Kaash and Delu to assemble on the grassy fields of the Tournament Grounds. Twenty thousand men stood in their gleaming armor to hear what I had to say. I told them that we could count on no allies among the Valari; I said that I still intended, however, to answer Sajagax's call and join with the Kurmak tribe in drawing swords against the Red Dragon. Anyone, I said, who did not want to make this fight was welcome to return to his home, without penalty or shame. It touched my heart that not a single man declined to march with me.

Two hundred miles lay between Nar and the appointed meeting place on the Wendrush. I led my army up the Nar Road for sixty of these miles at a bone-bruising pace. Summer rains found us passing through pastures, and soaked us to the skin. A few score of my men, suffering from chafing boots and bleeding feet, had to drop out of their columns and ride in the wagons. But then, after we crossed over the Culhadosh River into King Danashu's realm of Anjo, I had to order that every spare inch of space in the wagons be cleared. Indeed, I asked Lord Harsha to use the last of the gold that we had brought with us, jangling in little chests, to purchase more wagons – and great quantities of aged birch. I set our arrow makers to fashioning as many thousands of killing shafts as they could, sitting in their workshops inside jostling wagons. The wood of the white birch, especially from the upland forests of Anjo, was famed across Ea for making the straightest and truest arrows.

King Danashu declined to meet with me, although our route took us down through Onkar and the barley fields of Jathay, where King Danashu held court at Sauvo. He sent an envoy to inform me that he could not possibly consider leading any of his warriors against Morjin at this time. This did not surprise me. After King Danashu had conspired to take sides with King Waray against Ishka, King Hadaru had forced him to yield to Ishka the duchy of Adar and the barony of Natesh. Everyone knew that King Danashu feared that King Hadaru would soon send his entire army against Anjo, though King Danashu's envoy did not speak of this. For a long time, many had ridiculed King Danashu as a king in name only; now, with two great pieces of his realm broken off and the rest of it under dire threat from Ishka, he seemed less a king than ever.

His greatest lords, however, in consequence had taken upon themselves more and more of the royal prerogatives. Two of these – Duke Rezu of Rajak and Duke Gorador of Daksh – I had met on my first journey to Tria on the Great Quest. When I pointed my army across the high pastures of Daksh, with its small stands of trees and many herds of white sheep spread across rising green hills, both of these lords led the knights and warriors of their small domains out to join us. As Duke Rezu, a man with a face as sharp as flints, put it: 'Who, in their right senses, would fear King Hadaru above Morjin?'

Although the thousand men that these two dukes brought with them increased the size of our army only slightly, we could take good cheer that now three of the Nine Kingdoms would be represented in the coming battle.

We had a hard time crossing the mountains. The ice-capped peaks of the great Shoshan range rose up like a fortress of white and blue before us. The road through these rocky heights had crumbled nearly to rubble, for few came this way anymore, and no one kept it in repair. An early snow caught half my army coming down the side of a jagged mountain in the Goshbrun Pass; nearly all of the Delians suffered from frostbitten toes, for they had no footwear suitable for such harsh weather. Master Juwain managed to heal all of them with the warm green flame of his varistei, and so no one spoke of gangrene and amputation. Even so, it was a harbinger of more bitter assaults to the flesh soon to come.

At last, early in Ioj, my small army made the descent down to the vast steppe of the Wendrush. These sun-seared grasslands opened out to the west for what seemed an infinite distance. As before on our passage of the Mansurii's lands, we trod here with great care. Although Sajagax's Kurmak warriors would certainly greet us as allies, even if dangerous ones, the same could not be said of the Adirii, at least not some of this fierce tribe's clans. I remembered too well, two years before, leading a force of knights through country not far from here. Warriors of the Adirii's Akhand clan had crossed the Snake River to attack us, and had tried to steal the Lightstone. Sonjah, guiding us across the Wendrush's rolling eastern hills, explained that the Akhand's own chieftain had long since punished these treacherous Akhand; she assured us that *all* the Adirii had gathered to Sajagax's banner and would welcome us as brothers in arms. I wanted to believe her. Still, it grieved me to march nearly blind into this open land, for I did not know how far south Morjin had moved his army. And worse, I did not know if he might have sent out the warriors of the Marituk tribe, or others, ahead of his main force to harry us and kill us from afar with arrows.

And then the next day we came upon the Rune River, flowing here on a winding and westerly course. We marched to the north of this shallow brown water. It had not yet come time for my men to strap on their ankle bells, yet even so, the great noise of my army passing through the short yellow grass flushed many animals: antelope and ostrakats and huge herds of shaggy, bellowing sagosk. Lions we espied in their prides hunting these beasts; vultures circled in the sky high above the lions' kills, though they would not come down to earth to fight over the lions' leavings until we had passed by. How many more of these dreadful birds, I wondered, waited beyond the edge of the world to cover the field where my men must inevitably line up to face Morjin's?

Three days later, we came upon the Detheshaloon where the Rune turned south across the desiccated grasslands, even as Sonjah had said. This great mound, topped by a pile of rocks that looked something like a human skull, rose up some five miles to the north of the river and four hundred feet above the surrounding plain. Indeed, as no other feature of the earth here for many miles loomed more prominently, the Kurmak had named the nearby steppe after it. For ages the Kurmak warriors had come to this place to hunt. As far as Sonjah could tell us, though, the Sarni had never made battle within sight of these ominous-looking rocks.

In looking upon them, Abrasax declared: 'There is a great earth chakra here. I have seen few other places of such power.'

Sajagax had encamped his army down along the river. As we drew nearer, I looked in vain for the herds of animals and the rows of circular felt tents that made up much of the movable city in which Sajagax usually took up his residence. Sonjah informed us that Sajagax had left his tribe's women, children and old men – and their dwellings – farther to the southwest, on the banks of the Snake a few miles from where it joined the Poru. Should Morjin defeat Sajagax, such a safeguard would not really protect his people, but at least it would give them time to flee across the Snake into the open steppe to the south.

The warriors of the Adirii tribe, under Xadharax, had likewise arrived unencumbered by most material or familial possessions. They made their campfires to the west of Sajagax's warriors farther down along the river. Sajagax had apportioned to my army many acres of ground to the east of his army. We Valari and Delians immediately set to erecting our tents close – but not too close – to the Rune's muddy banks. The Kurmak warriors, watching us work, let out little whistles of scorn that the famed Valari should be so soft as to take tents with them to war. But they, I thought, had not just marched five hundred miles on foot across two great mountain ranges, where the snowy heights would freeze a Sarni warrior huddled beneath a smelly old sagosk robe.

That night, after Sajagax had returned from a lion hunt, he invited my captains and me, with my friends, to hold council. Though the Sarni at war might eschew the luxury of tents, they did not altogether refuse shelter. At the center of the Kurmak encampment many stiff hides had been erected as a windbreak around a huge firepit and several smaller ones. More hides over-hung the top of this circular wall, providing some protection against rain while allowing a clear view of the sky. The sky, as I remem-bered, was one of the three things that the Sarni revered.

Sajagax waited with other Sarni warriors in front of the blazing main fire to greet us. Of all the men I had known save one, he was the largest, not in size, for that distinction belonged to Aradhul of the Ymanir, but in his character and his vast, soaring sense of himself. It seemed that the entire steppe, stretching from the Morning Mountains to the Nagarshath range of the White Mountains, could not contain him. And as for his person, he was no small man. He stood taller than even myself and most Valari; bands of muscle bulged out from his bare, massive arms, encircled with gold. He had the neck of a bull and hands as strong as a bear's paws. As he crushed me close to him in a ferocious embrace, I smelled lion: in the black fur that trimmed his gold-embroidered doublet and upon his breath. Earlier, as I learned, Sajagax had put an arrow into a huge, black-maned lion at the unbelievable distance of four hundred yards. To celebrate this feat, he had eaten the lion's uncooked heart. Streaks of blood still stained the gray mustache that drooped down beneath his rocklike chin; his harsh face had split open with the widest of smiles. His eyes, as brilliantly blue as sapphires, seemed to take delight in all life's zest and cruelty – and most of all that night, I thought, in me.

'Valashu Elahad!' he shouted in a voice that rolled out like a clap of thunder. 'King Valamesh, now, Victor of the Battle of Shurkar's Notch, Vanquisher of the Enemy at the Seredun Sands – and Warlord of the Valari!'

For a while he stood calling out my other successes, mainly those won through force of arms against Morjin or his allies. Then he turned to greet those who accompanied me: 'King Viromar! Duke Rezu! Duke Gorador! Prince Thubar! Lord Tomavar! Lord Tanu! Lord Avijan! . . .'

And so it went, Sajagax stepping forward to clasp hands and welcome us. When I presented Abrasax and the rest of the Seven, he cocked his great head to one side as if looking for secrets that he thought they must conceal. And he said: 'Master Juwain, we are well met again, wizard! If the others of your order have such prowess as you with the magic crystals, then they will surely work marvels against our enemy.'

Then he came up to Bemossed. For nearly a minute he remained motionless as if caught by the deeper marvel of Bemossed's soft brown eyes. He reached out a blunt finger to trace the lines of the black cross tattooed on Bemossed's forehead. And he called out, 'This is the one that we have been waiting for! The Shining One – I know it is he! With him riding with us, I care not if Morjin commands a million men!'

Most of the Sarni warriors, gathered in close, looked upon Bemossed with awe lighting up their harsh faces; but others did not. Although the Sarni could be the most hospitable of people, several of Sajagax's captains seemed not to approve of their chieftain's open touching of men whom they scorned as outland *kradaks* – even if one of them happened to be the Maitreya. They stood back in their fierce pride as Sajagax remembered his duties and in turn presented them: 'Urtukar! Baldarax! Yaggod! Braggod! Tringax!'

Although none of these famed warriors could be said to have been made from quite the same mold as Sajagax, each seemed cut from the same cloth. They were big men bearing scars on their faces and the naked limbs of their thickly muscled bodies. They wore a great wealth of gold in the chains hanging down from their necks. To all, and especially each other, they glared out a challenge in their cold blue eyes and fearsome countenances.

'Braggod, look!' a giant named Yaggod called out as he pointed past Bemossed. 'He returns, as I said he would! It is Five-Horned Maram!'

Braggod, a red-faced man with a thick yellow mustache hanging down to his chest, nodded his head to Maram with a quick snap of his neck and a sullen stare. He did not need Yaggod – or anyone – to remind him how Maram once had downed five great horns of beer to defeat him in a drinking contest.

'It *is* Five-Horned Maram!' Tringax said. 'Though who would recognize him, so thin and wearing a suit of Valari diamonds?'

'Thin or not,' Yaggod said, 'I'd bet that he could still hold enough beer for any three men.'

Tringax, a handsome young man with a saber cut marking his chin, smiled coolly at Braggod and said, 'Perhaps three such as Braggod.'

Braggod glowered at Tringax as if he contemplated stringing his great, double-curved bow to put an arrow through Tringax's mouth. Then he cast Maram a haughty look and said, 'It was luck that the *kradak* remained standing when I tripped. Fortune will favor me the next time we hold horns together.'

'*I* would bet against that,' Yaggod said.

'*Would* you?' Braggod shot back. 'What would you bet, then? Your second wife? Now Tala is a stout enough woman, and she breeds well, as I'll admit, but I have wives enough and –'

'I would bet my horse,' Yaggod broke in.

'Your sorrel?'

'Are you mad? Jaalii is worth any ten of your horses, and like my own brother. But I would bet my white, Basir, whom I won in battle with the Marituk. Against my pick of *your* horses.'

While Braggod stood considering Yaggod's wager, he looked doubtfully at Maram. My best friend waited just to my left to see how this mostly amicable testing would play out. He licked his lips in anticipation of another deep taste of the potent Sarni beer – or so I thought.

'*I* say,' Sajagax called out, stepping up to Maram, 'that the Champion of the Five Horns could drink down any man – maybe even myself! But I also say that this is no night for duels. Such things can wait until we defeat the Red Dragon!'

'Does that mean,' Maram asked him, 'that we are to sit with you and there is to be no beer?'

'No *beer*?' Sajagax cried out. 'Does the sky have no sun? Of course we shall have beer tonight! And meat, and the best of company – and we shall talk of the Shining One's coming among us and how to put our arrows and swords through the Red Dragon's filthy heart!'

And so it was. I sat in close with Sajagax to his right around the main fire, as did Bemossed, whom Sajagax insisted take the place next to him on his left. King Viromar and a few of my captains joined us there, too, along with Sajagax's captains and the Seven. A fat old warrior with saber scars splitting his gray mustache and cheeks positioned himself straight across the fire from Sajagax. Sajagax presented him as Xadharax: the chieftain of the Adirii tribe. Xadharax, as I saw, had gained his great girth from his love of beer, buttered bread and huge portions of fatty meat which he downed with quick stabs of his knife and great gusto.

Sajagax, true to his word, provided us with much meat: roasted antelope and hams of wild pig; sagosk steaks and ostrakat wings and the much-prized livers of the red gazelle. And yellow rushk cakes, too, and salted milk curds, and as much beer as a man could reasonably want to drink – even such as Maram and Braggod. I listened as Yaggod made a wager with Tringax as to which of their new wives would bear children first, and to other bits of conversation. And then, when we had finished our feast, it came time to discuss more important things.

'Morjin has certainly marched south after burning Tria,' Sajagax told me in his great, rumbling voice. 'We've had reports out of Alonia. The Dragon army moves along the Poru, and not the Nar Road, and so his first objective must be to attack us here before falling against the Nine Kingdoms.'

I nodded my head at this. 'But how far south has he come, then?'

'That, only the eagles know. But I have sent Atara and the Manslayers up the Poru to watch for his army.'

At the concern that gathered in my chest like a great, knotted fist, Sajagax slapped my shoulder and said, 'Do not worry about my granddaughter. She is a Manslayer, and none can move across the Wendrush with such stealth. Or, if discovered, flee with such speed.'

'Morjin,' I said, smiling grimly as I remembered his invasion of Mesh, 'can strike quickly, if pressed.'

'Perhaps. But the Dragon might have been slowed by a rebellion in the Aquantir. We had a rumor of this, too.'

'With half a million men behind him,' Tringax put in, 'the Dragon's army will move as slowly as a sagosk herd.'

'But he cannot have a half million men!' Yaggod said. 'He cannot feed so many!'

'He can if he slays every sagosk and antelope between the Long Wall and the Detheshaloon!'

'No – that's impossible,' Braggod countered. 'I'd wager that his army will starve coming across the Wendrush.'

'Will you? What will you wager, then? Your third wife?'

Sajagax allowed his captains to argue on in like manner for a while. Then he raised up his great bow, so thick with wrapped sinew and stiff that almost no one except himself could bend it. And he called out, 'I care not about our enemy's numbers, so long as we have arrows enough for each of them!'

At this, I nodded at Lord Harsha, sitting farther around the edge of the firepit. And Lord Harsha said, 'We had hoped to help with the matter of arrows.'

Then he told Sajagax of the wagon loads of birch and arrows that we had brought with us to his encampment.

'That is good!' Sajagax cried out. 'Anjori birch – the best, for arrows! We will give you much gold for this wood!'

'Keep your gold,' I told him. 'And give us instead an arrow storm that will drive back the Sarni who ride with Morjin.'

'We will give you a tempest!' Sajagax said, shaking his bow.

While his captains passed around huge horns full of frothy beer, he and I discussed strategies for the coming battle. It turned out that we had each, on our own, come to the much the same conclusion about our enemy and how he must be fought.

'Morjin,' I said to him, 'will concentrate his forces on killing the Valari. Therefore he will have his Sarni allies make as many armor-piercing arrows as they can. But you must have your fletchers make as many long range arrows as *they* can – as Lord Harsha has asked of our own arrow makers.'

Sajagax nodded his head at this. When Morjin's army formed up to face mine, our lines of foot would clash in the center of the field, with cavalry riding against each other on either wing. To protect our extreme flanks, I planned to station Sarni warriors, riding their quick steppe horses and wielding bow and arrow. Our only hope of victory, as both Sajagax and I knew, would be for the Sarni whom he commanded to drive off Morjin's Sarni allies.

'The long range arrows will help with that,' he said, 'if we have enough – and if your Lord Harsha can help keep us resupplied.'

Lord Harsha turned his single, bright eye on Sajagax. 'I will keep you in good wood, if I must, though I would rather cross swords with the Red Knights who ravaged my home.'

Lord Tanu, who would fight on foot along with his warriors, remained very concerned with protecting our army's flanks. And so he asked Sajagax: 'How badly will the Sarni who ride with Morjin outnumber your warriors?'

Sajagax shrugged his shoulders at this. Again he said, 'I care not about numbers – of the Sarni. Morjin will have the Marituk, Zayak, Siofok, Janjii and Danyak, certainly. And almost as certainly, the Usark, Tukulak and Western Urtuk. And perhaps the Mansurii. And I shall have who I have. If all answer my call, then as many as forty thousand warriors will ride with me against Morjin's Sarni – probably no more than sixty thousand of them. Those are good odds, for we are Kurmak and Adirii and the Manslayers! I'd wager all the grass and the whole sky of Wendrush upon them. But Morjin's armies out of the Dragon Kingdoms are a different matter. If he truly has a half million men against Valashu Elahad's twenty thousand, then I *must* care about those numbers.'

He cast me a penetrating look, and I said to him, 'If all the Valari answer my call, we shall many more warriors than twenty thousand.'

'But will they, Valashu? Will they truly come?'

I let my hand rest upon my sword's swan-carved hilt, and I said, 'Yes, they will come – I know they will.'

'They *must*,' Sajagax said. 'I have sent out the call to all the Free Kings to gather here under your banner.'

Tringax obviously resented what Sajagax had just told me, for his fair, handsome face contorted in a scowl, and he said to his chieftain: 'As things stand now, *you* command more warriors than does the Elahad – with more Sarni to gather and follow you. And we fight on the Kurmak's land. And so *you* should be warlord of this army.'

'A man has one fate only, and that is not mine,' Sajagax called out. 'I know nothing of fighting on foot with spear and shield, as the *kradaks* do. But Valashu Elahad knows a great deal of fighting on the Wendrush. With the Manslayers' help, he defeated the Akhand clan not far from here.'

Xadharax, staring at Sajagax across the firepit, did not remark upon this. He just sat with his chin buried deep within his jowls. But he must have felt shame for what his rogue warriors had done and a desire to redeem the Adirii in choosing the right side in the coming war.

'And at the Battle of Shurkar's Notch, with *my* help,' Sajagax continued, 'Valashu Elahad defeated an Alonian duke and a greater force of knights. And lost no man, Kurmak or Valari, killed! And at the Battle of the Asses' Ears, he led Manslayers and Danladi warriors under Bajorak against the Zayak *and* the Red Knights. And defeated them as well.'

'Three battles,' Tringax scoffed. 'You have led us to victory in thirty-three.'

'But never so great a one as the Seredun Sands. I have not the Elahad's brilliance in battle.'

'You *do*!' Tringax protested. 'It is wrong for you to elevate this Valari king at your expense and those of the warriors who –'

'Enough!' Sajagax roared out, slapping his hand against his great bow. 'I am Sajagax, chieftain of the Kurmak and victor of thirty-three battles, even as you say, and no one will call me a modest man! But the Elahad is to be warlord! *I* say. It was he who first dreamed of making an alliance against the Red Dragon.'

'And he who destroyed our main chance of it with his lie that he was the Maitreya!'

'He was only mistaken,' Sajagax said. 'Sometimes the world takes time to reveal a man's fate. And it is the Elahad's fate to be Guardian of the Lightstone and Protector of the Lord of Light. Is that not why we gather here, to fight for the Shining One?'

At this, Sajagax laid his hand on Bemossed's shoulder. And Bemossed stared into the fire's writhing flames.

'I, for one, fight because a warrior must fight!' Tringax shouted out. 'And to make Morjin's men bleed their guts out, and to see the Crucifier's eyes eaten by the ants!'

The Sarni, I knew, revered the truth – and the speaking of it – even above their horses.

'I fight to make my children safe!' Yaggod called out. 'My sons *will* ride freely beneath the sky hunting lions if I have to kill a thousand of our enemy!'

'I fight for plunder!' Braggod said. 'How much gold will Morjin's army bring to the battle?'

'And I fight for glory,' old Urtukar told us. 'A man can never have enough of it, and it is good to go back to the earth with his sons honoring his name.'

Sajagax nodded his head at this as he stroked his bow. 'Those are all good reasons. But what good is gold in a world of the dead? How will our children ever be safe unless we make a new world? And how shall we ever accomplish *that* unless we bring the Law of the One to all lands?'

'My father,' Tringax said, staring at Sajagax, 'taught me the Law of the One: "Be strong! Bear no shame! Seek glory! Live free or die!"'

For a while he went on reciting truths that he had learned as a child. When he had finished, Trahadak the Elder, the headman of the Zakut clan, rubbed his leathery old face, then declaimed as if speaking for Sajagax himself: 'There is a new Law now! Or rather, an old Law that we understand in a new light. And Sajagax was born to bring it to the Wendrush and to all peoples: "Be strong and protect the weak! Bear no shame of any evil act! Seek the glory of the One!"'

As he continued speaking, Tringax seemed to want to open himself to this new way that Sajagax strove to bring to his people. But as with a stone immersed in water, little of what Trahadak said really penetrated Tringax's heart or touched his savage sensibilities. Seeing this, a young warrior named Darrax shouted at Tringax: 'What is wrong with you? Can't you see that there is more to life than slaying your enemies and gathering gold and women to yourself? Is your glory more important than that of your tribe? Or the glory of the One?'

Parthalak, another young warrior, nodded his head at this as he said to Tringax: 'I will teach my children that a man is the greatest who controls himself and gives his life that his tribe might have greater life. And that the Light of the One should shine upon the world!'

'And I will teach that, too!' a warrior named Alphax called out.

'And I!' another shouted. 'He who brings the Law of the One to the world will bring alive the One's light in himself. How can such a light ever die? So Sajagax has taught us! So I believe!'

And so, I thought, did most of the fearsome warriors who would follow Sajagax into battle.

Then Sajagax looked across the fire and said to Tringax: 'I have only one fate, and no man will keep me from it. So it is with Valashu Elahad and what he was born to do. It is *good* for a warrior to fight, Tringax. And even better to slay our enemy. But it is best of all to shed our blood on thirsty soil and to die for the Shining One and what he will bring to the world. Such a warrior, I say, is *imakla* and dies *not* when he dies.'

As Tringax knelt by the fire considering Sajagax's paradoxical words, Bemossed rose up to his feet. Although slight of build and soft in his manner – and worn with exhaustion – within him blazed a fierceness that put to shame even the most warlike of the Sarni.

'Blood nourishes only when kept in one's veins,' he told everyone. 'I want men to *live* for me. That is, not for *me*. Only for that which passes through me and truly quenches parched soil.'

And with that, a brilliant light gathered in his eyes, and he looked at Tringax. The savage young warrior froze as if a hammer had struck his head. And in that moment, I sensed, Tringax's heart finally opened, and he found himself wanting to die for this gentle man.

Seeing this, Bemossed's face fell heavy with an immense sadness. He turned to Sajagax to thank him for his hospitality. Then he excused himself and walked off into the night.

And Sajagax called out in his huge voice: 'Let us then live for the Shining One, even as he has said! And how better to accomplish *that* than by killing as many of our enemy as we can?'

He called for everyone's horn to be filled afresh with bubbling black beer. Then he raised up his horn and said, 'Death to Morjin, and all who bow to him! Victory to Valashu Elahad and all who follow him! Victory, and life!'

The Sarni warriors sitting on their sagosk skins clinked horns with each other – and with the Valari lords who accompanied me. They spilled much beer onto the ground and drank even more. The sound of their exultation echoed onto the steppe, as did their accolade: 'Live free and long, King Valamesh – Warlord of the Valari and the Sarni!'

The next day, the warriors of the Eastern Urtuk rode into our encampment, and the day following that, all the fighting men of the Central Urtuk tribe. And then on the 18th of Ioj, the Niuriu under Vishakan arrived from the southwest, swelling the numbers of the Sarni who would fight beneath Sajagax's standard to nearly thirty-five thousand. Vishakan had once aided me on my journey home to Mesh with the Lightstone, and he greeted me as he might one of his own sons. He told us to look for the Danladi, keeping pace across the steppe only a day's ride behind him. When the sun rose above the blazing grasslands the following morning, many cheered to see the five thousand warriors of the Danladi tribe making their way toward us just south of the river. And I cheered when the Danladi's new chieftain urged his horse between the long lines of campfires toward my pavilion, for I saw that it was Bajorak, my old friend.

Although rather short for a leader of the Sarni, Bajorak commanded his warriors' intense loyalty through his keen intelligence and fierce fighting spirit. Three scars marked his face, which many would have called handsome. When he saw me waiting to greet him, he dismounted with great dignity and came up to me. He clasped my hand and said, 'Greetings, Valashu Elahad! When last we parted after killing the Zayak and Morjin's knights, you told me that we would meet again in a better time and place.'

'I always hoped we would,' I told him, squeezing his hand.

'I doubted it not.' He looked up at the rocks of the Detheshaloon and added, 'Though I must wonder if this is truly a better place.'

'Any place is good where two friends can stand together against the Red Dragon.'

He flashed me a bright smile, but due to the scars cut into his face, it seemed more of a scowl. And he said, 'Look at you! The hunted wanderer I knew has become a king!'

'And you,' I said, 'a chieftain.'

His scowl suddenly deepened. 'And there are many Danladi who did not want to see a headman of the Tarun clan lead them. But in the end, the warriors followed me.'

I remembered that after the great Artukan had died, his son, Garthax, had become chieftain of the Danladi. But many of the warriors hated Garthax for dealing with Morjin and pocketing the Red Dragon's gold; they even whispered that the Red Dragon had paid Garthax to assassinate Artukan, who had died in a terrible agony.

'It was finally proved!' Bajorak told me. 'Garthax got drunk one night and bragged to his third wife of what he had done. He poisoned his own father! They put a hot iron to Garthax's liver, and he finally confessed. Then they cut off his eyelids and his manhood, and staked him out in the sun. The yellowjackets ate at him all day. I was not there to hear it, but they say he died screaming louder than his father.'

He fell silent for a moment, then added, 'And so the Danladi warriors now ride with me, and I ride with Sajagax – and so with you.'

Again we clasped hands, and I said, 'And I am glad for that. As will be my men.'

Bajorak's blue eyes sparkled at this. He turned to look farther down the river, where the rows of my army's tents stretched off to the east.

'But how many men are we speaking of?' he asked me. 'I do not see an army as large as Sajagax promised would gather here.'

'That is because the men of the Free Kingdoms have not yet arrived. And neither have the rest of the Valari.'

Bajorak must have heard something in my voice that troubled him, for he asked me, 'But will they come, Valashu? Do you truly think they will come?'

I nodded my head to him, and told him, 'Yes, they will come – I know they will.'

Bajorak's spirits brightened the next day when one of Sajagax's outriders galloped into our encampment with the news of an army marching toward us from the east. But this proved *not* to be the warriors of the Nine Kingdoms, but rather the combined forces of Nedu, Thalu and the Elyssu, who marched with more than ten thousand outcast knights from Alonia – under Belur Narmada, Baron Maruth of the Aquantir, and others – and a few hundred from Surrapam. As well came King Hanniban, who claimed to reign in exile. Upon the fall of Eanna, he had assembled a fleet to lead five thousand of his countrymen and the others of the Free Kingdoms on a great voyage around the Bull's Horn and through the dangerous Straights of Storm into the Alonian Sea. They had put to shore at Adra, in Taron, and then marched into Anjo and crossed over the mountains through the same Goshbrun Pass as had my warriors. And so found their way here.

King Hanniban, thick in his body and heavy with years, had once exercised all his ruthlessness to keep me from being acclaimed as leader of the Free Kingdoms. But now, having been chastened at losing his realm and nearly his life to the armies of the Red Dragon, he desired vengeance upon Morjin. I sensed, too, that he wanted to see the Lightstone reclaimed and placed in the hands of the Maitreya. As he said when he met with me in my tent: 'This is the time when the world must be reborn – or die for all time. It is said that men, too, will be reborn, if they stand beneath the radiance of the Cup of Heaven. But if they do not, if they take from the gold gelstei darkness instead of light, as Morjin does, then they will surely die – for all time. The Great Darkness is so close now, is it not, King Valamesh?'

King Aryaman of Thalu, a great warrior as tall and blond as even the largest of the Sarni, patted his huge axe as he put things more simply: 'If we cut the Lightstone from Morjin's hand, we shall win. If not, every one of us will die – and the whole world along with us.'

Altogether these two kings – along with King Theodor of the Elyssu and King Tal of Nedu – had added almost fifteen thousand more men to my army.

'But that is not enough,' Maram said to me later as he quaffed

302

down a horn of Sarni beer when we were alone together. 'Not nearly enough.'

And then, on the 22nd of Ioj, we gained a great and unexpected ally – great in the spirit of battle, if not numbers. From out of the west came a band of warriors whom the Sarni at first mistook for animals walking on two legs. They had never seen, as few had, the extraordinary men called the Ymaniri. All of them stood more than eight feet tall and were thick as boulders in limb and body. Silky white fur covered them from head to unshod feet. I rode out to greet these five hundred giants, led by my old companion, Ymiru. A mesh of a metal too fine to be steel covered a leather armor encasing him. With his single hand (for a dragon had torn off his left arm in Argattha) he gripped a huge, iron-shod club called a borkor. His ice-blue eyes looked out above a broken nose, and they filled with great warmth as he saw me riding across the steppe toward him.

'Val!' he shouted at me in a voice like a volcano's rumble. 'We meet again!'

I dismounted and stepped over to him. I let my hand be engulfed within his huge fingers. Then I looked behind him at the shaggy men gripping their borkors and I said, 'Yes – to fight Morjin together, again.'

'It be my fondest hrope!' he told me. 'That, and seeing your furless face once more before I die.'

I smiled at this, then said, 'I never expected to see you here. It must be four hundred miles from the mountains across the open steppe – and through the country of the Zayak and Janjii at that.'

'And bad country it be. Nothing but grass and more grass, without a single mountain to hold the eye or point the way back hrome. And no place to hide when the little yellow-haired men attacked us.'

Some of my knights and a handful of Kurmak warriors, including Tringax and Braggod, had ridden out with me to behold the strange sight of the Ymaniri marching into our encampment. At Ymiru's characterizing of the Sarni as 'little,' Braggod's face flushed an angry red. He said nothing, however, as Ymiru stood nearly at the same height as Braggod sat on top his horse.

'I think they were Zayak,' Ymiru added. 'They loosed arrows at us as if they were hunting sagosk. But the arrows broke against *this*.'

So saying he ran his finger across the tiny links of his armor, which he called *keshet*. It seemed that the Ymanir had made this marvelous material – which proved to be nearly as soft as woven silk and bright as silver – with the aid of a purple gelstei.

'And then we charged them,' he went on. 'The yellowhairs didn't know that we Ymaniri can run as fast *as* sagosk, for a short way. They were too late turning around their hrorses. And so we went to work with *these*.'

He seemed deeply sad as he raised up his borkor, as did many of the men behind him. Then he said, 'But can we not go somewhere we can hrold council? There be much we need to discuss.'

We went back to my tent, where we met with our companions of old, along with Estrella. This magical girl proved to be even more of a wonder to Ymiru than he was to her. When we told of her talent for finding concealed things and summoning rain from a cloudless sky, he laid his huge hand on top of her head and said, 'It be too bad that she can't summon an earthquake to swallow up Morjin's army in a fiery hrole. And so I suppose we'll have to fight.'

A sudden enthusiasm blew through him like a wind. He patted his borkor and added, 'But that, I suppose, be why we came here, yes?'

'But how *did* you come here?' Maram asked him. He gave Ymiru a great beer-filled horn, which Ymiru drank down like a cup of milk. 'How could you possibly have known to come to this forsaken place?'

Ymiru smiled at Liljana, and I caught a flash of his big white teeth. 'It was the Materix of the Maitriche Telu who called us here. Through Audhumla.'

I remembered well this seven-foot-tall woman who sat with the other elders of Urdahir who ruled the Ymanir. It had been Audhumla, through the virtue of her blue truth stone, who had verified the story of my companions' and my quest to find the Lightstone – and so saved us from being put to death as unwelcome strangers to the Ymanir's land.

'The truth stone be a powerful galastei,' Ymiru told us, 'though not so deep as Liljana's blue crystal. Audhumla can use it to hear the truths or lies that people speak, though not to eavesdrop their thoughts. Not usually. But Audhumla has been open to Liljana's thoughts, spoken across the world through the virtue of *her* galastei. It was Liljana – late in Ashte this was – who called the Ymanir to war against the Red Dragon.'

At this, Maram and my other friends stared at Liljana in amazement. And Master Juwain said to her, 'But that was before we set out for Kaash and Delu! How could you have known to call the Ymanir to war when *we* didn't know yet that there would be a war – at least, not when and where the war's great battle would be fought?'

'She knew,' Kane growled out as if Liljana were a thief caught with a stolen jewel, 'because she has looked into Morjin's mind! Is that not so?'

Liljana met Kane's furious gaze with the softness of her round, pretty face, as with the moon throwing back the sun's fire. And she said to him, 'I only looked into his mind for a moment. And *not* the Red Dragon's mind – only that of his High Priest, Arch Yadom. Morjin has entrusted him with a blue gelstei.'

Kane stared at her as if the heat of his gaze might burn away her words to reveal the truth or a lie.

And Master Juwain said to her, 'But you shouldn't look into *anyone*'s mind. Even those of your sisters. Morjin might be waiting for just such a move. And so it is a peril to *your* mind. And even more, to your soul.'

'And even more perilous *not* to look!' Liljana shot back.

'But think of what he took from you in Argattha! And what he might take still!'

'I am not so afraid of Morjin as you might think. Perhaps it might avail us more to consider what *I* might do to *him*.'

'But, Liljana, the Dragon still has the Lightstone, and you have only –'

'I have what I have. We all must fight Morjin in our own way.'

Her words disturbed all of us, and myself not the least. I remembered back in Mesh asking her to use her gift against Morjin in much the same way as she obviously had. I said to her, 'But if you knew that Morjin would march on Sajagax before falling against the Nine Kingdoms, why didn't you tell me?'

Liljana shrugged her shoulders at this. 'I would have, but we were moving west in any case. And then Sajagax sent Sonjah to find you, and made the matter moot.'

'Perhaps,' I said to her, 'but you should have told me even so.'

Her voice softened as she said, 'I know I should have – I am sorry.'

But this wasn't good enough for Kane, who growled out, 'She'll give our plans away, damn it!'

'No, I won't,' Liljana told him. 'But what is there to give away, really? Morjin knows that we wait for him here to do battle.'

'But he does not know our numbers, yet, or our order of battle!'

'I don't know that myself,' Liljana said. 'Neither, I think, does Val.'

I rubbed my aching head. 'Nor will I, until I receive report of Morjin's numbers and how his army is composed. But when I do set the order of battle, Liljana, Morjin must *not* know.'

Again Liljana shrugged her shoulders. 'Of course he must not. And that is why, before the Seredun Sands, I did refuse to look into anyone's mind, even as Master Juwain has said.'

'And that be a good thing,' Ymiru put in, 'for a man's mind be a private place and hroly.'

He sighed, letting out a great breath like the wind. Then, looking at me, he added, 'Still, I'd like to know what be in the minds of the Valari kings. Will they draw swords against Morjin? You once promised me they would, Val.'

'And they will,' I reassured him. 'I know they will.'

'Well they had better come soon,' Ymiru murmured with a sad shake of his head. 'Otherwise, I don't think there be much hrope.'

But the next day dawned and dusked without a hint of any Valari marching forth to join us. Then, on the day following that, one of Atara's Manslayers rode into our encampment to report that Morjin's army approached from the northwest. Although the Manslayers, she said, had still not made a good count of our enemy's numbers, Atara estimated that Morjin's army might fall upon our position here within ten days, if they moved quickly enough.

'Ten days!' Maram called out in dismay when he heard this. 'Even if I could drink ten horns of beer each day, that would make only a hundred horns until *the* day, when there will be no more beer. A hundred horns – it seems too, too little to fill a man such as I.'

For eight days, as Ioj ended and Valte took hold of the Wendrush with warm weather and clear blue skies, Maram drank a great quantity of beer, though no one kept track of the number of horns. And then, on the third of Valte, just after dawn, one of Sajagax's outriders galloped into our encampment shouting out the news: 'They come! The Valari – they come!'

From thousands of tents strung out along the river, and from around thousands of campfires, men hurried forth in a great multitude to look out across the steppe. I stood with Sajagax, Vishakan, Bajorak, King Hanniban – and many, many others – gazing toward the red, rising sun. We waited perhaps half an hour, and then a great glitter brightened the sere grass of a rise some miles to the east. I watched in wonder as columns of men, some on horses and others on foot, came pouring over this hump of ground and drew closer. The slanting sun showed the standards of six armies: the blue horse of King Mohan's line, which had ruled Athar for centuries; the white Tree of Life sacred to Lagash; King Sandarkan's two crossed silver swords; the gold dragon worn by King Danashu of Anjo; King Waray's white, winged horse; and most marvelous of all, the great white bear of Ishka, resplendent against a blood-red field. I did not have time to wonder if King Hadaru had finally died and Prince Issur had taken command of my countrymen's most ancient enemy. For just then, Ymiru pointed his furry finger at the sparkle of lights in the east, and his vast voice boomed out across the steppe: 'Look, it be the bright ones! The diamond warriors – they come!'

A thousand others picked up his cry as they called out, too: 'The Valari! The Valari! The diamond warriors are coming!'

Maram pressed his hand against his head, which must have throbbed from many days of drinking beer. In a voice still thick with sleep, he muttered to me, 'Ah, well, six more armies of your Valari. With Mesh and Kaash that makes eight, only eight, too bad.'

He stood with everyone else watching these thousands of warriors covered in bright diamond armor march closer. Then he said to me, 'Your Nine Kingdoms are strangely named, for there are only eight of them, or I have forgotten how to count. One of them must have been annihilated in some ancient war and lost to history.'

I looked on as the vanguard of the Ishkan army drew within a hundred yards of our encampment. I could now see plainly that King Hadaru himself, and not Prince Issur, sat on a large white warhorse leading the Ishkans – and the other armies. I smiled at Maram and told him: 'No, the ninth kingdom was not lost. It is *here*, on this field today.'

Maram rubbed his bleary eyes then cast me a puzzled look. 'I don't understand.'

My hand swept out toward the warriors approaching us, and then I pointed at the crowded lanes between the tents of the Kaashans and Meshians. And I said, '*We* are the ninth kingdom. Eight kingdoms there are, truly, as you have counted – as there have always been. But as it was at the Sarburn, when the Valari come together there is only one kingdom, and we call that the ninth one. For once, the Nine Kingdoms defeated Morjin, and we might do so again.'

'The diamond warriors,' Maram muttered, looking out to the east. 'The damned diamond warriors.'

I smiled again, this time more deeply. I touched the two diamonds of the ring that sparkled around Maram's finger, and I told him: 'Do not forget that *you* are Valari, now, too.'

That evening, after the six arriving armies made camp along the river on ground that Sajagax had reserved for them, I called a meeting of the Valari kings. We gathered with our captains in my tent, and for the first time since the disastrous conclave in Tria, we sat at table to discuss how we might fight Morjin. And so we finally had the miracle that Maram had prayed for.

It took some time of arguing matters of war before I learned how this had come to pass. It turned out the King of Athar had been the first of the six Valari sovereigns to have a change of heart. Soon after I had left King Mohan and his army arrayed along the Nar Road, he had ridden without escort up into Lagash. Alone, he had climbed Mount Ayu, where he found King Kurshan sitting in meditation, and he told King Kurshan of his intention to lead the Atharian army out to the Detheshaloon – and so leave Athar defenseless against Lagash. He then asked King Kurshan to suspend the formalities of Sharshan and join with him in waging a much more serious kind of war, against the Valari's true enemy. King Kurshan had then surprised King Mohan in calling for a peace between Lagash and Athar. As the singular King Kurshan had said to King Mohan: 'I would have spent my army in making war against Athar only because Athar made war against Lagash. But it is my navy that must be the glory of my realm. Someday, when we have defeated the Red Dragon, my ships will sail through the waters of the Northern Passage to the stars, where there is no war.'

King Mohan's act, I thought, took more courage than any deed that this fearsome warrior had ever done on the field of battle. With both the Atharians and Lagashuns ready for war, the two kings had immediately led their armies up the Nar Road and into Taron. When King Waray rode down from his palace and saw yet more columns of Valari marching west, his heart finally opened. Across his realm – and those of the other Valari kingdoms – warriors in their thousands called for their kings to honor Kaash's and Mesh's victory at the Seredun Sands by fighting for a more lasting triumph against Morjin's main force. King Waray, still in awe of how Bemossed had healed his daughter, finally gave in to this call.

And so had King Sandarkan. After King Talanu and I had out-maneuvered the Waashians by the Rajabash River, King Sandarkan had been consumed by shame – and it grieved him the most sorely that he had failed to join with the Kaashans and Meshians in annihilating Morjin's armies on the coast of Delu. As he told us over dinner in my tent: 'One time only a man might turn away from doing what is right and be forgiven, but not twice.' And so, at King Waray's invitation, he had led the Waashians into Taron, where they gathered with the armies of Taron, Athar and Lagash. And then the combined forces of these four kingdoms had crossed into Anjo, toward the Wendrush.

Upon beholding these columns of diamond-clad men flowing through his realm like sparkling rivers, King Danashu had felt a great stirring of his blood, and he had wanted to join them. But the King of Anjo never made a move without first looking to the King of Ishka. At last, King Hadaru, giving in to fate, had called up the entire Ishkan army – the largest in the Nine Kingdoms – and had marched out of Lovisii up the North Road into Anjo. There the Ishkans had joined with the five other Valari armies, and King Hadaru had insisted on leading them over the mountains and down across the steppe to the Detheshaloon.

'I was wrong,' he told the other kings and me as we sat at my council table, 'not to have come to Mesh's aid when the Red Dragon invaded two years ago. We all were wrong. We might have stopped the Red Dragon then and there. Instead of having to fight a much more desperate battle – and a much stronger enemy – here.'

He sat very straight in his chair, with his great, bearlike head turned toward me. A mane of white hair, tied with many battle ribbons, fell down to his massive shoulders. His jet-black eyes sparkled with little lights like the those of his ring's five diamonds. I had seen few men as powerful in body and spirit as he. If the wound that he had gained in battle with the Taroners truly festered, he gave no sign of distress, and he appeared utterly unready to die.

'It is a strange thing,' he said to me, 'for an Ishkan king to take the field as Mesh's ally and not its enemy. I remember too well the day that your father killed my brother.'

'As *we* remember,' Lord Harsha said, 'the day that you and yours killed King Elkamesh at the Diamond River!'

In that very same battle, Lord Harsha had lost an eye futilely defending the life of my grandfather.

'There have been many grievances between our two kingdoms,' King Hadaru admitted. 'But the blood of the coming battle shall wash things clean. Finally, we Valari *will* fight, as one – even as King Elkamesh dreamed. And as his grandson, Valashu Elahad, has dreamed.'

He paused to rub at his weary old face, then continued, 'There are those who have said that *I* should lead this alliance. I have said that, myself. But I have also said that if it is to be the Elahad who is to lead us instead, he must prove himself in battle. That he has now done, no Valari king more so. And so I am willing to surrender precedence and accept him as our warlord.'

In the way that he looked at me then, I felt his pride give way to a deep and overflowing strength, and his bitterness evaporate beneath a bright purpose. Somehow, I thought, his greed had become a hunger for something more than diamonds or land or glory in battle.

'I, too, accept King Valamesh as our warlord,' King Danashu called out.

This burly, long-armed man had proven himself as one of the greatest Valari warriors – and the weakest of kings. Although it might have been thought that he only followed King Hadaru's will, I sensed in him a fierce desire to regain the respect of his peers by distinguishing himself, and Anjo, in battle against our enemy.

'King Valamesh *will* lead us!' King Mohan said as he squeezed the hilt of his sword. 'Let no one speak against this!'

'I speak *for* it,' King Waray said, looking at me. 'Our fate is our fate.'

'I speak for the Elahad, too,' King Sandarkan said.

'And I,' King Viromar Solaru agreed. 'King Valamesh, as the Valari's warlord!'

King Kurshan, long of limb and gray of hair, had a face so cut with scars that many found him difficult to look at. I found him, at heart, to be the most faithful of men. With a nod of his head, he smiled at me and called out: 'Then with the Elahad in command, let us vanquish our enemy! And when that is accomplished, we shall ask him to lead the Valari back to the stars!'

The other kings looked at him strangely, though none gainsaid his wild dream. And then King Hadaru, sitting across the table from me, told me: 'Your father and I disputed many things, but he was a worthy enemy, and I was sorry that the Crucifier's men cut him down in his prime. If he looks on, from the stars, he would surely say that he has a worthy son to succeed him.'

These words, coming from the great Ishkan bear, made me swallow against the knot of memory tightening in my throat.

'When I was a boy,' I said to King Hadaru and the others, 'I never wanted to become king, much less warlord. Any of my brothers, I thought, would have been more worthy than I. Even after the Culhadosh Commons, where each of my brothers . . .'

I could not go on, and I listened as my voice choked off into a whisper of pain. I made a fist, and pushed it against the table. I could not look at King Hadaru just then, with his bright, black eyes laying me open, for somehow this hard, hard man seemed to suffer my hurt as his own.

He stood up suddenly, and walked around the table to stand at my side. Then he laid his hand on top of mine, and told me: 'I am your brother.'

'So am I,' King Danashu said, reaching his long arm across the table to cover King Hadaru's hand.

'And I,' King Waray said, also extending his hand.

'And I am your brother,' King Kurshan affirmed.

The wildness of his eyes touched something deep within my own.

'And I,' King Sandarkan said, coming over to us.

'And I,' King Viromar told me.

'And I,' King Mohan said to me with a fierce smile, 'am your brother, too.'

Their hands pressed down upon mine with a weight like that of tens of thousands. Finally, I withdrew my hand and clasped it to each of theirs in turn. I fought back tears as I said to them: 'I am your brother – and I will die rather than let the Red Dragon spill your blood upon this field.'

The kings of the Valari, who feared death no more than any man, smiled at me with great purpose lighting up their faces. The crackling campfires of our army cast an incandescence into my tent. From somewhere nearby, Alphanderry's strong voice carried one of his songs out to the world. I sensed then that each of these warrior kings carried a bright sword, and not a kalama. It was a moment of great, shining hope.

After that we spent the rest of the evening discussing strategy and tactics. We strove to devise an order of battle that would result in few Valari being cut down to the earth, while spilling whole rivers of our enemy's blood.

And then, the next morning, Atara led the whole Manslayer Society into our encampment and provided a good count of our enemy's numbers: true to the worst of rumors, Morjin led an army at least half a million strong. And they poured across the grasses of the Wendrush, in rivers of horses, oxen and wagons – and whole oceans of steel and bloodthirsty men.

19

For three days, the Red Dragon's army marched toward the Rune River. Sajagax led his Sarni warriors on a long maneuver to circle behind the columns of our enemy and harry them from their rear. But the Sarni under Morjin – led by the Marituk and the Zayak – parried each of Sajagax's attacks and covered the Dragon's advance. In truth, they nearly fell into full battle with Sajagax's warriors. This did not discourage Sajagax. As he told me on a bright Valte day, with the sun baking the grasslands: 'It is as we hoped: our enemy seems short of long-range arrows. And their warriors seem badly led, for I think that each of the tribes' chieftains honors none as a great chieftain, but looks only to Morjin to tell them what to do. And what does Morjin, surrounded by his Dragon Guard and his wagons, know of the contingencies of battle far out on the steppe and how we Sarni really fight? And so I care not that his Sarni outnumber mine.'

Still, as even Sajagax admitted, the true test of things would come only when our two armies faced each other in full strength on the field. We could not stop the Red Dragon's men from drawing nearer and setting up their tents in a vast encampment opposite ours four miles to the north of the river. In back of our enemy's line of campfires, the stark rocks of the Detheshaloon loomed like a vast, cracked skull. A much smaller prominence rose up two miles to the south of it and nearer to our encampment. Sajagax's warriors called this mound of earth the Owl's Hill, for one night they had heard a great horned owl hooing from its heights. When battle finally came, I thought, Morjin's armies would advance upon the river and form lines just beneath this little hill. Perhaps Morjin would ride up its gentle, grassy slopes and survey the field from its rounded top. If my warriors prevailed in driving back our enemy, they would have to attack uphill, at least on this one small sector of the field. I accepted this slight hindrance. For we held a much greater advantage in being able to draw up *our* lines with the river to our backs. In the heat of the day, with the sun beating down upon us like a fire iron, my men would have access to fresh water while Morjin's men would not.

At dusk on the seventh of Valte, with the Dragon army's camp-fires filling the northern horizon with a hellish orange glow, I took a moment to stand outside my tent with Altaru so that I might comb down my huge horse. Joshu Kadar and a few of my Guardians waited in front of one of our campfires nearby – but not too close. They knew that even a king sometimes needed a space of privacy.

'Old friend,' I said to my mount as I drew the brush across his shiny black coat, 'have you had enough grass to eat? Enough oats? Tomorrow will be a hard day.'

I continued working the brush along his flank, speaking to him in low tones. He nickered softly, and I felt the great muscles along his back and hindquarters fairly surging with life as if in anticipation of a great work soon to come.

'A *hard* day,' I said again. 'Our enemy has no honor, and they will try to pierce you with lances and swords.'

He turned his head to regard me with his great, dark eye as if to tell me that he would never let me down.

'And there will be elephants – they will try to knock you to earth and trample you. The Sunguruns have fifty of them and the Hesperuks at least two hundred more.'

I went on to inform him that we would unlikely to encounter any of the Hesperuk elephants, as we would take our post at the head of the Meshian, Waashian, Kaashan and Atharian cavalry on our right wing, with Sajagax leading half his Sarni farther to the right to protect our flank.

'I am sure,' I said, 'that Morjin will place the Hesperu army at his center to break *our* center. Other than the Dragon Guard, they are his best men. And so I shall place the Alonians and Eannans opposite them, for they are my weakest warriors. The Hesperuks will break though, I think, or at least push the Alonians back. And then, when half of Morjin's army has poured into a space too small, I will send in our reserve and command the Valari to close in from the sides to slaughter them.'

I felt my heart beating in time to Altaru's. I sighed because I had employed a similar stratagem to defeat our enemy at the Culhadosh Commons, and I thought it unlikely to work again.

'Morjin,' I told him, shaking my head, 'did not take the field at the Commons, but he will have studied deeply on what happened there. And at the Sarburn. Tomorrow, I think, he will make no major mistakes. It will not be a day for brilliance in battle – only bravery, or not.'

Again, Altaru nickered, and I smelled the thick, fermy scent emanating from him. I stroked the long, muscular column of his neck.

'Are you brave enough for one last battle, my friend?' I asked him. 'Just one more time of the steel screaming madness, I promise you, and then we can rest.'

As the afternoon's last light bled from the sky, I kept working the brush over this great animal. I assured him that there must be a way to victory – but only if each man and horse in our lines fought with a heart of fire. I lamented, for the thousandth time, the smallness of my own heart, which I had too often had to keep closed lest the sufferings of others crush me under. What would it be like, I wondered, not only to give my blood to Altaru and my other friends, but the deepest blaze within me?

I might have stood there all night whispering my doubts to the world, but just then Atara rode her lithe red mare down the main lane leading up to my tent. Her white blindfold flashed in the deepening gloom. She sat straight and grave beneath her great lion-skin cloak, lined with satin and trimmed with black fur. But I could feel the great effort that it cost her to hold this proud posture, for her side ached with a fierce, throbbing pain from a saber cut taken in battle with the Marituk.

'Val,' she said as she drew up close, 'Liljana will serve dinner in an hour – and after that you will have much to do. Can we not go somewhere where we can talk?'

In truth, with all the councils over the past days, I had not had a moment alone with her.

'Where, then?' I asked her.

She pointed south, past the river. 'Out there, on the grass.'

I nodded my head at this. I did not think my Guardians would like me to ride alone out onto the barren steppe where Morjin might have sent outriders to circle around and spy out our encampment, especially since I wore my tunic only and no armor. But some risks had to be taken.

And so I nodded my head to Atara, and quickly saddled my horse. Then we turned to ride past the rows of tents; we splashed across the river, which at this time of year wound its way across the grasslands as a brown trickle scarcely deeper than a man's knee. It did not take us long to gallop a couple of miles out onto the open steppe, where we found a gentle rise of ground and took shelter in its lee. We dismounted, then Atara removed her cloak and spread it out over the rustling grass. We sat upon it, looking out at the darkening world.

For a while we spoke of the starry sky and the soughing west wind, which promised hot, clear weather the following day. Then our talk turned toward the battle: 'You take a chance,' she said to me, 'in engaging Morjin with the river at your back.'

I shrugged my shoulders at this. 'We have discussed this in council. The river is shallow enough that we can retreat across it in good order, if we must. But if we *must* retreat, then the battle will in any case be lost – and then it won't matter.'

Atara, sitting next to me with her knee pressing against mine, slowly nodded her head. Her blindfold gleamed in the starlight.

'Have your kings and captains decided what to do about the elephants then? I'm sorry I missed the council earlier, but I wanted to verify that the Hesperuks really have two hundred and twenty of them.'

'Kane,' I said to her, 'faced war elephants long ago. He has told the warriors what they must do to fight against them.'

She smiled grimly at this. 'I am glad that I will lead the Manslayers against men only tomorrow, and not elephants.'

She took out her scryer's sphere, and sat rolling it between her long, lithe hands. I felt in her a quaking fear as if she had seen in her crystal some great and dreadful beast.

'You didn't invite me here,' I said to her, 'to talk about elephants.'

'No,' she said squeezing her crystal. 'Tomorrow, Morjin will unleash something upon us – some terrible, terrible thing.'

'What, then? Is it a firestone or a new kind of gelstei?'

'I don't know,' she said, lifting up her glimmering sphere. 'He keeps it from me. I look and look, in here, but all is dark.'

'Well, whatever it is, we'll destroy it! As we will the Red Dragon.'

The wrath she heard in my voice must have alarmed her, for she removed her right hand from her crystal and laid it on top of mine. 'You will seek him out on the field, won't you?'

I shook my head at this. 'Only if fate puts him in my path. It will be enough if we can drive off the Ikurian Horse, and circle around the Dragon's army from the right.'

On our right I would charge with the Guardians and the best of our knights against the Ikurians. On the left, I told myself, King

Hadaru would have a very hard task leading the combined Ishkan, Anjori, Taron and Lagashun cavalry against Morjin's heavy horse if they were to break through and complete the double encirclement that I envisioned.

'You seem sure,' she told me, 'that Morjin will set his Ikurians against our right.'

'As sure as I am that tomorrow will not be a day for my vengeance alone.'

'Truly?' she said. Her lips pulled up into a cold smile. 'Lie to me, if you will, Val, but not yourself.'

'What would you have me do?' I asked her. With one hand, I squeezed her fingers, while I rested my other hand on top of the hilt of my sword, which I had set down in the grass beside me. 'I cannot turn away from him.'

'No, you cannot. But Kane will keep by your side, through all the Ikurians' lances and swords – even through fire. Can you not let *him* slay Morjin?'

I turned to look toward the north, where the rising ground behind us blocked most of the glare of the Dragon Army's encampment. And I said, 'You are brave to talk of us slaying *anyone* with our enemy outnumbering us more than four to one.'

'What should I talk of then? What I *have* seen in my kristei? It is no different, here and now, than it was in Argattha.'

I lived again, in a blaze of memory, the anguish in the words that Atara had cried out to me in Morjin's throne room soon after he had taken out her eyes: *If you kill him, you kill yourself!*

'Didn't you once tell me,' I said to her, 'that no scryer can see all things?'

I remembered, as well, the ancient prophecy that 'The death of Morjin would be the death of Ea.'

'No scryer *can* see everything,' Atara said to me. Then her hand suddenly tightened around mine. 'But all scryers see *something* they know will be – unless something else is done to make it *not* be. But it never is, Val, never, never. Because men like you believe that whatever is, *is*, and always must be – and so go rushing madly toward their fate.'

I let her soft, grave voice play over again and again inside me. Then I said to her, 'My fate is my fate. So many will die tomorrow. It can't matter if I am one of them.'

'Can't *matter*?' she cried out. 'It matters to those who follow you, as it does to all Ea. And to me – it matters so terribly, terribly.'

316

I remembered another thing that she had said to me in Argattha: *If you kill yourself, you kill me.*

She began shaking then, deep tremors that rose up from her belly and ripped through the whole of her body. Her hand suddenly opened to seize hold of mine, and she dropped her sphere, which rolled a few feet across the grass. Upon realizing how careless she had been with this priceless gelstei, she turned her head right and left, as if trying to orient herself toward it. But I sensed that her second sight had left her, at least for the moment, and so she sat utterly blind.

She reached out to pat the grass around her. I placed my hand on her arm to stay her, then bent to retrieve her crystal. In the instant that my fingers closed around the cold white gelstei, I cried out in agony because it was as if I had grasped hold of a lightning bolt. A fierce white flash tore through me, and I beheld the same fearful thing that had terrified Atara: the great Tree of Life that grew out toward the future in all its infinite branchings. And each branch, I saw, every one of the tiniest shoots and sprigs, had been charred, as if by dragon fire. The whole of the tree stood utterly blackened beneath the dying light of the stars.

I gave this accursed crystal back to Atara. The touch of it seemed to reawaken her sight, as horrible and unwanted as it might be.

'Morjin!' I cried out. 'He will win tomorrow, won't he?'

'Val, I –'

'You always spoke as if we had a chance! But we never really did, did we?'

'Please don't be angry with me,' she told me as her hand tightened around mine. 'But I had to act as if there really *is* hope, don't you see?'

'Why, then?'

'Because hope is our *duty*. It is the deepest courage – truly, truly. And then, of course, you, with your beautiful, beautiful eyes and all your dreams . . .'

Her voice softened to a whisper, then failed altogether. It took her a few moments to gather in her breath again and say to me, 'I couldn't bear to see *you* lose hope, Val. Should I let the sun lose its light?'

I sat listening to the crickets chirping nearby and the roaring of a lion farther out on the grass. And I rapped my diamond ring against her crystal and said, 'But you can't keep *this* future from happening, can you?'

'Can't I? Don't we, in the end, choose our futures?'

'I always thought we could. But if every path leads only to destruction and doom, what is there to choose?'

'But I can't see *everything*! There must a chance – at least one beautiful, beautiful chance.'

'There must be,' I said, feeling the quick pulsing of the vein along her wrist. 'But what if there isn't?'

'If there isn't, if the tree is truly withered beyond hope, then the One *must* be able to breathe life back into it. Somehow, this impossible grace – it must be possible. I *have* to believe that. And so must you.'

I touched my sword's scabbard, which covered the inscription etched into the silustria. I asked her, 'Have you seen all of what is written here?'

'No, I haven't,' she told me, shaking her head. 'But I have seen *you* seeing it. There will come a moment – I know there will.'

'And then?'

'And then I don't know!'

She began shaking again as if from cold, although the evening continued warm. The wind, moving slowly across the earth, carried the distant booming of our enemy's war drums. I lifted up Atara's hand to press my lips to her skin, and I could almost hear the deeper drumming of her heart.

'Tomorrow,' she told me, 'when I lead the Manslayers against the Marituk, our arrows will sweep them from the field – I know they will. But we will have to ride far afield, so very, very far. I can't see how our paths will cross during the battle, Val.'

'No – neither can I,' I said, kissing her fingers.

'And after the battle, it will be . . . after.'

I suddenly could not bear the sight of her crystal sphere, nor the visions that she saw within it. And so I took it from her and buried it beneath the edge of her cloak.

'And now,' she murmured, 'it is now. For you and me, this is the only moment that ever *is*, don't you see?'

And with that, she kissed *my* hand, then pulled my arm around her to draw me closer. She kissed my mouth, my nose, my eyes, then returned to pressing her lips against mine with a fierce desire. She pulled at me with her hands and the force of her quick, hot inhalations as if she wanted to breathe my very soul into her.

'I want your child, Val,' she murmured. 'At least, its beginning inside me.'

'A child you will never live to see?'

'I don't *know* that,' she said. And then, 'Do you really love me?'

I felt her hands all warm and urgent against mine.

'Atara,' I finally said to her, sitting back to gasp for air, 'we only ever have *this* moment – that is true. But if we win tomorrow, we will have millions of moments – all the nights of our lives – for love.'

'Are you asking me, then, to keep inside what I can't *bear* to keep inside . . . as a faith in victory?'

'Faith, yes,' I said to her. 'We've come so far on almost nothing else. And we will need all our faith tomorrow.'

'I know you are right: we must at least *act* as if we can win,' she told me. I felt the chill of duty and acceptance begin to take hold of her. 'What could love possibly matter at a time like this?'

She folded her hands across her lap, and held her head utterly still. I listened to her deep breathing, even as I knew she listened to me. I sensed the hurt of her side where she had been wounded and a deeper pain within her chest. Her dreadful visions, I thought, had hollowed out her heart, nearly emptying her of hope. I felt this in *my* heart as a coldness and a darkness that sent terror shooting through me. I wanted to grasp hold of her then and never let go; I wanted to fill up this black nothing with all the fire and light I could find.

Without either of us speaking a word, at the same moment, our hands reached out toward each other. They met in the space between us, and our fingers twined and then suddenly locked together in the shock of knowing what we must do. I pulled at her, fiercely, even as she pulled at me; the force of our tensed limbs and bodies drew us together with a greater shock of lips bruising against lips in a kiss so savage with years of longing that it seemed that we were trying to devour each other. I smelled myrrh and musk in her hair, and tasted blood on her tongue. Her hand tightened around mine with such a terrible need that I thought our fingers might break.

Then we let go of each other, she to lift off my tunic and I to tear away the leather armor encasing her belly and breasts. When we had made ourselves naked, we fell at each other again in a fever to press skin against skin as if our desire could sear our flesh together as one. She lay back against her furry cloak and opened herself to me: her arms, her legs and that bright, beautiful thing deep inside her that had pierced my heart the moment I had first set eyes upon her. I knew I had to be careful lest I aggrieve the raw, red wound still seaming her side. But she didn't want me to take care, and she had none for herself. And so we pulled at each other like ravenous beasts, sweating and moaning and breathing in each other's breaths as if we could never get enough of each other. But we were like angels, too, for in our blaze of passion, we called each other higher and higher, where the deepest radiance pours as from an inexhaustible source.

For a moment, we returned to our star. It pulled us straight into its fiery heart, burning away time and the grasses of the steppe all around us, annihilating whole armies and the very world itself. And then we both screamed together as one: I because I could not bear the ecstasy passing back and forth between us like a lightning bolt, and she to feel me filling her up with love and light and burning raindrops of life.

Afterward, we lay holding each other. The soft beauty of her body, no less the sweetness of her soul, held me as within a dream that I had never quite dared to dream. It came to me that I had been a fool: wasting my blood and breath fighting a war to end war and living for a higher purpose. What could be more exalted, I asked myself, than the wild joy that Atara and I had made together? Was this not the will of the One and a song to all of creation? Was it not the One's deepest desire to pour itself out through us in a brilliant blaze of divine love?

Lions, Atara told me, when it comes their time, mate nearly continually for most of a day. We did not have a whole day together, only part of an hour. And really, only a moment: it was all anyone ever had. We spent it loving with all the fire and delight we could find. Then, after our hour was done and we had to ride back to our encampment, we both wept because it seemed that we would never come together as a man and a woman again.

When we walked through the opening to my tent, Liljana had just finished setting out dinner on the council table. Our friends – all except Kane – stood by the chairs there, as did the Seven. Liljana took one look at Atara and me, and seemed instantly to sniff out what had happened between us. Her manner was one of deep concern, but warm and welcoming, too. She beamed her blessings at us, and then insisted that we fill ourselves with some good food.

'I was afraid that your duties would keep you elsewhere,' she said to us as we took our places at the table. 'But I'm so glad you are here. After tomorrow, who knows when we'll have a chance to sit down to a meal together again?'

Liljana set out before us yellow rushk cakes with honey and

muffins made of fine white flour. She had roasted three kinds of meat: some little steppe chickens and a tenderloin of sagosk and a whole ham that she had reserved just for this night. She had also used a few jars of strawberry preserves to bake some pies. Daj loved strawberries, and so did Maram.

'I made a blackberry tart, too, for Kane,' she told us. 'If he ever arrives.'

'Ah, well,' Maram said, 'he probably had business elsewhere.'

'He has had all day to take counsel with captains and kings. But what could be more important than spending this evening with his friends? If Val and Atara can come to dinner on time, why can't Kane?'

For a long moment, I stood staring across the table at Atara. Then I looked at Liljana and said, 'Not two hours ago, fifty men rode into camp. They had escaped out of Alonia, and I'm sure they are of the Black Brotherhood – and maybe the last. A man named Idris led them. He said that he would speak only with Kane.'

Liljana let her irritation radiate out of her like heat from one of her frying pans. 'Well, if that is true, then Kane should speak with him later. There will be time enough for dealing with spies after we've eaten. It would be a shame for Kane to let all this food go to waste.'

I looked at the feast spread out on the council table. 'Kane said that if he came late, we should begin without him.'

'Well, perhaps we *should*. Since he is absorbed in such urgent matters.'

Liljana then bade us all to sit down, and this we did. It was good to share such a meal on such a night with good friends. Maram, of course, ate with great appetite, as did Daj and Alphanderry, to say nothing of Ymiru, and their eager consumption of the dishes that Liljana had set before us pleased her greatly. Abrasax and the other masters showed more restraint, according to their way, and they would not overfill themselves. Abrasax said that soon the Seven must retire to prepare themselves for the next morning, and they could not let indulgence in food clog their bellies and brains. As for me, I could scarcely eat. I kept gazing across the table at Atara. I could feel her concentrating all her desire upon me instead of her dinner. Never, I thought, had I seen her look so beautiful – and yet so sad. I had only to glance at her to feel the wildest of hope burning through me and the most desperate of despair, too.

Our anguish must have communicated itself to Bemossed. All during dinner, he hardly put more than a crust of bread into his mouth. He drank none of the black Sarni beer that Liljana poured into our cups. I felt something inside him growing tighter and tighter, like a bow bent too far and about to snap. Even so, he would not let any distress interfere with the enjoyment of our company. He tried to smile as often as he could, especially at Estrella, with whom he had always shared a silent understanding. He watched as Atara sat with her hands folded across her belly, and her great joy of life became his. He seemed to find some singular essence within each of us and to savor it the way another man might the richness of a sagosk steak or the sweetness of honey.

Maram, who must have sensed the terrible sorrow welling up out of Bemossed, finally pushed a cup of beer at him and said, 'You'll find that your food slides down more easily if you first lubricate your throat with a little of this.'

To please Maram, I thought, Bemossed took a sip from his cup and then ate a bite out of a muffin. But he said nothing.

Almost immediately, Master Juwain spoke out to Maram in order to fill up the silence: 'And you'll find that too much beer encourages stuffing yourself like a pig.'

'So what if it does?' Maram countered. 'I'm only fortifying myself for tomorrow. And as for beer, truly, I've had only a little.'

'You've had three cups worth,' Atara put in.

I stared at the clean white cloth encircling her face. Despite her blindness and preoccupation with me, she could be the most observant of women.

'Three small cups, to a man such as I,' Maram said, 'is like three drops to another.'

'Hmmphh – you overestimate your resistance to this drink. Just as you underestimate the importance of your resisting.'

'Well,' Maram said, pulling at his beard as he studied her, 'resistance *can* be a difficult thing, can't it?'

I felt Atara suddenly soften within the cloud of silence that came over her. She sat as if staring straight at me.

'And as for importance,' Maram added, 'I'm no more needed here than anyone else so foolish as to have come so far to face an army of half a million men.'

Atara slowly shook her head at this. 'But you are, Maram. I should tell you that a great, great deal will depend on you tomorrow.'

'Upon *me*? What, then? What do you possibly think I can do

against so many? And what have you seen in your scryer's crystal that you should tell me?'

Atara, however, would say no more, and Maram knew her well enough not to press her in this matter. Instead, he rapped his double-diamond ring against his cup and said, 'All right, then – I will drink no more beer tonight. And not another drop, I swear, until Morjin is defeated.'

Liljana looked at him curiously then, and she stood up to begin setting fresh cups onto the table. When she had finished, she brought out a bottle of wine and told us: 'King Waray sent this over earlier, with his compliments. It is Galdan, and should go well with our dessert.'

As Estrella began cutting one of the pies and serving us, Liljana uncorked the bottle. Maram, sitting across the table from where Liljana stood, held out his cup so that she might fill it more easily, or so he said.

'No,' she told him, 'you've just promised to forgo spirits.'

'I promised to forgo beer only – not wine, and a special vintage at that.'

'Would you drink before Val does?' she scolded him. She moved over to me and poured a stream of the dark red wine into my cup. 'This is a gift from one king to another, and you should count yourself fortunate to share in it.'

Liljana made no move to fill Maram's cup – or anyone else's. She stood watching me as if she wished me to praise her for acquiring the wine for what might be our last meal together. She waited for me to sip from my cup and indicate that the wine was good.

I reached out to lift up the cup. Just then I heard the hoofbeats of a horse pounding against the turf outside the tent. A moment later, Kane rushed in. He looked from my hand to Liljana, standing above me gripping the bottle of wine, and then quickly back at me. And he shouted out: 'Don't drink that – it is poisoned!'

Liljana stared at him as if she didn't want to believe what she had just heard. So did Master Juwain, and so did I.

'Poisoned!' I called back to him. 'But King Waray sent us this wine! He would not have come so far with his whole army just to poison me!'

'Unless,' Maram observed, 'he wished to replace you at the last moment as warlord.'

'No,' I said, looking down into the dark wine, 'no Valari king would ever poison another.'

Even as I said this, I remembered Salmelu Aradar, who had born the son a king.

'So, maybe no *Valari* would,' Kane growled out. He stepped closer to me, and the fury filling his thick body made me think of a tiger ready to kill. 'But I did not say that the poisoner was Valari. Who knows more about poison than she who trained to detect such filthy things, eh?'

He fixed his savage gaze upon Liljana, once King Kiritan's food taster, who had saved him from more than one poisoned meal. The force of Kane's blood pulsing through his throat impelled me to jump up and grab hold of him.

'You are speaking of *Liljana*!' I told him. 'How can you say this of her? She has been a good friend to you, and like a mother to me!'

'She is first the Materix of the Maitriche Telu!' Kane said. 'Those women would sacrifice their own sons and daughters to make what they will of the world.'

He told us then what he had learned from Idris, who had ridden from Tria with the knights of the Black Brotherhood to deliver this news: that the scryers of the Maitriche Telu had prophesied that Valashu Elahad would be the one to lead Ea into a new age. The Maitriche Telu hoped that this would be the Age of the Mother reborn, and so when I first came to Tria on the quest to recover the Lightstone, Liljana had attached herself to me in order to help nurture, guide and protect me. But because the Maitriche Telu also feared that the coming times might see a new Age of the Sword, or worse, the very destruction of the earth, Liljana stood ready to murder me should I prove to be the long-dreaded King of Swords.

'So,' Kane said to me, looking down where I had rested Alkaladur against the side of the table, 'you have proved *that* in summoning the Valari armies here and making yourself warlord. And in much else.'

His logic, however, failed to persuade Master Juwain. Although the Brotherhood and the Sisterhood had long been estranged, Master Juwain did not want to think such ill of Liljana, for he said to Kane: 'If Liljana wished Val dead, then she might have made him so a thousand times these past years. Why should she wait until *now* to poison him?'

'Because,' Kane said, 'it took her time to determine that Val must *be* the king her Sisterhood has feared. And because at no other moment would his death wreak such havoc. Think, Juwain! The Valari kings would renew their old quarrels, and fall at each other's throats. Perhaps they'd even draw swords against each other here on this field, eh? Sajagax would then be forced to try to take command, but the Valari would never yield to him. Never! Instead of one army facing Morjin, there would be ten. They'd be like fingers clawing about with no head to guide them. And so Morjin would cut one away from another, and destroy them – utterly.'

As he glared at Liljana, she glared right back at him with resentment, anger and a great sadness filling up her soft, round face. And then Atara pulled herself away from visions of the future to the tragedy of the present moment. In a cold, commanding voice, she called out to Kane: 'Put away your doubts – Liljana is no poisoner! How could you think that she would want Morjin to triumph?'

'So, how could I?' he snarled at her. Then he whipped about to face Liljana. 'How could *you* want that, eh, witch? *This* is how, I say: what Morjin would bring to the world is not what the Maitriche Telu has schemed for ten thousand years to make be. Not nearly. But it would be better than Ea's utter destruction in war. There would be a kind of peace, eh? All men and women would be slaves, or worse, Morjin's ghuls. Almost all. Your sisters would still try to work their plots and poisons in secret. They'd try to wait – another ten thousand years, if they had to. They'd wait and wait and wait, and someday they'd hope to murder Morjin and make the world their own.'

I stared at Kane, horrified by his terrible words, and so it was with Maram, Ymiru, Master Juwain and Abrasax. Bemossed seemed frozen within a vast silence. I sensed Estrella wanting to weep in outrage and hurt at Kane's attacking Liljana.

And then Kane continued his diatribe: 'You must think Morjin is a fool, eh? A *man*, who can be twisted about and won to your ways, like other men. Fool, you! You've deceived yourself, Liljana. You've looked into Morjin's mind once too often, and so he has deceived *you*. So. So – he's put his filthy poison in *your* mind, eh? How long have you been his ghul? Long enough, I say, to have betrayed us already. It was you, wasn't it, who gave away the Brotherhood's school? And not by mistake, but of your own will? And now you would murder Val. But *that* will never be.'

He moved to break free from my grip on him, and to draw his sword. But I clamped my hands on him with greater force, even as Liljana calmly picked up my cup and took a drink from it.

'You're wrong,' she said to Kane. 'So very wrong – there is no poison in this wine.'

Maram watched her as if waiting for her muscles to seize up and her face to turn blue as she choked and died. But she just stood there breathing deeply and glaring at Kane.

And then he shouted: 'It *is* poisoned, I say! You would have prepared the antidote and taken it, against just such a moment as this!'

Liljana shook her head with great sorrow. Then she turned to me and said, 'Kane's spy told truly about the prophecy concerning the King of Swords. And you *are* he – I am certain of this. But even if I knew that you would bring ten million years of war to the world, how could I ever poison you? How could I hope to see a new Age of the Mother if I must bring it in by murdering the man who is like my own son?'

Through the tears filling her large brown eyes I felt her love for me like a burst of warm sunlight. I let go of Kane's arm, and reached out to take the cup from her. Before Kane could stop me, I drank from it deeply, down to the last drop of wine.

'It is *not* poisoned!' I said to Kane. I felt the wine, sweet and good, warming my insides. 'Come, forget what has happened! Sit with us and eat. Liljana has only wanted to make us the best meal that she could.'

Liljana fought hard not to break out weeping openly. And Kane waged a much deeper war within himself, for he stood there grinding his jaws together as the tendons popped out on his neck. A dark light blazed through his eyes. He seemed like a mountain about to crack open and to touch the whole earth with his fire.

Then Bemossed stood up and came over to him. I looked on in amazement, for it seemed that he held in his hand a small golden cup. It caught the light of the candles in a soft shimmer. Bemossed gazed at Kane as he touched the fingers of his other hand to the side of Kane's head. Almost immediately, the agony tearing through Kane seemed to drain away. His eyes cleared to a deep black, all sheeny with tears.

'I . . . am sorry,' he said, nodding to Liljana. 'So damned sorry.'

Without another word, he turned and stormed from the tent. I heard him ride away into the night.

When I looked back at Bemossed, I could make out only air cupped within his hand. And he said to me, 'Do you see, Valashu? This battle is driving us mad even before we fight it.'

'And that is why,' I told him, 'we must never fight another.'

He glanced at my sword leaning against the side of the table, and said, 'Kane, I fear, believes he is damned to fight forever.'

'Kane will be all right now. I know he will.'

'Will he? Will *you*?'

I thought of all that had happened between Atara and me scarcely an hour before and the blackened Tree of Life that I had seen within her crystal. *Was* there truly any hope, I wondered? This question, and Bemossed's, filled my mind as I turned to stare at my sword. Alkaladur's blade, buried within its scabbard, burned with etched characters that I could not quite read.

'It will all be over tomorrow,' I murmured.

Bemossed laid his hand on mine and asked, 'Can you think of nothing except this murder you make in your heart, again and again?'

'Morjin,' I told him, 'must be destroyed. You know that.'

'I know that he is a man, like you. Like me.'

'No – he is nothing like you! You hold light in your hand, always, even when you hold nothing! And Morjin blackens the brightest and most beautiful thing in all the universe. Even as he has devoured himself.'

'Kane, too,' he said, 'is sure that Morjin is damned.'

I did not like the note of longing that filled his voice just then. I said to him, 'No man knows Morjin as Kane does.'

'Does he, really? Does he know himself?' He smiled painfully, and squeezed my hand. 'You should go to him, Valashu. He'll be waiting for you.'

'Can we speak later, then?'

Again, he smiled at me. 'Yes, later. Now go and speak to the man who has fought so hard to see you made king.'

We clasped hands, and I felt his blood coursing deep within him. His eyes, strange and sad, filled with a piercing light.

Then Atara stood up and moved over to the end of the table. She took hold of my sword, and held it out to me.

'You will need this,' she told me. 'As we need Kane. Without *him* tomorrow, I can see no chance at all.'

I strapped on my sword, and squeezed her hand. And then, after promising Liljana that I would return soon for a taste of her pie, I turned to walk out into the night.

20

Outside my tent, Joshu Kadar and Sar Jonavar, with Sar Kanshar and Sar Shivalad, stood keeping watch over me. I told them that I must walk alone through our encampment. I asked after Kane, and Joshu Kadar informed me that he had ridden east, along the line of campfires stretching for two miles down the river. I moved off through the lanes of tents in that direction. The music of flutes and men singing flowed out into the air. I greeted my warriors, who bent over little fires roasting sausages on spits or sagosk steaks or whatever else Lord Harsha had managed to procure for their dinner. Greasy plumes of smoke spiraled up into a sky glowing blue-black. The moon, waxing full, reflected a silver light onto the grasslands about us, and set the river's waters to sparkling. I looked up at Aras, Solaru and Varshara, outshining all the other stars in the heavens and so bright that they seemed to blaze like little suns. They pointed the way toward that place on earth where I thought that Kane might have gone.

This was a small hill to the east of the Meshian tents and just to the north of the river. This nameless hump of ground rose up almost in line with the distant Owl's Hill across the steppe and the much greater rocks of the Detheshaloon. Other warriors I queried confirmed that Kane had indeed ridden his horse up the hill's grassy slopes. I followed him, on foot. It did not take me long to hike up to the top, where I found Kane standing beneath the stars.

He held a diamond-dusted sharpening stone, the one that had once belonged to my brother, Mandru, and that I had passed on to Kane. He drew it down the edge of his sword in long strokes that set the steel to ringing. As I came up close to him, he said to me, 'Have you come to help me prepare for tomorrow, then?'

'Is that what you are doing up here?'

He looked at me through the thin light. 'I am sorry for what passed with Liljana – will you forgive me?'

'Ask that of her.'

'I will,' he muttered. And then, 'There are always battles to be fought, eh?'

I pointed toward the camfires to the north and said, 'Yes – and that is our enemy.'

'So they are,' he muttered again. 'The Ikurian horse, at least, have good armor: some of the best mail made outside the Nine Kingdoms. If Morjin places them on his left wing, as you think he will, we'll have a hard work cutting through it.'

'Everything,' I said to him, 'will be a hard work tomorrow.'

'At least you'll have a chance to take your revenge for the Ikurians killing Asaru.'

'Bemossed,' I told him, 'would not like to hear you speak like that.'

He looked down the hill, back toward the Meshian encampment, where my pavilion stood out in the light of the moon and stars. He muttered, 'He is like a flower, the most beautiful of flowers. So easy to trample or cut. Morjin would pluck him in a moment just to watch him wither.'

'Bemossed is stronger than you know.'

'There is strength, and there is strength. The sight of a perfect cherry blossom can make even the mightiest of warriors weep, eh? But for how long does a blossom hold its splendor of perfection? A day, Valashu. No more than a single day.'

'If what you have told of the Maitreya is true, then Bemossed's day has not yet come. At his quickening, when he finally holds the Lightstone in his hands, then –'

'That is why we must fight tomorrow,' Kane broke in. 'Despite what Bemossed would have us do.'

I turned north, toward the great blaze of our enemy's camp-fires spread out beneath the Dethcshaloon, and I said, 'Half a million men – Maram believes we have no chance against so many.'

I said nothing of what I had seen inside Atara's crystal.

'So – we have *a* chance.' Kane paused in his scraping his diamond stone against his sword in order to look across the steppe's starlit grasses. 'He is out there, somewhere, Morjin is. He can be killed, with steel, like any other man. You have forced him out of Argattha to take a terrible chance. You and Bemossed have. And that is *our* chance.'

I smiled grimly and said, 'Who is it who wishes to take revenge?'

He smiled, too, and his white teeth shone in the moonlight. 'I would as soon see your sword pierce his heart as I would mine.'

I drew Alkaladur then, and watched the heavens' radiance play upon its long blade. How many men, I wondered yet again, had I slain with this shining sword? How many more must I cleave and send bloodied to earth?

'I have hated this kind of killing,' I said to him, 'as I have hated nothing else.'

'So – but you have loved it, too, eh?'

Kane's savage gaze locked onto me in a silent understanding. Who knew better than he the terrible joy of fighting for one's life that made a man feel so utterly alive?

'Yes, I have loved it,' I admitted. 'And that is why I have hated it. And why war must end. There must be another way to such exaltation that does not degrade us so.'

Kane did not dispute this. But he growled out to me: 'Worry about being degraded *after* you've killed Morjin!'

'A chance,' I told him, staring at Alkaladur's silvery blade, 'one chance more slender than the edge of this. Master Juwain was right when he told me that swords alone will never be enough. Tomorrow, the Seven will have their work to do, too. And Alphanderry – and of course, Bemossed. Even Maram.'

I drew in a deep breath smelling of sunburnt grass and roasting flesh. Tomorrow, I thought, the day would wax long and hot, for tonight the air blew too warm across the glistering steppe. Then I said to Kane, 'And you – you must do what you were born to do.'

'So,' he said in time with a long rasp of stone against steel, 'so I must.'

'I do not mean killing men, Kane.'

'No? What is it that you think *I* must do, eh?'

I looked up at the bright constellations standing out like diamonds against the black silk of the sky. Their onstreaming light pointed toward mysteries long lost to the ages, the great ages of the universe that the angels called satras. Kane, I thought, was himself a mystery nearly as deep as the other universes beyond the stars.

I lifted my sword higher, and I willed the words etched into its blade to flare forth. Alkaladur's silustria suddenly shone with fiery white characters: *Vas Sama Yeos Valarda Sola Paru* . . . And I said to Kane, 'You made this sword, and you cut these letters into it – what is the rest of the inscription?'

330

Kane stared at the blade that I held gleaming beneath the sky, and he shook his head. 'I told you, I have forgotten.'

'Have you really?' I asked him. 'Has *Kalkin* forgotten, then?'

His hand locked around his sword's hilt as he shouted at me: 'You promised not to say that name!'

I drew in a deep breath to slow the beating of my heart. I said to him, 'You are who you are. And you –'

'I am no longer *he*, I say! I am this one, whom you see standing here, and no one else!'

The wind, blowing down from the Detheshaloon, whipped his white hair about his savage face.

'But how is it possible,' I asked him, 'to forget?'

'How is it that you don't remember the day your mother breathed life into you and named you Valashu?'

Now it was my turn to shake my head. 'But you have lived through . . . so much. Kalkin has. It was he who took the lead in the war against Angra Mainyu, wasn't it? Over Varkoth and Marsul – even Ashtoreth? Why, then? Why did one of the Elijik order take precedence over the greatest of the Galadin?'

'Why do the stars shine, damn it!' he growled at me. 'Who set the world turning day into night, you tell me!'

He stared at my sword, and it seemed to flare even brighter. I said to him, 'You know. I know you know.'

'I know nothing!'

Now I stared back at him, looking for the bright being that he had never quite been able to hide from me.

'Tell me,' I said to him.

'Don't look at me that way, damn it!'

'Don't lie to me – we've come too far for that!' I lowered my sword, slightly, in case the madness seized Kane again, and he saw me as his enemy, as he had Liljana. 'At the beginning of the War of the Stone, you journeyed to another world. The angels name it Agathad, yes? And we call it Skol, where the Galadin dwell. And you led Ashtoreth and Valoreth, all the others, in forging the true Alkaladur, didn't you? To heal Angra Mainyu. This is *told*! As you love me, tell *me* why!'

Kane put away his sharpening stone, and stood away from his horse. He held his sword with both hands, then ran his finger down the flat of the kalama's long blade. He looked at me. The stars' light set his hair ashimmer, and his eyes. I saw him searching for something within me, and within himself. His heart beat, hard – once, twice, thrice, a hundred times. It swelled with the hurt of trying to contain the great force of life that surged through him. I could almost feel his breath burning over his lips like the warm wind that blew across the steppe.

'So,' he finally said in a strange, deep voice, 'once there was a king: you know his name. On Erathe this was, oldest of the Civilized Worlds. Long ago. Long past long ago, for the king came to his throne at the end of the Valari Satra, at a time when some men had put away their swords to polish bright their spirits, but before the first men became more than men. He called himself Valari, for in his youth he had been a traveler among the stars, bringing Civilization to the worlds of the stars. He became great, in his body and being. In his *spirit*, Valashu. He ruled Erathe by right of all that was true and good. So, he thought of himself as good. Others did, too.'

He paused to gaze at his sword, and it seemed that he was peering straight through its steel into another world.

'And so one day,' he continued, 'the Lightstone's guardian returned the Cup of Heaven to Erathe, where it had first appeared within our universe, long past in the Ardun Satra. Ramshan, they called this guardian. A descendant of the first guardian, Adar, who was *your* ancestor, eh? And with Ramshan, Dauidun, the Maitreya of that time. For all of that age, the Maitreyas had journeyed from world to world, so as to quicken Eluru's barbaric peoples and raise them up to be worthy of joining what we called Civilization. Daiudun journeyed to Erathe to see if its king might be worthy of being raised up to a higher order of beings that had never quite been – at least not within Eluru. And so the Shining One used the Cup of Heaven to test this great and glorious king.'

Kane's hands tightened around the hilt of his sword, and then he broke off staring at it to look at me.

'The king,' he murmured, 'opened his heart to the Lightstone's splendor. His whole being, eh? I have said that the Lightstone holds no power to make anyone immortal. So, this is true. But the king – *he* held such power within himself, do you understand? He had gained it, through a long life of discipline and deeds so hard they would have broken most men. And so the Lightstone only quickened what he had called forth to quicken. In the end, with the blessings of the Ieldra, *he* raised himself up to become the first of the Elijin.'

'Kalkin,' I said, heedless of the wind that blew that name toward Kane's ears.

'Yes, he,' he said. 'The Law of the One, for greater beings, demanded great things of him. His first charge was to vow never to take human life. And his second charge was to help others to gain his high estate. And so he left Erathe to journey out to the stars, so as to carry out this noble mission. Many were the Valari whom he guided into the Elijik order. So, even the great ones: Valoreth, Ashtoreth, Arwe, Urwe and Arkoth. And Varkoth, too, and Manwe and Marsul. And the greatest of all these Elijin, the one called Asangal. He, who would become the first and greatest of the Galadin.'

I looked up at the heavens for the star that shone down upon the world of Damoom, where Angra Mainyu had been bound. I wondered if any of the damned Galadin and Elijin who followed him could see the once-bright being called Asangal bound within this Dark One.

And then Kane went on: 'For a long time, the Elijin went among the stars, helping to awaken the most advanced of the Star People so that they could join their order. Too, the Ieldra sent the Elijin as messengers to troubled worlds. They had to work by the power of persuasion, or by touching men's auras with theirs and strengthening them – even as the Seven do with their little stones, eh? So, to the world of Kush the Ieldra sent the one named Kalkin. One of its kings, a proud barbarian, would not heed Kalkin's counsel. He drew his sword and commanded Kalkin to kneel to him. To abase himself to this small, small *man* whose life would soon blow out like a candle in the wind! But Kalkin himself burned with pride, and none more so, eh? And so a madness seized him, and he fell upon this barbarian king and killed him with his own sword.'

Kane drew in a deep breath, held it, then let it out. I felt a quick and terrible pain slice through him. Then he said to me, 'Kalkin was not the first of his order to fall, but he was the greatest. Because his remorse was also great, the Ieldra did not cast him out of the Elijin. And so he lost only his grace and not his immortality. But upon him the Ieldra laid a doom: that of all the Elijin then walking the stars, he would not be the first to be raised up to the Galadik order, but the last – and not in any case until the ending of the ages. It should have been a sentence of death, eh? But Kalkin vowed not to die.'

Again, Kane broke off speaking, and he stood nearly motionless in the starlight. His large hands still gripped his sword; I thought that they were shaped no differently than the hands of any other man. The features of his fierce face reminded me of the portraits of my forebears hanging in my father's hall, while the colors of pride, longing, wrath and exaltation that brightened his being were as my own. His eyes, however, blazed with a vast and fiery will that did not seem quite human.

I could hardly bear to look at him as I shook my head and whispered: 'It cannot be possible! The great ages were hundreds of thousands of years long, perhaps millions – I do not know! You cannot have survived so long. Chance alone –'

'It is not *chance* that rules me!' he suddenly roared out, cutting me off. 'It is the One!'

He took his hand away from his sword, and he glared at it as if looking through the dark for his lifeline. Then he added in a whisper, 'And it is myself. I could not *allow* myself to die, do you see? Kalkin couldn't. And so he, who should have been first, had to wait and watch through an entire age as the Elijin satra ended and Asangal advanced to the Galadik order. And then Ashtoreth and Valoreth, all the others, by dint of strengthening their spirits, and through service and the Ieldra's grace. Indestructible they became, as well as immortal. And great, beyond any glory that you can imagine. And yet. And yet. They still remembered Kalkin, who had helped them become who they were. Kalkin, whose remorse at slaying the barbarian king had shaken the very heavens! That proud, proud angel who never quite turned his face away from the One. Only he, the Galadin said, the king who knew the way of swords, could ever really understand the even prouder Asangal's fall into evil and so take the lead in the battle to heal him.'

As if to assuage the burning inside him, Kane pressed his sword's blade to his forehead. I did not know what to make of what he had said. His words hinted at madness and marvels and truths almost too terrible to tell. I felt sure that he had not, in any way, lied to me. And yet I sensed that he had left out some vital part of his story.

'I have often wondered,' I said, probing him, 'what it would be like to be immortal.'

'So – to be immortal *how*?'

'But how many ways are there?'

'There is *this* way,' he said, thumping his hand against his chest. 'To live forever, in one's body, on and on and on. That is Morjin's way, and Angra Mainyu's. And as with power, those who most desire it are the least worthy to possess it. Fools, all. In their pursuit of it, they are like men swimming across the ocean for a million years in search of water.'

334

'I have always thought,' I said to him, 'that Morjin searched for something more.'

'So, he would *like* to. But he could never quite apprehend, thus believe in, the realm of the soul.' His hand swept up toward the heavens' millions of lights, shining down as they did every night upon their sons and daughters still living on earth. 'Not for Morjin the immortality of the stars, or in doing great works, or in children, or in people's remembrance of their ancestors. And not even in the One's own remembrance of all that has been created and passed on.'

'So it is written in the Saganom Elu,' I said. 'In the most beautiful of words. But Morjin, I think, would need much more than words.'

'So – so would you, eh? But this, at least, is proven. What other meaning can we make of Alphanderry's return to us? You *saw* him die in the Kul Moroth. Has he come back from there, or from some other place?'

I thought about this as I gazed up at the fiery furnace called Aras. The brilliant spirals of stars whirling around it seemed to point toward a deep mystery at the center of all things. And I said to Kane, 'Most men when they die, they die. They do not come back.'

Even as I said this, I could not help thinking of the words of the angels, which one of the Urudjin had spoken in King Kiritan's hall:

> *The Fearless Ones find day in night*
> *And in themselves the deathless light,*
> *In flower, bird and butterfly,*
> *In love: thus dying do not die.*

Kane looked at me as if he could peer into my soul, if not my mind. 'And most men when they live, they do not truly live. And so like Morjin and his master, they are already as ones dead. There is only one *true* immortality, Valashu. I have spoken of this before: it is the breath that holds the winds of all worlds within it, the stillness between heartbeats, the joy of a flower. The perfect moment, bright as ten thousand suns, that goes on and on forever. *This* is the indestructible life that the Shining One would show us.'

I thought of other words that the Urudjin had spoken about the universe's Maitreyas, and I now recited them to Kane:

They bring to them the deathless light,
Their fearlessness and sacred sight;
To slay the doubts that terrify:
Their gift to them to gladly die.

Then I said to Kane, 'The Shining Ones *are* that they might thus help the Galadin, and others, overcome their fear of death, yes?'

'So, they *gladly* die – and thus truly live, eternally.'

I stepped closer to Kane, and pressed my hand against his chest. 'This one, whom I have called Kane – I have not seen *him* quail before any enemy, in any battle, not even when it seemed certain that he must die.'

'Ha!' he called out. 'When one of the Blues swings an axe at my head, my heart beats as quickly as any man's!'

'But you never panic. You never think of running when you must fight. And you do not, do you, dread the dark? The neverness. When the light dies and there is only a cold nothing forever.'

'But the light cannot die, Valashu. And so, no, I do not fear *that*.'

'But what of the other one, then? Was Kalkin so afraid of being cast out of the Elijin that he had to make a vow never to die?'

'No – fear was never Kalkin's failing.'

He thrust the point of his sword upwards, then called out: 'He *dreamed* of the day when he would become one of the Galadin. So bright they are! Like fireflowers that never dim, like stars come down from the sky. The Galadin make the whole earth sing! Songs of glory, Valashu, such a ringing splendor that I cannot say! And yet in the end, as I've told, they must die – like the Shining Ones, gladly so, to die in their bodies. Into light! *This* splendor, bright as all the stars from the Seven Sisters to the Great Bear, the fire that breathes into being whole new universes of stars, I have only imagined. So it was with Kalkin. And so no, he did not fear such a fate.'

I stood listening to the crickets chirping in the grass and the breath that fell heavy and quick from my lips. From below our little hill, the sound of thousands of Valari chanting out the old epics had given way to a single voice flowing out across the steppe:

Sing ye songs of glory,
Sing ye songs of glory,
That the light of the One
Will shine upon the world.

I knew then that my friends had finished their dinner and that Liljana must have used her blue gelstei to cast Alphanderry's music out along the river for all to hear.

'Kalkin did not fear death,' I said to Kane, 'and yet he still vowed not to die. Why, then?'

But Kane did not answer me. He stood staring off at the stars as if remembering a time when he had walked upon them.

I turned my gaze toward the sword that he had once made. The Sword of Fate, men called it. The Sword of Sight. Within its shimmering silustria I suddenly saw a thing.

'There was more to Kalkin's vow, wasn't there?' I said to him.

He slowly nodded his head to me. 'So – there was.'

'Tell me, then.'

Again he nodded his head, and I felt a terrible anguish working at him. And he said to me: 'I have spoken of flowers and music and other prettinesses, eh? The One's light that shines through all things. But the world is also swords and blood and fire. Sheer hell, I say. It can be a torment to live through a single moment, let alone a day or a whole lifetime – or more. It is *hard* just drawing a breath. And harder still for one to breathe life into oneself as an Elijin or a Galadin, for as an angel's being is vastly greater than a man's, so is his suffering. So, Kalkin had many flaws and did many wrongs, but he had one great virtue, eh? He was *strong*. And so he vowed to remain within life as long as he had to. To walk through the deeps of the world, where all is filth and fire, nails and screaming – so to find light in the darkest of places. *Not* to bring this light to others, for so the Maitreyas come forth with the Cup of Heaven. But only to help men and women, even the lowest, walk the path from the earth to the stars. Not until all who could had become Elijin and Galadin would he be free to leave the world. And so the first would truly be last – so Kalkin vowed to the sun and the earth, and to the Ieldra who had sung them into existence; so he promised himself and even the One.'

He fell into silence, and I could not help staring at him. The world turned no more quickly toward the east than it ever did, and yet for a moment the stars seemed to whirl past me in a blur of light. Kane stood within this radiance staring back at me.

'That was a noble vow,' I finally said to him.

'So, it was,' he admitted, nodding his head. 'Much later, during the War of the Stone, the Galadin said that through the very act of making it, Kalkin had healed himself – and so he might find the way to heal Angra Mainyu.'

I thought about this, then asked him the same question that I had Ondin in the Vild: 'But in the end, he failed, as the Amshahs who followed him failed. Why, then?'

'*That* I have journeyed across the stars for half a million years to this place to understand.'

I pointed my sword out toward the fire-brightened rocks of the Detheshaloon, and I said, 'I thought you came here to kill Morjin.'

But Kane made no response to this. I felt his eyes burning like coals as he looked at me.

From the direction of the Owl's Hill more than a mile away came a sound that might have been the howling of a wolf – or perhaps the battle cry of one of the dreadful Blues who had climbed to its top in order to demoralize our encampment: **OWRULLL!** And I said to Kane, 'Swords and axes hold no terror for you, nor fire nor crosses, nor even death. What is it you *do* fear, then?'

I knew that he did not want to answer me. His jaws clamped shut with such force that I felt his teeth grinding together. His hands locked around the hilt of his sword.

'Tell me,' I said to him as the sword that I held suddenly glistened.

There is a force, like a river of light, that runs through all things. I felt it rushing inside me, sweeping both Kane and me away.

'Tell me,' I said again, gazing at him.

'Damn you!' he finally growled out. 'I fear nothing! Nothing except that bright one – do not speak his name! He is *too* bright, eh? Too damn blessed and beloved of the One. He can dwell in the stillness so *easily*. In the light, Valashu. Far from all the dark and desperate things that must be done in this world if such as Morjin is to be defeated!'

He seemed to fight against the immense pull of the world in order to keep from falling; I felt an immense tiredness working at his bones and every part of him. How was it possible, I wondered? How, for untold ages of men, had he lived fearing that the angel would break out from the walls of forgetfulness that he had built around himself? And year after year, century upon century, found the will to renew the war against himself and do battle yet again? He dreaded beyond any dread I had ever known that the unbound angel would weaken and destroy him. But this was his deepest hope, too, because the angel was a much greater and more powerful being.

'Kalkin,' I said, sensing a deep light streaming through the sword that he had once made.

'Be silent!' he growled at me. 'And do not look at me that way!'

I shook my head at this, and called to him again: 'Kalkin.'

'Damn your eyes! And damn that sword of yours!'

I felt every muscle in his body burning so as to move him to strike his sword into me.

'Kane,' I said to him, 'is the greatest warrior ever to have been raised up from any world, and he would never desert me. But will *Kalkin* ride beside me tomorrow, too?'

This question seemed to hang in the air like the ringing of a silver bell. So did the music that Alphanderry gave to the world:

> *Be ye songs of glory,*
> *Be ye songs of glory,*
> *That the light of the One*
> *Will shine upon the world.*

My savage friend stood there listening to Alphanderry's singing. He gazed at me in a silent desperation. He saw me, I sensed, as I saw myself: like a still lake that might gleam as brightly as a silver mirror, but mist-enshrouded. Where, I wondered, was the sun to burn away the mist?

I looked down the length of my shining sword at this anguished man who had slain so many. It would be easy to hate him, as I did killing and war. But I could not hate him – not even the darkest and most terrible parts of him. It was just the opposite.

'Kalkin,' I called out for the third time. 'Will Kalkin take the field against our enemies?'

I felt something bright and warm burst open within me – and within the man who stood by me at the top of the hill. His black eyes shimmered in the starlight; so, I thought, did mine. Then he saw himself in me. And I saw *him* come alive with a blazing purpose. He seemed like a great silver bird released from a cage and soaring into the sky. His gaze opened like a window to the deeps of his being, and there gathered suns and moons and whole universes on fire. His face shone with a terrible beauty. In the way he suddenly held out his hand to me, with such strength and grace and a wild joy, it seemed that all the immense suffering of the past and the infinite promise of the future were as one.

'Val,' he called out in a strange, deep voice, 'is a great warrior who would never desert *me*. But will Valamesh, the King of Swords, ride beside me tomorrow and do whatever he must to defeat the enemy? Will he? I *know* what he fears.'

339

This question, too, hung in the air. For a long time I stood listening to the whispering of the wind and my heart's wild beats. Then, in answer to what he had asked of me, I moved forward to clasp his hand.

A great smile broke from his face like lightning from the sky. And then there, at the top of the hill, in the sight of tens of thousands of campfires and millions of stars, we went to work practicing swords with each other one last time. As the night deepened toward morning, our blades clashed together in a ringing of steel and bright silustria. And all the while Alphanderry continued singing for all the earth and heavens to hear:

> *Be ye songs of glory,*
> *Be ye songs of glory,*
> *That the light of the One*
> *Will shine upon the world.*

21

I walked alone back through the lines of the campfires toward my pavilion. The great noise of our army had quieted as men finished their dinners and lay down to try to sleep, most of them outside their tents beneath the stars. As I made my way along, I greeted those warriors who had remained awake, calling out their names: 'Yuravay; Sharam; Durrivar of Ki; Naviru Elad . . .' There seemed almost no end to my homeland's ten thousand warriors whom I had led here, nor to the hours of the night. I came upon one man, Sunjay of Godhra, who sat trying to tie a battle ribbon to his long black hair. It was only his second ribbon, for he had fought at the Seredun Sands but had been too young to take up arms at the Culhadosh Commons the year before. Usually, ribbons were awarded only *after* a battle, but because I feared that none of my warriors might survive the coming day, I wanted them to be honored for their valor in merely showing up on this field to fight. All knew what a desperate fight it would be. And so young Sunjay's fingers trembled as he tried to work his red-colored ribbon into a knot.

'Sunjay, son of Torshan!' I called out to him. He was a rather gangly youth whose smooth, comely face still bore a look of innocence. 'Here, let me help you.'

I stepped over to him, moving around the sleeping forms of his companions. He bowed his head to me, and I quickly knotted the ribbon in his hair. And he told me, 'Thank you, Sire.'

'Thank *you*,' I said to him, 'for marching with me down such a long road. But tomorrow, we'll come to the end of it.'

'Yes, tomorrow,' he said, bowing his head again.

I sensed the emptiness of his churning belly, and said to him, 'Have you not had anything to eat?'

'We were given given antelope livers and steaks for dinner,' he told me, 'but I had no stomach for meat, if you know what I mean. Before I sleep, I shall try to eat a few battle biscuits.'

I asked him if he might have more of an appetite for pie, and his eyes brightened. I promised him that I would send out some of the strawberry pie that Liljana had been saving for me. And then I told him, 'Don't worry, lad, you will do well tomorrow. When the time comes, don't be afraid of yourself.'

He smiled at me as if astonished that I could sense his deepest fear. I set my hand on his shoulder, on the steel plate reinforcing his diamond armor, and I felt our regard for each other passing back and forth like a torch. Then I bid him goodnight, and moved off toward my pavilion as I spoke the names of other countrymen: 'Darshur the Bold; Telamar, son of Zandru; Suladad Yuval; Shanidar of Silvassu . . .'

Too many of my men, I though, were barely men who had yet to see their twentieth year. How cruel, I thought, that they should be cut down in the finest flush of life before they had the chance to marry and sire their own children. I must have greeted two hundred of them before I realized with a shock that I, too, was a young man with hopes and dreams.

When I finally reached my pavilion and lay down, I could not sleep, and so I spent the few remaining hours meditating instead. Just before dawn, Abrasax came inside my pavilion to lay his hand on my arm and shake me into a painful consciousness.

'Valashu,' he said in a low, grave voice, 'I must tell you something.'

I sat up from my sleeping furs to see Abrasax's great, white-haired head limned in the glow of the candles.

'What is it, Grandfather?' I said to him.

'It is Bemossed – he is gone, and no one can find him.'

He went on to explain that an hour before, Bemossed had left the tent that he shared with Abrasax and the Seven. Bemossed, too, as Abrasax related, had been unable to sleep, and so he had gone outside to look upon the last of the night's stars.

'When he did not return,' Abrasax informed me, 'Master Virang and the others helped me to search for him – helped in vain.'

'But he must be somewhere!' I said. 'He cannot have left the encampment!'

But neither could Abrasax and the Seven, as Abrasax admitted, search the entire grounds where the warriors of sixteen kingdoms and six Sarni tribes gathered for battle. But I, as their warlord, could. At least I could pass the word to the kings who followed me to order their captains and company commanders to make a search. Such was the virtue of an army.

The sun was rising over the steppe in the east as their reports came to me: no one seemed able to locate Bemossed, not my Meshians near the center of our encampment, nor anyone else from the Ishkans in the west to the Atharians in the east. And then, even as our enemy's great war drums began booming out the challenge for battle, Lord Tanu came into my pavilion with five sentries: Gorvan of Lashku; Sorashan; Vikadar, son of Ramadar; Barshar of Ki; and Karathar Eldru. It seemed that they had been stationed ten paces from each other along a picket line to the north of our encampment. Lord Tanu's sour face grew bitter as he informed me: 'All of these men were found sleeping at their posts! They tell that Bemossed gave them coffee to help them stay awake – and that the coffee must have been poisoned with a sleeping potion! They remember speaking for a while with the Maitreya, and then nothing more!'

Kane, who stood listening to this report along with my other friends and the Seven, ground his jaws together and then growled out, 'Bemossed employed the same stratagem in Hesperu to make me sleep and so escape into the wilderness.'

'Well, then,' Lord Tanu said, 'it seems that it is no fault of my men that he has escaped his duty on the eve of battle.'

And Bemossed's duty, according to Lord Tanu, was to inspirit the warriors to face what would soon come. Although he did not quite call Bemossed a coward, the word seemed to hang upon his tongue like a curse.

'But where did he escape *to*?' Maram asked. 'If he wished to flee, why did he poison the sentries to the *north* of our encampment? Why not flee across the river to the south, or east, away from our enemy?'

'Perhaps,' Lord Tanu said, 'he has gone over *to* the enemy – though I would not have wanted to believe that of him. But then the Lord of Lies has a way of turning men, doesn't he?'

I, too, feared that Bemossed had crossed the broad strip of grass separating our encampment from Morjin's. But I found myself hoping with a blood-pounding desperation that he had, in fact, gone off into the steppe because he could not bear to face the horror of another battle.

'I have asked Sajagax,' I told everyone, 'to send out riders to search for Bemossed. If he *did* flee, he cannot have gone far.'

As the sun rose even higher, however, and my warriors finished their breakfasts and gave a last polish to their armor, Sajagax's outriders returned one by one to report that they had been unable to find any sign of Bemossed. It seemed that he might really *have* gone over to the enemy – either that or simply vanished into the grass.

Finally, Sajagax himself, accoutered for battle and clutching his great bow, strode into my pavilion and announced to me, 'We cannot find him! And the word of his desertion spreads among the men like a plague. What are we to do, Valashu?'

'What *can* we do?' I said. The distant tattoo of our enemy's drums seemed to boom out with even greater force. I thought I heard the sound of trumpets blaring along the wind. 'Let us form up for battle.'

I clasped Sajagax's huge arm, and told him that after he had driven off or defeated the Sarni tribes arrayed against him, I would meet him upon the center of the field over Morjin's corpse. Then he struck his huge fist against my shoulder and stormed out to gather up his warriors.

All along the river, our trumpeters began sounding the call to assemble. The Valari – along with the warriors from Thalu, Nedu and the other Free Kingdoms – began crowding between the rows of tents in thousands as they took their places in their companies and battalions. Just before we marched out away from our encampment, I lingered inside my pavilion to say farewell to the Seven, and to Liljana, Daj and Estrella.

'Promise me,' I said to Abrasax, 'that if the battle goes ill, you will flee with the children before it is too late.'

I repeated my request to him that the Seven should try to take refuge in one of Ea's Vilds, where Daj and Estrella might possibly live out a good part of their lives even if Morjin destroyed the rest of the world. Although Abrasax would make no promises, he at least nodded his head in acknowledgment of my concern.

Just before I donned my great helm, with its crest of white swan plumes, I bent down to embrace Estrella. Her warm, dark eyes seemed to reach out to hold onto me. I knew that she would choose to remain here and die by my side if we were defeated. This lovely child who had journeyed so far with me through so many dangers seemed suddenly not so much of a child at all. I felt within her a great movement, as with a mass of charged air before a storm. I had always marveled at her deep and mysterious accord with life. Could she now foresee, I wondered, her own death? Or mine? It had been prophesied that she would show the Maitreya, and I wished that she might now point the way to where Bemossed had gone and tell me that he was safe from harm.

'Take care of the children,' I said to Liljana. I kissed Estrella's forehead, then clasped Daj's hand. 'Do not let them out of your sight.'

I embraced Liljana, and kissed her, too. And then it was time to go.

I led the way up from the river at the head of a column of the Meshian knights. Our horses' hooves beat against the earth, and the morning sun set our diamond armor on fire. Kane kept pace by my right side, with Maram at my left, followed by Lord Avijan, Lord Sharad and hundreds of others. We rode east, just past the hill where I had crossed swords with Kane only hours before. Slightly to the north of this little hump of ground, we met up with the mounted knights of Athar, Kaash and Waas, led by King Mohan, King Viromar and King Sandarkan. We massed together in long lines of stamping horses bearing warriors with long lances and gleaming shields. The rest of our army formed up with us as their anchor point: to our left and west, stretching out across the golden grasslands, the foot warriors of Athar took their places in glittering ranks five deep, followed by those of Waas, Kaash and Mesh. The white-haired giants called Ymaniri, led by Ymiru, framed the Alonians and Eannans at our center with the Thalunes farther to the west. Then came the Valari of Taron, Lagash, Anjo and Ishka. At the end of our lines, King Hadaru gathered with the combined cavalry of those same four kingdoms to anchor our army in the west. The distance from the swan and stars that my banner-bearer held aloft to the flapping red cloth showing the white bear of Ishka, as I estimated, must be nearly five miles. Behind our lines, in two groups, stood our archers; between them waited the scant reserves from Nedu, Surrapam, Delu and the Elyssu. Beyond the lines of foot and cavalry – spread out over the steppe even farther to the west – the warriors of the Niurui, Urtuk and Danladi tribes assembled in one of the much looser and more flexible formations favored by these horse archers. So it was with the Kurmak, Adirii and the Manslayers just to the east of my cavalry. I saw Sajagax on top of his stallion a few hundred yards away waiting at the head of eight thousand warriors; Atara, her white blindfold flashing in the sun, led more than three and a half thousand women of her Sisterhood.

'It will be a hot day,' Maram said from beside me as he looked

345

up at the sun, 'if we have to wait too much longer to engage. This is the part of battle that I hate most of all, the waiting.'

Even as he spoke, the drums of Morjin's army thundered with even greater force. Trumpets blared, and the cries of war elephants bellowed out across the steppe. So did the eerie howls of the Blues. I watched as, more than a mile away, our enemy formed up for battle. So many men, however, could not so quickly assemble into their lines.

'Half a million men,' Lord Sharad said from off to my right. He shook his head, encased in a shining steel helmet. 'Let us see if Morjin packs them twenty ranks deep.'

'Or extends his lines,' Lord Avijan said, 'miles to either side of us.'

For a few moments, they reopened the debate that we had argued during our councils. Lord Noldashan, with Lords Manthanu and Jessu the Lion-Heart farther back, sat on their heavily armored mounts listening to them speculate. So did Joshu Kadar, Siraj the Younger, Sar Vikan, Sar Shivalad and my other Guardians. Sar Jonavar, I thought, would not be able to lament after today that he had missed the greatest of battles. Farther along the front line of our cavalry, I saw King Sandarkan and King Viromar waiting to see how things would fall out. King Mohan, sitting beneath the standard of the blue horse of Athar, also looked our way.

'So,' Kane growled out into the warm morning wind, 'Morjin has enough men to build his ranks ten deep *and* to flank us.'

But so long as Sajagax's Sarni could rove the grasslands on either of our flanks firing their long-range arrows, as Kane observed, Morjin would be unlikely to extend his lines *too* far and so expose them to a hail of death.

'Sajagax will hold his own against Morjin's Sarni,' Maram said. 'Ah, he *must*. And if he does, I suppose it will be our fate to ride against those damn Ikurians again.'

We all waited to see how Morjin would set his order of battle. Soon I watched the black eagles of the Ikurian standard bearers move forward at the head of a great mass of armored knights, who took their places on Morjin's left flank opposite us. Morjin's heavy cavalry, I guessed, would outnumber ours by more than three to one. To the west of these fierce warriors with their broad-bladed swords and fur-trimmed helms, stood the phalanxes of Sunguru, broken at intervals by fifty great, trumpeting elephants. And then came the impressed soldiers of Eanna, who were almost like slaves, and the Sakayans in ranks twenty deep and seventy thousand strong. Their battalions formed just beneath the slopes of the Owl's Hill to their rear. I could not see clearly the army of Hesperu lined up beyond them on a swell of grass farther to the west. But riders brought me a report of the hundred thousand Hesperuk soldiers in bronze, fish-scaled armor. King Arsu, these messengers said, sat inside a kind of castle perched on the back of a great bull elephant with bronze-shod tusks more than ten feet long. Other lords and knights, with archers, rode atop other elephants at the front of the Hesperuk phalanxes. Then came the tiny armies of impressed Surrapam and Alonian soldiers, and the vastly larger army of Uskudar, led by King Orunjan. A horde of Blues with their fearsome axes gathered next to a great mass of more heavy cavalry from various Dragon Kingdoms; these thousands of heavy horse formed the Dragon Army's anchor in the west. As with our army, Morjin's Sarni would range across the steppe on either flank, fighting Sajagax's warriors. Behind our enemy's lines, Morjin had stationed archers and reserves, as had I. Most of these, it seemed, were Yarkonans: some of the very same men that Count Ulanu had led against my companions and me at Khaisham. I knew that Kane longed to take vengeance for the Yarkonans' burning of the Great Library and massacre of the people trapped inside. I did, too, but I had more concern for Morjin and his Dragon Guard. My messengers could not tell me on what part of the field they might be waiting for us. They guessed that they must be hidden by our enemy's lines, perhaps behind the Owl's Hill near the center of the field.

Where is he? I wondered as I set my hand upon the hilt of my sword. I remembered the saying that the silver gelstei would lead to the gold. *Where is the Great Beast who stole the Lightstone*?

Maram, beside me, ran his finger down beneath the mail covering his neck. His face was sweating, and he seemed to want nothing more than to drink a horn of cool beer. He gazed out at the great multitude of our enemy arrayed upon the Wendrush's trampled grass, and he said, 'So many – if the gates of hell had opened to disgorge a swarm of demons, I do not think there could be so many.'

'They are only men,' I said, pointing out across the field. 'And you are forgetting one thing about them.'

'Ah, what is that?'

'In all their multitude, there is not a single man named Maram Marshayk.'

This caused Maram to laugh, a sound that the warriors around him picked up and passed back and forth along the lines as they recounted the deeds of my best friend. They badly needed such encouragement. Bemossed's desertion, I sensed, had worked at their spirits like a leech draining a body of blood.

My stallion stamped his hoof against the turf, and I reached down to stroke his tensed neck beneath the armor that covered it. And I murmured to him, 'Just one more time, old friend. Just one more charge.'

Kane, to my right on top of the Hell Witch, stared out at our enemy with an immense will to destroy them. And I said to him, 'Such great numbers – not even at the Sarburn did Morjin and Aramesh command so many. I have never stood at a place of such a great battle as this.'

For moment it seemed that Kane's blood ran through his veins as cold as ice water. Then his black eyes flashed in the sun as he looked at me. 'No, you are wrong. For you have stood at the center of the Tar Harath.'

'The Tar Harath?' I said, puzzled. I remembered with a bitter pain that sun-seared hell at the heart of the Red Desert. 'Men do not even go into that place. No battle ever could have been fought *there*.'

'You are wrong about that, too. For once the Tar Harath was a grassland such as this. And it had a different name, taken after the site of the great battle.'

'What battle?' I asked him.

'So – we called it Tharharra.'

Tharharra, I thought, *the Tar Harath*. Could it be possible? *The Battle of Tharharra*, that had been the greatest of all the ages? There, once a time, a host of Galadin, Elijin and Star People led by Kalkin and Marsul had defeated a vast army of Daevas under Angra Mainyu. Marsul had wrested the Lightstone from Angra Mainyu himself, while Manwe and other Galadin had bound the Dark One on Damoom.

'But the verse we heard in the amphitheater,' I said in astonishment, 'told that Tharharra was fought on *Erathe*, out in the stars!'

Kane pointed up at the sun and said, 'We dwell, always, in the stars.'

Then his hand swept out across the grassy steppe east and west as he added: 'This *is* Erathe. That is what we named our world long ago – long, long ago. I was its king, Valashu. When I was born, the White Mountains stood lower and the Morning Mountains higher. The stars were different, too.'

He looked up at the sky, whose deep blue shimmer hid the great spirals of lights spread throughout the universe. Then he sighed and said, 'But men are not different – and so once again we must fight. But this will be my last battle.'

I turned to meet eyes with him in a silent understanding.

'Your time is coming, too,' he added.

I tightened my grip around my sword to draw strength from it. Then I drew Alkaladur and gave the command to advance. Trumpets rang out. In an unbroken line stretching five miles across the steppe, the men from the Free Kingdoms marched toward our enemy. Our cavalry kept pace on either flank, while Sajagax ordered his Sarni warriors to begin maneuvering for advantage on both wings even farther out across the grass. The terrible jangle of silver bells worn by sixty-five thousand Valari warriors seemed to shiver the air; the thunder of our drums shook the very earth. We drew within half a mile of our enemy, but their massed formations remained unmoving, like immense blocks of bronze and steel upon which we must surely break.

And then, as we narrowed the distance to four hundred yards, there came a great and hideous howl from the Owl's Hill. At precisely that moment, a terrible pain ripped through the center of my right hand, and I nearly dropped my sword. I looked out above our enemy's lines to see a band of Blues gathered upon the hill's top. A second howl split the morning's peace as my left hand, fastened around of the straps of my shield, burned as if pierced with a heated iron. Upon the third howl that fell upon my advancing warriors like an evil breath, I nearly fainted from the spike of agony that tore through the bones of my feet. Then I watched in horror, as did tens of thousands of my men, as the Blues at the top of the hill raised up a lone wooden cross.

'It is Bemossed!' I gasped out to Kane. My eyes burned as I stared across the field, trying to make out the face of the tiny figure nailed up on crossed beams for entire armies to behold. 'I know it is he!'

And Kane, I thought, knew it, too. His jaws clamped shut with such force that it seemed he might have bitten through steel plate; the fire in his eyes and shooting through his trembling body might have caused him to sweat blood.

'So,' he finally growled out. 'So.'

I sheathed my sword, and took hold of his arm. I was afraid he might fall into a fury and charge alone straight toward the Owl's Hill. And I was afraid that I might join him.

349

'It is the Maitreya!' one of my warriors down the line to the west cried out, pointing up and out. 'Look – it is the Shining One!'

There comes a moment when we know that doom is upon us, and cannot be averted. Even so, we try to deny it. As Kane shook his head in bitterness and despair, I sat on top of Altaru trying to stop tears from flooding my eyes. I did not want to believe what my heart knew must be true.

'The Maitreya!' hundreds of voices cried out all at once. 'It is Bemossed!'

I called for a halt then, for at that moment, a herald bearing a white flag rode out from our enemy's lines across the field. I sent out a herald of my own to meet with him. This man – his name was Sar Garash –soon returned to report that Morjin had requested a parlay.

'A parlay!' Maram called out to me. 'A trap, more likely. You can't let yourself get close to that crucifying snake, Val. Don't go!'

'Ha!' Kane shouted as he laid hold of his sword. 'If it's to be a trap, then let *us* spring it and put an end to Morjin for all time!'

'No, Kane,' I told him. 'You know we cannot.'

And we couldn't, I said, because if we slew Morjin, then surely Morjin's men would finish off Bemossed. Too, the one who met with us at the center of the field might not be Morjin himself, but only one of his droghuls whom we could not distinguish in appearance from the real Morjin. And last, I told Kane, we could not murder Morjin here beneath the sacred banner of truce because I was now a Valari king who could not do such a thing.

'Six counselors are to ride out with Morjin,' I said to Kane, 'and I am to bring as many.'

I turned to Maram, sweating in the building heat of the morning, and he huffed out: 'Not I! You have kings at your command, Val.'

'But you are a prince among men,' I told him, 'and a hero whom the minstrels will sing of for ages. Come, friend, and let us finally write the ending to this song!'

Maram was weeping as he nodded his head at me. I did not know if he shed tears for himself or for Bemossed – and all of Ea.

'Kane,' I said, turning to my right, 'you will come, too, yes?'

The blaze in Kane's dark eyes told me that nothing could stop him.

For my other counselors, I choose Ymiru, Atara, Sajagax and King Hadaru. It took some time for my messengers to ride forth and summon them to me. Then, beneath a white flag held aloft by one of my heralds, we moved out to confront our enemy.

350

We met Morjin and his counselors at the center of the field. Atop a snow-white horse, the Red Dragon rode easily and with an air of authority, as if the very grass and all the earth beneath him were his to command. I could almost feel the force of his fell desires emanating from him with a terrible heat. He wore an armor of mail and steel plate stained a bright carmine and encrusted with glittering rubies, in mockery of the diamonds that we Valari bore. Two of his retinue were similarly accoutered: a great, squat, black-bearded Ikurian named Zahur Tey, who proved to be Lord of the Dragon Guard, and my old enemy, Prince Salmelu of Ishka – now named Arch Igasho. Two other Kallimun priests hung by Morjin's sides: Arch Uttam, who had nearly put my companions and me to death in Hesperu, and Arch Yadom. Both had the gaunt, hollowed-out look of cadavers that had been eaten at by wolves; they wore long yellow robes in place of armor, for they were no warriors. The fifth of Morjin's followers, however, in his youth, had been a great warrior who had fought his way to become chief of the Marituk tribe. But over the years Gorgorak had grown nearly as great in girth as in reputation due to his fondness for food and beer. His once-golden hair had gone gray, and his little blue eyes buried deep within his puffy red face stared out at me in challenge. Right behind him rode Count Ulanu, now acclaimed as Yarkona's king. He had a hard, foxlike face framed by a neatly shaped beard. Ulanu the Handsome he had once been called – until Liljana had cut off the end of his nose in a battle preceding the siege of the great Library. As he drew closer, he glared at me with poisonous dark eyes as if to transfer his hate for Liljana onto me.

I did not need to look at Morjin to feel his great malice burning him up like a disease. I had not seen him, in the flesh, since I had put my sword through his neck in Argattha. Through the grace of his kind he had recovered from this mortal wound, and more, he had called upon the darkest of sources to invigorate his body with a terrible new life. Through the power of the illusions he cast, others saw him as a golden-eyed angel. But I would always see him as an old, old man whose sagging skin had gone gray with corruption. His smell was all foulness and fear, rage and hate.

He halted far enough away that I could not easily hurry forward to strike at him with my sword, but close enough for me to make out the webwork of broken veins that made his eyes seem like pools of blood. The others drew up behind him.

'King Valamesh!' he called out to me, formally and politely. 'I would like to thank you for making parlay with me!'

351

His voice, like a battering ram, struck straight into my chest with a power I had not remembered. Save for Alphanderry, I had never heard anyone put tone to words more beautifully.

'Morjin!' I called back to him. 'I do not know what we have to discuss – unless it is your surrender!'

I could almost feel Kane smiling savagely at this just behind me. But what I had said, and even more the manner in which I had said it, only infuriated Morjin.

'I did not give you leave to call me familiar!' he shouted at me. 'I am King Morjin of Sakai, Lord Emperor of Ea and Lord of Light!'

'You are the Lord of Lies!' I said. 'Why should I listen to anything of what you have to say here?'

In answer, Morjin turned to point at the cross rising up from the Owl's Hill and framed by the great, skull-like rocks of the Detheshaloon. I could not call out to Bemossed, nailed up in the air so far away, but my whole being burned to ask him a single question: *Why did you go to our enemy?*

'The Hajarim slave,' Morjin said, turning back to me, 'is a false Maitreya. I promised you he would be punished, and his agony has only begun. But it is upon you to end it.'

'How so . . . Lord of Light?'

Morjin could not abide sarcasm, and his face darkened with rancor. 'Surrender to *me*, here and now, your sword. Command your men to lay down their swords. Their bows, too. Command them then to return to their encampment. Do these things, and despite what I have written to you, I will spare their lives. I will see that the Hajarim is taken down from the cross and given to your healers.'

He lies! I told myself. *He is the Lord of Lies, the Crucifier, the Red Dragon, the Great Beast*!

And upon this thought, as I gazed up at Bemossed with his hands stretched out to the world, I knew why he had deserted in the dead of night. Out of a strange pride that knew nothing of vanity and conceit, but only the foolishness of compassion, he had gone to Morjin with a desperate hope that he might somehow heal this dark angel.

'Do as I say,' Morjin told me, 'and we can avoid this battle that no one wants. And I will let even *you* have your life.'

Could Morjin, I wondered, really think that I might believe him and set up my men to be slaughtered? Why had he *really* called this parlay?

'I, for one, *do* want battle!' Sajagax suddenly shouted, shaking his bow at Morjin. 'You have laid waste Kurmak lands and ravaged my people! We *will* have our revenge! I care not for any of your threats and lies! Nor your slave army: the One will give us strength today and keep our sight true. If Valashu Elahad had not asked otherwise, right here I would put an arrow through your eye!'

Sajagax's fierce words caused Morjin's pallid face to drain of all blood. I imagined, however, that Morjin's men perceived him through the colored glass of illusion as a mighty and sanguine warrior who stared down Sajagax with a vast self-assurance beaming from an implacable countenance. Morjin had only to nod at Gorgorak for this great chief of the Marituk to speak in Morjin's stead:

'You will do nothing if I put an arrow into you first!'

'Brave words!' Sajagax shouted at Gorgorak with a voice like a lion's roar. Then he pointed out into the steppe. 'Let us see if your deeds can match them! Within the hour, my warriors will ride against yours. Let us first, at a distance fit for Sarni chieftains, loose our arrows at each other. Let him who survives take the other's horses, wives and lands, and thus settle matters between the Kurmak and the Marituk!'

But Gorgorak, usually so bold, made no answer to this. He just sat staring at Sajagax with his little blue eyes. On all the Wendrush, it was said, no one could outshoot Sajagax.

Now Morjin turned the force of his will upon Arch Uttam, and his overawed Red Priest could not help but deliver more of Morjin's words:

'If it is battle you seek,' Arch Uttam told Sajagax, 'then it is battle you shall have! And at the end of it, when you are brought before the Lord of Ea in chains, we will tear out your liver and you will watch us feed it to the dogs before you die!'

Kane, who had liked Sajagax from their first meeting, growled out to Arch Uttam: 'Ha! Save your words for when you *do* have him in chains!'

Arch Uttam's skull-like face fixed on Kane. 'We should have put *you* in chains when we had the chance! I would have torn out much more than your liver!'

He said this with a seething glee, then turned to stare at Atara. She sat on her red mare, gripping her bow and remaining quiet behind the white blindfold that bound her face.

'And you,' Arch Uttam said to her, 'this time we will flay you alive. We will make a puppet of your skin to display in Lord Morjin's hall!'

Arch Yadom, who looked almost like Arch Uttam's evil twin, had been the chief of the priests who had tortured my companions in Argattha. He smiled at Atara and added, 'But you, unfortunately, will *not* be able to watch as we strip you to the meat.'

His cruelty proved too much for Ymiru, who stood behind me gripping his borkor in the only hand that remained to him. He raised up this fearsome weapon, and shook it at Arch Yadom as his huge voice boomed out: 'This, to you, if we meet again on this field, though you be no warrior and hide behind your ugly robes! And you be mistaken if you think you will ever return to Argattha. It belongs to the Ymaniri, and it be a hroly place. After your master surrenders, we will wash it clean with fire and build it anew!'

Now Count Ulanu, who called himself King Ulanu, took his turn to speak Morjin's spite. He glowered at me and snapped: 'It will be *you* who surrenders – and right *now*, or we will slaughter all of you, as it was with the Librarians at Khaisham!'

Before I could respond to this, Kane called out to him: 'Have you wondered, Ulanu, as you stared into the mirror, what you will look like without any nose at all? If a *woman* could disfigure you, what do suppose an army of Valari warriors will do?'

I could feel the blood pounding through Count Ulanu's face and flushing it purple. And he shouted to Kane, 'I am *King* Ulanu! And I, myself, will cut off Liljana Ashvaran's nose – and her ears, eyes and evil mouth! And carve up the children she now protects, as well!'

Kane stared at him as if regarding a piece of offal. 'A king who takes pleasure in massacring innocents is no king but only a butcher.'

'Do you remember the Kul Moroth?' Count Ulanu snarled at Kane. 'It was with *pleasure* that I had my Blues chop down your minstrel and crucify him! And even greater pleasure, after you fled the Library, that we took his body out of the crypt where you had deserted him. I gave *his* liver to –'

'Every abomination!' Kane suddenly shouted out. 'Every degradation of all that is human!'

For a moment, Count Ulanu watched Kane carefully as he might a chained tiger. He glanced at Morjin, in confidence that his master would somehow keep Kane from springing at him. And then he continued his taunts: 'Some parts of your minstrel's body I gave to my Blues to do with as they would. But I put his head in a jar of wine, that I might look at it from time to time. After Lord Morjin crucifies *you*, it will be my pleasure to show it to you.'

Kane's eyes blazed black as burning pitch; for a moment I thought that, truce or no truce, he might draw his sword and fall upon Count Ulanu. But he surprised me, for an icy calm came over him, like clear air in the deep of winter. In a strange voice he said to Count Ulanu, 'One man thinks he is the slayer and another man the slain. But both might be wrong, eh? When *you* die, though, Ulanu, I think you will truly die.'

None of our enemy seemed to know what to make of his mysterious words, not even Morjin, for he must not have learned of Alphanderry's return to us. The Red Dragon waved his hand at Count Ulanu as if brushing him aside, and he said to Kane: 'A cat has nine lives, and how many have *you* had . . . Kane? You must know that you have lived your last one. I, however, shall give it back to you on the sole condition that you persuade your friend to surrender.'

As Morjin turned to look at me with his dreadful red eyes, I wondered yet again why he had called this parlay. It could not be, could it, just that he hoped to strike terror into my men and weaken them for the coming battle?

One of those, at least, who had ridden with me, would not be terrorized. King Hadaru had lost all patience with such talk. He drew himself up straight on top of his horse, then he patted the hilt of his sword and called out: 'Why do we waste words? We all know that there will be no surrender – *before* the battle. And as for after, when the Valari's kalamas have done their work, let us see who still stands to call for surrender!'

'It will not be *you*!' Salmelu shouted at him. He sat within his red-tinged armor glaring at the man he had once called father. I had always thought Salmelu, with his great beak of a nose and weak chin, almost as ugly in his person as in his soul. 'And when you stand no more, Lord Morjin will give me Ishka to rule, and *I* shall sit on your throne in the Wooden Palace!'

I felt a great sadness, like a shadow across the moon, come over King Hadaru. He would not speak to his son, nor even look at him, for to him Salmelu had long since joined the dead. And so instead, he said to Morjin, 'I should have burned my palace before I marched from Ishka. As on the Raaswash I should have slain the one you turned away from me.'

'Do not despair, King Hadaru,' Morjin told him. 'When all is done here, we'll march east and *I* shall burn your palace – and all the Nine Kingdoms, as I did Tria. The lands of the Morning Mountains, I will then give to my faithful priest, Arch Igasho, to build anew and rule as king.'

At this, Salmelu beamed like a boy given a prize at a fair. Could he not see, I wondered, that Morjin lied to him? That even the Great Beast hated a traitor, and after the battle had been fought, would not give Salmelu even the dirt clotted to his horse's hooves?

'He will use you,' I said to Salmelu. 'After you have helped fight your own people, he will cast you aside like a broken arrow.'

Salmelu's gauntleted hand clenched into a fist, which he shook at me as he cried out, 'It was only evil chance that *my* arrow did not pierce you to the quick! But you still feel the burn of the kirax, don't you?'

I stared straight into his beadlike eyes as I told him: 'What I feel is nothing against the shame of seeing a Valari prince serve the Red Dragon.'

His hand clamped onto the hilt of his sword. 'It was evil chance, too, that you cut me in the circle of honor. But when we next meet in battle, I shall serve *you* with cold steel!'

At this, Maram whipped free his red gelstei and said, 'Not if I serve you with fire first!'

I wondered if he had forgotten his vow never again to use his firestone against human flesh? More likely, I thought, he counted on Salmelu – and Morjin – not knowing that he had made such a vow.

At the sight of the ruby crystal, Morjin's face tightened in fear and hate. With a peculiar edge to his voice, he said to Maram, 'Let us see who burns here today.'

I couldn't help gazing up at Bemossed, naked to the heat of the waxing sun and the anguish ripping through his body.

'Surrender,' Morjin said to me, 'and I will give you the slave.'

'No,' I told him, shaking my head. 'You will never do that.'

'Surrender to me, Valashu, or I will make *you* my slave. Here and now, as we speak.'

'No – you do not have that power.'

'Don't I? I will make you my ghul – the most beloved of all those I command. And the first thing you do will be to kill that vixen you call your woman!'

At this, he turned his poisonous gaze upon Atara, sitting quietly on the back of her horse.

'No,' I told Morjin, 'you are mad.'

'Am I, Valashu?'

'Let Bemossed go,' I said, looking up at the top of the Owl's Hill. 'Perhaps he can help you.'

For a single heartbeat of time, I wished this impossible thing that I had said might be true. I could feel Morjin feeling this desire within me. It caused his face to contort with rage, and he snarled at me: 'I will help *him* to die in agony!'

Yes, I thought, *he would. How long will he try to keep Bemossed alive?*

'As I will make *you* die,' Morjin cried out to me, 'this very day!'

Atara nudged her horse a few feet closer to Morjin, then turned her face so that she seemed to look him straight in the eye. I sensed her choosing her words carefully so as to discompose him: 'I have *seen* you here, Morjin. You and Val. It will be as it is and always was: you and he, chained to the same terrible, terrible fate. In your spite for each other, and even more in –'

'Have you seen *this*?' he cried out, cutting her off.

He reached into his saddle's pocket and drew forth a plain, golden cup. I gasped to behold once more the Lightstone's splendor, and so did Maram, Ymiru, Sajagax and others gathered there at the center of the field. But Atara seemed to sit within a cloud of confusion, for she had no eyes with which to perceive it and no scryer's vision had ever encompassed this loveliest of all things.

'Now who claims the Cup of Heaven!' Salmelu shouted out with all the cruelty he could command.'

'So,' Kane muttered, staring at the brilliant gold gelstei. I could feel him aching to draw his sword and cut it from Morjin's hand.

Then Morjin called out, to him and all of us, but especially to Atara: 'Valashu Elahad and I *are* chained together! And *this* shall be the hammer that forges the links!'

With that, he held out the cup toward me. Its soft golden hue suddenly flared to a deep and angry amber. The silver gelstei might seek the gold, but it seemed that the gold could also seek the silver. The long blade strapped to my side fairly quivered; I sensed the Lightstone pulling at my sword's silustria as a lodestone draws in iron. I had always hoped that the Lightstone, though it might command every other kind of gelstei, would have no power over the silver.

'Can you feel it?' Morjin said to me.

Despite myself – or perhaps *because* I wanted to deny the truth of things – I clasped my hand to Alkaladur's hilt. I had always called upon this marvelous sword to give me strength to bear the death agonies that I dealt out to others, and even more, to cool the heat of the kirax that poisoned my blood.

'Can you feel *him*?' Morjin asked me, pointing with his other hand toward Bemossed.

At that moment, with his golden hammer, Morjin battered down the walls of aloneness protecting me, and all Bemossed's agony came burning into me.

'There is a cure for the fire of the kirax,' Morjin said to me. 'A cure for all that grieves you. Do you remember what it is?'

To inflict my own suffering on others, I thought. *But how can I do such a thing?*

'You must open your heart to me,' he told me. 'You must direct that sword you keep inside toward those who defy me.'

'No,' I gasped against the pain tearing through me.

'You *will* serve me, Valashu!'

'No!'

I stared up at the Owl's Hill, and I felt Bemossed weakening in his final fight for life, even as Morjin's hold over the Lightstone grew stronger.

'Valashu, together you and I can –'

'No!' I shouted at him. 'Never!'

My voice seemed to fall upon my friends and Morjin's counselors with the force of a storm wind, for their faces grew grave with distress and they clung to their horses. But it left Morjin untouched.

'And *still* you deny me!' he thundered at me. He pointed behind him at the vast army lined up across the steppe. 'In the face of death and the destruction of all you hold dear, you deny me! So be it. If you won't accept the cure for what mars you, you will have the curse!'

Then his hand tightened around the Lightstone. I felt myself hurled as if into a pool of boiling oil. Its bubbling heat stripped the flesh from my bones and ate away my mouth and my eyes. I could not see, nor could I draw breath. Morjin had warned me that Bemossed's death throes would become mine, multiplied a thousandfold. I did not know if the immense pain piercing me to the core was only a tenth of that which Bemossed suffered – or ten thousand times as great. But it seemed to go on and on forever.

'Let go of your sword!' Maram called out to me.

I could not let go of my sword. I sweated inside my armor from every pore as my whole body shook; I gasped for air and bit my tongue and tasted blood. I did not want to let go of my sword. How could I fight Morjin without it?

'Do *not* let go!' Kane called out to me. 'Do not!'

I gripped Alkaladur's black jade hilt, carved with a great swan and set with diamonds, even more tightly. Then the torture unmanning

358

me eased, a little. I did not know if Bemossed, nailed to his cross, found just enough will to contend with Morjin over the mastery of the Lightstone and all its powers. Or if I might hold a strength of my own to resist Morjin.

'This parlay,' I gasped out to him, 'is over!'

Morjin smiled at me, and I knew with a searing certainty why he had called me to meet with him here between our two armies. An inextinguishable agony – to say nothing of Morjin's hate for me and mine for him – clung to me like a robe of fire.

'It *is* over,' Morjin said to me. His red eyes gleamed like pools of blood. 'And now it is time for you, and all of yours, to die.'

Without another word, but watchful of Atara's and Sajagax's bows, he wheeled his horse about and rode back toward his army. His counselors followed him. I heard Sajagax mutter: 'It is too bad I filled my quiver this morning with long-range arrows and not armor-piecing ones. Truce or no, I would slay that snake!'

'If you did,' Atara said to him, 'then Morjin's men would surely slay Bemossed.'

I sat gasping for breath as I fought for the will not to fall down screaming; it was like breathing in pure flame. I looked up at the top of the Owl's Hill. How much longer, I wondered, did Bemossed have to live? How much longer did any of us?

Then, with these thoughts trying to work their way through the blaze of pain that clouded my mind, I led my friends back toward our lines and battle.

22

Just as we reached that place where I had to part with Ymiru – he, to return to the center of our lines and I to our wing – I paused to tell him what he and the Ymaniri must now do. Then I rode back with Kane and Maram to rejoin our cavalry, while Sajagax and Atara continued on to take their places leading their Sarni warriors.

'King Mohan!' I cried out as we drew up to the massed knights on our right flank. Our enemy's drums had begun beating out the challenge to war once again. 'Lord Avijan! Lord Sharad – to me!'

Those I had called for, with Lord Manthanu, Lord Noldashan and others, galloped over to me to hold council. And I gasped out to them: 'We must change our order of battle! King Mohan, you will take command here of our cavalry.'

This fierce man, resplendent in his diamond armor, nodded his head to me. Although obviously pleased – and honored – he waited for me to say more, for he did not understand my decision.

'Lord Avijan, Lord Sharad!' I called out, turning to my cavalry lords. 'We will lead the Meshian knights back behind our lines to our center.'

Both of these great warriors seemed puzzled. According to all the Valari knew of making war, heavy horse had no place at the center of the battlefield hemmed in by masses of spear and shield men.

'We must break through,' I said. 'We must lead a charge up the Owl's Hill, and rescue Bemossed.'

'Sire,' Lord Sharad called back, looking at me deeply, 'you are not yourself!'

Now King Mohan cast me a penetrating look as if to wonder if what had transpired with Morjin had driven me mad. With the

360

robe of fire searing my soul, I wondered that as well. I had no time to explain that the fate of much more than Ea might depend upon keeping Bemossed alive. All I could say to my warriors was: 'The Maitreya cannot die!'

'But, Sire,' Lord Avijan said to me, glancing up at the lone cross towering over the battlefield, 'surely Bemossed is as one already dead.'

'No!' I shouted. 'There is still much life in him – I can *feel* it!'

'But even supposing we break through, when the Red Dragon perceives our objective, surely he will give the command to slay him.'

'No!' I shouted again. 'Anything might happen in battle. We might throw the enemy into confusion. Morjin himself might be killed, or wounded, and the command never given.'

Maram wiped the sweat from his face, and said to me: 'But can't you see it's a trap? That is just what Morjin will want you to think, and do!'

'It can't be helped, Maram.'

'Can it not? Morjin uses Bemossed just to get to you! And if we lose you, we lose everything. Don't let him kill you! If you must attempt this madness, choose another to lead the charge!'

'No,' I said to him, shaking my head, 'it must be me.'

At my obduracy, Maram looked at me in anger and frustration as tears filled his eyes.

Kane, staring up at Bemossed, said to me more tersely: 'So – it *is* a trap. A terrible chance.'

'It is our *only* chance!' I said to him. 'Will you ride with me?'

At this, Kane grimly nodded his head. So did Lord Sharad, Lord Avijan and Lord Noldashan – and others. And then, finally, so did Maram.

'Into the Dragon's jaws,' he muttered to himself. 'Well, my friend, I suppose I always knew this would be a day for fire.'

After sending messengers galloping to speak with Lord Tanu and Lord Tomavar, I gave the command for my army to renew its advance. Now, up and down our lines, our war drums began booming out their dreadful thunder. On our far right, out across the steppe's wind-rippled grasses, I saw that Sajagax had already begun the battle. Companies of Kurmak and Adirii warriors, with the Manslayers, rode upon the Janjii, Mansurii, Zayak and Marituk tribes loosing a hail of arrows. It was no easy work of logistics to cut out my Meshians from our other cavalry massed too near the enemy Sarni. It took some precious minutes of horses whinnying and stamping, and men shouting in confusion, to reform them behind our lines. And then, even as our thousands of foot marched upon our enemy and the tinkling of millions of tiny silver bells rang out into the air, I led my eight hundred knights back behind the advancing Atharian and Waashian infantry toward the center of the field.

Our enemy, however, remained unmoving. Phalanxes of pike men packed twenty ranks deep and locked together shield to shield do not easily advance in good order over uneven ground across a front of five miles. Why *should* the Dragon army move forward when they had only to wait for my warriors to impale themselves on the acres of steel-tipped pikes sticking out from a long wall of shining shields?

Soon our army came within range of our enemy's archers. Clouds of black arrows, with an unnerving whining, streaked up from behind our enemy's lines and fell upon my advancing warriors. At this distance, most broke upon or glanced off their armor with a clatter of steel against diamond that was dreadful to hear. A few shafts split the diamond seams and penetrated through the under-lying leather to skin and flesh beneath. Men cried out and fell; others hurried forward to take their places. Our archers, keeping pace behind our lines, paused every half minute to stand and loose volleys of their own. A great number of their arrows found their marks, punching through the poorer strip armor worn by the soldiers of Sunguru and the Eannan's thin mail. The screams of wounded and dying men merged with the cacophony of trumpets, drums, shrieking elephants and jangling bells into a single, terrible sound.

I rode quickly along, at the head of my companies of knights, whose heavily-amored mounts beat at the ground and churned up the earth. I looked to my right, at the glittering ranks of the Kaashans closing the distance to the great Dragon army. Through the gaps between my men, marching in loose formation, I could now see the faces of the front rank of our enemy. Thousands of pairs of eyes stared out in dismay at the approaching Valari warriors. I felt their fear like a wave of sick heat emanating from them. Although they badly outnumbered us, they must have heard the stories told of the Valari's long, steel kalamas and the pitiless men who wielded them.

My warriors' spirits held true and strong, though I felt how keenly Bemossed's torture grieved them. Spirit, in battle, was always such a delicate thing. A man's urge to risk his life for those of his compan-ions could become a dread of death; the natural fear that caused one's heart to send streams of blood shooting like an elixir through mind and limb could easily explode into a full panic.

'The Valari!' I heard someone from within the Sakayan phalanxes cry out. 'The Valari come!'

Just as our army drew within javelin distance of our enemy, another of the Sakayans called to him in answer: 'The Dragon will burn them! Let the Dragon burn all the Valari!'

More arrows streaked down from the sky. One of them clacked off the armor covering Altaru's neck; another broke against my shoulder's steel reinforcement. At last, my knights and I had come up behind Lord Tanu's battalions. Meshian javelin men darted forward between our lines, hurling their spears at our enemy. Javelins in hundreds struck deep into wooden shields with a great thucking sound. As our lines drew even closer to the massed phalanxes, warriors in our front ranks loosed spears of their own; almost all found their marks in the long shields that covered the Sakayans' bodies.

'Death to the Valari! Let the Dragon burn the Valari!'

Then, from Lord Tomavar's fourth battalion, one of my warriors let loose a cry of alarm. He stood some thirty yards ahead of me, and although I could see only the side of his stricken face, I felt sure his name was Garadan of Lashku. Sar Garadan thrust his spear into the air in the direction of Morjin's army, and he cried out, 'A dragon! A dragon has come to earth!'

I turned to gaze up toward the great, looming rocks of the Detheshaloon. So did ten thousand of my men. A black spot above the massif blotted out a tiny bit of blue in the sky. In only moments, however, it grew larger as it flew straight toward us like a flock of crows. But the thing that loosed a terrible cry into the air like a crack of thunder could be no bird nor bat, nor any other of the world's flying creatures, for it was not of the earth.

'A dragon!' hundreds of my warriors cried out. 'A dragon is come!'

Now I knew what dread thing Atara had warned me of.

'Oh, Lord!' Maram muttered, pointing out and up.

Just before my army closed with our enemy, the dragon – for such it truly was – bellowed out again. I could now see it clearly as it streaked closer, beating the air in quick whumphs with its leathery wings. It must be nearly forty feet, I thought, from its iron-like snout to the knotted tip of its tail. Red-black scales covered every inch of its massive body; its great, golden eyes gazed out with what seemed a desire to burn and rend. A long, sinuous neck turned its huge head right and then left as if the dragon was searching for something.

'Yormungand!' Maram suddenly cried out from beside me. 'The dragon's name is Yormungand!'

His distress caused me to call for a halt. I stared at Maram in amazement. So did Kane, Lord Avijan, Lord Sharad, Joshu Kadar and the other Guardians closest to us.

'But how do you know?' I asked Maram.

'Because I can feel *his* mind burning *my* mind!' Maram told me. He shoved his long lance down into its holster, and with his free hand, he grabbed his head. 'The dragon is looking for me!'

'So,' Kane growled out, staring up into the sky.

In Argattha, Kane had destroyed the six dragon eggs that we had found in Morjin's chambers. But Daj, I remembered, had warned us that Morjin kept seven eggs as an assurance that the dragon who had laid them would do as he commanded.

'Morjin must have hatched Angraboda's seventh egg,' Maram said, sweating. And raised Yormungand, he added, on human flesh and an inhuman hate of Morjin's enemies.

'Yormungand wants revenge for his mother's death,' he told me. He glanced down at my sword, which I had struck through one of Angraboda's weakened scales into her heart. 'Yormungand is looking for you, too, Val.'

Just then the dragon reached a space in the air above our lines. He opened his jaws to reveal rows of great pointed teeth, nearly a foot long. Then he coughed out a stream of a reddish liquid called *relb*. This thick, sticky substance burst into fire as it touched the air, and rained down upon the men of Lord Tomavar's third battalion. Most got their shields up quickly, and so protected themselves from the worst of the dragon fire. But at least ten of them screamed out as if they had been drenched in boiling oil.

'Yormungand,' Kane said to me, 'is looking for much more than *revenge*, Val. Dragons *like* to kill.'

Then Yormungand suddenly dove down toward the ground with a thunderous beating of its wings. It fell on top of Lord Tomavar's third battalion with a crash that crushed men screaming to the earth. Other men tried to put their spears or swords into Yormungand, but their weapons broke against the dragon's rock-hard scales. Then Yormungand savaged about, up and down the lines, snapping his jaws and crushing men's heads between his teeth, pulping their faces with the knotted tip of his tail, stamping them and tearing at them with his claws – and breathing out a fire hot enough to melt steel.

'Maram!' I cried out. 'You will not fight *men* with fire – but you must fight fire with fire!'

Maram had already taken out his great red gelstei. But with the

Guardians and other knights packed so closely about us, he had no clear line along which he might direct its flame at the dragon without also burning up our knights.

'There!' I cried out again. I pointed behind us at the little hill upon which Kane and I had stood talking the night before. 'You must go up there! You must stand and fight!'

'But the dragon will see me!' Maram cried out.

'He will see you in any case, once you loose your stone's fire.'

'Then maybe I shouldn't! I never want to burn anything, ever again!'

At that moment, Yormungand sprang off the ground and left a refuse of crushed and bloody bodies. He took to the air, even as hundreds of arrows loosed by our archers broke against his scales. With a great roar, he flew straight toward my knights and me. His golden eyes seemed to sear open the air. Then he dipped down his head and spat out a stream of flame that fell upon Sar Elkaru Barshan. Sar Elkaru cried out in agony as the burning relb spilled over his small shield and melted his face. I was not the only knight in my army to sport white plumes upon my helm. I noted that the white crane of the Barshans might look very much like the Elahads' silver swan, especially to a young dragon not familiar with the insignia of the Valari.

Then the dragon flew along my column of knights, closer to Maram and me.

'Go!' I said again, pointing at the hill. 'It is your time, Maram.'

Maram, sitting on his horse next to me, hesitated as he gazed up at the rapidly approaching dragon. He cried out, 'Why? Why must I always do precisely what I don't *want* to do?'

He gripped his firestone in his sweating hands with such force that I feared he might bruise his own flesh. Then, with a great sigh, he raised up the gelstei. The crystal caught the rays of the sun; it flared to a deep and angry red, and a bolt of crimson fire streaked out of its point. This flame shot up through the air and scored the dragon's bulging underbelly. It must have burned the dragon, if not pierced his scales altogether, for Yormungand let loose a great and hideous roar. I waited to see if Yormungand would now try to fall against Maram – and me. But Yormungand suddenly dipped down his wing, and veered off toward the right, back toward Morjin's army and the rocks of the Detheshaloon.

'He will return!' Kane called out to Maram. 'You've wounded him, I think, but like his mother, he will return.'

Maram sighed again as he looked at me. I felt his essential fear give way to an immensely greater love of life. He couldn't keep the tears from flooding his eyes, and neither could I.

'Farewell, Val,' he said to me. He tucked his firestone beneath his left arm as he held out his right hand to clasp mine. 'As long as I remain near you, I'll draw that damn dragon, won't I?'

Likewise, he bade Kane goodbye and clasped his hand, too.

'Whatever happens,' Maram told him, 'stay by Val's side.'

He swallowed, twice, hard, and adjusted his helmet. He sat up straight on his horse, looking out at Lord Avijan and Sar Shivalad and all the Guardians watching him. And then he drew in a huge breath of air and bellowed out: 'All right! I'll go! And let that dragon beware! King Valamesh is right: in all the world, there is only one Maram Marshayk!'

So saying, he wheeled his horse about and galloped off toward the little hill above the river. Soon – and ever after – it would be known as the Hill of Fire.

A great clashing of spears against shields and men screaming alerted me that the lines of my army had finally come up against our enemy. There would be much more to this battle than fighting one dragon, no matter how deadly or terrible. At first, up and down the field for miles, my warriors engaged Morjin's men carefully, and almost delicately, for it is no simple thing to go up against a phalanx. My javelin men kept coming forward through the loose Valari formations with fresh spears, and hurling them at our enemy. The javelins' long, soft, iron heads embedded themselves in wood, and since they would bend before breaking, they could not easily be ripped free. Soon the shields of the soldiers in our enemy's front ranks grew so heavy and cumbersome with javelins sticking out of them that they had to be cast down. Then the warriors in the front rank of Lord Tomavar's and Lord Tanu's battalions – and those of Kaash, Waas and Athar farther down the lines – went to work with their tharams and long spears, probing with great precision, stabbing them into our enemy's faces or the weak points in their armor. It was a long, brutal business, for even as we Valari struck down one rank of our enemy, another moved forward to take its place. With men packed twenty ranks deep, I feared it would take hours to tear open our enemy's phalanxes. Only then would my warriors rush into the great holes in the wall of metal before them with their kalamas. But once these long swords began flashing in the sun, the Red Dragon's soldiers would fall like hacked barley stalks and begin fleeing in panic – so it had always been, and so I hoped it would now be.

There were so many thousands, however, to cut down. And my men were too few, and I could feel them tiring beneath their weight of diamond and steel with every stab of their spears and chop of their tharams. I wondered how things went on our flanks, for the fog of battle had now closed in, and I could not see the Sarni warriors far out on the steppe to the east and west. How fared King Mohan in his charge against the Ikurians? Did he and his knights hold their own against the fierce horsemen of Sakai and keep Morjin from extending his lines so as to flank us? Did King Hadaru and *his* knights succeed in this task, on our west wing? It was hell, I thought, not knowing. And worse dreading the dragon's return and having to imagine what other nightmares Morjin might unleash upon us. And worst of all, being compelled to ride forward into the center of the field to rescue Bemossed before all was lost.

I led my knights to that place where Lord Tomavar's first battalion faced the joint in the Sakayan and Hesperuk lines. Just to the west of Lord Tomavar's warriors, Ymiru's five hundred Ymaniri had gone to work trying to batter down the Hesperuk phalanx. I could not tell who fought more fiercely: the eight-foot tall Frost Giants, with their marvelous keshet armor and their fearsome borkors dripping blood and brains, or my own Meshians, now forcing cracks in the Hesperuk and Sakayan lines with all the fury of their slashing kalamas.

'They will break!' I called to Lord Avijan. 'Our enemy must soon break!'

'Let us hope that we don't break first!' he called back to me.

To the west, I saw, the Hesperuk phalanx had now moved forward, pressing back the lines of Eannans, Alonians and Thalunes. Farther in that direction across the corpse-strewn steppe, King Waray's Taroners fought desperately against the end third of the Hesperuk phalanx – and their elephants. These strange, savage beasts nearly struck a panic into my men. Valari warriors – and those of Alonia and Eanna – up and down the field, struggled to effect Kane's counsel on how to contend with this new terror. Closer to us, in the lines of our enemy ahead of my massed knights, the Hesperuks brought to bear five more mountains of gray, raging flesh against Lord Tomavar's men. Lord Tomavar sent forward archers shooting arrows at the elephants' drivers, even as his javelin men hurled volleys of spears at the elephants' vulnerable bellies and eyes. A few brave warriors rushed in close to the elephants to slash through the trunks with their kalamas.

But the maddened elephants had stratagems of their own. They raged about the field, trumpeting ferociously, grabbing up men with their trunks and then dashing them to the ground, knocking them over and stamping them to a bloody mess. One elephant – a great bull – rammed his sharpened tusk straight through Sar Nolwan's neck, and so died Makarshan of Ki as well.

Duty demanded that I wait and watch these massacres. That, too, was hell. Bemossed remained nailed to his cross on top of the hill just behind the Hesperuk and Sakayan phalanxes, and it seemed that every moment he grew weaker, even as the agonies of all the wounded and dying men and beasts across the battlefield flooded into me like waves of burning pitch. Kane counseled me to keep a grip on my sword and let all this incredible suffering pass through me and into it. But that was something like telling a man cast adrift at sea that he should drink the ocean to keep from drowning.

'Be ready!' Kane called out to me. He clasped hold of my arm and shook it, as if to pull me out of the cloud of pain nearly choking me. 'It won't be long!'

After the elephants had been killed, the Ymaniri and the warriors of Lord Tomavar's first battalion fell upon our enemy with renewed fervor. They drove like a wedge deep into the Hesperuk phalanx. One face of the wedge consisted of the great, white-furred Ymaniri swinging their borkors with wild abandon, splintering shields, caving in helms and pulverizing bone. On the other face, my Meshians' kalamas whipped through the air in a brilliance of steel and blood. Their razor-sharp blades slashed through the Hesperuks' bronze armor. I gritted my teeth against the sight of the hacked limbs and cleaved men falling to the reddened earth.

Then, from the very point of the wedge, where Ymiru had met up with Lord Tomavar, I heard Ymiru's great voice bellow out above the din of battle: 'A hrole! For King Valamesh, let us make a hrole!'

I could almost feel, however, the exhaustion burning into Ymiru's great arm and body – and those of his men and Lord Tomavar's. Lord Tomavar himself fought like a fury, cutting through one soldier's chest, stabbing his kalama through the throat of another, and then ripping free his sword with a quick stroke to decapitate a Hesperuk lord. I sensed in him not only a fierce will toward victory but a desire to redeem himself for his wrongful pride in challenging me as king. But I did not know how much longer he or his men behind him could go on fighting this way.

Then Kane looked back behind us toward the river, and so did I. There, the Seven had come up from our encampment. Abrasax's snowy hair and beard gleamed in the bright sunlight, and so did

Master Juwain's bald head. The Masters of the Brotherhood stood gathered in a circle on the grass, with their hands held out toward each other. I knew that each held one of the great gelstei. Arrows fell around them. How they maintained their almost tangible calm in the midst of the great noise and death all around them I did not know.

But I soon saw the fruition of their efforts, or thought I did: the ground, from the river to the rocks of the Detheshaloon, suddenly seemed to grow transparent, as if dirt had been cleansed from a window pane. Deep within the darkness of the earth, a great wheel of light spun with a varicolored radiance. Somehow, the Seven called upon the great earth chakra's flames to feed the life fires of the men doing battle on the field above. They could not direct this force with any kind of precision, favoring the men of my army over our enemy's soldiers. But the flames found their way into those most open to them; they especially enlivened the blood and beings of the Valari warriors, who had sat each morning and evening for many years practicing the Brotherhood's meditations.

'A hole!' I heard Lord Tomavar call back to Ymiru. 'If we must slay a thousand men, we'll make a hole big enough to march an army through!'

I blinked then, and the vision of the earth opening to a deep splendor vanished before my eyes. I felt, however, a terrible new strength flowing into me. Its fire drove back the burning of the kirax and the agony of men dying near me. I sensed this same onstreaming force in Kane, and in Lord Avijan and Joshu Kadar, and in all the Guardians drawn up close behind me. It seemed that the earth was pouring into us her very life.

'Look!' Sar Shivalad cried out as he pointed with his lance ahead of us. 'They have broken the line!'

To the dreadful sound of iron-shod clubs crunching in armor and kalamas chopping through bronze and bone, the wedge of warriors ahead of us worked at the hole they had ripped into the Hesperuk phalanx. Ymiru and his men fell against one end of the ragged Hesperuk line, while Lord Tomavar directed our Meshians against the other. In the course of two minutes, as our enemy fell in tens and twenties screaming to the ground, the wedge widened to a funnel into which I might lead my eight hundred knights.

'Now!' I cried out to the men behind me. 'Let us ride!'

And ride we did. Altaru's great muscles hurled us forward almost without my prompting him. It was dreadful working through the hole in the Hesperuk lines, for Altaru's hooves crunched against the bodies of the dying and the dead. Too many of my men, I saw, had been compelled to sacrifice themselves, and they lay on the bruised grass like lumpy carpets of diamond or white fur. When I came to the point where the funnel of my still savagely fighting warriors opened out behind the Hesperuk lines, Ymiru pointed with his bloody borkor, and cried out, 'This is hrorrible, Val! I didn't know it would be so hrorrible!'

When Altaru and I burst into the space beyond the killing zone, fewer corpses littered the ground. Few men, for the moment, opposed us, but those who did fought for their lives. A hundred skirmishers came running at us and casting their javelins. And three score of the Hesperuk infantry who had panicked and broken, suddenly ceased their wild flight across the grass to turn and make a desperate stand. One of these – a giant with blood and brains dripping from his bronze fish scales – planted the butt end of a long pike in the grass in hope of impaling either Altaru or me. I cast one of my throwing lances straight through his eye, and I screamed as he died. Sar Shivalad and the Guardians close to me fell upon other Hesperuks, running them through with their long lances or using their kalamas to cut them down.

Archers, gathered nearby, loosed their bolts at us. Many broke against my knights' armor. But many, at this range, ripped through the diamond seams and found out the places where our mounts had no covering. Men gasped at arrows sticking out of their faces or embedded in their chests; horses screamed and stumbled, crushing their riders under. Then my men fell into a rage. They charged the masses of archers, and soon killed all of them, for the archers had but leather tunics to protect them against our terrible swords.

There came a moment when no enemy stood nearby to threaten us. My knights milled about, sticking their lances through the bodies of our wounded enemy, and I did not stop these executions. I looked off to the left; it seemed that King Hadaru's cavalry and the battalions of Ishka and Anjo might have pushed back the Uskadans, but it was hard to see, for clouds of dust obscured much of the battlefield. Likewise, I could not tell what was happening on our right flank. But at the field's center, the Hesperuk phalanx had pushed deep into the Alonian and Eanna lines, just beyond that place where Lord Tomavar's and Ymiru's men still fought savagely to keep open the hole they had made, and widen it, if they could.

Then I looked up to the right at the Owl's Hill ahead. Bemossed hung upon his cross like a carcass drained of blood. Breath still stirred within him, however, for somehow he managed to lift up

370

his head and gaze out toward me. I sensed within him, even deeper than his pain, an immense disappointment. And a fear for me. I thought I saw his throat working and his lips moving as if to tell me: 'Go back, Val! It is a trap!'

A pack of Blues, thirty strong, stood at the top of the hill around the cross as if waiting for me. Their broad-bladed axes gleamed in the sunlight.

Where is Morjin? I wanted to shout. *Where is the filthy Crucifier?*

Just then, to our left, from behind the ridges of rocky ground close to the Detheshaloon, men in great numbers began to pour forth. They bore bright, steel-jacketed shields, long spears and good armor, of mail and plate. Two thousand more Blues marched out with them, and light and heavy cavalry in the hundreds. I recognized the hawk and bear standards of men that my companions and I had fought at Khaisham. I did not want to wait as the forty or fifty battalions of Yarkona formed up. I knew that Morjin would throw most of them against the hole that my warriors had torn in his lines, and so block our retreat.

Where is the Dragon Guard? I asked the wind. *Where are Morjin's best men?*

As if in answer to my question, more cavalry burst forth from around behind the Owl's Hill. The famed Red Knights bore a heavy burden of thick, crimson-tinted armor that weighed down their huge horses. Although they could not move very quickly, Zahur Tey and their other captains at the front of their column were closer to Bemossed than my knights and I. I remembered Atara putting the count of the Red Knights at three thousand.

'We must reach the Maitreya before they do!' I cried out to my men, pointing ahead of us. 'Charge!'

Altaru, in a surge of mighty muscles, leaped forth almost to a full gallop in a single bound. Wind whistled through my helm, and my eight hundred knights and their mounts thundered across the ground behind me. Our course took us nearly straight up the gentle slopes of the Owl's Hill. The Red Knights had to work up and around the curving sweeps of grass to our left.

Even so, the foremost of them cut across our line of assault. They should have been able to intercept us and throw us back. But a rare spirit blazed through our hearts. Perhaps the earth fires that the Seven unleashed with their gelstei filled us with a terrible joy for killing; perhaps we all knew that only the most desperate hope remained of saving Bemossed – and the world. In the first seconds of this battle, I hurled five throwing lances at our enemy, and five of the Red

Knights fell dead or dying with wooden shafts sticking out of their eyes, mouths or necks. So it was with Kane, loosing his lances with a terrifying aim, as with the hand of an angel – and with Lord Avijan, Lord Noldashan. Sar Jonavar, Sar Shivalad and my other Guardians who came forward to try to protect me. But it was the Red Knights, at that moment, who needed protection from us.

I drew Alkaladur, and our enemy before us on the slopes of the hill seemed to shudder at the sight of this brilliant blade. I cut down a huge Red Knight, then thrust Alkaladur's point through another's chest. I wrenched my blade free, and crimson blood spurted from the hole in his crimson armor. A thrown lance slammed into my side, but did not pierce me. Then three more men rode at me, and I killed them with three lightning slashes, and I gritted my teeth against the sounds of silustria tearing through steel and men shrieking in agony. Kane, to my right, with a single sweep of *his* sword, struck off the head of a captain of the Dragon Guard, then sliced through the arm of a Red Knight trying to push a lance through my side. And then, unbelievably, as if Kane could sense the movement of every man on the field with an impossible precision, he whipped about to thrust his sword's point straight through a third knight's eye.

Close around us, my Guardians fought with scarcely less fury. Their diamond-tipped long lances drove through the plate armor of our enemy; their kalamas flashed forth, and keen steel edges cut through steel and bone. Founts of blood filled the air, and rivers of pain. Men screamed and died in hundreds as metal clanged against metal and horses collided and whinnied horribly.

Where is Morjin?

There came another moment when all the enemy knights closest to Kane and me either lay dead on the grass or hung back in fear. A brightening of my sword caused me to look uphill again at Bemossed. And there, just beneath the cross where the pack of Blues gathered, I saw Morjin standing and looking down at me. I knew him as I did the smell of death itself. My sword flared even more brightly, and the kirax burned up my blood. Morjin held the Lightstone shimmering like the sun in one hand and a lance in the other. His golden eyes fixed on me, in challenge and in hate.

'Why does he let the Maitreya live?' Joshu Kadar called out. He sat on top of his panting horse, which bore my standard of the silver swan and seven stars. 'Why does he give us this chance?'

Even a child, though, I thought, could see that we had almost no hope of continuing our charge uphill and taking Bemossed down from his cross. The Blues stood in a tight formation and shook their axes at us; more hundreds of Red Knights streamed out from behind the hill to ride up and put themselves between Bemossed and my companions and me. Farther away, toward the Detheshaloon, cavalry led by Count Ulanu galloped out to join them, even as his infantry marched forth at double pace to reinforce the Dragon Army's broken line and fall against Ymiru's and Lord Tomavar's men.

'A chance!' I cried out. 'A single chance – if we ride *now*!'

But even as we made ready to renew our charge, or at least fight our way uphill, I felt Bemossed's strength failing him. And Morjin's power grow. Suddenly, high in the air over the Detheshaloon, a black spot appeared. At first I thought it might be the Ahrim coming for me one last time. Then the spot began to widen and deepen, like a whirl of dusty wind eating up sky. I thought I could see little lights twinkling from its inky center.

'So, it is the *true* Skadarak,' Kane said, pointing up with his bloody sword. 'The stars reach their moment. Morjin opens the way to Damoom!'

From behind us, one of my knights cried out: 'Sorcery!'

'Illusion!' another said, looking up toward the cross where Morjin stood holding up the Lightstone. 'Morjin is the Lord of Illusions!'

As we attacked the Red Knights and our swords began their terrible work once more, a new enemy rose up before us. With a horrible ripping sound, our kalamas cut through flesh and bone, even steel, but they could not touch the dreadful things that Morjin sent to destroy us. I heard my men scream out that demons had joined our enemy. Sar Kanshar loosed a throwing lance against a monster, half horse and half man, that galloped toward him shooting arrows – or so he said. Siraj the Younger was trying to cut down a Red Knight whose face and limbs were made of sand. I looked on in a helpless rage as Siraj's sword passed right through this phantasmagory even as a very real Red Knight thrust a lance through Siraj's neck. I felt a terror seize hold of my men, not just upon the Owl's Hill, but for five miles all along our desperately struggling lines, from King Hadaru's cavalry in the west to King Mohan and Sajagax's Sarni in the east. I could almost see what my warriors cried out in panic at what they desperately did not *want* to see: twelve huge dragons appearing from behind the rocks of the Detheshaloon and soaring toward us as they roared out their disdain and spit fire into the air; winged tigers and apes in hundreds that flew after them; a pack of Blues whose faces were those of wolves; elephants with scales and serpent trunks; and a great beast, bigger than ten elephants, which was spotted like a leopard and had the feet of a bear. Out of each of its seven, lionlike heads there grew ten horns, each of which bore an iron crown set with seven fire-stones casting out black flames. These burned my men, their minds if not their bodies, but not so badly as the worst of the illusions Morjin sent to madden us. It infuriated me to see great warriors such as Lord Jessu the Lion-Heart hesitate to strike at our enemy because they perceived the Red Knights as having the faces of their fathers or mothers – or even as Bemossed or me. How long could they go on fighting, I wondered, if they couldn't tell what was real from what was not?

'Don't lose heart!' I cried out.

Beside me, Kane's sword split the helm of a Red Knight who had tried to brain me with a mace. Then he drove his horse into the mount of another man, nearly knocking him from his saddle. With the man unsettled, Kane reached out to grab hold of the joint in the armor covering his shoulder and threw him down from his horse. Immediately, the hooves of Lord Avijan's horse trampled him, and so with Lord Manthanu's mount and many others.

'Let us do our work,' I called to my warriors, 'and the Seven will do theirs!'

Then, as before, the ground beneath us seemed to grow trans-parent. The wheel of light turning deep within the earth grew brighter. I could almost feel it drawing down the rays of the sun and the much stronger radiance of the Golden Band as the stars and planets approached their moment of alignment. I could almost behold the splendor that spread out across the steppe and drove Morjin's illusions away.

'They are gone!' Sar Vikan shouted with a shake of his head. He suddenly leaned forward to thrust his lance through the face of a Red Knight who had slain Sar Yulmar, who had been Sar Vikan's best friend.

'All gone!'

'No – one of the dragons remains!' Jurald Evar shouted back to him. 'Look! It comes!'

No power of the Seven could cast back the thing of crimson and fire that flew out from the Detheshaloon roaring in malice, for Yormungand was made of flesh and blood, even as were my men. The dragon beat the air with a thunder of wings, and streaked straight toward Maram where he now stood on top of the Hill of Fire.

'So,' Kane growled out with a savage thrust of his sword. He had less care for the man he had just killed than for the blackness growing in the sky. 'The Dark One comes, too!'

The Seven likewise could do nothing to stop Morjin from tearing open a great hole in space that Kane had called the Skadarak – certainly not so long as Morjin commanded the Lightstone.

'Let us at least finally kill *him*!' Kane said to me as he glowered up the hill at Morjin.

Now Kane and I made circles of death around us with our swords. None could stand against Kane's kalama, for in his hands, it became almost a thing of light: spinning outward to cut through a Red Knight's neck; streaking like a ray of the sun straight into another's eye; flashing through flesh and steel as if no man or material thing could withstand it. I wielded Alkaladur with no less terror, for the Sword of Flame burned past my enemy's defenses and cut through good plate armor to strike home death. As the battle drew on and the sun climbed higher in the sky, Alkaladur flared ever hotter and brighter until it shone a hellish fire-white. Men screamed to feel it cutting them open or even just to behold it. In my wrath to slash and slay, the Red Knights began to hesitate and hang back from me, muttering beneath their breaths that *I* was a demon. So it went with Lord Avijan and Lord Vikan, who battled near me, and with Sar Kanshar and Sar Shivalad and Joshu Kadar and many others. They fought that day, if not like demons, then as killing angels whom nothing could hold back.

And yet I did not think that we could cut our way through our enemy to reach Morjin. In the thirty yards between us and the hill's top, hundreds of Red Knights now massed and pointed their lances down at us. Those highest up near Morjin had begun dismounting and standing together, shoulder to shield, to form a wall protecting him. Behind them awaited the howling, murderous Blues with their axes. And soon the hundreds of Red Knights still riding out from the Detheshaloon would fall against my warriors' flank and begin working up behind us.

'Damn you, Morjin!' Kane suddenly cried out. 'Damn you and the one you call master!'

Morjin, however, must have feared that we *might* reach him – or at least fight our way to free Bemossed as Morjin led a retreat down the backside of the hill. And so, smiling at me in utter triumph, he raised up his lance and plunged its gleaming point into Bemossed's side. He twisted it, causing Bemossed to writhe on his mount of wood and to cry out in agony. Blood flowed from the mortal wound torn into his naked flesh. Morjin caught the red stream with the Lightstone, then pressed the golden cup to his lips.

'Every abomination!' Kane thundered up at him. 'Everything that fouls the human spirit!'

Then he wept to see Bemossed so helpless against the anguish tearing through him.

'Come!' Morjin suddenly called to Kane and me, with lips stained carmine like his armor. At the sound of his voice, the Red Knights nearby hung back in their assault on us, waiting. 'Come to him now – if you can!'

Bemossed, looking down from his cross, pulled like a madman at the spikes nailing his hands to the crossbeam. More blood ran in rivulets from his palms and down his arms. He stared at the Lightstone in utter desperation, and I felt him burning to take hold of it for just one moment.

'Valashu!' he cried out to me. 'I am sorry! I thought I was so . . .'

His words died into the spasm of writhing that tore through his naked body. What had he wanted to tell me? That he had thought himself untouchable? And blessed and beloved, of the angels and men?

'I thought I was . . . beautiful!' he finally gasped out. 'I thought Morjin could see me . . . and so himself. But I was wrong. I am nothing.'

Another spasm seized hold of him as more blood ran out of the hole in his side. Then, with the last of his strength, he raised up his head like a king so that he could gaze out above the masses of men and horses gathered on the hilltop to meet eyes with me.

'It is all for nothing, Valashu. It is all *nothing* . . . so dark.'

Those were the last words he spoke to me. I watched the light go out of his eyes. Then, as if an axe had cut the muscles at the back of his neck, his head dropped down toward his chest. So died Bemossed, the man I had called the Shining One and Lord of Light, who was no blood of mine, but in spirit was truly my brother.

'NO!' I cried out as my heart broke open.

Flame and lightning flashed to the south, from the Hill of Fire. High above us, the spinning black thing blighted the blueness of the sky. It grew vaster and even darker, like a funnel cloud's whirl-wind about to descend and sweep everything away. A freezing cold fell down upon the earth.

23

I could barely keep seated on top of my horse; only Altaru's great hold on life, it seemed, kept me from plunging down to the bloodstained grass and joining Bemossed wherever he had gone. The world before me and everything in it fell black; I had to fight just to go on breathing.

NOOOOOOOO!

The scream inside me, that *was* me, seemed to go on forever. Then I felt Kane's iron fingers clamping around my arm and pulling at me.

'Let it pass through you!' he said to me. 'Let it go into your sword!'

I raised up Alkaladur then, and I felt all my anguish emptying into it. I swept it out in front of me. The sound of men screaming drove back the blackness filling my eyes, and I beheld an incredible sight: on the hill above us, the Red Knights were clapping their hands to their chests or heads and crying out in their own agony. Many dropped their lances and swords; some fell from their horses and lay writhing on the ground. Closer to Morjin, the Blues howled in pain and weakness, unable to lift up their axes. Just above them, at the foot of the cross, Morjin stood as if stunned by the blow of a hammer. He blinked his red eyes as the lance slipped from his hand and Bemossed's blood dripped down and spattered off his helm. Then he staggered about like a man drunk on too much wine.

'*Now* is our chance!' Kane shouted out.

Through the waves of grief sickening me, I saw that we *did* have a chance – but to do what? With Bemossed dead, there could be no hope of ever defeating Angra Mainyu.

'Now, Val – now!'

I nodded my head, and clamped my hand more tightly around the hilt of my sword. Then I led forward, straight into the Red Knights massed in front of us. I cut down everyone in my path; few managed even to raise up their weapons to defend themselves. My Guardians, those who hadn't been stricken too badly by Bemossed's death, followed. As for Kane, beside me, I had never seen him fight with such a furious will to strike his sword into men and murder them. His black eyes blazed with the heat of madness. He had no pity for the enemy, for they had none for him, or us. With every yard that we battled on, higher up the hill, it seemed that the Red Knights recovered a little more and counterattacked us with an increasing savagery and desperation. But it was not enough. Again and again, Kane's sword flashed out to rip through flesh, and so it was with mine. We, and the warriors who rode with us, worked a slaughter upon any and all who opposed us. We slew the Red Knights still seated on their horses, then mowed down the line of men protecting Morjin. The thirty Blues then flung themselves at Kane and me. Their axes, though, were like lead weights in their hands, and their hands and limbs had lost much of their terrible strength. One of them – a man as thick as a bull – managed to work in close to me and let fall his axe against my leg. But the blow failed to penetrate the diamonds sheathing me, or even break my thigh bone. I killed the man with a quick slash to the side of his bare neck. I had never really understood why the Blues went into battle naked. When they failed to chop down men with their fearsome axes, their enemies might work a horrible butchery upon them, as Kane and I did now: swinging our swords to slit open bellies and split their faces, severing arms and heads, slashing and thrusting and cleaving through their cyanine-tinted skin to cut them to pieces. At last, Kane and I, with the help of Lord Avijan and Joshu Kadar, had killed them all. And there, beneath the bloody cross, stood Morjin.

'To me!' he shouted out. 'To me!'

Around the curve of the hill, to the left, men pushed their horses galloping up toward him. Zahur Tey led fifty Red Knights, and with them rode the Red Priest known as Igasho.

'To me!' Morjin shouted again, this time in my direction. 'Come to me, Elahad, and I will make you my ghul!'

Now Morjin stood up straight and found the strength to draw his sword. I could feel the power returning to him, as a pulsing artery fills a limb with life. With Bemossed dead, it seemed that nothing could keep Morjin from wielding the Lightstone to command all the other gelstei – and the world. He thrust this small golden cup out to me as if to seize control of my sword.

'Do not let go!' Kane shouted at me. 'Alkaladur is *yours*!'

It seemed, however, that Morjin hadn't fully recovered or gained enough power to work his will though my sword's silver gelstei. As at the parlay before the battle, he could not make me use my sword to do his evil deeds. And neither could he keep me from wielding it.

And so I called Altaru to charge forward, and in almost a single motion of my bounding horse and my own inflamed body, I leaned out and swept my sword against Morjin's outstretched arm. The blade's silustria, hardest substance on earth, cleaved through a great ruby affixed to the gauntlet protecting Morjin's hand and wrist. I heard it crack, like a lightning bolt. My sword drove down through Morjin's wrist, severing muscles, tendons and bones, and the force of the blow struck off Morjin's hand and sent the Lightstone flying from his fingers. I watched in amazement as Kane, coming up quickly, reached out and snatched the golden cup from the air.

'To Lord Morjin!' Zahur Tey called out from twenty yards away as he and his Red Knights charged toward us. 'Protect our king!'

Blood spurted from the arteries I had opened at the end of Morjin's arm. He gasped from the shock of it, and staggered. I swung my sword again, this time to kill him, but by some miracle or terrible instinct for survival, he got his sword up in time to parry mine. Steel rang out against silustria, once, twice – and then Zahur Tey came up and pushed his horse almost straight into Altaru. I had to sweep out my sword against Zahur Tey's stabbing lance, or he would have impaled me. And then, with a splintering of wood, immediately to beat back the lances of two other Red Knights as they fell against me, too. I killed one of these with a thrust through the throat, and the other by splitting open his forehead. I turned back toward Morjin then, but it was too late: the Red Knights had closed in on him to protect him and bear him back away from me. I saw Salmelu pull him up onto the saddle of a riderless horse, even as another man twisted a cord around Morjin's arm.

'BEMOSSED!' I cried out.

I nudged Altaru over to the foot of the cross, and I reached out to lay my hand on the spike piercing Bemossed's feet. His flesh, exposed to the blazing sun, was still warm. His head hung down upon his chest; I could not bear the sight of his empty eyes. I lamented then that I had lost a friend while all the world had lost a Maitreya.

'Sire!' Lord Vikan shouted at me from ten yards down the hill. He pointed back toward the center of the battlefield. 'They have broken us!'

I turned to see a great mass of Hesperuk spearmen pushing through a huge fracture in the Alonian and Eannan lines. All our reserves, it seemed, had been thrown in to stop this advancing block of bronze and steel, to no avail.

'Lord Kane!' I heard Joshu Kadar call out. His shout drew my attention back to the top of the hill, where the Red Knights protecting Morjin had formed up into a half-circle facing my knights and me. 'Give the cup to King Valamesh!'

It is said that the Lightstone can be all things to all people: a talisman drawing good fortune; a vessel containing the secret of life; a golden mirror showing one's soul. Kane sat on top of his horse, unmoving, as he had remained since taking hold of the Lightstone. He stared at the little cup as if transfixed by its beauty. A radiance shone upon his face, and from deep within. Any of the Red Knights might have fallen against him then and knocked him to the ground. But I did not think they would have been able to tear the Lightstone from Kane's grasp.

'Surrender!' I called out. I pointed my sword at the Red Knights sheltering Morjin. An unspoken truce had befallen the men gathered beneath Bemossed's dead body – I did not know why. 'We have broken your lines! We have dismembered you! And we have the Lightstone!'

I tried to speak these words without laughing in bitterness. For Morjin had broken *my* lines, and my deepest hope, too. And soon, because he was Morjin, an angel of the Elijin, he would recover from his wound.

'*You* surrender!' he shouted back at me. The knights ahead of him moved aside so that he could face me. Now on top of his great white horse, he sat up straight as any king, one arm bound with a bandage while with the other he shook his sword at me. 'We still have four men to every one of yours! And a dragon!'

Although I could not turn away from him just then, a flash of flame from the Hill of Fire down by the river caused me worry that Maram could not last long doing battle against Yormungand.

'And we,' Morjin continued, looking at Kane, 'will take back the Lightstone!'

'No!' Kane shouted at him. 'You will never touch this again!'

380

Although he feared to charge Kane, Morjin did not shrink from gazing into Kane's terrible eyes. No man, I thought, could match Kane's strength, but Morjin was the Red Dragon, and the claws of his covetousness pulled at the little cup with a dreadful, ripping force. I felt Kane being drawn into something even more terrible than himself. High above us, the whirling blackness grew even blacker. I sensed a door to a deeper darkness begin to open.

'*You*,' Morjin snarled at him, 'will not keep me from it!'

Then Kane's immense will, like the calling of the earth, pulled him back to the world. He pressed the Lightstone to his lips. Its radiance caused his face to shine like a star. He turned to look me.

'No, not *I*!' he shouted back to Morjin.

Then he rode closer to me, and gave the Lightstone into my hand. 'You are its rightful guardian,' he told me.

Truly, I was – but who was I to guard it *for*? And how could I possibly guard it? In looking up at the black hole in the sky about to touch down to earth, I knew that neither I nor Kane nor even the Seven could stop Morjin from opening the door to Damoom, for it was already too late.

But Morjin, now looking up at the sky, too, suddenly cried out: 'I *could* free him – but I will not! No man is my master! Who should rule the stars? Only he who can command their very light and make it his own! Who is meant to be the Marudin and rule all of the Galadin and Elijin and the other orders? *Not* the one whom the Galadin defeated and bound like a slave, but only he who has the *power*.'

For the benefit of the men who followed him, no less me and mine, he declaimed that he had assembled upon this field an invincible force. He would win the battle, he said, and reclaim the Lightstone for the last time. Then the rightful Lord of Ea would go forth to lead all of Eluru into the Age of Light.

In looking about the war-torn steppe, I feared that he *would* win the battle. From our vantage on top of the hill, I could see most of the field. On our left flank, it seemed that the enemy's Sarni had pushed back ours, while the heavy cavalry of Uskudar and Hesperu tore into the arrays of knights led by King Hadaru. The Hesperuk phalanxes had cracked open our center, and the Yarkonan battalions had moved up against Ymiru's and Lord Tomavar's men. My Meshians were too busy working their spears and kalamas against these thousands of reinforcements to turn against the Hesperuks, as I had originally planned. On our right, although the warriors of Kaash, Waas and Athar held strong against the great

381

numbers massed before them, the Ikurian horse had nearly over-whelmed King Mohan's cavalry, which were already weakened. Soon, I thought, they would turn our flank, unless Sajagax and his warriors could come to their aid. But I had cause to worry that they too had been decimated.

'Surrender the Lightstone to me!' Morjin shouted. 'Surrender, Elahad, and I will spare all who followed you here!'

The thousands of Red Knights, those my warriors and I hadn't killed, massed behind Morjin and deployed around the curves of the hill. When it came to combat again, I did not see how we could defeat them.

The man for whom I should have guarded the Lightstone could do nothing against Morjin or the atrocities he had wrought. But *I* could. I could use the Lightstone as Morjin had, to bend men to my will and force them to give me their allegiance. I would persuade some of our enemy's captains and kings to come over to me, and to fall against those who did not. I might even wield the golden cup to strike death into the most willful of my enemies, as Morjin would have done his – but for Bemossed. I would certainly slay Morjin. I would put to the sword all who remained to stand against me, here on this battlefield and across Ea. I would claim dominion over the world, and I would become the King of Swords and Lord of War. But men would call me the Silver Swan, and that name would become more dreaded than the Red Dragon. And all that I did to reorder the realms of men and women to make a paradise on earth, no matter how terrible, would be for those I loved and for Ea. I told myself that I *might* not fall so far into evil as Morjin had.

NO!

The hardness of the Lightstone hurt my fingers; its brilliance burned my eyes. I ached to keep a grip on it and force from it all that was good and bright and beautiful. Aryu, I thought, must have told himself the same thing when he had slain Elahad and stolen it so long ago.

'Val!' It was Atara's voice. She shouted out my name and jolted me free of the Lightstone's spell. Thirty Manslayers came charging up the hill with the stout Karimah riding in front of Atara, holding the reins of her horse.

How had she come to be here? With a broken-off arrow embedded in the leather armor near her shoulder and a half dozen feathered shafts sticking out of her horse, it seemed that she must have fought her way behind the enemy's lines to this hill. Could it be that the three thousand woman warriors of the Manslayer Society had been reduced to the thirty riding with her?

'Estrella!' she called to me. '*She* is the Maitreya!'

I stared at her in astonishment. Her words made no sense to me.

'I have come here to tell you this!' she said, pushing her horse up to me. She fumbled through the air and finally managed to lay her hand on my arm. 'I have *seen* Estrella, with the Lightstone!'

'But no scryer has ever seen the Lightstone in any vision! *Or* the Maitreya.'

'But *I* have!' Atara said.

'But all the Maitreyas have been male. All the prophecies speak of the Maitreya as "he."'

'I don't care about the prophecies! Estrella *is* the Shining One!'

Morjin, from behind the wall of Red Knights protecting him, glared at Atara with a strange silence. His face seemed a mask of corruption and hate.

'He knows!' Atara suddenly cried out. '*He* can see her, and it burns his mind!'

I sat on Altaru, holding my sword in one hand and the Lightstone in the other. Once a time, before I had lost the cup to Morjin, Estrella had often stood in its presence and had even held it in her hands. She had seemed to take as little interest in it as she might a teacup. My sword suddenly flared a bright glorre, and lines from the ancient verse flashed through my mind:

> *The Shining One*
> *In innocence sleeps*
> *Inside his heart*
> *Angel fire sleeps*
> *And when he wakes*
> *The fire leaps*

> *About the Maitreya*
> *One thing is known:*
> *That to himself*
> *He always is known*
> *When the moment comes*
> *To claim the Lightstone.*

A dying scryer had told me that Estrella would show me the Maitreya. Was it possible, I wondered, that a thousand times she had?

I felt in my heart that it was true, and all at once it seemed the hardness of the Lightstone that had hurt my fingers fell away; its brilliance that had burned my eyes became an exquisite light that bathed them. The ache of my grip vanished as the image came to me of another hand reaching out with unique power to bring forth from the Lightstone all that was good and bright and beautiful.

'Estrella is coming,' said Atara, 'to claim the Lightstone.'

I felt in my heart that it was true, and so did Morjin.

NOOOOO!

From behind the protection of his knights, Morjin screamed at the sky.

Kane had once told me that Morjin kept a black gelstei. But this dark angel kept inside himself dark fires as well, and he now unleashed upon us all the force of his black and bottomless hate:

VALARI! DIE VALARIIII!

Morjin's droghul had assaulted my companions and me with a voice that chilled the blood and froze the limbs unmoving with terror – and killed. This Morjin, it seemed, the real Morjin who had come to earth so long ago, wielded this weapon with an even greater rage. He bellowed out in a voice of death:

DIEIIII! AIYIYARIII!

Something hard as iron struck a blow to my forehead; blood spurted from my nose, and, I feared, my very brains. I felt an acid eating through my stomach into my heart, and I could not breathe. Images came to me, not as memories but as sights and sounds and smells assaulting all my senses and my deepest self: the anguish in my grandmother's eyes as she pulled at the spikes that Morjin's men had driven through her hands; the screams of men dying at the Culhadosh Commons; the stench of hundreds of corpses rotting in the hot Yarkonan sun. I knew that I had to fight off the burning poison of Morjin's malice – either that, or die.

AIYIYARIII!

But others proved more vulnerable to Morjin's murderous voice. In Hesperu, his droghul had been able to direct it at only one man at any moment; now I feared that the real Red Dragon might find a way to strike down half my army. His breath seemed to burn out like thunder and fire. It fell upon Sar Kanshar, Sar Iandru and Jurald Evar, formed up in front of me. Sar Kanshar, maddened, threw himself onto the lance of Jessu the Lion-Heart, sitting next to him. Then Sar Iandru and Jurald Evar plunged from their horses to the ground, screaming as they grabbed at their chests. So did Manathar the Bold and Sar Jurgarth and a dozen other knights. And all the while Morjin's voice built louder, deeper and even more full of spite.

AIYIYARIII!

Soon, I thought, as I sweated and bled and fought to breathe, Morjin would slay all of us. His army, I feared, *must* be about to break mine. How long could Maram stand against a great dragon that could turn circles in the air and swoop down upon him vomiting out fire? How long could my knights bear up, here at the top of the hill, once the Red Knights had completed their encirclement of us and added the killing power of their swords and lances to Morjin's voice of death? I suddenly despaired that I *could* not use the Lightstone to slay our enemies . . .

And then, as from another world, I heard Alphanderry's voice rising in song above the crucifier's howl, filling the air above the hilltop. While we had stood tortured by the power of Morjin's black gelstei, Estrella and Daj had ridden up between my massed knights toward me, followed by Liljana and Alphanderry, and the Seven. They appeared to be untouched by the killing sound of Morjin's hatred. Alphanderry sat on top of his horse facing Morjin, and this strange, beautiful being who had been born in Galda and reborn in one of the earth's Vilds, chanted out a beautiful music.

Kane moved his horse closer to Alphanderry. His face had lost its savage lines and taken on almost an innocence. He seemed to drink in Alphanderry's song with his ears and his heart as if it were elixir recalling him to his youth. Something, with the weight of the whole world, moved inside him.

Alphanderry's throat and golden lips formed no words, but only the most pure and powerful of tones. His song rang out like millions of perfectly attuned bells. It resonated with the varicolored crystals that Abrasax and the Seven held vibrating in the palms of their hands; the great gelstei picked up the sound of Alphanderry's voice and gave it back to the world, amplified a thousandfold. The melody that he summoned from some shimmering and infinite source built ever higher, deeper and sweeter until it drowned out Morjin's death voice and utterly negated it. For Morjin screamed out all his hate of the world, while Alphanderry poured forth precisely the opposite. And so, as Morjin glared at Alphanderry in a wrath of bitterness, the golden minstrel sang out joyously, even as I imagined the Ieldra must once have sung the planets and stars into creation.

There is a chance! I thought as Morjin fell silent. *There must always be a way.*

'Now, Val,' Atara called out to me. 'Give the Lightstone to Estrella.'

Estrella had ridden up close to me but she sat frozen in her saddle, gazing at Bemossed. The way she looked at him nearly tore out my heart. I felt her longing and love, and something more, a deep, driving desire that he should return to life. And even deeper, a kind of dream that a part of Bemossed always *would* live, as did some inextinguishable essence within the rippling grasses and the bloodstained rocks beneath the cross, for that was how she saw the world. I wondered then if the Lightstone *could* be used to revive Bemossed? Could the Seven, through their gelstei, find their way into the center of the Cup of Heaven and release its nearly infinite powers?

I called to her, and Estrella tore her gaze from away from her murdered friend. A great change had come over her. It was as if she stood fearless before a burning, infinite sea.

> *When the moment comes*
> *To claim the Lightstone.*

Inside *her* heart, I thought, *she* wakes. In looking at Estrella then, she seemed to exult in all life's beauty – and in its horror, too. I suddenly remembered thousands of impressions and acts, like seeds of light, that Estrella had planted in me over long years of struggle, terror and war, her quick, wild eyes which saw so much and so deeply. On top of her little pony next to me, she radiated a beauty like that of a star. For the first time, I saw her not as a girl but a lovely young woman. I could almost feel her calling the Lightstone to her. In this silent song of her soul, as clean and natural as the wind, I sensed no hunger for fame or power, or even any desire, for herself. Rather, I thought, she saw the Lightstone as a *part* of herself, like an arm or an eye or a hand.

'So,' Kane said, his eyes blazing. 'So.'

Then Master Juwain, for once dwelling in the knowingness of his heart rather than the strife of his head, nodded to me.

'I agree,' Abrasax said from behind him.

'And I,' Master Matai said. 'Give her the cup.'

An incandescence of flame filled the sky above the Hill of Fire. What, I wondered, could even a Maitreya do against a dragon and all the forces of the Great Beast who had unleashed it?

As I reached out to set the Lightstone into Estrella's hand, it seemed that all time and history was an arrow streaking straight toward one moment and one place.

NOOOOOO!

The moment that her fingers touched the golden cup, a dazzling radiance began pouring from it. Like a fountain it streamed straight up into the sky. It fell into the whirling blackness as water into a hole, and suddenly the great vault of the heavens grew clear and blue again.

Then the radiance began pouring from Estrella. It swelled out like a ball of fire that did not burn, until both Estrella and the cup itself seemed to disappear within. Brighter and hotter it grew, like the sun, until I thought it might incinerate the whole top of the hill and all who stood upon it.

And then the blazing splendor grew utterly clear, like the air on top of a mountain. Estrella came back into view, sitting quietly on her horse. She seemed the same happy being that she had always been, but something more, too, for her face and every particle of her radiated a deep and inextinguishable light. With her eyes so bright and open, she seemed utterly awake, utterly aware – and at one with the whole world and even all the terrible things taking place on the battlefield.

Kane suddenly cried out to me, 'Val! Your sword!'

He pointed at Alkaladur, which I held shining in my hand. His eyes lit up as if he suddenly remembered why he had been born.

'Look!' he shouted. 'Look – and you will see the lines that I inscribed there!'

The fiery glyphs burned into my sword appeared exactly the same as I had seen them in the Vild:

> *With his eye of compassion*
> *He saw his enemy*
> *Like unto himself*

Then, in the brilliance streaming out of the cup in Estrella's hand, the last three lines suddenly flared out and burned themselves into my mind:

> *And he knew love*
> *And his enemy*
> *Was vanquished*

'No!' I shouted out. 'It cannot be!'

Morjin, thirty yards from me and protected by lines of his Red Knights, raised his sword as if to signal someone. On the east side of the hill, Count Ulanu signaled back to him that his Yarkonan cavalry was almost ready.

'It *must* be!' Kane shouted back to me. 'And you must find the way.'

'No – there is no way! How can you, of all men, ask this of me?'

Kane made no answer to this. He nudged his horse close to Estrella. He gazed at her for an endless moment and at the Lightstone she held close to her chest. Then she reached out to touch her fingers to the lids above Kane's black, blazing eyes. I felt the golden cup's radiance pouring into him like a river of light. It seemed to soothe the burning deeps of him and yet also to vasten him, his eyes and his hands and his great heart, every fiber of his body and the very sinews of his soul. I could almost hear the chains that had bound him for so long, with an unbearable pressure, suddenly burst. Then a man who was much more than a man turned his shining face toward me. He had wings, this being did, and he laughed out with a wild joy that shook the very sky because at last he was free.

'How *can* you, Kane?' I said to him again.

'It is not Kane,' he said, looking at me, 'who asks you.'

Because I could not bear the brightness of his eyes, I bowed my head to read again the words inscribed into my sword.

'In Hesperu,' he said to me, 'you almost found the way. But you held back.'

'Yes – because not even the Maitreya could do what you want me to do!'

'Is that so? You *can* do this thing!'

'No,' I murmured, staring down at the blade that I clenched in my hand. 'I am the King of Swords.'

His face fell fierce as of old and blazed once more with his relentless will. And he told me: 'And Alkaladur is the Sword of Love!'

'*This*,' I said, pointing my flaring blade at Morjin, 'I will strike into the Dragon, if I can!'

'So you will, Valashu Elahad. For the two swords *are* one and the same.'

Then he told me why he had forged a bit of silustria into the blade called Alkaladur so many thousands of years ago.

'I have been waiting,' he said to me, 'for the one who can wield it.'

And upon his words, the silver gelstei of my sword blazed a more brilliant glorre than I had ever seen.

Morjin, behind his massed knights, beheld it, too. I felt waves of dread washing through him. He raised up his sword as he stared out at me.

'All right,' I finally said to Kane. 'I will!'

But I did not know how I could do such an impossible thing. I thought it the cruelest turning of my life that I, who had hated Morjin so utterly, must now find a way to love him.

24

I was not, however, left alone to complete this task. The Seven, assembled near me, held their colored crystals out toward me. Alphanderry had never ceased his marvelous singing, and now the seven great gelstei sang back as if with the voices of the Ieldra themselves. Kane, his face shining like a star, gazed at me with a will toward utter triumph, and I sensed Ashtoreth and Valoreth and the greatest of the Galadin looking out through his brilliant eyes. Liljana and Daj, too, seemed to know what must be done. Atara sat on top of her red mare as if staring straight into my heart. *Her* heart beat in perfect rhythm with mine, fast and hard and full of sweet hurt. She could not contain her ardor for me, and for life itself. So it was with Maram, standing on top of a hill a mile away, as he desperately battled a dragon. I knew that he would let loose every bit of fire within him and do even the most loathsome of things in order to save me. As for Estrella, she smiled at me with all the warmth of the sun. She moved closer to me, cupping the Lightstone in her hands. Within its golden hollows gathered the flames passed on by all my friends and many beings, in colors of crimson and orange, yellow and green, blue and indigo and the deepest and brightest of violet.

'You will die, Valari!' Morjin shouted out to me. 'Now you will die!'

Once, outside of a tumbledown cottage in Hesperu, I had held within my grasp the greatest weapon in the universe. Why had I been so afraid to use it?

Because, I told myself, *you fear the same thing Morjin fears.*

I remembered the Elijin queen, Ondin, advising me that I must wish for Morjin's healing and all good things for him – he, who was the worst man I had ever known! Such a desire, I knew, if it could be summoned at all, must come from my heart. It must take life not only as a force, conscious and willed, but as a feeling as poignant as breath and as urgent as the blood burning through my brain and every part of my body. But I could not feel such a thing for anyone unless I opened myself to feeling my way into *him*.

But he is all foulness and filth! I thought. *He is vomit and pus and poison*!

'Be strong!' Kane called out to me. 'Strong as silustria, I say!'

He grasped hold of my arm, and I felt ten million years of his will to triumph against the most terrible of foes streaming into me.

He is a torturer! I thought, staring at Morjin. *A crucifier, a blood-drinker, a murderer*!

I could not open myself to the valarda without, in some way, finding myself alive and aware within another. And worse, letting him live and draw breath within me. But how could I ever do such a thing?

Because, I told myself, *I am a murderer, too*.

Inside myself, like everyone, I had always held a dragon's egg waiting to hatch. And I fought with all the fierceness of my breath to keep it from eating the best part of me alive.

With his eye of compassion
He saw his enemy . . .

In looking at Morjin across a few dozen yards of the battlefield's bloodstained grass, what did I see? That long ago before the Dragon had consumed him, this hateful and hideous man had been born a gentle soul – the gentlest and sweetest. And that, with all his heart, he wanted this bright, self-murdered being to be reborn.

But he cannot bear it! That which he most desires, he most abhors.

Then Estrella, with Bemossed's torn body still hanging from the cross above us, held out the Lightstone to me. The little cup seemed to draw down the sun's golden radiance and the blueness of the sky with an ingathering of colors. Stars shone there, too, in all their dazzling millions. Their radiance built, hotter and ever brighter, like unto the very splendor of creation itself. It was said that the Lightstone could hold the whole universe inside, but I did not know how much longer it could contain this brilliant angel fire.

'Strike, Val!' Kane called out to me. 'Only you know the way!'

What is it to love a man? Surely this: that your blood interfuses with his blood, in fire. That despite his terrible crimes, you want with all your heart and the force of your spirit for him to live as he should have lived, and all should live: bright, joyous and whole.

'Valari!'

Then Estrella, through the Lightstone, poured into me a resplendent and indestructible force. To call it love was to say everything about it, and yet too little. It was the shining hope of countless Galadin, Elijin and Star People watching and waiting on their spinning worlds throughout the universe; it was Atara's dream of bearing our child, and the very breath of the Ieldra, too. Within its overflowing radiance there gathered the primeval impulse of the stars to shine upon each other and call all of creation to a vaster and deeper life. It held a promise that no man or woman lived in vain and that all would be remembered and redeemed. And that no one, not even the most vile and estranged, could ever be alone.

'Valari!' Morjin cried out to me again.

I could not keep within myself this terrible and beautiful force. The sound of spears clashing against shields and men screaming out their death throes made it burn ever brighter; the agony in Morjin's voice ripped it out of my heart. Straight through my blood it blazed and into my hand. As with other swords, I knew I must wield it truly, cutting apart Morjin's shield, beating back *his* sword, driving it through armor. Alkaladur, the bright length of silustria that Kane had forged so long ago, shimmered with a perfect and clear light beyond glorre. Then the *true* Alkaladur, forged by the angels in the heart of the stars, streaked out like lightning and struck deep into Morjin.

The great Red Dragon fell silent as he twisted about with a bone-jerking violence on top of his horse. He coughed and gasped and let go of his sword. He let go of others' minds then, too, for Zahur Tey and many Red Knights near him cried out in dismay as Morjin lost the power of illusion over them. Horrible he was to behold, with his blood-red eyes and dead gray skin, and Zahur Tey's face screwed up in disgust. And yet something beautiful dwelled within Morjin, too, like a candle lit up inside a dark cave.

'Valashu,' he said to me.

With the angel fire still streaming from my sword and the clangor of battle splitting the air, I heard his voice like a whisper upon the wind. It held all the pain in the world and a plea that I might somehow take it from him. Years fell away from him then. His hideous face relaxed and softened, and flashes of gold brightened his eyes. I could almost see him as the beautiful being that he had once been: a man who would wish that hate should leave him and Atara be healed and deserts made green again. I felt within him a longing to call me his brother, as brothers we truly were. He seemed to want to hold out his hand to me.

There is a way, I wanted to tell him. *There is always a way*.

Then he looked deep into my eyes, and he cringed, as if looking into the sun. He gnashed his teeth together as he shook his head at me.

Why, I asked the wind, *can he not bear it?*

Fear, like a drink of poison, seized hold of him. His face tightened and began burning with his old malice, toward me and everything that might forge a bond with others and weaken him. No man, I thought, could resist the sword that I pushed through his heart. But the Red Dragon, through the force of his will, twisted it and transmuted this healing light into the most terrible of flames.

'No!' he shouted out to me. 'I will not let you make me your ghul!'

Then one of his knights handed him back his sword, and Morjin pointed it at me – or perhaps Estrella – as his head lifted backward and he screamed out into the air:

VALARI! AIYIYARIII!

He kicked his spurs into his horse's flank, and blood reddened the beast's white hide. His horse leaped forward with a terrible scream; so did Zahur Tey's mount next to Morjin, and so with Salmelu, and hundreds of other Red Knights. On the east side of the hill, Count Ulanu led a charge against the warriors I had deployed in a circle protecting Bemossed.

I pushed at Estrella's horse, urging her closer to the cross from where Liljana was calling to her and Daj. There, too, Master Juwain and the Seven, with Alphanderry, took shelter behind my knights.

Our forces came together in a clash of lances against shields, swords clanging against swords and horses whinnying in terror as they kicked against the earth and drove themselves against other horses in a great collision of flesh against flesh. To the west, below the hill, Lord Sharad led our rear guard in a hopeless battle against the Red Knights trying to cut off our route back to the hole that Ymiru and Lord Tomavar's men had torn in the Dragon Army's lines. But our way back no longer existed, for the Yarkonan phalanx had marched straight into it like a great steel plug. Soon the Red Knights and Count Ulanu's cavalry would complete their encirclement of my knights. There could be no escape for us so long as

Morjin lived and kept shouting out his command that his men should destroy us.

I turned to meet the attack of the Red Knights riding ahead of Morjin. The foremost of these – a big man with a great scar seaming his black beard – I killed with a quick thrust, driving my sword through the rings of red steel protecting his chest. Alkaladur might be the Sword of Light, but it still had terrible uses, too, and the needs of battle drove me to wield it in order to protect Estrella and those I loved. Two more times my bright sword flashed out, and two more of my enemy plunged to the ground. And then others, many others, pressed forward in a rage to kill me.

Kane, slightly ahead to my right, drove his horse forward to put himself before the Red Knights coming at me. I did not know what had happened to his sword. He had hold of a broken pike, which he used like a staff to protect me. It was a poor weapon to wield against heavily armored knights. Kane, in fighting to kill, had often fallen into a fury so terrible that his enemies had bitten off their own tongues in fear of him. And now, in fighting *not* to kill, as I realized he did, he had to call upon an even wilder and fiercer force. His speed and strength stunned me; I had never seen him move with such certainty, fire and grace. The end of his pike became a blur of wood as he whirled it past his enemies' lances and swords. He drove it straight into their chests, unhorsing them, and with savage blows he broke arms and elbows and even men's faces. But he would not slay them. The killing angel had at last become a true Elijin lord, and of all the great feats of arms I had witnessed upon any battlefield, I had never beheld such a marvel.

Joshu Kadar, Sar Jonavar and Sar Shivalad tried to come up on my left and push ahead to protect me. They hated it when I led the way straight into the lances and swords of our enemy, but expected it, too, for I was a Valari king. Sar Shivalad cast the last of his throwing lances at a Red Knight trying to stab a spearpoint into me, while Joshu fell into a vicious combat with Zahur Tey.

Then Atara pressed foward. I had commanded her to remain close to the cross with Estrella and the others, but she would not wait out the last of the battle helplessly. With Karimah guiding her horse, Atara was sighting the last of her arrows at a large Red Knight who was calling out curses and preparing to hurl a mace at me. He died clutching his hand to the shaft buried in his throat, and I heard Atara cry out: 'Ninety-nine!' At that moment, Salmelu bore down on both women swinging a bloodstained kalama. He killed Karimah with a quick slash that nearly cut off her head. And then he turned on Atara.

I did not see how she could withstand his attack. He had the longer sword and good steel armor against her Sarni saber and leather corselet; he cried out his rage to cut her to pieces so that he could get to me. As I chopped through the lance of yet another knight trying to impale me, I drank in the terrible sight of the bare-armed and blind Atara slashing out with her saber in a desperate struggle to keep Salmelu's sword from cutting her open.

'Atara!' Daj cried out. He, too, had disobeyed my command to wait with the others. Wielding a long lance that he could barely hold, the youth drove his horse almost straight into Salmelu, all the while stabbing with his lance. 'Val! I'll save you!'

It was upon me, I thought, to save him – and Atara. But I could not move to my left just then to engage Salmelu. For Morjin, still kicking his horse's flanks bloody and screaming out his hate, fell upon me from straight ahead.

'Die, Valari!'

Altaru whinnied out a challenge and reared up to strike his hooves into Morjin's white stallion. His teeth gnashed the air as he tried to bite Morjin or his stallion – I could not be sure which. It took a moment to steady him and position him next to Morjin's huge mount, side by side. Then Morjin's sword smashed down against mine. A shock of pain ran up through my arm bones; I did not know how Morjin called upon such a terrible strength. Again and again, we swung our swords against each other, slashing and parrying, thrusting and trying to cut our way through. My sword's silustria rang from the quick, powerful blows that he rained down upon me.

'Elahad!' I heard Salmelu shout out from my left. Steel clashed against wood as Daj furiously parried Salmelu's sword with his lance. 'I will cut off your woman's head and hand it to you! The boy's, too!'

I had no time to take in the battle raging next to me. I gasped and sweated and grunted with the great effort of keeping Morjin from splitting my flesh. Our horses screamed and pushed at each other, and our swords burned the air. I should, I thought, have been able to vanquish him. I had the better blade; I had youth and fire and recent practice in such deadly duels from all the combats that my war with Morjin had forced upon me. Above all, I had Kane as my teacher, and every lesson that this matchless old warrior had ever drilled into my nerves and bones lived on with every lightning stroke and thrust of my sword. But Morjin, some legends told, was the greatest swordsman ever to walk upon Ea. He had killed thousands of his enemy, sword to sword. He had a fount of power that only the Elijin could call upon. And he had his hate.

'Valari!' he shouted to me. Our swords slammed together and then sprang back. 'I will kill you and everything else on this world before I will ever become your ghul!'

We battled on with hundreds of other knights cutting and cursing at each other in a great circle at the top of the hill. The muscles in my arm burned from the great effort of swinging my sword; the sun's rays stabbed like daggers into my eyes. Morjin threw himself at me with an almost reckless rage, as if he did not care that I might slash him open so long as he could slaughter me. And Estrella. He kept looking over toward her, standing beneath the cross. I felt his furious will to tear her apart. With a ringing of steel, he managed to slide his sword away from mine and slice it down against my shield arm, nearly breaking it. Then he stabbed it at my face. I jerked back my head in time to keep him from piercing my brains – but his sword's point drove into my cheek and scored the bone beneath. I gasped at the jolt of pain that shot through my head, and I blinked against the blood that worked its way into my eye. I counterattacked with all the fury that I could find, but it was not enough. Why, I wanted to shout to the wind, could I not kill this man?

And the wind whispered back: *Because you do not want to see something beautiful perish from the earth.*

Love, I knew then, could destroy as easily as it could create. If I let it, my regard for Morjin would slow my sword and steal the blood from my heart. Then he would slay me. His men would overwhelm the nearly defenseless Kane, and cut down Atara, Joshu Kadar, Lord Avijan and all my other knights fighting so heroically upon this hill. They would slaughter Abrasax and Master Juwain and all the Seven. And Alphanderry and Liljana, too. After Morjin had clawed the Lightstone from Estrella's fingers, would he then put her on a cross next to Bemossed?

'No!' I called out him. 'It is *you* who must die!'

I knew that he must. He seemed to know it, too. I saw it in his red, anguished eyes and felt it in his blood as an unbearable burning that had grieved him for too many thousands of years. His whole being trembled as if haunted with his life and all the dreadful deeds that he had done. He fell at me slashing his sword in a frenzy and a fearful will to seize his fate.

'One hundred!' Atara cried out to the sky. Her duel with Salmelu had carried her ahead of me, and I caught sight of her jerking her bloody saber from Salmelu's throat. It seemed that somehow Daj had directed her precisely where to cut him. Then she called to me: 'Val! If you kill him . . .'

I did not hear the rest of her words, for her vision of what would befall me had long since found its home inside my heart: *If you kill him, you kill yourself!*

I knew that I would. It did not matter. My grandfather had once told me that some men are marked out to make their own fate.

And so I called upon all the radiance still pouring from the cup in Estrella's hand and the light coursing through my sword. A vast will, as fiery as Kane's, blazed through me. I swung Alkaladur at Morjin, once, twice, ten times, seeking for advantage with a controlled fury that Kane had burned deep into my soul. I finally beat aside Morjin's sword in a ringing of silustria against steel. His eyes opened wide, drinking in the light in mine. Love, I knew, might be the most beautiful force in the universe, but it was also the most terrible.

'Strike!' Kane shouted as from a million miles away.

And then a closer and deeper voice as Atara called to me in despair: 'Val!'

I rose up, standing in my stirrups as I lifted the Bright Sword toward the heavens. Then, before Morjin could move his sword back to cover himself, I swung Alkaladur's blade down against Morjin's shoulder with a tremendous force. The silustria split his armor and sliced through his body at a slant, cracking bones and tearing his lungs. With a shock of agony, I felt it cleave his heart. Then it drove down through his belly toward his opposite hip, nearly cutting him in two.

No Elijin, not even Kane, could survive such a wound. Morjin died in a torrent of blood, staring at me. Then his torn body plummeted from his horse to the ground with a great crash.

I gasped as I waited for the agony to sweep me away. Strangely, however, I felt no pain. I gazed down at the ground, and there, hovering over Morjin's still form, a dark cloud took shape as a man. It had a head the size and shape of Morjin's, and so with its legs, torso and arms. I could not make out any feature of its face, lost within a black nothingness. The Ahrim – for such I knew it was – suddenly reached out its hand to me and grasped hold of my hand. I could not let go, and neither could I resist it. I felt Morjin calling to me from wherever he had gone, and Bemossed,

397

and my father and my mother, my brothers, too, and all the thousands of men dead or dying upon this field. Down, I fell, down and down through a dark hole that opened through the ground. It seemed to have no bottom.

And as I fell through a terrible cold, faces appeared, glowing out of the gloom. I stared into the eyes of Raldu, the assassin, and at a shaggy hill-man of Alonia and at one of the hideous Grays. There must have been hundreds of these men: all those I had ever put to the sword. I had not realized that I had slain so many. And then, as I fell and fell, I saw that there were really millions of them. For the One had brought me forth – some flaming part of my soul – as a warrior countless times on countless worlds. And I had killed uncountable multitudes since the beginning of time. When I looked at the dead more closely, it astonished me to see that each of their faces was really my own.

And then I looked no more. There was nothing to see, nor did anything exist by which it might be seen. I heard nothing and I felt nothing, for I was nothing. The darkness deepened down into an even more utter blackness that went on and on forever.

Valashu.

And then there was light. As hate contains the seed of love and the black gelstei holds a firestone's flames, the neverness that had devoured me gave birth to a dazzling darkness. Faint, at first, it slowly grew brighter. And then quickly brighter and still brighter until it swelled outward and blazed like a sun. And then ten thousand suns, ten million of millions and all the stars in the universe pouring out an impossibly perfect splendor. I could not perceive it, as the eye takes hold of a flower's beauty. I could only *be* it, utterly interfused, for as it opened out and out into an infinite glory, the light and I were one.

'Valashu.'

I heard Estrella calling to me, but I thought that I must be dreaming, for Estrella could not speak. I felt a hand pressing down upon my chest, and my heart beating against it. My breath burned past my lips like a fiery wind. Then a fierce light filled my eyes. The sun – Ea's sun, warm and bright – sent its golden rays streaming down upon me. I blinked my eyes and squinted and gasped. Bemossed's blood-streaked body hung upon the cross just above me. I tried to sit up, but several hands pushed me back to the earth. Breaking metal and a terrible screaming filled the air.

'Val!' Atara called to me. She knelt by my side, while Estrella crouched down next to her.

'You live!' Master Juwain cried out from above me. 'You were dead, but now you live!'

He explained that after I had fallen from my horse, the Seven and Liljana had dragged my body to the foot of the cross. My heart had stopped, and so had my breath. No skill of Master Juwain nor even the life-strengthening powers of the Seven's gelstei had been able to revive me. But Estrella had.

'She called you back!' he said to me. 'She put her hand upon you, and your heart started beating again!'

As I looked up Estrella, smiling at me, Master Juwain went on to declaim that this was a miracle and irrefutable proof that she was the Maitreya. I could hardly hear him, for the sound of clashing steel and men screaming drowned out his words. I forced myself to sit up. All around us, at the top of the hill, the Red Knights and the Yarkonans had finally encircled my warriors and pressed them inward into an even tighter ring. With Morjin hacked to pieces, his Red Knights worked even more ferociously to exact revenge. So did Count Ulanu. He led his Yarkonans against my knights. His ugly face contorted in wrath as he tried to cut his way through in order to kill all of us, and his old enemy Liljana first and foremost. But just then, Liljana brought her blue gelstei up to her head. She must have put something into his mind that maddened him, for he suddenly looked at her and screamed and fell from his horse. His own men trampled him under, crushing him to death with another hideous scream. But it was not enough to keep his men from pressing on.

Nor could Kane turn back the tide of battle. Now fighting on foot, the better to protect Estrella, he whirled his broken pike about like a magician's staff, felling many, but he could not beat back an entire army. Neither could the bloody kalamas wielded by Lord Avijan, Joshu Kadar – and many others – as they sliced into the masses of men pressing them. Soon, I knew, the Red Knights would close in upon the cross and annihilate me and mine.

'My sword!' I heard my voice croak out. 'Where is my sword?'

Atara pressed Alkaladur's hilt into my hand, and my fingers closed around it. A surging of blood through my veins, like the Poru in flood, gave me the strength to stand up. Then Atara swept up her saber and turned to face our enemy.

'No,' I told her, laying my hand on her arm, all bloody from the arrow that had pierced her and her butchery of Salmelu. 'You have slain your hundredth man.'

I looked out across the war-torn steppe below the Detheshaloon, and I saw many thousands of men still slaying each other, pushing spears and swords past shields. And women, too. At the center of the field, where the enemy poured through the broken Alonian lines, I saw a battalion of Valari knights appear as if from nowhere and ride forward into the gap. The diamond armor of these hundreds of knights sparkled in the sun. I caught sight of a great blue rose against a white surcoat and other emblems that I did not recognize; I suddenly realized that somehow Vareva Tomavar and the woman warriors she had trained had found their way to the battle. Their kalamas gleamed like shards of silver. The tremendous tumult nearly deafened me; the sun's red flash off bronze and steel nearly burned out my eyes. I could not tell who was winning the battle.

'Estrella!' I called turning to this lovely young woman who had shown me so much. 'Will you help me again?'

Her smile was like a warm ocean washing through me. She nodded her head as if she had been waiting all her life for me to ask her this question. He hands grew bright from the radiance pouring out of the cup that she held.

I raised my sword up to the sky, aligning it with stars that I could not see but only sense. I pointed it toward the Seven Sisters and Agathad, where the Galadin dwelled, and Ninsun, source of the Golden Band at the center of all things. Then I brought Alkaladur down and swept it out across the battlefield, from our lines of knights and warriors in the west to the trampled grass in the east, where Sajagax's Sarni had now nearly routed the enemy's tribes. It was strange to think that Morjin's death had done nothing to dismay the men whom he had led here but had only caused them to fall against my men with an even greater savagery.

But I will give them dismay, I thought. *That – and much, much more.*

For I had brought back from the land of the dead a great gift.

'Val!' Atara cried out from next to me. 'Your sword!'

Once again, the Lightstone poured out an impossibly bright radiance. So did my sword. All the fire of life that blazed within me flashed out of it. The valarda was that force which opened one man or women to another, heart to heart. At the heart of all things, I knew, there shimmered but one light. It was *this* splendor that interconnected all beings together as one.

There is nothing to fear.

Truly, there was not. But so long as flesh burned with life, there would always be much to suffer. Now, as men battling in both the Dragon army and mine thrust steel through flesh, they suffered themselves the terrible agonies that they inflicted on each other.

The screams of the wounded and dying, in thousands, were joined by the shrieks of those who would cleave or slay them. No man could strike another without feeling the white-hot pain of a spear or axe or arrow or sword ripping through him. So it has always been with me. And so now I gladly – but with great grieving – shared my gift with them.

They cannot bear it!

Who, I wondered, could? For I, who had called upon my sword to help me endure the torments of those I had slain, had in the end driven myself down into death. Perhaps only Kane, I thought, of any man on earth or the stars, had the strength to drink in the anguish of those he struck down and keep on fighting.

But our enemy – and my warriors – could not keep on doing battle themselves. Sar Shivalad, after slashing open a Red Knight's neck, grabbed his own neck and fell gurgling from his horse. So it was with Lord Manthanu after he had swung his mace to brain a man, and with Lord Avijan, Joshu Kadar and many others. And so with our enemy. Zahur Tey, after he had stabbed Sar Zenshar, shook his head and cast down his lance. He did not mean it as an act of surrender – only that he would not, and *could* not, fight anymore. A dozen of his men followed his lead. And then thirty more, and then three hundred and a thousand. My knights began throwing down their weapons, too. And suddenly, like a wave spreading down and outward from the top of the hill where Bemossed hung crucified, the ringing of steel against steel slowly faded and died as all of the tens of thousands of men on the battle-field ceased fighting.

'Val!' Atara cried out again. Her face radiated a deep joy. 'I never *saw*!'

Truly, I did not think that she had ever looked upon this moment. But she had willed it to be, with all the force of her soul and the sacrifice of her flesh and the power of her white gelstei.

Then Estrella held the Lightstone high above her head. Its splendor, like unto that of creation itself, neither dazzled the eye nor burned but seemed to illuminate all things as from within. The golden cup grew even brighter, and its radiance fell across the miles of warriors spread across the plains; it fell across the whole world in a clear, numinous flower of light that blossomed outward and connected earth to the heavens.

There came a moment when no one moved. It seemed that it was no longer possible for anyone to move again, if their motions should be the stabbing of spears and the swinging of swords. All the men gathered beneath the Detheshaloon, almost, turned to look up at the Lightstone. Awe shone upon the faces of my Valari warriors and those of our former enemies, too. I felt them burning with a new will toward life. In the Lightstone's onstreaming glory, even the blood-soaked earth and the bodies of the dead and dying seemed transformed with a luminous and terrible purpose. Men and women gazed at the shimmering Lightstone as if wondering why they had been called into life and called into battle. I saw great warriors such as Lord Avijan, Sar Shivalad and Zahur Tey break down weeping, for the men whom they had killed and for each other – and for themselves.

Then the kings and chieftains who had fought that day, as if called to the top of the Owl's Hill, rode out away from their armies to the foot of Bemossed's cross, where I stood with Estrella and my friends. King Angand of Sunguru, his bloody blue surcoat showing a reddened white heart with wings, kept pace next to King Thaddeu. Hesperu's new sovereign had succeeded King Arsu, killed when the elephant he had been riding fell upon him. No king came forth from the nearby Yarkonans, for none would claim Count Ulanu's illicit crown. But King Orunjan, one of the greatest of the Dragon Kings, approached the cross to speak for Uskudar. He had reddish-brown skin and a nose as straight as a ruler; he stood tall, straight and proud. The chieftains of the Sarni tribes who had fought for Morjin made their way up the hill, too, but not Gorgorak, for Sajagax had sought him out during the battle, and had put an arrow through his heart.

It gladdened *my* heart to see that the great Sajagax, by a miracle, had survived the battle. He rode up to the cross with five broken arrows sticking out of various parts of him: two through his shoulder and one through each thigh while a fifth had embedded itself in his neck. I did not know how he managed to climb down off his horse and to stand next to Vishakan and Bajorak and the other Sarni chieftains who had followed him here. I did not know – then – that during the battle the warriors of the Janjii tribe in the east and the Siofok in the west had gone over to Sajagax, and that *all* the Sarni would soon be persuaded to make him their Great Chief, as Tulamar had been before him long ago.

Of the Valari kings, all came forth save for King Sandarkan and King Hadaru, who had died trying save one of his knights from the axes of the Blues. Prince Issur had immediately taken command of the Ishkans as their new lord. A pike had pierced King Mohan's arm and a saber added yet another wound to King Kurshan's fearsome face, but the two of them stood side by side on the hill looking up at me in anticipation. So it was with King Viromar, King Waray and King Danashu.

Others mounted the hill as well: King Hanniban and King Tal and King Aryaman of Thalu, who would be known hereafter as Aryaman Bloodaxe for the terrible deeds that he had done at the Detheshaloon that day. Great warriors who were not sovereigns stood with them: Thaman of Surrapam and Vareva Tomavar and Ymiru, whose white fur the ferocious combat with the Hesperuks and Yarkonan phalanxes had soaked almost completely red. And perhaps the greatest of warriors, and of all those who had fought upon the battlefield: Sar Maram Marshayk. For he had slain a dragon.

I watched my best friend slowly make his way through the parting Kaashan and Sakayan lines from the Hill of Fire. There, the great body of Yormungand lay where it had fallen, broken and burned. Maram himself had been burned, and badly, for Yormungand's flames had singed off his eyebrows and incinerated his beard and blistered much of his face a bright red. His left arm hung encased in charred leather and diamonds, and he could not use his blackened left hand. But in his right hand, he still clutched his bright red gelstei. As he drew closer to me, he held the great firestone high above his head as if showing me the sun itself.

'We're alive!' he cried out to me. 'O Lord! blessedly and beautifully alive! And dragonslayers, now, the both of us!'

He looked down at Morjin's hacked body, near the cross. So did Zahur Tey and King Angand, and many others. All seemed disgusted to perceive Morjin's true face: old and withered and ugly beyond anything they had ever imagined. And yet I thought that perhaps they could see in him, too, a terrible beauty for having finally found peace in death. The sight of the great Red Dragon lying so still, I sensed, shocked everyone gathered at the top of the hill into waking up, as from a bad dream.

'I was a fool,' Zahur Tey called out, 'for thinking that Morjin could have been the Maitreya.'

He turned his gaze from Morjin's body to look up at Estrella, standing beneath the cross, and so did thousands of others.

'We were all fools,' King Orunjan said.

Then King Angand, like a hawk alert to the shifting of the wind, called out: 'We followed Morjin because we thought he could unite Ea. But we were wrong.'

King Angand, a cunning and calculating man, did not speak the whole truth, for men had mostly gathered to the Red Dragon's standard because Morjin had terrorized them. But it didn't matter. King Angand, and others, seemed finally freed from Morjin's spell, and that was a very great thing.

'Many of us were wrong about many matters,' King Mohan called out. This fierce warrior had matched swords with King Angand's Sunguruns that day, and he gazed at King Angand in a silent understanding. Then he spoke of his hope for Ea, and his new dream shone forth in words that astonished me: 'I have fought in battles nearly every year since I was seventeen. I am tired of war. I long for peace. Once, in the time of Godavanni the Glorious in the Age of Law, Ea had a High King – and peace reigned across the world.'

Kane, standing next to him, drew his sword and raised it up toward me. In his rich, powerful voice, he called out: 'King of Ea! Let us recognize Valashu Elahad as Ea's rightful High King!'

Then he stepped foward to lay his sword at my feet, for he would never wield steel in war again.

'King of Ea!' King Mohan shouted, drawing his sword. 'King Valamesh! King of Kings!'

'King Valamesh!' King Viromar called out, also raising up his kalama to me. Then all the remaining Valari kings drew their swords, and added their voices to his: 'King Valamesh shall be our king!'

'Valamesh, High King!' King Angand acclaimed me. 'Let all who stand here now make it so!'

His will to see Ea united under one banner persuaded King Orunjan and King Thaddeu of Hesperu and others who had followed the Red Dragon. King Hanniban and the Free Kings likewise seemed swept away by the magic of that moment. They knelt before me, and set their swords on the ground at my feet. And they cried out with one voice: 'King Valamesh! King of Ea!'

Bajorak, however, although my friend, would not call me his king, for no Sarni chieftain would ever call *any* man king. But he, like Vishakan and most of the other Sarni chiefs – even Gorgorak's son, Artamax, the new leader of the Marituk – clearly saw that no Sarni tribe could now stand alone. Even as no alliance of tribes could stand against Sajagax and the High King of more than twenty kingdoms. And so, then and there, at the top of the Owl's Hill, the Sarni chieftains made Sajagax their Great Chief. And then Sajagax, with arrows sticking out of him like a porcupine's quills, came up to me.

'There *will* be a High King for Ea!' he called out in a voice that shook the earth like thunder. 'And a new law for Ea, that is just the Law of the One! Let none oppose it, or else be prepared to oppose all the Sarni! And let all the Sarni, who kneel to no man, even a king, honor one who must be a lord to even the greatest of kings!'

So saying, with a great struggle and will to overcome pain, he dropped down to one knee on the slope beneath me. Then he looked up and cried out, 'Lord of Light!'

At first I thought that he must have forgotten that I could not be the Maitreya; then I realized that he was looking past me, up at Estrella, who stood behind me holding high the Lightstone. Her face shone with a lovely radiance as the voices of kings and Sarni chieftains – and many others – rang out into the air: 'Lord of Light!'

Then I, too, turned and knelt before Estrella: a twelve-year-old girl holding a plain golden cup in her hands. I pressed my sword to the bloodstained grass beneath her feet as I added my voice to the multitudes crying out: 'Lord of Light! Lord of Light! Lord of Light!'

At last, when Estrella could bear this acclaim no longer, she motioned for me, and everyone else, to stand back up. She set her hand upon my hand and gently urged me to slide my sword back into its sheath. Her face lit up with the brightest of smiles. Then she fell against me weeping, hugging my hard armor close to her, kissing my palms and fingers and then standing up on tiptoes to press her lips against my lips, my face and my hot, hurting eyes.

The war, I thought, weeping too, was finally over.

25

T hen Estrella set her hand over my heart, and the pain that pierced me there went away. She touched the wound that Morjin had torn into my cheek; she turned to lay her hands on Maram's charred hand and upon Atara's bloody shoulder and her face. After that, Estrella went among the wounded, touching men's pierced bellies, hacked limbs and smashed heads. Many of these found their wounds suddenly healed; many of the dying, she kept from going over to the land of the dead. But she could not, it seemed, bring anyone back from that mysterious place, as she had me. Even a Maitreya, I thought, could work only so many miracles. And with tens of thousands of men and women lying upon the grass, it must have broken her heart that she had the power to help only a very few of them.

We began the burials that day. With such a great death coming upon the steppe, the sky above the battlefield filled with clouds of carrion birds. I had to ask Sajagax to set his warriors driving off the lions, wolves and jackals that would have taken away those who had fallen. The Sarni, of course, preferred such a fate and found great honor that their bodies should nourish other living things. But even the Sarni saw that too many of their warriors had died and could not be disposed of in such a way. And so they worked as hard as anyone, from the Dragon's army or my own, digging down through the steppe's tough sod. We arrayed the graves in ever widening rings of mounded earth and stone that spread out down the gentle slopes of the Owl's Hill. Near the top, we buried Morjin where he had died. And at the very top, after we had taken down the cross and wrapped Bemossed's body in a shroud that Liljana made, we set our friend deep into the earth. Maram used his red gelstei against the rocks of the Detheshaloon to cut a great stone in the shape of a cross. We mounted it over the head of Bemossed's grave to mark what happened here. Because I thought both Bemossed and I, in the end, had found the same truth, I asked Maram to burn into the stone the same words that the battle had burned into my soul:

> With his eye of compassion
> He saw his enemy
> Like unto himself;
> And he knew love –
> And his enemy
> Was vanquished.

A great many animals – mostly horses and elephants – had perished along with the men who had ridden them here, but these we did not bury. No one wanted to dig a grave large enough to accommodate an elephant. Then, too, Morjin had driven his vast army hundreds of miles across the Wendrush far from his base and easy supply, and it seemed that his men had gone to short rations and had nearly starved. They reluctantly butchered the mounts that had carried them into battle. I overheard one of my men say with great bitterness that if Morjin's followers could drink a man's blood, then surely they could eat a horse's flesh.

One beast we could not bury, nor could anyone think of how we might cut up the corpse and dispose of it. In truth, the dragons that had come to earth from Charoth could hardly be considered animals, and Yormungand had proved as cunning as many men. A terrible enemy he might have been, poison-hearted and vengeful, but I did not want to see this huge being rot inside his iron-hard scales beneath the hot sun.

And so Kane, now recalling long-forgotten lore, instructed Ymiru in some of the deeper properties of the purple gelstei that Ymiru had inherited from his father. Ymiru then used the lilastei against the dragon's body as Jezi Yaga had with the purple crystals set into her eye hollows: to turn flesh into stone. For ages to come, travelers and pilgrims would espy from afar a great dragon rock at the top of the Hill of Fire.

On the evening of the day following the battle, Lord Harsha brought me a report of the dead. A final count of those slain of the Dragon army had not yet been made, but Lord Harsha, with a face as heavy as stone, informed me that Ishka had lost 3,000 of her 15,000 warriors, while the Atharians had suffered nearly

407

as grievously. As for the Meshians, Lord Harsha said, we who had sacrificed so much to cut a hole in the Hesperuk and Sakayan phalanxes, the casualty list was even longer. He told me of the thousands killed in Lord Tomavar's battalions alone, and I held up my hand to stop him, saying, 'Bring me not numbers but names!'

Lord Harsha did, and the names of those Meshians who had died beneath the Detheshaloon's rocks would forever burn in my mind: Sar Kanshar; Lord Ramjay; Shakadar Eldru; Juvalad the Fair . . . There seemed almost no end to them. Lord Sharad had fallen in a heroic attempt to keep the Red Knights from cutting off our rear guard, and it saddened me to hear of Lord Tanu's death, beneath the Sakayan's spears. This crabby old man had challenged me for Mesh's kingship and had been hard to like, but easy to respect, for he had been a great warrior who had given everything for Mesh. Many wept at his demise, and surprisingly, Sar Jonavar was one of these, though he could not say why. With Lord Tanu in mind, I ordered more stones cut from the mound of the Detheshaloon. On the slabs set above the graves of the men of the Nine Kingdoms, I ordered names inscribed, and these words: *Here lies a Valari warrior.* Then, upon gazing up at the Owl's Hill and all the graves of the soldiers who had fought for Morjin, I ordered the names of our former enemy to be inscribed on their headstones, too.

It finally came time to decide the fate of those who had followed Morjin. Many of my warriors, Lord Tomavar foremost among them, still saw the men of the Dragon army *as* our enemy. At the least, they held them to account for unleashing a terrible war upon Ea and committing countless atrocities. Atara agreed with him. On the second night after the battle, she said to those gathered above the river to advise me: 'Many of Morjin's captains are murderers. And the kings who swore oaths to him have much blood upon them. How can we just send them back to their lands?'

'I am a murderer, too,' I said to Atara. I pointed out at the thousands of white stones marking the graves dug out of the Wendrush's yellowed grass. 'And upon my hands, there is an ocean of blood.'

'But, Val,' she said to me. 'It is not the same. You never ordered a child crucified! Or a man mutilated for refusing to acclaim you as the Maitreya. Or . . . a thousand other crimes. And so how can you suffer the criminals to live?'

I looked across the starlit steppe at the thousands of campfires of the men from Hesperu, Sunguru, Sakai and the others who had worn the Dragon's colors. And I said to Atara, and to my other friends: 'I am less concerned with punishing the guilty than with protecting the innocent.'

I told her that any campaign to root out the worst of Morjin's torturers and executioners would only ignite the war anew and tear apart the former Dragon Kingdoms.

'King Angand and the others,' I said, 'did not surrender to me as criminals to a magistrate but offered their allegiance as kings to a High King. I will hold them to their oaths.'

'They *should* have surrendered!' Sajagax called out hoarsely. A great white scarf bound his wounded neck. 'We *would* have won the battle! It was the arrows that made the difference.'

He nodded his head at the one-eyed Lord Harsha, and thanked him for keeping his Sarni well-supplied with the long range arrows that his warriors had used to gain advantage over the Marituk, Zayak, Mansurii and Janjii tribes in the east and the other enemy Sarni tribes in the west. Then he went on to say that his warriors surely would have turned both the enemy's flanks, while the timely arrival of Vareva Tomavar and her thousand Meshian women shored up our army's center.

'And so our enemy,' Sajagax went on, 'should be treated as vanquished. Too many of them, I think, care not for their kings' oaths and care nothing for the Law of the One!'

At this, I laid hold of the sword strapped to my side. And I told Sajagax: 'They will come to care. I will hold *everyone* to the Law.'

I went on to say that, in the time to come, I would require all of Ea's kings to stand before their people as I had. The wicked ones, along with their captains and counselors, would be cast down. And new kings would be chosen.

Ymiru, who had lost three hundred of his five hundred warriors in the gap torn into the Hesperuk phalanx, sadly shook his head at this. 'But, Val, what of Morjin's blood-drinking priests? They are *unhroly*!'

Kane, standing up straight and tall next to Ymiru, looked at him with eyes as old as time. He nodded his head as he rested his hand on Ymiru's great, furry arm. 'The Red Priests are that, and worse. And so the evil that they have done will not be undone overnight.'

No, I thought, the new age that Atara had dreamed of but never quite believed in would not come upon Ea fully realized in a year, or even a hundred years. But it would surely come, I said, even as a great and irreversible change had befallen the world and those who lived upon it.

It was to explain the new way for Ea that I called a council of kings and chiefs the next day. We met in my pavilion, and I stood to address King Angand and King Orunjan, King Mohan and King Aryaman and Vishakan and Bajorak and all the others. And this is what I told them:

'For all the ages of recorded history and the Lost Ages before them, there has been discord on Ea – ever since my ancestor, Aryu, slew Elahad and stole the Lightstone. How many lives had to be paid to atone for this murder? Millions. How many more men, women and children shall suffer death due to the evil of a world that was not of their making? Not a single one, I swear, if I can help it.'

For the Lightstone, I said, had at last been delivered into the hands of the great Maitreya, and the terrible chance that the Galadin had taken in sending the Lightstone to Ea had been redeemed. We could at last begin building the great civilization that the Star People had been sent to earth to create. Toward this end all the kings in every land and all Ea's peoples must direct their efforts. All who had fought upon the plains below the Detheshaloon, even those who had followed Morjin, must pledge their swords to fulfilling the Law of the One.

It surprised King Mohan and Sajagax that I would allow our former enemy to keep their arms and armor, but I explained that there might be discord in the realms to the south and that brigands and outlaws would need to forestalled. Just as we Valari would hold on to our kalamas in case any king or rebellious lord tried to turn back toward the Way of the Dragon. It was a paradox, I said, that we had fought a war to end war. And that now we must keep our swords to keep men from *using* their swords.

The greatest sword of all, of course, I held sheathed inside me, and no one wished to feel it cut them open again as it had here at the Detheshaloon. The valarda, I thought, *would* now awaken in all people across the world – but not overnight, as Kane had observed. I wished with all my heart that men and women should come to take delight in each other's joy rather than suffering the agony of another's wounds in battle. But I must stand ready to use Alkaladur's double-edged blade to cut, as needed, either way.

'I shall,' I said, nodding at Kane, 'send emissaries into all lands. The Brotherhoods will open new schools again. And the Sisterhood will raise up Temples of Life and teach alongside the Brothers. We shall build roads: from Alonia in the north to Karabuk in the south; from Galda in the east to Hesperu in the uttermost west – and everywhere.'

410

Then I told the assembled kings of the fate of the Kallimun, which had concerned Ymiru: 'The Red Priests' fortresses and torture chambers shall be torn down, stone by stone. And the Red Priests shall take the lead in cutting new stones and laying down the new roads.'

I summoned to my tent Arch Uttam, as evil a man as I had ever known. Many wished for his death. So, once, had I. But now I forced myself to wish that his life should make that of others better. And so I also summoned Sar Ludar Jarlath to stand with kings. Sar Ludar had been a stonecutter in Silvassu, and he had shaped many of the headstones pushing up from the grass of the battle-field. I asked him to show Arch Uttam his hands. Ludar's knuckles were nicked and bloodied from the hard labor of swinging a mallet against a chisel and, from time to time, inevitably missing and striking iron across flesh.

'You,' I said to Arch Uttam, grabbing hold of his hand, 'have cut a young woman's throat and drunk her blood. Now you shall cut stone instead and give your blood that women and men shall travel freely among Ea's kingdoms.'

Arch Uttam bowed his head at this, and so did Arch Yadom and the other Red Priests whom I had called to my tent. Although they obviously hated being sentenced to such lowly work, they must have expected a painful execution as payment for their terrible crimes.

'And all people *shall* travel freely,' I went on. I turned and bowed my head to Estrella, standing next to me. 'For a time, the Maitreya will reside in Tria, with the Lightstone. Any and all who wish will make the pilgrimage to stand before the Cup of Heaven. And when it is safe again, the Maitreya will journey with the Lightstone's Guardians into all lands.'

I gazed out at Ea's proud kings and chieftains to see how they received my words. All of them, I thought, even the most murderous of them – especially they – must long for a better world in some quiet chamber of their hearts, even if they still did not quite believe in it. Could I *make* them believe? No, I thought, I could not. But Estrella could. For her, and just such a purpose, the Lightstone had been sent to earth.

The next day, the armies began dispersing to the four corners of the world. Sajagax promised to help provision them and to escort them across the plains of the Wendrush. He assigned warriors from various tribes to march with the various armies, north, east, south and west, to ensure that they did not forget what had

411

happened at the Detheshaloon and did not fall into mischief along the way. By the time morning dawned on the fifth day following the battle, only Sajagax's Kurmak warriors and the armies of Alonia and the Nine Kingdoms remained, encamped along the river.

On a cool, clear afternoon, I called another meeting, this time on top the Owl's Hill. I wanted to take council with my friends, that we might see our way into an unknown world and discuss the hundreds of tasks that must be done if it was ever to take shape. And even more, I wanted to understand what had occurred upon the battlefield.

We gathered in a circle on the torn grass between Bemossed's grave and Morjin's. Atara grasped hold of my arm, and I helped her take her place beside me. Abrasax and Master Juwain, with the rest of the Seven and Ymiru, positioned themselves nearest to Morjin's headstone while I sat across from them, with Atara, Maram and Daj to my right and Estrella, Liljana and Alphanderry on my left. Kane, who had never liked sitting, stood silently just behind me, with his back nearly touching Bemossed's huge headstone. In the days since the battle, he had wandered about the Detheshaloon saying almost nothing to anyone, and I wondered if he might ever speak again.

'Thank you for coming here,' I said, looking out at my friends. 'And thank you . . . for everything. If not for each of you, in a hundred ways, I never would have lived to see this day.'

From the top of the hill, I had a clear view across the golden Wendrush for miles in every direction except to the northwest, where the rocks of the Detheshaloon blocked out a good part of the sky. On almost a straight line with this skull-like mass and our hill, to the southeast, I could plainly make out the dragon rock on top of the Hill of Fire. I marveled yet again that Maram had somehow slain Yormungand. Even as I marveled at him. Estrella's magic touch had restored his burnt hand and face to his usual ruddy hue, and the beginning of a heavy new beard shaded his chin and cheeks. He seemed happy. And proud. He took advantage of the moment to recount his great deed.

'Ah, Val,' he said to me, looking toward the southeast, too. 'I wish you could have seen me! I stood my ground on top of that damn hill, though any sane man would have run away. And I wanted to run, a thousand times, as you must know. But a thousand times more, I wanted to kill that damn dragon. For if I hadn't, he surely would have killed *you*.'

He told me, and all of us, that during his battle with Yormungand, the dragon kept trying to burn Maram's mind even as he flew at him spitting out fire. Yormungand, Maram said, hoped to terrify Maram into dropping his red gelstei so that he might incinerate Maram and then turn upon me.

'That thought consumed him,' Maram said. 'He wanted to see you – ah, please excuse me, my friend – he wanted to watch you fry like a chicken. For your slaying his mother, yes, but also because Morjin commanded him to. The Red Dragon had some kind of poisonous hold over the real dragon's heart. I felt it, as surely as I did the dragon's flames. Yormungand would have burned you, or crushed you to a pulp. And then turned on Estrella. I *saw* this in Yormungand's mind! When Estrella rode up to you in the middle of the battle, Morjin must have realized that she was the Maitreya – and commanded Yormungand to kill her, above all others on the field.'

As everyone looked at Estrella, Daj slapped his hand against Maram's arm, and said, 'But the dragon couldn't get to her, could he? He didn't dare to! Tell us how you kept Yormungand away from Estrella and burned the dragon's wings!'

Daj, I thought, perhaps many times over the past few days, had heard Maram tell his story. But I had been too busy to sit down with my friend over a horn of beer and listen to him.

'Well,' Maram continued, showing everyone his red crystal, 'for a long while, I *couldn't* lay any fire at all upon the dragon. He kept circling above the hill, flying away and then coming back to dive at me. Each time he did, I cast a thunderbolt at him – at his damn wings! His scales are hard to burn through, but his wings are no tougher than leather. My plan was to burn them off entirely, and then finish the dragon after he fell. But with each bolt of fire, just before I took aim, Yormungand saw it in my mind – I know he did. And so he veered, right or left, up or down, and pulled his damn wings out of the way.'

'And each time you tried to burn the dragon,' Daj said, 'the dragon tried to burn you!'

'Ah, so he did,' Maram said. He made a motion as if to pull at his beard, and then seemed to remember that the dragon had singed the hairs from his face. 'And he *did* burn me, too bad. If I hadn't cast down my knight's shield on the way up to the top of the hill and picked up a great shield dropped by some poor Waashian infantryman, he would have burned me to the death. As it was, the dragon fire melted the steel right off my shield – and nearly melted the skin off *me*. I was sure, then, that he was going to kill me.'

413

Maram paused in his story and looked at me as if in expectation that I might ask him what had happened next. I obliged him, saying, 'What saved you, then?'

'Liljana did,' Maram said, glancing across the circle to bow his head to her. 'She put some fire of her own into the dragon's mind.'

Liljana's soft, round face lit up as if in remembrance. She showed us her little blue figurine. 'Oh, I would hardly call it *fire*. I only had to distract the beast at a critical moment.'

'And distract him she did,' Maram told us. 'Then I burned the wings off that dragon! It was the fall, I think, that killed him.'

He paused to turn his head back and forth as if shaking himself out of a bad dream. Then he looked over at me as he cried out: 'We won, Val! We really won!'

With a loud grunt, he pushed himself up to his feet and crossed the circle to stand before Liljana. With a great puff of air, he leaned down to plant a loud kiss upon her forehead. He smiled so hugely that I wondered if it hurt his raw, red face.

And then, to my astonishment and that of nearly everyone else, Liljana smiled back at him. She, who had lost the ability to smile, or so we had all thought, somehow managed to do this impossible thing.

'Liljana!' Master Juwain spoke out, smiling too. 'It is good to have you back!'

Although Liljana's lips remained turned up to brighten her face, she began weeping without restraint. We all bowed our heads in honor of this miracle.

'What I would like to know,' Maram finally said, directing his words at Atara, 'is how *you* recognized Estrella as the Maitreya? The dragon didn't let that slip into your mind, did he?'

'Hmmph – he had no thought of me at all, I'm sure.' Atara sat next to me with a fresh white cloth binding her face. Another bandage padded her wounded shoulder, which Estrella had been unable to heal. She spoke to us in a calm, clear voice that rang out over the hill's many graves: 'But something did burn me, like the hottest of fires. That is, it burned away a *part* of me. This . . . is hard to talk about. Hard to explain in a way that will make sense to you. But this seeing that a scryer does has everything to do with her will. And no scryer has ever *seen* the Maitreya, or the Lightstone, because both dwell at the center of time, which is all fire and flame, like the heart of a star. And so terribly, terribly bright. It seems that no scryer can ever journey there. I don't think any scryer ever had: it would be like staring and staring at the sun. And burning, as flesh melts beneath fire. During the battle, with my sisters falling in the arrow storm, I thought of Val and I looked where I shouldn't have. Where I couldn't, really. But I *did*! Somehow. Then I melted. I found myself . . . not looking into the star and seeing, but *being* it. Pure flame, I was. And then everything grew clear, so impossibly clear. I *saw* the Lightstone shining in Estrella's beautiful, beautiful hand. But I knew that Val couldn't see this, and so I had to ride to tell him.'

Of that heroic ride, blind, at the head of the Manslayers across the battlefield, she would not speak, for almost all of her sisters had been slain and the Manslayers were no more. It seemed a horrific price for warning me that I must give the Lightstone to Estrella. As did Atara's plunge into darkness. For she told us that her gazing at the brightest thing in all the universe had destroyed her second sight once and for all, and that she would never have visions of the future or faraway places again.

I could not bear to think of her as utterly and hopelessly blind, but she had no pity for herself. She reached across my chest and extended her fingers to Estrella, sitting on my other side. And she said, 'I saw the Lightstone in this young woman's hand, and that is vision enough for ten lifetimes.'

While Estrella held the Lightstone shining like a little sun, she clasped hold of Atara's fingers with her other hand. It pained me that although she had healed many warriors of many dreadful wounds, she had not been able to restore speech to herself.

'Ah,' Maram said, looking at her, 'I still can't quite believe that the Maitreya could be a *girl*.'

At this, Master Juwain rubbed the back of his bald head, and looked at Estrella, too. His ugly face grew so bright that it seemed almost beautiful. Then, with much embarrassment, he said, 'I'm afraid that I am partly to blame for that. We of the Brotherhood are. Many verses, in the *Saganom Elu* and other sources of the ancient prophecies, speak of the Maitreya. And always as 'he' or 'him.' But in the ancient Ardik from which the prophecies have been translated, the pronouns referring to the Maitreya are always of the indeterminate gender, for which there is no really good translation. And so, considering that the known Maitreyas have all been male, it seemed most logical to choose the masculine pronouns.'

'*Your* logic,' Liljana said to him. 'But didn't I hint, more than once, that the Maitreya might be a woman?'

'You did,' Master Juwain admitted. 'But I am sorry to say that I thought you were joking.'

415

'Joking!' she said as her face fell stern again. 'When have I ever made light of such matters?'

They might have reopened one of their old arguments if Abrasax had not held up his hand for peace. And then said to them, 'Logic is logic, and everywhere the same, but the results of reasoning can only be as valid as one's premises. There is much that we have assumed that is clearly not true. And foremost of these assumptions, as pertains to this matter, is that man and woman are so different from each other as to require different pursuits of knowledge, and even different ways.'

He went on to say that now that the true Maitreya had come forth, the Brotherhood and Sisterhood must find a way to unite and lead the way for all of Ea.

'Very good, and I am all for *unions* of men and women, as everyone knows,' Maram called out. 'And I suppose that the Maitreya will bring in this luminous age that everyone hopes for. But what *makes* one a Maitreya? Why *Estrella*? And why didn't we see the signs that she was the Shining One?'

None of us, not even Abrasax or Kane, had any easy answers to his question. Master Matai, the Brotherhood's greatest diviner, spoke of the designs of the stars under which Estrella had been born and fate, while Master Virang attributed Estrella's deepest nature to the Ieldra's grace. Then Atara, always practical, squeezed Estrella's hand again and said to Maram: 'But of course we did have signs – and many of them. But as Pualani told us in the first Vild, people look at many things they fail to see.'

'Ah, I suppose so,' Maram murmured, eyeing Estrella. 'But didn't Val once say that on our journey to Tria, he gave the girl the Lightstone to hold? And that it had absolutely no effect upon her?'

'No effect that I could *see*,' I said.

'It might be,' Abrasax observed, 'that this contact with the Lightstone proved crucial to Estrella – and all of Ea. It might have been the sunlight that quickened the seed of who Estrella was meant to be.'

'The great Maitreya,' Master Yasul said, staring at Estrella as if he had waited his whole life for this moment. 'The greatest and last of all the Maitreyas.'

Liljana, sitting next to Estrella, rested her hand on her leg and smiled as if she, too, had long looked forward to this fulfillment of the ancient prophecies. Then her face fell sad and thoughtful as she looked at me. 'We should all be amazed at the way things have unfolded. We all wondered if the world would have been better if the Lightstone had remained buried in Argattha for another thousand years. How many times, Val, have you regretted that you recovered the Lightstone – only to lose it back to Morjin? And then lost your whole family? And so many of your people? Of course, nothing can ever justify such murders or take the pain of them away – how could it? But if what Abrasax says is true, then everything depended on our rescuing the Lightstone out of Argattha – *everything*. And so I have to wonder if things happened just as they were *meant* to happen.'

It was a strange thing for her to say. I considered her words as I gazed out at the thousands of headstones pushing up from the grass all around us. For the moment, I found myself transported back to another battlefield, upon which my father and brothers had died.

Then Maram, looking past me at the greatest of all the carved stones adorning the Detheshaloon, called out: 'But what I still don't understand is Bemossed. He *was* the Maitreya, too, wasn't he? A *true* Maitreya, and not just another man of talents who wanted to be more than he was.'

'I am sure that he was,' Master Matai said. His golden-hued face pointed past Bemossed's stone cross, up toward the sky. 'Just as I am sure that more than one Maitreya was born at the end of the Age of the Dragon. But here, too, language has misled us. We speak, most often, of *the* Maitreya, prophesied for this time. But, of course, there have been many Maitreyas throughout the ages. In the ancient Ardik, there is no distinction between the definite and indefinite article. And so we might reasonably translate the prophecies as referring to *a* Maitreya, who will bring in the new age.'

Abrasax nodded his hoary head at this, and told us: 'I, too, am sure that Bemossed was a Maitreya. As time went on, his aura flared like that of no other man I have ever seen. But it did not blaze, as Estrella's now does. I think we asked too much of him. It is most logical to assume that he never quite reached the moment of his quickening, when he would come into his full power.'

'And yet,' Master Storr said, tapping his finger against his freckled cheek, 'he found power enough to keep Morjin from using the Lightstone until almost the very end.'

'And *that* is another thing I don't understand,' Maram broke in. 'Once Bemossed had gone to Morjin, Morjin might have killed him whenever he pleased – and so gained full control of the Lightstone. But he waited. Why?'

'Isn't that obvious'?' Atara asked him. She patted the grass beneath Bemossed's headstone. 'How else could he have drawn Val into the trap upon this hill?'

'But Morjin hesitated even once Val had fought his way up here. Why did he not strike sooner?'

I waited to see who might respond to this. The answer, I thought, shone out as clear as starlight from Estrella's lovely face. But because she remained mute, I had to speak for her.

'Morjin,' I said, 'should never even have touched his hand to the Lightstone. It truly is like a star, as Atara has told. I can feel . . . how it burned him. How its brilliance blinded him to many things. And rather than nourishing his soul and illuminating him, *his* soul fed it. I do not think he could bear the darkness. And the emptiness. And that is why he could not quite bear to murder Bemossed. He hoped, until the very end, that Bemossed might find a way to heal him.'

'But he *did* murder Bemossed!' Maram said. 'And would have murdered Estrella. Why? Since he recognized, before anyone else, that *she* was the Maitreya, too?'

'Because,' I told him, 'Morjin was also the Red Dragon, and *that* one did not want Morjin to be healed.'

At least, I went on to say, the great Red Dragon, missing scales over his heart, would never expose that tender place to such as Estrella or Bemossed. Then I admitted one of my worst fears of the Beast that I had fought for so long: that Morjin would have tried to torture out of Bemossed the mystery of what it meant to be the Maitreya. But one might as well torture a flower to reveal the secret of its beauty.

'Morjin,' I told everyone, '*could* have chosen life. But that was his deepest flaw, that he always found it so painful to live.'

I did not add that in this, if nothing else, Morjin and I were as brothers.

'And that is what we have always taught,' Abrasax said. 'That in the end, our hearts are free.'

Master Storr nodded his head at this. 'And freely it was that Morjin chose not to unbind the Dark One. The door to Damoom stood almost open. We all *saw* that. Another moment and . . .'

He sighed as he looked up at the sky above the Detheshaloon. If Morjin hadn't seethed with a fury to be lord of all creation, one who was vastly more powerful than he would have destroyed half the universe in pursuit of just such an insane ambition.

'Morjin *could* have won,' I said. 'But in wanting to win so much more than the world, he lost everything.'

I stared across the hill at the small stone marking Morjin's grave. Did he, I wondered, now walk the land of the dead as I had? Did some bright part of him dwell with the infinite splendor beyond death, forever?

Maram, who always sensed so much about me, looked at me and said, 'He lost his soul. But you would have helped him find it again, wouldn't you, Val? With your *heart* of compassion. Though I still don't see how it is possible that you could have loved him.'

'I didn't, Maram – not as I love you,' I told him. 'In truth, I never stopped hating him. But in the end, I *did* see that he and I are not so different from each other, and that is a kind of love.'

I noticed Maram staring at my sword where I had set it down beside me on the grass. I drew the blade from its scabbard then. Alkaladur's silver gelstei, so near the Lightstone, blazed a deep and fiery glorre.

'And in the end,' Maram said, gazing at it, 'you killed him with that sword. As in a way, if I understand things right, you killed a part of Morjin just before the end with that other sword of yours. But I still don't see the connection between the two. Daj said that Kane told you that the two swords are one and the same.'

Maram looked up at Kane as if hoping he might shed more light on this matter. But our mysterious friend stood unmoving and staring at the granite cross above Bemossed's grave as if his bright black eyes could bore through solid stone.

'Kane!' Maram called out to him. 'What did you mean by that?'

There came no answer from this greatest of all swordsmen who would never take up a steel sword again.

'Kane!' Maram said once more.

And then a deep and powerful voice cracked out like a bolt of thunder: 'Do not say that name!'

The one we had called Kane edged into the circle between Estrella and me. The late sun caught his torn diamond armor, and seemed to set it – and him – on fire.

'I am Kalkin!' he shouted out. His hand pointed at Bemossed's gravestone and then swept out around the top of the Owl's Hill. 'Kane died here – and long, long past his time. You will not find his body, but you must bury him all the same.'

He stomped his boot, hard, against the earth. Then he reached out toward Estrella and held his hands over the Lightstone as if warming them before a fire. Without asking my permission, he took my sword from me, though with grace and gentleness, as if he knew that I would not mind.

'*This*,' he said, pointing Alkaladur at the Lightstone, 'Kalkin forged so as to focus the power of *that*. *I* made it so, long ago, as a spectacle focuses light.'

In his hands, my sword's silver gelstei blazed brilliantly – though, in truth, no more so than it had at *my* touch, many times. Kane, or Kalkin, as I must now call him, suddenly gave the sword back to me. He rested his hand on top of Estrella's head, then told us:

'Once, long, *long* ago, from the end of the Ardun Satra through the Valari and Elijin Satras and even into the present great age, the Maitreyas brought the Lightstone to the universe's worlds. Ashvar, we called the first of these Shining Ones, and the first of the ancient Valari to act as the Maitreya's and Lightstone's Guardian was named Adar. The Maitreyas, through the Lightstone, brought illumination to people and helped them overcome their fear of death. And so helped them to walk the path of the angels. Liljana has spoken of how things were meant to unfold. But what *should* have happened, in Eluru, as in other universes, was that men and women would awaken to our purpose as stewards of the earth and heavens. Then, through time, even the dirt beneath our feet would shimmer as through an enchantment and the very stars would come alive.'

Kalkin paused to drink in the Lightstone's radiance through his deep, black eyes. Then he sighed and went on: 'Asangal's fall over-turned the natural order of things. When he became Angra Mainyu, he brought a darkness to match the Maitreya's light. To *overmatch* it, almost – or so I feared for too long. We tried to heal Asangal once, in the time leading to the Battle of Tharharra. We failed. The Amshahs did. Solajin and Set, Varkoth and Varshan and Iojin: all the Galadin, Elijin and Valari led by Ashtoreth and Valoreth. And with them, the Maitreya of that time, Dawud Mansur. Thousands and thousands of years before I made the blade that Valashu holds, we tried to strike the true Alkaladur into Angra Mainyu. Through Dawud, we tried. But Angra Mainyu twisted the Sword of Light into the Fire of Death, and turned it back upon the Amshahs to slay millions.'

Kalkin stood close to Estrella, looking into the golden cup in her hands as if looking down through countless ages, dark and bright. Then Daj asked the question to which I thought my life must prove the answer: 'But so many angels – and a Maitreya! *Why* did they fail?'

'Because,' Kalkin said, 'although most people who stand before the Maitreya and Lightstone are ravished by their radiance, Angra

Mainyu has made himself as impenetrable as stone. And so with Yama and Kadaklan and Zun. And Morjin. These, who will not open themselves to the light, must be pierced by it – straight to the heart. And *that* is why I forged the sword that Valashu holds, to strike Alkaladur true and deep.'

As I raised up my bright sword to the sun, Kalkin told of what had happened here at the top of the Owl's Hill: at a crucial moment in history, millions of beings across the stars – including even the Seven and my companions – had fired the furnaces of their hearts and forged anew the Sword of Love. This great soul force they had passed to Estrella, who gathered it within the infinite golden hollow of the Lightstone and then poured it into me.

'On the day of the battle,' he said, 'Master Matai tells us that the stars and planets perfectly aligned with Ea. But this world had to await another conjunction, too: the Lightstone had to find its way into the hands of the Great Maitreya – and one who could wield the Silver Sword had to find the way to strike Morjin.'

Daj thought about this for a moment, then asked, 'But why couldn't Estrella wield the Lightstone *and* Val's sword? She is the *Maitreya*! If Val found a way to love Morjin, couldn't she?'

'So she could have, lad,' Kalkin said. 'But still she could *not* have wielded Val's sword. It was made for the hands, and heart, of a warrior.'

'But *you* are a warrior! *Kane* was. The greatest warrior who has ever been! Why couldn't he wield the very sword that he had made?'

Kalkin stood gazing down at Morjin's gray headstone. Then he said: 'Because Kane could never have opened his heart to the Red Dragon.'

'But Val could!'

'Yes,' Kalkin said, looking at me. 'Indeed, he could. Val is not the source of the true Alkaladur, but in him the valarda is *strong*. His blood burned the same as Morjin's blood, and so he knew how and where to strike. Too, he is the descendent of Adar, and therefore fated to be a Guardian of the Lightstone. A *true* warrior, of the spirit, and thus far greater than Kane.'

He smiled his old, savage smile, and his white teeth flashed in the sunlight. Then he bowed his head to me and called out: 'He is Valamesh, King of Swords!'

For what seemed a long while, he gazed at me, and my other friends did, too. I listened to the roaring of a lion out on the steppe and the wind whispering through the grasses from out of the west.

421

I stared at the thousands of stones pushing up from the steppe, and I thought: *I am the King of Swords, yes. And I will never have to slay another man again!*

Then our talk turned toward the difficult days that lay ahead of us, in Tria and in lands across Ea. Finally, with the sun melting a golden-red across the far horizon, Liljana stood up and invited us all to eat dinner together. Everyone joined her in making the short journey back down the hill and across the battlefield to my pavilion near the river – almost everyone. For Atara, still sitting next to me, clasped my hand in hers, and asked to remain a few more moments.

'Val,' she said to me when we were alone, 'I am blind now, but I think I was even blinder when I had my vision. I *saw* you kill Morjin a million times! And a million times more, I saw you dead. But never – never! – that you would return to me!'

I pressed my fingers to her wrist, and felt the blood pulsing there. And I told her, 'I *had* to return. Life is . . . so sweet.'

'And so sorrowful, too. I never *knew*, until the terrible, terrible moment after you came back, at the end of the battle, how hard it must have been for you to bear the valarda all these years.'

I touched my lips to her wrist, then said to her, 'But it was a joy, even more. Do you know what it is like to sit beside your beloved and *feel* every sweet and good thing inside?'

'Oh, Val,' she said, pulling my hand up to her mouth to kiss my fingers, 'I *almost* do!'

I looked down at the glowing tents of the armies still encamped by the river. And I said, 'Tomorrow we'll leave for Tria. Who knows what we will find there? Not all the Alonians have acclaimed me, and it might be hard to persuade their countrymen that a Valari should sit on Alonia's throne.'

'You,' she said, squeezing my hand, 'could persuade almost anyone of almost anything.'

'Could I persuade you of what I have dreamed of since the moment I first saw you? The King of Swords, they call me. The king needs a queen.'

'The Queen of Alonia,' she said.

Her face fell grave and bitter. She had always held a troubled love for her father, King Kiritan, and for his people, and she must have wondered if the Alonians really would accept his daughter as their queen.

'Are you suggesting a marriage of *expedience*?' she asked me.

'No – you know I am not,' I told her. And then, 'Only a marriage of the heart.'

'But I can't marry at all, now, no matter what my heart might wish.'

'Why not? A hundred men you set out to slay in battle, and you have fulfilled that vow. You are free.'

'Am I free from *this*?' she said, touching her fingers to the white cloth binding her face.

'Only if you want to be,' I said, resting my fingers there, too. Then I laid my hand on her belly and asked her, 'And what of *this*? What if you are carrying our child?'

'What if I *am*?'

'Have you seen that, Atara? You must have – you saw almost everything.'

'Perhaps I did. But now I can see nothing.'

I tried to feel through her leather armor and the flesh beneath for that tiny seed of life that might be quickening inside her. But no matter what Kalkin had said about the valarda being strong in me, I did not have that power.

'In the Valley of the Sun, you promised to marry me,' I told her. I took out the handkerchief enfolding a single strand of one of her golden hairs, and I pressed it into her palm. 'It is time.'

'Is it, truly?' she asked, squeezing the handkerchief.

'*Will* you marry me?' I asked her again.

Now she pressed her hand on top of mine. She turned her face toward the north, perhaps orienting herself by the warmth of the setting sun's rays upon her cheek. I thought that she must be listening to the wind – and perhaps for a faint pulse of life from within her womb.

'I would *love* to marry you,' she said. 'So much that I almost can't bear it.'

Then she shook her head sadly and added, 'But I just don't know if it really *is* the right time. Let us go to Tria, and we shall see.'

She kissed me then, and fire leaped through me, but we did not lie together as we had before the battle. If she would not marry me, after all, then such ecstasy would all too soon become a torment. But if she *did* consent to be my queen, we would have the rest of our lives to return to our star and dance beneath its light. Until we reached Tria, I would have to content myself with this bright and beautiful hope.

26

Historians would record that on the tenth day of Ashvar in the year 2815 of the Age of the Dragon, the victorious army of King Valamesh entered the City of Light. It should have been a radiant moment of bells ringing and people rejoicing in the streets. But it was not.

The Red Dragon had visited all his fire and wrath upon Ea's oldest human habitation. His soldiers had almost completely razed three quarters of the city, putting to the torch anything constructed of wood. They had used a stonecrusher to shatter granite houses to rubble and great buildings, too: the Tur-Tisander; the Tower of the Morning Star; the Old Sanctuary of the Maitriche Telu; the Hastar Palace; the Sarojin and Eluli Bridges – and many, many other structures. The wall surrounding the city, they had smashed in several places. From the Poru River west, past the once-great Varkoth Gate and then north toward the Manwe Gate, the whole wall lay in ruins. The docks along the river, both its east and west banks, had been reduced to a broken black char. Miraculously, however, one of the greatest works of architecture ever cast up on Ea remained unharmed. The Star Bridge – also called the Golden Band – still spanned the Poru in a single, glorious arch made of living stone. Perhaps Morjin's stonecrusher had no power to pierce to the heart of this marvelous substance, fabricated during the great Age of Law. Or perhaps Morjin, with time pressing at him, had felt himself forced to march from the city before he could wreak his full vengeance upon her.

On the day we entered the city, the foul weather of late autumn moved in over Tria from the Northern Ocean in a mass of gray rain clouds that would block out sight of the sun for days on end. Then too, the Trians would not easily come to welcome a Valari as their High King.

424

King Kiritan had once told me that I might marry Atara when I brought the Lightstone into his hall. This I had once done, but too late for Alonia's great king to give me his daughter's hand, as one of Morjin's creatures had murdered him. Even if King Kiritan had lived, however, he could not have presided over any such union within his hall, for Morjin had reduced the huge Narmada Palace – and all the buildings on its grounds – to broken bits of stone. With some regret and much reluctance, I ordered my army to encamp there, at the top of the highest of Tria's seven hills. The Trians, I reasoned, had become used to casting their gazes in that direction to behold the seat of Alonia's power and glory. It might comfort them to see that Ea's High King, although an outlander from Mesh, had at least restored law and order.

With winter soon coming on, both were badly needed in a place that had fallen nearly into lawlessness. And even more, the Trians – those who hadn't fled the ruins of their city – required food, shelter, clean water and the other necessities of life. Too many of them shivered beneath crude coverings of animal hides draped over blackened poles as their only protection against Ashvar's icy rains. The cries of babies wailed out day and night from these acres of squalid half-tents as their mothers' milk dried up. Long before spring, I feared, many men, women and children would begin starving to death.

'So it must have been in Surrapam after the Hesperuks devastated it,' Maram said to me late in Ashvar as we stood on the scorched grass of the palace grounds looking out over the city. 'I've always regretted having to flee that poor land and leaving the Surrapamers to such a fate.'

I had, too, and so before King Thaddeu had marched away from the Detheshaloon, I had made him promise to send aid to Surrapam to repair a part of the damage wrought by his father's murderous ambition. All Ea's peoples, now, I told Maram, would have to help each other.

Toward that end, I asked Lord Harsha to oversee the rebuilding of Ea's docks. This practical farmer and proud warrior had a great talent for dealing with almost anything of the material world. He sent his quartermasters galloping across the countryside outside the city to locate supplies of lumber. Soon, along both the Poru's muddy banks, the sound of saws tearing through wood ripped out into the cold, wet air. The new quays and docks, smelling of sap and tar, took form and pushed out into the river. Then bilanders and barks and other sailing ships made their way in from the sea and past the rocky island of Damoom to tie up in Tria's new harbor. They came from Delu, the Elyssu, Nedu and even faraway Thalu, and brought with them grain, oil, salt, furs, iron, wood – and a thousand other needful things. King Kurshan, still encamped with his warriors and the other Valari at the heart of the city, nevertheless managed to get word to his kingdom's people that the Lagashuns should send out a small fleet of ships to Tria. That did not prove so grand or impossible a venture as sailing through the waters of the Northern Passage and up to the stars. But the sacks of barley in the holds of the Lagashun ships kept many from starving – and that seemed a miracle enough.

On the darkest day of the year, Atara informed me that she was carrying our child. I wanted to rejoice and call for a thousand bottles of brandy to be emptied in celebration. I wanted to set a date for our wedding, too. But Atara, her voice heavy with sorrow, said to me, 'Let us wait, Val, for winter to end, and then we shall see.'

When Triolet came and spring beckoned, we began to build Tria anew. On a cool, blustery day, Kalkin stood with me on top of the rubble that had once been King Kiritan's palace. He stamped his boot against the pulverized stone and said to me, 'The new city will rise up out of the old. Just as your ancestors built Tria on top of an even more ancient city.'

'But I thought that the Star People founded Tria,' I said to him.

Kalkin's gaze seemed to tear open the ground. 'When Elahad led the Valari here to what he supposed was a virgin world, Ea was already old beyond old, as I've told you. Erathe, we once called it. And if we dug down deeply enough through *this*, we would find the ruins of Trialune.'

He went on to say that it was in Trialune that a great king had ruled the world before he had become the first of the Elijin.

'Build well,' he said, looking up at me. 'Make yourself a city that will be a glory to the earth and stars.'

And build we did. True to his admonition, I called to Tria architects, stonecutters, masons and sculptors from across Alonia, and indeed, the whole world. Once we had the roads repaired, teams of oxen drew forth carts of white and silver granite cut from the quarries to the southwest of the city. As well, ships brought into port cargoes of fine Delian marble, dragonstone from faraway Nedu and the very best Galdan glass, in dozens of colors. Such materials would have sufficed to restore Tria to its former splendor. But I wished for something more, and toward that end, I asked Ymiru for the help of his people.

Late in Triolet, from out of the fastness of the White Mountains, Ymiru summoned forth a host of Ymaniri, who journeyed across the Wendrush bearing iron mallets and chisels and a great knowledge of the art of shaping stone. And making it, as well. For the Frost Giants, as the incredulous Trians thought of these massive, white-furred men, had used purple gelstei to grow the huge crystals that gone into the building of the beautiful Alundil, the City of the Stars. Or rather, the Ymaniri's ancestors had, for they now possessed only a single lilastei, kept in trust by Ymiru. They would need dozens of such to accomplish the great work that I, and Ymiru himself, envisioned.

And so once again, Kalkin shared with Ymiru the ancient lore of the Star People, and Ymiru used his violet stone to create out of dragon ore another, and then fifty of these powerful gelstei. They made as well new firestones. Then the Ymaniri went to work, molding hard stone as they might clay, cutting flame through granite and raising up houses, inns, temples and other buildings. They fabricated sheets and blocks of living stone, in all its shimmering iridescence, and they crystalized out of water pure *shatar*, as clear and hard as quartz. One of the Ymaniri – the Elder named Hramjir – even succeeded in making glisse: a crystal nearly as adamantine as diamond and invisible to the eye. It would be many years before the Ymaniri, along with the Alonians and others who had come to this ruined place, set the last stone and called Tria complete. But by the first day of Ashte, with the fields outside the walls greening, flashes of ruby fire filled the air over the city from the Arwe Gate in the east to the Urwe Gate in the northwest, and its light spilled over the beginnings of new spires, towers and great bridges arching across the Poru River.

All this construction would take a great deal of time, and treasure. Many people paid for Tria's splendor with their sweat, blood and life fire freely given. But I sent gold to Galda in payment for their glass, and so to other kingdoms for other materials. Much of this coin – good, solid Alonian archers, as the shining round disks were called – came from King Kiritan's hoard, divided up by the Narmadas after he had been murdered. That half of the clan led by Javas Narmada surrendered this wealth gladly, while Belur Narmada, who had supported neither Morjin nor myself in the war, made great complaint. But I proclaimed that the Narmadas' treasure belonged to the true Narmada heir, and that was Atara. Furthermore, I told Alonia's great lords that they must all contribute to Tria's rebuilding, and indeed, that of the entire world.

I summoned them to the city late in Ashte. We met on the lawn outside of the new palace rising up from the Hill of Gold, as the Trians called this residence of their most powerful families. I commanded my army to draw up in all their thousands; my warriors' suits of diamond armor glittered beneath the sun in an eye-burning brilliance. Before them, in their finest tunics, embroidered with jewels and gold, stood Count Muar of Iviunn and Duke Malatam of Tarlan, who had both marched with Morjin's Dragon army. And Harkin Kirriland, scion of one of the ancient Five Families, which had ruled Alonia since time immemorial, and Duke Parran of Jerolin. All those who had answered my call to battle gathered there, too: Young Baron Narcavage, Baron Monteer, Javaris Narmada and the Eriades brothers, Julun and Breyonan. They looked uneasily upon their countrymen who had done nothing either to help or hinder Morjin, but preferred to stand back and hope that Morjin's army and mine might destroy each other. The most powerful of these were Belur Narmada and Baron Maruth of the Aquantir. Bringing Alonia's great lords together, I thought, was something like herding tigers, for it had taken a strong sovereign such as King Kiritan to keep them from falling with swords on each other and tearing Alonia apart.

I stood before them, with Atara at my side and my warriors behind us, and I told the lords that the time of war among the Five Families and the various dukedoms and baronies had come to an end. They would spend their wealth rebuilding their kingdom, and not on spears, shields and swords.

'You ask too much!' Count Muar shouted out. He was a thin man with angry green eyes and deadly-looking, like a cobra. 'I must be responsible for Iviunn: many estates were destroyed when the Aquantir fell against us during the war.'

Here he glared at Baron Maruth, whom I thought he would gladly have murdered, if given the chance.

'You *do* ask too much,' Belur Narmada said to me. 'You know nothing of the realm that you would rule.'

'No *Alonian* king,' Old Duke Parran said, tapping his finger against his cleft nose, 'has ever taxed us so!'

For a while I let him, and others, speak out as they would. Then I held up my hand for silence. And I told them: 'It will not be a *king* who taxes you. I shall rule Ea from Tria, but the ordering of Alonia I shall leave to her rightful sovereign. I have called you here today that you might acclaim Atara Ars Narmada.'

428

Atara stood quietly next to me, wearing her lion-skin cloak over a long, formal tunic that did little to hide the great swell of her belly. Although her white blindfold bound her blond hair instead of a crown, I thought that no woman could have looked more of a queen.

'A *woman*, and a blind one at that, to rule Alonia!' Duke Parran called out. 'Never!'

'She is with child,' Belur Narmada said, 'and will be too busy suckling him to bring succor to the realm.'

'And she is half Sarni!' Davinan Hastar observed.

And Count Muar added, looking at me, 'I knelt to *you* on the battlefield, as High King, but I will not kneel to *her* as Alonia's ruler. Choose another!'

Although Atara had spent her first sixteen years at her father's court, none of these lords really knew her. They each thought of themselves as rich, powerful and noble. But Atara, through many battles that they could not imagine, had gained a grace and fire far beyond them.

She stepped forward, and her words rang out strong and clear: 'I will not become your queen for my sake, nor will you kneel to me for your own. But you *will* kneel. Only in this way can we bring peace to Alonia.'

Where Morjin had compelled obedience through a voice that seized the sinews of one's will and filled the soul with terror, Atara evoked a much deeper force, as if she had beheld the shape of the future a million times and none could deny what she had willed with all her flesh and dreams to be. Alkaladur blazed within her, too. So did all her goodness, beauty and devotion to the truth. It was her covenant with life in all its onstreaming inevitability, I thought, that finally took hold of the nobles' hearts and swept them away.

It didn't hurt, of course, that she stood in front of the entire host of the Diamond Warriors. Or that Estrella came out to walk among the nobles, letting them gaze upon the Lightstone. They must have experienced something of Estrella's dazzling hope for the future. And my own. The sword I would always keep bright and shining within myself could tear them open to all the agony of battle, yes, but also to the joy of feeling within themselves a bright flame that could never go out.

And so, in the end, they did kneel to Atara. And then, with a cold clarity of will, but with compassion, too, she told them: 'You are Alonia's greatest lords and enjoy great wealth and repute, and so upon you the burden of bringing justice to our land will be the greatest.'

She turned in the direction of Duke Parran, and to him, she said, 'It is *hard* being taxed, is it not? As *you* have taxed the peasants who work your lands. They give you a three-quarters share of the crops they cultivate for the privilege of living in the hovels that you provide them.'

She told him, and the other lords, that henceforth they would be entitled to only a quarter share as rent and that they must build for their peasants houses of good, clean stone. Furthermore, over a span of years, they must allow these poor people to buy the lands that they worked for their own.

'All Alonians shall be free,' she said to them. 'As *you* shall be free from the burden of oppressing men and women whom you have made almost slaves. But free *for* what? Only to create. It stands written in the *Valkariad*: "They shall make themselves wings of light and fly across the stars."'

Here she paused to lay her hand over her belly, and she said to them: 'My son will never be what he should be until *you* become what you were born to be.'

She went on to tell them that on the site of the destroyed Tur-Tisander she would order a great granite stone to be set into the earth. And on this Victory Spire, as it would be called, the names of those who worked the hardest to remake Alonia would be inscribed.

I could not tell if the assembled lords would strive to attain such an honor with the same zeal they had devoted toward the acquisition of wealth, power and glory. They gazed at their new queen as many now looked toward the future which had come upon the world so suddenly: in fear of the unknown, but with a new hope, too.

Later, after the nobles had gone off and my warriors had stood down, I walked with Atara arm in arm along the edge of what had been the Elu Gardens. Morjin had burned these acres of flowers and trees down to char; now gardeners and others whom Atara could not see worked planting seeds and tending new shoots of gold and green.

Finally, she stopped and said to me, 'It is strange. Our struggles these past years nearly killed us, so many times. And *did* kill you! It has all been so terribly, terribly hard. Battles, though, even the worst, all have an ending. But *this* battle, to create this impossible world we both have dreamed of, will go on for the rest of our lives. And that, in its own way, will be infinitely harder than suffering wounds and risking death.'

'But it will also be a joy,' I said, resting my hand upon her belly. 'And haven't we proved that nothing is impossible?'

She clasped my hand, and pressed it more firmly against her. 'I wish I could believe that, Val. I know only that now I must be a queen, as I was born to be.'

She did not speak of either her blindness or the child growing inside her as a burden, but I felt a great heaviness pulling her down. And I said to her, '*My* queen – and *that* you were born to be as well.'

'Yes, I suppose I was. And I suppose that I shall *have* to marry you now. I won't have such as Count Muar calling our son a bastard.'

At last, we set a date for our wedding: the seventh of Soldru. In my happiness, I swept up Atara in my arms and kissed her deeply. But I, who had struck pure angel fire into the worst of men, could not find the way to drive back the darkness afflicting the woman I loved.

The following afternoon on that same lawn, Lord Avijan – with Lord Tomavar, Lord Harsha, Lord Jessu, Lord Noldashan and all the surviving captains of Mesh – came to me and asked to return to their home.

'Can we not persuade you, Sire,' Lord Avijan asked me, 'to reopen the Elahad castle and rule Ea from your own kingdom?'

I would as soon live inside a dungeon as my family's ancient castle, but I did not admit this to Lord Avijan. Instead, I told him, 'Elahad made his residence in Tria, and long before the Star People came to Ea, so did a very great king. And so I shall, too.'

I added that it made good sense to set my throne here in Tria, as ships could come and go through her harbor and Ea's seas, more easily connecting all lands with each other. And now that Ea's sovereigns had made me High King, I belonged to Ea.

'But, Sire,' Lord Harsha said to me with much sadness, '*we* belong to Mesh. Most of us left wives and children there. I, myself, miss my land and must return to tend my crops.'

'So you must,' I said to him, grasping his arm. 'Go back then, old friend, and plant your barley.'

I told my lords that they could return home after my coronation.

'But what of the other Valari kings and their armies?' Lord Tomavar asked me. 'Will you let them go, too?'

'I will. But from the best of their warriors, as from our own, I will choose knights, a thousand altogether, who wish to remain here as Guardians of the Lightstone.'

'A small enough force,' Lord Avijan said, 'to protect the golden cup – and yourself.'

'I will not need more. And if I do, the Valari will stand ready to march, to the end of the earth.'

'To the end of the stars!' Lord Avijan said.

'Faithful Lord Avijan!' I said, clapping my hand to his shoulder. 'You shall be Regent of Mesh, and your sons after you. Care for our land. I shall return there, when I can.'

Lord Avijan beamed as he bowed to me, for I did not think that he had anticipated such an honor. Lord Tomavar, watching him, might have burned with envy, for he had nearly become Mesh's king and now must defer to his rival. But I had honors to bestow upon him, too.

'Lord Tomavar!' I called to him. 'Of all Mesh's warriors, none fought so fiercely or well at the Detheshaloon as you. If not for you, I think, the battle would have been lost.'

I brought forth my brother's diamond-dusted sharpening stone, which I had passed on to Kane, and Kalkin had given back to me.

'Take this,' I said, handing it to him, 'that you will always keep your sword sharp and bright.'

Then I told everyone gathered there that the soul of Lord Gorvan Tomavar shone more brightly than any steel and that he was the truest of Valari warriors.

'Tomavar the True!' I called out to him.

His long, horsey face broke into a great smile as he bowed to me. 'Thank you, Sire,' he told me. Then he turned to gaze at his wife.

Vareva Tomavar stood beside my lords and captains with a proud sureness, as if she had earned her place among them – as indeed she had. Her raven hair spilled down across the diamond armor that still seemed so strange to see encasing the body of a woman. No spear, arrow or sword, during the battle, had touched her flawless, ivory skin. Her large eyes fixed on Lord Tomavar, with great love, as if she had at last forgiven him for abandoning her to Morjin and challenging me for Mesh's kingship.

'Vareva,' I said to her, 'if not for you and the women you led into battle, our enemy surely would have broken our lines beyond repair. Accept this, in honor of your service to Mesh.'

Then I presented her with a silver ring set with four large, brilliant diamonds: the ring of a Valari lord. She pushed it down onto her finger, in place of the warrior's ring that she had worn into battle.

'Thank you, Sire!' she told me. 'But you have already given me more than I dreamed.'

'Yes?'

'Yes, indeed: Morjin's death and peace for Mesh.'

'That was no more my doing than yours. You fought as hard as anyone.'

'Perhaps,' she said, gazing down at her ring. 'But I am glad that I shall never have to fight another battle.'

She went on to say that now she desired nothing so much as to return home and live happily with her husband.

Lord Tomavar inclined his head in agreement with this. 'I, too, am done with war. I would like to spend the years left to me siring sons worthy of becoming the Lightstone's Guardians. And teaching them to keep sharp not only their swords but their souls.'

He moved up to Vareva, and kissed her full on the lips. It was a shocking thing for a Valari lord to do in sight of his peers, but then Lord Tomavar had always been the most recklessly bold of warriors.

Then Vareva walked over to Behira, standing with my other captains and wearing her diamond armor molded to her rounded belly and full breasts. Most of my men, I thought, would have a hard time perceiving this plump, pretty woman as a warrior. But during the battle she had slain a Hesperuk lord, and now Vareva brought her to me to be acknowledged, too.

'Without Behira,' Vareva said to me, 'I never could have formed our women into a battalion and brought them here. She is as worthy as anyone of being honored.'

I grasped Behira's hand and said, 'Then you shall wear a knight's ring.'

Before I could motion to my ring bearer, however, she shook her head and said to me, 'It is not a *knight's* ring I wish for, Sire.'

She told me that she had only one boon to ask of me: that I would speak to Maram in favor of him marrying her.

'As I recall,' I said to her, 'before we left Mesh, you weren't sure that it was Maram whom you wanted to marry.'

I noticed Joshu Kadar, standing with my Guardians, looking on with an intense interest. I wondered if he still desired to make a wife of Behira, as Lord Harsha had once felt compelled to promise him.

'In truth,' I added, smiling at her, 'you weren't sure that you

433

wanted to marry *anyone*. You said that you wanted to serve me, instead.'

'And I *did* serve you, Sire. And we *did* win the war. And if war is good for anything at all, it is to clear away all our foolishnesses and remind us of what we really desire. And I desire nothing more than to marry Maram.'

Lord Harsha came over to his daughter and wrapped his arm around her back as if to protect her. And his single eye fixed on me. 'You said, Sire, that we should put off the question of Behira's marriage until greater matters were settled. And now they are.'

'Very well,' I told Lord Harsha and Behira, 'then I *shall* speak to Maram.'

Lord Harsha might have simply thanked me and left this matter to my discretion, for I was his king, whom most lords would never have presumed to importune. But Lord Harsha was something like a hound that would not let go a bone once he had taken hold of it. And Maram had evaded him – and Behira – once too often.

'*When* will you speak with him, Sire?' he asked me. 'You have many duties, and Maram has buried himself in that tavern down by the river.'

In truth, I had hardly seen Maram for most of two months. But I knew well enough that he had taken to spending his days – and nights – near the docks at a little stone tavern near the Inn of the Seven Delights.

With the Lords of Mesh looking on to see how I would respond, I said to Lord Harsha: 'We are finished here, and I have no duties now. Why don't we go and pay a visit to Maram?'

I decided to use this as an opportunity for Estrella to take the Lightstone into one of the city's poorest districts, as she already had gone among the refugees in the eastern half of the city. And so I asked Estrella to accompany Lord Harsha, Behira and me – and Vareva and Lord Tomavar, as well – and I commanded the Guardians to saddle their horses. Then I led the way down from the Hill of Gold past Eluli Square and the Battle Arch toward the river. We found Maram's tavern among blocks of old, crumbling buildings that Morjin must have thought too shabby to bother destroying. It would take some time, I thought, before my architects destroyed them themselves and rebuilt new houses here. Most of the Guardians rode or walked with Estrella down the streets as she showed the Lightstone to the poor Trians who came out of their tenements and shelters to marvel at it. But Joshu Kadar and Sar Shivalad went into the tavern ahead of Lord Harsha, Behira and me.

'Val!' Maram cried out as I pushed my way into a room that was all smoke and noise. 'Look! – Morjin left the finest part of Tria untouched! But what are *you* doing here?'

He sat at a wooden table with Ymiru and two of Sajagax's captains, Tringax and Braggod. A couple of hard-looking sailors and a merchant from Galda had joined them.

'It is the King!' a man at one of the other tables cried out. 'It is King Valamesh!'

Every head in the room, almost, inclined toward me. But Maram, looking upon Lord Harsha as he advanced on his table, called out, 'Oh, Lord! Whatever it is you think I've done, I haven't!' Then he turned to take a long pull from the mug of frothy beer sitting on the table before him.

We drew up to the table, and Lord Harsha's hand, by habit, fell upon the hilt of his sword. There was a time when Lord Harsha would have slaughtered Maram in a duel. But that time had passed, for Maram had become one of Ea's greatest warriors. So, in truth, had the time passed even for fighting duels.

'It is just what you *haven't* done that concerns us, Sar Maram,' Lord Harsha said. He let go his sword and waved his hand at the air to shoo away a cloud of smoke, then set his single, dark eye upon Maram. '*When* do you intend to marry my daughter?'

'Ah, soon,' Maram said, looking at Behira, 'very soon.'

'Yes, but *how* soon?'

Maram glanced at me and then back at Behira, and he coughed out, 'Ah, let us say when Val marries Atara.'

He smiled and took another pull of his beer. And I told him, 'That date has been set: the seventh of Soldru.'

'It *has*?' he cried out. He banged his mug down upon the table with such force that a good deal of the amber liquid sloshed out of it. Then he stood up and embraced me, pounding his hand against my back as he cried out, 'At last! At last! Congratulations!'

I smiled as I pulled back from him. 'Shall we say that I will stand with you at your ceremony, and you shall stand with me at mine?'

'Ah, *shall* we say that?' he said, looking at Behira.

And she told him, 'You promised you'd marry me after the war – if any of us survived it.'

'And you swore to me,' I said, looking at him, 'the same thing.'

He fell silent as he gazed down at his beer.

'It is time, Maram.'

'Ah, I suppose it is,' he muttered. Then he turned to Behira again and said, 'But I didn't know if you would still have me.'

'Still *have* you?' she asked him. 'Would a flower have the sun?'

Maram grew quiet again. He looked from Behira to Lord Harsha and then at me. He nodded at Lord Tomavar and Vareva, standing behind us. Then he turned to Braggod, whose long, yellow mustaches gleamed with beer foam, and he sighed out, 'A man can't win all battles, can he?'

He did not, I thought, refer to Braggod's and his ongoing contest to see who could hold the most beer, for Maram always prevailed in this. In truth, I had only seen one man who could outdrink Maram, and that was Ymiru.

'Most women,' Behira said with the heat of anger shading her voice, 'would wish for their beloved to fight battles to *win* them!'

'And so I have,' Maram said. He stood up, and clasped hold of Behira's hand. 'I can see that you don't understand. Ah, I'm not really sure that I do myself. But here it is: all my life, almost, I fought *hard* to take as much pleasure as I could, wherever I could. So that I could know that I was *alive*. And I succeeded – too well, really. I lived, such as few men have, but I did not really *live*. And that is because I have been afraid of the greatest pleasure of all. There came a moment, just after the Dragon had burned away my shield, when I knew that I *had* to marry you, if by some impossible chance I lived to tell you how much I love you.'

'But why *didn't* you just tell me then?'

'Because,' he said, 'love burns infinitely hotter than dragon fire. It's beautiful, yes, but terrible, too. And so I was afraid.'

Behira bowed down her head to kiss Maram's fingers, and she told him, 'You are a prince of Delu who became a Valari knight. And the only man on earth who could have slain that dragon. Don't tell me that such a *warrior* can't win at love!'

They suddenly pulled closer together to kiss each other – and so with the fire of their lips and hearts, they finally sealed their troth to marry. When Maram leaned back to gaze at her, I had never seen him smile with such happiness.

'Let us drink to marriage, then!' he shouted. '*Ours* – and Val's and everyone's!'

As the men at the other tables all looked on, Maram called out for mugs of beer to be set before everyone. I made the first toast, and Lord Harsha the second, and Ymiru the third. It did not take very long for everyone's mug to be emptied.

'Ah, but it's brandy we need!' Maram said, licking his newly-grown mustache. He thumped his hand against his chest. 'Now *there's* a fire that lingers here!'

He went on to lament the shortage of brandy in the city. Then he presented the man sitting next to him: Demarion Arriara, the merchant from Galda. Maram, it seemed, had arranged to buy wine from Demarion's vineyards and have it shipped to Tria.

'I shall build a distillery,' he announced, 'and make the best brandy in the world. Too many times these last years I've gone without it – but never again.'

'And I'll gladly help you drink it!' Ymiru said to him. 'But does that mean that you plan to make Tria your hrome?'

At the look of concern that befell both Behira and Lord Harsha, Maram again thumped his chest and assured them, 'Don't worry: there's more than enough room here for brandy *and* for love! And as for home, we'll have those five hundred acres in Mesh that Val has given us – and other places, too. With the Red Dragon defeated, the whole damn world will be our home!'

Later, that evening, after everyone had returned to the palace grounds, I stood on the new grass alone with Maram looking out at the city's lights.

'I am glad,' I said to him, 'that you and Behira will remain here for at least a part of the year. And the city *is* short of brandy. But I hadn't envisioned you suffering through two quests and twenty battles just to wind up a happily married merchant.'

'What *have* you envisioned, my friend?'

'Your father,' I said, 'will not rule Delu forever. Truly, he will not rule at all if I ask him to abdicate. You could help me there, Maram.'

'I would rather help you *here*.'

'But you could become a king!'

He looked at me and smiled hugely. 'I already am – and have been since the day that you called me your friend.'

My eyes burned into his as I smiled back at him. Then I said, 'But Delu is weak and needs a firmer hand than your father can provide.'

'That is true – but one of my brothers can certainly do better than I.' He pulled at his beard, and added, 'I have no liking to rule anyone, and even less to be ruled.'

'And yet, you would remain with me, who must be *everyone's* king.'

'You never ruled me, Val. You never told me what I must do.'

'But what *will* you do, then, aside from putting brandy in bottles where once you emptied them?'

Again, Maram smiled, and he waved his hand in a great circle out toward the city and the dark world that lay beyond. 'What *won't* I do! I will write poems that will burn in women's and men's hearts for ten thousand years! I will take up the mandolet and play duets with Alphanderry. I will father a dozen sons, and as many daughters – as many children as Behira wishes. I will make journeys: to talk to the Sea People by the great ocean and to walk through Galda's vineyards. And into the Vilds to eat the sacred timana again and marvel at the Timpum. I would look once more upon Jezi Yaga's eyes and even the sky of the Tar Harath. Somewhere, the Librarians who fled Khaisham will build the world's greatest library, and I will spend ten years there reading every book that I can lay my hands upon. I will climb mountains. Perhaps even Alumit, when the Morning Star rises and the whole mountain turns to glorre. And I will go down into Senta's caves to behold the music crystals buried in the earth and to listen to the angels sing. I will take ship and sail again to the Island of the Swans, and beyond, where the heavens light up like . . .'

He spoke on in a similar manner for quite a while. Then he looked deep into my eyes. 'I have lived as no man has ever lived, and now I will love as no man has ever loved – almost no other.'

He clasped my hand in his, and we both smiled. Then I told him: 'Behira will be happy to help you.'

'Yes – even as oil helps fire to burn more brightly,' he said. And then he added, 'But the flame must burn straight and true, like a fire arrow, and for that I will ask the help of Master Juwain and Abrasax.'

'And they will be glad to give it, though *they* might ask difficult things of you.'

'Well, I must make my peace with the Brotherhood. I must finish what I began, when I joined their order.'

'To walk the way of the serpent?'

'To walk to the *stars*, Val. As Kalkin once did. And as some day I will, too, when it comes time for *you* to lead the way.'

He squeezed my hand so hard that I thought my bones might break. Then he laughed and told me, 'I have written another poem, a bit of doggerel, really, but I thought you might like to hear it.'

'I *would* like to hear it, Maram,' I told him.

'All right, then. This is the logical completion to the other verses I wrote when we we looking for the Brotherhood's school. Listen:

The highest man rules all below:
The wheels of light that spin and glow,
The heart and head, ketheric crown:
The mighty snake goes up or down.

It's love that turns the world each day,
Sets stars to shine, makes men of clay,
But in light's aim, desire of dust,
All things do blaze with blessed lust.

And so I praise the thrust of life
To rise beyond the body's strife,
But also women, war, and wine,
For all that is, is all divine.

I am a seventh chakra man
Living out the angels' plan,
My pleasure 'turns where it began;
I am a seventh chakra man.

It was not to be, however, that Maram found his way back to the Brotherhood, for the Great White Brotherhood had ceased to exist. As Abrasax said to me on a cool, cloudy day in early Soldru: 'Over the course of too many years, too many of our schools have been destroyed, and we will not rebuild them. That is, we won't rebuild as before. Our Order had grown *old*, Valashu. Our ways set, as if in stone. But we have entered a new age – the Age of Light! – and so we will need new ways.'

Toward that end, he told me, the Brotherhood would join with the Sisterhood, and what once had been sundered into two far back in the Age of the Mother would again become one. Their new order would be called the Preservers of the Ineffable Flame. As in the ancient times, they would build Temples of Life and Gardens of the Earth. And the Lokilani of Ea's seven Vilds would help them. Together they would take the emerald varistei crystals into all lands, and turn even the deserts green. All the world would be made more fertile and fruitful, and the joining of man and woman would be exalted. People would speak once again with the animals, and sing the grasses and flowers into ever greater life. But in each garden there would grow a great tree toward the sky, reminding women and men that they must reach ever higher, even while keeping themselves rooted in the earth. And on top of each temple, the Brothers and Sisters would build a great spire pointing at the heart of the heavens. As Abrasax also told me: 'We must never forget that it is our destiny to return home to the stars, where we have always been.'

Beneath a low sky showing only a few patches of blue between huge white clouds, Maram, Ymiru and I walked with Abrasax across the grounds of the new temple being built in the eastern city on the ruins of the ancient one. Master Matai and Master Juwain and the others who had called themselves the Seven accompanied us. But now Liljana, and several other Sisters of what had been the Maitriche Telu joined us, too, and these wise men and women as yet had taken no special name for themselves.

We moved slowly among workmen chiseling away at blocks of white granite and sending stone chips and dust out into the air. Others cut stained glass and glisse for the windows, while ten huge Ymaniri worked with their lilastei shaping and growing the huge crystals that would form the substance of the temple. Much of this immense structure had already been set into place, with its six glittering walls made of living stone and its golden domes sweeping up into the sky. I called that a miracle, too. For even in the Great Age of Law, such buildings had taken fifty or a hundred years to complete. But they had not had the Ymaniri to build them.

At the center of the grounds lay an immense ruby crystal, more than two hundred feet in length. It was the greatest red gelstei ever fabricated on Ea, exceeding in every dimension even the powerful crystal that had once surmounted the Star Tower. I did not know by what art the Ymaniri could possibly raise it up and set it in place on top the temple's highest spire.

'Now *this* is a firestone!' Maram said as he paused before it to run his hand along its cool, gleaming surface. 'What flames it will gather inside!'

'What flames will *you* gather inside?' Liljana asked, moving up to him. 'If you come to us to do this work that you say you wish to do?'

'Only the hottest!' Maram said with a smile and waggle of his hips.

'Do not joke about that!' Liljana said, her face as stern as stone. But I could feel her fighting back a smile. 'Abrasax and Master Juwain can help you open what they call the body's chakras, as they offered to once before. But as I told *you* once before, when a woman awakens the Volcano, as Behira will under my guidance, it will take a true man coming alive to his whole being in order to bear such a heat.'

'Ah, a *true* man, you say? Taking to himself a *true* woman in this blaze of passion that you speak of? Are you trying to discourage me?'

Now Liljana did smile, with great kindness and warmth. And she told Maram: 'I'm only trying to prepare you for the sort of marriage that hasn't been seen on Ea since the Age of the Mother, and perhaps not even then.'

'Well, can anyone *really* prepare for marriage?' He smiled again at her, then turned to bow his head to Master Juwain. 'It will be enough that both of you help me as you can. And I can't tell you how grateful I am for that. Over these past years, I've given you a thousand reasons *not* to help me.'

'But ten thousand more,' Master Juwain said, 'that we want to see you happy.'

'Of course we do!' Liljana told him. 'How should you think that we wouldn't do all that we can for one who is like our own son?'

With Abrasax, Ymiru and the others looking on, she leaned forward to kiss Maram, which caused his red face to grow even redder. Then he said to her and Master Juwain: 'And you are like parents to me. My mother is dead and my father would not come to my wedding, even if I wished him to. Will you stand in their place when Behira and I make our vows?'

Liljana looked at Master Juwain as if she could see into his mind without really looking. With one motion, almost, they reached out and took hold of each other's hand. Then they looked at Maram, and almost with a single voice, they said: 'We would be happy to.'

Then they both offered to stand at my wedding, too. As Master Juwain put it to me: 'Now that Tria is on the mend, you deserve to put your own life in order and to be happy, Val.'

As I gazed out at the city in which Atara would soon reign as my queen, I could not find any reason to dispute him. Soon, at last, I would take up my flute and make music again – and for the rest of my life. I would play to the star that Atara and I called our own. I only hoped that, somehow, I could find a way to make Atara happy, too.

27

It was a season of weddings and talk of such even for those who weren't quite ready to make such a union. Joshu Kadar told me that he wished to journey back to Mesh and ask Sarai Garvar to be his wife. With Lord Tanu fallen in battle, he could see no impediment to marrying the woman whom he had never stopped loving, and neither could I. The war had made many widows who would desire new husbands and widowers who mourned their wives, not just in Alonia or the Nine Kingdoms, but all across Ea. If spring could bring new life to the world, then why shouldn't men and women bring a little happiness to each other?

On a bright day in Soldru, in sight of thousands, I married Atara, even as Maram did Behira. Alonia's great nobles gathered to witness the ceremony and bring us gifts. So did Sajagax, who gave Atara and me a great weight of gold and a lesser amount to Maram and Behira. Lord Harsha looked on proudly as his only daughter finally gained her heart's desire. I wished, of course, that my father and mother, and all my family, had lived to share such a triumph with me. But Master Juwain and Liljana stood with me, as they had promised, as did Ymiru, Daj, Estrella and Alphanderry and Kalkin. No man, I thought, could ever have a more devoted or beloved family. They watched with great gladness as I slipped a silver ring around Atara's finger, and so at last made peace between the lines of Aryu and Elahad and rejoined them as one.

Just before midnight on the ides of Marud, Atara gave birth to our son. We named him Elkasar, after my grandfather. Liljana said that he was long and a little too lean, but he seemed possessed of a great health and zest for life, and he grew quickly. His eyes, as Liljana described them to Atara, soon took on a bright, black sheen like those of his father, and his hair grew out almost pure sable. But he had Atara's square, open face and her long hands and her sportive temperament. She took to calling him her 'little lion,' for he roared fiercely when he grew hungry and seemed to eat with a ferocious appetite. And Atara nursed him with great gladness, holding him against her breast and pouring her milk into him. She sang to him in her clear, beautiful voice, and used her fingers to comb back his dark hair, and I thought that I had never seen a mother love a child with such sweetness and fire.

And yet, as the days passed, a deep sadness seized hold of Atara and would not let go. Liljana spoke of the mothers' melancholy which often befell a woman after she had given birth, but this was something different. Atara, warrior that she would always remain, tried to be brave and so she stopped lamenting that she would never lay eyes upon our son, for there seemed no help for her fate. She did all that she could to raise up her spirits: going riding with Sajagax through the Narmada Green in the morning; singing with Alphanderry in the afternoon; lying with me on the grass of the Elu Gardens at night as I called out the names of the stars. She even took the first taste of the first batch of Maram's brandy, though drink of any sort no longer pleased her and she put tooth to food only because she needed to keep up her milk and her strength. I did not know what could done for her. Neither did Liljana or Master Juwain, who had no potions or magic to cure such a malady. Estrella often held the Lightstone near Atara's heart, and seemed sad herself that its radiance failed to touch her.

Toward the end of summer, as Atara grew thinner and ever quieter, I went to Ymiru to speak with him about her, for I thought that he was a man who might understand her, suffering as he did from sudden and deep glooms. His white-furred face knotted in concentration as I described how Atara wanted to stop eating. And then he told me: 'My moods come and go like the storms of the earth herself, and sometimes dark clouds and snow blacken the world, but afterwards, there always be blue skies and the sun shining brightly. But it be something else with Atara. I think her soul be sick. And that be a hrorrible thing, like being sucked down a dark hrole. I want to believe that the Maitreya will find a way to heal her. I suppose we can only wait and hrope.'

Kalkin's advice to me was more succinct, for he told me: 'Give it time.'

Time, as Atara knew, was strange, for sometimes it streaked toward the future like an arrow while too often creeping along more slowly than a tortoise. At certain rare moments, it seemed to stop altogether. The Maitreya, I thought, possessed the gift to make it do so and to touch men and women with eternity, and for that reason laid claim to the Lightstone. But I, as a king, must live in the world and attend to a hundred duties each day, and I could no more hold back events and the seasons' turning than I could the tides of the sea. And so there came a time in early autumn when I had to prepare formally to be acclaimed as Ea's High King.

We held the coronation on the lawn outside of my half-completed palace on the eighth of Valte – exactly a year from the date of the Battle of the Detheshaloon. Kings, nobles and chieftains from every land came to honor me and bear witness to my vows to rule Ea according to the Law of the One and renew their own vows to me. King Thaddeu of Hesperu and King Angand brought me jewels to set in silver: rubies and black opals, sapphires and topaz and sardonyx. The new kings of Galda and Karabuk also presented me with rich gifts, as did King Hanniban and even King Santoval Marshayk, who had miraculously recovered from one of his convenient illnesses to make the journey to Tria. Sajagax gave me even more gold, and great beads of lapis and a magnificently illuminated copy of the *Saganom Elu*. Bajorak bestowed upon me a great bow, worked all in gold and lapis, and a golden arrow tipped with a brilliant sunstone. So it went with King Aryaman of Thalu and King Orunjan of Uskudar and the others. The Valari kings, of course, showered me with diamonds while my friends gave me more personal things.

The greatest gift of all, however, came from Kalkin. I had entrusted him with the great diamond that the Star People had given to me as proof that I had really journeyed from one of Ea's vilds to another world. Once, this perfect jewel had been the centerstone in the crown of Adar, first of the Lightstone's Guardians. And now Kalkin had set it into a new crown: made of silver gelstei which he had newly forged. With the entire Valari host drawn up in their thousands for the last time, their armor sparkling brilliantly in the sun, as the kings of Ea's lands and the Sarni chieftains and my friends all looked on, I stood before Kalkin and he placed the crown upon my head.

'So,' he called out in his rich, deep voice, 'the Age of the Dragon has ended and the Age of Light has begun!'

And upon these words, from the Temple of Life across the river, the great firestone surmounting its highest spire let loose a bolt of lightning that streaked straight up in a blinding incandescence that split open the sky. On and on this beacon would blaze, I thought, until its radiance reached the end of the universe.

'Let all acclaim King Valamesh, High King of Erathe!'

Katura Hastar, long ago, had prophesied that the death of Morjin would be the death of Ea. And so it had been, truly, for after the Detheshaloon, the old world had perished and given birth to the new. Kalkin, by right, had chosen a new name for the world that was really quite old. Erathe, the ground beneath our feet would always remain for him. But many others would come to call it simply 'Earth.'

After that we held a great feast on the palace grounds. A dozen kinds of roasted meats and a hundred good foods were served to the thousands gathered there. Maram supplied the guests with whole rivers of brandy, while Sajagax had ordered barrels of black Sarni beer brought up from the Wendrush. Alphanderry played his mandolet and sang songs of glory, and nearly everyone seemed happy.

Toward dusk, I finally managed to break away from the many people who wished to honor me. I sought out Kalkin, who stood alone by the edge of the Flu Gardens gazing out across the river. The immense gelstei on top of the Temple continued pouring out a fountain of light. Kalkin's bright, black eyes seemed to drink it in as if he would never fear any radiance ever again.

He nodded his head to me, and his beautiful face grew both sad and triumphant, all at once. I sensed some great new thing come alive within him. And he said to me, 'I will leave Erathe soon. In another year, or perhaps ten. But first, I will walk the world, and look upon her mountains and rivers so that I never forget.'

'I know you must go,' I told him, 'though I don't want you to.'

I looked across the lawn where Atara stood holding our son and talking with Master Juwain, Maram, Behira and our other friends. If anyone could assure me that Atara might be brought back to herself, it was Kalkin: the man whose soul had finally been made whole again after ages and ages of time.

'I will miss you,' he said to me. 'But at least I will know that my world and her peoples are safe in your hands.'

I looked at my hand for a moment, then held it out toward Atara. And I said, 'Safe, I can only hope, from the wars that might have been, though not from the atrocities that we failed to help. But I *have* to believe that there is hope for Atara. Can you help me, Kalkin?'

He looked at the diamond set into the front point of my crown, and then down into my eyes. And he said, 'Only the Maitreya can heal her.'

I gazed at Estrella, holding high the Lightstone, and said, 'But she has failed.'

Now Kalkin's voice fell deep and strange as he asked me: 'Has she failed, Valashu? Or have you?'

'I? I don't know what you mean.'

'Yes, you do – and you have known it since the Detheshaloon.'

I wanted to shake my head violently at this, but I was afraid my new crown would go flying off my head.

'Don't tell me,' he said to me, 'that since then you haven't thought long and deep of the verses that you first heard in the amphitheater from the Urudjin. Recite them for me now!'

I knew exactly which verses he meant; they told of the Amshahs' failure to heal Angra Mainyu and the hope that yet someday they might. Because I could no more refuse Kalkin than I would wish for Joshu Kadar to disregard me, I spoke the verses out into the cool twilight air:

> And though the dark was not undone
> A light within the darkness hides;
> While Star-Home turns around its sun
> The Sword of Light, and Love, abides.
>
> Alkaladur! Alkaladur!
> The Sword of Fate, the Sword of Sight,
> Which men have named Deliverer
> Awaits the promised Lord of Light.

'And that,' I told him, 'is Estrella!'

'But it was *you* who wielded Alkaladur!' He reached out to touch the hilt of the sword strapped to my side. 'Why do think that Morjin failed to seize control of this?'

'Because the Lightstone has no power over the silver gelstei.'

'The Lightstone has power over *everything*!' He lifted his hand off my sword, then pressed it to my chest. 'And here it abides.'

I couldn't help remembering the famous words from the *Beginnings*: *The Lightstone is the perfect jewel inside the lotus found inside the human heart.*

'And you,' he told me, 'are King Valamesh, the King of Swords – *and* the Lord of Light!'

446

I shook my head at this. 'No, I am a Valari, and we are never Lords of Light! The Urudjin confirmed that, too. You told me so yourself, and berated me for ever supposing that I might be the Maitreya!'

He fell silent as he stared at me; he seemed to be looking through the centers of my eyes to the end of the universe.

'Kane told you that,' he finally said to me. 'But he did not know. Not even Kalkin knew, not really, until this night.'

Again, I shook my head. 'But Kane could not have been so wrong! Neither could the Urudjin!'

'No, they could not have been *so* wrong. And they weren't: as regards the ages that have passed. But in the Age of Light, *all* will become as Maitreyas.'

'No,' I said, turning my head back and forth, 'it cannot be!'

Kalkin nodded at Estrella. 'She tried, a hundred times, to show you yourself. But you would not look.'

'Because there is nothing to see!'

'No, that is not why. There is something that you dread more than once you did death.'

Beneath his fierce gaze, I stood up as straight as I could, until I imagined the points of my crown pushed up against the very heavens. And so I tried to pretend that there was nothing I still feared.

'During the battle,' he said to me, 'you saw just how like Morjin you truly are. And so you think that the Maitreya could not be touched with such evil.'

'She could not!' I said, motioning toward Estrella.

Kalkin's large, hard hand reached out to seize hold of mine. And he told me: 'We are all born of the same mother. And for all of us, acting in the world, it is not possible to be wholly good. You know this, in your heart. And it is there that you must fight your last battle.'

Then he told me, not in words, but in the fire of his eyes, what my heart knew to be true: that I feared in being less than perfect I would become sullied and broken and wholly evil, and thus lose all restraint and fall as far as Morjin and Angra Mainyu had. And so I would kill my soul.

His hand pressed against mine, and his eyes caught up the shimmer of the evening's first stars as he said to me: 'But at the heart of everything there is only one Light, and it can never die.'

'No, perhaps not,' I said to him. 'But men and women can. And men can do such terrible deeds . . . so easily.'

447

'So they can,' he said to me. 'But so they also can find the strength to do such marvelous things.'

I felt an infinite and indestructible force coursing deep within his hand. It seemed unstoppable, too, like the bright rising of the sun after a long, dark night.

I looked at him and said, 'Why couldn't *you* have put your sword into Morjin? Why couldn't *Kane*? He was a thousand times stronger than I.'

'Because,' he said to me, 'slaying Morjin was *your* fate.'

'Yes,' I said, glancing at Estrella, 'I slew an angel to save the Maitreya. I did evil in a good cause like any tyrant.'

'No – you slew a beast to save a little girl. You did what you had to do, like any true man.'

We stood there on the lawn in sight of many thousands, gripping each other's hand and searching out the truth in each other's eyes. And then, in a low, deep voice, he said to me: 'A *true* man, Valashu. A king of kings. A greathearted being who, in the end, came to have the highest regard for his enemy. How could such a man deny who he really is?'

And then he added:

> With his heart of compassion
> He knew himself
> Like unto a star . . .

No, I thought, *it could not be possible!*

How could I accept the truth of what he had told me? What if he was mistaken? The Elijin, after all, made errors just the same as other men.

Then he looked up along the fiery beacon still shooting up through the sky. And he said to me, 'The Galadin are waiting to welcome you, Valashu. As they are all of Erathe's peoples.'

I looked at him deeply. Who, I wondered, was my fierce and flawed friend to speak for the Galadin?

He smiled as he let go of me, then held out his hand before me. I looked down at his open palm. There, one moment, it held nothing more substantial than air. And in the next, I saw a small golden object gleaming next to his skin. It was a timana, and I did not know how Kalkin had come by one of these sacred fruits. But I felt certain that his summoning of it had not been a trick of legerdemain but a much deeper magic.

'Take this,' he told me.

Maram, looking on from across the grass, called out, 'Do I see what I *think* I see?'

He led my other friends over to us with an easy assurance that I would always welcome his company. Then he touched his finger to the golden fruit and said, 'It *is* a timana!'

And Ymiru said, 'That be a pretty thing – almost too pretty to eat.'

'How did you obtain it?' Master Juwain asked Kalkin. 'I did not think the trees that the Lokilani planted could bear fruit so soon.'

But my mysterious friend did not answer him. He produced another timana, and then another and yet others, and gave one to each of my friends, even to Daj and Estrella who had now come of age to eat the flesh of the angels.

'Thank you, Lord Elijin,' Lord Harsha said, holding up his timana before his gleaming eye.

Alphanderry, cupping his timana lightly in his fingers, looked at Kalkin as if seeing him for the first time. Then he spoke out in his beautiful minstrel's voice, which also rang with the much deeper tones of those who had sent this strange being to earth: 'You are mistaken, Lord Harsha. This one is no longer of the Elijik Order.'

Lord Harsha gazed at Kalkin in wonderment, as did we all. I did not know what my friends saw then. But I suddenly perceived Kalkin as I imagined that Abrasax could: a great angel whose substance and soul poured forth bright flames of purest glorre. They encompassed him like a robe of fire, yes, but even more like a luminous cloak billowed out by the wind. Valari kings wore diamonds, as I did in the great gleaming stone set into the circle of silustria that Kalkin had given me. But he stood crowned in starlight and bearing bright jewels of grace and goodness shining upon his soul. A vast wisdom blazed within his eyes.

'Three times,' Alphanderry said to him, 'you surrendered the Lightstone to an heir of Adar where you might have tried to keep it for yourself. And now the Elahad guards it for the Shining One, and we have come to the ending of the ages, when all shall be restored. And so it has finally come time for the last to become the first.'

Kalkin bowed his head to Alphanderry, and the splendor of Aras, Varshara, Solaru and all the heavens' brightest stars seemed to gather in his countenance. Then he looked at Estrella, and told me, 'The Lightstone is to be kept by her. But its light belongs to everyone.'

Estrella smiled at me as if I could no longer refuse to see the bright being that she had tried for so long to show me. A soft radiance

449

streamed out of the golden cup in her hand and warmed my heart. I felt it all sweet and good inside me, and I knew that I held the power to say yes or no to the terrible beauty of life – and to myself. And so I held within myself another power as well.

'Atara,' I said, stepping over to her. She stood cradling our young son in her arms and turning her head left and right as if seeking for the source of my voice. 'Atara, Atara.'

I moved up close enough that I could feel her breath upon my face. Then I laid my hands over the white cloth binding her. All that was within me came pouring out in a bright blaze that warmed my hands. I felt it filling up the hollows where her eyes had once been. Then suddenly, with a murmur of astonishment, Atara gave me our son to hold. Her fingers, always so sure and steady even in the most desperate of battles, trembled as she worked to pull off her blindfold. Now it came my turn to cry out in wonder – and in delight. For Atara gazed straight at me through a pair of perfect eyes, all beautiful and blue and sparkling like diamonds, just as I had remembered them to be.

'Val!' she cried out to me. She worked her fingers across her eyelids, pressing almost frantically, as if only by touch could she confirm the impossible thing that had happened to her. 'I can see . . . so much!'

She laughed as she clapped her hands to the sides of my face, then looked deep into my eyes. She kissed me. She turned to smile at Estrella, and at Kalkin, and our other friends, and then laughed again as she saw Maram gripping Behira's hand. Her gaze drank in the thousands of people gathered on the lawn and its many bubbling fountains. She stared out, across the river where the ruby beacon continued streaking out from the firestone that Kalkin and Ymiru had made. Buildings constructed of living stone and stained glass cast their colors at each other in a brilliance that lit up the whole city. Tria's many new towers and spires, pointing up toward the heavens, caught the radiance of the stars, now coming out in all their millions from within the depths of the blue-black sky. But the greatest of all glories resided here, on the lawn in front of the new palace where Atara stood shaking her head in awe.

'He *does* have your eyes!' she called out to me.

She took back our son from me, and laid his head in the crook of her arm, and stood smiling down at him.

'Oh, Val!' she cried out. 'He is so *beautiful*!'

She kept looking at him as if she couldn't quite believe in such a miracle, looking and looking and laughing with a happiness that almost hurt to hear. And the new bit of life that was Elkasar Elahad looked up at her. And in the meeting of their eyes, mother and child, life reached out to life in all its glory, anguish, hope and love.

'Elkasar,' she sang out to him, running her fingers through his dark soft hair. Her joy was boundless. 'Elkasar, my little lion, my bright, beautiful star.'

She began weeping then, weeping and laughing and singing to our son, all at once. Her tears fell down and moistened his face. I watched as the corners of his mouth twitched and then pulled up into his first smile. Then tears welled up from his eyes, too, for he could no more withstand the force of Atara's love than I could – or Estrella, Daj, Maram or any of my friends. Even the man I had once called Kane blinked against the water filling his dark eyes, and that astonished me, for I had thought that his kind could not be touched by such things.

After that we all ate the fruits that Kalkin had given us. And I took Atara's hand and told her, 'There is something I must show you.'

I led the way down from the lawn and into the Elu Gardens. We walked among its many flowers and new trees, which had taken ten years of growth in a single season. A small, brown-skinned man named Danali, whom we had met in the first of the Vilds, appeared as if by magic from behind the oaks and elms. He held a bright emerald crystal in his hand; Elan, Iolana and other Lokilani who came forth to greet Atara also each kept one of the green gelstei. Atara seemed amazed at their presence here, for although she and I had rested among the garden's flowers nearly every night since the spring, the Lokilani had remained hidden from her, as indeed they had from most people.

After I had told Danali why we had come here, he called out: 'Come, come, Queen Atara! Let us go deeper into the trees!'

We all walked down the stone-lined path that wound around a patch of lilies and a small hill sparkling with starflowers. And there, at the center of the garden, grew a single tree. It was a new astor, with silver bark and leaves of gold: the first that the Lokilani had planted outside of their magic wood. Although still too young to bear fruit, the whole of it – bark, branches and leaves – shone with a soft light that spilled out into the garden.

'Val!' Atara cried out, hurrying over to it. 'Why didn't you tell me the Lokilani had come to Tria and had managed to grow an astor here?'

I moved over to her side, and said to her, 'I wanted you to see . . . for yourself.'

She stood beneath this beautiful tree, holding up our son to show him all the wonder of the world. The astor's radiance filled his bright, black eyes.

'But how is this possible?' Atara asked Danali. 'I thought astors only grew in the Forest and other enchanted places.'

Danali proudly swept his hand around the garden and said, 'But the Forest is *here*! Finally, finally here, as it will now come to all the earth! There is only *one* Forest, as we once told you.'

We all gazed at the growing trees and plants around us. Bursts of blue-eyed daisies, goldenrod, trillium and sunflowers brightened the evening. The sweet smell of life filled the air. Then Ymiru, standing nearly as tall as the trees, suddenly laughed out in a voice as deep as thunder: 'This be a *hroly* place! The Timpum have come here, too! I know you told me that they lived in such woods, but I almost thought that they must be a hroax!'

But the bright beings that everywhere lit up the garden were neither hoax nor hallucination but only the realest and loveliest of luminosities. They seemed to have faces, of a sort, playful or compassionate, as Flick had once had, and to speak in quick flashes the language of the angels. They touched the trees with white and silver sparks and filaments of fire. The whole garden glimmered with a living light. Alphanderry, too, stood staring out past the astor in wonder. In looking upon the Timpum in all their shimmering millions, he seemed for a single moment almost transparent to the deeper radiance that formed him.

'And now the Ellama will come here, too,' Danali said to me, 'just as Pualani once told you. And the Galad a'Din will walk the earth again!'

He paused to gaze at Kalkin, who gazed right back at him. And then he added, 'Soon, soon, they will come – go out on the grasses and see!'

And Alphanderry said to him, 'Will you come with us?'

'No – we will wait here, with the Timpum.'

I smiled at this, for the Lokilani had been waiting thousands of years for the beings they called the Bright Ones to return to their woods.

Because Atara wanted to find Sajagax and look upon his face, too, we said goodbye to Danali and went back up to the lawn. There we rejoined Joshu Kadar and Sar Shivalad and other Guardians of the Lightstone, who always fell a little anxious when

Estrella and I walked away from the protection of their swords for too long. Word of what had happened with Atara spread quickly across the palace grounds. Sajagax came limping up to us, accompanied by Tringax, Braggod and Bajorak, and Sonjah and Aieela and a few other women who had once called themselves the Manslayers. King Mohan and King Waray – and the other Valari sovereigns – pressed up to us as well. So did Abrasax and Master Matai and many others.

'Look!' Sonjah called out, smiling at Atara. 'The *imakla* one has been healed!'

From farther out in the throngs surrounding us, a blond-haired giant from Thalu added, 'The Maitreya has healed the blind Queen!'

A thousand men and women, it seemed, turned toward Estrella to look upon her and the Lightstone. Neither I, nor any of my friends, corrected this man, for in truth I could have done nothing to help Atara if Estrella hadn't helped me.

It was Sonjah who asked Atara the question that many must have wondered at: 'But, my dear one, can you still *see* the faraway things as you once did?'

Atara hesitated only a moment as a darkness clouded her eyes, and I wondered if she thought of Angra Mainyu, still bound on Damoom. But then she hugged Elkasar against her breasts and smiled brightly, and she said, 'I don't have to be a scryer to see what *everyone* can now see: that the future will be such a happy one. So beautifully, beautifully happy.'

After that, almost everyone seemed to want come up close in order to speak with Atara. And to celebrate the miracle of the restoration of her eyes. Maram saw to the distribution of hundreds of glasses of brandy and the speaking of toasts. Alphanderry played his mandolet, making a lovely music. He seemed to direct his words at Atara and Elkasar as he called out into the night: *We are songs that sing the world into life.*

And as he sang, his voice built higher and deeper and ever brighter. No bell could have sounded out with a purer or more perfect tone. It pealed like struck silver, and moved the air with its power. Then, as from far away, a ringing filled the sky. It seemed that the wind was singing back to him with a much vaster sound. It held something of the low, mournful melodies of the great whales and of the eagle's cry as well. Louder and louder it grew until it set the stones of the palace to vibrating and shook the very earth.

'It be Alumit!' Ymiru cried out. 'It be the hroly mountain!'

I did not know how he could have known such a thing. Or how

the great crystal mountain, the highest on earth, could have come suddenly alive with a ringing that carried hundreds of miles across the world to our land, and perhaps into others. Did the fishermen in Galda, I wondered, turn their heads to look for the source of this sound? Did the Lost Valari on the Island of Swans, who did not know war, hear this deep calling? Did the Avari, who knew too much? All the men and women around me stood listening as if struck to their core. Many of them, later, would speak of a rising wind that rang with sacred songs and the voices of grandmothers and great-grandfathers who had long since passed on.

And then, even as Estrella held the Lightstone above her head, thousands of points of light began piercing the inky blueness along the eastern horizon. All at once, the whole of the sky from east to west lit up with a vivid glorre.

'The Star People are coming!' Daj cried out, pointing upward.

'They *do* come!' Ymiru said, looking up, too. 'At last, they come hrome!'

We of the earth had been waiting eighteen thousand years for the Bright Ones to return, but we had not been able to open the door in order to welcome them.

'So,' Kalkin said, smiling up at the sky. 'So.'

We all watched as the points of light grew bigger and brighter; each one opened out like a luminous flower falling down to earth. They drew closer and closer until they floated down toward the bridges and buildings of the city. Now each dazzling sphere seemed more like a dolphin cutting the surf along the crest of a wave, only instead of gleaming with water, they blazed with a flame that opened the sky and moved back the air. I thought I could perceive, at the centers of these thousands of bursts of angel fire, radiant beings who looked much like Valari: men and women of the Star People, and Elijin led by the beautiful Ondin, and even the Galadin themselves.

'Look, Val!' Atara said to me, pointing her finger like an arrow up toward the deepest part of the sky. 'Do you see the star?'

I saw the star. I did not know how that could be possible. Against a shimmer of pure glorre, it flared more brilliantly than any other light in all the heavens, even Aras and Solaru. I knew that Atara must have descried it in the same moment that she had Estrella on the battlefield, but only now could be certain that what she had beheld then would actually come to be.

I listened as Atara told our son that someday he would journey out into the stars. He would bear a great sword, and guard Estrella and the Lightstone. He would fight the same battle that his father had, and so the Dark Angel, Angra Mainyu, would at last be defeated. And healed. And then Asangal, whole once again, would gladly find his ending as the greatest of the Galadin. The ending that was only a beginning: for out of the incandescence of his being would blaze a whole new universe, the light of which Atara and I now perceived as the brightest of stars.

'Oh, Val!' Atara said, pressing closer to me. 'My love, my life, my beautiful, beautiful king! – we really *did* win!'

I did not know how Atara and I – and Kalkin and Maram and Estrella and everyone else who had fought along with us – had brought into being this impossible world illumed by such a perfect light. And yet we had. Some would call it a miracle, and others fate. My grandfather would have said that a few valorous warriors had made their own fate, and that of the earth and the stars that shone down upon it. Through our blood and tears, we had done this great thing, through the risk of our lives and our hopes and our songs and our deepest dreams.

And so on a perfect autumn evening I stood on a lawn on top of the highest hill of the earth's greatest city, looking up at the sky and dreaming, along with the woman I loved and my son and my friends – and the many thousands of warriors who had fought to make me a king. Millions of lights brightened the heavens. I found my grandfather's star among them and whispered to him, in fire and in love, that the promise of life had been fulfilled. And one day, I told him, when his great-grandson had grown to be a man, we would venture out past the Great Bear and the Dragon and the other constellations to the bright heart of creation. Always as warriors, yes, but as angels, too, born of fire, burning for life and forever blazing like beautiful stars.

APPENDICES

Heraldry

THE NINE KINGDOMS

The shield and surcoat arms of the warriors of the Nine Kingdoms differ from those of the other lands in two respects. First, they tend to be simpler, with a single, bold charge emblazoned on a field of a single color. Second, every fighting man, from the simple warrior up through the ranks of knight, master and lord to the king himself, is entitled to bear the arms of his line.

There is no mark or insignia of service to any lord save the king. Loyalty to one's ruling king is displayed on shield borders as a field matching the color of the king's field, and a repeating motif of the king's charge. Thus, for instance, every fighting man of Ishka, from warrior to lord, will display a red shield border with white bears surrounding whatever arms have been passed down to him. With the exception of the lords of Anjo, only the kings and the royal families of the Nine Kingdoms bear unbordered shields and surcoats.

In Anjo, although a king in name still rules in Jathay, the lords of the other regions have broken away from his rule to assert their own sovereignty. Thus, for instance, Baron Yashur of Vishal bears a shield of simple green emblazoned with a white crescent moon without bordure as if he were already a king or aspiring to be one.

Once there was a time when all Valari kings bore the seven stars of the Swan Constellation on their shields as a reminder of the Elijin and Galadin to whom they owed allegiance. But by the time of the Second Lightstone Quest, only the House of Elahad has as part of its emblem the seven silver stars.

In the heraldry of the Nine Kingdoms, white and silver are used interchangeably as are silver and gold. Marks of cadence – those smaller charges that distinguish individual members of a line, house or family – are usually placed at the point of the shield.

Mesh

House of Elahad – a black field; a silver-white swan with spread wings gazes upon the seven silver-white stars of the Swan constellation

Lord Harsha – a blue field; gold lion rampant filling nearly all of it

Lord Tomavar – white field; black tower

Lord Tanu – white field; black, double-headed eagle

Lord Raasharu – gold field; blue rose

Lord Navaru – blue field; gold sunburst

Lord Juluval – gold field; three red roses

Lord Durrivar – red field; white bull

Lord Arshan – white field; three blue stars

Ishka

King Hadaru Aradar – red field; great white bear

Lord Mestivan – gold field; black dragon

Lord Nadhru – green field; three white swords, points touching upwards

Lord Solhtar – red field; gold sunburst

Uruk

King Mohan – gold field; blue horse

Lagash

King Kurshan – blue field; white Tree of Life

Waas

King Sandarkan – black field; two crossed silver swords

Taron

King Waray – red field; white winged horse

Kaash

King Talanu Solaru – blue field; white snow tiger

Anjo

King Danashu – blue field; gold dragon

Duke Gorador Shurvar of Daksh – white field; red heart

Duke Rezu of Rajak – white field; green falcon
Duke Barwan of Adar – blue field; white candle
Baron Yashur of Vishal – green field; white crescent moon
Count Rodru Narvu of Yarvanu – white field; two green lions
   rampant
Count Atanu Tuval of Onkar – white field; red maple leaf
Baron Yuval of Natesh – black field; golden flute

FREE KINGDOMS

As in the Nine Kingdoms, the bordure pattern is that of the field
and charge of the ruling king. But in the Free Kingdoms, only
nobles and knights are permitted to display arms on their shields
and surcoats. Common soldiers wear two badges: the first, usually
on their right arm, displaying the emblems of their kings, and the
second, worn on their left arm, displaying those of whatever baron,
duke or knight to whom they have sworn allegiance.

In the houses of Free Kingdoms, excepting the ancient Five
Families of Tria from whom Alonia has drawn most of her kings,
the heraldry tends toward more complicated and geometric patterns
than in the Nine Kingdoms.

Alonia

House of Narmada – blue field; gold caduceus
House of Eriades – Field divided per bend; blue upper, white lower;
   white star on blue, blue star on white
House of Kirriland – White field; black raven
House of Hastar – Black field; two gold lions rampant
House of Marshan – white field; red star inside black circle
Baron Narcavage of Arngin – white field; red bend; black oak lower;
   black eagle upper
Baron Maruth of Aquantir – green field; gold cross; two gold arrows
   on each quadrant
Duke Ashvar of Raanan – gold field; repeating pattern of black swords
Baron Monteer of Iviendenhall – white and black checkered shield
Count Muar of Iviunn – black field; white cross of Ashtoreth
Duke Malatam of Tarlan – white field; black saltire; repeating red
   roses on white quadrants

Eanna

King Hanniban Dujar – gold field; red cross; blue lions rampant on
each gold quadrant

Surrapam

King Kaiman – red field; white saltire; blue star at center

Thalu

King Aryaman – Black and white gyronny; white swords on four black sectors

Delu

King Santoval Marshayk – green field; two gold rampant lions facing each other

The Elyssu

King Theodor Jardan – blue field; repeating breaching silver dolphins

Nedu

King Tal – blue field; gold cross; gold eagle volant on each blue quadrant

THE DRAGON KINGDOMS

With one exception, in these lands, only Morjin himself bears his own arms: a great, red dragon on a gold field. Kings who have sworn fealty to him – King Orunjan, King Arsu, King Mansul – have been forced to surrender their ancient arms and display a somewhat smaller red dragon on their shields and surcoats. Kallimun priests who have been appointed to kingship or who have conquered realms in Morjin's name – King Mansul, King Yarkul, Count Ulanu – also display this emblem but are proud to do so.

Nobles serving these kings bear slightly smaller dragons, and the knights serving them bear yet smaller ones. Common soldiers wear a yellow livery displaying a repeating pattern of very small red dragons.

King Angand of Sunguru, as an ally of Morjin, bears his family's arms as does any free king.

The kings of Hesperu and Uskudar have been allowed to retain their family crests as a mark of their kingship, though they have surrendered their arms.

Sunguru

King Angand – blue field; white heart with wings

Uskudar

King Orunjan – gold field; $^3/_4$ red dragon

Karabuk

King Mansul – gold field; $^3/_4$ red dragon

Hesperu

King Arsu – gold field; $^3/_4$ red dragon

Galda

King Yarkul – gold field; $^3/_4$ red dragon

Yarkona

Count Ulanu – gold field; $^1/_2$ red dragon

The Gelstei

THE GOLD

The history of the gold gelstei, called the Lightstone, is shrouded in mystery. Most people believe the legend of Elahad: that this Valari king of the Star People made the Lightstone and brought it to earth. Some of the Brotherhoods, however, teach that the Elijin or the Galadin made the Lightstone. Some teach that the mythical Ieldra, who are like gods, made the Lightstone millions of years earlier. A few hold that the Lightstone may be a transcendental, increate object from before the beginning of time, and as such, much as the One or the universe itself, has always existed and always will. Also, there are people who believe that this golden cup, the greatest of the gelstei, was made in Ea during the great Age of Law.

The Lightstone is the image of solar light, the sun, and hence of divine intelligence. It is made into the shape of a plain golden cup because 'it holds the whole universe inside'. Upon being activated by a powerful enough being, the gold begins to turn clear like a crystal and to radiate light like the sun. As it connects with the infinite power of the universe, the One, it radiates light like that of ten thousand suns. Ultimately, its light is pure, clear and infinite – the light of pure consciousness. The light inside light, the light inside all things that *is* all things. The Lightstone quickens consciousness in itself, the power of consciousness to enfold itself and form up as matter and thus evolve into infinite possibilities. It enables certain human beings to channel and magnify this power. Its power is infinitely greater than that of the red gelstei, the firestones. Indeed, the Lightstone gives power over all the other gelstei, the green, purple, blue and white, the black and the silver – and potentially over all matter, energy, space and time. The final secret of the Lightstone is that, as the very consciousness and substance of the universe itself, it is found within each human being, interwoven and interfused with each separate soul. To quote from the *Saganom Elu*, it is 'the perfect jewel within the lotus found inside the human heart'.

The Lightstone has many specific powers, and each person finds in it a reflection of himself. Those seeking healing are healed. In some, it recalls their true nature and origins as Star People; others, in their lust for immortality, find only the hell of endless life. Some – such as Morjin or Angra Mainyu – it blinds with its terrible and beautiful light. Its potential to be misused by such maddened beings is vast: ultimately it has the power to blow up the sun and destroy the stars, perhaps the whole universe itself.

Used properly, the Lightstone can quicken the evolution of all beings. In its light, Star People may transcend to their higher angelic natures while angels evolve into archangels. And the Galadin themselves, in the act of creation only, may use the Lightstone to create whole new universes.

The Lightstone is activated at once by individual consciousness, the collective unconscious and the energies of the stars. It also becomes somewhat active at certain key times, such as when the Seven Sisters are rising in the sky. Its most transcendental powers manifest when it is in the presence of an enlightened being and/or when the earth enters the Golden Band.

It is not known if there are many Lightstones throughout the universe, or only one that somehow appears at the same time in different places. One of the greatest mysteries of the Lightstone is that on Ea, only a human man, woman or child can use it for its best and highest purpose: to bring the sacred light to others and awaken each being to his angelic nature. Neither the Elijin nor the Galadin, the archangels, possess this special resonance. And only a very few of the Star People do.

These rare beings are the Maitreyas who come forth every few millennia or so to share their enlightenment with the world. They have cast off all illusion and apprehend the One in all things and all things as manifestations of the One. Thus they are the deadly enemies of Morjin and the Dark Angel, and other Lords of the Lie.

The Greater Gelstei

THE SILVER

The silver gelstei is made of a marvelous substance called silustria. The crystal resembles pure silver, but is brighter, reflecting even more light. Depending on how forged, the silver gelstei can be much harder than diamond.

The silver gelstei is the stone of reflection, and thus of the soul, for the soul is that part of man that reflects the light of the universe. The silver reflects and magnifies the powers of the soul, including, in its lower emanations, those of mind: logic, deduction, calculation, awareness, ordinary memory, judgment and insight. It can confer upon those who wield it holistic vision: the ability to see whole patterns and reach astonishing conclusions from only a few details or clues. Its higher emanations allow one to see how the individual soul must align itself with the universal soul to achieve the unfolding of fate.

In its reflective qualities, the silver gelstei may be used as a shield against various energies: vital, mental, or physical. In other ages, it has been shaped into arms and armor, such as swords, mail shirts and actual shields. Although not giving power *over* another, in body or in mind, the silver can be used to quicken the working of another's mind, and is thus a great pedagogical tool leading to knowledge and laying bare truth. A sword made of silver gelstei can cut through all things physical as the mind cuts through ignorance and darkness.

In its fundamental composition, the silver is very much like the gold gelstei, and is one of the two noble stones.

THE WHITE

These stones are called the white, but in appearance are usually clear, like diamonds. During the Age of Law, many of them were cast into the form of crystal balls to be used by scryers, and are thus often called 'scryers' spheres'.

These are the stones of far-seeing: of perceiving events distant in either space or time. They are sometimes used by remembrancers to uncover the secrets of the past. The kristei, as they are called, have helped the master healers of the Brotherhoods read the auras of the sick that they might be brought back to strength and health.

THE BLUE

The blue gelstei, or blestei, have been fabricated on Ea at least as far back as the Age of the Mother. These crystals range in color from a deep cobalt to a bright, lapis blue. They have been cast into many forms: amulets, cups, figurines, rings and others.

The blue gelstei quicken and deepen all kinds of knowing and communication. They are an aid to mindspeakers and truthsayers, and confer a greater sensitivity to music, poetry, painting, languages and dreams.

THE GREEN

Other than the Lightstone itself, these are the oldest of the gelstei. Many books of the *Saganom Elu* tell of how the Star People brought twelve of the green stones with them to Ea. The varistei look like beautiful emeralds; they are usually cast – or grown – in the shape of baguettes or astragals, and range in size from that of a pin or bead to great jewels nearly a foot in length.

The green gelstei resonate with the vital fires of plants and animals, and of the earth. They are the stones of healing and can be used to quicken and strengthen life and lengthen its span. As the purple gelstei can be used to mold crystals and other inanimate substances into new shapes, the green gelstei have powers over the forms of living things. In the Lost Ages, it was said that masters of the varistei used them to create new races of man (and sometimes monsters) but this art is thought to be long since lost.

These crystals confer great vitality on those who use them in harmony with nature; they can open the body's chakras and awaken the kundalini fire so the whole body and soul vibrate at a higher level of being.

THE RED

The red gelstei – also called tuaoi stones or firestones – are blood-red crystals like rubies in appearance and color. They are often cast into baguettes at least a foot in length, though during the Age of Law much larger ones were made. The greatest ever fabricated was the hundred-foot Eluli's Spire, mounted on top of the Tower of the Sun. It was said to cast its fiery light up into the heavens as a beacon calling out to the Star People to return to earth.

The firestones quicken, channel and control the physical energies. They draw upon the sun's rays, as well as the earth's magnetic and telluric currents, to generate beams of light, lightning, heat or fire. They are thought to be the most dangerous of the gelstei; it is said that a great pyramid of red gelstei unleashed a terrible lightning that split asunder the world of Iviunn and destroyed its star.

THE BLACK

The black gelstei, or baalstei, are black crystals like obsidian. Many are cast into the shape of eyes, either flattened or rounded like large marbles. They devour light and are the stones of negation.

Many believe them to be evil stones, but they were created for a great good purpose: to control the awesome lightning of the firestones. Theirs is the power to damp the fires of material things, both living and living crystals such as the gelstei. Used properly, they can negate the working of all the other kinds of gelstei except the silver and the gold, over which they have no power.

Their power over living things *is* most often put to evil purpose. The Kallimun priests and other servants of Morjin such as the Grays have wielded them as weapons to attack people physically, mentally and spiritually, literally sucking away their vital energies and will. Thus the black stones can be used to cause disease, degeneration and death.

It is believed that that baalstei might be potentially more

dangerous than even the firestones. For in the *Beginnings* is told of an utterly black place that is at once the negation of all things and paradoxically also their source. Out of this place may come the fire and light of the universe itself. It is said that the Baaloch, Angra Mainyu, before he was imprisoned on the world of Damoom, used a great black gelstei to destroy whole suns in his war of rebellion against the Galadin and the rule of the Ieldra.

THE PURPLE

The lilastei are the stones of shaping and making. They are a bright violet in hue, and are cast into crystals of a great variety of shapes and sizes. Their power is unlocking the light locked up in matter so that matter might be changed, molded and transformed. Thus the lilastei are sometimes called the alchemists' stones, according to the alchemists' age-old dream of transmuting baser matter into true gold, and casting true gold into a new Lightstone.

The purple gelstei's greatest effects are on crystals of all sorts: but mostly those in metal and rocks. It can unlock the crystals in these substances so that they might be more easily worked. Or they can be used to grow crystals of great size and beauty; they are the stone shapers and stone growers spoken of in legend. It is said that Kalkamesh used a lilastei in forging the silustria of the Bright Sword, Alkaladur.

Some believe the potential power of the purple gelstei to be very great and perhaps very perilous. Lilastei have been known to 'freeze' water into an alternate crystal called shatar, which is clear and as hard as quartz. Some fear that these gelstei might be used thus to crystallize the water in the sea and so destroy all life on earth. The stone masters of old, who probed the mysteries of the lilastei too deeply, are said to have accidentally turned themselves *into* stone, but most believe this to be only a cautionary tale out of legend.

THE SEVEN OPENERS

If man's purpose is seen as in progressing to the orders of the Star People, Elijin and Galadin, then the seven stones known as the openers might fairly be called greater gelstei. Indeed, there are those of the Great White Brotherhood and the Green Brotherhood

467

who revered them in this way. For, with much study and work, the openers each activate one of the body's chakras: the energy centers known as wheels of light. As the chakras are opened, from the base of the spine to the crown of the head, so is opened a pathway for the fires of life to reconnect to the heavens in a great burst of lightning called the angel's fire. Only then can a man or a woman undertake the advanced work necessary for advancement to the higher orders.

The openers are each small, clear stones the color of their respective chakras. They are easily mistaken for gemstones.

THE FIRST (also called bloodstones)
These are a clear, deep red in color, like rubies. The first stones open the chakra of the physical body and activate the vital energies.

THE SECOND (also called passion stones or old gold)
These gelstei are gold-orange in color and are sometimes mistaken for amber. The second stones open the chakra of the emotional body and activate the currents of sensation and feeling.

THE THIRD (also called sun stones)
The third stones are clear and bright yellow, like citrine; they open the third chakra of the mental body and activate the mind.

THE FOURTH (also called dream stones or heart stones)
These beautiful stones – clear and pure green in color like emeralds – open the heart chakra. Thus they open one's second feeling, a truer and deeper sense than the emotions of the second chakra. The fourth stones work upon the astral body and activate the dreamer.

THE FIFTH (also called soul stones)
Bright blue in color like sapphires, the fifth stones open the chakra of the etheric body and activate the intuitive knower, or the soul.

THE SIXTH (also called angel eyes)
The sixth stones are bright purple like amethyst. They open the chakra of the celestial body located just above and between the eyes. Thus their more common name: theirs is the power of activating one's second sight. Indeed, these gelstei activate the seer in the realm of light, and open one to the powers of scrying, visualization and deep insight.

THE SEVENTH (also called clear crowns or true diamonds)

One of the rarest of the gelstei, the seventh stones are clear and bright as diamonds. Indeed, some say they are nothing more than perfect diamonds, without flaw or taint of color. These stones open the chakra of the ketheric body and free the spirit for reunion with the One.

THE LESSER GELSTEI

During the Age of Law, hundreds of kinds of gelstei were made for purposes ranging from the commonplace to the sublime. Few of these have survived the passage of the centuries. Some of those that have are:

GLOWSTONES

Also called glowglobes, these stones are cast into solid, round shapes resembling opals of various sizes – some quite huge. They give a soft and beautiful light. Those of lesser quality must be frequently refired beneath the sun, while those of the highest quality drink in even the faintest candlelight, hold it and give back in a steady illumination.

SLEEP STONES

A gelstei of many shifting and swirling colors, the sleep stones have a calming effect on the human nervous system. They look something like agates.

WARDERS

Usually blood-red in color and opaque, like carnelians, these stones deflect or 'ward-off' psychic energies directed at a person. This includes thoughts, emotions, curses – and even the debilitating energy drain of the black gelstei. One who wears a warder can be rendered invisible to scryers and opaque to mindspeakers.

LOVE STONES

Often called true amber and sometimes mistaken for the second stones of the openers, these gelstei partake of some of their properties. They are specific to arousing feelings of infatuation and love; sometimes love stones are ground into a powder and made into potions to achieve the same end. They are soft stones and look much like amber.

WISH STONES

These little stones – they look something like white pearls – help the wearer remember his dreams and visions of the future; they activate the will to manifest these visualizations.

DRAGON BONES

Of a translucent, old ivory in color, the dragon bones strengthen the life fires and quicken one's courage – and all too often one's wrath.

HOT SLATE

A dark, gray, opaque stone of considerable size – hot slate is usually cast into yard-long bricks – this gelstei is related in powers and purpose, if not form, to the glow stones. It absorbs heat directly from the air and radiates it back over a period of hours or days.

MUSIC MARBLES

Often called song stones, these gelstei of variegated, swirling hues record and play music, both of the human voice and all instruments. They are very rare.

TOUCH STONES

These are related to the song stones and have a similar appearance. However, they record and play emotions and tactile sensations instead of music. A man or a woman, upon touching one of these gelstei, will leave a trace of emotions that a sensitive can read from contact with the stone.

THOUGHT STONES

This is the third stone in this family and is almost indistinguishable from the others. It absorbs and holds one's thoughts as a cotton garment might retain the smell of perfume or sweat. The ability to read back these thoughts from touching this gelstei is not nearly so rare as that of mindspeaking itself.

Books of the Saganom Elu

Beginnings
Sources
Chronicles
Journeys
Book of Stones
Book of Water
Book of Wind
Book of Fire
Tragedies
Book of Remembrance
Sarojin
Baladin
Averin
Souls
Songs
Meditations

Mendelin
Ananke
Commentaries
Book of Stars
Book of Ages
Peoples
Healings
Laws
Battles
Progressions
Book of Dreams
Idylls
Visions
Valkariad
Trian Prophecies
The Eschaton

The Ages of Ea

The Lost Ages (18,000 – 12,000 years ago)
The Age of the Mother (12,000 – 9,000 years ago)
The Age of the Sword (9,000 – 6,000 years ago)
The Age of Law (6,000 – 3,000 years ago)
The Age of the Dragon (3,000 years ago to the present)

The Months Of The Year

Yaradar	Marud
Viradar	Soal
Triolet	Ioj
Gliss	Valte
Ashte	Ashvar
Soldru	Segadar